TERRAN COMMAND

TERRAN COMMAND

QUEST FOR FREEDOM

JOHN DANIEL PONTIUS

To my heroes
Chief Warrant Officer 3 Daniel Jonathan Pontius, U.S.A. Ret.
Sergeant First Class Nathaniel David Pontius,
Arkansas N.G. God bless you.

Copyright @2020 by John Daniel Pontius

All rights reserved. No part of this book may be reproduced in any form or by any electronic or mechanical means, including information storage and retrieval systems, without permission in writing from the publisher, except by reviewers, who may quote brief passages in a review.

This publication contains the opinions and ideas of its author. It is intended to provide helpful and informative material on the subjects addressed in the publication. The author and publisher specifically disclaim all responsibility for any liability, loss or risk, personal or otherwise, which is incurred as a consequence, directly or indirectly, of the use and application of any of the contents of this book.

WORKBOOK PRESS LLC
187 E Warm Springs Rd,
Suite B285, Las Vegas, NV 89119, USA

Website: https://workbookpress.com/
Hotline: 1-888-818-4856
Email: admin@workbookpress.com

Ordering Information:
Quantity sales. Special discounts are available on quantity purchases by corporations, associations, and others. For details, contact the publisher at the address above.

ISBN-13:   978-1-955459-80-8 (Paperback Version)
                978-1-955459-81-5 (Digital Version)

REV. DATE: 20/01/2021

CONTENTS

Holcron
Cassaria
Tigra
Katusium
Denta
Cayton
Jarro Nebula
Tratana
Terra
Betarus Minor
Ithcar
Gamora Prime
Mentarus
Risor
Herrac 2
Horvathian
Sepious Minor
Laylar
Earth
Oterrac

Tigra
Holcron
Cassaria
Denta
Katusium
Jarro Nebula
Ithcar
Cayton
Terra
Tratana
Fraken System
Betarus Minor
Mentarus
Gamora Prime
Risor
Herrac 2
Evar's End193
Horvathan
Earth
Sepious Minor
Otterac
Laylar System
Uvarian System

PROLOGUE

With a brisk cadence, three senior military officers in brown, highly decorated uniforms proudly marched in lock step formation down the long palace hall. The rhythmic metallic tap…tap…tap of their highly polished dark brown boots on the glistening, black marble floor echoed through the grand hall announcing their approach to the throne room guards. The large hallway windows allowed beams of sunlight to illuminate the richly grained, wood paneled walls spotlighting great artistic treasures of the empire. Displayed were intricately woven hanging tapestries and ornately gilded, hand carved picture frames accenting centuries old paintings by the empire's greatest artists.

Decorating the entrance to the throne room were pieces of the finest marble and bronze statues in the empire.

When the trio stopped at the throne room entrance, they presented their written announcement to the herald. The herald retreated to the throne room to inform the emperor of their arrival.

The four royal guards stood at attention in ceremonial uniforms with blaster rifles shouldered. The facial tendrils of the guards sensed the fear in the air from the two more junior officers and gave each other a knowing glance. Their highly developed senses were not fooled by self-importance and rank. However, they sensed something very different in the most senior officer. They sensed no fear or guile in this officer but rather a supreme confidence in himself. Something very lacking in those serving in the palace. The guards sensed that same quality in the Emperor.

The assassination of the previous emperor during the rebellion, opened a power vacuum only an enterprising and ruthless tyrant could fill. The High Council member, Bon Zeenoff, was just the man to fill the void and so much more.

Proclaiming himself as Emperor and Grand Protector of the Uvarian Empire, he formed a coalition of supporters that quickly seized all reins of power. In the ensuing blood bath, thousands of political and business leaders were murdered for as much as wavering in their support of the new emperor.

The emperor sat on his large golden throne with the spread golden wings of a large eagle protecting him. A marble stand was nearby with a glass bowl of several, finger length, silver fish calmly swimming in circles.

The chief advisor stood before the emperor. "Sire, Do the nominations from the fifteen tribal councils for the governors meet your approval?"

Emperor Bon Zeenoff nodded approval. "I see the tribal leaders have wisely chosen more loyal replacements. A very wise move on their part. Make sure the new governors get the support they need and remind them their failure has consequences."

"As you command, sire." The advisor replied as he bowed and took three steps backward to leave the throne room.

Finally, the large, hand carved, gilded twin doors opened. The herald appeared and beckoned the three senior military officers to follow him. Once in the throne room, they paused at the end of the red carpet and waited to be called forward. A planetary governor in front of them stepped forward and bowed.

"Governor, do you know why you have been summoned?" the emperor asked.

"Sire, I realize the taxes collected are insufficient, but I remind you our industrial capacity has yet to be restored to pre-rebellion levels. Industrial output will be very slow to recover under the circumstances. In addition, a terrible crop blight has caused severe food shortages. Our best efforts to increase food production will still fall short," the governor declared.

"Are you telling me you killed so many people in putting down the rebellion that there is not enough manpower to maintain industrial and agricultural output?" the emperor asked already knowing the answer.

"Yes, sire!" the governor weakly replied with his head hung low.

"Then you have been a most foolish servant," the emperor angrily charged with a pointed finger. "By recklessly and brutally suppressing a rebellion you all but wiped out the highly skilled manpower needed to recover and grow the economy. You caused great damage to the empire. You do not put down a rebellion by wiping out half the population on one of the most industrialized planets in the empire and turn most of the remaining people into subsistence farmers. I sent you there to make peace, instead you commit genocide.

'As you sowed so will you reap," the emperor charged.

"…but sire! the governor interrupted begging for mercy.

"Enough!"The emperor roared as he rose to his feet. "Captain of the Guard! Remove this man. Seize all his property and send him and his family to the mines on Mintose."

"Your will be done, sire," the captain acknowledged as he motioned two guards to seize the now former governor.

To assuage his anger, Emperor Zeenott paused to deftly snatch a small silvery fish from the fish bowl with his bare hand. With a dramatic flip into the air, he caught the fish in his mouth and swallowed it whole."

He gave a loud belch and scowled as the prisoner was handcuffed.

There was a fearful pause in the room as the guards dragged the distraught prisoner screaming from the room. His echoed pleas for mercy faded as the doors closed behind him.

The emperor turned to one of his political advisors, "Notify the elders of the Sarsan tribe the governor's replacement is approved and they had better not fail to support him.”

“Yes, sire!” The advisor replied and excused himself.

The herald announced, “Your Royal Highness, Grand Viscount Zinge Horthnot, Vice Admiral Baya Mutaka, Chief of Operations, and Rear Admiral Quat Simmor have arrived.”

“Zinge Horthnot, what great news have we from our glorious military?” the emperor asked anxiously.

Grand Viscount Zinge Horthnot, stepped forward, gave a slight bow of obeisance and replied, “Sire, you summoned me, remember?”

Emperor Zeenott smiled, “Ah, yes I did indeed. You have been the empire’s greatest military leader and my most trusted advisor.

‘I wish your advice and it must be completely candid. If you cannot do that just say so. I won’t hold it against you.”

“Sire, we have worked together for many years while you were on the High Council. You have been emperor for a year now and I haven’t wavered in my counsel. It is my duty to advise you as forthrightly and honestly as I can. How may I advise you today?” Zinge asked.

The emperor stood up from his throne. “Come walk with me in the garden while we talk. I so need to stretch a bit.”

Leaving the throne room, the two men walked past two guards and out two glass doors into the beautiful grand garden. A stone path meandered around a garden with multi-colored flower beds, manicured lawns, hedges and fruit trees of various kinds. From a rock waterfall, a brook gently flowed through the garden. Periodically, a foot bridge allowed access to different areas. Benches and low stone walls were placed throughout the garden to allow people to rest and enjoy different views of rare flowers, plants and fruit trees. The entire garden was lined with a high stone wall with only one iron gate and a steel security door covered over with vegetation. There were guards posted on the other side as well.

"Zinge, tell me what is your assessment of the state of the empire?" the emperor asked in a subdued voice.

Zinge paused for a long moment before answering. Not that he was afraid to answer the question but to consider how much detail the emperor wanted to know. "Sire, I will tell you what you need to know, not what you want to hear. The empire is in the throes of death. The centuries of corruption, brutality, and greed has bled the empire to exhaustion and the people to despair, poverty and desperation. This last rebellion was the result of a failure in leadership from this throne down to the lowest local politician."

"Wait, you blame me for the last rebellion?" the emperor asked.

Zinge looked the emperor straight in the eyes. "You are the emperor and our supreme leader. It does not matter who did or did not do, to cause the rebellion. You are responsible for all good and bad that happens. That is why you sit on the throne. Accept it and you will rule better than any emperor we have ever had. A billion lives were lost and yet the next rebellion is not far away. It is guaranteed to exceed the number of lives already lost."

Bon paused for a second. "If any other person in the empire had said that, he would be executed before sundown. Coming from you, I must agree with your brutal assessment. Sometimes I question what I was thinking when I seized the throne but it was for the people I did it in the end. I'm under no illusion there are already those who would kill me for a short life of power before someone takes it from them as well. Your wisdom is appreciated. What can the military do to prevent this disaster?"

Zinge shook his head. "Raw military force cannot be relied upon to stop what is happening. An army must eat to fight. Many of our forces stationed on nine of the planets are already on three quarter rations. This is not sustainable.

'You seized the throne ten years too late to save it, I'm afraid. Of the fifteen planets of the empire; five are on the verge of planetary famine and five are already in an agricultural collapse. Disease, massive crop failures and politically created food shortages are the main causes. Replacing the corrupt governors was desperately needed but again too little too late. Only two planets are capable of producing enough food for export. Even so, not nearly enough to save even one other planet from collapsing. The other three planets are in industrial collapse as they move people to agriculture to survive. It is the right move but it will take three decades or more to return them to their former glory."

The emperor held up his hand. "I grasp your assessment and had already come to the same conclusion. So, what can we do to save our people?"

"Sire, I have served under four emperors and you are the first to be more concerned about the people than the empire. I've been working on a plan to save most of our people but I can't find a way to save all of them. I've come up with a plan to not only save the empire but, in time, make it the most powerful empire in the galaxy."

The emperor scoffed. "That is impossible!"

"It is true, sire. One of our scout ships in the Delta quadrant reported finding two sources of zannite and have worked a deal with some local pirates for it to be mined. There is enough to use for a hundred fleets. They also found six inhabited planets with sufficient labor and food resources capable of meeting our empire's demands. It will require the plundering of resources and enslavement of those planets."

"You didn't learn all this from one report. Tell me how long you have been planning this?" Emperor Zeenott demanded as his eyes narrowed and he began sniffing the air for deception.

Zinge didn't flinch as he explained. "Forty years ago, Emperor Crossbit tasked my father to conduct an exploratory mission into the Delta Quadrant. He discovered the planets and their abundant food and resource potential. The emperor set in motion a plan to subjugate them.

'My father came across the pirates and formed an alliance with them to cause havoc throughout the quadrant, learn more about the planets, and weaken them. We inserted teams to infiltrate and set up underground cells to prepare for our invasion. They use an implant to control the useful minds of thousands. They are totally unaware of their control yet obedient, serving with guile and ruthlessness. It was at this point the first of the rebellions took place and Emperor Crossbit assassinated. My father was also killed and the plan forgotten for a time.

'I discovered the plan and continued to keep it a secret until there was an emperor who had the vision to carry it out. You are that emperor. I kept sending out scout ships to continue collecting intelligence, direct our spies, and sew intrigue and confusion. A year before you came to the throne, a huge source of the mineral, zannite, was discovered in the Delta quadrant. Since then, a smaller deposit was also discovered. These two discoveries made the invasion plan even more vital and success more imperative."

"Now I understand the smell of deception I detected from you some months ago. It was puzzling since it was deemed nonhostile," Emperor Zeenott nodded. "So how much of the fleet will you require?"

"The entire Grand Fleet of thirty-six cruisers and five long range scout ships. It will also require an invasion force consisting of over 150 transports and heavy freighters with 500,000 soldiers and equipment," Zinge declared without flinching.

Emperor Bon Zeenott gasped as he staggered to sit on a

section of the low stone wall. "We don't have those resources!"

Zinge beamed. "Yes, we do, sire. The resources have been carefully built up over the years. Now we are ready."

The emperor's eyes gleamed at the whole plan. "How soon can you be ready and when do you expect to complete the mission?"

"The voyage to the first planet is nine months and once we have possession of the zannite and the first planet is captured we will be self-sustaining. You can expect the first shipments of food and slaves shortly after that. I believe if all goes according to plan we could conquer the Delta Quadrant within two years and the crisis will be behind you. We leave when you give the order," Zinge declared.

"Then by all means go as soon as possible. In the meantime, what do I do? The people will grow more restless and see our lack of strength an invitation to rebel, will they not?" the emperor asked with deep concern.

"Do what all politicians do. You promise utopia and glory, make grand speeches, and if necessary, make opponents disappear to buy time. Deliver what little you can and above all else, raise an army motivated by a full stomach to keep the peace until I return," Zinge answered.

"So, what happens if you fail?" the emperor asked.

"You will be assassinated, the empire will cease to exist, billions of people will be dead and no one to bury them. The survivors will be wishing they were dead," Zinge declared.

"You certainly paint a tragic picture," Emperor Zeenott said.

"Don't worry, neither of us will be around for the worst of it if we fail," Zinge grimly replied.

CHAPTER 1

Major Adam Eastman stepped out of the International Space Station on his first spacewalk. Russian cosmonaut Yorgi Gorgorian was right behind him securing the hatch. Adam was mesmerized by the view of Earth.

"Fantastic, isn't it?" his partner asked.

Adam smiled. "Wow, Yorgi, you're right. The view of Earth really does grab you out here. It's impossible to describe! The sun's bursting rays and the glow of Earth… never seen so many vivid colors. The Earth's glow wants to light up the universe yet it's quickly swallowed by darkness. I feel I can touch God's handiwork yet it's just beyond my grasp."

"You won't enjoy it for long when you run out of oxygen," Yorgi said. "Let's get to work?"

Adam nodded working his way hand over hand along the ISS railing to the site of the first task on the work schedule.

Six hours later they finished the last task of replacing the high resolution Earth Survey Camera. Yorgi placed the broken camera in a bag, securing its tether to his line before working his way back to the air lock.

Adam contacted Houston. "Houston, we are wrapping up here. As soon as you complete the system check, we're done," Adam said checking his oxygen supply.

"I have time to squeeze in repair of the power coupling thermal blanket before calling it a day if you want?"

"Roger that, Adam. It's up to you. Five minutes to complete system check," the Houston controller said.

The senior controller cut in. "Abort! Abort! Abort! Return to station immediately! We have a satellite visual of five unidentified objects approaching the ISS at a high rate of speed.”

“Copy, Houston. Returning to station.” As Adam headed to the air lock, he saw Dr. Chika Takaki through the lab viewport waving at him to hurry. Adam understood the urgency but nothing happens fast in a spacewalk.

Halfway to the air lock Adam twisted around to see two brilliant flashes streak past the ISS about 800 yards away. During the sudden movement, Adam lost his hold and began tumbling wildly. In an attempt to stabilize himself Adam attempted to catch the hold rail with his foot. He missed but on the next rotation managed to catch the rail. He stopped the tumbling but ended up tangled in his tether.

Calmly Adam called out. “Yorgi, I need help. I’m tangled up.”

“On my way,” Yorgi said.

Collecting his wits, Adam focused his helmet camera on the spacecraft activity.

“Houston, are you getting this?” Adam asked.

“Roger that,” Houston said. We have very limited on board camera view. Relying on your helmet camera. We only have visual on two of the craft. Can you see the others?”

“I see four craft maneuvering in pairs. I don’t see the fifth one. The pairs are in formation circling one another. I can’t get all of them in the camera’s view at the same time.” Adam said.

“Pan your helmet camera as best you can and describe everything you see,” the Senior Controller ordered.

“Roger, Houston. The ships are definitely alien. They are identical, oval shaped and approximately sixty feet long by half as wide. There is one twin engine mounted pylon to each aft side of the ships. I see only three figures in the cockpit of the nearest ship. These ships are extremely agile. The ships are firing some kind of bright yellow energy bolts. They seem evenly matched, taking as much damage as they are inflicting. They’re circling around for a third pass at each other head on.

'The lead craft are showing damage. Wait a second. A wingman just took a hit shearing off his starboard engine pylon. That ship is tumbling out of control. Oh wow! It just exploded. Three ships left.

'The fifth ship is coming into view. It's much larger. I guess about 200 feet long by 50 feet wide. It's firing at the remaining two-ship formation. The third ship is looping around out of view. The two small ships are trading fire with the larger ship while attempting to close the distance. They are inflicting obvious hull damage to the larger ship. The other damaged small ship has returned into view trailing some kind of green gas. It's attempting to use the larger ship as a shield.

'One of the attacking ships just took a direct hit to the cockpit exploding into thousands of pieces. The wingman is now behind the large ship firing at the stern. There must be some kind of shield because there is no visible damage.

'That pilot is insane! He is dangerously close and now directing his fire at the damaged smaller craft. The damaged craft is now breaking apart.

'Ouch! Did you see that? Debris just shredded the pursuing craft. Just the large ship now. It's trailing some kind of green gas. It is approaching Earth's atmosphere. Is anyone tracking the ship?" Adam asked.

"Negative, Major. Our radar is being jammed. The high resolution camera just came online. The ship is moving too fast to maintain visual for much longer," the Houston controller said.

"NORAD? Adam asked.

"Negative. They're jammed too. So far there is only a trail of jammed radar systems to follow," the controller said.

"How about Space Force?" Adam asked.

"They aren't talking," the controller said.

Adam shook his head in disappointment. "I bet this incident goes viral on the Internet before I get inside the station."

Finally, Yorgi finished untangling Adam's feet and they retreated to the ISS airlock. Neither of them spoke a word as they removed their suits. Thoughts raced through Adam's mind. Who are they? Where are they from? What were they fighting over and did the good guys or the bad guys win?

Lieutenant Colonel John Braxton watched the cargo handlers offload the cargo pallets from the rear of the C-5 Super Galaxy. The sense of their urgency was evident and so was their frustration. He wasn't pleased with the stalled offloading of the PAC-4 missile launcher from the nose ramp. John looked at his watch.

"Let's go. Let's go. Pick up the pace. We've got to get this aircraft out of here!" John shouted above the din.

"Sir, for some reason the launch vehicle won't start. As soon as we get a tow bar we'll get it offloaded." Master Sergeant Jacobi said.

John shook his head. "We don't have time for that, push it off."

"Yes, sir!" MSgt. Jacobi said as he began motioning to one of his fork lift operators.

Spotting the wing commander's staff car approaching John groaned, "This is not the time to get in our way."

A forklift with a loaded pallet braked hard then swerved to avoid striking the staff car as it crossed in front of it. The wing commander seemed oblivious to the forklift. The staff car came to an abrupt stop next to John. The driver rolled down the window.

"How come this aircraft is still on the ground?" Brigadier General Pickering asked.

"Sir, we can't get the vehicle to start. As soon as we get it offloaded we're done. I've got everyone working as fast as we can," John assured her.

"All right, but that aircraft must take off in five minutes."

She warned before speeding off.

No sooner was the vehicle rolling down the aircraft ramp than the wavering shrill sound of the early warning attack siren began echoing across the flight line.

"Nuts!" John announced over the radio net.

Looking at the aircraft, John noted the last forklift cleared the rear of the aircraft and the ramps began retracting.

"Sgt. Andrews!" John shouted above the noise as he waved at the driver. "Get your load clear of the aircraft and take shelter."

Yes, sir!" she said turning off the engine before leaping off the forklift.

Hearing a screeching of tires, John looked to see the general's staff car come careening around the front of the C-5 at a high rate of speed almost striking the launch vehicle and nearby airmen. The general sped on for another fifty yards before skidding into some sandbags in front of the bomb shelter entrance. She was last seen diving out of her car and disappearing into the shelter.

The launcher now clear, the C-5 nose door began lowering into place. The engines roared to life as the ground crew scurried to pull the wheel chocks away and get clear of the aircraft.

John looked up and realized the early warning proved not early enough. The giant C-5 Super Galaxy made a short taxi then raced down the runway. *At least they got a chance.*

"Forget the launcher. Get to shelter now!" John yelled over the radio net. It was a futile effort as John realized his people were too far away to make it to the nearest shelter. He also realized he wasn't going to make it either. John dived behind a pile of nearby sand bags as Russian missiles began raining down all around the flight line.

Blinding flashes, searing heat, deafening explosions and

flying shrapnel engulfed his surroundings. Sensing everything happening in surreal slow motion around him, John was lifted up into the air like a ragdoll then body slammed to the ground. Despite his stunned senses, he knew everything was happening with instantaneous violence. He could feel the air rushing out of his lungs from the impact. Dazed and numb, it seemed an eternity before his senses began working again.

Looking around, his eyes began stinging from the acrid smoke. He closed his eyes and the stinging went away but returned when he opened them again. For a brief moment, John thought his only injury was having the wind knocked out of him. It was an illusion.

A voice moaned for help.

"Hang on," John called attempting to stand. His legs wouldn't cooperate. In desperation, he used his forearms to drag his body several feet to the young sergeant. The voice fell silent. John checked for a pulse. Nothing. To his left, he saw movement from Sgt. Andrews and dragged himself to her.

"Sgt. Andrews, where are you hurt?" he asked.

"My left arm. I can't move it," she moaned.

Assessing her injuries, John noted the left side of her face and body were badly burned. There was nothing below the left elbow. He applied a tourniquet made from a torn part of her uniform as best he could.

"Andrews, try not to move. I'll get us some help," John said. He reached for the radio on his belt but found it gone. Instead, he discovered a piece of the radio sticking out of his hip. When he attempted to remove it, a tremendous pain shot through his body. *On second thought, I'll leave it alone for now.*

Now another scream not of pain but of horror was heard. He looked over towards the shelter. The general came running out of the shelter screaming at the top of her lungs, flailing her portable radio in the air. The staff car was a pile of twisted wreckage. The last he saw of the general was her running down the cratered flight line away from the carnage and disappear into the smoke.

John looked around to where he last saw several airmen. The C-5 aircraft was gone but the PAC-4 missile launcher was a pile of smoldering wreckage half buried in a crater of debris and dirt. There were also the remains of several lifeless cargo handlers.

"Oh God, please no!" John begged. "I've killed them," he cried out trying to crawl to them.

He thought he saw some movement. "Someone's still alive!" John cried out forcing himself to crawl to the airman. He struggled to crawl faster. Checking the airman over as best he could, John tore off a strip of shredded uniform making a bandage to cover a head wound. He said something of comfort to the airman before crawling to the next person.

It became progressively harder and harder to move among the dead and wounded. His breathing became more troubled. Finally, John rolled over on his back and willed himself to inhale.

"I killed them. I killed my people. God, please forgive me," John sighed as his senses began fading. Above the cacophony of noise of secondary explosions in the direction of the munitions storage facility he heard the distinct sound of an ambulance. He felt the tender hands of someone touching him. He barely opened his eyes before feeling the stinging sensation of blood. He saw the beautiful vision of his wife, Victoria, hovering over him like an angel. He tried to call out her name but couldn't. Slowly she too faded into a white cloud and bright light. A tear rolled down his cheek as he slipped into unconsciousness.

Startled, John bolted upright. His body was shaking, lungs fighting to breath.

"Where are my people? I've got to save them!" Beads of

sweat rolled off his forehead.

"John, It's OK. You're home. You're safe now," Victoria said soothingly while guiding him to lie down again. "You did all you could, John. It's over."

"Never over," John whispered as Victoria gently caressed his forehead. The warm, moist touch of her kiss, reassured him the nightmare was over for the moment at least. His rapid breathing began to subside.

"John, will you please tell me your nightmare? Maybe I can help," Victoria asked.

"I told you before, I don't want to talk about it!" John snapped. "It's better you don't know. It's a dark closet no one should ever look into. It is better nobody knows."

"John, your nightmares are getting worse and more frequent. You scare me when you have them. Why don't you go to the VA for help?" Victoria asked.

John struggled to calm down. Victoria was his lifeline and soul mate. He feared driving her away more than anything else. How do you tell the one you love you're a murderer? This was his shame and needed to be carried alone.

"Honey, please!" John pleaded. "I don't need some production line shrink telling me I need a drug that gives me even more horrific nightmares. If you think I have problems now, you haven't seen anything. Their drugs almost drove me insane in that hospital in Germany. I'll never let them touch me again."

Victoria gently rubbed his back. "I understand, I really do but we both know you can't handle this alone. Would you consider talking to Pastor Boyle? Both of you served together on the same base during the war and became good friends. Maybe he could help?"

"I'll consider it," John said. "For now, just drop it, please?"

"Ok, John, but please go see him, soon will you?" Victoria asked.

"All right, all right. Now get some sleep," John said.

"All right then, good night!" Victoria replied rolling over upset.

John reached over and gently rubbed her shoulder. "Honey, I'm very sorry I snapped at you. If you want me to see Pastor Boyle I'll see him, I promise!" John relented.

"Thank you. Now go back to sleep or you'll be too tired to go hunting with the boys," she said.

John said nothing more as he lay in bed deep in thought. The War of Russian Aggression abruptly ended for Lt. Colonel John Braxton half way through the two-year war. After months of surgeries and physical therapy John was medically retired from the Air Force with eighteen years of service. His career began as a nuclear missile launch officer. After the Start IV Treaty, the military closed the last of America's missile bases. After a string of logistics staff assignments, he spent two years as a logistics squadron commander.

The war changed everything for him. After rehabilitation, and against his better judgment, John took the first job offer that came along as a salesman for Primacy Global Logistics, Inc. In his gut, John knew it was a mistake, but he was desperate to feel useful again.

A year and a half later after refusing to take part in a kickback scheme involving a foreign government contract, he parted ways with the company. Yesterday was his last day. He began praying more earnestly than ever before. He needed to trust God. John knew God had a plan and in time all would be revealed. As he lay praying in the darkness he once again sensed the vision of green pastures and the peacefulness of lying down beside still waters. Slowly, peacefully, he drifted back to sleep.

It wasn't long before John awoke again. He rolled over and looked at the glowing red numbers on the digital clock. It was 4:30 a.m. He now felt wide-awake. The eerie resonance of moonlight beaming through his bedroom window showed Victoria still asleep. Her skin glistened like pearls giving her an irresistible beauty. The faint scent of her favorite perfume filled the air. Despite her physical aurora, something deeper attracted John to this exotic, raven-haired beauty.

Victoria exuded heartfelt warmth John discovered long ago he couldn't live without. After twenty-seven years of marriage he was more in love with her than ever before. Her comforting words and gentle ways repelled the dark clouds that haunted him. She made home a refuge from the stressful outside world. She couldn't make his nightmares go away, no one could, but her abiding love helped him through the pain. Victoria was always there, keeping him from slipping into the dark abyss.

I might as well get up and make the boys breakfast. John got up and quietly put on his hunting clothes and left the bedroom. In the kitchen, he set about making his sons' favorite breakfast: pancakes with blueberries, sausage, scrambled eggs, and hot chocolate with a shot of strong coffee.

John smiled as he added cinnamon to his drink.

It was nice having Jonathan, now twenty-four years of age, home for the weekend. He was almost finished working on his Master's degree in aeronautical engineering and decided to take a break. It had been awhile since he was home last. Oddly enough John missed the cloud of good-natured mischief that always followed him. Jonathan was short in height and medium build, brown eyes and hair. His swaggering smile was a perfect match for his quick wit and sharp mind. His fiancée, Katrina Nevins, was a registered nurse in Washington State. They were planning a June wedding next summer.

David was nineteen years old. He was in the Air Force

ROTC Program at a nearby university and doing very well. The numerous models of fighter aircraft decorating the bedroom with a prominent picture of him receiving his private pilot's license left no doubt he was serious about being a fighter pilot. His quiet nature earned him the moniker, Ghost. John or Victoria often had to call his name out just to know if he was around. A faint voice of "Here!" was the usual reply from some remote quiet corner of the house. Always quietly going about his business, David was comfortable in a crowd or alone. He was also the frequent target of his brother's playful pranks yet they were the closest of siblings. His shy, handsome stature, thick blond hair and bright blue eyes often attracted female attention much to his embarrassment. He was three inches taller than either John or Jonathan, but there was no mistaking he was a Braxton.

John and Victoria wished their daughter, Susan, was home for the weekend but she was deep in her medical studies. She was a year younger than Jonathan and in her fourth year of medical school in Toledo, Ohio. Only about two hours away, she often came home on weekends. Ever the studious one, she was mindful Jonathan had a mischievous way of altering everyone's plans. There was never a dull or quiet moment when they were together. She dearly missed her brother's mischief but her studies had to take priority this time.

Jonathan and Susan started homeschooling together in kindergarten and continued all the way through high school. They posed a very striking resemblance and shared such strong mannerisms most people assumed they were twins. In their junior year of college Susan introduced Jonathan to her roommate, Katrina. She was excited to see her best friend soon to become her sister-in-law too.

"Smells good!" Jonathan said as he joined John in the kitchen.

"Morning! Is David up?" John asked.

"Yep, and as slow as ever," Jonathan said. "He's always had two main gears in his transmission. Park, and Slow. Overdrive only kicks in when playing video games or basketball."

"How about setting the table?" John asked. "By the time you're done he'll smell breakfast and be along."

"Hey breakfast smells good. Is it ready?" David asked sniffing the air as he entered the kitchen.

As soon as the table is set," John smiled.

Before Jonathan got the plates out David was already setting the rest of the table. John brought the food to the table and everyone took a seat. Jonathan reached for a serving spoon.

John cleared his throat and shook his head at Jonathan. "Come on, you know better. Since you are the most eager, how about you saying grace?"

"Yes, sir. Dear Father, thanks for fellowship, the food and your loving grace. Bless our hunt, keep us safe, send the biggest buck ever our way and help our shots be true. Amen!"

"Wow! You sure asked for a lot with your shooting skills," David said poking Jonathan in the side.

"Anyone check the weather report since you got up?" John asked passing a platter of pancakes around.

Jonathan raised his hand while waiting to finish a bite. "We have a big storm front coming in. We should get heavy rain and good dose of thunderstorm activity around daybreak. Looks like we won't be out very long."

"Well, we could catch them moving to bed down before the storm," David said.

John smiled. "That is a good possibility. Better be on your toes. If the deer are in a hurry you'll miss them."

"There was something on the headline about the space station astronauts on a spacewalk and seeing alien ships collide," Jonathan said.

David shook his head. "Everyone knows there is no such

thing as space aliens. I bet it was some Russian space junk entering the atmosphere. Since the war ended there's been a lot of that stuff happening."

"You never know, David. They once said Earth was flat but it isn't. They once said the sun revolved around the Earth but it doesn't. They once claimed people couldn't breathe if they went over one hundred miles an hour but now we go into space. We don't know half as much as we think we do. Can you even begin to imagine the panic if space aliens really showed up?" Jonathan said.

"You can debate aliens later we'd better clear the table and get to our hunting stands," John said.

"Good point!" Jonathan agreed.

A few minutes later they were in the beat up four-wheel drive pickup truck heading to the old Buckner farm.

"Dad, you believe in space aliens?" David asked.

John smiled. "I don't know one way or the other. For sure I'm not going to limit what God chooses to do much less when, where, or how.

"Did NASA report an alien meteorite like in the movie War of the Worlds?" John asked winking at Jonathan.

"No, it was just a breaking news headline. One thing for sure, at least we won't be like those three poor guys at the Martian landing site," Jonathan noted.

"What three guys?" David perked up. "What are you talking about?"

"What? You never saw War of the Worlds?" Jonathan asked a bit incredulous.

"No, I don't like science fiction, remember?" David grumbled. "So, what happened in the movie?"

John explained, "The Martians landed near a small town in a spaceship disguised as a meteor. The townsfolk asked a group of scientists at a nearby fishing camp to study the meteor.

The scientists made a bunch of excuses but agreed to examine it in the morning. The sheriff suckered three townsfolk into doing his job and had them guard the meteor till morning."

Jonathan continued. "During the night, a Martian slowly rose out of a hatch in the fake meteor. The three guys were scared but tried to welcome the Martian to Earth. In a grateful gesture of peace, the Martian zapped them with a ray gun killing them deader than door nails," Jonathan emphasized by pretending to swat a bug on the dashboard.

"Yep, nothing left of them but three smoking piles of ash," John quipped.

"Oh, great!" David sighed realizing they had strung him along.

A mile down the county road, John made a right turn onto a gravel road and drove another half mile to a turnout into a field, and parked.

"When you get to your stands keep in contact with our cell phones but don't play with them, got it?"

The boys nodded but obviously not happy.

"Good! At the first sign of lightening or thunder get out of the tree stands fast. We'll meet back at the truck. Let's go."

Just as the three of them got settled into their stands it began a light misty drizzle. As daybreak came a large buck passed right in front of David but there was no shot. John, looking through his small field glasses, saw David on his cell phone and never looked up to see the deer. The deer continued on his path and crossed in front of Jonathan's stand. John looked at Jonathan busy on his cell phone too.

John texted, "Hey guys, are we playing games or what? The biggest buck I've ever seen around here just passed in front of both of you. Get your heads in the hunt."

"Sorry, I was just reading that four alien space craft fought it out and blew themselves up near the space station. Another entered the atmosphere and disappeared," David replied.

"There is a storm cell about to hit us any moment!" Jonathan answered.

"All right, let's get back to the truck," John replied in frustration. No sooner did they climb down from the stands than the rain began falling heavily. Two lightning strikes crackled in the distance.

"Come on, boys! "John waved. "Hustle before we get dumped on." As they joined up, another sound was heard. It was a loud whining sound similar to a turbine jet engine. The clouds were so thick and low John couldn't see a thing even when the sound seemed directly above them. In the field six does jumped up and scampered in several directions.

"Oh great!" David said. "They were in the middle of us the whole time."

The low clouds began madly swirling and the tall brown grass began blowing wildly as the sound got louder. Out of the swirling clouds a large alien ship descended. Heavy gray and green smoke poured from a long, jagged hole near the top of the ship close to the engine section. The ship violently wobbled for a moment then recovered. As it leveled off the ship extended several landing skids and eased to the ground.

"Take cover!" John shouted above the din.

In the middle of the field loomed the silhouette of a spaceship. It was three stories high, two-thirds the length of a football field long and half as wide. Its shape resembled a space shuttle on an overdose of steroids minus wings and rudder. John noticed a slight rotten egg smell as the smoke drifted in their direction. As the smoke ceased billowing from the gash in the top of the hull the damage was more visible. Through his binoculars, John could see the cockpit fifty yards away. The rain was falling very heavy now with thunder booming and lightening flashing in the sky. Through it all John couldn't get a clear view of anyone aboard.

Carefully crawling through the weeds and mud, John tried to get a closer look at the ship. A pair of flashing red lights and humming sound announced the opening of the access ramp. Located mid-length on the starboard side, the wide door swung out from the bottom of the ship then extended out before lowering six feet to the ground. The dimly lit cargo bay made it difficult to see inside.

At the top of the cargo bay ramp appeared two figures about six feet tall, barrel-chested, with spindly long arms and legs. They had long necks, round, heavily scarred faces, and bald heads. The pig-like ears and wide flat noses completed the cartoonish appearance. They wore dirty earth brown jumpsuits patched in various places, quilted silver fabric vests and dark brown leather boots. Both aliens held weapons similar to a large semi-auto pistol with long slides and optical sights. The tallest alien wore a red sash across his chest and barked orders to someone inside.

John gripped his shotgun more tightly. Slowly he turned his head to see his two sons close by. They were well hidden behind a clump of thick brush but John couldn't help noticing their mouths were wide open in shock. They too held their shotguns at the ready. The leader gruffly shouted more orders to the alien beside him.

He scurried inside and a moment later reappeared. Another figure followed behind wearing a silver protective suit and hood carrying an extendable ladder. Two more aliens similarly dressed in brown jumpsuits followed behind him carrying a large metallic box. They walked down the ramp to where the hull damage was and set up the extension ladder. With a safety line hooked to his waist, the hooded technician climbed up to the damaged area.

Standing near the top of the ladder the hooded technician shined a flashlight inside the hole to survey the damage then climbed down. He removed his hood revealing a human like being with short, graying hair. The left half of his face was covered with a black mask hugging the contour of his forehead and cheek. John surmised from his angry exchange with the leader they were definitely not on friendly terms. The man in the suit seemed to understand them but replied in a different language that reminded John of the Gaelic tongue.

One of the aliens by the ladder went back inside the ship for a moment and returned with some parts. The masked technician gestured they were not the right parts. Another exchange of angry words and gestures ensued until the alien disappeared inside once again. The scarred aliens remaining by the ladder spoke between them in a slurred gruff language, nodded agreement, and drew their pistols. A moment later the alien reappeared forcefully prodding and pushing three young human-like females. Their hands were bound behind them and their feet hobbled with rope. The leader on the ramp barked an order before shoving the females tumbling down the ramp.

Next to the ladder the two guards squealed in laughter. One of them raced over to the females to assist the other guard. They forced the groaning, bruised women to kneel as if preparing for execution. One of the guards grabbed the youngest female by her long golden hair; blood seeped out the side of her mouth from the fall. The guard began shaking, slapping and hitting her. The other two females struggled against their bonds but to no avail. Speaking the same Gaelic-like language, they pleaded for their captors to stop beating her.

The leader shouted more commands at the technician. When the technician nodded understanding the beating stopped. The technician held a hammer in his right hand and gesturing with his left, indicating what parts he needed. The leader quickly disappeared inside the craft.

John again looked back at his sons. The anger on his face said it all. He pointed at David and then at the scarred alien at the base of the ladder.

"If I know Dad, deer season's over. Alien season just opened," Jonathan whispered to David.

"No kidding!" David whispered back.

Signaling Jonathan, John pointed at the two guards near the females and the leader at the top of the ramp. Jonathan nodded. The three men crawled closer to their targets. The noise of the storm masked their movement through the tall grass.

The blonde-haired woman, groaning in pain, attempted to stand up. The guard shouted an order at her but the woman gave a glaringly defiant look in return. For just a second her eyes flashed a cold cobalt blue glow. This set off another series of violent kicks. With a wicked laugh, he stepped back leveling his gun at her head.

"Nuts!" John shouted instinctively as he jumped up, leveling his shotgun. As he sighted his shotgun he froze. The vision of injured and dead airmen on the tarmac, hearing groans and screams, once again smelling the acrid smoke returned to over power him. All John could do was yell, "No! Not again."

Jonathan looked over and saw John frozen like a statue and knew what was happening.

"Dad, snap out of it!" Jonathan shouted then fired at the alien aiming at his father. A deafening roar rang out. The guard's cruel smile changed to speechless horror as a heavy 12-gauge slug struck his shoulder spinning him around.

The roar of the shotgun snapped John out of the flashback. Realizing what had happened, he fired and the guard crumpled to the ground.

Jonathan stood and fired at the second guard dropping him where he stood.

Swinging to his left John rushed towards the guard at the ladder to get a clear shot. When John fired the first shot the guard ducked down in the tall weeds preventing David from firing. A few seconds passed before the guard popped up from a different position. The guard fired a snap shot at John just missing his head. John didn't even flinch as he swung his gun to return fire. At the same moment, David fired and struck the guard knocking him against the ladder.

As the ladder fell away, the technician, still holding a large hammer, leaped on top of the guard. With a raging scream he struck the guard a final blow.

"Dad! You OK?" David called out.

John waved he was OK and pointed at the ramp opening.

Now the alien leader re-appeared at the cargo bay entrance with his pistol drawn. He was about to open fire at John when David and Jonathan fired two quick shots that sent him tumbling down the ramp and into the mud beside one of his fallen comrades.

Jonathan and David rushed over to free the drenched and muddy females. John verified all of the aliens were dead and collected up the weapons.

David knelt down to cut the bonds behind the back of the injured blond-haired woman. Her rain drenched white silk blouse and black loose-fitting slacks were tattered and bloody from several lacerations. As he rolled her over onto her back her rich blue eyes gave off a sharp glow before fading away.

"Hey!" David shouted in surprise as he leaned away. Quickly recovering, David brushed aside her long wavy golden hair revealing a face of ivory porcelain skin of rare beauty. The golden cross necklace sparkled against her skin. The brothers glanced at each other at the discovery but said nothing.

"You're safe now!" David reassured her hoping she understood.

The white-haired woman behind him held out her bound hands gesturing to be freed.

"Can you cut me loose?" she asked.

Turning towards her, David stood in surprise. "You speak our language?"

The white-haired woman ignored his question. "Please free me so I can tend to my sister?"

"Sure!" David said cutting her bonds. To his complete surprise, she lashed out a powerful left punch. It struck David just below his left eye staggering him backwards. His assailant then raced over to tend to the injured sister. As David recovered, she motioned him to stay back. David quickly shouldered his shotgun and aimed it directly at her.

The white-haired female was five feet, ten inches tall and athletically built. Her straight shoulder length white hair outlined an oval face with high cheeks, slender nose and dark brown expressive eyes. Her clothes consisted of a red silk blouse with black loose-fitting slacks. David noticed both women wore highly polished mid-calf black riding boots.

"Nobody touches our sister, you got that?" his attacker said.

The injured woman spoke softly to her white-haired protector who then seemed to calm down.

"OK, OK! You didn't have to sucker punch me to make your point," David said rubbing his cheek.

Jonathan's attention turned to the third female standing nearby with her bound hands held out gesturing to be freed. She also had an athletic build, long red hair and sea green eyes. The red hair was rolled up into a bun. Her facial features were similar to the others. She wore a pair of low-cut work boots and a tan mechanic's jumpsuit with old grease stains. He also noticed this sister was wearing an identical golden cross necklace.

"I promise not to hit you. I'm Estron. My sister, Aycana, is the hot headed one not me. Siyana is really injured. I can help." A bit reassured, David lowered his shotgun as Jonathan cut her bonds.

Once freed, she raced over to join her sisters.

By now the downpour slightly eased up and the lightning

and thunder had moved on to the east. The man in the suit now joined the group. Aycana exchanged a few words in their language between them and he nodded agreement.

John went up the ramp and looked inside the cargo hold and came back down. He saw David holding his hand over his left eye.

"We just rescued them and out of the blue this one punches David." Jonathan said pointing at Aycana. "He forgot to duck. He's going to have a beauty of a shiner for it too!"

"There's a lot we don't know yet so let's be on guard, OK?" John warned. The two brothers nodded.

Aycana came to attention and bowed. "Thank you for rescuing us."

"You speak our language? Are you from Earth?" John asked.

"No, we are from the planet Cassaria. I'm Aycana Toburg, these are my sisters; Estron and Siyana. The man with the mask is a family servant and crewmember, Dexter. Our stepbrother, Gavin, is half-Earthling. He taught us your language using a book his mother called the Bible."

"We are Christians. Do you know Jesus Christ too?" David asked.

"Yes, we do," Estron smiled.

"That is unreal. Bible believing aliens that look humans," Jonathan said. "So where is your brother?"

Aycana winced at the remark. "He's on the bridge with a pirate guarding him. Another pirate is doing repairs in the engine room but could be anywhere by now."

"I'm John Braxton. The one you punched is my youngest son, David. The wise guy is my oldest son, Jonathan. OK, I'll go get them and bring your brother out. David, stand guard over them. Jonathan, you stand guard at the top of the ramp."

"Dad, are you sure you can do this?" Jonathan asked.

"Thank you back there, it won't happen again. I can do this," John assured him.

"OK," the boys said.

As John started up the ramp, Aycana stopped him. "You'd better use one of these weapons. They are very simple to use. That long gun of yours will be very hard to use in the tight confines of the ship." She quickly demonstrated how to use the weapon.

"It operates very much like a semi-automatic pistol. I got your back. Be careful, Dad," Jonathan said. "I'll never be able to explain this to Mom."

Holding the pistol at the ready, John again surveyed the cargo hold as he entered. A quarter of the bay was filled with crates of various shapes and sizes strapped to the floor. Smaller containers were placed on special racks to keep them from shifting. There were also two large 2000 gallon tanks secured to the side of the rear bulkhead.

Next to the main access hatches on the fore and aft bulkheads were elevator platforms going from the cargo bay deck all the way to the upper third deck.

"See you in a bit!" John grimaced as he opened the creaking forward hatch.

When John was out of sight, Jonathan looked sternly at David. "David, no matter what, no one is to ever know about Dad. We watch him like a hawk but no one knows. We give him the chance to work this out. He needs to conquer his demons, you got it?"

David gave Jonathan a puzzled look. "We took out the bad guys as far as I'm concerned."

"Good," Jonathan said patting David on the back. "Braxtons stick together."

John found a dimly lit passageway with three doors on each side and a seventh door at the very end. John worked his way down the passageway clearing each of the rooms as he went. The first room on each side of the hall was for storage of tools, parts, and spacesuits.

The other two rooms on each side of the passageway were crew quarters. The stench of sweaty, dirty clothes was bad enough but the low table in the middle of the rooms displayed a sight far worse. On each table was a food platter piled high with what looked like rotted fish and vegetables covered in a brown lumpy sauce. The foul smell reminded him of chicken manure. It was all he could do to fight back the gagging sensation wracking his throat. Each room was equipped to quarter six crewmen but by the trashed and foul conditions, John couldn't believe anyone would want to use them.

When he came to the end of the passageway the seventh door opened to a forward compartment containing two racks of missiles, weapons consoles, weapons storage lockers and other electronic equipment. Inside the room to the right of the doorway was another four-foot square elevator platform. It showed no obvious controls, just a glowing green light.

John scratched his head, puzzled as to how it worked. Above the platform, he spotted a row of small bright white lights outlining the closed hatch above but nothing more. He stepped onto the platform and touched the green light. There was a whisper of compressed air as the platform began to move upward. The trap door above the platform slid open. Nervously, John brought his pistol to a firing position and carefully swept the bridge as it came into view. The sounds of humming equipment and cooling air drowned out the sound of the elevator's operation.

The bridge was larger than John imagined, except for the glowing lights from several consoles, the bridge had a dimly lit appearance. As he stepped off the platform, John had a full view of the bridge. He spotted two individuals with their backs to him on the opposite side of the bridge. A human was sitting at a console with another pig faced alien guard armed with a blaster behind him.

The guard glanced over his shoulder, realized John was not one of his mates and wheeled about to face him.

John shouted, "Drop the weapon!" The absurdity of giving an alien a command in English flashed through his mind, but it was all he could think of at the moment.

The guard failed to comprehend John's order, pivoted and raised his weapon.

Two rapid shots flashed from John's pistol striking their target. The alien was able to get off a wild shot that glanced off a nearby console. It ricocheted off and grazed the shoulder of the man at the console. The alien fell back against a nearby console and slid to the floor. Mortally wounded, he gasped for breath and struggled to move but couldn't. Smoke emanated from the two cauterized holes in his chest. The smell of burnt flesh began to drift throughout the bridge. Within a few seconds, he closed his eyes and slumped over. The blaster fell from his hand onto the floor.

With his one good arm raised the injured man had a surprised look. He slowly stood and acknowledged John's act then coldly glanced at the guard's lifeless body.

Keeping his gun aimed at the alien, John eased his way across the bridge and retrieved the guard's weapon. The man nodded approvingly to John.

"OK, Mr. Brilliant, what am I going to do now?" John muttered out loud.

The man smiled, "I speak your language. My name is Gavin. Are my sisters safe?"

"Ah, yes, my sons are with them and an older man."

Gavin smiled. "Good. Thank you for rescuing us. There is a blue first aid kit on the wall behind you. I could use a bandage to stop my bleeding."

John retrieved the kit and found a large bandage.

"There is a packet of yellow powder that you can use to

stop the bleeding before you put on the bandage. It also numbs the wound for a while."

"Interesting how it forms a seal over the wound," John said as he generously sprinkled the powder onto the wound. When the foaming stopped, he applied the dressing. As he did so, John kept glancing at the dead alien. "Five of these guys are dead. Are there any more?"

"They are Gamoran pirates. We were captured while on a diplomatic mission. There were six of them on board taking us to meet up with another ship. The last one is in the engine room doing repairs. The ship is fairly sound proof so I doubt he is aware of anything. Shall we go get him? He is a rather harmless fellow but who knows how he will react if he sees you alone."

John shook his head. "No thanks! I can handle it."

"Please allow me to assist you. Despite being a pirate, he was helping us in our escape." Gavin said.

"You trusted a pirate to betray his friends?" John asked.

"This one was not always treated much better than we were by his fellow pirates," Gavin answered.

John thought about it but still didn't like the idea. He removed the power magazine from the dead alien's pistol and handed it to Gavin. "OK, I'll go half way with you. Sorry, but until I know what's really going on this is the only deal I'm offering."

Gavin shook his head in disgust but took the pistol. "All right. I understand."

"OK! Let's get this guy. You lead," John said pointing out the bridge hatch.

Gavin led John through a short passageway past four rooms to another elevator. John noticed it was similar to the elevator he used earlier. Gavin waved his hand over the green light and the elevator took them up to the third deck. The elevator opened to face a large open lounge area.

Behind the elevator was a longer passageway leading about half the length of the ship and past six passenger cabins along the way. The two men quickly cleared them. At the end of the passageway, they came to another elevator that lowered to the rear of the cargo bay.

"Jonathan, don't shoot," John called down.

"OK!" Jonathan replied.

Once back down by the loading ramp, John introduced Gavin and Jonathan, and explained the situation. With Gavin still leading, the two men entered the reactor room.

The low humming of pumps and smell of ozone greeted them as they cleared the sterile room. Only the pulsating milky blue glow from the viewing port of the transfusion reactor illuminated the room.

Suddenly the engine room hatch opened revealing a very short pirate carrying a large heavy toolbox. As he stared at Gavin's gun pointing at his heavily scarred face, a look of sheer horror and shock registered. The diminutive pirate, in a reflex act of surrendering, dropped the heavy toolbox and threw his hands in the air.

Gavin screamed in agony as the toolbox fell on his feet.

The pirate, taking advantage of the moment, now reached for his sidearm.

John shoved Gavin out of the way with his free hand, while thrusting his gun against the alien pirate's flattened nose. With his free hand John negatively wagged his finger shaking his head.

Gavin was momentarily stunned as he bounced off the bulkhead and collapsed on the deck.

The frustrated pirate gave a sigh of defeat, dropped his pistol and raised his hands in final surrender.

John picked up the pistols and stuffed them into his coat. Helping Gavin up, John put one of Gavin's arms over his shoulder for support, and motioned the diminutive pirate to move forward. With their prisoner in the lead and Gavin limping, they rejoined the others. Aycana was arguing with David demanding to enter the ship for an aid kit. Estron was shouting at Siyana to remain still.

When Dexter saw the alien pirate, he rushed after him with his hammer held high.

Gavin barked a command twice before Dexter dropped the hammer and angrily stepped aside. The shouting sisters fell silent.

Angrily, Gavin glared at his sisters and Dexter. "What's going on? Have all of you gone mad?"

"The pirate must be executed," Dexter demanded.

"I understand your feelings but we don't murder prisoners. This prisoner actually helped us and will not be harmed!" Gavin firmly declared pointing at the short pirate.

John and his sons listened to the scene unfold silently taking it all in. There was a moment of silence, as everyone tried to comprehend what transpired.

Finally, Gavin knelt down next to Siyana. He looked over her wounds and shook his head. He asked Aycana to prepare her to be moved to the ship's sick bay. As Gavin stood up, Estron began sobbing against his chest in a language unintelligible to the Braxtons.

Gavin put his arms around Estron comforting her. Looking to the Braxtons he explained, "The past few months have been harrowing for all of us. First the betrayal by a crewmember, subsequent capture, and all the crew murdered except Dexter. It has been stressful beyond belief yet my sisters stood strong. Our escape failed and we were about to be executed when you came along and rescued us. Thank you for saving us. We are indebted to you beyond our ability to repay."

John gave an understanding nod. Then pointing to David,

"Gavin, this is my youngest son, David. Jonathan you've already met."

"Welcome to Earth," David said.

"What's with the pirates?" Jonathan asked.

"We're from the planet Cassaria on a diplomatic mission for our father, King Adrian Toburg. We have been at war with Gamoran pirates for over thirty-seven years. The people of the planet Holcron are allies. We were seeking alliance with the people of the planet, Tigra. The pirates found out and captured us. Three months later we are here on Earth," Gavin said.

"So how did you learn about us?" Jonathan asked.

Gavin smiled. "It is a story of tragedy and miracles. Thirty-four years ago, Gamoran pirates kidnapped two hundred Earthlings from a ship at sea, including my mother, intending to sell them as specimens to a Gamoran science cartel. Later they got greedy and attacked a large Cassarian freighter. It was actually a Cassarian military decoy.

'The Cassarian captain, my father, defeated the pirates and freed the Earthlings. Father fell in love with my mother and they soon married. I was born a few years later. My mother died when I was five years old. She left many recordings about Earth cultures, your language, history, her faith and her Bible.

'Because of her and other freed Earthlings, Christianity spread rapidly across Cassaria. Not all Cassarians reacted well to the new faith. Converts largely became regarded as second-class citizens. Many found a home and future in our military where they were free to worship. Because the military is dedicated to space defense and exploration, we are largely isolated from most of Cassarian society. We are kind of like out of sight, out of mind. Despite our treatment, we proudly serve to protect all Cassarians.

'It shocked everyone to find there was another, though very distant, planet with people like us. Because Earth is technologically behind and by our standards aggressively war like, Cassaria and other space traveling planets signed an agreement forbidding official contact. Crashing here is one thing but we must leave as quickly as possible to avoid complications."

"I see," John said. "We will do our best to protect and help you with repairs as best we can."

Aycana stood up and reached out with her right hand in a palm up gesture and head slightly bowed. "David, I'm very sorry for striking you.

You risked your life for us. I was afraid for Siyana and not thinking of your rescue of us. I see now you were trying to help her. Please accept my apology?"

David repeated the hand gesture and slightly bowed his head, "Aycana, your apology is accepted."

John now realized the character of those they rescued. Aycana possessed a frank demeanor, yet exuded a grace that befitted a royal family upbringing. She was not afraid to take responsibility for her actions.

"Very good. We don't want bad feelings to prevent making new friends," Gavin said.

Siyana looked up at David and held out her hands. "Could I ask my rescuer to help me to sick bay now?"

David blushed. "Sure."

As David helped Siyana, it was all Jonathan could do to keep from laughing. No one couldn't help notice the soft glow of her blue eyes when David gently helped her up. With the help of Aycana they gently helped her up the ramp.

Jonathan rolled his eyes, "Well the hook is set already."

"Jonathan, don't start that," John cautioned.

Gavin pretended not to notice and gave some instructions to Dexter.

There was no mistaking in John's mind Siyana was the

most poised princess of the three sisters. Just as outgoing as Aycana, but there was no missing the grace and charm that exuded from her demeanor and petite frame despite her pain and injuries. Estron was just the opposite. From the stained mechanics jumpsuit and nervous gum chewing, it was obvious she did not attend the same charm school.

"What's our prisoner's name," John asked sizing up their diminutive prisoner.

"His name is Deze. He has learned a little of your language but he knows a lot about Gamoran pirate operations that can prove helpful," Gavin said.

"Ok," John said."Make sure he understands the consequences of crossing us even once. One mistake and he joins his dead shipmates!"

Gavin conveyed the terms to their prisoner.

Deze's face got very animated and vigorously nodded agreement.

"I don't think he'll cause any trouble, but Estron will guard him and protect him from Dexter," Gavin replied handing his pistol to Estron.

"I understand," Estron agreed. "Dexter will surely kill him if given a chance."

Turning to John, Gavin explained, "Estron will escort Deze to the engine room and supervise repair work."

"Gavin, you mentioned your mother was from Earth. Do you know where from?"

Gavin paused for a moment. "I was taught your language from a book she always kept close to her. She called it the Bible. She taught many of our people Christianity. There are many believers now including all our family. She said she grew up on a farm in a place called Ohio."

"Really?" John asked. "That's not too far from here. Our country is called the United States of America."

"Yes, I remember her speaking that name. She taught so much on video before she died," Gavin said.

Excuse me," Dexter interrupted. I'll begin the repairs immediately. I'm not sure how we can fix some of the damage though."

"We are glad to assist you," John assured him. "Your presence will draw unwanted attention very soon. How long will it take to get the ship air worthy?"

After talking to Dexter, Gavin became obviously worried. Dexter returned to the ladder to examine the damage in more detail a second time.

Gavin and the Braxtons, in the meantime, began putting the alien bodies in some makeshift body bags.

Dexter returned to the group and explained the damage to Gavin.

"Dexter says the damage seems minor to the oxygen exchanger and engine coolant systems. The damage to the booster relay system and the hull breach are more serious. The pirate mother ship took most of the parts and tools we normally carry. We can probably get it air worthy in about a day but space is out of the question without at least four or five days of repairs with the right tools and materials," Gavin explained shaking his head.

John grimaced, "You can't stay here that long. As soon as the storm passes the government will be out in force looking for you. They will think they have your best interest in mind and won't harm you.

'However, they will take you away and seize the ship supposedly for your safety. Other less friendly elements will be right behind them and not have such benign interests. They will view your technology as a gateway to fame, power and riches. You will be expendable if you don't give them what they want. The fear mongers are the real danger. Their fear will be infectious and that will lead to unpredictable chaos. The sooner you can get this thing airborne the better. I know a location with the right tools where you can finish repairs with no interference. Worry about everything else after we're out of here!"

Gavin asked a few more questions and Dexter nodded agreement.

"Dexter thinks he can get the ship flyable sooner as long as we stay at low altitude. It will take about three to four hours to fix the necessary systems."

"Good. Gavin, if you oversee the repairs, the rest of us will finish putting the bodies on board and clean-up to avoid attracting attention. Victoria can bring some supplies," John stated.

Uh, Dad?" David said rejoining them. "They have a weird sick bay. It has stuff like you can't imagine and Aycana says the only person who knew how to use it was killed by the pirates. The only other person that even knows how to turn it on is Siyana and her condition is worsening."

"So, get our first aid kit." John said.

"That's just it. I thought it was in the truck but it's missing. It's still at home."

"Great, you'd better go get it. I'll call and ask Victoria to come help," John said.

"Yes, sir," David said taking off for the truck.

Noticing the dark clouds moving in and the wind picking up, John checked the weather forecast on his cell phone then gave his wife a call.

"Victoria, just calling to let you know the boys and I are fine."

"That's nice. Did you bag a deer?" she asked excitedly.

"Not exactly. An aircraft made an emergency landing in the field behind Buckner's woods and they need our help with repairs."

"Anyone hurt?" Victoria asked.

"Uhh, well, uhh," John hesitated not to say too much over the phone. He knew Victoria would not believe his story unless she saw it. "One could use your help. David left the first aid kit behind so he is coming to get it. Five others are a little exhausted from the ordeal. Could you whip up something to eat? I'm sure they're famished. You can come back with David."

"Sure, I'll be glad to help. See you in a bit." Victoria said ending the call.

The thunderstorm passed on leaving a misty drizzle. Another thunderstorm rumbled in the distance. Standing at the top of the ramp expecting Victoria's arrival, John smiled. . The roaring of a pickup truck's engine announced Victoria's arrival. As the truck came to a stop at the bottom of the ramp an awestruck Victoria sat staring at the craft.

"What do you think?" John asked while helping Victoria out of the truck.

Victoria blurted, "No one is going to believe this!"

"You'd be surprised," John said.

Exiting the driver's side, David laughed. "I bet the Coast to Coast fans would."

"Let's get out of the rain, another storm is coming," John said pointing up the ramp.

Once at the top of the ramp, Victoria noticed the five long plastic bags nearby. The bloodstain on one of them caught her attention. Visibly shaken, Victoria could barely speak. "What … what happened?"

Before John could answer, David unzipped one of the bags.

Victoria shrieked. "What did you do?"

"David!" John shouted.

David realized his mistake, "I'm sorry, I wasn't thinking,"

Victoria shuddered, "David, don't ever do that to me again!

'John, what have you done?" Victoria shrieked.

John looked her in the eyes. "Victoria, calm down. They are Gamoran pirates who badly beat one of the women and were about to execute all of them. There was no choice. We had to —"

A voice behind them interrupted, "John and your sons had to kill them or my sisters, Dexter, and I would most certainly be dead by now."

Victoria turned around to discover two strangers, half way up the ramp behind her. A rather handsome young man reached out to take her hand. As he did so he gave a slight bow and kissed the back of her hand.

"I am Ambassador Gavin Toburg of the planet, Cassaria. We are most humbly appreciative of their bravery."

However, the tall, gaunt, masked man behind him captured Victoria's attention. He reminded her of something out of a 1950's horror movie. It was all too much at one time. Victoria let out a piercing scream then fainted into John's arms.

John managed to catch her and sat her down on a near-by container. He shook her a few times before she regained consciousness. He gently whispered in her ear, "Honey, everything is OK. We're all safe."

"This is just too much at one time," Victoria said.

"I'm so sorry if we frightened you," Gavin said.

"Yes, the ambassador can be a very engrossing figure," Dexter innocently noted.

Victoria studied Dexter's face for a moment. Now she saw the man behind the mask differently. She sensed a man covering his own pain barely aware of how people saw him.

Victoria laughed at the accidental humor. "Gross is the proper word to use but we'll leave it there, big guy."

"As you wish, madam," Dexter nodded.

"John, we need more time to get the ship air worthy. Our best guess is it will take eight more hours to make reliable repairs. We're finding more damage as we go," Gavin explained."

"With the thunder storms approaching I think we are safe for now. I doubt they would fly drones into such weather," John said.

"If they do, our jamming system will blind them. Your technology is primitive to ours. They might get a general location fix but nothing more," Gavin smugly replied.

"I see. Is there anything we can do to help?" John asked.

"Not really. We just don't want any visitors for now," Gavin said.

John nodded agreement. "I think we can handle that with our … primitive means," John said.

A forward hatch opened and Aycana and Jonathan entered the cargo bay.

Gavin pretended not to notice John's irritation, however he just couldn't ignore the pain in his shoulder. "How is Siyana?"

Aycana noticed the flinch as she placed her hand on Gavin's shoulder. "So how did that happen and why didn't you tell us about it?"

Gavin tried to brush it off. "It's nothing and there is way too much to do right now. Now, how is Siyana?"

"She's stable for now but I can't figure out how to use the medical equipment," Aycana said while continuing to inspect Gavin's wound.

"You mean two of you are injured?" Victoria asked.

John nodded. "She got roughed up pretty bad by the Gamoran pirates. He caught a ricochet from one of the pirates. He'll live but both should see a doctor."

"I can take her to the hospital," Victoria offered.

Gavin and Aycana looked nervously at each other. "That is not acceptable," Gavin said. "We must stay together."

John sensed they were not trusted quite yet. "Gavin, she could have internal bleeding for all we know. She needs medical help and so do you."

"Could Susan help?" Victoria asked.

"Who is Susan?" Gavin inquired.

"Susan is our daughter and fourth year medical student. She's really smart. I wish we could do better but with the hospital ruled out, she is the best option we have at the moment," Victoria said. "I can call her but it could be a couple of hours before she gets here."

"All right," Gavin nodded, "that will have to do."

Victoria pulled out her cell phone. "OK, I'll make the call."

John nodded agreement. "OK, folks, we need a volunteer as a lookout covering the south end of the road."

Jonathan volunteered, "I'll take it."

"Great, we need another lookout post on the hilltop on the other side of the field to detect unwelcome visitors from that direction."

Aycana raised her hand, "I'll do it."

"Thanks, Aycana. I appreciate the spirit," John smiled. "David, you get the north end of the road.

David nodded agreement. Then his eyes lit up. "Hey, I got an idea. How about we take the Road Closed signs from Edison Street, and put them at each end of the road? That way we only need one lookout post and can get back to the ship faster if we need to bug out."

"Great idea!" Jonathan said.

"You and Jonathan can work on that. It won't stop the authorities but it should help keep locals away or at least slow them down. If you spot anything suspicious contact me on the radio net," John explained.

Victoria looked confused. "Why are you worried about people finding us?"

"I think our government will act with their best interest in mind before the interests of our friends. That can be good or bad. Do you want to find out the hard way or control the meeting on our terms? No doubt authorities around the world are flooded with UFO sightings. Despite Gavin's jamming, once the thunderstorms pass, we can expect the authorities to go into a full search mode. It's all a matter of time," John explained.

"OK, I get that," Victoria said. "So, what has that got to do with us anymore?"

John paused for a moment before answering. "This is a game changing event for mankind. We are in the middle of it. The technology in this ship and what our friends know will change everything on Earth. Some people will do anything to possess this knowledge, or, out of fear, destroy it.

'Victoria, our new friends are not the only ones in danger. We're the good Samaritans who just killed five alien pirates and captured another. As strange as it seems, we saved people from another planet who still need our help. I don't believe we can turn our backs on them. The way I see it we still have a Christian duty to protect them. When word gets around we helped them, we'll be targets for information too. Whether anyone likes it or not, we are in this together for the time being."

Victoria shuddered. "John, what have you gotten us into?"

John shook his head. "Quite frankly, my dear, I have no clue. All I can do is trust God and follow his lead."

CHAPTER 2

Frantically a hand fumbled in the dark, searching for the lamp switch as the phone continued ringing on the nightstand. An alarm clock thumped onto the floor and a glass of water nearly tipped over. Finally, the hand found the ringing phone and picked it up.

"Whoever you are, this had better be extremely important!" National Security Advisor, Russell Long warned.

"Sir," the White House aide replied. "NASA just notified the chief of staff of an incident in space. The space station crew reports a firefight between five UFOs..."

Russ bolted out of bed and again fumbled around trying to turn on the nightstand light.

"Ouch!" he yelped as he blindly stubbed his foot against the stand.

"Mr. Long, are you all right?" the aide inquired.

"Yes, yes, I'm all right." Russ painfully groaned. "Has President Leatham been informed yet?"

"Yes, sir. Chief of Staff Edward Cox informed President Leatham a few minutes ago. The president is calling an emergency meeting with key members of the administration.

'We are giving you a head start to get here and get up to speed on the event. He wants you to do the briefing in one hour."

"OK, gather all the video, pictures, transcripts, intel, whatever we have, and have it ready for me when I arrive. I'll be there in less than thirty minutes," Russ replied as he hung up the phone and replaced the clock on the nightstand. It was 4:00 a.m.

Ten minutes later Russ raced to the apartment lobby still trying to get an arm through one of the sleeves of his sport coat. His flapping sleeve caught on the door with a ripping sound jerking him backwards knocking him to the floor with a heavy thud. Russ grumbled to himself as he stumbled back to his apartment for another sport coat.

Two building security guards manning the residential tower's security camera console burst out laughing.

"Once a nerd, always a nerd," the first guard quipped.

"Dr. Long gets caught on that door at least once a week. You'd think he would have figured it out by now," the second guard jeered as he handed his partner a five spot. "Bet ya double or nothing he doesn't do it again for the next week."

"You're on!" the first guard snickered. "He's not the only slow learner around here."

As Russ drove to the White House his mind was more focused on the news than the road. *This could be the most important event in human history. If handled right, it could lead to a second term landside for the whole party in the upcoming election. It would certainly be a feather in my career cap too.* The thought of having a treasure trove of technology and information that could put the United States light years ahead of the rest of the world was intoxicating.

With less than an hour to prepare his briefing, Russ was ushered into the meeting room by Chief of Staff, Edward Cox. Vice President, Gary Koppel; Secretary of Defense, Larry Longstreet; Chairman, Joint Chief of Staff, General Raymond Turnbull; and Central Intelligence Agency Director, Mike Richards were already seated. Everyone stood when President Leatham entered.

"Please be seated," President Leatham gestured. "Russ, what do we know so far about our UFOs."

"Mr. President, at 2:55 a.m. Eastern Standard Time, the space station crew observed and videoed five alien ships in and around Earth's orbit. Four of the ships destroyed each other in a firefight, but a fifth larger ship sustained damage and struggled to maintain orbit. It finally entered Earth's atmosphere where visual sighting was lost."

The president interrupted, "Do we have the video footage?"

"Yes, Mr. President. This is the footage recorded by Major Adam Eastman who was just wrapping up a spacewalk when the event occurred.

'His helmet camera footage is about all the footage that exists."

The NASA footage of the battle sequence came up on the large screen. When the video was done playing the president asked for a replay and a third. Once satisfied he signaled Russ to resume the briefing.

"A trail of jammed radar showed the ship's general flight path to south central Michigan. For a few seconds during a severe storm it reappeared on local radar in Jackson, Michigan. NASA believes this alien ship possibly crash landed west of Jackson. They are requesting to send a team to investigate. Time is of the essence. I suggest we keep this out of the press for now. However, with NASA's history of leaks I suggest someone else do the investigation for now," Russ concluded.

"Wow! I never dreamed..." Vice President Koppel stammered as he fell back into his soft leather chair. The room fell silent as everyone gathered their composure.

"You're right," President Leatham agreed. "Suggestions?"

"Sir, we must find these visitors, discover their intentions and secure the ship ASAP!" Secretary Longstreet urged. "We need a total news blackout on this event until we have some answers. We have to get on top of this."

Edward Cox nodded agreement, "If the press wants a comment, we remind them that the tabloids have printed bloodsucking space monster stories for decades. We'll investigate and inform the public when we have all the facts."

"I like that approach," President Leatham said.

"Mr. President, I suggest the Air Force Office of Special Investigations handle the investigation. They can put together an investigation team out of Selfridge Air National Guard Base in the area within a couple of hours and are better equipped to keep things under wraps." General Turnbull added.

"Perfect," the president agreed. "The Air Force OSI will handle the investigation. It will keep leaks to a minimum. If this is for real, I don't want this technology getting into the wrong hands.

'I leave for the G-20 summit in Moscow this afternoon, which will give me a chance to talk to the Russian president. If I cancel the trip it will alarm the press and public."

"Mr. President, do we really need the Russians? After all it did land on American soil." Russell implored.

"I see your point. However, we share the space station, so Russia already knows and will not be silent if we freeze them out. We can promise to work together and share any technology from the space debris. Let me be clear, what lands on American soil stays in American hands. It has to be absolutely secured air tight.

'I want a plan of action for securing the ship and technology. I also want a proposal dealing with exploiting and developing any technology and avoid destabilization effects both internationally and domestically. The chief of staff will task the various agencies for their input.

'I'll call President Speerov before I leave to set the tone of our meeting."

Russell was irritated with the decision. "What about the Germans, French and Chinese? Do we give them everything too?

The CIA Director interjected, "Good question. The new French and German leadership need to get past their knee-jerk opposition to everything NATO members propose. The Chinese provide their pawns the cover to acquire nuclear weapons and terrorize peaceful people. They are not trustworthy on any issue."

"I agree," the president concluded. "China needs to abandon its bullying and thieving behavior.The new governments of France and Germany can't forge military ties to China and expect us to trust them any better than China. They made a conscious decision and with it comes consequences. I'd rather destroy all the technology than a single piece of it fall into evil hands. Am I understood?" President Leatham looked around the room at each person to make his point.

"Gary, as the V.P., I want you to oversee this while I'm gone. Everyone is to give full cooperation and support. The Director of Homeland Security is in California and will need to be briefed. Folks, I stress again, no leaks! Keep need to know to the barest minimum."

Everyone agreed and the meeting ended. As Director Richards was leaving the president took him aside.

"Mike, send your best team to Michigan. Be on guard for foreign interests showing up. Your agents must make first contact at all costs. Do whatever you have to do to keep the UFO technology secure. I'll brief Vice President Koppel but no one else is to know of this plan.

'Once the press is told the Air Force is investigating the UFO it will become a circus, let the OSI be the decoy."

"Yes, Mr. President, I understand. Fortunately, my best team is undercover in Toronto. They have a plane at their disposal. We can have them on scene in two or three hours."

"Toronto?" President Leatham asked with a surprised look. "It's part of a legitimate mission with Canadian Intelligence. The rest you don't want to know for now, trust me."

The loneliness on the bridge combined with the lightening, and thunder were hypnotic as John starred out the bridge view ports. Memories of those who died while he survived came back. The faces of each and every one of them cried out and pleaded not to be forgotten. *How could I forget?* John told himself. *I know each and every person's name and face. I won't commit the mortal sin of forgetting them.* Quickly he closed the closet door in his mind to prevent anyone seeing into this secret place.

As the storm tapered off, John slowly regained his senses. The two hours of wind and pouring rain had given way to fine droplets of water now trickling down the canopy. John sighed in relief as he returned to going over maps planning their escape route to Nevada. The low cloud cover and mist made it more difficult for discovery by locals but not by drones and satellites.

John was well aware of Air Force drone and satellite capabilities but those assets have to be moved to a general area to be of use. That bought some time but not much. Only the severe storm could help to hold them off. Once their location was discovered things were definitely going to get rough.

Thoughts of fight or flight were quickly dismissed. Their only real hope was getting airborne. A fight of any kind would be unacceptable unless fired upon first. The road barriers succeeded in detouring the couple of cars attempting to access the dirt road. Aycana, David and Jonathan monitored potential approaches. Dexter, Deze and Estron continued making progress on repairs. With Gavin's wounded shoulder, supervising was all he could do. Siyana continued resting in sick bay.

Meanwhile, Victoria returned home to gather clothing, blankets and food supplies. Once discovered, a circus of government officials, marauding press and souvenir hunters would descend on the tranquil neighborhood. John shuddered at the thought of what would happen to his friends and wonderful neighbors. The only thing he could do was leave them in absolute ignorance. It was their best protection. Victoria and John realized a meeting with authorities was inevitable but wanted it at a time and place of their choosing. Controlling the situation was paramount to everyone's safety.

Our whole family must be together to prevent anyone being used as a bargaining chip. Victoria decided, *I must persuade Susan to come home but how? Tell the truth about the UFO's and aliens? No! How about a family emergency? After all, there was a shooting and several bodies! Siyana could use some attention too. Yes, that will do nicely.* She made the call.

With the worst of the storm past, Victoria was sliding the last box of food supplies onto the pickup bed. Susan eased her compact car onto the gravel driveway. She jumped out, rushed over and hugged her mother. A fourth-year medical student in Toledo, Ohio, Susan had chestnut brown shoulder length hair, dark brown eyes, a slight athletic build and an extremely intelligent mind.

"Mom, what's this big emergency," Susan blurted staring at the truck loaded with supplies. "You said something about a shooting! Why all the groceries? You said something about a weird accident? Where is everyone? Mom, what's going on…?"

"Hey! Slow down, girl. Grab your bags and hop in. I'll explain on the way." Victoria said.

Minutes later, the truck pulled up to the ramp of the alien craft.

Susan, who had been listening incredulously at her mother's story, now sat speechless staring in disbelief at the space ship.

"O… K! Now, I believe you," Susan conceded.

"Don't feel alone. I didn't believe your father at first either. I thought he was out of his mind until I saw this for myself."

"People are going to go bonkers when they hear about this!" Susan exclaimed.

"That's why we have to get out of here. It's not going to be safe for any of us," Victoria cautioned.

John appeared at the top of the ramp and welcomed Susan with a big hug.

"Hey, Sunshine! Look what I found. Want to go for a spin?" John teased.

"From the looks of that damage, you didn't pick this thing up at a yard sale, did you? You sure it can fly?" Susan bantered back.

"Ha! Ha! I'll take the truck inside. Victoria can make the introductions. Siyana really needs your help. We're about to go on the ride of our lives," John announced.

"For an hour or two?"

"Sorry, but this ride will be for a few days at best," John nervously smiled.

"Well Dad, I'll meet your new friends, but I am not going anywhere. Can't become a doctor by going on extended joy rides," Susan declared.

"But can't you see it will not be safe for you to stay behind?" her mother asked with deep concern.

John shook his head. "Not now, dear."

"I have dreamed of being a doctor since I was a little girl and nothing is going to take that dream away!"Susan stated emphatically.

Victoria paused for a moment. "You are stubborn. Must have got that trait from your father. No way you got it from me. Well, come meet our friends and see what you can do for Siyana."

Susan agreed, "But I must head back early tomorrow. I have a project that must be completed for my class on Monday."

John cut them off. We can talk about this later. We called you to help with two injured people. Let's take care of that first and talk later, okay?"

The two women nodded.

"Great, Victoria, show Susan to sick bay and our most injured patient. Siyana is our priority for the moment."

Gavin and Dexter entered the bridge finding John still studying maps of Nevada, Idaho and Montana. Seeing an Earthling on his bridge irritated Gavin but he put the thought aside for the moment.

"All temporary repairs are completed for low altitude flight. We'll get under way once Dexter finishes several system checks," Gavin announced.

John smiled "Great, it should be dark in about an hour. You can lift off when ready. I marked your route on the maps. If we follow this course we should avoid detection. Just fly due west out over Lake Michigan at 6000 feet.

'Once you get over the middle of the lake, turn due north. After we enter Canadian airspace, we'll drop down to 300 feet, turn west again. We should stay below 300 feet following the terrain to avoid detection. We call it flying nap of the earth or NOE. Can this bucket handle it?" John teased.

Gavin was visibly annoyed at the question. After looking the maps over, he scanned the data into the navigation computer. Once Gavin punched a command key, a holographic projection appeared next to the Captain's chair.

"Thanks, but with the holo-projector we don't need such primitive maps," Gavin said tossing the maps back to John. "And yes, I will take off when I'm ready and system checks complete."

"Whoa! That is a really cool system how does it work?" John asked ignoring Gavin's slight.

"This is the navigation console, Gavin explained. "Navigation coordinates are set by keypad or touch screen. When in orbit the ship's sensors automatically map the surface and terrain for possible future use. All I have to do is activate the holo-projector and I get a 3D holographic display. It automatically adjusts to altitude and I can control the detail as desired. It is advanced beyond your ability to understand but that is how it works."

"That's fantastic. The route it's projecting flies you directly over three military bases. It sure won't take much to figure out where we're going you think?" John said. "I have no interest in stealing your ship if that's what your worried about. When we get to those coordinates we can contact my dad. He has a machine shop in Lovelock, Nevada. We'll hide the ship in a nearby canyon while he helps with the final repairs."

Gavin sighed, "That's all well and good but we also discovered a very serious problem."

"Really? What's wrong? John calmly asked. "With my primitive mind, I'll try to understand as much as possible."

Gavin grimaced realizing his insult was out of line. "A coolant line to the warp engines ruptured. We fixed the line, but all the warp drive coolant is gone. Earth hasn't developed the technology yet to even make it. We only have sub-light capability. Getting back home is now impossible."

"One problem at a time, good friend. For now, let's just get you to Nevada. OK?" John reasoned.

"Yea, one problem at a time," Gavin winced as Dexter began his system checks. "By the way, the road signs are working. That was clever."

"Thanks. That was David's idea. The hand of providence is amazing," John declared. "Out of curiosity if your father is king, are you and your sisters more properly prince and princesses?"

Gavin shooked his head. "A year after my mother's death father remarried. His second wife gave birth to Aycana, Estron and Siyana. Father called them his jewels. Though we are children of the king, the throne is not inherited. The king's wife retains the title of queen because of her many duties of state but the rest of us have no titles except the ones we earn.

'The Council of Unity elects the king for life unless removed by a no confidence vote for failure to protect the people. The title of king is an ancient one but now only allows him to command the military and cast tie-breaking votes on the Council. They make sure he never has to cast his vote. Because of tradition the public holds the kingship in high esteem and expects him to make appearances and periodically address them on issues of public interest. There hasn't been a planetary war in two hundred years, so the kingship has become largely ceremonial. That is until the pirates came along.

'In the past, the Council of Unity regarded the pirates as a nuisance and just bribed them off. After the attack on the planet Holcron two years ago, my father persuaded a majority of the Council to stop the tribute payments. A very heated debate ensued and I'm afraid father made many unforgiving enemies."

"So how long was this diplomatic mission to last?" John asked.

"General Tayer, father's best friend and advisor, proposed I lead the mission to Tigra as a show of trust and give me some experience.

'My sisters were added to the mission at the last moment. Looking back, I think Father was trying to protect us from dangers on Cassaria. This was my first diplomatic mission and I really messed it up.

'The pirates intercepted our ship and took us hostage. They not only demanded a ransom for our freedom, but tripled the tribute as well. This kidnapping was meant to greatly undermine my father's support. I have no doubt some Council members are scheming to replace my father. We have no idea where the pirates plan to take our ship or why we should be near your planet. Earth is so distant from the other inhabited planets it makes no sense. Earth is the last place to ever look for us," Gavin explained.

"Maybe that is exactly what someone wants. Is there a connection between the pirates and a faction of the Council of Unity?" John asked.

Gavin continued, "There are rumors to that effect but, unfortunately, I have no evidence of such a link. Our captors even made a few comments of such a conspiracy. Without proof though, we can do nothing.

'I have no doubt Father has spies and ships looking for us. Until we are free, he dares not confront the pirates or expose the traitors. Conversely, if he pays the ransom and tribute, he will be removed from office in which case they will have no further need of us."

"I see," John said trying to put the pieces together. "If it wasn't the Cassarian military last night, who was trying to rescue you?"

Gavin smiled, "Pirates manned those corvettes. One of our crew betrayed us to the pirates leading to our capture. Afterwards the traitor was executed along with all the crew except Dexter. Fortunately for Dexter, they did not know he was a pirate hunter. Because he is a highly skilled engineer on the ship's unique engines and support systems they spared him.

'The pirate flagship loaded their cargo onto our ship a couple of weeks ago while they went on another mission. The corvettes were left to escort us the rest of the way to Earth and wait until the pirate flagship arrives. We are supposed to rendezvous with another ship where the four of us will be sold into slavery and the cargo transferred. In desperation, I devised a plan to free us.

'I bribed two of the corvette crews to destroy the other corvettes. The surviving corvette crews would help us overcome the pirates on this ship. The plan failed."

"What went wrong?" John asked.

"Well," Gavin winced. "Their targeting was awful. All four corvettes were destroyed in the firefight. The plan quickly unraveled from there.

'After being forced to land on Earth, all I could do was wait for an opportunity to overpower my guard. That was when all of you showed up. The rest you know."

"Sorry the plan didn't work so hot. We were glad to be of assistance though," John smiled.

David's excited voice boomed over the radio net. "Hey, Dad! A dark blue step van is creeping down Cochran Road! It has some short antennas on top!"

"That's it folks. This is not good. Everyone get back to the ship fast!" John replied.

"Gavin, we really need to get moving. As soon as everyone gets aboard, I strongly suggest you take off," John urged.

"I understand." Gavin took the pilot's seat and began buckling himself in. "Dexter…"

"All equipment is stowed away. Already canceling system checks and powering up the reactor to full power," Dexter hurriedly pushed a series of buttons at the engineering station. "Let's hope she holds together! Engines will be on line in less than two minutes."

In sick bay, Siyana pointed out the locations of pain on her side and chest where she was kicked several times, as Susan examined her.

"Siyana, you need to get lots of rest, OK?" Susan urged.

"I don't have an x-ray machine but you probably have a couple cracked ribs and a couple more bruised."

"Yes, I think I need to lay down here for a bit. Thank you for taking care of me," Siyana said as she winced from a spasm of pain.

"You have some really neat equipment here. You know how to use it?" Susan asked.

"Not really," Siyana said. "The computer is not that hard and if you tell it what is wrong it will direct the recommended treatment, but I don't know how to use the diagnostic equipment or grasp all the nano cell technology. It's very new and the pirates killed the only person who knew how to use it. If you want to try figuring it out go ahead."

"Thanks, I'll give it a try," Susan replied.

"So how did all of you end up on Earth?" Victoria asked.

Siyana explained. "Three months ago, we were sent on a diplomatic mission to Prime Minister Nikola Penasee of the planet Tigra. We were captured by the pirates. Gavin came up with a crazy escape plan but it failed. I thought we were all going to die. Thankfully your husband and sons rescued us.

'All of us are good pilots but no combat experience. This was our first deep space mission. Our lack of experience got us in trouble and most of the crew killed. I can still see the look in the captain's eyes when the pirates executed him. It haunts me every night..."

"Siyana," Susan interrupted. "It wasn't your fault. Pirates murdered them, not you. Don't blame yourself for what evil people do.

Gavin's voice announced over the ship speakers, "Everyone strap yourself in for emergency takeoff."

Susan rushed for the exit. "Mom, I have to get off now! I can't possibly go! I have ..."

Victoria grabbed her and pulled her to the nearest seat.

"I'm sorry Susan. There is nothing we can do now. We'll sort this out later when we meet your grandpa in Nevada," Victoria reassured her.

"I can't go!" Susan cried out in frustration. As Victoria struggled to strap her in, Susan felt her life's dream shatter and her future out of control. There was nothing she could do as the seatbelt and her world tighten around her.

OSI Special Agent Raya Alomar drove the step van slowly down the dirt road while Special Agent, Nicholas Hill, electronically surveyed the area. The equipment would detect any large metal objects or electronic signals within range of a half mile. Even at that range, there were plenty of large twisted sheets of metal roofing, metal roofed buildings, discarded appliances, derelict farm equipment and vehicles cluttering his screen. Increasingly heavy rain and now, lightening, prevented the use of low altitude drones. Still, he knew he was on the right track.

According to radar and a few phone calls from residents to law enforcement, the UFO had to be in this general area. Orders were to quietly secure physical evidence and investigate the UFO site. Any aliens or persons involved were to be taken into protective custody. Driving up and down every dirt road in the township seemed like a waste of time to Raya.

"Raya, turn right onto Cougar Road up ahead and stop while I adjust the ground signal," Nicholas directed.

Raya slowed to a stop. Blocking the dirt road to the right was a "Road Closed" sign. Nicholas looked at his map then at the sign.

"What the…? This is Cougar Road but the sign says Edison Street. Something isn't right. Go around it. Let's see what's up ahead."

"You got it," Raya replied.

"Raya, there is a gigantic metal object up ahead! Either someone erected a huge metal building in the middle of a field or we have located our UFO. On the left about a third of a mile ahead!"

"There is a turnout ahead and lots of fresh tire tracks too," she announced.

"Take it!" Nicholas replied.

Daylight was fading quickly but the fresh tire tracks were easy to follow. In the distance the agents heard a low but steadily increasing whine reminiscent of multiple jet engines powering up. Raya stepped on the gas knocking Nicholas off his feet and throwing him into the equipment in the back of the van. Mud spewed in every direction as the van struggled to gain ground.

"Remind me to requisition off road tires when we get back to the office," Nicholas quipped struggling to his feet. The van whipped past the woods, and swerved right. Crashing through a metal gate, the van came to an abrupt halt. The van's spinning tires began digging deep into the muddy field.

David and Aycana could hear the racing engine of the approaching van as they reached the loading ramp. Jonathan was running as fast as he could but his heavy hunting boots and the slippery mud made for a comical race to beat the approaching van.

"Come on, Jonathan! You can make it! Hurry up, they're almost here!" David and Aycana shouted.

Splash! Jonathan's feet flew up in the air as he landed flat on his back in a mud puddle a few yards from the ramp.

Jonathan struggled to get up only to fall flat on his face. In desperation, he started crawling the short distance to the ramp. David and Aycana rushed to his rescue, each grasping a muddy arm to help him to his feet.

All three raced to the ramp as David laughed at his brother, "You run like a dork in those boots!"

"Good observation, Sherlock!" Jonathan replied as they reached the top of the ramp. He removed one boot. As he held it upside down water gushed out. "You try running in water filled boots in that muck."

Straight ahead a huge spaceship, reminiscent of a giant wingless space shuttle, hovered while retracting its landing pads. Nicholas jumped out of the van frantically flashing his OSI badge. Racing after the spaceship, he slipped in the mud and fell flat on his face.

The ramp to the ship was closing but Nicholas could clearly see a young man covered in mud laughing and waving good-bye. *Whoever is flying the ship is obviously not very impressed with my badge.* Nicholas grimaced watching the spaceship disappear in the dark clouds.

Rushing back to the van, Nicholas radioed base command post. "Command post. This is OSI Agent Nicholas Hill. We need a scramble in pursuit of a UFO over Jackson County heading due west. You should be seeing it on you radar now. Also request recording the radar tracking data for later review. Also send a tow truck. We're up to the axle in mud."

"Roger, Agent Hill. We are tracking now and will have two fighters scrambled in fifteen minutes."

"Fellas, at the rate that ship is moving, good luck catching them."

Once airborne, David and Aycana arrived on the bridge and took seats to watch the action. John carefully watched every move Gavin and Dexter made at the controls.

When it came time to drop down below 300 ft. and fly NOE nothing happened.

John cleared his throat to get Gavin's attention. "Before you turn west you must drop down to fly NOE or they will easily find us and attack."

"I told you we don't need your advice. Our shields can protect us from any attack your people can throw at us." Gavin snapped.

"Actually, that is not accurate," Dexter declared. "Without coolant, our reactor is not able to go warp. It can only keep the shields up at half strength for a very short time without over heating the system in atmospheric conditions. That would not be healthy for us. We will have no problem using the ship's auto-pilot to fly NOE."

"All right, do what John says," Gavin grimaced.

John smiled and continued to explain, "By now the Air Force has scrambled fighters in an attempt to intercept us. Once you drop below radar, they will hopefully assume we are still heading to Canada. This should cause momentary confusion as the Canadians debate granting flyover permission or scramble their fighters to pick us up. By then, we'll be long gone. You have to fly nap of the earth the whole way. They will never find us until we want to be found."

"That is clever, but that location is in the middle of barren mountains. How will we get repairs there?" Aycana asked.

"That's the easy part," David assured her. "My Grandpa's machine shop is there. If he can't fix it, you're toast."

"Is he that good?" Aycana asked.

"Yep, Grandpa has a saying, 'If it doesn't fit, get a bigger hammer.' You've got nothing to worry about," David proudly reassured Aycana.

Dexter, Gavin and Aycana had a look of horror on their faces, but the Braxtons broke out laughing.

"Don't worry, Gavin, Dad will get you fixed as good as new," John promised.

By midnight the Mobile Response Command Center (MRCC) team arrived at the UFO landing site. Agents Hill and Alomar cordoned off the area, while others setup floodlights, power generator, the command center and canopies over evidence to protect from the rain. Nicholas was not surprised to learn that the UFO was lost on radar and the scrambled fighters never made contact.

Agent Philip Blackmund arrived with the MRCC team

and began mapping every piece of evidence on his computer in the command center. When finished, he gathered the other two agents together.

"We are beginning to form a picture of what transpired. Tire tracks are of a well-known manufacturer, commonly used on pickup trucks. It appears the vehicle came and went from the site at least three times. One set of tracks end where the craft's ramp touched the ground.

'Where the bottom of the ramp would have been, a myriad of footprints, two shotgun shells and four blood-soaked areas were discovered but no bodies. Samples of blood were collected for analysis. Several shoe and boot casts were made but there was so much movement in the area it is hard to tell at this point how many people were at the site."

"So where did the truck come from?" Raya asked.

Agent Blackmund smiled. "That is a good question. The tire tracks are most likely from a pickup truck, and the fact it came and went a few times, shotgun shells, and it's hunting season, I suspect some local hunters came across the UFO."

"We will need to do a house by house search. I bet we find mud tracks in someone's drive that match these tire tracks," Nicholas surmised.

"We will start searching the western and northern sectors, then cover the eastern and southern sectors," Raya announced.

"Sounds good," Agent Hill agreed. "Agent Blackmund, take the evidence back to base for further processing and keep us posted."

A security police sergeant approached the OSI agents. "We found something you need to come see."

"We're kind of busy at the moment, Sergeant. Take a couple of photos, tag it and bag it for now, please?" Raya replied.

The sergeant motioned them to follow. "I don't think that's going to work."

The agents followed him to the edge of the field where a couple of airmen were setting up a floodlight. When the light came on everyone stood in awe.

"You're right, sergeant. We're not going to bag that any time soon," Nicholas said staring at a four-foot diameter maple tree.

About fifteen feet up the trunk was a deer stand with a fresh two-inch hole burned through the side of the stand and into the trunk.

"I doubt that is a natural anomaly," he stated.

Lynn Jung Lee's instructions were to follow the MRCC convoy from the base. I wonder how my handler knew that piece of information? Lynn asked on her first assignment.

When the convoy stopped at a traffic light, she pulled up beside the last vehicle, reached out and attached a small magnetic tracking device to its side. It was easy to hang back a mile or two and follow them to the UFO landing site. Taking advantage of the initial confusion in the darkness, she had no problem planting her listening device. The electronic bug attached to the MRCC trailer was working superbly. Lynn Jung Lee, with little effort, now knew about as much as the American agents.

Driving around the local area, Lynn discovered muddy tracks leading to a driveway, but no pickup truck. Cautiously, she drove past the house twice. Seeing nothing to alarm her, she drove up to the house and knocked on the door several times. No one answered. She walked around the back of the house and peered through a window. Seeing no one, Lynn deftly picked the lock to the back door.

The pantry and refrigerator were empty giving the impression the occupants would not be back anytime soon. Lynn found an email on the office computer indicating the family planned to visit a brother in Canada the next day. Beside the computer, a file basket held mail addressed to John and Victoria Braxton. She snapped pictures of the family portraits. The message app. showed the last message was made to a George Desjardin in Trenton, Ontario.

Suddenly the phone rang. After three rings a voice message began, "You've reached the Braxton residence. We are not available to take your call right now. Please leave your number after the tone. If this is George, see you soon with a big surprise."

She was headed to the master bedroom when she heard a knock on the front door. Lynn pressed herself up against the wall next to the door and carefully peeked out the window.

At the door was a middle-aged man in blue jeans, a flannel lined canvas jacket and John Deere baseball cap. He called out, "Hey anybody home!" He knocked twice more then stuck a piece of paper to the door. After the car pulled out of the drive, Lynn checked the note. The note read, "I'll be by shortly to harvest the corn in your field."

Time to leave. I have all I need to find them in Canada. Lynn carefully made sure no signs of her presence were left behind.

CIA Agent Jeff "Slick" Prewitt and his partner Agent Roberta "Cat" Saunders spotted Lynn when she planted the bug on the command post trailer. A vehicle license check revealed valid plates, her name and address. It didn't take long for Langley to relay all he needed to know about her.

Lynn Jung Lee, a Hong Kong native, came to the United States to obtain her automotive engineering degree. She later landed a job with General Motors in Detroit, Michigan.

She was likely recruited and trained as a sleeper agent twelve years ago before re-entering the country under a work visa. Slick smiled like the fox about to toy with a field mouse.

"Well, Cat! The game is a foot and we have home field

advantage. Why would the Chinese use an untested sleeper to work alone on such a vital mission or is she just the first of more to come?"

Cat licked her lips. "I don't know but she's all mine to take down."

They followed Lynn to the Braxton home. Slick didn't want Lynn getting too nosy in the house so he decided to rattle her cage a bit. While Cat placed a locator device underneath Lynn's passenger seat, he sauntered up to the front door, knocked several times before sticking a note to the door.

When Lynn drove off, Cat used the tracking device to follow at a distance while leaving Slick behind.

Slick entered the house the same way as Lynn and carefully worked his way through the house. He noticed a small Canadian flag in a room with a drafting table and computer station. As he looked around the room he saw a Ph.D. in Architecture diploma hanging on the wall for Victoria Desjardin. There was a note pad with a Canadian phone number and e-mail address. A search of the computer showed a recent message about an upcoming trip to Canada.

In the boys' room were two pictures of them in a desert mountain area on ATVs with a person Slick assumed was their grandfather.

Opening the phone bill on the desk with his folding knife, he noticed the Canadian phone number was not listed. However, several calls were to Lovelock, NV. He photographed the bills, and returned them to the basket.

Slick's cell phone vibrated. New message: John Braxton former Air Force officer, Canadian wife, Victoria, whose brother works for Canadian Agriculture Department in Trenton, Ontario. They have two sons, Jonathan and David, one daughter, Susan, grandfather, Henry Braxton, owns Desert Metal, a machine shop in Lovelock, Nevada.

Slick texted back: "Braxtons and friends could be going to either Trenton, Ontario, Canada or Lovelock, NV." He also included the addresses. A moment later another text message instructed him to await further instructions.

A further search of the house revealed the lack of household supplies and an empty gun safe. Slick noticed a cabinet with several martial arts trophies and a picture of a college age girl. "Hello Susan. I guess you know how to take care of yourself."

Family photos lined the living room walls giving him faces to go with the names. A book case held a variety of literature on different topics but were mostly Christian based. On a second larger bookcase were a collection of military books on history and theory. Slick spotted a Bible on the coffee table. It was Victoria's personal Bible. *Odd, they seem like devout Christians so why would she leave her Bible behind?* Bookmarked at Isaiah 55 were two pictures. One picture showed John, his two sons and the grandfather, standing in a desert landscape with a mountain range in the distance. The other picture showed two boys with their grandfather on ATVs in the same desert mountains.

He called Cat. "Break contact and come get me."

Slick grabbed the Bible before leaving the house. *I'll bring it along. It could make introductions easier when we find them.*

CHAPTER 3

The morning sun peeked above the cold Humboldt Mountains of Nevada painting the sky and desert with glowing shades of gold and copper interspersed with receding slate blue shadows across the valley floor. John could see his breath in the cold crisp air while standing on the ship's ramp spotting for Jonathan as he backed the pickup truck out of the cargo bay. Once on the ground Gavin, Dexter, John and Jonathan gathered to see them off.

"Jonathan, Dexter insists on going with you," John said.

Jonathan winced. "It's bad enough he'll stand out as a stranger but with his mask, he'll stick out like a neon sign?"

"Yep, I said the same thing. He insists on inspecting the quality of Henry's work before letting him help. Keep Dexter out of sight as best you can."

Gavin handed Jonathan a device similar to a large cell phone with a cover. "Here's a flip communicator. It can contact us anywhere, even in orbit. Press the blue star icon and speak my name. This ear bud gives you hands-free communication. Just touch and command "Sync" and then the name of the person you want to speak with."

"Thanks!" Jonathan said slipping it into his jacket pocket. 'Dad, I'll bring the ATVs too."

"We don't need them for now, concentrate on what we need. You have the list."

"A couple of Grandpa's buddies use some army surplus camo as shade cover for their hunting camps. I'll try to borrow as much as I can."

"Some is better than none. We don't need a lot, just enough to hide two security outposts from the air," John said.

"Got it! Catch ya later then," Jonathan waved.

Before Dexter got in the passenger side, Jonathan pulled out his dusty work hat from behind the truck seat and flipped Dexter's jacket collar up. "Dex, put this on and slouch down in the seat when we get to town."

"Thank you, Jonathan Braxton!" Dexter said.

Everyone watched Jonathan and Dexter bounce and rattle across the desert canyon. Once out of sight, John and Gavin returned to the bridge where Aycana began teaching David the flight controls and flying basics.

"When will they get back?" Gavin asked.

"Hopefully before dark," John said. "How much time do you think we have before the pirate flagship arrives?"

Gavin rubbed his chin as he worked the data pad. "I estimate twenty-one days give or take a day or two. Their captain is not known for being punctual."

"Not a lot of time if you think about it. What kind of a ship are we expecting?" John asked.

"Let me show you." Gavin stepped over to the holographic display keyboard, typed in a few commands and a holographic 3D projection of an enormous battle cruiser appeared.

"Wow! That is one huge ship. How did they get their hands on that?" John gasped.

"Two years ago, the pirates attacked the orbital construction yards of the planet, Holcron. It's famed for its spaceship construction. This particular battle cruiser, the *Holcron Star*, was completed but not yet crewed when the pirates attacked. It's the fastest, most powerful ship ever built. The battle was ferocious. Uncle Usus fought like a lion and personally led the counterattack that drove off the pirates."

"Who is Uncle Usus?" John asked.

Gavin smiled. "Excuse me, I mean Admiral Usus Dever. He is High Admiral of the Holcron Navy. Uncle Usus is our godfather. We've always just called him uncle. Usus and my father are closer than brothers. They were the two that created the decoy ship to trap the pirates and free my mother and other Earthlings. "Because of their special friendship our two planets are such close allies"

"I'd like to meet him some day," John said. "Go on."

"Half the pirates were killed and thousands of Holcrons," Gavin continued. "The construction facilities were gutted but worse, many of Holcron's best and brightest scientists, engineers, and experienced crews were butchered before they could even arm themselves.

'Two years later, the Holcrons have not fully recovered. The pirates are more powerful and feared than ever. The ship's normal complement is 300 personnel. In a pinch, they can operate with a skeleton crew of seventy-five for short voyages if nothing major goes wrong."

"That's not much of a crew. Is that all it requires?" John asked.

"Much of the systems are fully automated and maintained by a couple hundred engineering droids. They can easily work in space and around the clock so a larger crew is not required. The longer the voyages, the more stress on the crew and thus the more crew needed especially if the air wing is on board.

'Hangar 1 holds three small or two large armored shuttles along with two freighters the size of this one. A common pirate tactic is to use corvettes to escort captured ships back to their hidden base. Hangar 2 goes the length of the ship and was designed to hold a fighter and bomber wing but the pirates don't have the resources to activate it."

"Lucky for us!" John quipped. "Any combat troops aboard?"

"The *Holcron Star* can also carry a company of 120 space marines plus four more large armored assault shuttles stored in hangar 2. According to this pirate data pad, there are no troops aboard but the armored shuttles are available.

'I estimate the pirates have no more than 150 personnel to run the ship until they return to base. Right now, they are at their weakest, but Cassaria neither knows nor can they do anything about it," Gavin explained.

John scratched his head in deep thought. "I see. Well, if we can land in hangar 1, I believe we can capture it and replenish your coolant. Then you're on the way home."

Gavin was taken aback by the proposal. "How do we dock without getting blasted into space debris?"

John confidently smiled. "If we can get Deze to cooperate, he can claim the corvettes were attacked and destroyed and several crewmembers were killed. Several are still barely alive needing immediate medical attention and request emergency docking. As for capturing the crew, I have to give it more thought. I have faith that problem can be solved too. I know people that might be persuaded to help us with the boarding party."

"Wow!" Gavin exclaimed. "Are all Earthlings as crazy as you?"

John thought for a second. "Most assuredly but without capturing the ship you will never see home, your father will be killed, and Cassaria will be defeated."

"Putting it that way there isn't a choice is there?"Gavin grimaced. "Bottom line is we get them or they get us."

"Precisely!" John nodded.

Over the next two hours, Gavin explained the battle cruiser's layout, docking protocols, security systems, and crew stations throughout the ship.

"So how do we get Deze to cooperate with us?" Gavin asked.

"We can beat it out of him but I'm not into torture, are you?" John grimaced.

Gavin shook his head. "No, I'm not into that either and Dexter would rather kill him outright."

John shrugged his shoulders. "That's the rub, how do we

get him to cooperate?"

Both men fell silent for a moment.

"I got it," Gavin exclaimed. We can't torture him but he doesn't know that. He does fear Dexter so let's use that. We need to pay a visit to the engine room."

When John and Gavin arrived at the reactor room, Estron was finishing replacing a sensor. Deze was nowhere in sight.

John's eyes instantly flashed with anger and his face turned deep red.

"Where is the prisoner?" Gavin growled.

"In the engine room." Estron replied sensing something was wrong.

John rushed into the engine room.

"He is a dangerous prisoner and you are not watching him?" Gavin shouted. "Are you crazy?"

"No!" Estron shot back.

"For all you know, he could be sabotaging the ship. You want stranded on this dump of a planet forever?" Gavin growled.

Estron lowered her head. "No!"

The clanking of tools falling on the deck echoed from the engine room as Deze tumbled through the engine room hatch. As Deze picked himself off the floor, his eyes flashed angrily at John.

John grabbed Deze with both hands by his jacket. "If you think you can sabotage this ship you got another thing coming."

"Mr. Braxton, stop it! He's harmless. Deze is on our side." Estron cried out.

"Yeah, right! Is that why he almost blew a hole in your brother? If I hadn't pushed Gavin out of the line of fire he'd be dead. I doubt you'd be defending him, then would you?" John asked.

"No! I guess not. But he's no danger to us!" Estron cried out.

"Nonsense, his loyalty is with the enemy," Gavin said.

"Listen, if Deze is going to be this much trouble, why not let Dexter finish him off?" John suggested.

Gavin growled. "John is right, we don't have time to mess around with him."

"I can't believe you would kill him," Estron cried out. "That's murder!"

"No, It's justice. He's a pirate in league with those who killed our crew. Estron, until we can trust him we must treat him as a prisoner. He can get us all killed. We must stay alive and get home if we are to somehow save our planet. Do you understand?" Gavin asked.

Estron exhaled a deep breath. "I understand. I will not fail in my duty again."

Deze's anger at John turned to instant fear when he realized what Dexter would do if he had the chance.

"I can be good!" Deze begged. "I don't want to go back to the pirates either. J…j…just give me a ch…ch…chance. I…I…I can help you. Please!"

"Gavin! You know this is wrong, come on!" Estron said.

"Not my planet, not my rules. This one is John's call.

"I've had enough of this drivel," John declared. He grabbed Deze by the back of his jacket collar and pushed him out of the reactor room.

Estron pleaded again. "Mr. Braxton, give Deze a chance, please. You are a better man than this! I know you are!"

"We will talk about Deze's future existence later. For now, I'm locking him up in his quarters," John replied.

Deze's pleas for mercy echoed throughout the cargo bay as John forcibly led him to his quarters.

"Estron, if Deze wants freedom he is going to have to earn it and fast," Gavin warned.

The elderly man dressed in faded blue denim clothes was intently working at the large metal lathe. The noise of the lathe masked the approaching footsteps of two men. They stood patiently silent until the elderly man noticed them and shut the lathe down.

"Well look what the cat dragged in!" the elderly man said.

"Hey Grandpa! How are ya?" Jonathan said giving him a hug.

Seventy-year old Henry, slightly bow legged and sporting a desert tan contrasting his silver hair was not accustomed to surprises in his desert lifestyle. All he needed was a burro to complete his sourdough image.

"Good as ever despite you trying to give me a heart attack. What's wrong, ya can't call ahead anymore?" Henry groused.

"It's a long story, Grandpa, but we couldn't risk calling you."

"Really? Told ya to stay out of trouble. So, who's after ya?"

Jonathan looked around before answering. "I'd rather not discuss it here. You'd never believe it."

"That can't be good!" a shocked Henry replied. "Who is 'we' and what's with the Lone Ranger here?"

"I wish I was kidding. The whole family and a few friends are at Seven Troughs. We really need your help to fix a few things. This is one of our friends, Dexter," Jonathan explained.

Henry smiled reaching out to shake his hand. "Well, welcome to Lovelock. Where ya from?"

Dexter gave the outstretched hand a puzzled look before shaking it. In a deadpan voice he declared, "Mr. Henry, how do you do? I'm from Kysandia. Jonathan failed to tell me you owned a working metalsmith museum. It is very quaint." Without waiting for a reply, he turned away and began exploring the shop.

Jonathan winced at the remark. "Sorry, he doesn't know American customs very well yet."

Henry waved it off. "That's obvious. It always takes a while for foreigners to catch on. So, where's Kysandia anyway? This guy's a little heavy in the drama department don't ya think? Is he one of those unemployed actors from Hollywood or something?"

"That's a long story. I'll explain it all later. I made a list of a few things we need. Oh, and we need the quads too," Jonathan smiled.

Dexter returned from his tour of the shop. "Despite your primitive equipment you do exceptional work, Mr. Henry. If you can assist us we would be most appreciative."

"I'll help under one condition." Henry demanded.

"What is that, Mr. Henry?" Dexter replied in his deadpan demeanor.

"Friends call me Henry."

"As you wish, Mr. Henry!" Dexter replied without emotion, Henry and Jonathan rolled their eyes.

"We got our work cut out for us loosening this guy up!" Henry said raising his eyebrows.

It was after lunch and David was standing guard over Deze as he finished cleaning up the cargo bay.

"Am I doing a good job, sir?" Deze asked.

"So far, yes," David said. "Why?"

"Sir, you are a nice man but your father wants to kill me."

"No, he'd rather not kill you but you give him a reason and he will. Give him a reason not to and he can be your greatest friend. You chose the wrong side. Now you have to earn his respect. Let's take a break," David said.

Confused, Deze replied, "OK, David sir. What would you like me to break?"

"No, no!" David laughed. "I mean rest for a little bit."

"I get it, thank you David sir."

A bit anoyed, David grumbled, "And don't call me 'sir'. I'm not in the military."

Deze nervously lowered his head. "I'm required to address everyone as 'sir' or be shot, sir," Deze replied.

"Deze, I'm not a pirate or military. I have no desire to harm you," David promised. "You seem like a nice guy. I'm only concerned for everyone's safety. Be on your best behavior and I'll treat you as a friend, not a prisoner. OK?

"OK! Are you my friend?" Deze asked excitedly.

"Deze, friends never betray their friends. It's a two-way street. You understand?"

Deze smiled for the first time. It was a big smile and the scars on his face only made the smile more pronounced.

"I like that. I've never had a friend before."

"Well, be a true friend and you will have many more before this is over," David promised. "I've noticed you're a very skilled engineer. How long have you been doing it?"

Deze proudly thumped his chest. "Since I first started walking."

"What?" David asked incredulously.

"I was born on an ore freighter my father owned. It was a piece of space junk so I learned a lot about spaceship engineering and repairs growing up. Six years ago, it broke down and we couldn't repair it. Father put out a distress signal and as our luck would have it a pirate ship responded. They blew up the ship after picking it clean of anything useful including us. My parents later died of a virus and I was only kept around because I knew how to fix things."

"I'm sorry to hear about your parents. I wouldn't worry. Things will get better for you if you're with us, just give it some time." David assured him.

David placed the ear buds to his mp3 player in his ears

and leaned back to relax.

Deze looked puzzled. "I've never seen people put wires in their ears before. What do they do?"

David laughed. "This is a mp3 player. It allows me to listen to my favorite music. The ear buds allow me to hear privately. We have wireless ones but mine broke. I'm just using these until I get new ones. On our world, we have all kinds of music. Don't you listen to music on your world?"

"I don't know. I've never been on my home world of Gamora. As far as I know there is no such thing as music and we definitely don't stick wires in our ears?" Deze replied still trying to comprehend the meaning of music.

"Here, try listening to this. It's country music," David offered as he placed the ear buds in Deze's ears. Deze immediately started tapping his toes on the floor to the beat.

"David, is talking funny part of the music?"

David chuckled, "Some people call it a southern twang and it's not country music without the accent. Dad and Grandpa call it singing hillbilly. You can listen to it for a while if you like."

"Thanks. By the way, can I have my pistol back," Deze asked.

"I seriously doubt it," David answered.

"OK. I noticed Estron carrying it. It belonged to my father. It hasn't worked since I was born. I just carried it as a keepsake."

"Really? I'll ask Dad. If you behave yourself and earn our trust you'll get it back I'm sure. Give it some time, you'll see."

"I understand if he wants to know me better first," Deze sighed. "I'm just worried about Dexter. He stares at me like a dog that can't remember when he ate last."

"Gavin ordered Dexter to leave you alone so we'll just have to trust him for now. OK?"

"O…K!" Deze nervously agreed. "Would you like to see some really cool stuff ?"

"Sure! What ya got?" David asked.

Deze showed David around the cargo bay like a little boy showing off his toys. When they came to three tall stacks of tied down large cargo cases he removed the tie down straps and opened container after container showing off contents of precious gems, rare earth metals, gold and platinum coins from different worlds. David was dumb struck. There was more treasure than he ever imagined. Next, Deze pointed out containers holding hundreds of blaster pistols, rifles, explosives, grenades, and other weapons.

Lastly, Deze opened one of twelve containers resembling very large metal footlockers. It contained fifty violet, florescent glowing crystals, each two-feet long, and eight-inches thick. He gently handed one to David.

"The zannite crystal you're holding is considered more valuable than all the other containers of gems and precious metals together. I'm not sure what the mineral does, but I heard whoever possesses the mineral can rule the galaxy," Deze explained.

David studied it before carefully returning the crystal to its container and sealing it shut. Together they re-attached the tie down straps and made sure everything was secured.

Deze pulled out a small leather bag from his pants pocket and produced a handful of alien gold coins.

"Can I buy the music player?" Deze asked.

David declined the offer. "Deze, you are my friend, aren't you?" David asked.

"Yep!" Deze nodded.

"Then I'll make a deal with you. If you tell me where the pirate base is, I'll let you listen to the music for the rest of the day. Deal?" David offered.

Deze's eyes lit up. "There are two bases, so how about for two days?"

"You got a deal!" David agreed.

Deze beamed with excitement declaring, "The moon of Betarus Minor. The other is a secret base where this mineral is found. It's on an inhabitable planet in an uncharted region halfway between Cassaria and Earth."

Deze clutched the MP3 player and began dancing his way to his quarters where David secured the door and returned to the cargo bay.

As David exited the cargo bay, he met up with Estron and Siyana coming down the lift from the bridge.

"Hi!" Siyana smiled coyly. "My turn to give another flying lesson. Are you ready?"

"Sure! Let's go for it," David smiled back noticing Estron's instant glare.

"Estron, you don't have to worry about Deze. He's in his quarters listening to music," David declared.

"Thanks for the update!" Estron glared again and walked off.

"What's her problem? Deze is just fine." David asked a bit confused.

Siyana's blue eyes gave a soft glow. "It's not about Deze but no need to worry. Let's go!" She said leading David by the arm.

John and Victoria were sitting on a large flat rock about forty yards from the ship surveying the area when Susan approached them.

"Hey, what are you doing?" Susan asked.

"Just showing Victoria how much has changed. The town was just north of here about a mile up the valley. The gold mines were active for about ten years then closed around 1918. A couple of flash floods wiped out a part of the town and the bank safe was washed a couple miles down the road. The last residents were an old couple that lived in a very dilapidated house down by the water troughs. They passed away years ago and the house burned down shortly after that. The water springs for the troughs dried up a couple years later and the local ranchers quit feeding their cattle in the area. Nothing but a ghost town now."

"Interesting, no wonder you wanted to come here. No one but ghosts around these parts," Susan said. "By the way, can Jonathan take me into Reno when he gets back? I really have to get back to school before they kick me out."

Victoria shook her head. "John, you know it's not safe. We already know they are looking for us. If Susan goes back, they will be waiting for her."

"Susan, you know your mother is right. I have no doubt even if Jonathan takes you to Reno, you'll never board the plane before you are taken away in handcuffs," John nodded.

"But I have to get back to school or everything is ruined. I worked all my life for this. It is all I ever wanted to do. Now because of some aliens, my life is wrecked? Dad, this isn't right!" Susan argued.

"I do very much understand your frustration. If you'd stayed behind you would be in an interrogation room right now, not in class. Once you convinced them you told them everything you know they might keep you in protective custody just to protect you from the mobs and press that will be shadowing you like a flea on a dog's back. So, tell me, is that what you want? John asked.

"No!" Susan sighed. "How am I going to ever be a doctor if I can't go back?"

"That is a good question for which we don't have a good answer," Victoria said.

John sighed. "All I can think of is you'll have to trust

God like the rest of us. I really don't have a better solution. I didn't plan this. It was thrust upon your brothers and I and we did what was the right thing to do. There was no time to weigh the pros and cons. We had a split second to choose the path of being good Samaritans. It's about who we are. Such a path comes with duties that transcend desires.

'Sorry you didn't get a vote in this. You are training to meet the needs of desperate people who have no one to turn to for help, yet here we are doing the very same thing. We have to follow God's leading and trust him. It won't be easy but it is the right thing to do. End of sermon!" John declared.

Susan thought for a moment. Tears began to roll down her cheeks.

"You are right. These people do need our help. We saved their lives. There are no other people they can turn to and trust. You are also right, we as a family are committed to this and no vote is going to change the duty we have to bear together. Forgive me for being so selfish.

'My problems are nothing compared to what they are facing. I can't even imagine being hundreds of thousands of light years away from home, stranded on a backward planet and no chance of leaving here alive except with the help of our crazy family. That's desperation."

John and Victoria laughed.

"Crazy is right," Victoria agreed.

For the third time that day strangers invaded the Braxton home. Agents Hill and Alomar found a message to Victoria's brother in Trenton, Canadian phone number, empty gun vault and pantry. Other items such as clothes and tools were missing. Family photos in the living room gave faces to names. The evidence pointed to the UFO escaping to Canada.

"There has to be something else," grumbled Agent

Nicholas Hill.

All the mail was unopened except for a phone bill, a credit card bill showing a refund balance and an electric bill. They were opened with a knife but there was no knife or letter opener. Envelopes in the trash had been torn open.

"Raya, please check all the doors. See if any were picked? I'm going to check the grounds. I don't think we were the first visitors today."

It didn't take long for Nicholas to form a picture of what transpired before their arrival. Two different entries were made. A petite woman's fresh footprint below the window and fresh work boot prints leading up to the back door were found. The note on the front door was bagged and tagged, plus the same print near the shed, probably of a man. One of the visitors must have opened the bills with a knife. Birthday card laid on a pile of recent mail from Lovelock, Nevada. Nothing from Canada.

Nicholas received a call from his supervisor who reported the Braxtons used their cell phones to call to Lovelock, Nevada three times in the last month but nothing in the last 3 days. There were no calls made to Trenton, Ontario in the last several months. He also discovered John Braxton's father lived in Nevada and John's wife, Victoria, was a Canadian citizen. The Canadian number belonged to her brother in Trenton, Ontario.

"Raya, how did these people beat us here? This investigation is barely twelve hours old and already others know more than we do."

"Well, we could have a spy among us or watching us."

"But that doesn't explain beating us to the house. They must have been here hours ago. How did they know?"

"Wait a minute that means someone had access to our information." Nicholas realized. "We're bugged! Raya, we need to go back to the MRCC and find that bug before we head to Lovelock, Nevada. Have the plane refueled and the pilot waiting. Tell him to bring his lunch."

"Let's go!" Raya replied.

Slick received a message from Langley informing him Henry Braxton was not in town and they should take up their search there. By six o'clock in the evening, CIA Agents "Slick" Prewitt and "Cat" Saunders landed by private jet in Reno then drove in separate vehicles to the old desert town of Lovelock. It was early evening when they arrived at the motel.

Cat looked at the motel and shuddered. Slick laughed. "What were you expecting?"

The old motel was made of weathered, tan brick with white paint peeling on the trim, revealing several layers of various colors. The shrubbery was spindly and unattractive, but suitable for desert life. The motel most assuredly saw its best days seventy years ago. The mom-and-pop establishment was clean, bug free and cheap. It also advertised such modern amenities as HDTV and Internet service. Since it almost never rained, no one cared if the roof leaked.

Slick looked out his room's window. A worn sign over the door on an old, white weathered cinder block building read: "Desert Metal Machine Company, Henry Braxton, Owner." A smaller "Closed" sign hung in the door window.

"Well, what do you know? I'll go to the front desk and inquire about a welding job," Slick chuckled.

The motel manager revealed that Henry Braxton's machine shop was the only one for ninety miles. Henry specialized in fixing machinery for the ranchers and miners in the area and the manager claimed if Henry can't fix it then it really is scrap.

"I noticed the sign on the door says he's closed. Is he on vacation?" Slick asked scratching his head.

The manager shook his head. "No, I saw Jonathan, one of his grandsons, in town this morning. He probably took the day off to spend some time with him."

"Will he be gone for long?" Slick asked. "I'm looking for some temporary work."

The manager shrugged his shoulders. "Can't say. They loaded up two pickup trucks with equipment and a trailer hauling three ATVs. They are most likely in the mountains working his gold mine south of town."

"Oh! Does he do good work?" Slick asked.

"He's a crusty old codger, but the best machinist you'll ever find. If he's open tomorrow you'll find him at the shop. You might want to check the café down the street before going elsewhere. Breakfast there is a morning ritual for old Henry."

"I'll take your advice, thanks," Slick said. Once outside, he called Cat's cell phone.

"Hi, Cat! Jonathan Braxton showed up this morning and Henry promptly closed up for the day. Finding them in these mountains is going to be like finding a needle in a haystack. We had better get some eyes in the sky at first light," Slick proposed.

"I'll call Operations and arrange it. Anything else?" Cat volunteered.

"Nope! Better get some rest while we can. It's been a long day and I get the feeling things are about to get busy around here. Later!"

Henry Braxton stood beside his pickup truck gawking at the sight of the space freighter. Jonathan parked the family pickup and ATV trailer beside him and began laughing at his grandpa's expression. Dexter tried to break a smile but still hadn't gotten the knack yet.

Victoria rushed down the landing ramp to welcome him and gave him a big hug.

"Victoria…ah …Hi…ah!" Henry stuttered.

"Henry, by the look on your face, you'd think you just found the mother lode," Victoria laughed.

Before Henry could reply, Susan and David appeared with everyone else close behind.

"Grandpa!" Susan shouted giving Henry a big hug.

"Hey, how'd ya get that shiner?" Henry asked looking at David's eye.

"It's a long story," David replied sheepishly.

"He wasn't keeping his guard up!" Jonathan teased giving a glance at Aycana standing at the cargo bay entrance.

Henry followed Jonathan's gaze and raised his eyebrows, "Trying' ta see stars the hard way are ya?"

David shook his head while everyone laughed at his expense. Jonathan noted John's irritated glare when he saw the trailer with the four-wheelers.

"You did say to concentrate on the important stuff,"Jonathan said.

"You need a hearing aid for Christmas?"John asked very irritated.

Jonathan just smiled as he grabbed David to help unload the equipment.

John introduced Henry to their new friends. Henry noticed Dexter's tenseness when introduced to Deze. Henry grinned looking at Dexter and Deze. "Well fellers, looks like we're gonna spend some time together."

Deze beamed.

Dexter scowled.

After a few minutes of conversation, Gavin and Dexter showed Henry the damage. It wasn't long before sounds of welding, grinding, and air hammers were loudly echoing off the canyon walls.

It was late afternoon when Secretary of Defense, Larry Longstreet received a call from the vice president for an update on the UFO Issue.

"Yes, Larry, what do we know so far on this UFO? Have we found it?"

'Well, Mr. Vice President, our agents tracked the space ship to a field in south central Michigan but it took off right before their eyes. No contact. It appeared to fly to Canada, but we believe the craft changed course and now is in Nevada.

Apparently, a local Michigan family name of Braxton is giving aid to the crew. We know there was a gunfight, and lots of blood but we have no idea how many persons were involved. Two separate individuals searched the Braxtons home before we arrived. Listening and tracking devices of Chinese origin were found on the National Guard's mobile command post supporting the site investigation."

"Good grief! They were quick out of the chute," Vice President Koppel sighed. "What about the other entry, do we know who they are?"

"Not yet, sir," the secretary replied.

"Well, find out and keep me posted. Pass the Chinese spy problem on to the FBI. That will keep our OSI agents free to do their mission."

"Will do, sir. Have a good afternoon!"

After supper, Jonathan returned with Henry to Lovelock for more tools and materials. They arrived just before dark. They decided to load up right away rather than wait for morning. Henry backed the truck inside. Before Jonathan could lower the door, a stranger approached.

"Is Henry Braxton here?" the stranger asked.

"I'm Henry, but who's asking?" Henry demanded as he slid out of the truck but shielded himself behind the vehicle's door.

The stranger looked over to Jonathan. "Jonathan Braxton, I presume? If you will allow me a few minutes of your time, I'll explain."

Henry pulled a revolver from a hidden pocket in the truck's door, "Mister, I'm not in the habit of asking questions twice. Tell me who you are, or get out of my shop while you can still walk.

"My name is Jeff Prewitt. Friends call me, Slick," Jeff said as he cautiously raised his hands. In one hand was a Bible in a burgundy zippered case. "In her haste, Victoria left this behind. I thought she might want it."

"You're no friend yet so let's just keep it formal for the time being." Henry demanded.

"Take it easy Grandpa," Jonathan said. Jonathan took the Bible from Slick's hand and opened it up. "It's Mom's Bible all right. Let's hear what he has to say? We don't like what he says, he can leave or you can shoot him. Your choice, OK"

Henry hesitated but finally lowered his gun. "Now you start talkin' fella. If I think you're jerkin' us around the buzzards are gonna have somethin' new on the breakfast menu."

It was late and John was still on the bridge looking over the 3D schematic of the *Holcron Star* when he heard the shuffling of feet entering the bridge.

"David, what's up? I thought you were sleeping? John asked.

"Your insomnia is contagious," David sighed.

John smiled. "So, what's bothering you?"

David shooked his head. "I never thought I'd kill a man. It's not easy sorting through all the emotions."

"David, that means you value life. You made a choice to save a woman from being beaten and executed in cold blood. You had no way of knowing who was good and who was bad.

It was a tough call but the right call. I had the same thoughts racing through my mind as well."

"Putting it that way I guess you're right. I could never live with myself if I'd done differently but still…"

John gave a reassuring nod. "Well, I never killed a man before now either so we'll deal with it together…"

"Whoa! That thing is huge!" David interrupted pointing to the holographic display.

"That thing," John pointed out, "is the pirate flagship, *Holcron Star*, and it's keeping me up with two puzzles I can't seem to solve."

"What do you mean?"

"The *Holcron Star* is over three fourths the size of an aircraft carrier. On each side of the ship is a massive engine mounted on an outrigger pylon. As you can see, it has five decks. The first three decks are crew quarters, several storage areas, a medical center, two dining rooms, workstations, and a recreation area. Most of deck 4 is dedicated to storage, fabrication and repair shops. The engineering station is here and two reactors here." John pointed out as he explained, "Hangar 1 takes up almost the whole rear third of the four main decks. It's used for docking supply freighters and similar sized craft.

The fifth deck is hangar 2 and stretches the length of the ship.

Though intended for an air wing, it was never activated. Now it is used for launching, recovery and maintenance of shuttles."

John changed the 3D view. "Six twin elevator shafts throughout the ship are used to transport personnel and supplies between decks. The elevator closest to hanger 1 also lifts to the bridge.

The ship was originally designed for long, deep space

missions with frequent resupplying of coolant. The Holcrons solved the coolant production problem, which allowed the construction of such a large ship. However, the pirate attack destroyed half of their coolant production capability. Coolant is as vital to a spaceship as gas is to a car.

"So how are they able to operate in deep space without a plentiful supply?" David asked.

John smiled."That is one of the puzzles that has me flummoxed." "In addition, at various points around the hull are defensive laser cannons, missile bays and magnum plasma cannons." John indicated as he spoke. "No matter how you look at it, there seems to be no easy way to capture a ship that large."

David gasped, "Capture? Dad, it's suicide to attack that thing much less capture it!"

"Well, we had better find a way because the *Holcron Star* is coming here to take possession of this spaceship and our friends. I doubt they will be friendly when they find out we killed their buddies."

"How do you know all this?" David asked.

John pressed a couple more buttons and a 3D regional map of space appeared. "Gavin filled me in. Look at this space map. Here are the different planets and star systems. Earth is located far from any of the other populated systems. They are all more advanced in technology, so why come here?

'This space between Earth and these populated planets are barely charted. On three occasions the pirates captured exploration ships approaching this region. Why? In fact, why would they even be there much less in our solar system if there is a scarcity of coolant?"

David asked, "Is that your second puzzle?"

"Yes, and a third just came to mind," said John. "Why did the pirates bring our friends here? In theory, they can't possibly carry enough coolant to go from here to the closest inhabited planet. All our answers are on the *Holcron Star*."

"I was going to tell you this in the morning but Deze told me the locations of the two pirate bases. One is the moon in Betarus Minor system. The bigger base is located in an unknown system halfway between Earth and Cassaria.

'Deze showed me around the cargo bay. There are some large tanks and a couple of containers with some extra-large grenadelike canisters containing what Deze described as a highly potent knockout gas. The pirates use the gas to capture ships. Would they work?"

"That should do the trick," John said. "I'll check with Gavin in the morning. What works for the pirates ought to work for us don't you think?"

John brought up the ship's schematic of deck 4. "If we can get to the Environmental Maintenance room, release enough gas simultaneously into the air supply, we could take the whole ship."

"You think that will work?" David asked.

"Yes, that will work perfectly. Good job, David. Did he show you anything else?"

"Oh, there are some crates full of rare earth metals, gold, silver, platinum, gems, and money from various planets. Just typical pirate treasure stuff, ya know," David joked. "There are also numerous crates full of different kinds of firearms, explosives, and what I assume are spare parts for the ship. The coolest things are kept in twelve large unmarked crates. Each crate has fifty of these, two-foot long, violet, florescent glowing, crystals carefully packed. Deze called them zannite crystals. He said they were extremely valuable. He has no clue what they are for though."

John queried the computer, "Let's find out."

David and John crowded around the screen as John read

the information. "Zannite, is the rarest and most valuable mineral known. It is found in very minute quantities on only a handful of planets throughout the known parts of the galaxy. When shaped by a special process into a crystal, zannite, in theory, could be used as an energy multiplier for anti-matter engines, large energy weapons and heat exchanger.

Zannite has the potential to boost the warp speed of a space ship, thus reducing space travel time by up to seventy-five percent. Zannite could also boost magnum plasma cannon performance, transfusion reactor efficiency, and eliminate need for coolant."

'That's it!" John said. "This solves the coolant problem enabling faster travel and longer space missions."

"How did the pirates get a hold of that much zannite if it's so rare?" David asked.

John called up the star chart again, and looked at the unexplored area. "I bet that is the reason three expeditions disappeared in the region of the unnamed planet Deze mentioned."

David sighed, "Now I'm wondering if our friends know and holding out on us? I was just beginning to like them too."

"This cargo is a galactic game changer for whoever gets their hands on it. Don't mention any of this to anyone until we sort out what's going on. Also, keep Deze distracted from rummaging through the cargo again or discussing it with anyone else. You understand?"

"No problem, but what about our Cassarian friends?"David asked. "We'll try to sort this out before the repairs are done," John declared "Nobody is going anywhere until we get the truth."

"Hey Sunshine, you're welcome to join us!" John called out.

"How did you know I was here?" Susan asked in a low voice.

"Someday when you listen to your children walk through the house you'll know. Jonathan can't enter a room without announcing himself. David softly shuffles his feet and you, my dear, walk as deftly as a ballerina. Anything else you want to know?"

Susan laughed. "OK, I give. I couldn't sleep either. I went to sick bay and discovered some really cool medical treatments involving nano cells…"

"OK, everyone, we need to end the science class and get some sleep," Victoria sternly spoke from the back of the bridge.

"All right, dear. Someone has to pull the security watch so the rest of you hit the sack," John said.

"It's already very late, Dad. How about I split the shift with you?" David offered.

"You got a deal. I'll wake you up in four."

As John sat gazing at the radar screen he dozed off. For the first time since the war, instead of a nightmare, he dreamed. A most unusual dream of flying through space racing past hundreds of stars. Upon arriving at a planet, a brief battle took place and out of the cloud of dust a small beautiful city sprang up. With Victoria in his arms they were sitting on a high hill looking down in a valley watching children playing and dancing in the fields. A warmth wrapped around them and he could sense all was as it should be.

When John opened his eyes, he realized a blanket was draped over him. Victoria was sitting in a chair next to him also wrapped in a blanket sleeping peacefully. It was soon time to wake David up but John decided to let him sleep. Everyone needed all the rest they could get.

CHAPTER 4

The next morning, after breakfast at his favorite cafe, Henry and Jonathan drove over to the machine shop. Henry, suspicious by nature, didn't trust the CIA agent.

When Jonathan explained everything to John, he wasn't surprised at the CIA contact and approved bringing the agent with them.

Jonathan began hitching up the trailer loaded with extra materials, a plasma welder and extra fuel cans.

Henry went to gather a few extra tools when he noticed his office light was on.

I don't remember leaving the light on. Oh well, wouldn't be the first time.

The sound of a toilet flushing in the adjacent bathroom caught Henry off guard.

"About time you guys showed up," a voice called out from the other room. Henry recognized the voice but it didn't make him feel any more secure.

"I was beginning to wonder if anyone worked around here," Slick announced, stepping into the office.

"This is my shop, sonny. I come and go as I please. You up kind of early for a government type, aren't ya?" Henry scoffed.

"Secret Agent Class 101, agents never sleep, it ruins our image," Slick deadpanned back.

"Yeah, right! I guess that's where the old saying, 'No rest for the wicked' came from," Henry parried.

'You guys always work with a partner. Where's your sidekick?"

"If I told you, I'd have to kill you. Since I'm not in the mood, let's just get going?" Slick urged.

"O–K!" Henry groaned fidgeting nervously as he opened an old worn safe next to his desk. Without looking, he reached for a pistol he kept inside. His hand flopped around inside not finding it.

Slick rolled his eyes. "You must think all government agents are dumb."

"Yep, pretty much," snapped Henry.

Slick shook his head. "You'll get it back later, I promise. I'll let you keep the one in your coat if it makes you feel better, just don't reach for it. I'd like to remain friends."

"You know about that one too?" Henry groaned.

'I'm a secret agent, remember? It's just a precaution. No offense, can we go now?"

"Nope!" Henry smiled.

"Why not?" Slick asked confused.

"Cuz you ain't goin' nowhere armed. You hand over the guns, we do a search for electronic devices and then we go."

"And if I don't?" Slick replied.

"Then like Grandpa said last night, the buzzards are going to have something new for breakfast!" Jonathan said standing in the doorway with a shotgun aimed at Slick.

"You win. Search away!" Slick agreed handing the two pistols to Henry and holding his arms out.

Cat Saunders stayed behind to watch their backs. To familiarize herself with the area, Cat took a tour of the town, airstrip and access roads.

The area boasted a very odiferous wild horse stockyard, several ranches, a state prison several miles away, a defunct armored car manufacturing plant and a couple gypsum and gold mining operations. There wasn't a whole lot else going on in the area.

Being raised in an eastern city suburb, Cat wasn't impressed with Lovelock's amenities. Three things struck her as most amusing about the town. First was a bumper sticker on the back of a rusty old pickup truck that read, "Real cowboys don't line dance!" The second was that not a single man wore a cowboy hat with feathers on them. Third, no one wore fringe on their leather jackets. No Nashville pretenders here, just the small town real deal. To Cat it looked like a dusty ghost town refusing to die.

Gavin bolted upright in bed. A new nightmare left him in a cold sweat. The idea of being marooned for life on a backward planet was beginning to consume his thoughts even in his sleep. Then the aroma of breakfast captured his senses causing his stomach to growl. Quickly showering and dressing, Gavin let the aroma of real food lead him to the galley. There he found Victoria and Siyana serving platters of home cooked food. Estron, Deze, David, Susan and John were already eating.

"Good morning everyone! What's for breakfast? It smells fantastic," Gavin said rubbing his hands together and taking a seat at the table. David poured Gavin a cup of coffee and passed it over to him.

"Oh, that smells so good," Gavin said before sipping the dark brew.

"Sure beats the burnt Bocar root tea back home," Siyana beamed.

Gavin nodded agreement as he contentedly inhaled the aroma. The freshly brewed coffee led to a spread of flapjacks, ham and eggs. It was a new visceral sensation for Cassarian and Gamoran senses.

Over the last couple days, Victoria introduced them to several new, exotic foods and drinks bringing their long dormant taste buds back to life.

"What is Bocar root tea like?" asked Susan.

"It comes from a very versatile tree back home. The dark umber colored wood is used for making fine furniture. The green nuts are roasted and considered gourmet fare, and the root bark is also roasted until a deep dark brown, coarsely ground then brewed like your coffee," Estron said.

"And it tastes like burnt sawdust too," Deze added.

"If we ever establish trade with Earth," Gavin said, "I'm thinking of exporting your coffee to other worlds. I could make a fortune. I noticed Earthlings cook with a wide variety of spices and herbs too. This is heavenly compared to the Stinkum gruel we've been eating for the past month in space. Just the thought of the gruel made me nauseous."

"Stinkum gruel? It even sounds gross," David said.

Siyana groaned. "It is gross. In the galley is a special processor. All food containers are made from food fibers. All food waste, containers, etc. are ground up in it, nutrients and flavorings added and then made into a dry ground meal. Once crews run out of frozen or fresh food and get desperately hungry, hot water is added to a measure of the meal and made into a soup. A crew can live off it indefinitely if they don't choose to starve to death first."

"I assume the smell is where the name comes from?" David asked.

Siyana continued, "Yes, experienced space travelers have a saying, 'The first things to die in space are your taste buds.'"

Susan shivered. "I think I'd go intravenous first.

"Speaking of that, I noticed you've been spending a lot of time in sick bay. You getting anywhere?" Estron asked.

"It took me a while to figure out the diagnostic routine but I finally got it working." Susan proudly announced.

"You figured it out? That's fantastic." Gavin said.

"I was her first patient too!" Siyana proclaimed.

"So how are you feeling today?" John asked.

"Sore all over but getting better. Susan used the scanner and discovered I had two cracked ribs and two bruised ones just like she thought. The doctor wrapped me up and gave me some pain pills with orders not to push it for a few days.

Susan laughed. "I'm a long way from being a doctor but the medical diagnostic computer is an amazing medical tool. I hope to figure out how the nano cell program works in a day or two. It's really awesome technology."

"I wondered what you were doing in sick bay," Gavin said. "I really appreciate you taking such great care of Siyana."

John stood up to leave, "Well, that was a great breakfast. I have some things to stow away in the cargo bay so I'll see you all later."

After Gavin finished eating, he headed to the cargo bay elevator. Aycana, Estron, and Siyana intercepted him in the corridor and motioned him into their cabin. It was obvious something was bothering them.

"Gavin," Estron asked. "Have you figured out how to get us home yet? We can't stay here forever. Earth is not ready for intergalactic relations. It's hard to trust these people with what we know about Earth's violent history."

"I agree," Aycana chimed in.

Siyana disagreed. "I am confused. Despite all we know about Earthlings, it doesn't match up with what we are experiencing."

"What do you mean?" Estron asked. "They killed the pirates, didn't they? They are trying to take our ship, aren't they?"

"Hold on a minute, Estron," Gavin interrupted. "To be fair, weren't we trying to kill the pirates too? Don't blame them for doing what we would have done if my plan succeeded. They gave us our guns and ship back after freeing us, didn't they? They are helping us get home, aren't they?"

"OK, fair point," Estron admitted.

"They saved our lives and we should be very grateful but that is as far as it goes," Aycana groused.

Gavin nodded agreement. "The longer we are together the more impossible it will be to avoid entanglements we might regret later."

Siyana shook her head. "Again, I disagree. Providence brought us together for a reason. We need to follow the path before us. Despite all that has happened we are still here. I think God knows what he is doing.

'The Braxtons have a dilemma too. What they know about us also threatens them. I don't think they can ever return safely to their home and live in peace."

"Is that our fault?" Estron interrupted.

"No?" Siyana challanged. "The reality is we need them as much as they need us. The bonds of trust will make us stronger. Is there any other realistic choice?"

Aycana groaned. "The bonds you speak could destroy us too. Gavin, you still haven't told us your plan. The last one almost got us killed. Remember?"

Gavin winced at the challenge. "Yeah, well we do need them. I wish I had a better plan but I don't. Anyone else have one? Mr. Braxton's plan to get us here and help with the repairs is working so well Dexter says we should be done ahead of schedule. Unless we can come up with the coolant we need we are stuck regardless.

"I think the way Siyana is making eyes at David, she has plans of her own," Estron teased.

Everyone laughed except Siyana who blushed. The effect lightened the air.

"Jealous much?" Siyana teased back. "True, David is handsome, but my life is complicated enough right now.

Besides I hardly know him.

"Right, don't let emotions get out of hand. Father is trusting all of us to respect our customs," said Gavin.

"Does Mr. Braxton have a plan to get us home too?"Aycana asked.

Gavin nodded. "John is working on a plan to capture the *Holcron Star*. Aboard is more than enough coolant to get us home. We are supposed to meet later this morning for more details.

'We talked yesterday about the pirate war. I believe there is a conspiracy within the Council of Unity and the military. A pirate attack occurred after each of the Military Budget Committee's meetings."

"So, what's that got to do with anything?" Estron asked.

Gavin explained. "Those meetings discussed ship refitting, moving up decommissioning schedules, canceling of new ship construction, but most importantly, redeployment of fleet resources to cover commercial shipping lanes. Every attack on our commercial shipping occurred when our cruisers were least able to respond. All of those redeployments were classified."

"Couldn't it just be a coincidence?" Estron asked.

"When pirate attacks succeed one hundred percent of the time?" Gavin asked.

"Now I smell a rat," Aycana snarled.

"Maybe, but I'm going to need more evidence before accepting some conspiracy theory," Estron insisted.

On that point, everyone agreed.

Dr. Russell Long waited at his favorite restaurant for his friend to arrive. He first met Dr. Loretta Sanchez at Georgetown University while they both were in graduate studies. They usually discussed foreign affairs and politics, challenging each other's ideas. After graduation, he proposed to her. She refused and made it clear she wanted nothing to do with marriage or children.

Though deeply wounded by the rejection, it was enough to silence him on the issue. Between what little he knew of her past and her single-minded obsession with her career, he counted himself lucky to be considered her closest friend. In the end, Russell settled for her friendship, but deep inside hoped she might someday change her mind.

Fifteen years later, they still maintained a close friendship as their careers kept both of them in Washington D.C. She was now Assistant Deputy Secretary of State, while he was recently appointed National Security Advisor.

"Sorry I'm late, Russell. I had to return a Senator's call. She just couldn't stop blathering about her self-importance," Loretta declared as she arrived at their usual table.

Loretta came from an immigrant family. Through hard work and determination, she rose to a position of accomplishment and professional respect. She came a long way from the barrios of Mexico City where she was born.

Her parents paid a smuggler to sneak the family into the U.S. when she was barely able to walk. Later, as a young teenager, the family became citizens under an amnesty program. She proved an exceptional student and won a full scholarship to Georgetown University. Eventually, she earned her Doctorate in Asian Foreign Affairs.

However, her most important lesson was not learned in the classroom, but from her father. She grew up despising him until the summer before leaving for college. All her life, she believed her father was lazy and foolish. He constantly spent his time after work chatting endlessly with the other farm laborers. They would talk for hours and hours about this and that, sometimes leading to big arguments. Her mother kept the children shielded away from it, so Loretta never understood what was going on.

One day, there was an altercation between a worker and his supervisor. Loretta's father quickly organized a strike. It just wasn't a strike against the offending farm but several other farms in the area as well. The workers won and overnight her father was catapulted to leader of a very powerful farm labor union in California.

The lesson learned was to organize, plan, make allies, wait for the right moment, then seize opportunity by the jugular. If patience is the mother of success, then ruthlessness is the father. She would never forget that lesson.

Russell rose to help seat her but she motioned him to stay seated.

"You're such a gentleman," she smiled. "Since Secretary Smith went with the president to Russia for the G-20 Conference, I've more paperwork to do and meetings to attend than usual. From what the newspapers and networks are reporting, I guess you've been busy chasing UFOs. Tell me, is Earth really being invaded by little green men?" Loretta teased.

Russell laughed. "There is no invasion by little green men. I can't say more than that though. Reporters all over Washington are searching for clues."

The waiter interrupted their conversation by taking their orders and quickly left, but Loretta never took her eyes off Russell. He seemed unusually nervous about the whole subject.

Loretta slipped off a shoe and began caressing Russell's leg with her foot. As usual, Russell became noticeably distracted while she skillfully asked questions about different subjects and the UFO. Russell really didn't pay much attention to her questions much less his answers. His mind was on her foot. By the time lunch was over, Loretta learned everything.

Few knew she was a rising star in another respect. Her position in the State Department allowed her to develop a network of global contacts as well as many like-minded Americans, in and out of government, who felt the super power status of the United States was the root cause of global poverty, corporate corruption and suppression of human rights. She kept her silence, but remembered those who might be useful either knowingly or unknowingly. Russell had always been in the latter category. The years of stringing him along were finally paying big dividends.

David and Dexter were on top of a high, large rock out cropping near the ship, installing a remote controlled high power camera and ground radar for security. As they finished, they spotted a cloud of dust in the distance.

Dexter opened a channel on his flip com. "Gavin, we have the radar and camera mounted. David is powering them up and ready for a system check. We also spotted a dust cloud coming our way about five miles out."

Gavin turned on the camera and performed a quick system check before zooming in on the vehicle. He quickly identified three people in the pickup.

"John, there are three people in the truck," Gavin said. "Thanks. Henry will signal us when he approaches if all is well. No headlights are the warning of a trap," John replied.

John radioed David to provide cover. Aycana took up a position behind some rocks on the opposite side of the clearing. Gavin alerted the others of possible trouble and joined John on the ramp.

Less than a quarter of a mile away, the truck's headlights turned on and John breathed a sigh of relief. The truck slowly rolled into the camp and stopped within thirty yards of the ship's ramp.

Jonathan got out first from the passenger side retrieved a box from the bed of the truck and handed it to John. Inside were two semi-auto pistols, a laptop, a remote satellite modem, and a cell phone. "I wrapped the electronic devices in tin foil to block tracking."

"Smart move," John winked.

Dexter waved an electronic device resembling an oversized cell phone over the large black duffle bag and a day shoulder pack looking for other listening or tracking device but didn't find any. When Slick stood outside the truck Dexter checked him as Slick starred at his mask.

"Clear!" Dexter announced.

"Good job!" John said handing the day pack back to Slick.

David and Deze appeared from behind the ship. Deze rushed over and picked up Slick's duffle bag.

John shook Slick's hand. "Deze will take your bag to Room 1 on deck 3."

"Thanks!" Slick replied.

John explained, "For security reasons, we'll hold on to your weapons and stuff for the time being. I know spies are supposed to be nosy but if you want our friends to be nice restrain yourself. They don't want any trouble but there are 5 pirate bodies buried nearby to prove you don't want to mess with them. Aycana will escort you at all times on the ship, OK?"

Slick Prewitt rolled his eyes. "Just my luck. I track you people all over the country in the name of peace just to attend a redneck 'Treki' convention in the middle of the desert."

"Thought you spies could handle anything after graduating from Secret Agent Class 101?" Henry sniped.

Everyone broke out laughing.

"Welcome to our galactic party. What's your name?" John asked.

"My name is Jeff Prewitt. You can call me Slick."

"This is the Cassarian Ambassador at Large, Gavin

Toburg from the planet, Cassaria.

'Ambassador, this is Agent Jeff Prewitt of the United States Central Intelligence Agency."

Both men quickly exchanged pleasantries before making their way to the passenger lounge to discuss business. Gavin motioned Agent Prewitt to a chair at one end of the table while he took another seat at the opposite end. John took a seat between Gavin and Slick. Siyana and her sisters took seats behind Gavin. Once Victoria served some coffee, she took a seat next to John.

Once everyone was settled in, John spoke. "Gavin, I give fair warning, Agent Prewitt is a spy for our intelligence service. I suggest being careful what you divulge," John said.

"I appreciate the warning," Gavin nodded.

'Slick, I'll give you the floor first," John offered. "Explain your presence."

"My assignment is to make contact, find out what is going on, and help prevent this ship from falling into objectionable hands. President Leatham wants our world time to adjust to the idea we are not alone in the universe. There is great concern over the introduction of alien technology. President Leatham wants to avoid global destabilization this incident could cause.

'As for finding you, that was a little tricky. A Chinese agent broke into Mr. Braxton's home and was last seen driving off to Canada. Once she figures out she was suckered by amateurs, she will be along and wanting to get revenge to save face.

'I played a hunch Trenton was a diversion. Lovelock seemed more logical."

Slick unzipped his day pack and retrieved a Bible. Handing it to Victoria, Slick smiled. "I thought you might want this."

Victoria nodded with a smile. "Thank you very much. I have missed it."

Slick continued. "I expect an OSI team to show up sometime today or tomorrow," Slick said. "They are a decoy team. We'll lure to search south of the town and continue searching further south."

"How did you know we were north of town?" Gavin asked. "Pure hunch. The pictures of Henry and his grandsons showed the mountains in the background. That put them north of town. Henry very recently sold a claim south of town but kept a much older claim north of town. It just made sense to me."

"Good guess!" John smiled with a wink at Victoria.

"Their orders are to peacefully protect the ship, its technology and all personnel involved. The problem is that once they find you, secrecy will become impossible."

"Well,"Gavin said, "this ship and crew are on a diplomatic mission. Any force used against us or our ship would be regarded as an act of war. Am I understood?"

Slick nodded. "Understanding you are on a diplomatic mission we fully respect your status. Since you're on American soil we will provide whatever level of protection and assistance you request."

Gavin winced. "When you understand the situation, your government might reconsider."

"Meaning?" Slick asked.

Gavin looked at John to answer. "Meaning in about seventeen to twenty-one days a Gamoran pirate ship the size of an aircraft carrier will show up looking for this ship. Once they find out their crew is dead and former prisoners free, they are going to get very violent. It is packing mean and nasty the likes you can't begin to imagine. Earth has no defense against it.

'This ship will be fully operational minus the warp drive in about 48 hours so long as everything goes as planned. To get back home to solve some very serious galactic issues, they must acquire the coolant on the *Holcron Star*. Earth is a long way away from any technology that can help them."

Slick rubbed his chin in thought. "So how can the United States of America help in this situation?"

Gavin gestured to John. "John has a plan to capture the *Holcron Star* and get the required coolant."

Slick smiled incredulously. "So what is your plan?"

John brushed aside the slight. "Our plan is to use this ship to insert a team to take the *Holcron Star*. First, the pirates are not expecting an attack. Second, one of their crew is held prisoner. We can use him to get us on the ship without raising the alarm. Though the ship is large, right now they have roughly 150 crew members. Once aboard the ship we can take it over, give the coolant to Gavin, send him on his merry way, and Earth avoids a battle it can't win."

Slick looked in disbelief at Gavin. "That is your plan? I will talk with my government but I think we can handle this for you."

"We appreciate your help. However, John will head up the assault. What we need from you is logistics," Gavin insisted.

"That is OK we can handle this without John. We have people specifically trained just for this kind of operation," Slick declared.

"Maybe so," Gavin replied, "but I want John to head up the assault. If you desire our help to save your planet then I insist you play by our rules. Oh, and let your president know trying to make diplomatic ties with the pirates is a disastrous idea. The last planet that tried that approach lost most of its population to death, disease and slavery."

"A Seal team could easily capture it," Slick offered in a last desperate effort to gain control of the situation.

Gavin looked at John who shook his head in disagreement.

John leaned over into Slick's face. "I'm afraid you're not getting it, pal. They really don't trust Earth governments. They view us as a violent, backward planet. They don't want some gung ho shooters to shoot first and ask questions later and most likely blow the ship to smithereens preventing them from ever getting home to save their planet.

'We have made friends with them. We understand them and share their plight. They don't completely trust us either but we aren't the government so they do trust us more. It is best you work with that for now."

"I see!" Slick said. "In that case, we will work through you and earn that same trust."

"Thank you! Can you start off by providing us the resources and supplies we need to capture the ship? I'm sure you can help us recruit veterans capable of doing the job. We just need the government at a distance so our friends don't get spooked," John said.

Slick thought for a moment. "It makes the mission riskier but if we recruit the right people it can work."

"I'm sure you know the right people. The other thing is we need a working fund. Can it be arranged for the government to create a bank fund in Reno?"

Slick, thinking he had them in a corner countered, "That is not a problem, what do you have to secure the loan with?"

John looked at Gavin.

Gavin looked at his sisters and after a minute of exchanging whispers nodded agreement. "The gold and platinum will be use as collateral. The rest of the pirate cargo goes to the Braxton family to do what they please save the spare parts and tools. Consider it a gift for you and your family's great help. We owe you that much for our lives."

"Are you sure, Gavin?" John asked. "That is quite a generous offer."

"I'm not sure what all they brought aboard but I do know there is more than enough gold and other metals to cover whatever you need. The rest is yours," Gavin nodded.

Victoria choked. "We appreciate your generosity, Gavin."

"Generosity?" Gavin asked. "Susan accidentally told me you recently lost your job and have drained all your savings to help us. You gave up everything for us. It is a debt we must repay."

"So how much are we talking about?" Slick asked.

John swallowed. "Oh, can we have the US Govt. hold $200 million in gold and deposit the equivalent in a bank of its choosing for now. I'm sure there is more gold to follow."

Slick winced at the offer. "You aren't planning on a leveraged buy of Nevada, are you?"

"Something like that but not Nevada," John smiled. "I have no idea how much we have but I'm sure we have more than that. Once we capture the *Holcron Star*, there should be a whole lot more."

"Well, I'll have to wake up some people in Washington but it can be done. How many people will you need?"

"You and I can work it out later but I believe about eighty ought to do it," John said. "That is about all the ship can carry in the cargo bay anyway."

"And if your plan fails?" Slick asked.

"If we fail, governments can claim non-involvement, even total ignorance, and hope to avoid destruction. If you take the ship from us and try a plan of your own, you'll have no one to fly it not to mention commit an act of war," Gavin reminded him.

Slick nodded in agreement. "I'll explain all this to my boss and make sure they understand the urgency. I'll need my electronics back."

"Sure, just be mindful time is of the essence," Gavin said.

"Yes, Mr. President, I will pass your message on to the Cassarian Ambassador. I'm sure he will be in agreement. However, I am very concerned about news leaks. The press is already reporting a battle in space and the crash landing of a UFO in Michigan. What about the press?" Vice President Koppel asked.

"Tell them we have nothing to report at this time. We are investigating the incident and will pass on what we know as soon as possible. Keep me posted of your progress; you're doing a great job."

"Thank you, Mr. President, and have a good night," the vice president said ending the call.

Vice President Koppel pushed the intercom button and asked his secretary to call the CIA Director for him while he made a few extra notes of his conversation with the president.

A couple of minutes later his phone rang with CIA Director Richards on the line.

"Yes, Mr. Vice President, what is the decision on the Cassarian Ambassador's request?"

"We are to give them all the initial support requested. After that they're on their own. Set up a Government line of credit account for them in Reno for $200 million guaranteed by the Treasury Dept.

We have no diplomatic relations with them as of yet so no diplomatic account. We need deniability so we have to act accordingly. Do whatever you need to keep the hounds at bay, collect as much intel as possible on the Cassarians, and let us all pray this crazy plan works."

"Yes, Mr. Vice President! What about my two agents?"

"Ask them to keep us updated otherwise, what agents?" Koppel said.

"I understand. Have a good afternoon," Director Richards said ending the call.

Mike Richards was not totally pleased. He understood the strategic necessity of the decision. Deniability of the alien presence is the only possible means of protecting an otherwise defenseless planet. If the military openly opposed the pirates, it would be a senseless slaughter. There is no way to oppose an attack from space. Cities, bases, ports, ships, even airplanes and missiles have no possibility of survival.

"At least we got the equipment, supplies, and list of former military personnel with the skills they need," Mike muttered. "I especially dislike cutting off my best field agents, but if Mr. Braxton is going to succeed, he needs them.

He called Jacob Wilkes, Director of Operations into his office. A few minutes later the DO entered. "Jacob, come in and have a seat," Mike said with a smile.

"I take it the president has given approval for support?" Jacob guessed.

Mike nodded. "Yes, but there are a few strings attached."

"Why do I get the feeling I'm not going to like this?"Jacob sighed.

"You won't but our job is to make the impossible happen," Director Richards reminded him.

The twin engine Cessna plane touched down on the tarmac runway and taxied up to an old hangar that could have used a coat of paint about fifty years ago. Three unmarked SUVs pulled up as the three OSI Agents stepped off the plane.

"So, this is the county airport. Good grief. You would think a plane hadn't landed here since the 60's," snarled Agent Raya Alomar wishing she were anywhere else.

"Actually, from the appearance and condition of the tarmac, I would say that it was resurfaced about three years ago and from the fresh oil stains in front of the hangar, a plane was probably repaired here about a week ago," Agent Philip

Blackmund stated.

"Simply amazing!" Nicholas Hill declared. "Are any of your observations germane to finding the Braxtons?"

"No, sir!" Phillip snapped like a raw recruit.

"I thought so. Well how about you expending your hypervigilant energy on the case?" Agent Hill growled.

"Yes, sir. Will do sir," Agent Blackmund said as he scurried to unload the luggage and equipment.

Agent Alomar tried to keep from laughing at the exchange but finally gave in.

Agent Hill just gave her a half smile and shook his head.

A Navy Petty Officer in civilian clothes stepped out of the lead vehicle and identified himself. After everyone introduced themselves the drivers helped the agents load their gear. A few minutes later, the convoy was on its way to the nicest motel in town.

After getting squared away in their rooms, Nicholas and Raya paid a visit to the local police department. The sheriff was cordial, but obviously not excited to see Feds, military no less, in his jurisdiction.

"What brings the OSI out here?" the sheriff inquired.

"We're conducting a routine investigation and need to speak to Henry Braxton. Do you know him?" Nicholas asked.

"Everybody around these parts knows old Henry. What you want him for, he forgot to pay his taxes or something?" the Sheriff smirked.

"No, the IRS handles that stuff," Nicholas deadpanned. "We understand he spends quite a bit of time in the mountains and hoping to enlist his help in searching for an object some witnesses claim came down around here. It's the usual meteorite sighting tin foil types claim is a UFO. You know how those turn out!"

"Good luck with that. You just missed him. He left for a

vacation with one of his grandsons this morning. I expect he'll be gone a few days. I was on patrol south of town when I saw him pass with their ATVs in tow. He was headed toward the Fallon area. Strange you should mention UFOs though."

"Why is that?" Raya asked.

"A camper called about three hours ago some thirty-five miles south of town, claiming a large, strange looking aircraft buzzed their campsite early this morning and almost choked them to death from all the dust it raised. They complained it even blew their tent down. They were not happy campers," the sheriff smiled.

"Where did you say the sighting was?" Nicholas inquired.

The sheriff walked over to a map on the wall and pointed to some hills southeast of the Lovelock Highway.

"They claimed they were camping in this area and doing some recreational prospecting. It is federal land and the Navy flies over that area a lot. I just assumed it was an experimental aircraft from the Fallon Naval Air Station and suggested they camp somewhere else if they don't like the air show."

"Why didn't you go check it out?" Raya asked.

"It's federal land, honey. It's your jurisdiction not mine. By the way the Feds are not very popular in the valley. Living in the desert is a tough life. Every time someone tries to do something to improve life around here, some elitist bureaucrat from Washington shows up. They proclaim some half-wit regulation to block it followed by an army of federal marshals and lawyers to enforce it. I tell you the locals would rather welcome a chain gang from the prison up the road than you folks."

"I see. Thanks for the information, sheriff. By the way, was Henry headed towards those hills?" Nicholas asked pointing to the hills on the map.

"I suppose he could be in that area but good luck finding him. There are not many roads out there. It's almost entirely off-road driving and he knows every inch of it.

"Henry used to be part of the county search and rescue team. If a plane crashed, it could take weeks just to find it much less get to it. Henry is your man if you need to find something in those hills."

"Thanks, sheriff. I appreciate the information and have a good afternoon," Nicholas cordially smiled and left the office.

"He called me honey! That condescending jerk," Raya fumed as they got to their vehicle. "Well, one thing for sure…"

"What's that?" Nicholas asked.

Raya poked his arm. "If Henry knows how to find something in those hills, he also knows how to hide it."

Slick ended his call from Director Wilkes and shook his head in disappointment. Dexter escorted him to the passenger lounge to join Gavin, John and Victoria. The look on his face told them the news was not all they wanted to hear.

Slick explained, "Well, the good news is your plan is approved. The airdrops with all the supplies you requested should arrive over the next 3 days. Some of the items you asked for caused a stir. Certain people wanted to know how you knew they existed. They were quickly told to shut up and send them. In addition, they are sending my partner a list of names of people with the types of experience you need. I took the liberty of requesting them. I have served with them during the war and they are the best. They also know how to follow orders and keep their mouths shut. You can reject them if you wish but you really won't find better outside of active duty. The OSI is going to serve as a decoy and roam around the desert South of Fallon all the way to Area 51. That should keep the conspiracies alive for months. You will be able to operate without further government interference. All you have to do is keep an eye out for snoopers. My partner and I will gladly assist you any way we can.

'The bad news is the government, for numerous reasons, doesn't want to be seen as being involved. Once the last airdrop is received, my partner and I will officially be considered having gone rogue and all official ties to the government severed. Because of the airdrops, we will be accused of misappropriating government property so they have deniability. I have numerous backdoor contacts to use so don't worry, we can get our job done."

"We could really use your expertise," Gavin said.

"Thanks, we are at your service," Slick assured them.

"Welcome aboard!" John smiled as he shook Slick's hand. "Glad to have you with us too," Gavin smiled with a handshake.

"Now about the manpower?" John asked. "I know a couple of friends formerly in the military that can help out with logistics and additional supplies. Jonathan has a friend who works as a NASA engineer. His skills will be helpful. Jonathan knows a few other people with support skills that might join us, but we really need some highly experienced special ops. types to serve as the tip of the spear. Go ahead and contact those on your list and help us screen everyone."

"Sounds good. I'll keep my partner, Cat, in town for now. She is the one having the OSI driving all over the desert looking for us. After the OSI is gone she'll join up."

John nodded in agreement. "Great! You and Jonathan take the truck to Reno and ask your contacts to meet us there in two days. Let them know we will cover their expenses for the trip. Set up a meeting place to screen them.

'I'll join you for the screening process. Those we select will be brought here. They can bring personal gear and two or three changes of clothes. We'll provide whatever else is needed."

Slick handed a note to John with all the banking information.

John smiled. "Thanks, we'll meet the bankers with the gold before noon tomorrow."

Victoria and John waved at the truck as it drove off with Jonathan and Slick. Susan was standing beside her parents blocking out the setting sun with her hands as the truck bounced and rattled along the desert trail until out of sight.

"Dad, you think they will be all right?" Susan asked.

"They'll be fine. I just hope the police aren't looking for our truck," John replied.

"I wasn't worried about that," Susan sighed.

"If you're wondering if Slick can keep your brother out of trouble, your talking even money," Victoria added.

Susan winced. "That is exactly what I'm worried about."

"Look out coming through!" Henry called as he slid a heavy case down the ramp to his truck. David and Dexter followed with similar heavy cases and in a few more trips loaded all the gold Henry's truck could carry.

John helped Henry lift the last container into the truck. "We'll meet with the banking officials and two Treasury officials first thing in the morning. They will take possession of the metal at the depository.

The government will hold the metal as collateral and a line of credit made available in a special bank account. We'll be in business by afternoon."

Gavin smiled. "Thanks for working this out for us. This makes our preparations a lot easier."

Deze walked down the ramp to where everyone was standing. "Mr. Braxton, can I speak to you in private for a minute?" Deze asked.

John pointed to some nearby rocks. "Sure Deze. Let's go over there and we can talk." Once they sat down John tried to smile and set Deze at ease.

"OK, Deze, you look worried," John said. "You've been doing a great job so far, what's on your mind?"

Deze hesitated a bit. "Well, Mr. Braxton, I'm not sure how to say this but I've been on the Outsider's ship. I don't know a lot but, other than Captain Gath, I'm the only one alive to have been on board."

John leaned forward and in a hushed tone said, "Deze, take your time. Tell me everything you know. Don't leave anything out."

Deze took a deep breath. "Captain Gath on occasion rendezvoused with the ship. He usually flew the shuttle alone to meet with them. One time I was taken along to handle a cargo container while Captain Gath was meeting with them."

"Really, tell me more?" John urged.

Deze began drawing a picture of the ship on the desert dirt. "The Outsider ship is shaped like a large submarine with the back end chopped off. The four engines are clustered underneath in a second hull half as long as the main hull, but twice as big around. In the front of the lower hull is a hangar bay for up to six shuttles. At the far end of the bay was a large generator with a red rocket sled attached to it. The whole machine was mounted on a rail leading out the hangar bay entrance. It looked like it was designed to jettison the whole generator in an emergency."

"That seems awfully stupid," John said.

"That's what I thought, unless…unless it is prone to being unstable," Deze surmised.

"If it's that dangerous why put it on the ship at all?" John asked.

"You wouldn't unless it gave you an incredible tactical advantage," Deze replied.

"Hmm! What advantage could that be?" John asked deep in thought."

"Well, when the ship would first appear, it was almost invisible." Deze asked.

"What do you mean almost invisible?" John asked.

Deze scratched his head. "It kind of shimmered like a hole in space out of focus. You couldn't tell what it was but if you looked carefully you could tell something was there. One of the sensor operators complained they couldn't get a targeting solution. Capt. Gath got very angry and almost executed him on the spot. The ship would slowly drift onto the sensor screen then just as slowly drift out of range. Shortly after that Capt. Gath would send a signal and we would meet up."

"So, tell me about the hangar?" John asked.

"It was full of storage containers on one side. The language written on them, I'd never seen before. On the other side of the hangar was the generator and in the middle of the hangar was one of their shuttles and enough room for our shuttle to land."

"Were there any crew? What did they look like?" John asked.

"Yes," Deze said. "There were two but they wore breathing masks."

We had to wear them too. The hangar had no atmosphere and it was very cold but we did have artificial gravity."

"Hmm, …I'm just thinking," John said. "What did the generator look like?"

"It was about the size of your truck and the two deck hands were anxiously aiming hoses at it and spraying what appeared some kind of coolant to cool it off. It was so cold it had frost all over the sides, yet steam was coming out the top like it was just used." Deze explained.

"So how long was the ship in the invisible mode?" John asked. Deze thought for a moment. I'd estimate no more than ten minutes from the time it first appeared to when Capt. Gath signaled it and it became visible again."

"Very interesting," John murmured. So, what was the cargo you were delivering?"

"The crate was a smaller scale container similar to the zannite cases but only big enough to hold one crystal. Oddly enough, Capt. Gath would not go within five feet of it much less touch the case," Deze explained.

"Interesting, very interesting," John declared. "Deze, I need you to keep this a secret between you and me for now. No one else is to know. I mean no one until I say so."

"Yes, sir!" Deze saluted.

CHAPTER 5

After wasting two days in Ontario, a humiliated and infuriated Lynn Jung Lee realized it was a wild goose chase. She discovered George Desjardin, Victoria's brother, worked for the Canadian government as a Livestock Inspector. It was a diversion and she fell for it like an amateur.

To top it off technical problems on the Chinese shuttle scrubbed the launch. It meant the Chinese and French could not reach the UFO debris field first. It was a setback for China, France and Germany but they were determined to gain control of Earth's future. It just made them more determined than ever. It was all on Lynn Jung Lee to secure the technology so desperately needed and now she knew where to find it.

Agent Hill and his team were frustrated. After searching every square mile between Lovelock and Fallon they hadn't one clue to the alien ship's location. Three helicopters and a CIA satellite failed to uncover any leads.

"A ship that big can't disappear forever in the desert much less in the mountain ranges of Nevada. There are only so many places you can hide a ship that size," Nicholas realized.

"Maybe we haven't looked far enough south," Raya exclaimed. "It seems like Braxton wanted us to follow, but not find him," Agent Philip Blackmund surmised.

"What do you mean?" Nicholas asked.

"Well, he knew who we were when we approached the ship in Michigan, but he took off anyway. He pretended to fly to Canada, yet, I keep thinking he knew we would figure out he went to Nevada. We get here and the only clue we find is an anonymous tip claiming a sighting south of town.

'The sheriff sees Henry Braxton's truck drive past him

heading south, but is never seen again. All the aerial drone searches yield nothing. I don't think they are south of us, but north," Philip said.

"You may be right but our instructions are to continue searching further south," Raya confirmed.

"But the rugged mountain terrain up north is far easier to hide a ship and far harder to search. We might as well post a message on the door of Henry's shop asking them to give us a friendly call rather than waste our time chasing them," Philip grumbled.

There was silence as everyone pondered what to do next. Suddenly, Nicholas grabbed a black marker and pad of paper and wrote furiously.

"No, your not going to do what I think you are going to do, are you?" Raya asked.

"Yep! What have we got to lose? We could be here for the next month and find nothing. Remember, Henry knows the mountains better than anyone else. Even if we did find them, they would just fly somewhere else. They have a whole planet to hide on.

'We don't want to drive them off; that would only make matters worse. Let's drive over and post this note and see what happens," Nicholas suggested.

Everyone starred as Nicholas walked towards the door.

Nicholas paused, turned around and asked, "Does anyone else have a better suggestion?"

Agents Raya and Philip looked at one another, shrugged their shoulders, and followed.

Cat returned to her motel room in Lovelock after assisting Henry and John with the gold transfer in Reno. As Cat exited her car, she saw the three OSI agents drive up to the front of Henry's machine shop. They posted a note on the door and drove off.

Cat left her room an hour later pretending to go jogging. On her way down the block she pretended to knock on the machine shop door. She stuffed the note in her pocket and resumed jogging around the block again. Back in her room, Cat read the note and called the number.

"Hello, this is Agent Hill. Who is this speaking?"

"You don't have a need to know. What do you want to speak to Henry for?" Cat replied in a fake drawl.

"I would like to speak to John Braxton, please?"

"I'm his personal secretary, darlin'. You can speak to me or forget ever makin' contact. One last time, what do you want?"

"No! Wait! Please don't hang up. How do I know you are the real deal and not some crank caller?"

"I'm the anonymous caller that told the sheriff a UFO was seen south of Lovelock. I know a Chinese agent beat you to Braxton's home. I also know she bugged the MRCC in Michigan. Is that proof enough for you, or do we need to end this conversation?"

Oh crap! We've been used all along, Nicholas grumbled to himself.

"OK! I get it. We were sent to make contact and secure the alien ship from harm. We just want to make contact and render assistance. We're not here to arrest or detain the Braxtons or any aliens nor steal the ship."

"We already know that. I'll relay your request to him. For now, you best keep searching further south and keep your little eyeballs peeled for strangers on the way here. Think you can get that part of your mission accomplished?"

"Thank you for the advice. How can I reach you again?"

"You needn't bother. I'll call you if I need you. By the way, I hope you're not wasting time tracin' this call. It will ruin your day," Cat said ending the call.

Cat laughed knowing they were tracing it anyway and how disappointed they'd be when they found out they couldn't.

"Did you get a trace on the call, Philip?" Nicholas asked.

"You are not going to believe this, boss. The call was encrypted and untraceable from a satellite phone. These people are using a government satellite to make their calls. How do civilians do that? I thought it was impossible," Philip said totally exasperated.

Raya put her hands on her hips and rolled her eyes. "I guess that explains why the CIA satellite photos were no help. We were sent on a fool's errand."

"The CIA is using us to run interference. The caller was right, she did ruin my day," Nicholas grumbled.

Nicholas called his commander and reported his findings. The commander was just as stunned. "So much for all the talk of joint intelligence agency cooperation," the colonel growled.

As the report made its way up the chain of command, the shock wave of anger followed.

When Secretary of Defense, Larry Longstreet heard, he made a personal visit to Vice President Koppel. Secretary Longstreet ignored the usual exchange of greetings as he was ushered into the office.

"Let me get to the point, Mister Vice President. When we sent the OSI team to investigate the UFO sighting it was with the understanding it was a legitimate investigation not a fool's errand. The president and you have played the military as fools and I resent being used in such a manner. I thought we were all on the same team?"

"Calm down!" the vice president urged. "Nobody is trying to make the military look foolish. We did send them on a legitimate investigation, Larry. A CIA team was sent to uncover any foreign assets and hedge our bets. In the process, they did discover a Chinese agent, who, at the moment, is on her way to Nevada.

'The CIA team uncovered the real trail and made first contact. I'm sorry your people were embarrassed. By letting them continue their mission, they provided cover for the CIA team. It's just the way things turned out."

"All right," the Secretary of Defense relented. "I guess I would have done the same thing."

"We are going to let John Braxton run with a long leash for now. If we go near that alien ship the media will turn it into a circus event. They'll take off and go somewhere else leaving us holding our hat. For now, that is the last thing we want. The president approved four C-17's full of equipment and supplies. Director Richards just briefed me the first drop is this evening; the CIA agents will then be cut off to provide us deniability.

'I suggest we back off for now and concentrate on preventing further foreign intrigue. The president doesn't want the aliens and Braxtons on the run. If you or your people have a better suggestion let me know."

The phone rang interrupting their conversation. After a short conversation the vice president hung up. He looked at Secretary Longstreet and paused to collect his thoughts.

"That was the Director of NASA. He reports the *Pegasus* has just been sabotaged and a computer virus has severely damaged operations. The launch for tomorrow is scrubbed indefinitely.

An investigation is underway. God only knows what we'll find but I'm sure things are about to get worse in foreign relations.

'The president returns tomorrow morning. I suggest you alert the OSI team to be on guard for foreign agents and avoid searching north of Lovelock. We have to trust our agents can handle their end while we keep everyone off their backs."

"Can do," Secretary Longstreet said, "but the CIA owes me one."

"OK, Larry. I promise I'll take care of you."

The last session of the G-20 Summit was a disaster. France, Germany and China announced a new economic trade union called the Triad. Efforts by the United States to address trade imbalances were countered by the Triad's demands for impossible trade concessions. Earlier in the day OPEC announced plans to reduce oil production by 12 percent over the next three years, ostensibly, due to declining oil field reserves.

France, Germany and China seemed totally unconcerned by the announcement. On the other hand, other world leaders went into a near panic, as they quickly realized the economic impact around the world.

President Leatham leaned over and whispered to Secretary of State, Dr. Noel Smith, "There has to be more to OPEC's actions than declining oil production. The timing is too obvious. True, there were concerns over declining oil field production levels, but new fields in Russia, the South China Sea, Brazil, Canada, and the Gulf of Mexico were just opening and domestic production and exports in the US are at a record high."

"There is trouble in the air and it's rooted in the Triad,"Secretary Smith whispered back.

"I think you're right. I bet they offer a deal to put a leash on the OPEC dogs if we meet their demands," the president wagered.

Just as predicted, during the next break, a French diplomat approached the Secretary of State. In very hushed tones, he offered the assistance of the Triad to broker a deal in which OPEC would agree to restore production levels. In return the

U.S. would agree to share all alien technology we uncover and throw in a few minor trade concessions.

Without indicating any of the disgust he felt, Secretary Smith agreed to relay the message to President Leatham. The meeting was back in session when Secretary Smith rejoined the president.

When Secretary Smith saw the president's expressionless face he knew something was wrong. "Mr. President, what's wrong?" he asked.

"The space shuttle Pegasus and NASA computers were just sabotaged," President Leatham whispered back.

"I think such perfect timing was no accident," Secretary Smith said. "They just offered to put a leash on OPEC if we share all alien technology and other un-named concessions."

President Leatham whispered back, "They just overplayed their hand."

The three Triad leaders watched intently for any visual response as Secretary Smith whispered the message in the president's ear. To their surprise, President Leatham showed no emotion until it was his turn to speak. He refused to take to the podium. Instead, he stood straight and tall with the American delegation. His stance and demeanor commanded the undivided attention of everyone present. With steely determination, he looked each of his opponents in the eye. Their faces betrayed feelings of intimidation as smirking smiles vanished and eyes looked away.

Out of the deafening silence, President Leatham calmly and firmly spoke. "You, sirs, in your greed and lust for world power are attempting to blackmail the United States. We will not stand for it. America will not sit idle while you destabilize the whole world and risk global conflict.

'The United States spent billions to land on the moon sharing our discoveries and technologies to benefit mankind.

We spent additional billions building the world's most powerful telescopes and radios to study the universe and shared our discoveries. We do not have frozen alien bodies and pieces of crashed alien spaceships at Area 51 despite what you see in the movies.

'The United States has no such alien technology. You blackmail us and bring us to the edge of war to demand something we do not have. You are insane. America is the most generous nation on earth. We gladly share with faithful friends and those in need but evildoers and blackmailers?

'Never!

'We looked upon all of you as friends. In return, you have betrayed us, attempted to blackmail us, and conspired to economically ruin countries around the world. America would rather burn candles in their homes than submit to your blackmail. There is a price for treachery and it will be you who pay it!"

Ending his speech, President Leatham defiantly exited the meeting followed by the American delegation. The meeting immediately descended into chaos as delegates began shouting at one another. When order could not be restored the conference abruptly ended.

That night the president's wife ordered the White House lights turned off and placed candles in the front lawn windows. Millions of Americans followed the First Lady's example.

Internet news sites buzzed with such headlines as: "World leaders demand little green men from U.S." and "Allies stand with America against blackmail." The world had changed in an instant and billions of people were frightened with not a single thing they could do about it.

Jonathan was busy assisting a friend at the registration table of the hotel conference room when a voice at the doorway drawled with a Texan accent, "Hey, is this where I apply for the Sasquatch Expedition?"

"Nicky, let me help the lost cowboy. We'll talk more later," Jonathan said.

"Sure thing," Nicky Stinson replied. Jonathan's former college roommate, snickered while giving the cowboy a strange lookover.

The burley Texan stood tall wearing a red flannel shirt, blue jeans, and brown denim jacket. A weathered chocolate Western style hat and saddle leather satchel completed the persona. The bulge in his left cheek betrayed the trademark Jonathan was warned to expect.

"Nope, the Sportsmen's Show is at the fairgrounds across town. We're the Trekkie Club looking for a few good people though. Sign in here." Jonathan deadpanned pointing at the sign in sheet.

"Slick tipped you off, uh? I should have known. What's going on?"

Jonathan verified the Texan's name before handing him a Non-Disclosure Agreement.

Jonathan shook his hand "Traven Rivers, welcome. We've been waiting for you to start the show. Please fill this in and sign. They're waiting for you down the hall in the Executive room with answers to all your questions."

Traven looked around the room. In a corner of the room was a table with a coffee station, cold drinks on ice, and a variety of finger food. The rest of the room was filled with chairs and tables for the 80 people filling out paperwork and chatting among each other in low voices.

Many of the men Traven recognized from his past.

They exchanged a few quick greetings before Traven signed the form and handed it back.

"Don't you want to read it?" Jonathan asked.

"Naw! All it says is I can't say anythin' about whatever." Traven snickered.

"OK, take it with you down the hall, first room on your left. Knock and they'll take it from there," Jonathan smiled. "By the way, best you get rid of the vegan snack before the interview. They want to make sure you know how to talk."

Traven chuckled. "Ok, you win the introduction round. What's your name?"

"Jonathan Braxton. Slick warned to be on the lookout for a Texas vegan and give you a proper greeting."

"I'll let him know you did a good job. I like guys who aren't intimidated. Will we be working together?"

"If you sign on," Jonathan nodded.

"Good." Traven smiled as he left the room.

Slick greeted Traven and ushered him into the Executive Room. Traven also noted there was a mahogany conference table pushed to one side of the room with a smaller selection of drinks on ice, a coffee pot and a half eaten pizza. In another corner was a laptop computer setup and printer on another table. In the center of the room were three club chairs and the very obvious metal folding chair hot seat. A middle-aged man in kaki slacks, open collar oxford blue shirt and dark blue sport coat stood to welcome him. Traven's years of training tipped him off to the slight bulge of a concealed carry gun under the jacket. Slick introduced Traven to John Braxton.

"I assume the wise guy greeter down the hall is your son?" Traven asked.

John smiled. "Glad to see you both hit it off. Lets skip the pleasantries and get to the rat killing. Have a seat."

"Slick told me much about you serving together in Delta, so tell me what you've done since then?"

"I was an operator for eight years. I was seriously wounded on a mission and decided after I recovered to start a security company. Six months ago I sold the company and started a solo consultant business.

"What made you sell the company?" Slick asked.

"Way too much government red tape and a desk with a choke collar and short leash."

Opening his satchel, Traven took out a couple letters. "Here are two references if you would like to check me out?"

John waved them away. "I already have the most important recommendation I need. I just need to know if you can capture a large tanker sized ship with about 150-armed pirates. This is a dangerous mission with global implications."

"Is that all? Don't get insulted for asking but is this operation legal?" Traven asked.

John smiled. "The White House is very aware. Slick was sent by the president to assist us."

Slick nodded in agreement.

"Now who is going to train these people? You don't seem to have the experience. Traven asked sizing up John.

"Right you are. I was an Air Force officer in missiles and later logistics not Special Ops. You do have skills needed to accomplish this mission. I need you to train and lead these people in capturing the pirate ship."

Traven paused for a moment.

John sensed Traven was wavering, "I was always told ten Delta operators could beat a hundred of anyone else's army. You think you're up to the task?"

Traven looked Slick in the eyes. "You really trust this guy? Can he really pull it off?"

Slick again nodded. "I would never have called you if I didn't think this is the right thing to do. Can he lead us? No doubt in my mind but it's up to all of us to pull it off.

"Everyone needs to know this is not a walk in the park. Some or possibly all of us may not come home," John said.

"OK, if Slick says it must be done, I'm in. One other question, you mentioned pirates and a ship. Where is the target located?"

Slick looked at John who shook his head. "If I told you now you'd never believe me. This evening I'll present the full situation and evidence. When we get to our training site tomorrow you will know everything. We have to maintain absolute secrecy for now.

"OK! I want in on the selection process. I noticed there are a lot of people out there that don't know crap about the military much less special ops."

"True, but they are an important part of the mission and will need training too," John said.

"So how many shooters do we need?" Traven asked.

"Thirty to forty if you can find that many out there. We are going to gas the ship then cleanup. More shooters won't be necessary if our plan works," Slick said.

"What if your plan doesn't work?" Traven asked.

"Then more won't matter," John said.

Traven paused for a moment. "Then we'd better get started. We got a lot to do fast."

It was an exhausting remainder of the day interviewing prospective team members. They interviewed 80 men and women of various educational, technical, and military backgrounds. The ten not selected were paid for their travel expenses and dismissed. It was late evening when the seventy recruits gathered in the conference room. John joined the anxious group and began to address them.

"What I'm about to tell you will sound like something out of Hollywood, so I ask your indulgence before calling the straight jacket squad. Five days ago…" John spoke of aliens, spacecraft and the imminent threat to Earth.

Many in the audience glared at Jonathan, Slick and Traven incredulously. John recognized the look of disbelief and signaled Jonathan to bring Gavin, Aycana and Deze into the room.

The three aliens walked among the audience in their home world clothing, shaking hands and greeting as many as they could in their native tongue.

Many reached out touching Deze's face to confirm his scars were real and not some Hollywood trick. Some of the audience brushed Aycana's hair aside checking for pointed ears. John also showed a video of the ship and a display of alien weapons to prove the authenticity of John's seemingly wild tale.

One of the recruits rose to ask a question. "I don't doubt anything you have told us, however, except for about forty of us, the rest of these people are just amateurs with college degrees. You need pros with military backgrounds and combat experience. Why isn't the military doing this?"

"A good and fair question," John countered. "Many in this room do not have operator backgrounds but are needed for other tasks. All the same, Traven Rivers will be your trainer and all of us will be ready to do their part in this operation. The problem is there are foreign governments and individuals who would exploit these people and their technology to change the balance of power in the world.

'President Leatham is very concerned this doesn't happen. He also needs deniability of the alien presence for obvious reasons."

"Well, aren't you exploiting the technology for your gain?" a woman asked.

"To some degree, you're right. Guilty as charged," John declared.

"The difference is I'm trying to prevent the destabilization, not create it. These people were taken hostage and on the verge of being executed by Gamoran pirates when my family intervened. If we sought wealth and power, we had opportunity to kill everyone, not just the pirates, while capturing the ship and contents for ourselves. That didn't happen, did it?"

"Guess not or we wouldn't be here. OK, I see your point," she agreed.

Another person asked, "Now who is going to lead these people? You don't seem to have the experience?"

"Right again. I was a missile launch officer and later a logistics officer in the Air Force, not a grunt. All of you were picked because you have skills needed to accomplish different parts of this mission. No one in our history has ever fought in space. It's new territory and you all will be the first to do it."

Slick stood up. "John is being modest. He was a Lt. Col. in the war. He was wounded in action and spent over nine months in a hospital. He was responsible for the saving of several lives. Look up his record if you like but don't doubt his ability to lead by example."

"Are you sure you have enough experienced operators?" a fourth person asked.

"I have a plan to put the whole ship in our hands without firing a shot. If the plan falls apart, you'll be the insurance policy. You believe you can do it?" John challenged.

Another veteran asked, "Traven and Slick, I've worked with you in the past. You really trust this guy? Can he really pull it off ?"

Slick looked the man straight in the eyes. "Ben, There's no other way. That's why we're asking for your help. Can he lead us? You bet! 'Will we succeed in the mission? That depends on all of us, not just him. Everyone needs to know this is not a walk in the park. Some or possibly all of us may not come home."

"OK, if you say it has to be done, I'm in. One other question. You hinted the pirates will return if we fail, explain?"

"If we don't capture the ship and expose their plans, every inhabited planet in this sector of the galaxy will be conquered or destroyed. Earth is defenseless against the firepower of that ship. This is the only chance to take the fight to them."

John paused letting that thought sink in. "I know everything presented is a shock, so take tonight to think it over. Please be mindful of the need for absolute operational security.

'If you decide to go with us, transportation will be out front of the motel at 0500 hours. If you wish to write letters remember security is paramount. We'll pay the postage; just leave them with Slick or Jonathan as you board the bus. We will leave at 0515 hours for those who wish to join.

"Those not wishing to join us, please respect your confidentiality agreement. If you meet us at the bus, you'll be paid for your passage home. I greatly appreciate your valuable time. At 1900 hrs. there will be a free all-you-can-eat buffet spread in this room. Relax, fill up and enjoy the camaraderie with old friends or meet new ones. Thanks for coming."

Everyone went to his or her room to consider their options. When they watched the news of the Economic Summit and the millions of lights out all over Reno, there wasn't any further persuasion needed.

When they came together to eat it was a somber reunion and making of new friends. That night some people were too nervous to sleep. Others wrote letters to family or loved ones to say they would be unreachable for a couple of months, but not to worry.

Nicky Stinson thought this situation was the irony of a lifetime. He just accepted a job as a NASA engineer, hoping in a few years to fulfill his dream of becoming an astronaut. Now he was walking away for an adventure in space beyond his wildest dreams.

As the sun settled, everyone at the newly established camp was engrossed in their duties. Victoria was making meal plans for the next several days. Jonathan's fiancé, Katrina, her brother, Joshua, and two others arrived that afternoon.

Katrina and Susan were roommates their senior year of college and became close friends. It wasn't long before Susan introduced the stunning black curly haired beauty to her brother. Jonathan was quickly mesmerized by her southern charm and quick whit. Two years later they were engaged and soon to marry. Susan rushed Katrina to sick bay.

"You would not believe all the technology they have," Susan said.

The Cassarian concept of practicing medicine is really different. Sick bay is equipped with a medical computer that shows you how to treat just about anything with nano cell technology."

"What? I thought that was just in movies," Katrina said.

"So did I until a couple days ago. Everything I just learned in med school is so outdated by this technology it's scary. Look at this." Susan turned on the computer and called up the treatment for pancreatic cancer.

"This is unreal! It makes our chemotherapy barbaric," Katrina gasped.

"No kidding and this just scratches the surface. Forget all you ever knew. This is like stepping out of the dark ages and into a whole new world of medicine," Susan declared.

On the bridge, David was getting more flying lessons from Siyana. "Gently! You need to pretend the flight controller is fragile. It will respond to your slightest hand movements so don't try to overpower the controls or the ship will respond violently. Watch the screen," Siyana explained as she placed her hand over his and gently moved his hand on the flight controller.

"I get it now. The response is a lot smoother," David said.

He looked at Siyana; their eyes locked on each other and feelings they never experienced before washed over them. Siyana's eyes took on a soft blue glow as both blushed. She kept her hand on his hand for a moment longer then withdrew it.

Siyana was a bit shaken by the contact and the feelings that overwhelmed her. "I'm sorry. I–I–didn't mean to... I mean..."

David nervously smiled. "What's wrong?"

"Ever since you rescued me I have resisted these feeling. When I was kneeling on the cold ground waiting to be executed, I begged God to rescue me. Suddenly you appeared out of the mist in answer to my prayer. I never felt this way before, honestly! It is enticing and terrifying."

David agreed. "Well, to tell you the truth, I know what you mean. I've never felt this way before either."

Victoria interrupted as she entered the bridge with a couple mugs of hot chocolate on a tray. "I thought all of this training might require a break. I see I was just in time."

David and Siyana were startled by Victoria's surprise entrance. "I'm sorry, Mrs. Braxton. Forgive me. I have been improper," Siyana exclaimed as she lowered her head.

"Nonsense!" Victoria softly replied, gently touching Siyana's shoulder, "It is understandable but let's stay focused on the task at hand."

"OK! Now, David, show me how well you can fly this ship?" Victoria asked.

"You asked for it!"David said as Siyana reset the flight simulator program on the flight console.

"Are you sure you got the hang of the controls?" Siyana inquired, not sure he was ready for another try.

"You just watch. It will be the flight of your life,"David reassured everyone as he started the simulated liftoff.

CHAPTER 6

The late Indian summer breeze whipped small swirling dust clouds through the hotel parking lot in the early morning. It would be another two hours before the sun bathed the bustling city of Reno in its warmth. By now the casino tourists and gamblers had retired for the night but the city had not yet begun the early morning rush hour.

Two old blue church buses screeched their brakes to a stop in front of the hotel lobby. Already the lobby was filled with men and women laden with travel bags. Some of the people were young post college types while some were hardened ex-military, all covering a wide range of ages and skills. Traven Rivers was speaking with a few of his men when Slick arrived.

"Glad to have you along," Slick said with a handshake.

"Hey, Dude, I'd toss a rattlesnake in your bed if you hadn't invited me," Traven teased. "It's been about seven years since I last saw you. As I recall, you were facing a court martial. How did you get out of that mess?"

Slick chuckled. "Not much came of it. I was on a mission to extract a CIA operative from an al-Qaeda stronghold in Yemen. I commanded the lead team and Major Dickenson insisted on leading the covering team. The enemy was tipped off. Everything went south from the get go with only two of my team and I managing to escape. We never did link up with the CIA operative. However, right in the middle of the trial, the Major developed a serious memory lapse when the CIA operative showed up alive with a very different story. It turns out the Major was passing information to an al-Qaeda operative he claimed was a Yemeni Intelligence officer. That story didn't wash when they found his hidden bank account. The last I heard, he was making gravel at Leavenworth.

Afterwards the CIA recruited me and the rest is blacked out history.

'I know John Braxton is former Air Force. He's a good guy trying to do the right thing. I suspect there is more to his motives but it really doesn't matter."

Traven rubbed his forehead. "Well, he may know how to saddle a horse but can he ride one?" I don't like a bunch of rustlers thinking they can blow into Dodge City and get rowdy. Whatever it takes to stop them, I'm all for it," Traven said as John joined them.

John handed each of them a large envelope. "Good morning gentlemen. Here are your orders with background information. Study these on the way to camp. Training starts when we step off the bus. We'll divvy up the recruits for the different assignments later this afternoon. Make every minute of training count. Failure is not an option. Got it?"

"Yep, the pressure's on now," Traven said.

"That's why you get paid double and I expect my money's worth," John winked.

'OK, everyone," Traven announced, "let's load `em up!"

Seventy sleep deprived figures climbed aboard the old school buses. John was pleasantly surprised to see not a single person backed out at the last minute. Two hours later, on a remote canyon dirt road, the buses came to a large, plywood sign greeting them, "Welcome to Camp Shangri-La."

"David!" John said as Jonathan nodded in agreement.

The recruits started gawking out the windows as the space freighter came into view. Traven and Slick were the first to step off the busses. Traven looked at Slick and shouted, "It's drill time, everybody off the bus and form up. Move it! Move it!"

"Slick, take the people from your bus and I'll form up the others. All you folks on the ramp fall in except the old lady. You can relax, ma'am," Traven said pointing to Victoria.

"Old lady? My name is Victoria, junior, remember that if you want to eat today," Victoria shot back like a lightening bolt.

"John winced. "That 'old lady' is my wife and she's run in the Boston Marathon four times. I doubt you could keep up with her without killing yourself."

"No offense, ma'am!" Traven smiled tipping his brown, dusty, cowboy hat. "It'd be an honor to run with you at your convenience."

"Sonny, glad to have company if you can keep up," Victoria laughed as she vanished back inside the ship.

Once formed up they were off on a moderately paced mile and a half run followed by breakfast. Afterward Traven had a short meeting to hand out assignments for setting up shelters and storage areas.

By noon, Gavin, Slick, Traven, Victoria and John sorted through short biographies on every person to select candidates for crew and support duties. Gavin, along with Dexter, Estron, and Siyana were assigned the crew training duties. Slick and Traven had the task of training the assault teams.

Because Aycana received a tour of the *Holcron Star* under construction while visiting Holcron, she and Deze were assigned to help train and advise the assault teams. Susan and Katrina were put in charge of the two medical teams.

Based on her experience, Robin Lefleur, a college friend of Susan's, was chosen to oversee the dining operation. Gavin was given the responsibility of training John and Alpha Team. Alpha Team's mission was to capture and take command of the bridge. The two assault teams led by Slick and Traven were to secure the rest of the ship.

Henry returned from his shopping spree in Reno with more supplies and joined the meeting.

"How did your visit to the bank go?" John asked.

"The bank president was suspicious about so much money

being transferred. I gave the bank president the phone number of that treasury fella Slick told me to call if I had any problems.

'When they were done talking, that banker was unusually polite. He even offered a special account with a higher rate of interest. He promised to personally handle all our future banking needs."

"Knowing my friend in the Treasury Department, he probably threatened to audit his bank until he was behind bars if he gave you any trouble," Slick added.

"I really like your friend. Ya think maybe he knows some good stock picks?" Henry asked.

"He probably does, but if he told you, you'd spend the rest of your life behind bars.

"Naw! At my age I'll pass," Henry grinned.

When Traven, saw Henry, he couldn't help comment, "Hey John! Kind of desperate for recruits, aren't we? This old geezer would croak on us before the first mile run was over."

John laughed. "This is my father, Henry Braxton. Henry this gentleman with the size 16 boot in his mouth is Traven Rivers. Traven is in charge of training the assault teams with Slick."

"Well, it sure is great to have ya along soldier boy even if ya don't respect your elders," Henry replied.

"OK, everyone, our working lunch is over," John announced. "From now on we'll meet after supper for a progress report in the passenger lounge to discuss any issues or problems we need to address. Let's get back to training. Not much daylight left."

Estron entered the maintenance tent with Deze under tow.

"Henry, I brought Deze for you. He's all yours. When you're done with him make sure you escort him back to his quarters."

"Thanks, Estron. I'll take care of him." Henry said.

"What are you going to do with him?" Estron asked.

"John asked me to solve a problem for him and I asked for Deze's help. Gavin approved it."

"Well, Deze will gladly help so good luck," Estron said and left the tent.

"What are we doing?" Deze asked.

"John has a problem and…"

Dexter entered the tent and immediately Deze tried to hide behind Henry.

"What is he doing here?" Dexter asked in his usual deadpan demeanor.

"Deze is helping us on a project," Henry replied.

"Do we get to experiment on him?" Dexter asked.

"No!" Henry replied. "Deze is part of our team and you will treat him as a partner. For our purposes, Deze is neither a pirate nor prisoner on this project," Henry demanded.

"Why?" Dexter inquired.

"Because we need him!" Henry replied.

"Are we going to kill pirates?" Dexter asked a bit more animated.

"No, we are going to capture them. A whole ship full and it is up to us to figure out how," Henry said.

Dexter cocked his head in bewilderment as he starred at Deze.

Deze wasn't sure what to make of it. "I'll make a deal with you. You quit threatening me and I will help get you home. Deal?" Deze asked.

Dexter didn't even flinch. "Does a sherpon have any say in who eats it? You are hardly in a position to make deals."

"Now see here!" Henry demanded. "Deze is goin' to work with us and you'll treat him with respect. You want to hurt Deze you'll have to go through me first. Understood?"

Dexter looked even more puzzled staring down at Henry noting the ten inches in height difference and considerably more difference in height with Deze. He stared for what seemed like an eternity at Henry and Deze.

Finally Dexter nodded. "As you wish, friend. This I promise, Deze helps us capture the *Holcron Star* and he lives. Fail us in the slightest and he will never leave this planet alive."

"Deze?" Henry asked.

"I want to defeat the pirates too. Okay by me," Deze agreed.

"Good," Henry said. "Now shake hands so we can get to work."

The three men shook hands and the partnership was formed. "By the way, what's a sherpon?" Henry asked Deze.

"It is the dumbest six legged animal on Cassaria famed for its tender meat and fine wool," Deze replied.

Henry looked up to heaven and whispered, "Well, that wasn't so hard for ya was it? Just hang in there, Lord, we're not done needing you yet!"

Dr. Loretta Sanchez lingered at the mall after her lunch with Russell. She was so glad to be away from the poor little fool. Russ was so easily manipulated she developed great contempt for him. It didn't matter how hard he tried to not discuss the UFO issue, she was able to glean everything he knew. There was a lot of information to digest.

We have multibillion-dollar satellites and multimillion-dollar spy drones that can track a car all over the country and read its license plates, but can't find a spaceship larger than a 747 airliner in the desert. It doesn't add up. Is it incompetence or a cover up?

Nope, They're just pretending they aren't real to keep everyone away.

Russell mentioned the OSI reported sightings of a UFO

south of Lovelock near Fallon. He also mentioned that the drone spy planes were sweeping the central Nevada area and coming up with nothing. Didn't President Leatham mention Area 51 in his remarks at the summit?

Yes, it all fits together now. Area 51 is much farther south. Coming up empty handed and the reconnaissance photos to prove it gave the president the deniability he needed.

I can put an end to that scam and weaken the president. The Russian president agreed to replace what OPEC cut off. If the Russians believed they were betrayed, it would be all over for the president's little scheme. All I have to do is cause enough fear and distrust so the nations will turn their backs on America.

She reached into her purse and pulled out a disposable cell phone and little black contact book. It contained names and phone numbers of useful political contacts. Now they were needed.

"Hello! This is the New York Daily Review. To whom may I direct your call?" the operator asked.

"May I speak to Thomas Kasill please?" Loretta responded with a handkerchief over the mouthpiece.

The phone rang several times until a voice answered, "This is Thomas Kasill. What can I do for you?"

Loretta tried to fake her voice. "I have some vital information you might want to know regarding President Leatham's remarks at the summit and the UFO incident. The president is lying and I can prove it."

"Listen lady, do you know how many crank calls I've gotten in the last three days? How do I know you are for real? What's your name and what information do you have?"

"I'm a very well-placed source in the administration so forgive me if I don't tell you my name. Just call me Isis for now. You can verify I'm a reliable source by checking out a John Braxton of Concord, Michigan. He and his family were helping the aliens hide the spaceship. They fled to Nevada and are now detained at Area 51 along with the aliens and ship…"

After she completed her call to Thomas Kasill, she placed three more calls to make sure the story was going to make the news.

She knew these sources would say anything to support her story if for no other reason than to advance their own careers by embarrassing President Leatham.

A couple calls to some activist sources would ensure the story was reported with lots of quotes from other sources. With her calls completed and the seeds of mischief planted, all she had to do was sit back and watch the fireworks begin.

The morning run started a very busy day for the recruits. Everyone managed to keep in formation. Teamwork and disciplined execution were an absolute must for the assault teams to succeed so that's where the training focused.

After breakfast, everyone assembled at the ad hoc firing range which consisted of a couple plywood tables, four wooden door frames simulating the entrances on the *Holcron Star*, and fifteen mannequins in different poses at various distances up to twenty-five feet away.

Dexter and Aycana issued a pistol to each person as they filed by. Experience with firearms ranged from absolute ignorance, to those with actual combat experience. After each was issued their weapon, Aycana instructed the recruits on handling the unusual weapons.

"This is the Quinn Industries Mark 12 Blaster pistol," Aycana announced. "It is simple to operate with a select fire dial to regulate the force of the beam fired. The '0' setting is the off position and is the only position allowed during training until further notice.

'Setting '1' renders a person unconscious for a short period of time. Setting '2' easily kills a human target and could severely damage or destroy equipment. Never use the '2' setting aboard a ship in space unless directed by the ship's captain. To do so without orders is considered a serious criminal act.

'The power pack fits into the grip like the magazine of a semi-automatic pistol. You have been issued three power packs. At the bottom of the power pack, you will find three small lights. The green light is thermometer shaped.

The green light shortens as the power pack is discharged. When the light goes out, the power pack is completely discharged. The amber light will flash to indicate the power pack is damaged and should be disposed of or turned in for repair.

'The power pack also serves as a stun and flash grenade by removing the base cover. The red light will flash for five seconds. If the cover is not replaced by then, it will explode with a blinding flash. The resulting explosion will leave anyone within a ten-foot radius stunned and disoriented for a couple of minutes. If you are holding the power pack when it explodes, you will have to learn to shoot with your other hand. One power pack is inserted in your blaster and you have 2 spare.

'You can expect to fire approximately forty-five bursts on the first setting and about twenty shots at the second setting. To reload, just press the button on the left side of the grip and the old power pack falls out. You insert another pack and slap the bottom firmly to ensure it is properly seated like so." Aycana demonstrated with her weapon so everyone understood the procedure.

"There are two types of sights on a blaster. There is the laser sight that is grip activated and the typical metal open sights as on your type of pistols. During training, the laser sight is used instead of the blaster beam. That is why the zero setting. I will now demonstrate the power of the different settings."

Aycana selected the first setting and fired at a rock about the size of a basketball. A short blast of white energy sent the rock rolling about five feet. When she fired again with the second setting, a much more intense beam struck the rock, exploding it. When the dust cleared, the rock was scattered into many gravel sized pieces.

"I now turn you over to your team leaders for further instruction. Thank you for your attention," Aycana announced.

Traven broke the teams up for practice and after an hour they began the half-mile run back to camp. About half way back to camp, one of the team members suddenly screamed and fell to the ground holding her leg as two recruits beside her shouted for help. Unseen along the trail, a six-foot Great Basin Rattlesnake struck Georgia Riggs, one of Susan's college friends, just above the ankle.

Susan and Katrina rushed to aid her. After examining the bite Susan looked at Traven. "We need to get her to the medic station aboard the ship immediately. We need a stretcher."

"I'm her stretcher but you'd better keep up with me." With that Traven scooped Georgia up in a fireman's carry and took off running the remaining quarter of a mile to the ship. Susan and Katrina were right on his heals.

Jonathan quickly captured the rattlesnake and carefully removed it to a new location.

"I've never seen such a creature before. Is it deadly?"Aycana asked.

"Rarely but their venom can do a lot of tissue damage," Jonathan explained. "These snakes are usually hibernating for the winter by now. The unusually late Indian summer has kept them up. These snakes prefer to avoid trouble but if disturbed can deliver a very painful bite."

"OK, Let's get formed up and finish the run," John called out.

The teams reformed and quickly finished the run back to camp.

Arriving at sick bay, Traven carefully laid Georgia on the table. Katrina began checking Georgia's vital signs and sterilized the wound while Susan went to the medical computer.

She took a small device about the size of a cell phone, attached a needle-like probe on one end and inserted the probe into one of the bite marks. In a few seconds a light flashed on the device. Susan withdrew the probe and read the computer screen report. Touching two screen buttons, they waited another few seconds until a nearby machine, resembling a single slice toaster on its side, ejected a small, slender, two-inch-long syringe tube. She placed the tube into a syringe gun and gave it to Katrina to inject into Georgia's wound.

"What are you injecting into her?" Traven asked.

"It is an injection of nano cells. The probe examines the wound and determines the nature of the injury and the makeup of the venom. The computer then programs the nano cells to attack the venom throughout her body. Georgia would normally have to be taken to Reno, given an anti-venom injection and spend the next several days in recovery.

'The danger of ending up with some long-term damage would normally be a real possibility. However, the nano cells will have her up and walking by evening with no side effects,"Susan explained.

"How did you learn that?" Traven asked amazed.

"Ever since Katrina and I came on board we have been learning medicine from this computer. I have a long, long way to go before I'm very proficient, but if we ask the right questions the computer is designed to teach us what to do in any emergency."

"I think something is happening in my leg. It's creepy. It's like a whole bunch of something crawling around inside," Georgia shrieked.

"Don't worry, Georgia. It's the nano cells doing their job.

In a few minutes you will feel noticeably better as the swelling and pain subside," Katrina reassured her.

Within fifteen minutes, Georgia's vital signs were back to normal. By the next morning, except for the bite marks, she was fit to return to duty to everyone's amazement.

Henry sped his truck through the camp and skidded to a stop beside the ship. He hurriedly made his way up the ramp straight to the bridge.

Gavin was training John on navigation and warp flight while Aycana and Estron just finished installing a security program and ground radar link to the ship's holo projector to improve camp security.

Henry burst onto the bridge and excitedly thrust a newspaper in front of John. Pointing excitedly at the headlines he exclaimed, "The fools are about to start a world war. Look!"

"OK, so Hungary, Poland, Greece and some other countries are pulling out of the European Union. I never thought the EU would last anyway, did you?" John replied.

"Read on. Poland has offered to accept all U.S. military forces from Germany."

"Bravo for the Poles. The way the Germans are behaving, I'd just as soon have our troops and their families where they are welcomed. The Poles have always been good and very noble people. What are you so alarmed about, Dad?"

"The world is breaking up into two factions and things are about to get real nasty. On the radio, they announced the Russian space shuttle was destroyed and three spies caught. Speculation is the Chinese and French were behind it.

'The news reporter was saying nothing could stop the Chinese ship from being the first to reach the debris in space and reap any technology recovered. Russia is threatening war on China if they go near the debris field. If this keeps up we won't have to worry about pirates."

"I see your point, but what do you propose we do about it?" Gavin challenged.

"Why not go up there and blast what is left of the debris so there isn't anything to fight over," Victoria said.

"Good idea but that only eliminates one part of the problem. We are still here and the other part of the problem," Gavin reminded everyone.

"I see your point, but if the Russians strike back, there will most assuredly be a world war," Victoria replied.

"A world war? Does that mean millions or billions of people murdered all because of us?" Estron asked visibly upset.

"It's not about us, Estron. Evil is everywhere and good people need to wake up and take action. Our world is being threatened too remember? We have to find a way to warn Cassaria before its too late," Aycana reminded everyone.

"This is getting hopeless!" Estron groaned.

"Hold on folks! With the ship fixed,we can easily protect ourselves. There is nothing to worry about," Gavin replied optimistically.

"I'm not talking about us, Gavin. I'm talking about the whole world. Governments are in a panic and nobody seems to be thinking rationally," Victoria retorted.

"You got that right, Victoria," Henry agreed as he fidgeted. "Change can be a scary thing when leaders offer no clear vision."

"People now know Earth is no longer a solitary island in space," John explained. "Almost everyone, honest or scoundrel, will want to be a part of the new age dawning. People have to change how they view the universe.

'Until then, our problems will continue to multiply. We need to make many friends and few enemies if we are going to get the support we need," John said.

"Enemies? We haven't done anything to make people

hate us. I don't understand," Estron sighed.

"It's no different from people on other planets," Gavin said. "Humankind has no lock on greed, jealousy, and hate. There is always someone who can't wait to hate you just because of what you have or who you pick for friends."

"That's right. Once we capture the *Holcron Star*, our manpower and logistic needs will greatly increase. No matter what we decide to do, we will need supplies of every kind and lots of people with a wide variety of skills. Some people are going to help us while others will oppose us.

'I'd rather choose my friends than my enemies. What say all of you?" John challenged.

"I feel we need to destroy the debris field now to buy everyone time to think seriously about the future. Our real friends will respect our decision while our enemies expose themselves," Gavin concluded.

Aycana and Estron nodded in agreement.

After dinner, Gavin and Dexter were on the bridge reviewing data concerning the debris field. David entered but did not interrupt. He wandered from one display station to another. His presence did not go unnoticed or his nervous demeanor.

Dexter glanced at David and then remarked to Gavin, "Well, I guess that completes the data review. Deze and I will get the engines prepped for the mission. See you later."

After Dexter left the bridge, Gavin turned and feigned surprise. "David, I didn't know you were here. Need some help with the flight control training?"

David struggled for words. "Well, I think…ah…I mean…no. Oh, man this isn't coming out right."

"I guess not. What are you trying to say?" Gavin smiled.

"It's about us. I mean Siyana and me. I've developed feelings for her. I don't want to dishonor her or violate your customs. So I'm seeking your advice," David said.

"David, I am pleased you recognize the importance of our customs and respect Siyana's honor. You both have known each other for only a week. Don't you think you might be rushing things a bit?"

"Well, I thought so too until last night. It was then that we both realized we felt the same for each other. That is why I'm here."

"I see. There is so much we have been through but there is so much more we are about to go through. The outcome is very unpredictable.

'We must focus on the *Holcron Star* for now or we will all be dead. If we succeed you will most likely never see each other again. If my father were here, he would ask you one question. Would you and could you call off this relationship if asked at any time?" Gavin asked.

David reflected for a moment before responding. "Because I respect Siyana, you and your family, I would and could break off the relationship if asked. Not only because you asked, but also because it's the honorable thing to do. However, I warn you my feelings for Siyana would not change."

"Spoken like a gentleman and man of true honor. My father would be proud to know you, so I will ask you to put your feelings aside for now. Let God direct the future. Understand, upon returning home our father's approval must be sought before the relationship goes any further. Agreed?"

"Agreed!" David smiled as they shook hands.

"Now, I understand from Siyana that you and Jonathan are fast learners and quickly developing into fine pilots. Is that true?" Gavin asked with raised eyebrows.

"I don't know about that, but we are doing well in the trainer program. I have successfully flown all the takeoff, landing and docking scenarios and got a perfect score on the

Callton Meteor Challenge."

"You have done well then, it took me two months to beat the challenge and I don't know of a single pilot who has ever gotten a perfect score. That is great news because at midnight you will be Siyana's copilot for your first mission in space."

"You're kidding? What are we going to do?"David asked excitedly.

"We are going to get rid of the spaceship debris before anyone starts a war over it. You had better get everyone rounded up so I can brief the mission in 30 minutes in the lounge. We will be taking off in about 4 hours."

"All right! Our first mission," David proclaimed. "This is going to be so awesome!"

Siyana and David went through the pre-flight checklist and found all systems functioning. The exchange of looks between the two betrayed more than an excitement for the upcoming mission, but they quickly focused their attention to the task at hand.

John was in the captain's seat for training with Victoria and Sean operating the navigation system controls. Molly and Georgia manned the communications center. Gavin was seated behind them overseeing the training. Aycana and Estron were in the Defense Control Center training Jonathan, Joshua and Nicky. The DCC was one deck directly beneath the bridge containing the fire controls, missile bay, and laser cannons.

Gavin knew for a trained crew this would be a routine flight. However, with half the crew just starting their training nothing was routine. Everything they were doing was very unorthodox to put in mildly. Gavin realized he was way out of his comfort zone but there was no other way with his original crew dead. His sisters were capable of doing the mission alone but it was vital the others learn everything possible about space flight before they confronted the *Holcron Star*. The sinking feeling in Gavin's stomach told him that would not be enough to survive.

Siyana reviewed the takeoff procedures with David. When they were completed, David asked what training was like on Cassaria.

Siyana explained. "On Cassaria, most cadets begin training at age 16. It takes six months to learn each of the four different crew positions. After a minimum of two full years the cadet was given a certification test. If he passes, he's promoted to Junior Lieutenant.

'After being commissioned, the new officer could apply for pilot training. If their score on the flight proficiency exam was high enough, they were accepted for a year of advanced pilot training. After a minimum of six years as pilot and receiving the highest of ratings, a pilot could apply to attend Space Command War Academy.

'After one year at the Academy, the best graduates were assigned as First Officers for four years. Those officers, selected by a Captains Review Board, are promoted to major and given their first command, usually an escort vessel of some sort."

"That is a lot of training," David said. "How are we going to learn all that?"

Siyana winced. "We have less two weeks to train all of you Earthlings. Sixteen-hour training days are the norm for now but what we are teaching you is barely enough to survive. There is so much all of you need to learn it scares me. You and Jonathan are particularly adept at the flight controls and weapons. John is proving a calm, bold leader on the flight deck with an uncanny ability to adapt to new situations. All of you are very fast learners and, in time, would turn into exceptional pilots if not killed in the process."

"Well that's encouraging," David muttered.

"Your dad has the hardest task of all," Siyana said. "Each

of you have so much to learn and so little time. Everyone has their small part but he has to make it all come together. If you do succeed in capturing the *Holcron Star*, John will have months to learn not only how everything functions on the ship, but also how to command such a large and complex vessel."

Gavin checked the ship's clock. Okay everyone," he announced, "Its time to start the mission." Gavin gave a nod to John.

John began calling out each step of the pre-flight checklist. When all stations reported ready, John gave the order, "Pilot, initiate launch." Although in total darkness, the ship's sensors collected all terrain data and projected the view onto the forward bridge canopy. This allowed everyone on the bridge to see everything like it was daylight. Siyana called out each step in the launch checklist while David worked the flight controls. Once the ship lifted twenty feet off the ground, Siyana raised the landing gear, while David carefully rotated the ship with its antigravity thrusters to ease away from the nearby rock outcroppings.

Clearing all the obstacles, David carefully advanced the throttle. The ship eased forward a couple hundred yards allowing David a chance to get the feel of the ship's controls and response to commands.

Once David felt confident, he grinned widely as he engaged the subspace engines, shooting the ship across the valley floor. Slowly, David lifted the nose and began to smoothly gain altitude. Within a few seconds the ship was airborne.

Siyana then announced, "Captain, Launch checklist is complete."

Gavin, impressed with David's takeoff, gave him a nod of approval.

John checked with the engine room. Deze reported all systems were at optimum performance. All other stations reported normal system operations.

David kept the ship in a climb as Siyana increased engine power while calling out speed and altitude until the ship attained proper orbit with the debris.

Georgia initiated a scan of the wreckage and sent a projection to the holo-projector next to the Captain's chair. John directed the sensors to sort through the debris and identify the larger pieces There were six nacelles with engines intact, two cockpits mostly intact and one plasma weapon intact that could provide valuable and salvageable technology.

Gavin confirmed the targets. David adjusted altitude to maneuver the ship into optimum firing position.

Meanwhile, Aycana and Estron showed Jonathan, Joshua and Nicky how to use the ship's sensors to program the targeting computer. Once the targets were confirmed as locked by the targeting computer, Jonathan, Joshua, and Nicky took turns independently firing the two magnum cannons. Since the targets were stationary, it was a simple task. Within a few minutes the targets were turned into molten slag.

"Captain." Jonathan reported, "All targets are destroyed."

Gavin smiled at John. Good job. The rest of the debris won't do anyone much good and will be burned up once pulled into the Earth's atmosphere."

Upon returning to their makeshift base, David winced at the stiff jolt when the landing gear touched ground.

"All stations secure all systems and report." John announced over the comm.net. Each station reported all systems safe and secured. With the last report, John announced, "All systems secured, mission accomplished. Congratulations on a job well done."

Down in the weapons bay, Jonathan, Joshua and Nicky introduced Aycana to the custom of a high five celebration.

CHAPTER 7

President Leatham looked around the conference table. Seated were the cabinet and key staff members. Only his National Security Advisor, Dr. Russell Long, was missing. He was giving a guest lecture at Georgetown University. His aide sat in his place. The air crackled with tension.

The president began. "Folks, when this UFO incident first started twelve days ago, I ordered absolutely everything on the strictest need to know basis with no leaks.

'Apparently, someone has made the mistake of not taking me at my word. Our national security is threatened. We have already come to the brink of war and I will not be pushed into it by a pair of loose lips."

"Mr. President, is it possible someone in the OSI leaked this information?" the chief of staff asked.

"It's possible, but I doubt it," President Leatham replied. "There are only a few people with any real knowledge. As a result of a highly classified, counter intelligence investigation, a warrant was obtained resulting in the recording of a cell phone conversation intercepted right here in Washington."

The president gave a nod as a NSA officer played the recorded call. Over the next two minutes a female voice told a reporter almost everything about the UFO and the Braxton family.

President Leatham took a sip of water from his glass and resumed speaking. "The saving grace is their source claims the Braxton family, aliens, and the UFO are presently held at Area 51. That bit of misinformation has allowed us to discredit the whole story. Press Secretary Melinda du Pont is arranging a tour of this facility for the press to prove the story is false. Let's hope it gets the press off our backs. No more leaks will be tolerated, period. Now for the next item of business…"

The sun began sweeping over the sleepy town of Lovelock when Henry pulled his truck up to the front overhead door of his shop. Henry looked around. This time of day, Lovelock is always dead quiet. What in the world is going on? The whole town is like a giant parking lot. All the hotel parking lots were full and many of out of state cars and television station vans lined the streets.

Henry pulled his truck inside and quickly closed the garage door behind him. No sooner did he exit his truck, then the office phone rang. He hurriedly shuffled into his office.

"Hello! Can I help you?" Henry asked cautiously. "Henry, this is Pete. What are you doing in town?"

"Pete, it looks like the motel business is booming. A circus blow into town?"

Pete was almost speechless. "Henry, where have you been for the last week? Haven't you read the papers or listened to the news?"

Henry stuck to his cover story. "Well, I've been working my claim with my grandson. Why?"

'Every paper, TV, and radio station in the country is talking about your son, John and his family under guard at Area 51, along with a bunch of aliens and a spaceship. The press claims an alien ship landed south of here and was hauled off by the military.

"Everyone thinks you must know something. If you don't get out of here fast, you'll be mobbed by a gaggle of reporters and nut cases. I'm telling ya, Henry, it isn't safe. You get out of town and don't come back till it all blows over," Pete warned.

"Thanks for the warning, Pete. Will you watch the shop for me?"

"Sure, Henry, no problem. Now get!" Pete pleaded and

hung up.

Henry went back to loading his truck. He finished loading a couple old fifty-five gallon drums and other supplies when he heard movement behind him. Henry turned. Standing ten feet away an Asian woman was pointing a Glock 19 with silencer at him.

"Move away from the truck and carefully raise your hands," she said motioning him with the gun.

"Hey, don't point that thing at me, I didn't do nothing. Who are you and what do you want?" Henry asked, as he fidgeted nervously.

"Are you Henry Braxton?" she asked sternly.

Henry nervously nodded, "What's this about? I paid my taxes."

"I chased your family from Michigan across Ontario, and now to this dump in the desert. I want John Braxton now!" she demanded.

"I don't know where John is. I've been in the mountains working my claim for the past week. What do you want him for?"Henry lied.

Pointing her gun at Henry's feet, she fired a shot. It ricocheted between Henry's legs sending small chips of cement flying. "I will ask you again, don't disappoint me. Where is the alien ship?"

"Aliens? I have no clue what you're talking about. I am telling you the…"

Another shot whispered through the air striking Henry's right arm. He fell back against the wall grasping his wound above the elbow. "Hey! No need to do that!" Henry yelped.

"You have just one more chance then I'll have to find John another way. Where is he?" she again demanded aiming the gun at Henry's head. Henry closed his eyes and tensed up.

"Not telling you anything," he groaned.

"Where?" she shouted.

"None of your business!" a woman's voice called out.

Henry opened his eyes to see a tall, slender, black woman swing a steel rod knocking the gun from his assailant's hand.

The pistol went flying through the air, struck a lathe and skidded across the floor.

"Get her," Henry shouted.

The two women charged each other punching and deflecting blows in quick succession pausing when the steel rod was knocked away from his rescuer's grip.

"Come on," Henry cheered. "Knock her lights out!"

The two women continued the fight kicking and punching each other again and again. Henry feebly shadow boxed with one hand rooting for his rescuer.

"Watch out for her kick!" Henry shouted.

The warning came too late as the assailant struck a high kick that sent his rescuer reeling against a workbench behind her.

"Look out!" Henry shouted as the assailant retrieved the steel rod.

His rescuer rolled to her left dodging the blow just in time. Several more swings missed her but another kick to the chest sent her falling violently backwards across the engine block on a pallet next to the hoist. She reached out to grab the hoist chain to break her fall but missed.

Henry winced. "Come on get up and fight or she'll kill us both," he groaned. The shock and blood loss caused Henry to slowly fall back against the wall and slide to the floor.

One more time the assailant swung the rod for a final decisive blow.

Henry's rescuer, seizing the dangling chain with one hand, she rolled to her left to avoid the blow. Missing its mark, the steel rod struck the engine block with such force; it sent a shock wave of paralyzing energy into the attacker's hands. The rod fell to the floor.

Still holding onto the chain, Henry's rescuer used the momentum to spin around and smash her elbow into the assailant's back, driving her head into the engine block.

"You got her now," Henry moaned.

Reaching out she wrapped the hoist chain and hook around the dazed assailant's neck. Henry could sense he was on the verge of passing out but found the strength to groan, "Finish it."

Grasping the dangling control box, his rescuer pushed the button raising the hoist. As the hoist lifted her body, the assailant struggled to free herself but to no avail. Within a few moments her struggles faded. It was done.

"Thank you, God!" Henry murmured.

Henry was on the verge of passing out again when his rescuer shook him and brought him around.

She was shaking from the rush of adrenaline. "You OK?" she asked while looking for something to wrap around the wound and stop the bleeding.

"Not feeling so hot at the moment. You must be Slick's partner. You hurt? There is a first aid kit behind the seat in the truck and a pile of clean rags on the bench," Henry said.

"I'm Cat. A bruise or two but otherwise I'm fine. Just a minute," Cat said retrieving the items and began treating the wound.

Henry sat on the floor looking up at the dangling body.

"I don't think she's doing so hot though," Cat said.

"Suppose not," Henry said. "Who was she, a friend of yours?"

"My friends put up better fights. She was a Chinese mole activated when the alien ship landed. They probably sent her to get whatever technology she could recover, or destroy the ship, including your son and his family if necessary.

'I was out jogging and saw her jump the fence and enter

the back door. I knew she was after you so…"

"The rest is history," Henry interrupted. "Thanks for saving me."

"We'd better get out of here before people start poking around. You can't come back until all this blows over," Cat explained.

"I got the hint. I'm all loaded up. Let's just get back to camp." Henry said.

Cat finished binding the wound and helped Henry to his feet. "There, I stopped the bleeding but we need to get you to the hospital."

"No hospital!" Henry said shaking his head. "I just need to get back to the camp. My granddaughter can take better care of me there."

"Okay, have it your way," Cat said.

"What about her?" Henry asked pointing to the lifeless body.

"Don't have time now. Leave her for the sheriff to figure out. It will give him something to do besides pass out parking tickets."

"Good point!" Henry groaned as Cat retrieved the pistol and laid it behind the pickup seat.

Cat made Henry comfortable as she buckled him in. Driving as fast as she dared down dirt roads, Henry guided her to the base camp.

Gavin entered the temporary storage tent joining John, Traven and Slick near several stacks of containers from the ship. They were sitting on large unmarked crates. John invited Gavin to sit on another one nearby.

As Gavin sat down, he noticed several more similar crates stacked behind John partly uncovered with plastic. "What's up?" Gavin asked.

"I just got a message Army intelligence was planning to

seize the camp and your ship. They planned to take over the operation. A three-star general and a few other officers have been arrested." Slick announced.

"Now you see why I insisted on no military involvement from your government," Gavin said. "The temptation is just too great."

"I agree. Who authorized this?" John asked.

"The general decided to take matters into his own hands. He was planning to use a special forces team and take over our camp by force," Slick nodded. "You were right. I have been assured there will be no further actions from our military. The general is in a cell wearing a straight-jacket and on suicide watch until a mental health evaluation and investigation are completed. I have no doubt other heads will roll. I'm told President Leatham is furious to say the least."

"Please, I wish no executions of these people. I really want it understood we just want to get home," Gavin assured them.

John smiled. "Gavin, it is just an expression meaning they are going to stand trial for their crimes. They may do jail time but they will most assuredly keep their heads."

Everyone laughed.

"I see you have your share of the pirate treasure already," Gavin said noting the crates.

"There wasn't much choice. We needed to make room for all the equipment and personnel for the assault," John said.

"I understand," Gavin agreed.

"We've been discussing the pirates and the *Holcron Star*," Slick said.

"That's right. Some things just don't seem to add up," Traven added.

"What do you mean?" Gavin asked.

John stood up. "I've been researching the ship's computer archives and captain's log. I found some information of interest but the implications will change our situation drastically," John said.

"Go on. I'm listening," Gavin nodded a bit confused.

John held up a map of the Central Region of space and pointed to a solar system. "Here is a habitable planet. It's virtually unexplored except by the pirates. Are pirates known for exploring or raiding freighters and colonies?"

"Now you have my attention," Gavin said.

"I've been wondering how the pirates are able to sustain deep space operations without severe coolant supply problems. I also asked myself why the pirates attack exploration missions in a region devoid of trade routes or colonies. I have a theory that might provide the answer. Are you familiar with zannite crystals?" John asked.

"Sure, but the stuff is so rare our scientists have just a few micro sized crystals to experiment with. They can only speculate as to its real potential. Besides there are no known quantities to mine. What samples exist were found in a meteorite cluster in the Jarro Nebula. Why?" Gavin asked.

"Could it be the pirates found a rich enough source of zannite to exploit, especially for warp engines?" John countered.

"That's preposterous!" Gavin scoffed.

"Yep, that's what everyone assumes, but, theoretically, what if they did?" John asked.

Gavin shook his head. "Our intelligence sources claim the pirates are getting their coolant from Gamora Prime. As for the zannite, in the wrong hands, the entire galaxy would be in peril. However, I can assure you that much zannite doesn't exist. It's pure science fiction."

"I'll take your word for it then. By the way, I want to clarify so there is no misunderstanding or ill will. You gave me all the pirate cargo in our possession, correct?" John asked.

Gavin smiled. "Yes, of course. I checked the cargo remaining aboard ship and except for the knock out gas tanks, you have what's yours."

"I just wanted to make sure. We are new at galactic friendships and I don't want any misunderstandings," John assured him.

"You've got nothing to worry about, John. Our friendship is secure. We do appreciate what you and your people have done and are doing to help get us home," Gavin said. "You and I are late for our training class on the bridge. Let's go."

As John and Gavin left, Traven and Slick stayed behind.

"If I didn't know better, I think our dear leader is hiding something from the clueless ambassador." Traven delared.

As Slick stood up, his foot kicked against the container he'd been sitting on. It made a hollow sound. Slick lifted the container lid and laughed.

"There's nothing but foam packing material with empty cutouts. Whatever was in it is gone."

Traven looked at Slick and inspected his container. "It's also empty." He knocked on the other containers. They were empty too.

"All twelve containers are empty. I remember them coming off the ship very heavy. It took a forklift to move them. I wonder what was in them?"

"Somehow I'm not surprised. John just told us what was in them," Slick said. "Gavin said that much zannite doesn't exist yet John has six hundred of them squirreled away somewhere in these mountains. John is thinking way ahead of everyone. It appears he doesn't know whom to trust."

"Can you blame him?" Traven asked. "If you were him, who would you trust? We have space pirates, alien diplomats, CIA agents, OSI agents, foreign spies, a Government that one minute wants to seize the ship or next minute wants to stay out of a galactic war, then there are a bunch of mercenaries getting itchy for some action. I'd be absolutely paranoid out of my mind. Yet, he's playing it so cool it's frightening. I doubt he'll show his hand until he's good and ready."

Slick shook his head in disagreement, "He at least trusts us to watch his back. He has to trust someone and he chose us. It isn't important we know everything so long as we stand by him. It appears John is not the fool some in Washington think he is. He's caught on to the game of galactic poker real fast. He just used us as witnesses and at the same time tipped us to what it's all about. The inexperienced ambassador foolishly fell for it and reaffirmed the deal and his ignorance. I think Aycana is the bigger danger. She is more than capable of holding her own in a fight and always seems to show up when least expected."

Traven scratched his head. "You're right. I was sparring with her yesterday. She whooped me good while never breaking a sweat. I can only guess the number of people who would not bat an eye to kill for whatever he's hiding."

Slick took a deep breath and paced around one of the containers starring at it. "This," he said pointing at the containers, "changes everything!"

"What do you mean?" Traven asked.

Slick lowered his voice to a low whisper, "Now we don't know who to trust either."

David stood outside the back of the tent listening attentively. *Dad was right to trust them. It was a risk but if we have to trust someone, they are the ones we need to trust.*

Russell looked at his watch impatiently. *Loretta is fifteen minutes late as usual. You'd think since we eat lunch every day at the same Italian restaurant and at the same time she'd at least call if running late.*

His cell phone buzzed an incoming message from his

aide. After reading it he put his phone away and reflected on it.

The president is concerned about UFO leaks. Well, he should. The opposition in Congress and their friends in the press are clamoring to control the narrative and it's backfiring. The world is changing and in a way out of their control making them desperate. I'll just mention President Leatham's concerns to Loretta as a friendly reminder.

Ah, finally she's here, Russell smiled upon hearing her voice talking to the restaurant hostess.

"Hello darling!" Loretta said kissing him on the cheek and quickly slipping into her seat before Russell could help her.

"Hello to you too," Russell replied. "Last minute problems at the office again?"

"You know foreign diplomats. They think my sole reason for existence is listening to their pompous, blowhard speeches. How has your day been?"

"Oh, my day started out with a lecture I gave at Georgetown. The rest of the morning was spent reading a stack of reports and studies that are so verbose and boring they should be classified as WMDs, Weapons of Mental Destruction."

"You mean you haven't read all the interrogation reports on the aliens and Braxton family at Area 51?" she teased.

"No, the OSI handles that stuff. Speaking of which, my aide told me President Leatham blew his top at the staff meeting this morning over UFO leaks and warned any further breach would be met with criminal charges."

"Wow! He really doesn't like leaks, does he?" she asked.

"Not really and this leads me to another issue. Loretta, I have a confession to make," Russ sheepishly announced. "I have been wrestling with this and I need to be up front with you."

"Russell, what's wrong?" Loretta nervously inquired.

"I haven't been totally honest with you concerning the

UFO incident. I'm deeply sorry. I never intended this to happen. I absolutely trust you but I can't violate the president's orders. Everything I told you was not necessarily true. You know how I feel about you and hopefully you feel the same way. I don't want to put you at risk." Russ pleaded.

Loretta paused a long while before speaking in order to play up the dramatic moment. "Russ, I'm deeply hurt you would lie to me. However, I deeply appreciate you caring for my security. We have a special relationship and I can't help feeling betrayed. At the same time, I know the security rules as well as you do. I apologize for putting you in such a predicament. I'm the one responsible for this mess, not you. I forgive you but more importantly, please forgive me?"

Russell sighed relief. "Of course. How could I not? You mean everything to me, Loretta."

"Good," Loretta said. "Let's change the subject to something more pleasant, shall we?"

"OK! What are you doing tonight?" Russell asked.

"Well, I was thinking of a long hot bubble bath and turning in early. I've been up late too much lately trying to finish that lengthy report on relief aid to Bangladesh. I hope to finish proofing it this afternoon."

"In that case can I treat you to a quick light dinner tonight so you don't have to cook?"

"That's so sweet of you, Russ. Let me see how much I get done this afternoon. I'll give you a call before I leave from work. How's that?"

Russell sensed he was being put off again but was too polite to say so. "Sounds fine. Just don't forget to call," he said.

John, Victoria and Gavin stood at the top of the cargo bay ramp overlooking the scene before them. The base camp was setup about a hundred yards away. The Army portable shelters, port-a-potties, showers, laundry and dining hall tents were located on the right side of the camp. Henry had scrounged up two used fourteen by seventy-foot mobile classrooms parked nearby. One had two classrooms.

The other had been modified for food refrigeration units and food storage.

There were three portable diesel-powered generators, several fuel drums, three large tents used for storage and several crates and containers stacked in various locations according to their contents.

Two used school buses, a van and a very old, rusty, beat up flatbed truck were parked in the motor pool area near the generators.

"Henry has proven a great scrounger," Victoria said.

John nodded, "Yes, he has. All the vehicles are local so they don't draw any attention with his trips. It all just looks like Henry is up to his usual scrounging."

"Well, John, I have to hand it to your father," Gavin declared. "If we need something, he knows where to get it. The camp may not be pretty but it meets our needs."

"Henry, Deze and Dexter are quite the team. Using a laser to dig the water well was brilliant. Without it we couldn't have lasted a week out here," John said.

"Actually, it was Deze's idea, they just put it together," Gavin pointed out.

John raised his eyebrows. "You're kidding? Deze came up with that idea?"

"You bet, and the waste filtration system as well. Quite a handy little fellow to have around, isn't he? You think Deze has earned some of our trust and drop the guard?" Gavin asked.

John nodded. "I agree he's come a long way but let's see if he goes through with his deception in capturing the *Holcron Star* first." Suddenly John and Gavin's flip coms beeped.

"We have a situation," Slick reported. "My partner, Cat is on the way in with Henry. He's been shot."

"What happened? John asked. "Is Dad in serious condition?"

"Cat says he was shot in the arm and lost quite a bit of blood." Slick said. "That's all I know at the moment."

"Okay, let's initiate Condition 1. Institute the security team procedures and see how everyone responds." John said.

"Done, out." Slick closed.

Gavin's phone beeped again as the alert warning sound resonated throughout the camp. "Yes," he responded.

"The security drone shows Henry's truck coming in and someone else is driving it," Estron announced.

We are expecting it." Gavin said. "Keep a sharp eye to make sure they are not being followed. Also, alert the medic team to respond. Henry has been shot."

As Henry's truck approached the camp entry point, Henry had Cat turn on the headlights for the all clear sign.

"It's OK!" Slick shouted over the comm. net. "She's my partner, Cat Saunders."

One of the security guards at the gate motioned for Cat to continue into the camp.

Cat pulled up to the ship's ramp and jumped out of the truck. "Henry's been shot and needs medical attention. He's lost a lot of blood. I wanted to take him to a hospital but he insisted I bring him here for help."

"We need to get Henry to sick bay." John shouted as Susan and Katrina came rushing down the ramp with their medical kit.

"Thanks for the help," John said shaking Cat's hand.

"Henry muttered something about his granddaughter being able to save him," Cat said.

"Susan and Katrina are our medical team and the sick

bay is equipped to heal him faster than any hospital," John explained.

Henry was rushed to the ship's sick bay's examination table where he regained consciousness again. Susan and Katrina were excited to use the wound treatment program they practiced for the last few days.

"You girls think this is a party?" Henry groused.

Susan looked at Henry and smiled. "Good, your conscious again. Stay with us, Grandpa." Katrina closed the sick bay door leaving John and Victoria watching through the door's window. Katrina checked his vital signs and inserted an IV while Susan cleaned the wound.

"The bullet passed through; that's a good sign," Susan said.

Katrina picked up a stylus probe and waved the sensor end an inch above the wounded area.

When the light on the unit stopped flashing red and went steady green, she fed the results into the computer. On the holographic projection, the results of the scan showed the extent of tissue damage and infectious bacterial readings. "Grandpa, we'll have you up and about in no time," Susan pledged.

Susan and Katrina reviewed and selected the recommended treatment activating the Nano cell processor. Lights flashed on the processor panel. Susan and Katrina were excited to see the processor working.

Katrina prepared an injection to numb the wound area and gave fair warning.

"This is going to sting but we need to numb the area to make the healing process more comfortable for you."

"Ha! I'm shot. You got me on an IV and you ladies are worried about me feeling pain from a tiny needle? Gals, give it your best shot," Henry boasted.

"Okay, here goes, Grandpa." Susan warned as she inserted

the needle.

"Ouch! Ouch! Ouch! That smarts." Henry yelped.

Katrina and Susan laughed.

"You old sourdoughs aren't so tough after all," Susan said.

Henry silently gritted his teeth struggling to put up a tough front.

About five minutes later a beeping sound came from the processor and a green light flashed showing the nano cells were ready. A slender inch long capsule rolled out onto the tray. Picking up an injector gun, Susan inserted the capsule and slowly injected its contents into and around the wound in several places according to the marked injection points on the holographic projection.

"Grandpa, we don't have to worry about surgery. Nano cells are a fantastic technology. Katrina and I are trying to learn the technology but it does have limits. If the trauma is too severe, an operation to repair damage is required before injecting the nano cells. We aren't trained for that yet," Susan declared.

Katrina taped the wound closed, placed a healing cuff over it and verified it was sending healing progress data onto the projection. The nano cell healing process was monitored for the next three hours.

Henry squirmed on the table complaining of the crawling sensation in his arm, but Katrina assured him it was normal and the sensation would subside. At the end of the three hours of monitoring the cuff and IV tube were removed. Henry now felt comfortable and fell into a restful sleep.

John felt a rocking sensation and heard the siren of an emergency vehicle. He opened one eye and saw the IV bag hanging above him. He also noted the bandage covering his other eye forcing him to move his head to see better.

"Relax, Colonel. You're in an ambulance on the way to

the hospital. Your injuries are severe but not life threatening. You'll be fine," the nurse assured him.

"Thanks," John whispered as he closed his uncovered eye. "How are my people?"

"It's a miracle anyone survived the missile attack but you survived and saved several lives. Without your actions they'd all be dead," the nurse confirmed.

"But I killed them, it's all my fault," John cried out. When he opened his eye again he saw the nurse but the face was that of Henry. "I even killed you. I killed my own father. I should have never let you go."

John sensed something cold against his face and looked around. He was sitting in a chair outside sick bay with lovely Victoria caressing his face with a cold wet towel wiping the sweat away. John gazed around and saw Traven, Slick, David, and Jonathan standing beside him trying to hold on to him.

"I'm sorry. How long was I out of it?" John asked.

"About ten minutes, you had another episode," Victoria said. "You're okay now, just rest."

"How is Dad doing?" John hesitantly asked.

"Grandpa is doing better than you right now," Jonathan said. "Just relax."

"Yes, Dad, please just relax. Everything is taken care of," David repeated.

John nodded and took a deep breath.

"Sorry I let you guys down with this," John said looking at Traven and Slick. "I didn't mean to hide…"

Slick interrupted. "You didn't let anyone down. Traven and I fought in the same war and fight the same ghosts your fighting right now. You are never alone. We are a band of brothers and you will never fight this alone again, ever, you got that?"

"Thanks fellas, but how can I lead all of you?" John asked.

Traven cleared his throat. "John, you have done a great job

so far and you will keep doing a great job. It's who you are."

Slick nodded. "I read the record on you, John. I knew about this before I ever signed on. You don't know how to lose, you don't give up and defeat isn't in your vocabulary. When they said you'd never walk again you proved the experts wrong. You found a way to save so many lives despite your own injuries. Now you need to find a way to defeat your ghosts and we know you will. That's why we're here. Everyone trusts you, even President Leatham. There is no other way he'd agree to all of this if he didn't trust you'd get the job done."

Traven nodded agreement and took John's hands and held them in his big strong hands. Slick covered their hands with his.

"Always together, never alone," Traven declared.

Jonathan, David and Victoria added their hands to the pile. "Never will you fight alone, ever," They repeated.

A tear rolled down John's cheek. "Thanks guys, that means everything to me."

Victoria gave John a hug as the sick bay door opened. Susan saw the hand pile and raised an eyebrow and smiled. "The walls are thin. Everyone, Grandpa is resting and healing well. He's asking for Dad alone. Dad, please keep it short. He needs all the rest he can get for now. Everyone else can visit in the morning."

John slowly stood up as Traven and Jonathan helped steady him.

"Thanks, everyone," John whispered as he entered sick bay.

Henry was resting on the patient bed with his eyes closed as John approached.

"Come closer to me," Henry moaned.

"I'm right here Dad." John said leaning closer.

"Good, I want you to listen carefully. I know you. I know what happened to you in the war and I know the nightmares that haunt you," Henry said as John tried to interrupt him.

"Shhh!" Henry scolded. "There isn't a tear you shed in your episodes that Victoria doesn't shed two so don't try to fool us. It's a lousy secret. I witnessed a couple episodes when I was visiting you at the hospital in Germany. You were unconscious then but I heard everything. I know you're going to blame yourself for me going to town alone and I'm not having none of that. It was my fault and no one else's. I thought I was tough enough to handle things myself. That was stupid on my part and God sent Cat to rescue me. I've been humbled by his grace. Just leave it there."

"I've been humbled as well. I thought I was always alone being haunted by ghosts. It turns out I was never alone. I was just too blind to see it, forgive me."

"Nothing to forgive. Let's just move on. There is a lot of God's business we have to get done and not much time. Pull up a chair and let's pray."

When Susan looked in, the two men were in deep prayer and holding each other's hands. She decided to leave them alone a bit longer.

About an hour later John appeared on the bridge. "How is Henry doing?" Gavin asked.

"He's fine and resting, thank you for asking." John said. "The Chinese sent an assassin to kill us and I can't help wonder how many more are on the way. It won't take long for them to start looking with their satellites. I have to assume more trouble is on the way. Revenge is not on my mind as much as realizing we need to send a message. We have to get these people off our backs and let them know who they are dealing with."

Gavin had a worried look on his face. He handed a data pad to John and shook his head.

"Sorry but I was thinking about your enemies using their

satellites to track us down so I had our ship sensors locate and tap into all their military satellite transmissions. It looks like a satellite is moving into a stationary orbit over Nevada. It won't take them long to find us," Gavin said.

"We think alike. That doesn't detract from our mission, does it?" John asked.

'I was going to propose another training flight and some target practice. At the same time maybe send a friendly warning of things to come if troublesome nations continue their unfriendly behavior. Does that sound acceptable?"

John grinned. "Hmm! More flight and weapons training, a sensor and communications exercise, and an opportunity for you to practice galactic diplomacy. I agree. Let's get the crew ready."

The crew quickly assembled in the passenger lounge looking for some payback for shooting Henry.

"Everyone is standing by for a crew briefing," Victoria reported.

Gavin announced the mission objectives and assigned the targeting data gathered to help Aycana identify the Chinese and French military satellites and civilian communications satellites. "Estron, I prepared a message for you to broadcast through their satellites. After the broadcast, we will commence destruction of several satellites to prove our capability. David and Siyana, the flight profile is already sent to your flight data pads."

An hour later the ship was in orbit. The ship's sensors tapped into twenty of the Chinese, French and German communications satellites.

John gave the order to begin transmitting. All three countries were receiving the transmission of a camera shot of the Cassarian freighter in space and Gavin's recorded message.

"This message is to the people and leaders of China, France and Germany. Greetings from the sovereign planet, Cassaria. You have foolishly tried to bring your world to the brink of war over possession of this ship and its technology. You assumed since it landed in the United States that the American government had possession of the spacecraft. Your assumptions are false.

'This ship and crew are on a diplomatic mission and such hostile acts can be interpreted as acts of war. You sent an assassin to kill us and our friends. We have committed no crime nor harmed anyone to warrant such behavior. You gave your assassin her orders. She has failed in her unfortunate mission. Her criminal acts are on your shoulders.

'Your acts of attempted theft, attempted murder, and violations of International and Galactic laws constitute numerous acts of war crimes against a sovereign nation. The goodness of the Cassarian people thus far have prevented interference in Earth affairs but you have now crossed the line.

'You are seeking a war in which you are totally defenseless. For the sake of the lives of your own people, we demand you cease and desist in your hostile actions or face the most horrible of consequences.

You have twenty-four hours to transmit your desire for peace or reap what you have sown. This demonstration will be your only warning." The transmission ended.

"OK, let's do it. I want just the twenty Chinese and French military communication satellites targeted and destroyed. Aycana, do a scan of each satellite to ensure there are no weapons aboard and report when ready to fire," Gavin ordered.

David and Siyana maneuvered the ship to give Aycana and Jonathan the optimum firing solutions as they approached the targets. Over the next few minutes they scanned and destroyed nineteen satellites. To those people on Earth able to see the explosions it was a gigantic display of pyrotechnics never seen before. The varying sizes of the explosions mixed with red, yellow, green, blue and white colors appeared like a planetary New Year's fireworks display.

An alarm went off on Aycana's scanning console. "I've found a Chinese satellite armed with five nuclear warheads."

"Cease fire! Ceasefire! Shields up. Helm, reverse course and back off 200 miles. Aycana, do sensors show weapons armed?" Gavin asked.

"Yes, sir!" she replied. "They are being armed now." "Communications, we need to jam all signals to and from the satellite." Gavin ordered.

"John, take the captain's chair and I'll assist you. You need the experience," Gavin said.

"Thanks!" John smiled.

"Estron, is it possible to reprogram the satellite computer to fire its engines?" John asked.

"No problem. Earth's computers are very simple. Our computer can make it do anything you want," Estron confirmed.

"Wonderful! Siyana assist Victoria, I need a navigation course plot for the satellite to break orbit on an intercept course with the sun. Estron, does the satellite have enough fuel to break orbit and complete the flight profile?" John asked.

Estron reported, "It barely has enough fuel to break orbit."

"OK, we will have to do it the hard way. David, place the ship on the intercept course for the satellite. Nicky will use the magnetic grappling cable to drag it out of orbit.

Once on its way, Nicky will release the tow and David will bank out of its path. Meanwhile, Estron will program it to fire its engines to complete its intercept course to the sun. There it will incinerate itself with no harm done. Does everyone copy?"

Everyone confirmed the plan.

After the third try Nicky was getting frustrated.

"I'm sorry, sir," Nicky said over the intercom. "I'll try harder."

John smiled. "Nicky, you can do it, just relax and give it a bit more lead."

"Okay, sir," Nicky said. He took a deep breath and aimed more carefully.

Jonathan leaned over and waited for the right moment and whispered, "Fire!"

The magnetic plate missed by about 3 feet. Everyone sighed as Nicky reeled in the cable for a another try.

"That was better, Nicky," John calmly said out over the com.net. "Don't worry about the misses. We'll be here until you get it. Take a deep breath and let me know when you are ready to try again."

"Yes, sir," Nicky sighed again.

"David, I want you to swing by as close as you can and let the ship drift past the satellite. OK? John asked.

"Understand," David answered.

"Something is happening to the satellite computer. It is trying to reboot," Estron called out.

"Keep trying to jam the signal," John ordered.

The ship made a loop and approached the satellite to within a few feet. As it drifted past, Nicky put the sight on the target and fired. The cable played out and the magnetic plate attached itself.

Nicky called out, "We got it!"

"Great job, Nicky. "Estron, what's the status?" John asked.

"Well, when the cable attached itself, the magnetic field blocked the signal. The Chinese are permanently locked out. It is all ours now," Estron replied.

"Thank you. Great job everyone," John said. "Now let's get this thing on its merry way and go home.

The Cassarian freighter safely returned to the Nevada desert. Upon landing, everyone gathered in the passenger lounge for a debriefing then to supper.

In the dining tent, the crew watched the news report on

the Cassarian Ambassador's telecast message and the world's reaction.

John and Victoria joined the rest of their family at the table. "What are they reporting?" Victoria asked.

Susan smiled. "People from all three countries are in the streets protesting their leaders' reckless behavior. World leaders are making the usual righteous indignation speeches demanding the three governments be held accountable for their actions and confirm support for the Cassarians. In France, the French president declared Cassarian actions as acts of aggression. However, the streets of Paris and other cities filled with protesters demanding the president resign or be removal from office. The military leaders responded by placing the president under house arrest pending the outcome of an investigation of his actions. They also promised elections for a new government within ninety days.

Jonathan added, "The German prime minister announced her resignation and was arrested before she could run. The Chinese military were confronting large crowds throughout the country. Thousands of civilians were being shot, but the harsher the military cracked down, the more people resisted. In desperation, the Chinese Communist Party leaders were removed in an internal coup. The new regime chose peace."

"Looks like it's all over for the bad guys," David said.

"Don't bet on it," Victoria said. "With these people, it's just a matter of time before they raise their evil heads again."

Working late in her office, Loretta caught a news segment about the alien visitors and ship. Earlier reports claimed the aliens, their spaceship, and a Michigan family were being held at Area 51.

"If Russ sees this he'll know I'm the leak. Time to put an end to this relationship once and for all," Loretta seethed.

Russ was irritated but not surprised. Instead of being upset he immersed himself reviewing the finishing touches on his latest tome, *Imperial Roman Contributions to Modern Concepts of National Security.*

It wasn't until the fifth ring he answered. "Dr. Long speaking!"

"Russ, it's Loretta. I didn't wake you, did I?"

"No, I was actually working on my manuscript. You forgot to call me after work."

Loretta feigned being tired. "Sorry, I just got home."

"You still could have called!" Russ scolded.

"Russ, let me make it up to you, please? I'll meet you at Nash's Diner. You know that all night, 50's diner two blocks from my apartment? My treat!"

Russ perked up. "The one with the Nash Rambler on display? Is the food good?"

"They claim the best Ruben sandwich in the metro area."

"Now you hooked me! Be there in ten minutes."

"I'm here and waiting!" Loretta said and hung up.

Russ's frustration dissipated. Russ raced to the bedroom, struggled into a clean polo shirt and splashed on some cologne. Snatching up his coat, he awkwardly plunged his arms into the sleeves, then hurried out the door.

True to form, the coat pocket caught the door knob pulling him off balance. Russell looked quite comical sprawled on the floor flat on his back.

Two security guards watching the monitor burst out laughing when they saw Russ hit the hallway floor. One of the guards noted the time on the security log.

"He's getting better. That's six days since his last stunt," the security guard said as his partner handed him a five spot. "Keep your money, you make me feel like a thief. Can't believe you keep betting on this loser!"

Their laughter stopped when the underground parking garage camera showed a woman in a flaming red wig, black mini skirt, stilettos and a long fur coat slip up behind Russell Long as he opened the driver's door to his green sedan. Russ appeared not to know the person at first. There was a brief discussion before Russ showed he was hesitant to get in the vehicle.

She placed her hand in her coat pocket and pointed it at Russ like she had a gun pointing at him. Russ held out his hands as a shield but slowly got into the driver's seat. Russ's response alerted the two guards.

Once the woman got in the back seat, they drove down the exit ramp.

The first guard looked at his partner, "Call the police. I'll try to intercept them," as he ran out the door. Russ's car exited the garage as the guard burst from the emergency exit. He was just in time to see the green sedan hang a left and speed out of view.

It didn't take long for the Metro police to locate his car ten blocks away, parked along the side of the road, engine running. Blood splatter covered the windshield. Russ was slumped over the steering wheel with a massive bullet hole through the head. The officer placed his fingertips on Russell's neck and shook his head. "No pulse, he's dead."

"Ya ready to order, honey?" the waitress asked.

Loretta angrily set her smart phone down for the fifth time. "Men! They want you to be on time but can't manage it themselves!" She heaved a sigh.

"Yes, I'll have a club sandwich and salad with Italian dressing to go."

"As you wish," the waitress answered.

CHAPTER 8

John, Gavin, Jonathan, Slick and Traven stood at the foot of the ship's ramp starring at a large cart covered with a tarp. Henry, Dexter and Deze were quite proud of their invention.

Henry explained. "John asked us to come up with a solution to gas the crew and take over the *Holcron Star*. We calculated we need to deliver way more gas than the grenades can deliver. I think we came up with a solution that is easy and guaranteed to get the job done fast. Fellas, remove the tarp."

Deze and Dexter removed the tarp to reveal a cart mounted with a large spool of high pressure hose with a special nozzle.

"This is our solution," Henry explained. "The one end is hooked up to the gas tanks in the cargo bay. We run the hose down the ramp to the hangar exit door then down the corridor to the air quality duct system compartment. Once the nozzle is attached to the duct, the gas is released and circulated, the crew gets knocked out, and the ship is ours. We calculated it will take eight of these hoses to deliver the gas fast enough to get the job done. You can use this one for your dry run exercise this afternoon. Tell us what you think and we can make whatever modifications you need."

"What are you using to pump the gas?" John asked.

"Estron routed a pressure line from the auxiliary pump in the engine room to the tanks. It can deliver all the pressure we'll need," Deze said.

John and Gavin looked at Slick and Traven.

"I think this will get the job done and a simple way to do it. We can assign two people to each line and once the gas is released the teams kick off," Traven said.

Gavin nodded. "This is just the ticket to pull this off."

Slick nodded agreement.

"By the way, how soon before we could remove our masks?" Traven asked.

"I have an air tester that will register when it is safe. I estimate about five minutes for the scrubbers to filter out the gas once the sensors are turned back on. They will be out for at least an hour. That leaves plenty of time to secure the ship and flex cuff the pirates before they recover. According to Deze, when they regain consciousness, crewmembers are going to have blurred vision, severe headaches, and very weak," Dexter replied.

"Ok, let's do it. Traven and Slick will work out the procedures to make sure it goes smoothly," John said.

After lunch, Estron began training Victoria and three others in space navigation and communications on the bridge. "Since navigation tasks are computerized, the most important skill for the moment is learning to use the navigation computer and gain familiarity with star system charts, symbols and input commands. The Communications console handles both deep space and sub space communication. You will master the basics of both. Once you have mastered the basics you will learn secure communications encoding and decoding procedures. Everyone on the bridge crew must learn both navigation and communications skills."

Georgia raised her hand. Isn't the bridge fully manned at all times?"

"Not usually," Estron said. "Most of the time the bridge has only three to four people on duty. When at a higher state of readiness, the bridge is fully manned. A fresh crew is usually used to replace the bridge crew especially if they have been on duty for several hours."

"Today we will review and practice receiving and sending sub-light video and messages. We'll also finish our phase 2 class in sub-warp navigation. Learning to plot a single course change on the fly at sub-warp speed is not too difficult but a series of warp course changes has to be carefully checked and rechecked to prevent gravitational drift deviations for example.

'In warp navigation each succeeding miscalculation or uncorrected course change multiplies the chance of crashing into a sun, planet or meteorite. To prevent that, the computer verifies the actual arrival point. It then calculates any necessary course deviations to avoid collisions with all known objects on the proposed flight path.

If the ship's sensors detect objects on the flight path it will automatically update the flight plan and alert you during the jump. The navigator's job is to verify the computer corrections before engaging each segment of the jump. Everyone's lives rests on your flawless performance."

On the deep space communications screen, an amber light flashed, a computerized voice announced an incoming message.

"Hold it, Victoria!" Estron cautioned. "Press the message record icon but don't open a channel reply or acknowledgment."

"What kind of message is it?" Victoria asked.

"It's a search message from the *Holcron Star.* Call Gavin and John to bridge," Estron said.

When Gavin and John arrived they played the message. "They are trying to establish contact." Gavin said.

Gavin and John replayed the message.

"But why do that if they know we are here?" Victoria asked.

Good question," John said. "Gavin, you told us they were coming here."

"I thought so. If there was a change, the lead pirate on our ship kept it to himself," Gavin said scratching his head. "Before the fight began this is where I was told we were meeting the pirate captain."

John rubbed his chin in thought. "Okay, so we wait until

the last possible moment then make contact. I'm gambling your ship is not at the correct rendezvous point."

"How do you know that," Estron asked.

"If we were at the correct location I don't think they'd be sending a search message. Obviously, they weren't expecting us here like I thought," Gavin said.

"So, does that mean Earth is not in the danger we thought?" John asked.

"Hardly," Gavin said. "Captain Gath has violent plans for Earth that he made plain. The details I know not, but it would be a first if he showed up and threw a party. There is no way around the facts when he discovers; the escorts are destroyed, we've taken our ship back, and we have his treasure. He will go on a rampage to find us. One thing I do know, everyone who had a hand in aiding us are all going to share in his wrath."

"Well, our goal is to get to him first. Let's get this set up." John said paging Deze to the bridge.

When Deze replayed the search message he immediately became frightened.

"Do…do you want me to reply now?" Deze asked.

"Estron, can you tell how far away the *Holcron Star* is?"John asked.

She donned an earpiece and verbally asked the computer the question. Within seconds the computer completed the signal analysis and cross-referenced the data to the astronavigation chart at the Navigation station behind her. A small red dot appeared on the chart screen giving the approximate location of the *Holcron Star*. "I'm transferring the data to the holographic projector now," Estron announced.

There was dead silence on the bridge as they studied the holographic projection.

The projection showed a sector of space including Earth and many other solar systems.

Gavin explained, "A faint white sphere shows the limit of the ship's sensors. Well beyond it you see a red blip of the computer's estimate of where the *Holcron Star* is and estimated course."

John broke the silence. "That's odd. They are on a course to Sepious Minor. It's more out of the way than Earth. Estron, how much time do we have before they are out of range of our reply signal?"

"Just a moment," Estron said as she queried the computer. A yellow ring appeared showing the maximum distance their signal could reach.

"Gavin, if we wait till they are almost out of range before sending a distress signal, how long before they would most likely arrive?" John asked.

"I would send the distress signal when they are about here," Gavin said pointing to an area on the map projection.

"They will slow down to sub-light speed once they approach your solar system and could arrive about six to eight hours later depending on their speed. I suggest we keep the moon between them and us. That way their sensors will not detect us until visual contact is made."

"Deze, you ready to put on your little play?" John asked.

"Yes, sir!" Deze pledged.

"Good, we'll send the distress signal in four hours. It is imperative you be convincing. I have every confidence you'll do a great job," John urged.

John's confidence bolstered Deze's courage. "You can count on me. I won't let you down."

Traven and Slick arrived on the bridge. "You are just in time," Gavin announced.

"Really, for what?" Traven asked.

"We just received a search message from the *Holcron Star*. If all goes according to my estimates, they will arrive in 32 days," Gavin replied.

"Correction, make that about seven days," John said. Everyone looked astonished at John's statement.

Gavin shook his head. "And how do you know that?"

"I said before there were things not adding up," John reminded him. "He is traveling way to fast to transit the distances in the pirate computer files. Your records show the ship was designed for Warp 4 speed. However, the pirate records have the ship traveling at Warp 6 transit times. He'll be here in four to seven days."

"I told you that was impossible!" Gavin declared. "We can only travel at Warp 4. No one has engines that can travel any faster."

"John swiveled the Captain's chair around and typed in a couple commands. A moment later one of the pirate files appeared on the Captain's screen.

"Here you go," John said. "Check it all out yourself. Estron, you too. You come up with a different answer let me know. Traven and Slick have an exercise I have to attend so I have to excuse myself."

With that John left the bridge. Traven looked at Slick with a shocked expression.

"I guess we'd better get going too," Slick said.

When they reached the bottom of the ramp Traven stopped. "What was that all about?"

"I'd say someone has been doing his homework and others aren't keeping up," Slick replied.

"It looked more like the student just took the master to the woodshed to me." Traven agreed.

Slick tugged on Traven's sleeve. "Come on, before the student takes us to the woodshed too."

All the boarding party teams were assembled and waiting when John arrived at the mockup training area. In the open desert were life sized wooden and canvas layouts of the four decks and the bridge. It didn't look like a space ship. However, it gave everyone a sense of the immenseness of the ship, what was located where and how to clear each compartment.

Slick had a few surprises for the assault squads along the way just to keep everyone from thinking it would be easy.

The teams assembled at the initial assault point, which simulated the freighter's cargo bay.

"Everyone ready!" Slick called out.

"Hooah!" Everyone cried out.

Traven blew the whistle to start the timed exercise.

Twenty minutes later the exercise ended and everyone assembled in the mockup hangar area.

Traven critiqued the exercise. "Assault Teams 1 and 2 did very well but still took too long to clear their assigned decks. Alpha Team failed to clear the Captain's Deck and thus were killed and that led to the rest of the teams being wiped out.

'In a few days, we will be doing the real assault. If Alpha Team fails we are all dead. For all our sakes, you have to work together. No mistakes. Tomorrow, we will practice this again and again until it is flawless. Breakfast is at 0600 hours. We will assemble at the mockup at 0800 hours. Dismissed!"

John held back Alpha team. "We aren't waiting until tomorrow. I apologize for not being a more effective team leader. I won't let you down again. It is now up to you to not let me down. The success of taking the bridge is paramount. I know killing someone is a foreign concept for you. However, if we don't overcome this fear we will not be the only ones to die. Everyone will die. That can't be allowed. We are it folks, now let's get this right."

"Yes, sir!" the team shouted.

"That's the spirit," John grinned. "Now let's walk through the plan and look for what can go wrong and how we are going to react."

After the walk through, everyone returned to the top of the simulated ramp.

"OK, does everyone understand their task and how to react to the changing situation?" John asked.

Everyone nodded.

"Well let's see if we do," John said blowing his whistle. Five minutes later they were at the simulated bridge. John looked at his watch.

"That was slow but everyone completed their tasks. Once the gas is released, we must get to the bridge as fast as we can without a single mistake. Do it again."

It took seven more attempts before Alpha Team finally reached their best time of two minutes, thirty seconds with no mistakes.

In the distance, Slick and Traven were observing the team go through their paces.

"Not bad, not bad at all," Slick said.

"For a bunch of amateurs, they got the choreography down. Let's see how they do tomorrow with pressure and someone shooting back," Traven said. "I expect they will choke when it comes to pulling the trigger."

Deze practiced his message but it did not go well. Long years of intimidation and fear of the pirate captain was so ingrained that his voice was totally unconvincing. With the reality of the pirates approaching, all those fears were returning to haunt him.

John and Gavin were concerned. The mission was on the verge of failure unless Deze pulls it together.

Victoria decided to take the matter into her own hands. She sat down on the chair next to an uncontrollably shaking Deze.

"Deze, have you ever thought about all the friends you

have made since coming to Earth?"

"Oh yes. I've never had so many friends before. Everyone here treats me like I'm needed and part of the family. I never had brothers or sisters. Growing up in space you don't make many friends either. I'm so different yet all of you act as if none of that matters," Deze replied.

"Because it doesn't matter," Victoria said matter-of-factly. "Deze, your past is forgotten. You have demonstrated loyalty, courage and resourcefulness. These are virtues of a warrior, but more importantly, you have proven a good and true friend. People will speak proudly of these virtues whenever your name is mentioned on Earth for centuries to come."

"Really? You really think so?" Deze asked feeling a bit of pride.

Victoria smiled, "Yes, I do, Deze. We all have faith in you. No matter how you might feel, you have friends that will stand with you. You have a home with us. You are one of us now."

Deze raised his head with new found courage. "I guess you're right. My friends are more important than my fears. This is something I have to do. Let's do it."

He stepped over to the communications console and selected the pirate-code frequency on the deep space communications screen and took a deep breath. John, Victoria, Gavin, Estron and David nodded silently, anxiously waiting for Deze to begin.

"*Holcron Star*, come in! *Holcron Star*, p-p-p-please come in!" Deze stuttered. He stopped, shook his whole body as a dog might shake after getting wet. Then clearing his throat announced with a wince, "I forgot to touch the mike icon."

"No harm. Go ahead, you can do it," John encouraged.

Deze took another deep breath, resolutely touched the mike icon and with a calm clear voice spoke.

"*Holcron Star*, please respond. This is Gamoran freighter 1-2-9-7. *Holcron Star*, this is Gamoran freighter 1-2-9-7. Please reply?" Deze paused for a minute and repeated the call.

On the third call there was a crackle of static then a voice replied,

"Gamoran freighter 1-2-9-7. This is the *Holcron Star*, standby."

There was a long pause, then a deep angry voice roared over the intercom, "Captain Togg Gath here! Lieutenant Pimish, you were supposed to meet at the rendezvous point. Where, by the gods of Gamora, have you been? I'll have your head for this if you don't have a good excuse."

"Sir! This is Shipmate Deze," was all he had time to say before being interrupted.

"I don't want to speak to the ship's bilge monkey. Put Lieutenant Pimish on now or I'll have you cut ear to ear. You hear me?" Captain Gath growled.

"I'm sorry, sir. Lieutenant Pimish and most of the crew were killed when we were attacked and our escort destroyed. Two other severely wounded crewmembers survived but later died as well. I am the only crew member left."

"Well, too bad for them," the pirate captain responded as if only inconvenienced. "Is my cargo secure?"

"Yes, sir," Deze replied. "It is secure. However, the ship is…"

"Are the hostages alive?" Captain Gath interrupted.

Deze cleared his throat. "Sir, they are injured but still alive. The ship was damaged and I have made some repairs but all the coolant has leaked out and warp travel is impossible. Request docking for coolant resupply and replacement crew."

"So, you fancy yourself the ship's new captain, hey? Well, I'll decide who gets to be the hero around here. We have a rendezvous to keep and will arrive in four days. After you dock, report to me. I will decide what to do next. Out!"

The communications screen confirmed the call ended. Everyone on the bridge cheered and patted Deze's back for his performance. John raised his hand to request silence, and then inquired, "Well, do you think he bought it, Deze?"

"Oh yes. He bought it all right," Deze replied. "He is probably setting up my execution as we speak, but not until he gets the ship and hostages back."

"Don't worry Deze, he'll never get the chance," Gavin reassured him.

"Deze, you did a wonderful job. Thank you!" Victoria smiled as she gave him a kiss on the cheek.

Deze's eyes went wide as his scarred face blushed in embarrassment.

Two hours after Dr. Russell Long's funeral, President Leatham, FBI Director Leon James and Director of Homeland Security Alan Bates sat in the Oval office.

"Gentlemen, how is the investigation going?"the president asked. "Sir, whoever did this was trying to be really clever," the FBI director stated. "The murderer meant us to believe a prostitute kidnapped him and shot him. My people aren't buying it."

"Explain?" the president inquired.

"It was totally out of character for Russell. There was no pornography found in his home or on his computer to connect him to that kind of lifestyle.

'We have questioned almost a hundred people in the area that night. Nobody recognizes a streetwalker or call girl matching the description the cab driver gave us. I think the killer wants us to waste time on this rabbit trail while the real trail grows cold. There has to be a motive but so far we can't find it. I promise we will keep looking, Mr. President," replied Director James.

"Please keep looking. I appreciate your hard work. Russell

was a good man. Whoever did this must be brought to justice. Is it possible that Russell was killed by a foreign agent?" the president asked.

"Mr. President, we have no indication of that, but we are exploring all possibilities at this time. Our intelligence sources can't find any connection with France or China, but it's still early in the investigation," Director Alan Bates said reassuringly.

The president sighed in frustration. "OK, gentlemen. Please keep me informed of any new developments. Thank you."

The president's phone rang. His secretary informed him CIA Director Mike Richards was on hold. The two men excused themselves.

"Yes, Mike, what's up?" the president asked.

"Mr. President, I just received a message from our rogue agent."

The Gamoran pirate ship is expected to arrive in four days.

"OK, I'll have the Secretary of State implement our global notification alert and pass along what intelligence they need. If the Cassarian Ambassador and the Braxtons fail, we play ignorant. If we have to do so, we do what we can to defend ourselves," President Leatham said.

"Yes, Mr. President. We'll do our part,"Director Richards agreed.

Darkness descended over the valley. The cold crisp, clear night revealing a brilliant star-studded heaven. There was a full house for evening prayer meeting. John and Gavin arrived late but just in time to hear Chaplain Boyle's message. Their families saved them each a seat.

"When I was a little boy," Chaplain Boyle began, "I heard the story of David and Goliath for the first time. One of the things that impressed me was why would David use a sling? More importantly once he saw the giant Goliath, why did he pick up five stones?

'If it was me, I'd have picked up a lot more than five stones I can guarantee you. Years later during the War of Russian Aggression I was at an air base in Poland when it came under a missile attack. As the missiles rained down on our base I was terrified at what was happening. There was nothing that could have prepared me for that attack. I was wounded and ended up in a hospital in Germany. As I laid on a gurney waiting to be rolled into the operating room, oddly enough, a question I had asked myself came back to me. Why did David pick up five stones?

'While you're on a gurney and numbed up really good with nothing to do but stare at the ceiling I guess your mind will dredge up all kinds of crazy things. I couldn't get those five stones out of my mind. There was no doubt of David's complete trust in God. No matter what danger David faced, he found courage in the knowledge that God was with him. He killed a lion and a bear so who was this Goliath to fear?

'Yes, what about the five stones? I realized he picked up five stones out of the brook because those five stones were just the right size and shape. Nice and round, not too small and not too big. They were just right to fall a giant. They were the perfect sling ammo and the first shot brought down a giant. Bull's eye!

'It was at that moment I realized it was the brook God wanted me to focus on. In the middle of a battle that was to change history God shaped those stones for just the right moment. It was a brook that shaped me too. I could hear the water gently soothing my wrecked body and soul. It brought peace to me in a moment of most desperate need just like it did David. As David prepared to go to battle the brook met his need.

The drugs brought nothing but numbness to me, but a gentle brook brought me peace. God was still with me and he promised to restore my soul.

'Let us visit Psalm 23. Over the centuries, many a soldier has found comfort in Psalm 23. As we prepare for the upcoming battle, let us be of good courage for God is with us …"

Afterwards, John strolled through the camp making his late-night rounds. The camp was quiet except for the hushed conversations and muffled humming of the power generator on the opposite side of camp.

Many people turned in for the night while others took a shower or wrote a final note to loved ones. Four people pulled security detail. Another person monitored the security system. John joined one of them for a few minutes as she did her rounds.

"Georgia, how's the snake bite healing?" John asked.

"Doing well, sir. It's all healed up as if it never happened," Georgia replied.

"Glad to hear it. When do you get off shift?"

"I'm on guard duty till midnight then two others have it for four hours. Traven doesn't want anyone to miss too much sleep so we are alert for tomorrow. The camp seems unusually calm and quiet tonight," Georgia observed as they rounded the corner of the motor pool. "Is it always like this before a battle?"

"I can't say as my personal experience was different but I imagine the last couple days and nights are different as people begin to steel their minds. Are you worried about what's coming?"

Georgia brushed a lock of auburn hair from her face and looked up into the starry sky. "You know it seems so strange. A month ago, the world seemed so absolutely set in granite. All this was supposed to be impossible. Then Susan called me and said she had the opportunity of a lifetime and to come to Reno. I couldn't imagine what she meant but curiosity got the better of me. You're paying for the plane trip made it impossible to refuse. At first I was scared to death but realized at least I have the chance to do something about it. I realize now everyone else is just as nervous. Chaplain Boyle was right. We just have to do our best and trust God for the victory. Are you nervous, sir?"

"Nervous? You've got to be kidding. My nerves are made of steel," John teased as he shook his body like he was having spasms.

Georgia giggled, "I guess it doesn't matter who you are does it?"

"No, Georgia. It's quite normal. I had a great uncle who fought in the Pacific during World War II. He rarely talked about it. He said he lost his best friends during the war. One time he opened up and told me of his first battle. It was his first night on Guadalcanal. He was trying to get some sleep in a foxhole half filled with filthy water. The stench of death filled the humid jungle air. Bullets, tracers and screams of the wounded and dying from both sides filled the dank jungle as the enemy probed along the front line. He was so scared he was petrified with fear. He was convinced if he closed his eyes he'd never open them again.

'Things seemed to quiet down and several men in his squad began whispering relief. Suddenly a trumpet blared and 200 enemy soldiers charged their position. Night flares filled the sky illuminating the battlefield as mortar rounds exploded everywhere. It wasn't until a bullet ricocheted off the top of his helmet that he came to his senses. He got indignant someone dared shoot at him. At that moment, his training and will to survive kicked in. Without even thinking about it, he started throwing grenades and firing his machinegun and yelling at the enemy, daring them to do it again. He dodged from one foxhole to another as the enemy pressed their attack. The next morning, he discovered he was the only man left alive in his squad.

'He never got over that experience. He just knew if he was ever going to make it home alive he needed to fight smart, keep on fighting and above all trust in God. Don't worry, Georgia, I have great trust in you. You'll do your duty just fine."

"Thanks for having such confidence in me, Mr. Braxton. I won't let you down, I promise."

John left Georgia to finish her security rounds and joined up with Jonathan, Katrina and Nicky as they sat around a small campfire.

"Nicky, how's it going?" John inquired.

"Just fine, Mr. Braxton." Nicky smiled.

"We're just talking about our college days, Dad," Jonathan said.

"We were reminiscing of the time we roomed together my junior year. That was the same year I met Katrina."

"Then indeed, it was a very good year," John said.

Katrina gave a soft laugh and nodded agreement.

"Nicky, Jonathan was telling me you were about to start working for NASA. How do you like space now?" John inquired.

"Well, sir, It's more than I ever dreamed it would be. I used to lie on the lawn at night and stare at the stars for hours wondering if I'd ever get to travel to them or if there really was life on other planets. I never dreamed this would happen. I wouldn't have passed this up for the world," Nicky exclaimed with excitement.

"Well, we're really glad to have you along, Nicky. The stars have always fascinated me too. You're not the only one who likes to star gaze here. I like to get out on a clear night and just enjoy the vastness of the heavens. It's always an opportunity for reflection, wonder and peaceful time with God. I really enjoy those moments."

"Yes, I know what you mean," Nicky agreed. One thing

does confuse me though. Most people thought life could only exist on Earth. Has this shaken your faith at all?"

"God didn't tell us everything he knows nor did he tell us everything he wants us to know. He gave us a lot to explore and learn. I think God gets a special thrill when we discover more of his creation. Kind of like opening a Christmas present," John said.

"I never thought of it like that before. It really isn't my faith in God that is shaken but my arrogance in thinking we could put God in this neat little box," Nicky agreed.

"There you have it in a nutshell. Well, everyone, get a good night's sleep. Tomorrow is going to be a long day," John warned.

As John returned to the ship he found Victoria, Susan, David and Siyana sitting at the top of the ramp. Siyana was describing her home and what life is like on her world.

"Just about all construction on our world is done by droids. Some droids are human like but only about half as tall. A few are as tall as people. Most droids are about knee high and rectangular. They carry a variety of tools and attachments to do a variety of tasks where the other droids are more specialized. They scurry about doing assigned tasks with great precision and very useful on space missions. Each one is programmed to do certain tasks during each phase of construction. The droids can work metal; weld, install electrical circuits and plumbing very quickly and efficiently even in space.

They work twenty-six hours a day, every day and only break for recharging or maintenance."

"Is your calendar like ours?" Victoria asked.

"Yes, very similar. Our weeks are eight days long, with ten months and our year is 360 days long. We have a leap year like you do but it is every ten years.

'We use a type of ceramic polymer concrete that cures

within a couple hours allowing construction to continue very quickly. This substance allows us to be more creative in shaping our buildings. A similar heat resistant, armor version is used in space craft construction. We used it to repair our hull. It can also be used in space. Metal is still used in some areas but as you can see on this ship it is used sparingly.

'For example, this ship took less than two months to build. People do some of the finish work but much of it is prefabricated by droids. The humans inspect everything during the construction process to ensure safety and quality.

'A ship like the *Holcron Star* with enough droids can be built in a year and a half. It then takes two months for humans to finish fitting and inspecting the ship.

'To build a large home like the ones on Earth takes less than a couple weeks with droids after the foundation is laid and the human finish work another week."

"Wow! That is fast. You miss your home?" Susan asked.

"Oh, yes. I think of home often. The gleaming white cities are so beautiful with a simple flowing style of architecture. With our technology, our cities don't experience the noise and crowding like your cities."

'Free enterprise was a core belief in our society for centuries until the planet came under one government, it gradually became more a collective than a free market. With the pirate wars, our economy has largely stagnated. Politicians control everything and at the heart of what is wrong with everything."

"So how does intergalactic trade work?" Victoria asked.

Siyana lowered her head. "Grandfather wanted to start a company but to do so he had to get permission from the Cassarian Corporate Commission. It is controlled by three of the most powerful families in politics. They refused to allow it. He sold almost everything he owned to bribe them.

They assumed he'd fail but he began trading with Holcron and became rich overnight. They tried to stop the trade but the public supported him so they had to back off. It was about then the pirates began attacking his ships with impunity. Father joined the military and rose thru the ranks quickly. When he rescued the Earthlings his popularity grew and he became king. I think the politicians thought they could control him but that backfired too."

"How does the military survive in a society like that?"John asked.

"Anyone can join the military but our Christ following families are heavily taxed and persecuted. To escape it, most of them serve in the military. We are at the mercy of the politicians who disdain us. Some of the public sector prefers we remain out of sight and out of mind. Thankfully, a majority of the public recognizes our sacrifice and appreciates our service. Sadly that majority is shrinking. Our military is allowed to be strong enough to keep our enemies at bay but not to defeat them. Thus the status quo," Siyana explained showing her frustration. "I hope someday our people are able to have the freedom your country enjoys. Everyone seems so much happier here than on my home world."

"We see our freedoms eroding as well but we are not as far down that road. I hope freedom comes to your world too, Siyana. Freedom is what the heart longs for, but there is always someone who just can't let people live their own lives," Victoria sympathized.

"I hate to break this party up folks, but we really need to turn in. It will be a very long day tomorrow. " John said as he helped Victoria up. "See all of you in the morning!"

Traven clapped his hands together and rubbed them excitedly. "Well everyone, now that the morning exercises have got you warmed up, let's get to work. Up to the mock up ramp and let's see if you got what it takes today."

Looking around, Traven signaled Henry and Deze to get ready. He blew his whistle and the drill began. As the teams raced forward smoke bombs went off and stun grenades exploded. Everyone charged on with lightning speed. Four minutes later everyone was at their finish marks.

Mission was declared complete.

Alpha Team reached its objective in record time. They then employed radios to direct the progress of the other teams smoothly and accurately.

John looked at his team. "You all did fantastic, great job."

Slick looked at Traven and both nodded approvingly. "Three weeks of effort brought the teams together as best as could be expected," Slick declared. "With the use of the knock out gas we can do it."

Gavin joined them. "Gentlemen, I was watching from the ship. I'm impressed. I didn't expect it to go so well. Your people are not the same people I saw three weeks ago."

Traven smiled. "You are right they have improved quite a bit. They have a long way to go but under the circumstances I hope we can get the job done without anyone getting killed."

"So, do I," Gavin agreed. "So, do I."

"So, does everyone else," Slick said. "I'm worried."

"About what?" Gavin asked.

"They are as good as we have time get them. The mission plan is as good as it can be. I've done missions that were flawless in planning but went down the sewer from the get go in action. We need to reinforce in the minds of our experienced people the need to keep the amateurs moving and engaged. If a firefight breaks out they are the ones who will bear the brunt.

Alpha Team has improved beyond my expectations but they are still the most vital yet weakest link in this operation.

They die so do we," Slick said.

"Good point," Traven agreed. "Let's run it again?"

The morning wore on and drill after drill proved they were as ready as could be.

After lunch, Gavin went to the bridge to find David and Siyana deep in their flight training. John and Victoria were at the holographic projector gazing at a star map.

"What are you looking at?" Gavin asked.

"Victoria and I were wondering what rendezvous Captain Gath was talking about. On the star map, I traced the flight path and it leads to a coordinate in the middle of nowhere. It's even more remote than Earth if you think about it," John explained. "It's even more concerning they must be traveling at warp 6 to make it to Earth in time."

"That's impossible! Something isn't right," Gavin said. He replotted the projected course and time of travel.

He looked at the result and recalculated it again.

"You're right. Gavin said. "Something is wrong. I don't know what it is but I can't explain it either. In two days, we will capture the ship and have an answer. In the meantime…"

"I know, don't worry about it. It's impossible!" John smiled.

Gavin just shook his head and left the bridge.

Victoria kept starring at the star chart in deep thought. "We have a bigger problem."

"What's that?" John asked.

"Whoever Gath is meeting most likely has warp 6 capability too or they wouldn't be meeting there," Victoria said.

CHAPTER 9

The arrival of a cold front during the night left a light dusting of snow across the canyon floor. The unusual Indian summer in November came to an abrupt end over the Humboldt range. For Braxton's little army, the clear cold sunrise was the last thing on everyone's mind as they stood in formation near the freighter.

Gavin and his crew were already aboard completing their preflight checks. Standing at the top of the ramp, John waited for Traven and Slick to complete their inspection of the teams. Once the inspections were complete, John addressed the group.

"A short time ago nobody dreamed the world would find itself at this moment in history. People from other planets, space pirates, and giant spaceships were reserved for science fiction books and Hollywood movies, yet here we are. This is the reality, losing is not an option! There are no second chances, no instant replays.

'Years from now when you are old and gray, children will gather at your feet and beg to hear the great stories of courage, loyalty, honor and sacrifice for humankind. We have the honor to tell of great deeds, the heroes we fought beside, weep for the fallen and of a great God who was with us.

'Many people will wish to tell our story but their words will fall silent. They were not here and did not earn the right. Only we who paid the price can speak of triumph, glory and the dawn of a new age for mankind. By God's grace we made it happen.

'Throughout history great heroes have lived and died. Sadly, many names are lost in the annals of times past and battles long forgotten. We will not be forgotten. We will overcome. We will be victorious. We have a world to save!"

"Hooah!" everyone shouted and charged up the ramp.

Once the boarding was completed, John started to raise the ramp. As he looked down the ramp he stopped. At the bottom of the ramp, a solitary figure stood, a forlorn look on his face. John walked down the ramp, and his arms around his father.

"Take care, son!" Henry pleaded. "I want my family back safe."

"Don't worry, Dad. We'll be back. Stay close to the flip com I gave you. Hold down the fort. I'll contact you when the ship is ours. I promise."

They patted each other on the back one last time before Henry walked a safe distance away.

John walked up the ramp, turned and waved a last farewell as the ramp door began to close.

A short while later, the freighter was in position using the moon to mask its presence. To monitor the approach of the *Holcron Star,* six military satellites in orbit around Earth were made available by NASA to help detect its approach while the freighter stayed out of view.

Everyone was eager for action. Some people waited in the lounge but still the cargo bay was crowded. The odors of nervous, sweating people packed into the cargo bay grew stronger as the hours ticked by. There was nothing to do but bear the agonizing wait.

"It's been six hours and still no sign of the *Holcron Star* Gavin whispered.

John nodded but said nothing.

"You think we should move the ship out into the open?" Gavin asked.

"No, we need to be patient and let them come to us. The less time they have to find and scan us the better. No, we just wait," cautioned John.

Two hours later, the pirates still hadn't made their appearance. The teams in the cargo bay were stretching, doing pushups, and even running in place to shake off the effects of the cramped space and stress.

Those crewmen on the bridge were not able to work off their stress. They were totally focused on their tasks. However, they did draw inspiration by the coolness John and Gavin displayed. John sat on a portable seat next to the holographic projector and the Captain's chair. In hushed tones, John and Gavin exchanged information with a calmness and confidence that told the rest of the crew everything was under control.

A red dot appeared on the holographic projector. It was the *Holcron Star.*

Estron was at the Navigation console and reported, "Gavin, the ship is at Warp 2 just passing Jupiter."

"They are coming in faster than expected," Gavin said.

"No problem," John declared. "It's less time for them to react."

A pulsing amber light flashed on the Communications panel signaling an incoming message. Deze was about to respond when John stopped him.

"Don't answer it yet, Deze. Wait till he hails us a couple more times. Let them get a little worked up first. It will distract them from getting suspicious," John cautioned.

Three more hails were sent and each succeeding message was angrier in tone.

"OK! Deze, reply now!" John said.

"*Holcron Star!* This is Gamoran freighter 1-2-9-7."

"Standby 1-2-9-7!" said the pirate communications operator.

Captain Gath growled over the comm. link "We will arrive in 15 minutes. Dock when we arrive and don't waste my time about it either."

"Yes, sir! Will dock immediately upon your arrival. Out!" Deze curtly replied.

"To all hands! We will be docking with the *Holcron Star* in about fifteen minutes. Make final team checks and prepare for the assault." John announced over the PA system while giving Deze a thumb's up sign and nod of approval.

"Gavin, they have dropped down to .5 sub-light speed," Estron announced.

"Well, Gavin, thanks for the ride. See you when we take the ship," John said as he shook Gavin's hand.

Victoria gave David a hug. "You two take care of each other," Victoria said giving Siyana a wink and followed John to the elevator.

Aycana also gave her brother a hug. She was a bit uncomfortable using the Earthling custom but she liked the sentiment it conveyed.

Gavin was surprised but accepted the gesture. "You take care!"

Aycana smiled, "I'm not the one you need to worry about. It's the other two."

Gavin smiled. "You're right. That's why you are going and they aren't. Father would kill me."

Aycana smiled and waved good bye.

"Captain Gath, our sensors have detected six satellites tracking us," a pirate at a console reported.

"Those puny people are able to track us?" the captain asked.

"Apparently so. We are also receiving a message from a space station. They declare they are an unarmed scientific station and welcome us to Earth in peace," the pirate sneered.

Captain Gath laughed. "The slaves welcome their future masters in peace, do they? Let's show them what peace is really like. Send a message thanking them for the hospitality. Target our forward plasma cannons on two of the largest cites you find and level them. Also, take out those satellites tracking us.

Save the station for last and take it out with a missile. Fire when ready," Captain Gath laughed.

The plasma cannons fired numerous times within a few minutes. When they stopped firing the two largest cities on Earth ceased to exist.

Captain Gath was euphoric. "See the glow of the cities? I love that glow. They look so warm and peaceful." In less than a minute the six NASA satellites were slag floating in space and the Space station was in thousands of pieces.

"Now that we have their attention, let's pickup our treasure and prisoners. Have a security team greet our diminutive fool and bring him in irons. I've had enough of his insolence," the captain scowled.

"But sir, Deze is the one who saved them. Shouldn't we honor him?" a pirate at the navigation console asked.

Captain Gath roared with anger. "You dare question my judgement? He's no pirate. He is a slave and a useless one at that. No one challenges my orders," With that he drew his pistol and shot the pirate dead. Turning to his First Officer he said, "Get that mess cleaned up and find a smarter replacement immediately."

"Yes sir," the First Officer said. I have one in mind who will meet your requirements. I'll have the replacement report immediately." He turned to the Communications officer and said, "Have the Chief of Maintenance send up Carla."

"You sure?" he whispered to the First Officer.

"Yes, I'm sure," the First Officer whispered.

"She's savvy enough to handle the captain."

As the *Holcron Star* came into view, everyone on the bridge momentarily stood aghast at the enormous size of the mighty ship. "The ship has slowed down to .1 sub-light speed."

"Excellent!" Gavin said. "David, maneuver the freighter to approach from behind. The *Holcron Star* is on a direct heading to the international space station."

Without a warning of any kind, the *Holcron Star* began firing its plasma cannons at two cities. When the cities were destroyed the *Holcron Star* fired at the six NASA satellites and a missile took out the space station. Everyone on the bridge of the tiny freighter gasped in horror at the act of cold-blooded genocide.

Gavin had little time to react to the incident. "Siyana, increase speed one half point. David continue your approach.

"Gavin that's too fast. We'll crash into the hangar!" Siyana replied.

Gavin nodded. "We might, but I have every confidence you won't let that happen. Execute!"

Siyana gave the rear thrusters a bump and the ship gave a slight lurch as the speed increased.

Suddenly Captain Gath's voice boomed over the comm. link screaming at Deze whom he assumed was piloting the freighter.

"Don't you know how to fly that stupid thing? You're about to ram the hangar. Your approach is too fast, break off immediately."

"Sorry, sir! I'm doing my best despite our damage," Deze replied.

By the time Deze finished speaking; David already maneuvered the ship to within a hundred yards of the hangar bay.

"Three, two, one, Now!" Siyana hit the reverse thrusters to cut the speed. The ship shuddered more violently as it struggled to rapidly reduce speed. Just as the ship was approaching the hangar entrance David extended the landing gear.

"This maneuver ought to clear everyone out of the hangar bay!" Gavin declared.

As the freighter skidded across the deck throwing a shower of metal sparks, Siyana punched the reverse thrusters a second time and the freighter came to a stop. For a second David and Siyana looked at each other in shock.

"We're alive!" Siyana said.

"At least I think we are," David agreed.

After the hangar re-pressurized, John opened the cargo bay doors and extended the ramp.

"Go! Go! Go!" John shouted as he started pushing Traven and Assault Team 2 down the ramp even before it was fully extended.

The first shots from the team took down five armed Gamoran pirates entering the hangar bay. The pirates didn't even know what hit them. John was right behind the team.

In one sweeping movement, Assault Team 2 finished clearing the hangar while Slick and Assault Team 1 dashed to the corridor accessing the Air Quality Circulation Room. They secured the far end of the corridor while Team 2 arrived and secured the other end. Alpha Team was supposed to be right behind them with the hoses. Where were they? John thought.

He turned around. "Come on let's go! Move it!" He shouted. The team members handling the hoses were pulling them as fast as they could go when Jonathan and a team member, Sean Miller, tripped over a hose and tumbled. The big burley Sean somersaulted back to his feet, grabbed the hose with one hand and lifted Jonathan with the other hand. Barely missing a beat, they were off and running with their hose again.

"Good recovery, keep going!" John urged.

John was right behind them making sure no one was left behind. When all the assault team members exited the freighter, Gavin dispatched two of his remaining crew to flex cuff the unconscious prisoners.

Alpha Team reached the Air Quality Circulation Room

as Team 2 took up their position. Alpha Team attached their hoses to the main air ducts and locked them in place. Jonathan signaled the emergency air quality sensors were turned off.

Standing in the corridor, John raised both fists high signaling everyone to don their masks. Traven held up one fist signaling his team was ready. Slick raised his fist a second later followed by Jonathan signaling for Alpha team as John donned his mask. Pointing at the hose operators, Alpha Team released the gas while Jonathan turned a dial that manually set the circulating fans to full speed. John looked at his watch. In three minutes either the gas worked or violence was going to break out. The seconds ticked by. *Come on!* John pleaded to himself as time seemed to stand still.

He looked down one end of the corridor. Traven signaled all was well at his end. John looked at the other end. Slick signaled all was well at his end too.

John looked at his watch again. One more minute to go, he muttered to himself. *Oh Lord, help us in our greatest time of need!* He silently pleaded one last time. Looking at his watch again he counted off to himself, …five, four, three, two, one. He signaled Jonathan time was up and the Air Quality Circulation System was restored to normal. Two minutes later Dexter's monitor device began beeping and flashing a green light signaling the air was again safe to breathe. John gave the all clear signal to remove their masks and Assault Teams 1 and 2 raced off to secure their assigned decks.

"Let's go team!" John urged. Alpha Team raced to the nearest elevator and ascended to the bridge.

When the elevator doors opened on the Captain's Deck three members raced off and secured the Captain's Quarters and escape pods but there was no Captain Gath. John punched the elevator button to the bridge.

As the doors opened John shouted "Charge!"

They burst onto the bridge. There was dead silence.

All about the bridge were unconscious pirates. The spacious bridge, the nerve center of the ship was normally manned by ten personnel. There were only eight bodies and Aycana could not identify any of them as Captain Gath or the First Officer.

Aycana looked at John, "Captain Gath and the First Officer are not here."

A sinking feeling in the pit of his stomach began to form. Aycana find them!" John ordered.

"The rest of you secure the prisoners then get to your posts." Aycana went to the ship's security console and began scanning for Captain Gath.

John looked around the bridge. Aycana had accurately described every detail. During combat operations, the bridge crew was increased to seventeen personnel. It was divided into two parts. The front two-thirds of the bridge was the Command Center (CC). Everything a ship's captain needed was virtually at his fingertips. The rear one-third of the bridge was the Air Operation Center (AOC). Since there was no air wing aboard the ship this area was not manned. On the port side between the two centers were two elevators having access to all decks. On the starboard side of the bridge was an elevator having access to all decks and an emergency stairwell to the Captain's Deck below where the Captain's Quarters and three large escape pods were located.

At the center of the CC was the Captain's Chair and command console on a revolving platform. Attached to the platform and capable of independent rotation was a large holographic projector. Surrounding the Captain's Chair was a configuration of stations.

In front of the captain's chair were two flight system consoles for the ship's pilots. In each corner of the bridge were Defensive Laser System Stations. On the port side of the CC was the Navigation and Communications Stations. Located to the rear of the CC were the Electronic Counter Measures

Station (ECM), Intel-Sensor Station (ISS) and the Deflector Shield Station. On the starboard side of the CC were located the Missile Combat Station and Plasma Cannon Fire Control Station.

The entire bridge was a low light environment and the large windows gave a 360-degree view of the ship and surrounding space. Armored shields could be raised for added protection and the windows instantly converted to large flat screens to maintain viewing. The smell of electronics, the whispering of the air conditioning, black console décor highlighted by the glow of various colored lights and screens added to an almost cave like appearance and feel.

Alpha Team quickly secured the bridge, disarmed and flex cuffed the unconscious pirates then dragged them to the open floor area in front of the port side elevators.

Once the pirates were secure, Aycana found the ship's internal sensor display and called up a holograph of the ship. With two assistants, she used the sensors to identify the locations of life forms on board and directed the squads to the location of pirates on each deck.

Siyana and David arrived and took over the pilot and copilot seats. Siyana, began setting the *Holcron Star*'s flight computer for a high orbit. Nicky and Jonathan were busy checking the life support and engineering status consoles near the starboard elevator and emergency stairs. The two Alpha Team members left to clear the Captain's Deck reported no pirates and arrived by elevator to guard the unconscious prisoners.

John surveyed the prisoners. "Aycana!' John shouted. "Have you located Captain Gath and the First Officer?

Aycana pressed a couple buttons on the console. "Sir, we are trying but there are so many unconscious crew we are having difficulty sorting them out. Just a few seconds more to…"

The door to the emergency stairwell slid open. In a flash of motion, the hulking figures of Captain Gath and the First Officer burst onto the bridge with a roaring shout and blasters drawn. Nicky and Jonathan were closest to them.

Nicky was the first to see Captain Gath. Realizing he had no chance to draw his own weapon, he gave Jonathan a shove and lunged in front of Captain Gath's fire using his body as a shield. The first blast struck Nicky in the left side of the chest, spinning him around; the second blast struck him in the back knocking him to the floor.

Nicky's shove gave Jonathan the split second he needed to react.

Captain Gath's next two shots whizzed past Jonathan's head.

In reply, Jonathan and John both drew their blasters and returned fire. Multiple stun blasts struck the pirate captain in the chest, knocking him to the floor unconscious.

The First Officer's shots went wild but John and the two team members guarding the prisoners returned fire. He was quickly immobilized.

"Nicky, Are you OK?" Jonathan called out. There was no response. Jonathan rolled over to his friend's motionless body. Finding Nicky on the floor in a pool of blood, Jonathan called for a medic and began giving aid.

"Man down! Man down! Medic to the bridge immediately!" John shouted over the comm.net.

Nicky lay on the floor unable to move. His breathing was rapid and shallow. Jonathan desperately tried to give first aid to his dear friend. With Captain Gath's weapon on the highest setting and firing at point blank range; Nicky Stinson never had a chance. Nevertheless, Jonathan frantically struggled to stop the bleeding.

Nicky, gasping for air, in a weak voice pleaded, "Tell

family… dream…came true…I…love them!" He grabbed Jonathan's arm with his last bit of strength, gave a sigh and was gone.

Jonathan sat on the floor holding his friend in his arms refusing to let go when Susan and Katrina stepped out of the elevator with their medical kits. John, kneeling beside Jonathan, looked up at them and shook his head.

"I'm sorry, it's too late. He's gone. There was nothing anybody could do," John sighed as he closed Nicky's eyes.

Katrina put her arms around Jonathan as they wept together over their dear friend.

The bridge fell silent as everyone tried to deal with the loss. John stood up. "A hero is dead. It's not over yet and no time to mourn. To your duties so no more die.

John removed his jacket and covered Nicky. The team refocused with resolve to the task at hand.

Captain Gath was flex-cuffed and searched for other weapons.

As he regained consciousness, Deze indulged himself with a swift kick to Gath's abdomen and spat out, "Bilge Rat am I? Not so intimidating now, are you? You'll pay for what you've done this day!"

"Take him away," ordered John.

"I'll be happy to show you the way to the brig, gentlemen," Deze said to the guards.

Cuffed and restrained by two guards, Captain Gath in a last attempt at defiance tried to spit at Deze but got a rifle butt on the side of the mouth instead.

"Hey, no more! Put them in separate cells. We need him to talk. Gag him for now," John said.

"Yes, sir! Sorry, sir." Sean Miller replied as they taped his mouth shut and prodded him to the brig.

Jonathan seemed stunned as John sat him on a nearby

chair. "Sit here for a minute."

John noticed the forward missile launchers were still powered up.

"Aycana, would you go over to the tactical weapons console and power down the forward missile launchers?"

"Yes, sir!" Aycana replied. Aycana was also struggling with Nicky's death as she wiped tears from her cheeks. With much effort, she and her two assistants continued to direct the assault squads to find and secure the pirates.

John contacted Gavin. "The bridge along with Decks 1 and 3 are secured. Captain Gath and First Officer are secured in the brig. We lost Nicky. Please send a team to care for him will you?"

"A tragic loss. We will take care of him immediately," Gavin sorrowfully replied.

Aycana called out, "Mr. Braxton, we are getting numerous readings indicating two storage areas on decks 2 and 4 contain approximately sixty life forms each. Sensors do not show them as part of the ship's crew," Aycana reported.

John looked around the bridge. "Thanks, Come with me. Have Molly take over your duties."

"Victoria, notify the team leaders. Have them post guards outside those locations. Begin moving the secured prisoners to hangar 1.

'Siyana, put the ship on autopilot to maintain proper orbit.

'Jonathan, you have the bridge," John ordered.

"What?" Jonathan asked. His face was pale. The shock of his friend's death left him numb.

John grabbed him by the shirt and shook him. "Jonathan, I need you with your head in the game. Nicky saved your life. Never forget that. Honor him. There is still more to do and we don't want to lose anyone else."

The shaking brought Jonathan back into focus. "Oh, yes,

right. Sorry, I got the bridge. We'll keep scanning the ship to make sure we got everyone."

"Good!" John said.

"Aycana, David and Siyana come with me. We'll investigate the storage area on deck 2. Victoria, inform Assault Team 1 I'm going to the deck 2 storage area and to join us with a squad as soon as they can."

Victoria passed the message to Slick. "AT 1, Alpha 1 is going to investigate deck 2 storage area. Finish removing your prisoners and meet him with a squad when finished."

"Sir, AT 2 reports starting to clear deck 4," Molly reported. "Great, thanks," John acknowledged.

The ad hoc team entered the elevator and made their way to deck 2. Being cautious, Aycana and David scanned the corridor and finding it clear, signaled John and Siyana to exit the elevator. They quickly made their way to the third storage area down the corridor where the guard was posted.

Aycana verified that it was the correct storage area on her sensor hologram and said the people appeared still unconscious.

John and Siyana stood on one side of the large sliding door and Aycana and David on the other side. John pressed the door access button, the door slid open with a whoosh of foul air. The stench from the room caused everyone to reel backwards. John covered his nose with the sleeve of his free arm. With his blaster at the ready he peered through the doorway while the others covered him.

The sight they beheld was worse than the smell emanating from the room. On the floor lay approximately fifty unconscious men, women and children in tattered, filthy, badly worn rags. The people were emaciated from a lack of proper nutrition and the whole room stank from lack of proper hygiene facilities.

Everyone lowered their weapons and stood transfixed at the sight. Siyana looked around the room and recognized some of the earth toned clothing and decorated shoes as Cassarian. Several wore the Green leather vest and square toed shoes from Holcron. She also saw the light bluish skinned people from Katusium. She let out a gasp and her blue eyes flashed as tears welled up and began running down her cheeks.

"What have they done to my people?" she cried as she sank to the floor.

"The lousy stinking animals! How could they treat people like this?" Aycana shrieked.

"Can we just shove the pirates out an air lock and be done with it?" David asked in disgust and anger.

"I wish we could, I really do, but we can't. We'd be just like them if we did," John said as he put his arms around Siyana and Aycana in fatherly comfort.

"Now I realize inhumanity is not a behavior unique to Earth nor is the universe as civilized as we imagine," Aycana cried.

John opened his flip com and contacted Traven who confirmed the same ghastly scene on deck 4.

John then raised Jonathan on the flip com. "Jonathan, when the decks are cleared and pirates rounded up in Hangar 1 continue monitoring. We don't want any more surprises."

"Yes, sir!" Jonathan acknowledged.

"Also dispatch Susan to direct medical assistance here and have Katrina sent to deck 4 for medical assistance there. Relieve Victoria on the bridge and have her come down here to lend a hand. These people are going to need a lot of help. David will remain here. Aycana and I are going to the storage room on deck 4."

"Yes, sir. Victoria, Susan and Katrina are already on their way," Jonathan acknowledged.

John then contacted Gavin. "We have real disasters on decks 2 and 4. Detail as many of your people as you can spare to assist and send someone with the video camera. We need to document this barbarism. We have approximately fifty to sixty people who were held prisoner in each of the two storage areas. These people are going to need a lot of medical assistance when they come around."

"Will do," Gavin replied.

Minutes later John and Aycana arrived at the storage room on deck 4 and saw an identically horrific scene. Dexter was already trying to help and Aycana jumped in to do what she could. The need was overwhelming. She gasped recognizing some of the Cassarian victims. Many others were Holcrons and a few from the planet Katusium. Gavin soon arrived and was appalled at the sight.

"They were mostly Cassarians, in the same condition as on deck 2," John said trying to control his outrage.

"Are there any officers?" Gavin asked not seeing any.

"Sorry, Gavin, the clothes are so tattered and soiled we can't tell. Once the people regain consciousness we will know more," John answered.

Gavin continued to look over the people and recognized many. "I can't believe this," Gavin declared. "I know the ship they were on. It was an exploration ship. I knew most of the officers, scientists and many of the families. It looks like all the officers are missing."

Gavin grasped his chest as he staggered to lean against the bulkhead. "They killed every officer they captured in cold blood. I…I didn't think such barbarism was possible!" Gavin fought back both the pain and anger.

"Take courage my friend. These vermin will pay dearly for their crimes, but for now we have to concentrate on the living," John reassured him.

"What do we do?" Gavin shouted angrily. "We can't treat this many…"

John put his finger to his lips to calm him down. "We'll get help, don't worry!"

Katrina arrived and looking over Gavin's shoulder shrieked in horror. John gently laid his hand on her shoulder and nudged her out of the room. Katrina took deep breaths to get her breathing under control, before calling Susan on her flip com. After a brief discussion, the medical teams took control.

"I'll start triage. The most serious get moved first," Katrina declared. "Susan is doing the same thing on deck 2. There is a sick bay on deck 2. We'll send the most serious victims there for treatment. Put all the other patients in whatever crew quarters you can find.

'We need to get some nourishment in as many as can hold it down. Many will require intravenous feeding for now. We don't have near enough medical supplies and proper food. We need a lot more. They also need to be cleaned head to toe, their ragged clothing destroyed and clean clothing issued.

'We also need lots of medical help fast. For the time being, this ship is a hospital."

"Yes, ma'am!" John and Gavin replied.

Back on the bridge, Jonathan reported all decks were now cleared and the prisoners removed to hangar 1, with the exception of Captain Gath and the First Officer. Jonathan had the First Officer moved to one of the Prisoner rooms after the people were removed.

"You can't put me in there! I'm the First Officer," He demanded.

"Why not? You thought it was good enough for your prisoners. It's good enough for you. Clean it up and we might even let you get some fresh air on occasion," Sean Miller said as he shoved him into the room.

Captain Gath struggled coming to terms with his new quarters. There was total darkness save a very small red light on the cell camera.

"Let me out of here, let me out now!" Captain Gath screamed. "Let me out while you still can. If you don't they will come. They will destroy you and turn your planet into ash and molten rock. You will all die."

There was no response, just dead, eerie silence. In the darkness, there was no sense of time, or space.

Cat Saunders continued watching the monitor and taking notes.

"Make all the threats you want Captain Gath. It won't matter what you say or do, you're all mine now."

Molly MacKay was at the communications console when John stepped onto the bridge.

"Captain on the bridge!" she announced.

John was surprised and a bit embarrassed by the announcement. "My father is retired Navy and I noticed they did that all the time when I was growing up; so I thought it appropriate to do it when you come to the bridge," she volunteered.

"I was never aboard a naval vessel, but I get it," John smiled. "I need to contact base camp. Can you patch me to Henry?"

"Yes, sir!" Molly replied.

"Hi, Dad," John greeted. "The mission was a great success."

On the bridge screen Henry could be seen shifting his stance. He was very visibly shaken. "Yes, they are breaking news some space rangers captured the ship that destroyed Beijing, Shanghai and the International Space Station. The death toll is estimated at forty-four million."

John shook his head. "It's almost impossible to imagine that many people could be murdered in a matter of minutes. We lost Nicky. He was killed taking the bridge. He saved

Jonathan's life by sacrificing his."

Henry wiped tears from his eyes. "In the short time, I got to know him I couldn't help but think of him as part of the family."

"I know what you mean and we are definitely going to miss his upbeat ways. He never gave up. We also have an emergency here. We found 105 men, women and children the pirates were holding as prisoners. They are in horrible shape, half starved, barely clothed and sick. I'm sending down a shuttle. Can you gather up all the food and medical supplies you can?" John asked.

You bet! See you soon," Henry said as he signed off. Slick, Gavin and Traven arrived on the bridge.

"Slick, I need you to contact Washington. Apprise them of our situation. We desperately need a medical team to help or some of these people aren't going to make it. I'm afraid to even transport them for now," John explained.

Slick contacted the Director of Operations at CIA Headquarters through a satellite patch and reported the successful mission. Jacob Wilkes requested John speak to President Leatham. Moments later President Leatham came on the line.

"Mr. Braxton! Since we are speaking I assume your mission was a success?"

"Yes, Mr. President, our mission was successful. The *Holcron Star* is captured. We lost one team member, Nicky Stinson. Two other team members sustained minor injuries in a fall. We have 125 pirates captured plus their captain, who is pondering his future right now," John reported.

"That's great news, Mr. Braxton. On behalf of the American people and those of many other nations, thank you for a job well done!" President Leatham replied.

"I'm very sorry about the destruction of Shanghai, Beijing and the space station. I wish we could have prevented it, but the pirates attacked them without warning. We'll try to recover the three bodies from the space station. Please pass on my condolences to the families of the astronauts."

"I will do that for you. It was a cruel, senseless act. Is there anything we can do for you, John?"

"Yes, sir! This ship is not designed for atmospheric travel. We rescued 105 men, women and children incarcerated by the pirates. They are in need of serious medical attention. They are in such a fragile condition we don't dare transport them at this time. Plus, many of them are sick and I believe should be quarantined until checked out. They are also very malnourished and in need of clothing. We need a team of doctors and nurses to assist us with the sick or I'm afraid several might not make it."

"By all means. Vandenberg Air Force Base is at your disposal. I'll have them notified to provide whatever you need immediately. I expect you are overwhelmed with tasks at hand, but I would like to meet with you at your convenience to discuss the future," President Leatham said.

"Yes Mr. President. Allow us to get things squared away here first. I agree there is much to discuss." John replied.

"Please thank your team on behalf of all Americans and the world. Look forward to meeting with you soon." The call ended.

John turned to Slick and Gavin. "President Leatham authorized use of Vandenberg AFB and a medical team to assist us. Gavin, prepare one of the shuttles. Take Slick, Aycana and Jonathan with you. Please take Nicky's body with you so they can prepare him. Bring back the medical team, food and medical supplies. Be careful, I suspect they will play games at first.

'Tomorrow afternoon Jonathan, Siyana, Victoria, and I will visit Nicky's family in person. We met his family at Nicky's college graduation two years ago. He has a younger sister and a very close-knit family. It's going to be really hard."

It was four hours after they captured the *Holcron Star* and almost nightfall when the shuttle, piloted by Aycana and Jonathan, landed at Vandenberg AFB.

They were directed to a large hanger that was originally built for the space shuttle program. The shuttle eased into the hanger and once inside, extended its landing gear and gently put down. Inside the hangar there was an ambulance and three staff cars.

The wing commander and two colonels were standing nearby, along with several security police, service personnel and the requested medical team.

Slick stepped out of the craft first followed by Gavin and approached the general and his small entourage.

"Sorry to disappoint you. Mr. Braxton will arrive sometime tomorrow. My name is Jeff Prewett; and this is Gavin Toburg, Special Envoy and son to King Adrian Toburg of the planet, Cassaria."

"Nice to meet both of you!" General Klinedecker said.

He introduced the two colonels and invited everyone to step into a nearby conference room for a few minutes.

"I have an Honor Guard detail standing by to transport the body to our hospital morgue. After that we'll load the cargo and medical supplies. I have orders straight from the White House to treat your fallen comrade with full military honors.

'Mr. Prewitt, I received a call from CIA Director Richards to be on the lookout for you. He is most eager to hear from you directly. He rather sternly requested you contact him as soon as you step foot on the ground. I have arranged a secure line in the next room."

As they entered the office, Gavin inhaled the aroma of coffee brewing in a pot nearby.

"Oh! That smells good," Gavin sighed.

"Here, I'll pour you some. It's a fresh pot. Do you want sugar or cream?" one of the colonels asked.

"I'd love some but make it black please. We don't have such a drink on our planet, but it would be a big hit back home for sure. Since I have been on your planet the last three weeks, I've gotten hooked on this drink."

"So it's your ship everyone's been chasing?" the general asked.

"Afraid so," Gavin nodded. "Mr. Braxton will arrive tomorrow evening. We need arrangements made for a meeting with President Leatham per his request. Suffice it to say, for the moment, Mr. Braxton and his family rescued us from pirates, captured the pirate's flagship to prevent an attack on Earth and our recapture. Unfortunately, that is not even the half of it. The young man who died was a good friend killed in the battle and a great hero to us all.'

"I will work with the White House to set up the meeting. Is there anything else we can do to help you?" the general asked.

"Well, general. We have a long list of needs. One pressing need is a highly secure detention facility to hold 125 pirate prisoners. They must be separated from their officers and kept in total isolation.

They must not be seen, interviewed, photographed or in any way communicated with until we can figure out what to do with them. Many of them are guilty of the worst of galactic war crimes and highly dangerous. They must be kept under heavy security at all times," Gavin warned.

"Not a problem. I think we have a place that will meet all the security requirements. We can secure arrangements by tomorrow afternoon. The mosquitoes there will surely welcome them to the new world. We will have more supplies ready for pickup whenever your transport returns."

After a few more minutes a chief master sergeant announced the requested medical supplies were secured aboard the shuttle and the medical team ready to board.

Gavin finished his coffee and escorted the team to the shuttle where Aycana and Jonathan helped buckle in their passengers. The doctors and nurses were nervous about traveling in space, but Gavin set them at ease.

"Relax folks, the Hummingbird class shuttle is the safest shuttle ever made. It's really, nothing to worry about. Flying in one of these shuttles is so safe we don't even bother with airbags. It can carry up to 24 passengers and more equipment than you can load. You only have the co-pilot to worry about. He is still in training so if you do get sick, you have to clean it up," Gavin teased with a big friendly smile.

Just as the new passengers were buckled in, Slick rejoined them and started up the short shuttle ramp. He turned to General Klinedecker. "Sir, thanks for the courtesy of the phone. I apologize for the inconvenience, but I hope those digital cameras your people took pictures of inside the craft with are easily replaced. Our security sensors don't like them."

General Klinedecker gave one of his colonels a stern glare, but said nothing.

"And thanks for the hospitality too. The coffee was great. We'll be seeing you real soon," Slick smiled with a wink and a wave of his hand as the auxiliary engine began warming up.

A short time later, the medical team found themselves standing on the *Holcron Star* hangar deck. Katrina welcomed them aboard. Without wasting any time they were escorted to sick bay. The two doctors and six nurses went right to work. In the midst of medical technology, the likes they couldn't even imagine, twenty-one emaciated patients lay in need of critical treatment.

Thoughts of their first time in space and being on an alien ship quickly vanished as they focused every thought and action on keeping their fragile patients alive. For the medical team, it was going to be a long, long night.

Susan and Katrina were briefing the team on their

treatment of each patient when John Braxton arrived to look in on them and greet the new arrivals.

"Doctor Hunter Grant, I'm John Braxton welcome to the *Holcron Star.*"

"Thank you! This is a unique experience to say the least. You were just in time for these folks. If you had captured the ship a day or two later, many of these people would have died. As it is, I think there is a chance we can save them," Doctor Grant said.

"I understand. I just hope and pray they make it. If you need anything ask Susan or Katrina. We will get whatever you need. I don't want to use up your precious time so I'll be on my way. Good night." John said with a tired smile.

As John continued his ship's tour, he took the time to ensure everyone was squared away and the security guards watching the prisoners were alert with plenty of coffee on hand. When he completed his tour, John returned to the bridge and turned the night watch over to David and Dexter.

"I'll be in my quarters if you need me," John stated as he made an entry into the ship's log. Wearily walking towards the elevator he turned to announce, "You have the watch, good night."

John entered the Captain's quarters for the first time. After being up for almost thirty hours he was exhausted. The rich appearance and opulence of the quarters surprised him.

I imagine Victoria will be doing some serious redecorating. John thought as he surveyed each room. The large living room was luxuriously furnished with plush burgundy carpeting, soft, leather covered, hand carved chairs and couches. The room was decorated with some of the most remarkable and obviously valuable paintings, vases, carvings and statues.

The beautifully crafted wooden bookcases lined with what John assumed were great works from various cultures. The tastefully designed tables finished off the room's grand appearance.

Beyond the living room was a study area with a computer terminal built into an ornately carved hand-finished desk with a fifty-inch viewing screen on the wall above it. To the right of the living room was the dining room furnished with yet another ornately carved table and four equally ornate chairs. Further along was a kitchenette.

The bedroom was around the corner of the kitchenette and accessed through the living room. Not quite as large as the living room, it was furnished equally in splendor. Two walls were lined with built in carved wooden drawers and a third with mirrored closet doors and most importantly, a large four-poster bed. There was a pile of used linen on the floor near by. A large bathroom and walk in shower was accessed from the bedroom. The quarters were meant as a place for a captain to rest and relax from the pressures of command and entertain small groups of guests.

Staggering across the bedroom, John kicked off his shoes and collapsed on the bed next to an equally exhausted but already sleeping Victoria.

CHAPTER 10

John Braxton bolted upright in bed. His body ached all over and his head was spinning. Collecting himself, he groggily looked at his watch and noted it was mid-morning. Slowly he did some stretches to help get his body moving.

I wish Victoria woke me up before she left. Oh well! I'd better get moving. It's going to be another long day.

After a hot shower and shave John put on the clothes Victoria unpacked for him. She also left a note letting him know there were fruit, juice, and a blueberry bran muffin in the refrigerator. If he wanted anything else just call Food Service and they'd bring it. Since he hadn't taken the time to eat in almost twenty-four hours anything tasted good. *Well, I'd better get to the bridge before I visit sick bay and get an update.*

Instead of choosing one of the three elevators, John opted to check out the stairwell Captain Gath used in his attempt to retake the bridge.

He quickly realized the stairwell was air tight at both ends with a closed air vent. The window on the door opening to the bridge allowed Capt. Gath to see what was happening. No wonder Captain Gath and his First Officer managed to escape the knockout gas. John paused on the stairwell and slowly smoothed his hands on the cold metal walls. As his hands moved across the walls the closet door opened in his mind and the faces reappeared. This time his vision was different. The voices called out to him that this was their place of remembrance. When John regained his senses, he saw the names and date of each person who died that horrifying day.

A separate date was also written with Nicky Stinson's name added. John touched his name. *A precious life snuffed out in a heroic attempt to save a friend. It's my duty to make sure it wasn't in vain,* John shuddered blaming himself. *I'm in command. Every life is my responsibility. They trust me to honor them in life and death. Nicky wasn't the first to die under my command and surely won't be the last. The burden of command is a sacred burden and I was chosen to carry it. They chose this place for closure.*

"Captain on the bridge!" Molly announced as John stepped onto the bridge.

"As you were!" John quickly followed.

John tried to hide his embarrassment but everyone still noticed and smiled before resuming their duties. Dexter, Traven, Slick and Susan were at the holographic projector along with Gavin and Victoria.

"Good morning, John. We are just starting a shift status report," Gavin said. "Go ahead, Dexter."

"The *Holcron Star* appears overall in good shape with no serious maintenance deficiencies noted in the engineering log book. The ship has a full load of coolant too."

"Great! Have we gotten clearance to transport the prisoners?" John asked.

"Traven, your cue." Gavin said.

Traven nodded. "The prisoners started getting restless last night but are now behaving themselves. We had ten of the officers try to stir things up early this morning. We separated them and things calmed down quickly. Security is alert to quell anything they might try to pull.

'An hour ago, we got approval from Vandenberg Command Post to begin transporting the prisoners directly to Guantanamo Bay. We are readying the prisoners as we speak. The base has enough space, very high security and isolated. They have separate facilities for officers and crew with no visitors allowed."

"Fantastic! I want them off this ship as soon as possible.

When you transport them, I want hoods over their faces with hand and leg restraints. It's vital we keep them from stirring up trouble during the transfer."

"Good points," Traven said. "Will do."

John turned to Dexter and Gavin, "Dexter, I know the *Holcron Star*'s engines are maintained by droids, but I think you'd better inspect them with a fine-toothed comb. Being shorthanded, no one knows what deficiencies the pirates overlooked much less what engine modifications went undocumented."

"Right on. We can't take their word for anything," Gavin said. "Slick, what do you have?"

"Bravo squad is assisting with the medical team. All other personnel are now reassigned to ship duties.

Deze and Estron are training them in the essential tasks. Captain Gath is under interrogation by Cat. It's only a matter of time before she finds a way to make him sing. He's not as tough as he appears. Here is her first report," Slick said handing it to John.

"Good. Please keep us updated," Gavin agreed. 'Victoria, what do you have?"

Victoria passed a folder to John.

"Robin has recruited four Cassarians with food service experience able to help. The number of people we freed was unexpected and overwhelming. With the extra help, she was able to get breakfast served this morning. Many of the people required special meals because of their condition. Breakfast was a bit late but everyone got all they wanted to eat. She is getting a handle on it and reports she's ready for your luncheon meeting."

"What luncheon meeting?" John asked confused.

Victoria laughed. "The one Jonathan said you wanted for his briefing and gave me a list of everyone needing to be there.

I took the liberty of notifying them.

"Well, hooray for liberties," John said sarcastically as he took a gulp of coffee. "I guess we're having our first power lunch in space."

Victoria continued. "Our manpower problem is severe, but we expected it. Henry messaged me he has received over thirty inquiries to join us since this morning."

"What? John asked. "We aren't even able to handle new recruits yet. They can send a resume if they want but tell Henry not to promise anything."

'The bridge shift and training schedule is posted. Jonathan didn't want to give up the bridge watch last night. We finally persuaded him to get some rest late this morning. He plans on going with us this afternoon to call on Nicky's family."

"I'm not surprised, He needs to be there," John said.

'Gavin, would you consider taking on Sean Miller to serve as your assistant in getting more supplies from Henry?"

"Sure," Gavin agreed. "Slick is going with me to drop off the prisoners. I can pick up the supplies on the way back."

"Thanks," John said.

"Susan, how are things in sick bay?" Gavin asked.

"Of the hundred and five people rescued, I'm sorry to report two died during the night. They were so weak from starvation and other medical issues we were too late. The nano cells are healing the twenty-three other critical care patients. The doctors report recovery will be slow but expect them to fully recover. The other eighty patients are doing very well. We are learning amazing treatment technology as we go along."

'I'm sure," John said. "Sorry to hear about the two deaths. You, Katrina and the medical team have done an incredible job."

"Yes, please pass on my people's appreciation as well," Gavin added. "We are grateful for their assistance beyond what words can express. The generosity and courage all of you have displayed is something my people will never, ever forget. We will begin the burial arrangements of our dead?"

"I understand," John said. "Whatever assistance you need let us know."

After the morning briefing, John, Victoria and Siyana went with Susan to sick bay. He thanked the medical team and made sure their needs were addressed.

John and Victoria spent time visiting as many of the patients as possible assuring them whatever they needed would be provided. They were now in safe hands. Siyana was instantly recognized and her demeanor and comforting words assured everyone all was well.

As they left, Victoria asked, "Siyana, I couldn't help notice the atmosphere changed in the room as you spoke to them. May I ask what you told them?"

Siyana blushed and her eyes took on a soft blue glow. "They know the parable of the Good Samaritan. I told them that in our darkest hour your family risked everything, even your lives to save complete strangers.

'That it was not enough, you brought friends who also risked their lives to save us all. One gave his life. All of them can thank God for the great Samaritans he sent. They wish to hold a memorial for him and thank all of you for your sacrifice."

John and Victoria were deeply moved. Victoria wiped away a tear. "I don't know what to say, Thank you!"

Siyana shook her head as her eyes continued to glow. "As I understand Earth customs, it is we who say, 'Thank you!' with most humility and gratitude."

John smiled. "Siyana, you are correct. In return we say, 'You are welcome! It was an honor to serve."

In a surprise show of emotion, Siyana gave Victoria and

John a hug and bowed before departing.

Back in their quarters, John and Victoria poured over the contents of the folder she gave him and Cat's report.

"Jonathan stayed up all night working on this? I asked him to find the answers to a couple questions but he really went all out. He researched the ship's records and message traffic collecting way more information. I had the same suspicions but he really dug deep." John said amazed.

"Well like father, like son. When you two hounds get on a scent, you don't stop until you have the answers. After digesting its contents, I understood why Jonathan took the initiative to call the meeting," Victoria said.

John shook his head. "I agree. This and what I uncovered tells us a lot but causes us to ask more questions. We just jumped out of the frying pan and into the fire. Let's get to the briefing."

Robin served cold cut sandwiches, a large vegetable tray and a fruit compote with a choice of iced tea or lemonade. After Chaplain Boyle blessed the meal, everyone began eating while Jonathan activated a holographic projector on the middle of the table.

Before the briefing started, John noticed Dexter whisper something in Gavin's ear. Gavin's composure changed to one who had just eaten a bunch of very sour grapes. John gave a knowing smile and thought. *Looks like Dexter took my bait. Well the cat is finally out of the bag.*

John looked around the room. "Jonathan, begin, let's hear what you learned."

Jonathan brought up a display of their sector of the galaxy and began his briefing.

"Our Cassarian friends already know this so please bear through some of this so the rest of us can get caught up. On the display observe the known inhabited planets of Holcron,

Katusium, Cassaria, and Tigra located at the top portion of the projection.

Earth is located at the far lower right corner. To the left of the map is Gamora Prime. To the center bottom is Sepious Minor which is not inhabited but worthy to keep in mind. Just below the top string of inhabited systems is a nebula cloud called the Jarro Nebula.

'The pirates have been doing far more than raiding commerce and destroying survey ships. Behind the Jarro Nebula is the central region with three significant star systems discovered by the Gamoran pirates.

'Tucked away just outside the middle of the Jarro Nebula, is the Betarus system. It contains a previously unknown pirate base on a small lifeless desert planet called Betarus Minor.

'Between the Betarus system and Gamora Prime is a much larger solar system known as the Mundary system. One of the largest planets, Mentarus, has six moons. The planet is uninhabitable. However, the largest moon, Risor, has a barely breathable atmosphere.

'To the right of the Betarus system is a system we discovered in the pirate captain's computer files. For discussion, I named it the Terran system and the habitable planet, Terra. Gravity and atmosphere on Terra are very similar to Earth. Terra contains a wide variety of plant and animal life, but is devoid of human life. It is now home to the largest pirate base and a very active mining operation. The moon also contains a smaller base used for making resupply and space repairs."

What are they mining that is so important?" Siyana asked.

John kept watching Gavin, who remained speechless yet even more visibly shaken.

"Wow!" Aycana said. "The pirates sure have been busy. They explored and charted three systems that have habitable planets or moons and established three bases of operation. Our expedition barely identified the Mundary system a year ago before being driven out of the region."

"There's more, Aycana," Jonathan said. "The question Dad has been asking and no one could answer was, how could the *Holcron Star* get to all these places without taking years to do so? We have been slowly putting the pieces of the pirate puzzle together. My research gives us a bigger picture of why they are so protective of the central region. More of the puzzle pieces are coming."

John nodded to David who produced an object covered with a table cloth. He placed it on the table and removed the cloth.

There, for all to see, was a two-foot-long crystal of violet glowing Zannite.

Gavin sunk back down in his chair in disbelief. Siyana and her sisters glared at Gavin in complete shock. Dexter, sat behind them trying to hide his frustration. The silence in the room was stifling.

Gavin stood up and pointed at John. "Stop, right here. You have known the answer for some time, haven't you? Why did you hide this from us?"

John stood up firing back. "I tried to tell you twice but you denied the possibility of zannite existing in sufficient quantity. I didn't know if what you said was out of arrogance, ignorance or design. So, I kept my silence until I knew the answer. Remember the meeting we had in the tent with Slick and Traven? You were adamant that it was impossible for any usable quantity of Zannite to exist and refused to even consider the possibility. Yet, you gave me six-hundred large zannite crystals along with other pirate treasure as a reward for our help. You assured me that all of it was mine to do with as I pleased. Traven and Slick were witnesses."

Traven and Slick looked at each other and winked.

Gavin sat down in defeat. "What you say is true. I'm

sorry. I was in denial. You had the right to be cautious under the circumstances. You deserve your reward for all you have done and my generosity is genuine. I was arrogant to dismiss what is now so glowingly obvious. There were no ulterior designs, I promise you. The problem is I have unwittingly broken Galactic law by making them available to you."

"Well, we are now a part of the galactic community, like it or not. Don't beat yourself up about it. Unfortunately, there are bigger fish to fry," John said taking his seat.

"What do you mean?" Aycana asked.

'We now know the Gamoran pirates are in league with the Tigrans just to survive as a warrior class. That connection led to our capture," Gavin surmised.

"There is one other tidbit we have learned," John announced. "In a message from several months ago, we found a pirate spy code named Digger. He claims Counselor Glaxis was manipulated in his activities to help their cause without realizing he was being used.

'Digger was able to persuade him to require the fleet be drawn closer to Cassaria and require decommission of three more cruisers ahead of schedule. At the same time, he bragged of canceling procurement of three new cruisers as a cost cutting measure to balance the budget."

"Why that little weasel!" Gavin groaned. "Digger is Council Assistant Willett Quiller. He works for Councilor Taxis Glaxis whose family owns Glaxis Global Energy Enterprises. He was the person who drew up the decommissioning and shipbuilding plans and helped Councilor Glaxis lobby them through the Council."

Aycana cleared her throat. "Quiller also works closely with General Nix Tayer, Father's closest advisor."

"We have to warn Father," Siyana pleaded. "We must get home as soon as possible."

"Not so fast,"Gavin cautioned. Rushing off without a plan could get us all killed. What else do you have to report?"

John opened up a folder. "Cat reported Captain Gath threatened others would be coming to free him. Jonathan, you have any leads on that?"

Jonathan nodded. "According to the message traffic the rest of the pirate fleet does not know where the *Holcron Star* is or its actual mission. They are off plundering and doing what pirates do."

"So, who are these people coming to free him or is he just blowing smoke?" John asked.

"The better question is who has the ability to get here with enough firepower to free him?" Estron asked.

And knows where we are?" Siyana added.

"Both of you are correct," John agreed. "I'll have Cat interrogate Captain Gath some more on that."

"I think there is a galactic conspiracy far greater than we suspected," Jonathan stated.

"How so?" Siyana asked.

Jonathan pointed at the Zannite crystal. "There are six-hundred crystals and probably more. Does anyone have a fleet large enough to use this many, much less, has the leverage over the pirates to trade them?

John looked around the room. "We need to gather more information to answer that and meet again. We need to get going on our visit to Micky's family."

"May I ask what are we going to do with Deze? He's earned his freedom don't you all agree?" Estron asked.

"I kept my word. Deze earned my trust and is completely free. I spoke with him last night and invited him to officially join our crew. He agreed," John announced.

"One last question. What are you planning to do with the *Holcron Star*?" Aycana asked.

"The *Holcron Star* is ours," John said. "I intend to

take this ship, train a crew and take the fight to the pirates. If another pirate ship shows up, who has the only chance of stopping them? We are not going to wait for another attack. Every Cassarian, Holcron, and Katusian is welcome to join us. Anyone who doesn't want to join is free to return to Earth or leave with you."

"You want take the fight to the pirates then I'm with you," Dexter said.

Aycana nodded. "I'm in too. I'm tired of playing defense with these scumbags."

"Scumbags? I think you are starting to sound too much like Earthlings," Gavin teased.

"Maybe so and maybe I'm starting to think like them too. Mr. Braxton's plan to take the war to the pirates may be just what we need to do to save Cassaria. We show up on Cassaria and we risk tipping our hand before Father has a chance to do anything to stop them," Aycana said.

"Good point!" Gavin agreed. 'Estron, what about you?"

"Aycana makes a good point but what about saving Cassaria and Father. I just want to go home," Estron sighed. "I'm all for killing every pirate we find along the way."

"I see," Gavin noted. "Siyana?"

"There has to be another way to warn Father while not making the situation more dangerous. After all we are supposed to be dead. There has to be a way to warn Father without tipping the traitors off. We show up and the opposition will move before Father can act. Taking out the pirates sounds like the best course of action for the time being. I'm in," Siyana said.

"What about your diplomatic mission?" Susan asked.

"Our government is already at war with the pirates. They are criminals under Galactic Law. My mission is already compromised.

We are free to do as we wish now," Gavin explained.

"Mr. Braxton, you have another ship."

Slick and Traven glanced at each other approvingly.

John nodded. "Folks, all is now out in the open among us. Let us be of one mind and one goal: freedom. There is treachery beyond what we are seeing. Let's get busy. There are worlds to save."

Everyone agreed and the meeting adjourned.

Siyana settled the shuttle down gently in a lightly dusted snow covered pasture behind an old barn on a central Indiana farm. Victoria, Jonathan, Siyana and John made their way to the house. The old two-story, wooden farmhouse was in sore need of a new roof and a coat of white paint but it still glowed with the warmth of a country home. The flowers in the hanging pots on the front porch had long dried up. The porch swing creaked as it slightly swayed in the breeze. To John it brought back memories from his childhood of his grandfather's farmhouse. The house may have been old but that just gave it a special charm.

The cold, winter breeze gave the visitors a chill as Jonathan knocked on the front door. A slightly heavy set, middle-aged black woman wiped her hands on her apron as she answered the door. The smell of fresh baked bread wafted past the door.

"Jonathan Braxton! I do declare, it's nice to see you again," Nola Stinson exclaimed as she gave Jonathan a big hug.

"Nola, you remember my parents, John and Victoria, and this is a friend of ours, Siyana. May we come in?" Jonathan asked.

"Of course. Come in. Come in!" Nola gestured. "Have a seat in the living room while I get Malcolm and Crystal. He's in the study doing some paperwork and she is working on a college resume on the computer. I didn't hear you drive in. Where did you park?" Nola asked looking out the window and seeing no car in the driveway.

Oh! We just dropped in and parked out back by the barn.No big deal really," Jonathan said grappling for a plausible reply.

"My goodness, you didn't have to park way out there," Nola exclaimed as she left the room.

A minute later, Malcolm, Crystal and Nola joined their guests.

After introductions were made and a little small talk, Malcolm asked what brought them to the area.

"Did you receive a letter from Nicky about three weeks ago? John asked.

"Yes, we did. It was the last we heard from him. He said he found a better job than the NASA position and was going to be out of the country for a few weeks and not to worry. Why?" Malcolm asked.

"Nicky was working with my family and some very important people. Have you been listening to the news of the UFO and the destruction of the space station yesterday?" John asked.

"Who hasn't? The whole world is buzzing about it. I thought all that UFO stuff was just silly, but I have to change my thinking now. Aliens murdering people in cold blood does not bode well. It seems like something out of a science fiction book, doesn't it?" Malcolm asked.

"But what's that got to do with Nicky?" Crystal inquired.

"Not only were the three astronauts on the space station killed by the space pirates. I'm horribly sorry to report that they killed Nicky too," John said softly.

The news hit the family like the world had just caved in on them. Nola and Crystal gasped in horror then broke down sobbing uncontrollably. Totally speechless, Malcolm fell back in his chair in shock, and just shook his head in his hands fighting back the tears. Victoria went to stand next to Nola placing her arms around her trying to give comfort. The grieving family didn't notice the soft blue glow in Siyana's eyes as she tried to comfort Crystal.

"I don't understand. How could Nicky have been killed? He couldn't have been on the space station," Nola cried with tears rolling down her cheeks.

"He wasn't on the space station. He was part of the force that captured the pirate ship moments later," John explained. "Nicky was a hero who helped save us and billions of lives around the world."

"Mister, you come into my home, tell me and my family our son is dead. You rip our hearts out then you insult us with some nutcase lie. What kind of man are you?" Malcolm snarled in pain.

"Nola, you asked about how we arrived and I offer this as proof of our story. Look out the window of your dining room. You will see an alien shuttlecraft. Kneeling before Crystal is the young woman who piloted the craft. Siyana is from the planet, Cassaria, and was a hostage of the pirates until we freed her along with her brother and two sisters."

Malcolm, Nola and Crystal made their way into the dining room and looked out the window. The second shock left them speechless. Malcolm put his big burley arms around Nola and Crystal to hug them. He closed his eyes to fight back the pain trying to understand the truth of what he was seeing. While huddled together he began praying fervently appealing to God to ease their pain and welcome their son into his house in heaven. Finally, they returned to the living room still struggling with their pain.

"Please tell us what happened?" Malcolm asked wiping away more tears.

Over the next few minutes John explained the whole course of events of the past three weeks from the first UFO sighting to the assault on the *Holcron Star* and Nicky's death. When John concluded recounting the events, Jonathan spoke up.

"I owe Nicky my life," Jonathan said choking back his own tears. "I brought a letter Nicky wrote before going on the mission. He wanted you to have it in case he didn't return," Jonathan said holding out the letter.

Nola shook her head and refused to take it. "Victoria, I can't read it. Would you please read it to us?"

"I would be honored!" Victoria said softly as she opened the letter and began to read:

Dear Family,

If you are reading this letter it means I have gone to be with the Lord. I know the next few weeks will be difficult for all of you and I deeply regret putting you through all of this pain and sorrow.

You always taught me to help others in time of need and do what was right no matter what the cost. Now, threatening us is the greatest danger to all mankind and I believe it would have been wrong to not try to stop it. There will be many more battles I'm sure before we are secure from this evil.

Please pray for those who will carry on the fight. They need all the help and prayers you can give them.

When Mr. Braxton would talk to us, he would end by stating, "There is a world to save." I can think of no nobler cause. One day we will be together again. I love you all.

God bless, Nicky

There was a long pause before Nola could find the words to speak. "Thank you, Victoria." Nola sighed wiping away more tears.

Now I understand. He did the right thing. We're so proud of Nicky. His sacrifice wasn't in vain."

"Where is his … body?" Malcolm asked.

"Nicky is at Vandenberg AFB in California being prepared for burial. The president has directed the Department of Defense make the funeral arrangements according to your wishes. They will contact you shortly. Here is a phone number you can call if you need anything. We will return his personal effects and do whatever we can to help you.

'President Leatham plans to make a special announcement on TV tonight to explain what's been happening and proclaim a national period of mourning for Nicky and those killed on the space station.

'Again, I'm so sorry for Nicky's loss. He was a dear friend to all of us and a true hero," John said struggling to hold back his emotions. A short while later as John, Victoria, Siyana and Jonathan were boarding the shuttle, Crystal came running out waving at them to stop. She was carrying a backpack with clothing dangling out the top.

"Please wait, I'm going too. I have to finish what my brother started. Please?" Crystal begged.

John stopped on the ramp and asked, "Don't your parents need you?"

"Yes, they do, but our world needs me more. I was taught that way too," Crystal replied.

John looked towards the porch. Nola stood next to Malcolm with an arm around each other waving good-bye.

"Welcome aboard!" John announced. He again looked at her parents and returned their waves with a salute.

Nola and Malcolm stood gazing into the sky as the shuttle circled the Stinson farm before swiftly disappearing into the clouds. After the shuttle was out of sight, they continued to comfort one another, pained by the loss of their heroic son and proud of the daughter who saw her duty and embraced it.

Cat grilled Togg Gath most of the day with little to show for it. He sat handcuffed to the metal chair across the table from her. He had not slept in over thirty hours. The beads of sweat dripped from his bald head and disheveled beard onto his sweat soaked gray undershirt, brown pants and bare feet. A puddle of sweat gathered under the chair. Still he would not answer her questions. All he would do is smile and demand to be called by his rank when addressed.

Cat looked at him with distain. "You are no longer anything. You are just an animal. Rats have no rank. Even your name will never be used again. Your new name is Rat.

'Now tell me where are you from?" Cat asked.

"I've already told you, I'm from Gamora Prime and my name is Captain Togg Gath," he moaned.

Cat calmly corrected him. "That is a lie, your name is Rat. Who were you planning to meet with?"

It won't matter what you call me. You are all going to die. Their heavy scout ship will destroy all of you. Their fleet is the largest ever seen and they will destroy this planet and enslave the survivors. They will do the same to all the other worlds and no one will stop them."

Cat smiled as if she had already broken him. "Rat, you will tell us who they are and where they are from or you will discover we are more ruthless than they are."

There was a knock on the door. On cue Dexter brought the evening meal of pulled BBQ pork, potato chips, a biscuit, and an apple. Togg Gath snarled at the sight of the food and demanded to know what it was.

Cat, in a moment of sarcasm, explained, "In our culture we eat the bodies of our enemies after a battle to draw on their strength and spirit. The meat is that of your First Officer cooked in a special blood sauce."

With her bare hands, she scooped up a bite of the meat.

"I'm amazed at how tender you Gamorans are. I trust the rest of your crew are just as tasty. The chips are a vegetable cooked in his rendered fat. It signifies his feeble struggle before being slowly bled to death. The biscuit is made from his bones that were baked hard, then ground into flour.

'The fruit is to mock his entry into an eternity of fire and torment, as his body will never again bear fruit. You will follow your crew as meals for the rest of our crew unless you start telling us what we wish to know."

Captain Gath's defiance began to give way. His eyes went wide with horror and his body trembled with cowardly fear. Captain Gath's vile and corrupt imagination began to play with his mind. In his fear and horror, his mind flashed with visions of himself being slowly butchered and cooked.

Cat didn't miss the fear in his eyes and the sweat that began to pour from his brow. Now she had him. Now he would tell her everything she wanted to know. It was always a matter of time.

"Come now, Rat. Eat up and honor your men," as she scooped another bite of the pork from his plate with her bare hand and shoved it into her mouth. "Come! Come, you stinking rat. Gamoran flesh is a new and tasty treat for us Earthlings. Enjoy!"

Quaking in fear, Gath fell over still handcuffed to his chair. As he lay there, Gath started babbling and crying like a baby. Cat threw his tray of food all over him and shouted, "Tell me everything or join your crew on a serving platter!"

For the next twelve hours, bit by bit, Togg Gath answered every question in great detail. He dared not lie especially after seeing Dexter and his grim, expression of revenge.

Cat got him to reveal the real name of Digger. She threatened that if he lied she would know. He believed her.

Hours later Estron sat at a computer researching and

verifying Captain Gath's confession. She was more than a little miffed at Gavin for asking her to help with the research.

By the time she finished, Estron could hardly contain her rage over the names of the revealed traitors and their plans for the destruction and plundering of her people and home world. The hatred of their faith was so great they were willing to sacrifice over a billion people to ensure this strange religion was wiped out on their planet.

She trembled at the realization of what needed to be done. Any lingering doubts about joining up with the Earthlings vanished. There were going to be many scores to settle. *So this is why Gavin insisted on me doing this assignment. He knew I had to discover the truth on my own.*

Estron entered Gavin's quarters and informed him the assignment was done.

Gavin called up the report on his data pad. "Thanks for your help."

"You knew all along I wasn't quite committed to our teaming up with the Earthlings? You knew, didn't you?" she began sobbing.

"Any doubts now it's the right thing to do?" Gavin asked.

"No! None at all!" Estron said collecting her resolve. "Thanks for making me see the truth," she sighed burying her face in her brother's chest.

Three days after the capture of the *Holcron Star* the Braxtons finally arrived at Vandenberg AFB. It was early afternoon when their shuttle settled with a gentle landing in front of the cavernous hangar. Many of John's team and some of those rescued had already arrived and were busy inside.

Siyana finished shutting down the engines as David lowered the rear ramp. A minute later the Braxton family stepped onto the tarmac. Standing by to greet them were

General Klinedecker and his aide.

"John Braxton, I presume?" the general inquired.

"I am," John replied, reaching out to shake hands.

"My name is General Jake Klinedecker. So, pleased to finally meet you."

"Sorry, I couldn't come sooner, we had much to get squared away," John replied after introducing his family and Siyana.

"I understand completely. If all of you will follow my aide, we have tailors waiting to alter and fit you for the uniforms you requested."

"Uniforms?" John asked puzzled.

"Oops! Sorry, dear," Victoria responded sheepishly. "I knew you were swamped with problems so I took the liberty of ordering uniforms for the memorial service tomorrow. I thought it would look better as most of those rescued have only rags to wear."

"Victoria, if there is even a thread of pink…"

"Don't worry John. Trust me!" I know what I'm doing," Victoria assured him.

General Klinedecker continued, "After you're fitted, we have a rehearsal for the service. There are some refreshments over on the tables by the side conference room.

'President Leatham, key congressional leaders and cabinet members are arriving in three hours. He wishes to meet with you and your people then hold a private meeting with you and your key team members. He wants to avoid the press, which will be swarming all over the place tomorrow."

"Fine with me. I'd just as soon avoid the press all together but I understand," John said.

President Leatham, staff, and congressional leaders

arrived on Air Force One on schedule. President Leatham insisted on informality for the meeting. He genuinely wanted to meet everyone especially Gavin, his sisters, Deze, Dexter and those rescued from the *Holcron Star*. After the meet and greet, the key people on Braxton's team made their way into a nearby room.

President Leatham, along with a couple of his cabinet leaders, Chairman of the Joint Chiefs of Staff General Raymond Turnbull, CIA Director Mike Richards, and two congressional leaders were ushered in. The Braxton and Toburg families, Dexter, Slick and Traven took seats around a table with a portable holo-projector in the middle.

"Thank all of you for taking the time for this meeting. This is an historic time like none other. Also, thank you and your people for a job well done as well as my condolences for Nicky's tragic loss. I pray those rescued who couldn't be here are recovering well?" President Leatham inquired.

Thank you, Mr. President. Two of the liberated Cassarians died before the next morning, but if it wasn't for the medical team from Vandenberg, we probably would have lost several more," John answered.

"Please tell us, just what is the galactic situation we are facing?" President Leatham asked.

Jonathan gave a quick overview of the portion of the inhabited galaxy as revealed so far on the holo-projector.

Following up on Jonathan's briefing, John explained, "From our interrogations of Captain Gath, we have learned of a faction on Cassaria that is in league with the pirates. We have also learned there is an invasion fleet preparing to invade the inhabited planets in this sector with the support of the pirates. For now, these people are only known as the Outsiders. We have intercepted and captured weapons far more powerful than anything known to mankind. There is an outsider scout ship due to arrive and take possession of them."

Gavin explained the danger to Earth, the other planets and the rough plan they worked out capable of stopping the pirates and Outsiders. As the conspiracy and the plan to defeat them was revealed, General Turnbull became increasingly disturbed taking copious notes. When the briefing ended, there was a momentary silence before President Leatham spoke.

"Tell me, where do we go from here? I assume from your plan, you don't intend on turning over the *Holcron Star* to the United States government or the United Nations for that matter."

"Sorry, Mr. President, I do not," John explained. "Please don't get me wrong. We are grateful for the support you've provided. Our mission would have failed without it. 'In my opinion the United Nations is ineffective, corrupt and does more to support tyranny than to rid the world of it. I will not have anything to do with them and at the moment the ship is ours."

"I see!" President Leatham acknowledged rubbing his chin.

John continued. "As for turning over the ship to my country, I could, but I won't. The issue of deniability is no longer necessary but the issue of destabilization is real. I admit I was idealistic and thought that somehow destabilization could be avoided. Recent events have made me realize destabilization is the price we're going to pay for entering a new age.

'Thankfully, we have a chance, however slim it might be, to determine our destiny and define that new age. People and nations must adapt and get on board no matter the sacrifice or join others on the ash heap of history. We must help save this part of the galaxy or lose everything we hold dear."

"That is quite ambitious. You are quite the visionary," The president smiled. "I see your point and many of us have come to similar conclusions. If it hadn't been for your actions, we would now be at the mercy of pirates. Don't quote me but as for the United Nations, I couldn't agree with you more. Earth will not have a global government, especially one run by maniacal dictators and socialist tyrants. I believe most Americans now realize freedom and peace are not synonymous. One must fight for freedom and always fight to keep it. Peace is but an interlude.

'One thing is also clear, we can't have a private citizen running around the galaxy with a giant warship at his disposal either."

The president looked at Gavin and asked, "Does your government allow private citizens to have such ships?"

"No sir! They do not," Gavin reluctantly agreed as he lowered his head.

"Then what do we do?" President Leatham asked with a baited question.

"I am proud to be an American, but most of us also desire to establish a colony on Terra," John said pointing to its location on the holographic map.

"Terra has to be taken and colonized to secure the zannite and prevent Tigran and pirate domination. In the meantime, we have to prepare to meet the Outsiders. It will be a daunting task and needs to be free of political infighting and squabbling. We might as well do it before anybody else does. A colony on Terra would gladly work closely with the United States and her allies for the cause of freedom," John pledged.

"That is a workable solution. However, until you capture the planet you have no legitimate status. Fortunately, I do have a solution to that problem. As a former Air Force officer who never resigned his commission, you give me a loophole.

'Two weeks ago, I had secret orders cut activating you back to active duty with your own command and appropriate rank. I also directed your crew to receive temporary military status. The alternative under the Geneva Convention would declare all of you as illegal combatants. You'd be no better than the pirates with whom everyone is fighting.

'May God bless you and your command, General Braxton," President Leatham proclaimed as he handed a small black velvet box to John. John opened the box. Inside were two gold stars.

"Thank you, Mr. President. I hope I prove worthy of them and your trust."

"I know it is highly unusual but with the grudging support of Congress it was approved yesterday. General Turnbull will give you anything you need to complete your mission. When Terra is liberated, we will meet again to determine the colony's future. I only have two requests."

"What are they?" John asked.

"Both of us were idealists concerning destabilization, but the flip side is it is also undeniable. Unless we make quantum leaps in technology and acquire the ability to defend Earth, grave danger will continue to threaten Earth's existence. We can't ignore these issues without serious consequences," President Leatham exclaimed.

"We will do what we can, Mr. President," Gavin pledged. "Cassaria and Holcron don't have the forces to win the war alone.

'If the pirates are neutralized, and the leaders of Katusium realize they are being played, hopefully we can turn the balance of power in our favor.

Earth's contribution to galactic freedom will not go unappreciated by your new friends and allies. I guarantee it," Gavin promised.

"Then we have a deal," President Leatham said as he took a deep breath. "Gentlemen, I've learned much today and I'm grateful for our new-found friendship. Thank you all for this opportunity to meet with you. I'll leave you with General

Turnbull. I'm sure there are many issues to be worked out. To paraphrase your words, General Braxton, we have a galaxy to save. Godspeed!"

With the meeting concluded, President Leatham left.

General Turnbull and his aide-de-camp remained behind.

"General Braxton, I'm going to assign my aide-de-camp, Lt. Col. Arlin Perry, to act as liaison for you. He is highly trustworthy and an expert at clearing red tape and getting things done. When he speaks, he speaks in my name. Let me assure you he is not here as a spy. He is your insurance policy.

'Anyone gives you garbage, he will make sure they clean it up. Earth's future is totally dependent upon your success. You can draw personnel from any branch of service or recruit your own personnel as you like."

"Well, sir, I do have one special request," John interjected. General Turnbull nodded. "Sure! Ask away."

"I need an expert in carrier and fleet operations as a temporary advisor as soon as possible. There is a lot I have to learn. It will be a pleasure working with General Klinedecker and Lt. Col. Perry."

"It so happens, the best in the business is a personal friend of mine and available. Admiral Stephen MacKay taught at the Naval War College until his wife passed away a few months ago from a battle with cancer. He is retired and I have no doubt bored out of his mind. I think he can be persuaded to work with you."

"That will do nicely," John said. "I look forward to meeting him."

General Turnbull laughed. "You won't have to wait long. He's here spending time with his daughter and plans to attend the service tomorrow. I understand his daughter is part of your crew. I'll give him a call."

"Molly MacKay! That answers a lot of questions." Victoria

smiled.

John shook the general's hand. "Thank you, General. We'll keep in touch."

After the meeting broke up, John Braxton and most of his crew returned to their temporary quarters on base for some rest and relaxation. Tomorrow was going to be a long day.

CHAPTER 11

"Tench-Hut!" Traven shouted. The command echoed through the cavernous open-ended hangar as the two squadrons of airmen snapped to attention. The whispering rush of a gentle breeze followed as Brigadier General John Braxton escorted the Commander-in Chief, First Lady, and bereaved families, as they entered and made their way to their reserved seats. The nation's attention now focused on the very unusual memorial service for Major Adam Eastman and Second Lieutenant Nicky Stinson.

Except for a single television crew, the memorial service was closed to the press at the request of both families. That didn't stop members of the press from covering the somber event at a respectful distance. They were kept from the hangar behind a roped off area guarded by security police. Two flag-draped coffins flanked by honor guards were front and center before the seated guests. Behind the coffins were two squadrons and to one side the Air Force band struck up a soft melodic rendition of *"Amazing Grace."*

The two squadrons were very different. The squadron next to the band was made up of Air Force personnel in their dress blues. The second squadron dressed in a similar dress uniform in black.

Several eulogies were given including one by Jonathan Braxton. The last eulogy was given by President Leatham.

Once the attendees left the hangar area, the new crew of the *Holcron Star* was fair game for the press. The news media and photographers swarmed around vehicles in a desperate effort to get the alien story.

Thomas Kasill wrestled with his conscience on the way to his motel room. His secret source, code-named "Isis," regarded John Braxton as a power-hungry opportunist trying to blackmail his own country. Fugitive, thief and murderer were terms Isis used when speaking of John Braxton.

"He's just another control freak seeking world power and wealth. Nothing new here or is there?" Thomas muttered.

What Isis told about him and the White House press release portrayal of John Braxton as just an average Joe, didn't match. Experience told Thomas things are never as they seem. Everyone in Braxton's family repeatedly refused interviews. Even friends and relatives refused to speak on or off the record about the Braxtons or any other crew member. He assumed they were helping cover up a dark past.

However, today's events revealed an interesting picture. There were strong ties of loyalty, trust and admiration from those who knew him. They didn't hesitate to form a wall of protection around the family. It appeared the Braxtons had a deep-seated distrust of the press, particularly those on the left .

I sincerely want to hear John Braxton's point of view but how do I penetrate the wall to make it happen?

The White House press release referred to him as Brigadier General John Braxton. Thomas assumed it was a cover story to help bury the whole UFO event in a cloak of national security. When John Braxton's fifteen minutes of fame dies out, Washington would, as always, resort to the politics of personal destruction. There would be no compunction among Washington power brokers to either own his soul or ruin this interloper and his family. The Washington power brokers were writing that script already.

"Thomas," his editor once said, "the fate of the world is too fragile to trust to the masses. Democracy is designed as an illusion to keep them pacified. The reality is, the elite run this country and the world. They alone are worthy to decide our future. Our job is to facilitate that while making sure they don't get too carried away."

As a young cub reporter, he came to Washington wanting to change the world into a social utopia. Twenty years later, Washington had corrupted him and he knew it. His quest to change the world had almost destroyed his soul. The manipulation of leaks, misinformation, and outright lies from scheming, egotistical politicians, sycophant aides, narcissistic activists, and self-serving news media became an all-powerful dog leash around his neck. Everyone was fighting over who got to jerk his leash the hardest to write their agenda driven view.

Deep down in his gut Thomas realized Washington was a cesspool of primordial ooze.

The silence of his motel room started closing in as Thomas starred glassy-eyed at his laptop computer. It was like starring at a 100,000 piece jigsaw puzzle in a fog. *There are too many questions and, so far, no answers. Isis obviously has a hidden agenda, but what is it? Why has her information gone sour lately? In fact, what interest would she have in the whole affair if she wasn't directly involved? Could her actions be nothing more than the usual beltway power games? Was Isis a setup or did her source dry up? The whole alien ship thing was the story of a lifetime but the intrigue behind it is an even bigger story? What is the real story behind John Braxton? They don't grab some guy off the street, pin a star on him and give him the most powerful space ship in the universe. Arrgghh! This whole thing's nuts!*

Thomas stormed out of the room in desperate need of fresh air. A fast walk around the block four times broke him out in a sweat and blew the fog of frustration away. Before returning to his room he helped himself to a cup of dark liquid from the hotel lobby coffee pot. He hadn't left the lobby when he took a sip.

"Gross. Whatever that stuff is, it's not coffee," Thomas choked as he threw it in the waste can. He took a copy of the newspaper and settled for a bottle of water from the pop machine.

Returning to his laptop and notes, Thomas again looked over the pieces of the puzzle. An hour later he was still clueless. In his mind, he could still hear his editor admonish him. "Thomas, there is a whole lot more to the alien story than anyone knows. Don't come back until you have the answers." *Here we go, more tugs on the leash.*

In frustration, he began pacing the room. Suddenly his eye caught the headline of the newspaper, "FBI clueless to White House murder."

"Could it be Dr. Long is the connection?" Thomas shouted.

The boss thinks there's a deeper, darker underlying story and here it is starring me in the face. She was right; this story smells of a Pulitzer Prize.

The more he thought about it the more the pieces started falling together. To verify Isis's information, Thomas listed other sources to ensure his informant was not singled out.

If Dr. Long were the primary source, it would explain why the sudden stop of reliable information. Could it be Long's murderer was Isis or an accomplice?

Drawing from previous research material and an interview he did on Dr. Long two years ago, Thomas listed names of known associates and friends. A process of elimination left him with the names of three men and two women.

During his interview, he found Dr. Long to be almost two different persons. When I asked questions about his personal life, he would blush, stutter and stumble through the answers.

If the questions were about foreign affairs, he would give a mind-boggling dissertation. He was definitely a geek and hardly the kind of person to make enemies.

Three names were of university professors. A few quick calls revealed; one was on a sabbatical in Europe, one was a visiting professor at Oxford for a year, and the other doing research in Japan. Another name was his book agent. The last name on the list seemed quite odd. Dr. Loretta Sanchez of the State Department. An internet search revealed they were in grad school together and very close friends. *Could she be the mystery source?*

In Washington D. C. the improbable is never dismissed.

Sanchez was known as a brilliant career diplomat. Some thought she was the most politically savvy person in the State Department. She was also called the "Witch of State" by former department employees foolish enough to cross swords with her.

"Yes, I need to know more about this relationship," Thomas muttered.

Special Agent Maxine Maxwell didn't buy the news story of Dr. Long's death at the hands of a street-walking prostitute for one minute. It didn't take much investigating to figure out the crime scene was a setup.

Dr. Long did not know his abductor but how did the killer know he was going out at that late hour? There was nothing stolen, not even his wallet, no fingerprints were found, and so far no witnesses.

The few clues she had were hair strands from a cheap red wig, a cab driver's description of a redhead with a French accent and a security tape of Russell being abducted. The woman in the video wobbled when she walked in the pointed stiletto shoes and fidgeted with her wig. She didn't seem comfortable wearing such clothes. As the car drove by the camera, she turned to hide her face. The woman knew every camera angle.

Maxine drew up a list of women associated with Dr. Long. For Washington D. C. it was a surprisingly short list. Instinct told Maxine someone on this list knowingly or unknowingly aided the killer. The problem was witnesses weren't coming forward. This case was going cold and something had to break soon.

After Air Force One left Vandenberg AFB, news broke of China's People's Liberation Army staging a countercoup. The tyrannical generals held secret military tribunals charging leaders of the new found Democratic Revolution with treason and declaring anyone supporting the group as enemies of the State. Enemies would be executed. The generals miscalculated the new determination of the people. Instead of cowering under threats of death, the people and their leaders grew in resolve and numbers.

The PLA showed no mercy as unarmed men, women and children were slaughtered wherever they found dissent. In some areas whole villages ceased to exist. Despite the terror, hundreds of millions of Chinese people were determined to have real freedom. Russian military forces were put on alert and several additional divisions were ordered to the border poised for invasion of disputed territories. Many Chinese commanders and troops refused to support the communist hard line generals and joined the democratic forces. This drain of PLA resources weakened their assaults allowing democratic forces to organize more effective military responses.

What began as a communist military countercoup degenerated into a full-fledged "fight to the death" civil war.

Jonathan, Katrina and Susan stepped off the shuttle onto the deck of the *Holcron Star*'s hangar. The duty officer was Katrina's brother, Joshua.

"Welcome back. How did the meeting with the president go?" Joshua asked.

"Good. Dad will brief us all tomorrow."

"You mean 'the general' don't you?" Joshua reminded him.

"Well, we're getting used to that. The president kept addressing dad as 'General.' Dad kept looking around the room thinking he was talking to someone else. It was funny to watch. Even the chief of staff struggled to keep from laughing. How were things here while we were gone?"

"It's been very quiet. Except for our pirate captain. One minute he's refusing to talk, the next minute he's sing'n like a jaybird. I had a visit from one of the Cassarian patients. Name is Dr. Khem Kremmel. He wants to help with the other patients. I told him I would pass his request to General Braxton."

Susan, a bit agitated, said, "Everything is under control. We don't need his help, besides, I'm not so sure he's healthy enough for duty yet."

"Isn't he that handsome guy that all but drools when you're in the medical ward?" Katrina teased.

"I'm too busy to notice. I think you're imagining things," Susan retorted. Her face flushed with irritation.

The group broke out laughing. David stuck his head out the shuttle door. "Hey, hold the party somewhere else. Siyana and I are heading out to the beach."

"OK, little brother. You two have fun." Jonathan chuckled as he herded the group out of the hanger. A minute later the shuttle was on its way back to Vandenberg AFB.

"I have a few things to take care of. How about meeting up on the Forward Observation Deck in two hours," Jonathan suggested.

"I have some patients I'd like to check up on too. Sounds like a plan," Katrina agreed.

A couple hours later, Jonathan and Katrina met up on the observation deck. The deck was a large open area on Deck 1 that gave a wide view of space. The main cafeteria took up the rear portion of the observation deck and could seat one hundred and fifty people comfortably.

On the left was a snack bar and a smaller upper lounge area. At the very front of the observation deck was a lower lounge area. It was four feet lower than the main floor and arched almost all the way around the inner hull with a ten-foot high viewing window. There were three staircases to access the lower lounge with tables, lounge chairs and sofas furnished for the crew's relaxation. The viewport had armored shields that closed in an emergency. Though the *Holcron Star* was a warship, the boredom and stresses of deep space travel made the observation deck a vital social hub for the crew.

Choosing a sofa in the center of the lower lounge, Jonathan and Katrina relaxed while taking in the breathtaking view of Earth. The swirling white clouds, blue oceans and colorful land formations were a constantly changing masterpiece of natural art.

"Every time I look at Earth I'm overwhelmed," Katrina said. "It is so gorgeous!"

"Not as gorgeous as looking at you," Jonathan smiled.

"Flattery like that might get you a couple of kisses before midnight," Katrina teased.

"Only two kisses? Well, so much for that book of one liners," Jonathan bantered back.

Katrina laughed. "We're engaged. You don't need one-liners anymore. Now that we've captured the ship, what's next?"

Jonathan let out a deep breath. "The last three weeks have

changed everyone's plans. Nobody planned this far ahead except Dad and he's slow leaking what he's thinking. I'm not sure how all this affects us."

"Jonathan Braxton! You're not going anywhere without me so get used to it, buster," Katrina said poking Jonathan in the side. "Just because circumstances change doesn't mean my heart changes. You got that?"

Jonathan was a bit surprised at her reaction. "Of course, but that's not what I was thinking about. I was thinking maybe we should move up our wedding plans."

Katrina's eyes lit up. "Now you're talking. I was thinking the same thing. Our plan to have the wedding back home next year doesn't seem possible or practical. What do you suggest?"

"I thought maybe we'd do it right here in about two weeks.

Chaplain Boyle would be glad to perform the service. I can ask Dad about it and see what he thinks."

"Two weeks! You don't give a girl much time to plan!"

Jonathan looked downward, "Yes, I guess that would be unfair…"

Katrina kissed him gently on the cheek, "OK, two weeks it is."

Jonathan reached out to embrace her as a double beep sounded on his flip com.

"Jonathan Braxton here. What's up?" Jonathan inquired.

"Bridge here, we have detected six missile launches from a remote area in China. The sensors identify them as hyper-velocity ICBMs with multiple warheads. Five missiles are aimed directly at us and will strike in less than three minutes."

"Sound general quarters and get the engines powered up ASAP!" I'm on my way!" Jonathan ordered.

Jonathan looked apologetically at Katrina, "Sorry, I've got to go!"

"Go on, save the world, but you'd better not leave me at

that alter in two weeks!"

When Jonathan arrived on the bridge a quick glance at the holo projector revealed the positions of the missiles and their projected flight paths. Joshua was powering up the deflector shields, but it would not do much if the missiles made direct hits.

Meghan McLeod, manning the Communications station, already alerted Vandenberg AFB and the duty officer, Sean Miller, aboard Gavin's freighter.

Georgia Riggs, at the Engineering station, was doing her best to power the engines up. Another crewmember, Scott Bower, studying navigation programming when the attack began, was now trying to input directions into the navigation computer but was so inexperienced he was having difficulty.

"Scotty, stop what you're doing, we don't need navigation. Power up the cannons on the aft starboard defense systems console," Jonathan ordered.

Scotty replied. "Yes, sir! That I know how to do."

"Joshua, once the deflector shields are fully up, power the forward starboard defensive systems. Meghan, take the other flight control seat and help me get this beast moving."

Meghan shook her head. "The warp engines are down for some maintenance. We don't have enough time to get the sub-light engines up."

Jonathan grimaced in frustration. "Doesn't matter, some power is better than none. We'll use the thrusters on manual for some extra boost.

Jonathan buckled himself into the left flight control chair and flipped a switch disengaging the autopilot. A warning light flashed and a computer voice warned the autopilot was disengaged. He flipped a switch cancelling the warning.

Disengaging the flight control yoke he activated the steering thrusters. Now he could use the thrusters controlled by the joystick on the right armrest to control the yaw, pitch and roll of the ship in sub-light speeds and docking conditions. On the left armrest was a set of controls for keeping stationary position. He switched those off.

He pressed the middle blue button on the flight control stick to engage both sub-light engines. As the engines slowly built up thrust he adjusted the sliding throttle switch for more forward speed and ever so slowly pushed the joystick forward. The ship sluggishly responded moving in so slow a motion Jonathan could hardly tell the ship was moving.

Meghan looked at Jonathan and shook her head.

"Maybe we should get out and push?" Jonathan said in desperation.

In a last attempt to save the ship and crew he did the unthinkable and pushed the throttle to full power and joystick into a dive.

To the astonishment of everyone on the bridge, the ship began to nose over into a steep dive. Gently Jonathan banked to starboard. This maneuver forced the missiles to change course. In doing so the ship was now distancing itself while at the same time exposing the missiles to an oblique starboard broadside.

"I get what you're doing," Meghan said and began reading out altitude and distance to reentry. "You're buying us time for a broadside firing solution."

As gravity increased speed, the *Holcron Star* began to rapidly close the distance to the incoming missiles. A computerized voice relayed distance and time of missile impact.

"Are you crazy? This ship can't go atmospheric," Georgia shouted at Jonathan.

"There's always a first time!" Jonathan groaned as he kept pushing the joystick. He quickly realized as he gained speed the joystick became more responsive and the more maneuverability he was gaining. Sensing what Jonathan was attempting, Meghan finished strapping herself into the other flight control seat. The *Holcron Star* gained speed and with every second the maneuvering ability Jonathan desperately needed to save the ship increased.

"Joshua, Scotty!" Meghan shouted. "Press the first two red buttons on the left top panel of your consoles. The computers will supply the targeting data to the fore and aft starboard laser banks for targeting solutions.

"When you have targeting solutions, hold the lower right target lock button next to the targeting screen until it glows green. Once it goes green all starboard laser banks will engage the missiles until destroyed."

Because Jonathan was maneuvering at a slight angle away from the five missiles, the *Holcron Star* was now less than fifteen-seconds from impact.

It took a couple more seconds for the computers to acquire target lock. Finally, the buttons turned green. At that moment, Jonathan completed the starboard maneuver and the ship was now in perfect position to fire. With less than five-seconds before impact, the ten starboard lasers erupted in a blaze of brilliant violet light that sliced into the fuel tanks of the incoming ballistic missiles. The resulting explosions destroyed the missiles without detonating the nuclear warheads.

For a split second, everyone sighed relief except Jonathan and Meghan. They were totally absorbed in a heroic effort to save the ship from making a fiery reentry. Jonathan took what speed he gained from the dive and pulled the huge lumbering ship into a climb while Meghan fired the docking thrusters to help boost control.

Everyone held their breath for what seemed an eternity. The ship seemed to teeter between climbing to a higher altitude and plunging into Earth's atmosphere in a huge fiery molten mass.

Georgia, Scotty and Joshua gazed out the port and starboard windows observing the surface edges of the outer hull begin glowing a dull red as the surface temperature rose.

The computer-generated female voice continued warning of atmospheric reentry. Ever so slowly the ship began to resist the forces of gravity as the engines picked up power from the reactors. Finally, Jonathan felt the flight controls ease their resistance.

An elated cheer followed the sigh of relief on the bridge as the computer warning system announced, "Atmospheric reentry threat canceled."

"We're not out of the woods yet," Jonathan declared leveling out the ship. "What's the status of the sixth missile?"

Meghan swiped her fingers across her console display screen calling up a new display. The projection flickered as the display changed and sensors showed the track of the missile with its calculated trajectory.

"It is headed for Vandenberg AFB," Meghan said.

With the increased speed, Jonathan changed course using the *Holcron Star* to block the missile's reentry.

"Joshua, setup the fire control computer like you did before on the missile. It will fire when in range. We must destroy it before it begins arming the warhead upon reentry."

'Aye, sir!" Joshua replied.

"Jonathan, sensors project we won't be in range for another minute but the missile will arm in forty-seconds,"Scotty announced.

"I really hate days like this," Jonathan grumbled as he put the ship into another dive straight towards the missile.

"Here we go again," Meghan groaned. I sure hope you can pull this maneuver off twice or we're toast."

"If we don't make it, we won't be the only ones," Jonathan grimly replied.

Meghan called out, "Missile will arm in ten seconds…

nine… eight…seven…six…five…four…three…two…"

Suddenly a flash of intense violet light knifed through space striking the missile warhead. The resulting destruction prevented nuclear detonation.

Once the ship returned to a higher orbit, Jonathan kept the ship at general quarters and all defensive weapon systems powered up. He also ordered all reactors brought up to standby power.

Georgia notified Vandenberg AFB the results of the attack and requested further orders from General Braxton. A minute later Jonathan got a call.

"Jonathan, I don't know how you did it but thanks for an outstanding job well done!" John exclaimed. I do need statements from each person on the bridge as to what happened in as much detail as possible."

"Yes, sir! Anything else?" Jonathan asked.

"You are ordered to take no further action except to defend the ship and begin acquiring targeting data on all PLA bases and ships and particularly the launch sites of the missiles. Ship personnel on the ground are being recalled as we speak," John said.

The moonlight sparkled off the ocean as gentle waves lapped the white sandy shore. Stars shined brightly in the cloudless sky and the aroma of the salty ocean filled the air. Siyana and David strolled in the darkness oblivious to the lights of passing ships. At a rock outcropping, they paused.

"It is so beautiful here. All these wonderful scents and sounds of nature get taken for granted until you've been in space for a time. There is nothing in space but silence, nothing to smell unless the air scrubbers break down. Then you wish you couldn't smell at all," Siyana said with a tone of experience.

"You don't like space travel?" David asked.

Siyana laughed. "Oh, don't get me wrong. I love space travel, especially visiting other worlds and meeting new people. It is the experience of a lifetime. However, memories of home are always in the shadows tugging at you. A voice keeps whispering, 'Come home! Come home! Come home!'"

"I understand. There is no place like home," David agreed.

The couple were gazing at the stars when a series of violet flashes and massive fiery bursts appeared low on the horizon. David and Siyana were at first awed then puzzled.

"What in the world was that all about?" David asked.

"Laser battery shots. Look!" Siyana said pointing at the faint streaks of light in the sky and secondary explosions. "See the glowing twin engines of the *Holcron Star?* Something is dreadfully wrong!"

No sooner had she spoken than their flip coms started chirping. "All personnel report to the shuttles for emergency evacuation immediately," the voice ordered. "This is no drill. Report immediately. We are under attack."

"Well, so much for a romantic date!" David sighed as he grabbed Siyana's hand to help her over a rock outcropping.

As they madly dashed down the beach to their car, another series of laser flashes streaked across the sky resulting in another explosion. The second series of flashes spurred them to run even faster.

Fifteen minutes later, David and Siyana arrived at the hanger. Many of the crew already reported. Gavin was directing them aboard the freighter. Siyana noticed Gavin made an addition to the freighter's side. Below the freighter's identification numbers the name *Halfling* was added.

"I like it!" Siyana smiled. "What do you want us to do?"
"Aycana and Estron are powering up the ship. You and David take Shuttle 1 and wait for John and Victoria. They should be along any minute," Gavin shouted above the noise.

"What happened?" David asked.

"The Chinese army attacked the *Holcron Star* with missiles.They targeted another missile at Vandenberg AFB. Jonathan destroyed the missiles. That's all I know."

"OK, we'll get Dad and Mom out of here as fast as we can. See you aboard ship," David confirmed.

David and Siyana boarded Shuttle 1 and began running the preflight checklist and powering up the engines. David called his parents.

"Yes, David, where are you?" John inquired.

"We are powering up Shuttle 1 now and awaiting your arrival," David replied.

"We are at the Guest House. Can you fly the shuttle over here? There are six of us. However, we are waiting on your grandpa to arrive. There is a field behind the Guest House. You can land there."

"Roger that! Call me when he arrives. I can be there in less than a minute. Can you mark the field?"

"We'll mark it with a triangle of three road flares. Out!" John confirmed.

Victoria answered the knock at the door. Molly MacKay and her father, Admiral Stephen MacKay, along with Lt. Col. Arlin Perry were quickly ushered in.

"You arrived just in time. John just talked to David. Shuttle 1 will be here shortly. If you need any other belongings we can get them later," Victoria said.

"Where's Henry? I can't raise him on his flip com," John said in frustration.

There was another knock at the door. "That's probably Henry now," John sighed. Victoria opened the door and gasped so loud it drew everyone's attention. In the doorway was Henry in handcuffs accompanied by two big burley security police officers.

"Henry!" Victoria exclaimed. "What's going on, sergeant?"

"We pursued this guy driving an old, beat up truck across the base headquarters lawn, through a parking lot, and the backyards of several homes in base housing. We finally caught him about a block away. He says he's being recalled to his space ship and was in a hurry. Traffic was all tied up so he decided to take a short cut. We didn't believe him, but stopped to see if you can identify him," the staff sergeant stated.

"He is one of us and I'm sorry for the difficulty, but we do need him aboard ship immediately. Was there any damage?" John asked.

"Yes, sir. He ran over two garbage cans and spread the contents all over a front lawn. He also tore up a couple shrubs in the housing area. In addition, the vehicle has so many safety violations it really ought to be towed to the junk yard."

"Now see here, sonny. That truck was just getting broke in when you were in diapers. It took me years to get my truck broke in," Henry declared rather indignantly.

"Henry, please! You're in enough trouble," Victoria urged with a soft voice and a finger over her lips.

Henry sighed and nervously shifted his feet some more as he conceded to Victoria's admonition.

"We'll gladly pay for the damage. I apologize for the mess. The vehicle will be towed as soon as possible. I can assure you, we will take corrective action so this doesn't happen again," John replied while glaring at his father.

"I'm sorry sir, the garbage cans are not a big deal but the shrubs are a serious problem." The staff sergeant retorted.

"Please, sergeant, it can't be that big of a deal. It's not like he ran over the wing commander's front lawn or something," Victoria said defensively.

"That's just it, ma'am. It was the wing commander's front lawn," the sergeant stated.

Henry hung his head in embarrassment while everyone broke out in laughter except the security police. Lt. Col. Perry intervened by taking the two policemen aside. After a few brief words they removed Henry's cuffs, apologized for the inconvenience and quickly left.

"Thanks, Arlin for your help. We need to get the signal flares deployed fast," John said hailing David on the flip com. and urging everyone out the door.

"Don't worry about the damage or Henry's truck. The security police will see to it his museum piece is well cared for," Arlin promised.

A minute later Shuttle 1 landed and six passengers quickly boarded. The whine of the shuttle's engines echoed in the night air as it lifted off for the flight back to the *Holcron Star.*

Upon arriving aboard the *Holcron Star,* crewmembers raced to stow their gear away and report to their stations. Henry was amazed at the enormity of the ship.

"Hey, general son, what can I do?" Henry asked.

"Dad, you never have to call me general, OK?" John said a bit embarrassed.

"Sounds good to me," Henry smiled.

"I must get to the bridge for now. You want to come with me or team up with Dexter for a while?" John offered pointing to Dexter across the hangar heading for an exit hatch.

"I'd just be in your way. I'll catch up to Dex and follow him a while. See ya later!" Henry waved shuffling off after Dexter.

Henry soon found Dexter well ahead of him and scurried to catch up while Dexter weaved around the crewmembers rushing to their duty stations. He was fascinated with the ship's complexity as well as how everyone seemed to know where he or she was going. One oddity caught his sharp eyes. Dexter was the only one wearing a blaster on his hip. Everyone else was unarmed. When Dexter came to the elevator he opted for the stairwell down.

That's odd. I've seen the floor plan of this ship. The elevator takes you to Engineering. Oh well, maybe he knows a short cut.

As Henry arrived on deck 4 he saw Dexter enter a room he knew was not Engineering. *This here's the Brig. The door lock has been jimmied.* Henry rushed in. In front of the cell stood Dexter, his blaster drawn.

"Dex, Stop! You don't wanna do this!" Henry shouted.

Startled, Dexter asked, "What are you doing here?"

"I should be askin' you that question." Henry replied slowly moving across the room to place himself between Dexter and Captain Gath still in his cell. "Don't be shooting this space scumbag! He ain't worth it!"

Captain Gath rattled the bars to his cell. "Stop that idiot! He's going to murder me in cold blood. The sick twisted nut is going to murder me!" Captain Gath screamed.

"Awe, shut your yap ya babbling coward. You deserve to die, just not right now," Henry snapped back.

"Dex, my friend, please put the gun away."

"Out of my way, Henry! I'm doing the galaxy a favor killing this scum."

"Ya got a point there, my friend, but it wouldn't be just him that dies."

"What?" Dexter asked confused.

"Well, first ya have to shoot me before ya can blast a hole in Captain Scumbag. After that, John will have to hold a trial and execute my friend. I don't have many friends in this world, Dex, but you sure are one I'd like to keep around a while. It would really pain me to have my son execute my friend."

"Henry, how could it pain you if you're dead? Get out of

my way!" Dexter growled.

"Never mind about that," Henry rolled his eyes, "You're confusin' the issue. I can't let you do this."

"You need me alive. Don't let him kill me!" Gath begged.

Henry took a deep breath in frustration. "We only need ya long as you cooperate and ya ain't cooperating. Now shut up ya coward and let me do the talkin'."

Dexter stepped to the side trying to get a clear shot but Henry moved to block him.

"I know you carry a lot of pain but this won't make it go away," Henry tried to reason.

"Pain? You have no idea the pain this man has caused me. You have no idea what real pain is!" Dexter shouted while sidestepping again for a better shot.

"Dex, I know your pain better than most. Since I first met you, I could see pain behind your mask. Ya think you're covering scars on your face but the real scars are in your heart ain't they?" Henry asked blocking Dexter's aim once more.

The revelation of Dexter's innermost secret took him by surprise.

Dexter reeled back and grasped his chest as if to keep the pain inside. Now he shifted his aim to Henry.

Dexter cried out, "He deserves to die for what he did. He murdered my wife and son and laughed as he did it. He left me for dead but I survived. I promised revenge for what this sick animal did and I will have my revenge. You don't have the right to stop me."

"Yes, I do!" Henry replied unbuttoning his shirt revealing scars covering his chest.

"How did you get them?" Dexter asked softly.

"My Beth was pregnant with John when a drunk driver plowed into us. I was knocked out with the broken steering wheel stuck in my chest. When I came to, I couldn't move.

Beth was pinned in her seat and blood everywhere. I wouldn't let them cut me out until they got her safe.

'It didn't matter. She was dead. The medics saved John. He was born right beside me in that wreck.

'I know your pain. I wanted to kill that drunk driver. Narry a scratch on the rascal. I was filled with hate and revenge."

"So why didn't you kill him?" Dexter asked.

"Something always held me back. I was wrestling with God and blamed him. I woke up, Dex. God was a trying to help me. Beth was with Jesus in Heaven lookin' down on me. I owed it to her to raise up John the way she wanted. At that moment, I started to see the world through God's eyes for the first time.

'From that day on I determined I'd raise John as best I could. I knew God spared him for something special. I have a family that loves me and looks out for me. I got friends like you. We are family on this here ship. Ya kill Captain Scumbag now and you'll undo everythin' good," Henry begged.

'Put the pain and hate away and live the life your wife wanted ya to live. Ya need to trust God not wrestle with him. Now, put the gun away. Here, you are part of a special family that loves and needs you. You have a home with us."

Dexter hesitated then slowly began lowering his blaster. "I'm sorry. You see though my mask and still want to call me friend?" Dexter begged as a tear appeared from under his mask.

"Sure. What are families for?" Henry smiled.

The look in Dexter's eyes pierced Captain Gath. "Today, I will not kill you. A day will come when you wish I did."

Henry put his arm on Dexter's shoulder and turned him towards the forced entrance. It was then Dex saw two security guards had been poised to intervene if necessary. They relieved Dexter of his weapon and allowed him to pass. Henry and Dexter walked together to Engineering. Not a word was said between them. They didn't need words to understand each other.

On the bridge, John and Jonathan stood in front of the Security console monitor. Jonathan turned the security warning light off and called up the video record file. They nodded to each other as John hit the Delete command key.

CHAPTER 12

Nations expressed their outrage at China's unprovoked nuclear and cyber-attacks. They were most horrified at the communist party's butchery of their own people. They also feared the anticipated American response. President Leatham gathered his remaining cabinet leaders, key staff and advisors at the White House. The vice president and other selected cabinet members were already evacuated to the remote shelter and linked by satellite to plan America's response. After a period of silence accentuating the gravity of the situation the president spoke.

"I can't put into words the anger and outrage towards those who attacked us nor express the depth of gratitude for the heroic actions of the *Holcron Star* crew. A heroic young man risked his crew and ship to foil an attack that otherwise would have led the world into nuclear chaos. God's providence spared the world a holocaust beyond imagination."

President Leatham paused again taking a deep breath to collect his thoughts. "Now we can pause and examine a different response. I asked the Secretary of Defense to update us on the Chinese military crisis."

Secretary Longstreet signaled an intelligence officer to begin her briefing. When the briefing concluded twenty minutes later, the Secretary of Defense spoke.

"Mr. President, it's clear the PLA is in a desperate position. Since the pirates wiped out over 40 million people and two major cities the government has been in chaos. They refuse any and all aid. In fact, they blame us and our allies for the pirate attack. Since the attack, they have been ineffective in responding to the disaster. Their infrastructure just can't muster the relief needed for the hundreds of millions of people affected in the region. Half of China is in open revolt.

'They want communist power restored at any price. The increasing defection of troops and growing civilian opposition is rapidly tipping the scale against them."

Secretary of State Smith asked, "Could it be the missiles were fired as a warning to stay out of their civil war? They keep the military advantage if they can isolate the opposition."

General Turnbull added, "Sir, Dr. Smith is partially right. If you want to fire a shot across the bow, you fire one shot not six followed with a full court press cyber-attack. The attack was obviously anemic.

Intelligence suspects this attack is a ruse to sucker us into attacking the wrong side and con us into doing their dirty work for them."

"How so?" Vice President Koppel asked.

General Turnbull used his laser pointer on the projected map. "This western region is where the mobile missile launchers fired the missiles. The territory is changing hands very rapidly. Two missile bases have already been seized and two more are under attack. If they can make us believe the missiles were launched from these two bases and we attack them not knowing they are now controlled by the rebels it is possible we could tip the scales in favor of the communists.

'No doubt the PLA was testing the *Holcron Star*'s defenses and maybe even hoping to take it out. Given the Cassarians have twice before foiled their plans, I'm sure they view our possession of the *Holcron Star* as intolerable. When starring defeat in the face, nations will often take desperate and even senseless measures to stave off the inevitable."

"Mr. President, I agree with General Turnbull," Secretary Longstreet chimed in. "In their minds, the Chinese Communists probably believe there was nothing to lose by attacking the *Holcron Star*. To save face and make sure no one interferes in domestic affairs is a very logical act on their part, even if it's insane from our point of view. They're counting on us not being trigger-happy and launching missiles in return. However, we can't give them a pass. There must be a painfully measured response or they will be tempted to attack again with more force."

The president thought for a moment then turned to General Turnbull. "A nuclear response is absolutely out for now. Such an act would kill millions of Chinese on both sides. The PLA is counting on their usual bully tactics. I will never be bullied. They also attacked the Cassarian diplomatic mission and that on its face is an act of war on the Cassarian nation. While under our protection it makes the situation even more serious. It can't be forgiven. Appeasement is an admission of failure.

'The cyber-attack that followed caused economic havoc. From that we will recover even stronger while their economy will be wrecked beyond repair. Their miscalculations are going to be our gain.

'I want those two missile bases verified to be in Chinese Communist hands then neutralized. Make sure none of the targets are in the hands of democratic forces when we respond.

'I need to assure our allies our response will be a measured response but not nuclear in nature. I'll also hold a press conference after our response to explain our actions to our citizenry and the world."

The meeting continued for another hour as further political details were hammered out. The rest of the country, indeed, the world, anxiously waited for the American response.

Most of the news networks vigorously interviewed opposition talking heads and self-proclaimed military experts attempting to influence the president. It didn't matter who the pundit was, the mantra was the same: it was almost the end of mankind and President Leatham's fault.

Critics also blamed John Braxton and the Cassarian aliens for their warlike provocation and willingness to exterminate mankind to protect their selfish hoarding of alien technology.

The people aboard the *Holcron Star* were not oblivious to what was being said in the news. It was like listening to an alternate reality far removed from what they experienced. The vast majority of Americans weren't buying the rhetoric and lies either. In fact, they were getting fed up. The Red Chinese launched a nuclear attack and a strong response was paramount to make sure it didn't happen again.

When a local TV affiliate in Chicago tried to get a "man on the street" interview near the downtown waterfront, the reporter had trouble finding anyone who would answer his question the way he wanted. Frustrated, the reporter finally saw a trio of construction workers walk by and seeing the union decals on their hard hats thought they would be good subjects to approach.

"Excuse me, may I ask a question for our evening viewers?" the reporter asked holding out his microphone while the camera zoomed in for a close-up.

"Sure!" one of the burley construction workers replied.

"Considering President Leatham's failure to bring about world peace, do you believe the United Nations should step in and force him to share alien technology to avoid further bloodshed?"

The construction worker paused for a second then exploded. "You mean to tell me it's the president's fault that Chinese leaders and generals attempted to blow us up and we need the United Nations to save us? Pass this on to your elitist screwball pals."

The worker grabbed the reporter's microphone and threw it in the freezing river before punching him to the ground. The two other construction workers joined in the fray. A moment later the camera operator lay sprawled beside the reporter as his camera sank beneath the floating ice.

The female camera assistant started screaming for help. Responding to her screams, several bystanders appeared only to join in pushing the news van into the river. When it was all over, police quickly ushered the news team out of the area to safety. When the police tried to interview witnesses, everyone claimed they saw nothing.

The bridge night shift crew of the *Holcron Star* were in the middle of briefing the relieving day shift crew when John Braxton stepped onto the bridge.

"Captain on the bridge!" Molly announced.

"Carry on! Please carry on!" John winced rubbing his forehead. "Jonathan, what's your report?" John inquired.

"We are maintaining higher orbit and reactors are on standby at one hundred percent. A lesson learned there. We won't get caught without maneuvering capability ever again. The crew is on standby alert. I thought it important to continue training where possible until we get further orders. Starboard defensive lasers are powered up in standby mode.

'Aycana is collecting targeting data on Chinese bases and ships. She is almost done with the survey. She also received targeting data transmissions from the Air Force.

'Susan reports six patients remain in sick bay and thirty-two remain in quarters. All twenty-six Cassarians released from medical care have volunteered to serve with us. Gavin has vouched for them and I assigned them light duties pending your approval. We also have fifteen Katusians requesting duty but Gavin said he'd check them out first.

Four Cassarian, Holcron, and Katusian mothers with six young children are in passenger status. Susan requests you visit sick bay to discuss a patient with her at your convenience.

'I went ahead and set up a duty officer schedule. Aycana is relieving me as duty officer and Joshua is assigned swing shift. I'll have night shift again tonight. I've already briefed Aycana and if no further questions, the captain's chair is yours."

"Great briefing and thanks for getting the schedule done. I was going to do that this morning. I want you to know you showed a lot of guts last night. I don't know where you came up with that maneuver but you saved many lives and the ship," John said proudly patting Jonathan's shoulder.

"To be honest, I don't know either. It just seemed the right thing to do at the moment. I had a great bridge crew with me," Jonathan said.

"I was thinking of something to honor all of you. Got any ideas?" John asked.

"Well normally I'd ask for pizzas for the whole bridge crew to celebrate but I do have another request as well," Jonathan said.

"You've got to be kidding?" John retorted.

"No, I'm serious. You taught me to cash in on favors when you can," Jonathan deadpanned.

"I never said…" John began but Jonathan cut him off.

I want permission for Katrina and I to get married aboard ship in two weeks," Jonathan declared.

John didn't hesitate. "Permission for both requests approved provided you wear your mess dress and tie for the occasion."

"That's dirty pool, but for Katrina it's a deal," Jonathan sighed.

The whole bridge erupted in cheers.

"As you were people!" John smiled.

Jonathan struggled to contain his excitement. "By the way, I did some more research like you asked. I sent you a folder on what I found. You're right. Some things aren't adding up. After you read it you'll know why I set up a special meeting at 1600 hours."

"Another one?" John teased. "Thanks, I'll look at it in a little bit."

Molly interrupted the conversation. "Sir, two messages just arrived from General Turnbull for you and one for Admiral MacKay and Lt. Col. Perry."

"Go ahead and forward the message to them," John ordered as he read the first message on his data pad and said nothing. Reading the second message, John rubbed his forehead and pondered its contents as well. Everyone on the bridge was curious but kept their silence.

"Sorry, Jonathan. You don't get to go off duty just quite yet. Go get some breakfast, then report outside the main briefing room in an hour for a meeting with Admiral MacKay. General Turnbull has ordered an immediate inquiry conducted by Admiral MacKay into the events of last night."

"Did I do something wrong?" Jonathan asked a little nervous.

"Not a chance in my book, son. I think they just want the details of what happened. I'll send them the statements from everyone. You have nothing to worry about. Go get some chow and report."

"Yes, sir!" Jonathan replied then disappeared in the elevator.

"Molly, please page Admiral MacKay, Lt. Col. Perry and Gavin. Ask them if they would join me in the briefing room on Deck 1 in thirty minutes. Also have Joshua, Meghan, Scotty, and Georgia report outside the briefing room in an hour."

"Yes, sir!" Molly acknowledged.

John read the report Jonathan gave him. Aycana handed him a memory stick and after a few words with Aycana left for the briefing room. Admiral Stephen MacKay, Lt. Col. Perry and Gavin joined him. As they read their messages Admiral MacKay began to chuckle.

"I take it you have received similar instructions?" Stephen asked.

"I did, but I'm a little surprised we are doing this." John

stated. "I'm not keen of putting people through an inquiry when they have barely begun training. We're combat experienced by default not training. To say we are raw recruits is putting it mildly."

"I agree," Gavin acknowledged shaking his head. "Are they looking for someone to hang or something? As far as I can determine it was a miracle the ship was saved at all."

Admiral MacKay smiled. "That's it in a nutshell, gentlemen. It wasn't a miracle or an accident. Some people conducted themselves way above the call of duty, something beyond expectation for their skill and experience. We are ordered to determine the facts of the event and report them to General Turnbull."

"This is done when the White House asks questions. John, they are looking for someone to decorate not hang," Arlin exclaimed.

"I see! I guess we had better get it done then. I took the liberty of retrieving the ship's video log of the bridge crew during and shortly after the action in question. It is about ten minutes long. I need to visit sick bay on another matter. If you need anything at all just notify the bridge. They will take care of it."

"Thanks, John. I'll let you know of our findings before we submit our report," Stephen reassured him.

"I appreciate that," John smiled as he left the briefing room.

Victoria helped two of the rescued mothers and a little girl sort through some racks of donated clothing from several clothing stores in Santa Maria. Victoria spotted a couple pairs of pants and t-shirts for the little girl and handed them to her Katusian mother. "Tierra, I think these are about Geddy's size," Victoria said.

"Oh, they should fit nicely," Tierra said. Tierra's physical features were very human like with the exception of slightly bluish skin and snowwhite hair. Her slender six-and-a-half-foot frame, and naturally exaggerated graceful movements gave the appearance of a delicate ballerina carried about on a gentle breeze.

"Your husband is most kind to provide these clothes for us. His kindness is truly appreciated," the Katusian mother said.

"All of you have been through such a horrible ordeal. We're glad to help any way we can," Victoria replied.

"When we were in sick bay, General Braxton came by to visit and gave Geddy, a large box. Inside was the most beautiful doll she'd ever seen. She began crying for the first time since witnessing her father's execution. For the longest time Geddy cried while clutching the doll in one arm and hugging your husband's neck with the other arm. You can't imagine how much the doll means to her. She will never part with it. The bedtime story was the icing on the cake." Tierra explained, choking with emotion.

"Yes, all of us are grateful for your people's kindness. We are not accustomed to such open displays of kindness and generosity," the other mother added.

"All of this brings back memories of a very evil time in our planet's history. We have no tolerance for a repeat of such despicable acts. This is the least we can do for you," Victoria said. "Here, Tierra. Try this dress on Geddy. I think she'll love it.

'Have you found anything, Sandi?" Victoria asked the Cassarian mother.

"I've found a couple pairs of slacks and blouses that will fit and a soft sweater that is absolutely gorgeous. I found some clothes for Teena too. These clothes are much better designed and durable than what we are used too," Sandi said admiringly.

"Yes, and such a variety of fabrics and colors I might add. Earthlings seem to enjoy variety very much," Tierra said in a soothing voice as she stroked the different fabrics against her cheek.

"Yes, having choices is important to us. It is an expression of our freedom and individuality. We have several changes of clothing to fit our moods, the type of work we do, special occasions, even what we wear to bed or around the house. Don't you have a closet full of clothes at home?" Victoria asked.

"Oh no!" Tierra blushed. "By custom we are rather utilitarian. Even the rich rarely have more than five or six sets of clothes. They are based on our class and profession. Two formal changes and a few changes of work clothes is all we need. Oooh! I really like this dress. I think I'll take this one," Tierra declared holding up a long sheer white negligee with a very deep plunging neckline.

Victoria gasped as she saw Tierra holding it against her body. "Tierra, that's what you wear to bed with your mate. You wear that around the ship and every man aboard will go absolutely insane."

Victoria held up a beige silk blouse and tan slacks. Try this instead? It's comfortable and attractive yet keeps the crew's minds on their work."

"Oh! I get it," she giggled. "I really don't need that kind of problem in my life right now."

All the women laughed.

"Tell me, Tierra. How was your group captured? I was led to believe the Tigrans and Katusians were allied with the pirates," Victoria asked.

"It is a long story, but to sum it up, Katusium's trade routes were being raided on a regular basis. The Tigrans brought evidence to us that the Cassarians and Holcrons were the real culprits. They persuaded us to join their alliance so the Cassarians and Holcrons would agree to trade talks. They guaranteed this could avoid war. Everything the Tigrans told us appeared true so our leaders agreed. The attacks ceased and our economy began to prosper again.

'After a year and a half still no trade talks and attacks on our trade routes resumed. The Tigrans told us they were being attacked too. They proposed a war against the Cassarians and Holcrons as the only way to restore peace and prosperity. We decided against war. In turn, we were urged to launch a science and exploration mission in hopes of discovering inhabited planets to open new trade. It proved a trap to force us into a war we didn't want."

"I don't understand," Victoria said.

Tierra became noticeably upset. "My husband owned and commanded the *Wymeria*, a private research vessel on an expedition to the central space region. Five months ago, we discovered an uncharted but habitable planet. As we approached, we discovered a pirate base with a previously missing Katusium freighter docked beside a Tigran warship. Realizing we were betrayed, we tried to make a run for it but couldn't signal home.

'We didn't get very far before being captured. My husband, along with all the other officers, were put in separate cells. The rest of the crew and survivors were placed in the makeshift security rooms you found us in. I have no doubt when the prime minister finds out what we know, a war is certain but not what the Tigrans are expecting."

Victoria shook her head. "Are you sure of that?"

Tierra proudly lifted her head. "I'm the prime minister's daughter and Geddy, his only granddaughter. My husband was the oldest son of the most prominent clan leader on our world. Losing some cargo is one thing, but the wanton execution of innocent people on a peaceful unarmed research mission is unforgivable. The Tigrans and pirates will pay dearly now that we know where their base is located. I can assure you."

"Oh, how so?" Sandi asked.

"We are a proud people and our families are everything to us. My people are a very gracious people and quick to forgive minor offenses.

However, you harm their families, your life is in mortal danger. We will hunt them down no matter what the price. My people are that way."

"I see. I can't imagine how Geddy has endured all those horrors," Victoria sighed.

"They beat me and tortured my husband unmercifully before they hideously beheaded him. I begged them not to force Geddy to watch but they forced her to and took great joy in her screams. It's something no child should ever witness.

'General Braxton helped bring Geddy back from the darkness. I am eternally grateful. For the first time, she sleeps all night without waking up screaming. After General Braxton's story time, she asked to sleep in her own bed for the first time. Later when I checked in on her the doll was still clutched in her arms."

Victoria wiped the tears from her eyes and gave Tierra a hug. If we can do anything for you please don't be afraid to ask. I promise we'll do all we can. There was a moment of silence before Victoria spoke again.

"Sandi, how did you and Teena end up in the pirate's clutches?"

"Our ship was also on a science expedition a little over a year ago. The pirates somehow knew right where to ambush us. Except for the officers, most of us were taken prisoner and spent ten months in the zannite mines. We were abused, beaten and nearly starved to death. The pirates later captured more people to replace us so they told us we were being sold as slaves.

'When the pirate crew with Gavin's ship didn't signal, they were at the rendezvous point, Captain Gath went into a frightened panic. He was very anxious to find the freighter before the Tigrans. He feared the cargo the freighter carried must never reach Tigran hands or the whole plan was ruined."

"What planets deal in slavery?" Victoria asked.

"That's just it, none of the worlds we know permit slavery. It hasn't existed for centuries. As for the cargo, the pirates were double dealing with someone but we don't know who," Sandi said.

Victoria sighed grimly. "We thought the zannite crystals were for the Tigrans, but this takes treachery to a whole new level. We thought the Tigrans were double-dealing the Katusians, but it turns out the pirates were double dealing everyone.

'Whoever the pirate's real secret partner is, it does not bode well for us. Just when you think you know the game you're playing, some jerk throws a joker on the table."

John arrived in sick bay just as Susan finished examining one of the Cassarian patients. He sensed right away there was frostiness in the air and realized it was between Susan and her patient.

"Susan!"John inquired."You wanted to see me about something?"

"Dad, this is Dr. Khem Kremmel. He is requesting permission to join the crew. I just finished his physical. He is still a bit weak from his ordeal but otherwise fit for duty," Susan said stiffly.

Dr. Kremmel shook John's hand. "I am at your service, sir. I notice you are short-handed and your staff inexperienced. I thought I could be of some use to you. You obviously could use the help."

John tried not to laugh as Susan's face began turning red with anger from what she considered an insult.

"Well, what services do you propose to offer?" John inquired.

"I'm a medical doctor and have rather extensive research experience in chemistry and biology. I would like to train your medical staff and improve their skills," Khem replied.

"OK! Excuse us for a moment while I confer with Susan. We'll be back with your answer."

Khem nodded with a smile as Susan and John stepped out.

Before John could say a word, Susan unloaded, "Katrina and I are doing just fine without him and we still have the nurses from Vandenberg. Besides, he keeps giving me the eye everywhere I go. I feel very uncomfortable around him."

"I can see he's an obvious burr under your saddle. Are you sure your objections are for the right reasons?" John asked.

"What do you mean by that?" Susan snapped.

"I think your objectivity just crashed. Gavin recognized Dr. Khem Kremmel the day we captured the ship. The Kremmel and Toburg families are very close. Gavin and Khem practically grew up together. Dr. Kremmel is also one of Cassaria's most brilliant doctors and outstanding researcher. He designed the computerized medical diagnostic and Nano cell treatment equipment you've been using.

'He was part of an expedition sent a year ago to explore Terra and the unknown region around it when attacked by Gamoran pirates. He and the entire expedition were never heard from until now. Don't you think you could learn just a little bit from him?" John challenged.

Susan thought for a moment. "That explains why Gavin and his sisters visit him so frequently. Yes, I could learn a lot from him, but he really does make me feel uncomfortable. I don't know why but I guess I'll learn to deal with it. What do you propose doing with him?"

"Gavin suggested asking Dr. Kremmel to temporarily serve as our medical team leader and train the medical staff until he returns to Cassaria. You and Katrina have done a fantastic job under the circumstances but I think it's a brilliant suggestion, don't you?"

Susan paused to swallow her pride before nodding agreement. John squeezed her hands to reassure her as they rejoined Dr. Kremmel.

"Dr. Kremmel, thank you for your offer of assistance. If you are willing to head the medical team we could really use your expertise."

"I gladly accept as long as Susan agrees. I've been watching her work. She has performed remarkably well despite her inexperience. Susan and Katrina will become a great medical team."

"I look forward to working with you," Susan muttered unconvincingly.

John smiled. "Wonderful, I'll leave you both to your duties then. I must make a visit to Engineering before I get back to the bridge. If you need anything let me know, Dr. Kremmel."

When John entered Engineering he found Dexter and Deze talking to a staff sergeant about the zannite crystal installation. From the looks of things, the conversation was getting heated.

"What seems to be the problem?" John asked.

The NCO realized John's presence and snapped a salute. "Sir, welcome to Engineering. We were discussing how the pirates rigged the zannite crystals wrong."

"We found the crystals were incorrectly installed by the pirates. Dexter explained. "However, he wants two more crystals."

"Yes, TWO crystals," Deze echoed.

"Does the system work with two crystals, staff sergeant?" John asked.

"Sir, yes it does but rather poorly. Other ship designs are set up in such a way one crystal can be used for the engines, another for the shields and a third for weapons systems. However, the *Holcron Star* is a different design. It has much more redundancy. The primary consoles are on the bridge. They are routed through the maintenance consoles next to each reactor room. Each console system separately controls either the port or starboard engines and shields. The weapons system has a separate bridge console and on the secondary bridge. A seperate crystal should be installed directly to the weapons power conduit to the weapons reactor.

'For the two main reactors, if any system fails or needs maintenance, the remaining maintenance console can assume dual control of the other reactor and engines. The pirates did a patch job with two crystals that could over stress it in sustained combat. One crack in the crystal and it is useless. They didn't know better. There should be two crystals per main reactor. For each main reactor one crystal routs power to the engines the other routs power to the shields for optimum efficiency. We need the redundancy if you want this ship to fight its best," the staff sergeant explained.

John rubbed his chin. "I see. You make a lot of sense. What is your name and what rank did you hold in the Holcron Navy?"

My name is Staff Sergeant Kieran Tossa," he replied. "I was a Senior Engineering Specialist.

John smiled. "So, Staff Sergeant Tossa, how do you know all this?"

"I helped design and build the power systems when the ship was being built. I know it inside out," Staff Sergeant Tossa replied with some pride.

Dexter and Deze suddenly turned red faced.

John cleared his throat. "Well, Dexter and Deze, I suggest you do what he tells you. Chief master sergeant of Engineering, you are out of uniform. You are assigned to oversee their work and notify me when it is completed to your satisfaction. You may begin the work after we stand down from general quarters. How long will the change take?"

"Less than four days," Tossa replied.

"Very good. I want the system humming to perfection," John ordered.

John left for the bridge leaving the three men a bit confused.

Chief Master Sergeant Tossa asked, "Why does the General want the system humming?"

"I have no idea what humming is," Dexter declared a bit puzzled.

Deze smiled. "It is an Earthling expression. It means to make the system sing to perfection."

"Okay, Deze. I don't know which song it is supposed to sing but I do know what perfection is so let's get the conversion planned out," Tossa said beaming with joy.

Returning to the bridge, Molly started to announce John's presence. John quickly cut her off. "Carry on!"

Estron was conducting training on the communications and engineering consoles with several of the crew while David and Siyana were at the flight consoles with four other trainees.

Aycana gave up the command chair and moved over to the Intel/ Sensor Console.

"Aycana, has there been any more activity from the Chinese?" John asked.

"No missile activity since the Air Force took out the two missile bases and their tunnel networks. Several air bases are launching fighters and bombers against each other.

'Several cities are experiencing extensive street fighting and uncontrolled fires but we can't determine who is on which side. It appears that except for the Chinese navy, there is a standoff at present. One Chinese submarine surfaced to surrender and was quickly seized by Taiwan.

'The biggest threat detected so far is a Chinese nuclear sub stalking an American carrier group for the last half hour. We transmitted the information to the carrier and an American sub is on its stern. I would not want to be in that Chinese sub if they want to start a fight," Aycana said.

"Sir! We have an incoming FLASH message," Estron announced.

She decoded the message and forwarded it to John Braxton's data pad.

John read it, and then handed the data pad to Aycana. The message reported the Chinese Democratic forces have captured the remaining nuclear missile bases. However, Braxton was ordered to continue patrol and respond defensively as needed to protect Allied forces.

"Sound general quarters! Power up the starboard weapon systems and continue tracking the Chinese sub."

John picked up his data pad and began to review attack options and capabilities against the Chinese sub. Aycana answered his many questions and showed him different ways to use the magnum plasma cannons, the laser cannons and missiles against air, surface, below ground hardened targets. In the situation they were now in, it would be a turkey shoot since the Chinese lost the element of surprise and the *Holcron Star* was prepared to instantly respond to any attack.

"Captain, the Chinese sub is making an aggressive run on the American carrier group and the nearby American sub just maneuvered into attack position," Aycana announced.

"We will let the American attack sub handle the enemy sub," John said. "If they launch any missiles or torpedoes we will take them out. Helm, adjust course and speed to maintain stationary orbit over target area."

"Aye! Captain. Adjusting course and speed to maintain stationary position now," Siyana responded.

A moment later she announced, "Captain, we are in stationary position above target area."

"Captain, the Chinese sub just launched four missiles on the carrier. The American sub just launched two torpedoes at the Chinese sub. The American torpedoes have acquired and locked on target. The Chinese missiles are on track and will impact the carrier in twenty seconds."

"Lock laser cannon targeting onto their missiles and fire when ready," John ordered.

A few seconds later Aycana replied, "Targets locked on and firing." The bolts of lasers streaked through the atmosphere towards their targets. The captain of the American carrier, U.S.S. Ronald Reagan, tracked the missiles through his binoculars as they homed in on his ship. The laser fire struck the missiles at four thousand yards from the carrier with a spectacular shower of cascading debris and burning rocket fuel.

"All targets destroyed, sir! The Chinese sub is taking evasive action but can't shake the American torpedoes. Contact in ten seconds. Torpedoes have detonated on target. Enemy sub is breaking up," Aycana announced.

"May God rest their souls! They were sent on a fool's mission that never had a chance. Resume original orbital course and speed. Secure all weapons to standby mode. Continue search for enemy ships and report them as previously directed. All stations resume "standby alert" and thank you all for a job well done," John announced.

"Now I know where your son gets his command presence and instinct for action," Admiral MacKay said while standing behind the holo projector with Lt. Col. Perry.

"Stephen, I didn't notice your entrance on the bridge,"

John commented.

"You weren't supposed to notice us," Stephen replied with a smile. "You know Jonathan is just like you. When I asked him why he didn't make distance instead of turning into the missile attack, he replied, 'It was the safe thing to do but not the right thing to do.' I told him he risked his ship and crew who were totally inexperienced and untrained. He said, 'So what? Our first duty is to save our country. It's what needed to be done.' It's hard to argue the results."

"Sir! We have another message from Vandenberg," Molly reported as she sent the message to John's data pad.

John called up the message, read it, and announced, "We are to resume our training program immediately. Chinese Democratic leaders report all Chinese nuclear forces are now secured. As long as the PLA doesn't have any nukes squirreled away, the *Holcron Star* has other urgent business to attend."

"I suggest we start the course on command training and combat tactics this evening,"Stephen offered."Who do you want attending?"

"Jonathan shows much promise, John," Arlin suggested.

"Yes, I agree," Stephen nodded.

"All right, let's have Jonathan, Aycana, Shawn Miller, Gavin and myself attend. I'm planning to assign Jonathan and Aycana as First Officers to the *Holcron Star* and Gavin is taking Sean as his First Officer on on the the *Halfling*."

"Good choices. Jonathan notified us of an Intel Briefing at 1600 hrs. We'll leave you to your work and see you then," Stephen replied and left the bridge with Col. Perry.

"Aycana! Have all hands resume normal operations and training.

Continue passing threat information and tracking data to the U.S.S. Ronald Reagan Battle Group. If there is another attack, go to general quarters and take only defensive actions until further orders. You have the bridge."

In the briefing room John, Victoria, and Jonathan were studying the holo projection of the inhabited planets. Gavin was helping himself to some coffee at the refreshment cart when there was a knock on the open door.

John stood to welcome Admiral MacKay and Col. Perry. "Come in, take a seat. Slick and Traven should be along any second…"

"Knock, Knock!" Traven announced with Slick alongside. "What's up?"

"Ah, the gang's all here. Let's get started. Help yourself to the refreshment cart in the corner," John announced.

'When Gavin and I first discussed their capture, we found several questions unanswered. We hoped the capture of the *Holcron Star* would fill the gaps in our knowledge. The key question is why is Earth, suddenly the focus of pirate attention when it's so out of the way?

Gavin added, "We now know the pirates double-crossed the Tigrans on the zannite shipment, leaving the pirates as the only ones to have zannite powered ships.

"We also learned those we rescued were to be sold as slaves as well." Victoria interjected.

"Could it be the pirates didn't choose Earth as the rendezvous point? Pirates are opportunists. They seek to attack when the advantage is in their favor. They either try to avoid superior opponents or make deals to keep them at bay," Admiral McKay said. "Could it be Captain Gath was trying to keep the people he was meeting with from discovering the main source of zannite?"

"I think you are on to something, Stephen." John said. "Jonathan did more digging in the ship's archives. He uncovered some interesting information. Whenever Capt.

Gath rendezvoused with a ship, the ship's computer log always recorded the name of the ship, date, time and coordinates. However, on four occasions he rendezvoused with an unnamed ship at the same coordinates. Cat tried everything she could to pump Capt. Gath for more information. All he could tell us was that they were an unknown race. He referred to them as Outsiders. She couldn't get anything more out of him."

"You mean he wouldn't provide any more information?" Gavin corrected.

"Cat's not so sure that's the case. She tried every interrogation trick she knew but nothing worked. She thinks his memory is blocked or suppressed," John said.

"This is getting mind boggling," Slick grumbled as he massaged his forehead. "We have a conspiracy on top of another conspiracy and everyone seems clueless as to who is pulling everyone's strings. On top of that the question still remains, why is Earth involved? In all the vastness of space why come here?"

"That's an important question but we have to deal with Terra first!" John declared.

"How are we going to do that with one battle cruiser and a dinky freighter?" Jonathan asked sarcastically.

"Hey, watch what you call my ship," Gavin retorted.

"Sorry, no offense intended. It's just that whatever they have will definitely out number and out gun us or I doubt they'd bother coming." Jonathan reminded everyone. "We need to do something to change the odds and sooner the better."

"Glad you brought up that point," Admiral MacKay said. "John and I have been forming some preliminary plans to take the Central Space Region. To say it is going to be difficult is putting it mildly.

'From the ship's message traffic, we know Proto is lightly manned. They are expecting the *Holcron Star* to arrive and use their manpower to strengthen its crew. Since we are expected, surprise is on our side. We can capture Proto and the base on Terra at the same time. The moon base is not going to be that difficult as it is short-handed and poorly defended with maybe forty maintenance and ten security personnel.

'The ship's computer data reveals a hundred captives or more working the zannite refinery and mines. There are also about a hundred and fifty Tigran engineers and Gamoran scientists. There are supposed to be roughly fifty Tigran and Gamoran security guards."

Everyone squirmed in their seats and gasped at the proposal. "No big deal, if I had special ops troops to pull it off. This assault requires split second timing and no margin for error," Traven warned. "We need highly trained pros for this kind of a dog fight."

"Precisely! Besides, I need our boarding teams for another mission. About how many troops will you need?" John asked.

Traven thought for a moment. "To be on the safe side, I'll need about a hundred experienced troops to get the job done, but why do you need the boarding teams? You plan on capturing another ship?" Traven asked.

"Good thinking," Admiral Mackay smiled. "The pirate ships come there quite regularly. We need to assume one or two ships might be docked on Proto when we arrive. We need to secure Proto before they have a chance to sound the alarm. I think with the element of surprise on our side it can be done.

Gavin nodded. "Yes! Do we want to destroy a warehouse full of Zannite crystals? If not, do we want to risk using plasma cannons? We don't even know what will happen if a container of zannite crystals were struck by a laser cannon. For all we know it could blow the planet to bits."

Everyone looked at each other in dead silence.

"Better make that two hundred and fifty troops," Traven

winced.

"I agree," Admiral MacKay added.

John grimaced. "I have no idea where to find that many troops."

Col. Perry interrupted. "Leave that problem with me. I can get enough volunteers to get the job done and find facilities for training too."

Can I trust they won't take the ship?" John asked.

"That was discussed some time ago. General Turnbull and President Leatham agreed If you were recalled to active duty and you accepted the terms it wouldn't be necessary. You passed the test so there will be no stunts," Arlin promised.

"Thank you, Arlin. The ultimate problem is keeping the capture of the *Holcron Star* a secret long enough to capture the pirate bases and help the Cassarian forces fight off the impending invasion five and a half months from now. We need to come up with a way to warn King Toburg without giving ourselves away," John explained.

"Why don't we turn the tables on the pirates?" Slick suggested.

"What do you mean?" Gavin asked.

"Well, the pirates capture other ships and we just captured their flag ship. They don't know what's happened yet. Why not pretend to be pirates, dock with a pirate ship and do it again? The *Holcron Star* can jam any signals so no one is the wiser.

'They have three heavy cruisers, seven light cruisers and three corvettes left at their disposal. The more ships we capture, the easier it will be to capture the next one. The biggest problem we have is getting enough crew to man the ships after we capture them," Slick explained.

There was silence as everyone pondered the idea and alternatives.

"The Holcrons have trained crews without ships. Some

of the ships belonged to them. Suppose we are able to contact Uncle Usus? He can provide the crews without raising suspicion and be trusted to discretely warn my father of the plot," Gavin said.

"So, you just exchange brain waves through space or give him a call on the cell phone?" Jonathan asked sarcastically.

"I can arrange a discrete rendezvous and explain the situation. I will meet him and convince him to join us and contact my father. They are so close his visit wouldn't even raise an eyebrow."

"That's great but you can't do that until the zannite module is installed on the *Halfling*," John noted. "Dexter and Deze are working on it as we speak. It should be completed within four days. There are plenty of highly experienced Holcrons and Cassarians ready to take over the engineering and reactor training."

Stephen gave a nod to John. "We will have to modify our plans as we go but this is a good start."

"Good enough then. How much time will it take to go to the rendezvous location, make contact and return?" John asked Gavin.

"With the engine modification, I estimate fifteen days or so to reach the rendezvous point and make contact."

"How long would it take the admiral to communicate with your father?" John followed.

"He should meet with my father within another fifteen days after the rendezvous, I would guess," Gavin replied.

John nodded. "That gives your father roughly three and a half months to counter the plot against Cassaria. That should do. Have your mission plan ready in two days. You leave in five days. Pick your crew and take Deze with you. He might come in handy if you run into pirates."

"Thank you, John. I'll complete the mission and return as fast as possible," Gavin pledged.

"Traven, while Arlin rustles up your army, begin working on detailed plans for capturing the two target bases. Jonathan will work with you and lead the boarding teams. Slick, I need you to remain for a few minutes. Are there any other issues to address?" John asked.

"Yes, now that we are done interrogating Togg Gath, what do you plan to do with him?" Gavin asked.

"He still might yet prove useful so we will hold on to him for a while longer. When this is over I thought, we would turn him over to the Holcrons. They seem to have suffered the most and I understand they are not shy about punishment," John replied.

"No, they are not. I have no doubt he would receive a very fair trial before being very fairly executed," Gavin grimly agreed.

John stood up. "That wraps up the meeting. You have your assignments and thanks for your time, folks."

John waited for everyone to clear the room before addressing Slick. "Slick, good intelligence is vital to any military operation. Sometimes, however, protecting an asset is even more important. I have a deep covert mission that needs a very experienced person. Are you willing?"

Slick cleared his throat. "Can you trust me to do that? In the world of spies, trust is an awfully fragile word you know."

"You are absolutely right, but without trusting someone we won't survive. This mission is of the utmost importance and there is no one I trust more than you to do it. As I said before, I trust you and Cat will honor our agreement."

"We made a deal and we'll keep it. What do you want done?" Slick agreed.

The secretary hung up her phone and looked over at Dr. Loretta Sanchez seated in the waiting area. "Secretary Smith is ready to see you!"

Loretta walked into the office. Secretary of State Noel

Smith greeted her from his desk and motioned her to have a seat. He maneuvered his wheelchair across the room to where Loretta sat and opened a folder.

"Loretta, I've looked over your proposal and agree with your concerns. It is entirely new ground in diplomacy and must be approached with caution."

"Dr. Smith, the small concessions and agreements made on the fly with the Cassarians or any other group of aliens could entangle us in an alliance we might regret later. The president may unknowingly be making deals with the Devil and no one the wiser until it's too late."

Dr. Smith squirmed in his chair, "I see your point, but we haven't signed any agreements with the Cassarian government. Wouldn't we be jumping the gun to send an ambassador before formal relations are established?"

"A valid point, but by sending an ambassador at large, we would be able to setup the necessary ground work while avoiding any unnecessary entanglements," Loretta argued.

"OK! I'll take it up with President Leatham and see what he thinks. There is merit in what you propose. Great work, I appreciate your thinking ahead."

Loretta smiled as she left the office. *John Braxton, you may have forced us to change our plans but your continued interference won't stop the coming revolution. You can't stop us even with the Holcron Star. You have no idea what's coming.*

CHAPTER 13

The *Halfling* arrived at the rendezvous point in the Tratana System in good time. Gavin expected the Holcron ship to arrive a day later. Gavin stared at the small lifeless planet before him. "OK, Mr. Miller. Let's see if you can put us in low orbit around this planet."

"Yes, sir. What altitude do you want?" Shawn Miller asked.

"High enough we don't burn up and low enough we are not easily detected will do just fine," Gavin grinned.

"But sir, is there a specific altitude you want?"

Gavin tried to keep a straight face. "Mr. Miller, if I had a specific altitude in mind I would have said so. I'm testing your judgment. Now impress me."

"Oh! I get it," Shawn replied.

Shawn went over to the navigation display and called up information on the gravity structure of the planet and of any orbital objects. With beads of sweat rolling off his forehead, he chose an altitude and issued the appropriate orders. A minute later the *Halfling* was in an established orbit.

"Very good, Shawn. You did your homework. Most students fail their first try. An orbit too high allows approaching ships to detect us first and an orbit too low could blind or limit our sensors. With experience, you will become more bold and comfortable taking an even lower orbit but this will do for our purposes," Gavin said.

After two days of silent drifting in orbit, the inexperienced crew was getting edgy. Everyone knew being discovered by the wrong ship could endanger the whole mission. Gavin was sure Admiral Dever received his carefully worded message and would make the rendezvous.

The crew continued training and running drills to take advantage of the time. Even though his sisters were needed on the *Holcron Star*, Gavin believed in time his new crew would work well together. Deze showed an energetic proficiency at training and the crew responded well.

Another thirty-six hours passed and still no ship arrived. Gavin was in his quarters attempting to rest when Shawn Miller's voice broke over the intercom.

"Captain to the bridge! We have an unidentified cruiser on long range sensors."

Gavin replied, "I'll be right there!"

After racing to the bridge Gavin studied the sensor display and decided to risk transmitting a voice message in the clear.

"This is Cassarian freighter, *Halfling*. Approaching ship, please identify yourself?

"*HSS Torrent* here. How are you, my Halfling?" the boisterous voice crowed.

Gavin sighed in relief. "Uncle Dever, so nice to hear your voice again."

"Halfling, everyone in the universe thinks you are dead."

"Thanks to some new friends that is miraculously not the case. Prepare for docking, I have much to urgently report."

"Agreed. See you shortly," Admiral Usus said signing off.

"Now I see what you were talking about docking," Shawn said.

"The ship's landing bay is way too small for a freighter our size." Gavin nodded. "The *HSS Torrent* is an older and smaller design compared to the *Holcron Star.* It can handle large shuttles but everything else has to use the docking port. It's what happens when a ship ages slower than the newest technology can be applied. This ship is over fifty years old. Its engines, weapons and sensor systems have been upgraded three times.

I knew Holcron was preparing to extend the length of the ship for deeper space missions but it obviously hasn't happened yet."

Once the small freighter was alongside the flagship a large docking tube extended out about ten feet and attached itself over the *Halfling*'s cargo ramp door. As the airlock doors opened, the dim ambient light revealed a tall, portly figure standing at attention. When the lights were brought to full brightness everyone saw before them an elderly gray-haired man with a well-trimmed full beard, and wearing a burgundy tunic, black pants with a gold stripe down the sides and a well-worn but highly polished pair of black, knee-high calvary boots. Tucked in the black sash around his waist was a curved, ivory handled dagger with a jewel-encrusted sheath symbolic of his station as Holcron Fleet Admiral.

"Permission to come aboard?" Admiral Usus Dever bellowed in a confident baritone voice.

At first sight, Shawn Miller thought he was standing before Santa Claus, the space warrior. That first impression evaporated quickly once Admiral Dever requested permission to come aboard. Just the manner, strength, and confidence he exuded told Shawn he was undeniably in the presence of a great charismatic leader. *Who in their right mind would deny the man's request?*

"Permission granted!" Gavin replied as everyone present came to attention with a salute.

When the Holcron admiral returned the salute, Gavin raced over to embrace his uncle.

Dever's uniform reflected a man humbly secure in himself and his position. His simple burgundy tunic was trimmed with a single gold braid on each sleeve. The four-star rank on his shoulders and his nametag above the right breast pocket were the only items displayed. The scar across his face spoke far more of his courage than the rows of medals and ribbons he refused wearing.

Although Admiral Dever possessed an infectious warrior spirit, it could not hide his jovial demeanor. He had an innate ability to equally awe, charm or threaten those around him. Usus, by his very presence, inspired people to trust him even with their lives. Once Usus Dever took the measure of a man's spirit and found him true, his loyalty was unshakeable. It was no surprise Gavin's father and he were such great friends. Officers fortunate enough to serve under him claimed his heart could just as easily win men over as utterly crush fools.

Gavin beamed with surprise, "Uncle, you look as fit as ever. It's good we meet again."

Usus roared a jolly laugh as the two men embraced in friendship. "We haven't met in three years and the first thing you say to me is a lie?"

"Would you rather I told the truth?" Gavin asked with a sly grin.

"No!" Admiral Dever quickly parried.

'I'm forced to look at myself in a mirror every day so the truth does not escape me. A little flattery is good for the soul, just not too much mind you," Admiral Dever teased shaking his finger.

"Getting on in years does have its challenges, doesn't it?" Gavin agreed as he patted his uncle's belly.

Usus smiled. "And some challenges we could do without. Now tell me everything that has happened. It's rumored you and your sisters were murdered. Obviously, all is not true. Are your sisters well too?"

"Yes, my sisters are alive and well. They are also, for the moment, very safe. It is a long story and why I am here. Both our worlds are in grave danger, more so than you can imagine. Let's make ourselves comfortable in the passenger lounge. I will explain everything."

Once they settled around a table in the lounge, the customary drinks and pastry were served, Gavin started explaining their harrowing adventures. He told of their capture, failed escape, planet Earth, their rescue, the Braxton family, zannite crystals, the planned sneak attack, the betrayals and the capture of the *Holcron Star*. Gavin also presented the evidence they collected and a zannite crystal as proof.

There was a long silence as the admiral examined the messages and evidence a second time. He kept glancing back at the large, violet glowing crystal. The implications of such enormous zannite crystals existing did not escape him. When he finally looked up his demeanor changed to utmost seriousness. For the longest moment, he starred into Gavin's eyes as if he could measure the truth of everything discussed.

Speaking in a very low, firm voice, "Gavin, I've known you all your life. You are as honest as your father with a bit of that special diplomatic tact your mother possessed. Your story and this evidence is overwhelming. How many of those zannite crystals are there?"

"There are six hundred I know for sure and no doubt there are more being made as we speak. These were promised to the Tigrans but the pirates double crossed them. Before we seized them, we suspect they were on the way to an invasion fleet from a people we only know as the Outsiders. It takes three to properly equip a space cruiser. Imagine the *Holcron Star* on steroids. Then multiply that by two hundred-fold. From the *Holcron Star*, we learned they figured out how to rig them for the engines.

The design was flawed but Dexter and a couple others figured out how to improve the system and install them for the cannons and shields. The accuracy of the cannons was marginally reduced but we're working on that. Can you imagine the power of over a hundred ships with these?" Gavin asked.

Admiral Dever fell back in his chair. "All I can see are billions of innocent people being destroyed, cities laid waste and a dark cloud descend upon civilization. The depth of evil is beyond my wildest imagination.

'These evildoers are from the burning Lake of Gadash itself and must be stopped, whatever the cost. This Braxton fellow must be a good man for you to trust your sisters to his care. What are the Earthlings like?"

Gavin smiled. "I found these particular Earthlings have a love for freedom that makes them greater in battle than any people I have ever met, yet they desire to live only in peace. Their generosity and kindness are even greater than their fierceness. However, I would be the last person in the galaxy to pick a fight with them. In John Braxton, you will find your equal in cunning. He sees events and plans so far ahead I can't keep up. I'm ashamed to admit I underestimated him too many times yet found him unshakably loyal, honest and, thankfully, forgiving."

"It sounds like we have found good allies just in the nick of time. Tell me, how big is their fleet? They must have hundreds of ships to have forced the *Holcron Star* to surrender without a fight."

"You want to know how many ships as of right now?"

"Yes, Halfling, of course now!"

Gavin took a deep breath and paused as he feigned counting on his fingers. "Let's see. If I count the *Holcron Star*, that brings the grand Earth armada to a total of…one," Gavin sighed with a disheartened face.

There was a moment of silence as Gavin tried to measure his uncle's disappointment.

"What?" Admiral Dever roared as he slapped Gavin on the back. "That's just great! Indeed marvelous!"

"I don't understand!" Gavin replied in shock.

"Oh, Halfling!" Usus bellowed. "You have much to learn. Do you not understand this is the stuff of great victories and legends that tens of generations from now will still sing and tell the tallest of tales about?

The greatest of evil conspiracies, planets of people unaware of the catastrophe about to destroy them, and a small ragtag band of warriors join forces to defeat the evil empire. Oh, I wouldn't miss this battle for all the gold in the universe. This is destiny in the making my Halfling."

The admiral took a swig of hot drink. His large frame suddenly shivered as he raised his eyebrows. "My stars!" Usus declared. "What is this you're serving? It's a heavenly brew like none other."

"On Earth, it's called a Chocolate Mocha Latte. I'm going to put beverage shops on every planet, and sell that stuff. I'll die a very rich man," Gavin proudly declared thumping his chest.

Admiral Dever's eyes widened. "I should say so! I've never encountered such a delicious brew in all my life. I just discovered some taste buds I never knew I had."

Gavin's eyes gleamed. "They have more wondrous things too. They are most anxious to open trade routes with anyone who will swear themselves a friend."

"Then we have much to do, Halfling. I assume you and this Braxton fellow have a plan. What do you wish of me?"

Over the next hour, Gavin explained the need for the admiral to secretly warn his father of the plot and of those who seek to betray Cassaria.

"You also need to contact the Katusians and warn them of the Tigran lies and betrayal," Gavin added.

The admiral burst out laughing. "Are you mad? They have shut off all diplomatic relations. My ship will be blown into scrap metal before they ever let me near their planet."

"Not with the Katusian prime minister's daughter and

granddaughter on board."

The admiral's eyes widened again. "What?"

"Yes, we rescued them from the pirates when we captured the *Holcron Star*. They will return with you to support all our claims. If everyone comes together to defend Cassaria, the Tigrans can be defeated.Then it will be a race to Earth to foil the Outsider invasion."

"Yes, I see. I will do all I can to warn Adrian and the Katusians," Admiral Dever pledged.

"One last thing. General Braxton has a business proposal. The details are contained on this data pad. If it is agreeable to the Holcron government, work must begin right away. I think you will find the offer much to your liking," Gavin smiled handing over his data pad.

The admiral read over the request and supporting documents. As he did so he drank two more lattes. When finished there were several more minutes of discussion before Admiral Dever rose to depart.

"Assure General Braxton I will accomplish all he asks of me as swiftly as possible. Based on his generous terms, I have no doubt his proposal will be swiftly approved.

"This is Aycana's gold necklace. Give it to Father. He will then know all you say is true and we are safe," Gavin stated handing the necklace to him.

Usus tucked the necklace in his pocket. "Gavin, do not worry about these Outsiders. They are seeking to divide us and let us whittle each other down before attacking in strength. We will isolate and defeat the Tigrans and remain strong enough to meet the Outsider's attack. I have no doubt we will be victorious and survive to enjoy our new friendships.

'You needn't worry about your parents, they refuse to believe all of you are dead though the people around them have long given you up. Adrian told me destiny would not permit such a thing."

Gavin smiled. "Tell Father we will be united soon. God has heard his prayers and his faith has been rewarded."

"Ah! That's the spirit, Halfling. Keep your wits about you and keep your sisters alive. There is much to accomplish," Admiral Dever cautioned.

"One last thing," Gavin said. "I have a team I need you to smuggle onto Cassaria."

Gavin called in two of the team. "Usus, I want you to meet Agent Jeff Prewitt of Earth and his second in command, Sandi Portello of Cassaria. I need you to smuggle the team to Cassaria. No one must know who they are or what they are doing."

Admiral Dever shook their hands. "It will be an honor to deliver you to Cassaria. If you need anything before we arrive let me know and you shall have it. Once on Cassaria we must never meet again. I have no doubt our Embassy staff and I will be under continuous surveillance. The rest of your mission I do not want to know. I wouldn't want you to have to kill me," Admiral Dever roared with laughter.

Slick didn't even smile.

Minutes later five passengers, their luggage, a container with 3 zannite crystals, a coffee maker and a supply of coffee beans were transferred to the Holcron flagship before the ships departed.

The first wedding in space was a grand event held on the observation deck of the *Holcron Star*. The family and close friends were transported to the *Holcron Star* along with many VIPs, a camera crew and three reporters for the event. Jonathan and Katrina were warry of such publicity but the White House Public Affairs people suggested it would be a great way for the public to be introduced to a new era in space and receive a tour of the *Holcron Star*. The whole world was starving for information about the people from different worlds making up the crew. After much discussion, Jonathan and Katrina consented to the public event.

The excitement and preparation also proved a great pressure release for the crew. The last few weeks of sixteen-hour workdays were wearing thin on everyone. The enormity of learning many new technologies, mastering the variety of duties on a starship, and the discipline of coming together as a functioning team were monumental. Realizing the dangers, they were facing, everyone pushed themselves to their limits.

The Observation Deck was decorated with silk orchids, artificial palm trees along the edge of the observation window. It gave the appearance of a tropical night under the picturesque backdrop of the glittering Milky Way. The seating area was in two sections towards the back of the deck.

Katrina's full-length white silk and lace gown accented her figure and made her appear to float as she walked down the aisle. Beautiful, white fragrant orchids adorned her luscious blond hair, which was pulled up to frame her lovely face with natural softly curled tresses. White satin slippers and gloves completed the picture of an angel who just stepped out of a dream.

Jonathan reluctantly looked debonair in his white mess dress uniform. Normally he chaffed at wearing such a getup but for the love of his life he'd wear anything. The most notable thing he wore was a broad, beaming smile. It broadcast to the whole galaxy he was the happiest of all men.

Chaplain Boyle performed the grand ceremony and proudly proclaimed Jonathan and Katrina husband and wife. The resounding cheers resonated throughout the ship. Minutes later the reception line formed and everyone got to meet and greet the newlyweds and families of the bride and groom. Afterwards, the guests began mixing about the observation deck as people from different worlds began learning about each other.

It was a colorful picture with men in their fine suits, ladies dressed in stylish outfits of every color and those of the military in their dress uniforms. David could not help notice how strikingly beautiful the three Cassarian sisters were. Aycana glowed in a long sparkly silver gown that accentuated her curves, her white hair glistening, contrasted by her eyes dark as night. Estron was a vision of femininity in a long lacy emerald green gown that complimented her flame red hair and matched her lovely eyes. However, it was Siyana who took his breath away in her floor length periwinkle satin gown that shimmered in the light, her long golden hair and those deep azure sky blue eyes, so captivating they invited him to swim inside. The hypnotic vision of Siyana caused the world around David to quickly fade.

Vice President Koppel shook hands with John. "Congratulations! The wedding was splendid. They are a most handsome couple."

"Thank you, Mister Vice President. They are a fine couple indeed. I'm so glad you could come."

"Nonsense, I wouldn't miss this event for anything. This is the third time I've met your family and I must say there is something about them that intrigues me. They have a presence about them that is especially uncommon. Where did they go to school?"

"Well, they actually didn't go to school in the usual sense. They were homeschooled all the way through high school. Jonathan is almost done with graduate studies in engineering. Susan is in her final year of medical school. David was just starting college until this detour appeared."

"They've done well!" the vice president said.

Victoria joined them with a worried look on her face. "John, would you go distract Henry? He's studying the beverage fountain with that look of mischief in his eyes.

In your absence, I'll bend Vice President Koppel's ear for a few minutes and introduce him to many of our new friends."

"Oh great! Please excuse me, Mr. Vice President?" John asked as he rushed off to find Henry.

"Who is Henry?" the vice president asked.

"Henry is John's father and the sourdough version of the mad inventor. He was the inventor of the machines we used to knock out the pirate crew and capture the *Holcron Star*."

"I see!" the vice president said raising his eyebrows. "Would you like a couple of my security team to watch him for you?"

"I doubt they could keep up with him," Victoria laughed.

As John looked around for Henry, a guest approached him. "General Braxton! Allow me to introduce myself. I'm Dr. Loretta Sanchez from the State Department."

"How do you do!" John replied as he shook her hand. "Welcome aboard. I'm sorry Dr. Smith couldn't attend."

"Thank you. It is an honor to be here," Loretta ingratiatingly replied. "I have proposed a diplomatic mission to travel with you to establish diplomatic contact with our newfound friends. I could use your support in getting this plan implemented."

"I am not a politician but I do see your point. However, we need to concentrate on winning this war first. The last thing I need is anyone creating political distractions that might divide us," John said.

"I understand. Military issues are important," Loretta agreed. "But it's important to make diplomatic contact as soon as possible don't you agree?"

"The Cassarian Ambassador is away on a diplomatic mission doing just that. When he returns I'll have him contact you and you can discuss it with him? I'm sure something can be worked out that is agreeable to all parties. The other worlds are as anxious to make friends with us as we are with them,"

John said politely.

"Yes, I see your point. The Leatham administration envisions a galactic United Nations based on Earth's model to instill a greater sense of peace and unity for all worlds," Loretta said with an air of superiority.

"Dr. Sanchez, I hope we have loftier definitions of peace and unity than what the United Nations has produced so far on Earth. Grand but empty speeches, useless symbolism, and double speak never secures peace.

'Talk by hollow-chested politicians never won a single war but have certainly started and lost quite a few. Please excuse me but I've been sent on a mission to rescue my father," John said as he smiled and moved on through the crowd.

Well, I know where he stands, Loretta thought. The Senator is right, I will definitely be on guard around that man. He can ruin everything.

"Hello! My name is Dr. Khem Kremmel and your name?" Khem asked.

"Dr. Sanchez, Dr. Loretta Sanchez. Where are you from?"

"I'm from Cassaria. What area of medicine do you practice?" Khem asked.

"Oh no! I'm from the State Department. I am planning a diplomatic mission to establish relations with Cassaria and other worlds. What do you do?"

"At the moment, I'm the ship's chief medical officer. I was taken prisoner by the pirates and freed when the Braxtons captured the *Holcron Star*. Before that I was a medical research doctor and microbiologist with the Skiven Medical Research Institute at the Imperial University on Cassaria."

"Impressive, if I ever need first aid for an amoeboid I'll be sure to look you up," Loretta remarked coldly while surveying the room.

Khem paused for a second not sure if he'd just been

insulted or missed a bit of Earthling humor.

Susan, standing next to him realized the awkwardness of the remark, whispered in Khem's ear that it was a joke.

Khem burst out laughing. "Dr. Sanchez, I would like you to meet Susan Braxton. Susan, this is Dr. Loretta Sanchez from your State Department."

"Nice to meet you Dr. Sanchez. I hope your plan works out for the best," Susan replied. "Please excuse us but I've been asked to introduce Khem to Vice President Koppel. We'll see you again later."

Thomas Kasill's editor pulled more than a few strings for Thomas to join the pool of reporters permitted aboard the *Holcron Star* to cover the wedding. In addition to the wedding coverage, the reporters were given a tour of the ship. It was the assignment of a lifetime by itself even though he had other motives.

In all his research of possible female suspects connected to Dr. Long, Dr. Sanchez was the stand out. He even found an old newspaper article reporting her father claimed aliens abducted the family when she was a teenager.

Granted, he was grasping at straws, but it was all he had to go on. Recalling an interview with her about three years ago, he pulled up all the video and audio recordings of his interviews. Thomas found a long, forgotten question left out of the published interview. During the interview, he slipped a question in drawing a response he hadn't expected.

"Dr. Sanchez, have you ever had contact with aliens?"

Her demeanor changed. She bristled like a cat cornered by its mortal enemy. "No!" she answered very curtly.

"You mean you dispute you father's published claim from years ago that the whole family was abducted?"

She appeared to choke on her drink. She patted her chest

and cleared her throat to restore her self-control then continued, "I'm sorry, I misunderstood your question. My father was a habitual drug user. Our family suffered mentally as well as physically from his abuse. We all made statements at the time to avoid his wrath. Now that he is dead, we are free to tell the truth. Thank you for allowing me the opportunity to set the record straight."

For the rest of the interview Thomas asked questions but got only stock answers. At the reception, he again encountered Dr. Sanchez. She clearly did not recognize him and didn't pay much attention to the conversation either as she continuously scanned the crowd of guests. During their casual conversation, Thomas again caught her off guard. After a couple of minutes of idle chitchat Thomas suddenly asked, "It seems so disconcerting to be among aliens, again doesn't it?"

"Yes, it is," Dr. Sanchez, muttered as she waved to a familiar face across the room. Suddenly she choked on her drink. "Pardon me, I miss understood the question. It does seem strange to be standing on a spaceship that not too long ago we denied could even exist. Excuse me, I see a friend from the White House I must visit." Dr. Sanchez deftly handed Thomas her finished glass as if he was a mere waiter and casually walked off.

Thomas smiled and muttered, "I'm not likely to get her off guard again." Then he recognized the person she started talking to wasn't from the White House. It was Senator Pickering's aide. He wasn't sure what her answer meant but the fact she covered it up proved again he was on the right track. Thomas smiled as he realized she had proven his instincts correct. All her phony coverups and evasive actions would not shake him off the trail now. Thomas smiled. *This hound has the scent. Let the hunt begin in earnest.*

After the reception was over the cleanup on the

observation deck began. Susan, still in her bride's maid gown, was on a stepladder attempting to remove decorations when Khem came up behind her to give a hand.

"Here, Susan, allow me to help you before you fall off the…" Khem's offer of assistance was too late. As Susan toppled from the ladder, Khem reached out in time to catch her in his arms.

"Thanks! I should know better than being on a stepladder in this gown," Susan said as Khem set her on her feet.

"I'll gladly give you a hand. Just tell me what you need and I'll do it for you."

"Why thank you, Doctor," Susan replied politely.

"Please, Susan, call me Khem. We work too closely together to play the doctor, doctor game.

"OK! Khem," Susan coldly agreed.

Khem stepped in front of Susan as she tried to turn away and held up his hands in a sign of surrender. "Susan, whatever I did to offend you so deeply, I sincerely apologize. I would never want to do something to hurt or offend you. Please, please accept my deepest apology?" Khem pleaded.

"OK!" Susan demurred. "Tell me then, why did you stare at me so much when you were in sick bay? I felt like some lecher was undressing me with his eyes. It felt humiliating."

Khem squirmed uneasily. "You will not slap me for answering this question truthfully will you?"

"No! I promise," Susan said.

"I was unconscious for two days before being rescued. When I first opened my eyes in sick bay, I was delirious with fever. You were the first person I saw and the perfect vision of an angel, standing over me. I could not take my eyes off you because the sight of you was like a healing spirit. I was so sick I had no idea I was being rude. All I could think of was you were my lifeline, an angel of mercy. I have not been able to get my mind off of you since. If you hate me for my behavior I am deeply sorry. I'll do my best to avoid your presence in the future, if you wish," Khem pleaded, his head hung low.

Susan reached out with her hand and tenderly lifted up his chin.

Gazing into his eyes she saw the pain and sincerity. "I do appreciate your honesty and I understand now. You didn't do anything wrong. If you are serious, you can make it up to me though?"

"Sure! Anything! How?" Khem begged.

"Meet me here at 2200 hours for some ice cream."

"You got it," Khem smiled.

"Great! Let's hurry getting the decorations down. I'm dying to get out of this itchy gown," Susan said as she scratched her side.

"What's wrong with the gown? You look great in it."

"Listen, you just got to first base, don't push it," Susan teased.

"A…h! Right, sorry. Very sorry! My lips are sealed," Khem replied in a feigned panic. He quickly scampered up the stepladder to remove the decorations.

At Vandenberg AFB, a hangar echoed with chatter of NCOs organizing three hundred and twenty soldiers in black fatigues into four platoons.

The soldiers were very carefully hand-picked from Australia, Canada, Great Britain, Russia, but mostly the United States. A few were from Japan and South Korea along with a dozen more Cassarians and Holcrons rescued from the *Holcron Star*. Everyone was a volunteer for the assignment. Those from Earth were almost all combat experienced in special operations. Their nametag above the right breast pocket was the only item found on their uniforms.

When everyone was formed up, a hangar side door opened and a tall, grizzled sergeant major entered. He looked like the tough drill sergeant who ate boxes of nails for breakfast and bricks with mustard for lunch. The gaunt face, the demeanor of a coiled spring ready to pounce, and fierceness in his eyes signaled every soldier's attention.

"Tench-Hut!" Sergeant Major Randall Stone bellowed. The whole hangar shuddered and boots clicked.

General Braxton briskly entered wearing his Black Watch fatigues. Major Rivers followed behind him. As General Braxton stepped up to the platform podium and clipped on the microphone, he paused to look at the soldiers standing at attention.

"At ease! My name is General John Braxton. Welcome. Some of you may have heard of me in obscure parts of the news."

The hangar echoed with laughter.

John pressed a button on a small control stick he pulled from his pocket. A twenty-foot holographic-projection appeared behind him showing the locations of their region of space with the various inhabited planets, major systems and the Jarro Nebula.

"All of you have been told of a vague mission of great danger and importance. I'm here to tell you what that mission is and why we must prevail. I want no one going on this mission without knowing the truth. Our mission is simple; save Earth and other worlds from conquest by pirates and an invasion armada from a people only known as the Outsiders. I expect the odds to be greatly against us in every battle.

'There is only one promise I can make. I promise as long as I am alive, I will do everything in my power to achieve victory. I will not waste a single life for the machinations of personal grandeur. We are on a mission like none other in history. I intend to take this fight to the enemy.

'We will be fighting on planets we never knew existed, fighting enemies we have never met. We will be fighting for our freedom, for our loved ones, for the soldier on your left and the soldier on your right, for the very survival of our worlds. We will do the seemingly impossible and be victorious. We have no choice. Whatever prejudices you have must be put aside. There can be no place for them here. Far too much is at stake. If you believe you can't do this mission or put your prejudices aside, please leave this hangar now. I won't blame you if you do."

John paused and looked around the hangar. Not a soldier moved.

"Thank you for staying. I'm honored and most grateful to serve with you. If you complete the training, you will be among the first to claim brotherhood in the Blue Watch."

There was a loud cheer as the name of the unit was announced and the Blue Watch flag unfurled. It consisted of a dark blue tartan shield with a gold lightning bolt in the center imposed on a skyblue flag. Just below the shield was a banner with the words, *First Guardians of Freedom.*

"We are from many nations and worlds. It doesn't matter where you came from or what rank you held. What does matter is that you unite and share your expertise and knowledge with everyone else in this unit.

Every moment must be spent learning something new, something useful, becoming a better warrior. Thinking outside the box is not good enough; you must perform outside the box. You must become as ferocious as a lion and wise as a serpent.

'Sergeant Major Randall Stone is the man to go to with any problems. If you can't resolve it yourself, see him before it's too late.

'On the first page of the Blue Watch Field Manual is our Code of Conduct. It will be strictly followed. It is simple. Memorize it, breath it, dream of it if you have too, but for all you hold dear don't test it. Simply put, we are family here. We do not lie, cheat, steal or bring dishonor to the family in any manner. I am not a tyrant; there is simply not enough time to waste on pettiness and foolishness. Billions of people on several planets are relying on you for their very survival. The clock is ticking, folks. We must save our part of the galaxy. I turn you over to your Blue Watch commander, Major Rivers."

Sergeant Major Stone again called everyone to attention as John handed the microphone over to Traven and left the hanger. As John stepped outside he motioned for the sergeant major to follow.

Once outside the hangar John paused, "Sergeant Major Stone, I allowed Traven to pick the people for this outfit and the first name on his list was you. He told me underneath all the grit and gristle is one of the most skilled, experienced and intelligent warriors he's ever known. That's what I'm looking for too.

'These people are already tough and know how to kill but I need smart, problem solving warriors too. Short of killing them, do whatever it takes to get them ready. I will make sure you get everything you need."

Sergeant Major Stone was expressionless with his gravelly voice, "Sir, I've worked with Major Rivers in the past and you couldn't have a better leader for the kind of troops you want. I promise you the smartest, best trained, combat unit ever in uniform as long as nobody gets in my way."

"Then we are of the same mind," John nodded. As he slid into his staff car next to Admiral MacKay. Sergeant Major Stone saluted and returned to the hangar.

"Where to, sir?" the driver asked.

"To the wing commander's residence, please," John replied.

"That was a good speech but can you deliver?" Admiral MacKay asked.

"You heard it?" John asked a bit uneasy.

"I snuck in just as you started. Wish I was that eloquent," the admiral said.

John chuckled. "I don't know about eloquent. If I was in their place I'd be very nervous about going to war against aliens I never heard about."

Steve looked at John. "Well, just for the record, I am very nervous."

John shook his head. "Get in line behind me. We've been absolutely lucky to have come as far as we have. Every step we take is a step into the unknown."

"That's the good part," Steve grinned. "So far the enemy has no clue what's coming either."

John gave a nervous chuckle. "Let's do our best to keep it that way. Col. Perry is at the wing commander's quarters for the meeting. I hope he has good news from the White House."

In sick bay, Khem was just finishing up a report on his data pad when Susan returned from making her patient round for the evening.

"What's up? You seem very deep in thought," Susan asked.

"I think we were visited by a spy. Well actually more than one," Khem remarked.

Susan looked puzzled. "What do you mean?"

Khem, sighed. "I discovered an unknown program in the medical system that was never accessed by the pirates. It seems they had no idea it existed in our medical data base. It can be cross shared with the security network too. That feature was not turned on either.

'One of the things this program does very well is medically screen everyone who comes aboard the ship and continues to monitor their vital signs wherever they go.”

“That sounds really invasive if you ask me,” Susan grumbled.

“You bet if on your home world. In space, one of the greatest worries is bringing unknown pathogens aboard that could incapacitate or wipe out a whole crew or taking it back to your home world without ever knowing it. This program can tell who is carrying harmful pathogens or who’s had recent surgery or even a transplant. It’s not perfect but on a ship this size and capable of deep space travel it is better than nothing. We know the security system can track the location of people but with this program tied together we can detect exactly who to isolate.”

Susan nodded. “I see. But for Earthlings it would be a serious violation of our privacy if not warned of its use.”

“I have learned that” Khem said. “I took the liberty of turning off the filters to the security system and set the program to just warn us of who has the medical issues. We can sort it out from there. When I set the new parameters, one person immediately appeared, Captain Gath. It showed he has a most unusual transplant in his brain and neck. The surprising thing is there is no medical reason for it to be there. When I turned on the security application, I discovered it is transmitting a very short range signal. It’s a code not encountered before.”

“Wow! Are there any more like that?” Susan asked.

Khem nodded. “Yes, there are three more aboard the ship and two recent visitors. Two are Holcrons and one of the Cassarian women. It appears her transplant doesn’t seem to be functioning.

One Holcron is working in food service and another is on the security team. I sent for them under the guise of a health follow up. The two visitors are a concern as both work for your government. One is Senator Pickering’s aide and the other is Dr. Sanchez from the State Department. They were aboard for the wedding."

"But how did they get those implants?" Susan asked in shock.

"That is the question we can't answer but someone had better find out real soon before news of our capture of the *Holcron Star* falls into the hands of the wrong people. What also concerns me is how many more are there on Earth?" Khem asked.

"Block all this off so no one can access it but us. Then we need to go see Dad. He'll figure out what to do, Susan declared.

The candle lights burned brightly in the White House windows. In a rare conference meeting going into the late-night hours, the president, his cabinet and congressional leaders met to discuss the latest alien intelligence.

"The news just keeps getting worse on the Gamoran pirates.

General Braxton reports an unknown empire from an unknown planet has worked a secret deal with the Gamoran pirates. They are referring to them as the Outsiders. Their goal is to start a war among the peoples in this sector of space. Once factions are weakened enough, they intend to invade, subjugate them or destroy the planets. Earth is the first target these outsiders intend to strike. Unfortunately, we are also the most vulnerable.

'General Braxton and Admiral MacKay have put together a plan to stop them. The Cassarian Ambassador has departed on a mission to turn the tables on the Tigrans enough they might be persuaded join us in the fight. We have five months to put together a planetary defense," President Leatham said.

"Mr. President!" Senator Francis Pickering interrupted. "Do you mean to tell us you have ruled out negotiations? Is war really the only option you want?"

"Don't you mean surrender?" Vice President Koppel retorted. "There's nothing to negotiate."

Senator Pickering was unfazed by the question. "You mean to tell the American people, indeed the whole world, we should prepare for global war against an unknown enemy, with unknown capability, and for all we know, with unknown intentions? Shouldn't we give peace a chance first?"

"Senator, are you proposing sending a greeting committee to meet with them before they attack?" the Speaker of the House asked.

Senator Pickering took a deep breath and stuck her chin up in the air. "Nothing of a kind, Mister Speaker. I am suggesting sending General Braxton to make contact and negotiate. Why not require him to solve our problems instead of initiating galactic bloodshed."

General Turnbull shook his head in disgust. "Senator, that's uncalled for. Let's not forget it was the pirates who took the first shot and destroyed the space station and murdered 44 million people in cold blood. Your proposal would just be a Custer's Last Stand in space. Like it or not, General Braxton's plan is the soundest option available. If the Outsiders show up before Gen. Braxton returns and we can get them to sit down and talk, great. However, if we don't prepare, we won't have a chance to protect anyone. It will be a global massacre.

'The cities, not to mention our military bases, are sitting ducks for alien ships shooting from space. We have no possibility of resistance until they land. Our ships at sea, and even our best fighters are nothing more than clay pigeons."

Senator Pickering was unmoved. "And how do you know all this about them, General?"

"If it is peaceful relations they desire, why send an invasion fleet? We're no threat to anyone. They are coming here to conquer," General Turnbull shot back.

"Let me make it clear," Senator Pickering declared. "There has been enough talk of war and bloodshed around the world in recent weeks. My party demands peace not war. How many more men, women and children must be slaughtered before your lust for blood is satisfied, Mister President?"

Many of the cabinet members bolted out of their seats in anger at the offensive remark. President Leatham, however, motioned with his hand for them to calmly return to their seats.

"Senator, I will not be goaded into doing nothing for the sake of political jockeying for power and partisan politics. You and your party had better start putting our country first. The threats to this country are far too dangerous for partisan politics. Our most solemn duty is to protect this great country and its people from enemies both foreign and domestic.

'Go ahead and call your press conference. Have your fellow party members stand behind you, go before the cameras and declare to the whole world the white flag of surrender is the solution to Earth's survival.

'Let's see how the people react to your sound bite on the evening news. I think the vast majority of Americans will take exception to you selling them out without a fight. I dare you to try it.

'If you do, your party won't have a single seat left in congress come next fall's election. Once the people realize you played cheap political games with their lives and the lives of their children, your party will be buried on the trash heap of history. Go on senator, just try it!" the president goaded back.

Senator Pickering reeled back in her seat from the verbal challenge. The president correctly saw through her ploy. She knew the president was right. The vast majority of Americans were not inclined to surrender their freedom without a fight no matter what the odds or political leanings.

Even if her party was right in advocating peace, the timing was not yet right. She needed more momentum to win this fight. For now, she bowed her head in defeat.

The silence hung in the room like a dense fog. Finally, the president spoke again.

"People, we need to break this to the public calmly and truthfully. This time everyone is in the war, not just the military. People tend to panic when they feel helpless so let's empower them. Where should we start?"

Special Agent Maxine Maxwell finally got a decent lead in her investigation.The taxi driver, in a second interview, remembered noticing the streetwalker was wearing a red wig. She remembered it because the streetwalker had almost jet-black eyebrows and it seemed really off. When the artist's picture was changed to black hair, the features revealed a very Hispanic appearance.

After interviewing taxi drivers on duty that night, Maxine found three taxi drivers who remembered picking up a woman of the same description and all within about an hour according to the time logs. The last taxi driver dropped off the woman about six blocks of where Dr. Sanchez lived.

On a hunch, Agent Maxwell drove around the area and noticed a homeless man wearing a red curly wig pushing a shopping cart with all his worldly possessions along the public sidewalk. Maxine's partner wheeled the car around and followed the homeless man for a short distance to a mall parking lot. The man was scared to death when Maxine and her partner approached him. He began pushing his cart as fast as he could to get away. He didn't get very far before Maxine stopped him.

"What's your name?" Maxine asked showing her FBI identification.

"Sam Casey but people call me Sammy. I didn't do nothin', honest!" he stammered.

"I just want to talk to you for a minute, Sammy. You're not in any trouble I promise you."

"You ain't lyin' to an old man are ya?" a frightened Sammy asked.

"No! In fact, it might even be profitable for you. Where did you get the wig?"

Sammy looked around suspiciously. "Four weeks ago, I was behind the gas station and this street walker wearin'it and a real short, black dress goes into the bathroom. A few minutes later she came out completely changed and throw'd her clothes in the dumpster. I fished them out thinking I might get sumthin' fer em someday."

"What time of the day was it?" Maxine asked.

"It was around midnight or so. Don't have no watch ya know," Sammy answered showing his bare wrists.

"You still have the dress?" her partner asked.

"Yep, I kept everything in the bag she throw'd away."

Maxine reached into her wallet and pulled out a twenty-dollar bill. "Look, I'll give you this twenty-dollar bill for all of her stuff. Is it a deal?"

"Ya tryin' to cheat old Sammy! I'd get more for just the dress ya know!" Sam stated pretending to be offended.

"You probably could get more but I could seize it as evidence and then you would get nothing," Maxine sternly warned.

"You got a deal!" Sam quickly agreed snatching the bill from Maxine and surrendering the wig and bag of clothes from his cart. "Nice doin' business with ya!" Sam said and quickly shuffled off.

CHAPTER 14

Kerra was having a difficult time getting the *Halfling's* long range sensors to work properly. No matter what adjustments she made, the sensors wouldn't present a clear screen image. In frustration, she gave the console a bash with her fist. That didn't work either.

Noticing Kerra was frustrated, Shaun Miller asked, "What seems to be the problem, Kerra?"

"I can't get the sensor screen to stop shimmering. I think it's going bad. I've tried all the checklist adjustments but the problem still persists. I can't be sure any of my sensor readings are accurate," Kerra exclaimed.

"Well, don't further damage the equipment by beating it. Call Dexter to come check it out. We need our sensors working properly to make this voyage," Shaun declared.

Kerra paged Dexter for assistance. A minute later Dexter arrived on the *Halfling's* bridge.

"What seems to be the problem, Kerra?" Dexter inquired.

"There is this intermittent shimmering on the screen and I can't clear it up," Kerra pointed. "It's there one minute on the portside edge of the screen, then disappears for a period of time then reappears again each time moving just a bit more to our stern. It's always on the bare edge of the long-range sensors."

"Oh really! I did a system check before we left Earth and everything was just fine. I'll run the diagnostic test again and see what we find. When did the symptoms first appear?"

"The problem started about an hour ago. It's happened four times since," Kerra explained.

Dexter ran the diagnostic test on the sensor programs. He then plugged in a hardware diagnostic device and ran several more tests. Opening up a rear access panel, he discovered a little corrosion on a power coupling that took a few minutes to clean.

"Except for a little corrosion on a power coupling, everything tests out just fine," Dexter noted. "Is it happening on your screen now?"

"No, it's fine now. Thanks!" Kerra said.

"If the problem returns, let me know right away."

"Will do!" Kerra answered.

The excitement was electrifying throughout the *Holcron Star* as the crew prepared for its first training exercise. Everyone was eager to prove their newfound skills especially John Braxton. As he surveyed the bridge crew performing their tasks, John was quite pleased. The checklist discipline and teamwork were starting to show the polished professionalism that only confidence in one's skills can bring. Training on a navy ship took months and even then, there was still much to learn that only experience could bring to the table. Under the circumstances there was no such luxury.

The training progressed well but John knew the crew had a long, long way to go before being truly combat ready.

The six-day exercise would identify the crew's strengths and weaknesses in skills, teamwork and leadership. The ten observers assisting Admiral MacKay were highly experienced *Holcron* and Cassarian technicians with much combat and deep space experience. A few of the Holcrons actually trained as part of the *Holcron Star's* crew before its capture. Their training proved invaluable, but now it was time to raise the pressure a bit and push the crew to a higher level.

"You launch in ten minutes, John. Remember, for the duration of the exercise I am, in essence, not here. Whatever happens, whether real or simulated, is subject to evaluation.

You may ask clarification of the instructions I give you, but nothing else. In case of a real emergency you can suspend the exercise. If my inspection team observes any major safety violations jeopardizing the safety of the crew or ship we will immediately halt the exercise and direct corrective action as required. Any questions, now is a good time?" Admiral MacKay inquired.

"No, I understand the parameters of the exercise. Let's do it!" John said.

Moments later John gave the order to lay in the course for Sepious Minor and break orbit. The exercise would take the *Holcron Star* on a triangular course.

Four days out towards Sepious Minor followed by a two-day leg towards the Mentarus System. Along the way, they would intercept the *Halfling,* complete a boarding and capture exercise, then escort the *Halfling* back to Earth.

A couple of hours after departing Earth the first exercise problem began.

"Sir! I have a report of a fire in hangar bay 1." Meghan reported from the communications console.

John picked up his data pad and brought up the appropriate checklist. "Alert Fire Response Team Alpha and medic team to respond immediately."

He then contacted the maintenance crew in hangar 1 for a report on the fire but got no response at first. On the third contact attempt the maintenance crew responded. Everyone continued his or her checklist tasks and two hours later the fire exercise was finished.

The bridge and medic crews performed well. The fire response team was too slow and a bit disorganized at first but effective in the end. More drills would develop the faster response and teamwork needed.

On the second day out, there was a simulated radiation

leak in one of the main reactors. Engineering responded very poorly mainly because they failed to follow the response checklist. There was a breakdown of command in Engineering so John sent Jonathan, as First Officer, to the reactor room to restore order. When Jonathan entered the reactor control room, he took command of the situation and restored the checklist discipline needed to correctly resolve the problem.

In reviewing the situation, it was found that without Dexter present there was little cohesion or confidence among the engineering crew. John ordered Jonathan to drill the engineering crew over and over until they performed flawlessly. Eight hours and seven drills later, the engineering crew finally pulled it together. When Jonathan reported to the bridge, he had been on duty for almost twenty-four hours. John sent him to his quarters for eight hours' rest while Aycana assumed duty officer.

The remaining exercises over the next few days went just as poorly. There were major problems but more drills and experience would correct most of the deficiencies.

Thankfully nothing that threatened the safety of the ship. The most noticeable issue was a lack of experienced officer and senior NCO leadership thanks to the pirate's policy of executing all captured officers. Several candidates, chosen as "officers in training," had a lot to learn in a very short time and competed for key positions. The pressure on them was intense but the best were rising to the occasion.

The hangar and bridge crews seemed to perform the best mainly because their training started even before the ship was captured.

During a hull breach exercise in the hangar bay, resourcefulness proved alive and well. The exercise simulated a laser blast breaching the hull making a twenty-four-inch hole in the hangar bay. To simulate the atmospheric venting, an air vent was opened in a controlled leak. The Cassarian officer in training immediately implemented the proper checklist and ordered the hangar evacuation. He shoved people out the hatch until he was the last man to evacuate.

Just before he evacuated himself, he grabbed a loose piece of titanium armor plate and shoved it over the air vent. That stopped the atmosphere venting until the suited-up response team could reenter the hangar. Though the officer's action wasn't on the checklist, his response was deemed appropriate in a combat situation. The response team was able to achieve simulated repairs in half the expected time.

While several more exercises were going on throughout the ship, each bridge shift was constantly undergoing navigation, long range sensor scanning, emergency and security responses, along with defensive and offensive targeting exercises.

Early during one watch, Aycana called John Braxton to the bridge.

Aycana, as the DO, was at the Sensor Console with Georgia.

"What's the problem, Aycana?" John inquired.

"Sir, for the last hour we had three instances of long range sensors detecting a shimmering anomaly on the edge of our maximum range. The system identifies it only as a visual distortion. I disagree with the identification. It doesn't act right for a system glitch. It changes speed to match us yet we can't get a positive fix either."

"Have you run a system check on your sensors to make sure they are working properly?" John asked.

"We did that when the problem first appeared. All software is at optimal efficiency."

"How about a hardware check?"

"We did that too. We followed all checklist procedures and Estron gave all the equipment a thorough check," Georgia replied. "She couldn't find anything wrong."

"Georgia, tell me how you came to spot it and about where does this shimmering appear on the scope?"

"It showed up during a routine sweep. At first I thought it was a smudge on the screen. I cleaned the screen and it was still there. I then implemented the checklist for a diagnostic system check. Maintenance was sent to check the scopes and sensors. The scopes proved clean with no defects. The sensors still showed the intermittent anomaly so I ran the sensor system failure protocols. When the system came back up, it showed everything operating at optimum levels.

'The first shimmering appeared a few degrees off our stern and just on the edge of our sensor range. It seemed to approach us then stop and drift off the scope again. The next two appearances were directly astern of us and just as before appeared on the edge of our sensors then drifted off again."

John paused for a moment."OK, Georgia, I want each occurrence carefully plotted as best you can and mark the time as well. Let's see what shakes out before we rendezvous with the *Halfling*."

"Sir, you don't really think it's the equipment?" Aycana inquired.

"No! I suspect we have a bashful visitor. We'll play dumb for now."

"I see, but why not reverse course and see what happens?" Georgia inquired.

"If we do that, we tip our hand. It could be an Outsider scout ship, or who knows what. One thing for sure, we can detect it before it can detect us," John nodded.

"How so, sir?" Aycana asked.

"The object is approaching us, but only to within a certain range before drifting off. If they could detect us sooner, they would not risk being within our sensor range, stealth or not.

They are relying on their stealth to keep us from getting

an exact fix and identification. Without a positive fix, we can't get a target lock so we must avoid a fight. Their stealth may not be perfect but it is effective. We are going to have to figure a way around their stealth technology or we're sitting ducks," John answered.

"What if it is the Outsiders and they're trying to make contact?" Georgia asked.

"Excellent question and a distinct possibility. We will just have to wait to find out," John said as he reached for his flip com. He paged Cat Saunders and got a sleepy reply.

"Sorry to wake you up, but your assistance is needed on the bridge as soon as you can get here."

"Yes, sir!" Cat moaned and signed off.

A few minutes later, Cat appeared on the bridge with a cup of coffee in hand. John briefed her on the problem and suggested that Togg Gath might have some information he would like to share. Cat nodded in agreement while relishing the thought of out witting Capt. Gath one more time. She had become very proficient at turning the cowardly Gath into an intelligence gold mine.

He was clearly afraid of the Outsiders but believed cooperation with his captors was in his best interest. Cat was confident she could convince him into volunteering additional information. Even on other worlds, bullies are the biggest cowards of all.

"I'll be back shortly with your information," Cat smiled as she stepped into the elevator.

"Aycana, I'll be in my quarters. Call me if the situation changes or Cat returns. In the meantime, this development is kept hushed except for Cat and the bridge crew. Make sure all bridge personnel get briefed."

"Yes, sir!"

Sergeant Major Stone was in his element giving the Blue Watch a real workout. The different nationalities of soldiers offered different skills and experiences. Each group was made up to maximize the experiences of each member. Slowly but surely, they were forming the teamwork and cohesion needed to build the kind of unit General Braxton wanted.

Traven was relieved to have Sergeant Major Stone. Serving with him in the past, Traven knew his leadership by example and knack for getting the best out of every soldier were invaluable assets. The soldiers were in awe of him as much as they feared to fail him. The rumor among the troops claimed Sergeant Major Stone was the result of a diabolical super soldier experiment. The sergeant major did nothing to dispel the rumor.

The exercises over the next few weeks were designed to build teamwork, develop problem-solving skills, and physically push those who weren't in the best of shape. One of the tests involved two steep rocky hills that were each about three hundred feet high and inside a three mile circuit. At each starting point was a six-hundred pound pallet of doughnut shaped cement disks, each about six inches thick by two feet in diameter, a length of rope, and three metal poles about eight feet long. On top of each hill were several small flags attached to a pole. Each team, in turn, was brought to the starting point while the other teams trained elsewhere.

Sergeant Major Stone briefed the exercise to each team. "The object of this exercise is to transport the wooden pallet of cement disks to the opposite side of the course while retrieving one of the flags on top of the hill along the way. You can use only the resources before you and the exercise must be done with full battle gear. Everyone must arrive at the destination as a team. You have one hour to complete the task.

'If you fail to complete the mission within the one-hour requirement, you will reassemble at the starting point with all the disks and start over until it is successfully completed. There are no other rules or restrictions. Any questions?"

Staff Sergeant Corky O'Brian led the last team. He was an American by birth but of Irish immigrants. His red-haired crew cut and playful humor made him standout in any crowd. Physically, he was one of the shortest men in Blue Watch at just five feet six inches. However, he had the build of a circus trapeze performer and was a tryout for the U.S. Olympic Men's Gymnastics Team before joining the Army. Corky loved a mental challenge as much as a physical one. This natural born leader relished difficult challenges that pushed his mental and physical skills to the limit. In the Blue Watch, Corky was definitely in his element and decided now was the time for his team to make their mark.

In previous exercises, he always wagered his team would finish first, putting up a box of Lucky Charms Cereal against the sergeant major's cigar, which he was fond of chewing all day but never smoked. Of course, O'Brian's team did an excellent job but always came up a point or two short of winning the cigar. His charming personality kept him from earning his teammates ire and his corny wagers became the comedic relief for the Blue Watch recruits.

True to form, he, again, bet the sergeant major a box of Lucky Charms against the cigar. Sergeant Major Stone, growing weary of his grandstanding, this time countered with a wager of his own. "Tell you what, wise guy. Your team wins this exercise and I will give each man a box of cigars."

"Ah, sergeant major, to make such a wager with an Irishman is good sport, but most of my mates are true Christians and such a bet is an obvious insult ya see. Can't ya make a more honorable wager for their sake?"

"O'Brian, your bets have become a big joke so why not up the ante? If you lose, you buy me a box of Cuban cigars. If you win, I'll give a weekend pass to you and each of your men."

"Now that's the spirit, sergeant major. It's a deal," Staff Sergeant O'Brian conceded with a big smile.

O'Brian gathered his team around him. One of the men, being a very accomplished free climber, received the assignment of going for the flag on top of the hill. The rest of the team would take care of the pallet of cement disks.

When Sergeant Major Stone fired the starting pistol, the team dashed off on their assignments. The man assigned to go after the flag scampered up the steep hill like a mountain goat. The rest of the team started removing the cement doughnuts from the pallet.

Shoving two of the poles through the forklift holes of the pallet, they then mounted the cement disks like wheels onto the poles. The rope was looped over the end of each pole to hold the wheels in place. The rope was then attached to the third pole to serve as a pulling harness.

Grabbing the harness pole in front of them they began pulling the pallet, now loaded with all the team's gear and remaining disks, the mile and a half distance around the hill to the finish line.

After retrieving the flag the soldier re-joined his teammates pulling the last couple hundred yards to the finish line setting a course time record. The team celebrated their record but Sgt. O'Brian was not quite done.

As a final tease, Corky reached into his pack. "Here, sergeant major.

You can have the box of Lucky Charms as a bed time snack just to prove there are no hard feelings," Corky declared with a wry smile.

"Well, staff sergeant smarty pants, just to show I harbor no ill will, you can repeat the exercise and return the flag to the pole and everything else to the starting point. It's double or nothing if you beat your record."

The team members glared and Corky's wry smile until they realized it was his plan all along. Once the starting pistol fired, the team reacted with excitement as they repeated their accomplishment. Corky's team beat the course record they just established and for good measure by going around the other side of the hill for a complete circuit. From that moment on the exercise was called the O'Brian Challenge.

Sergeant Major Stone masked his approval as always but inside realized not only had Staff Sergeant O'Brian played him fair and square but also set the standard for Blue Watch leadership and training.

During the next few weeks, twelve teams completed the exercise on the first try but couldn't break O'Brian's team record. Fourteen teams completed the exercise on the second try and eight teams completed it on the third try. The two remaining teams accomplished the exercise on the fourth try. No one ever figured out exactly how O'Brian's team accomplished their feat. The O'Brian team members proudly kept their secret.

Over the next few weeks each team trained hard as an independent team, as well as, with various combinations of teams according to exercise requirements. Four months later, only two hundred and fifty men and women completed the training.

Everyone was tense with excitement on the *Holcron Star*'s bridge as the intercept course brought the *Halfling* within sensor range. This signaled the beginning of the ship boarding and capture exercise.

Admiral MacKay, Henry and Victoria were also on the bridge to observe the exercise.

John appeared calm on the outside but was just as anxious as the rest of the crew. The team was, on the whole, shaping up well with the exercises revealing the good, the bad and the ugly of crew strengths and weaknesses. Everyone admitted there was a lot more training to do.

"David, bring the ship around to port and make an approach from the stern. Come up along the *Halfling*'s starboard side," John ordered.

"Will do! Turn to port and approach target from the stern, then come along the starboard side," David replied.

"Molly, signal the *Halfling* to come to a stop and prepare to be boarded," John again directed.

Before Molly could acknowledge the order, Aycana interrupted, "Sir, we have the stealth ship back on screen just on the edge of our sensors directly astern. There is also a new ship not cloaked, 65 degrees starboard. The ship's computer identifies it as the pirate heavy cruiser *Fire Hawk*."

The news caused everyone on the bridge to fall dead silent. "Sound general quarters! Molly, cancel that message to the *Halfling* and give me a secure comm. link to both Jonathan and Burt Armstrong in Security. "

The admiral, seeing the determined look in John's eyes, calmly inquired, "What are you thinking?"

"As far as the whole galaxy is concerned, we are a pirate ship. We need to maintain that illusion for our uninvited viewers or we will give ourselves away. If things go sour, I plan to fight it out here in the hopes we can contain the damage. On the other hand, if we can create the opportunity to capture either of the two ships, I will not hesitate to do so. I especially want that cloaked ship. We need to know how to get around that cloaking if we are ever going to defeat them," John explained.

"I was thinking the same thing, not that we have much choice. We don't dare cut and run. I concur, better to play the part and see what unfolds," Admiral MacKay agreed. "Lord help us, please!" he whispered looking upward.

"Amen!" John chimed in.

"OK! Everyone listen up. We are going to continue with our mock capture of the *Halfling*. That will give us the appearance of being a legitimate pirate ship. If we are convincing enough, the other pirate ship just might let its guard down. If it does, we will capture it, and if the opportunity arises, the cloaked ship as well. Any questions?"

Everyone on the bridge nodded in agreement.

Molly announced she had both Jonathan and Burt Armstrong on the secure comm. link.

"Gentlemen, we have a developing situation. There's a pirate ship and a suspected Outsider cloaked ship in sensor range. I want Jonathan to continue to carry out the mock capture of the *Halfling* while Burt prepares a team for the real boarding of the pirate ship. When the *Halfling* is simulated captured, both ships will land in the docking bay.

'Burt's team will assault the pirate ship if the opportunity arises. We will relay the ship's layout to you. Once back aboard, Jonathan's team will rearm and stand by for the assault on the cloaked ship if we have a chance. Any questions?"

Burt and Jonathan acknowledged and signed off.

"Aycana, fire a shot well in front of the *Halfling*'s bow and hope Gavin understands and plays along," John ordered.

Aycana acknowledged the order and fired a magnum Plasma shot across the bow of the *Halfling*.

"What in the blazing galaxy was that about?" Gavin stammered as the plasma bolt crossed in front of the *Halfling* lighting up the bridge with a violet glow. "That wasn't in the exercise plan."

"Maybe it isn't in the exercise plan but that is a signal to cut engines and prepare to be boarded on Earth," Sean replied.

"Gavin! The shimmering anomaly has returned 90 degrees starboard and a heavy cruiser is approaching directly ahead of us. Both are just on the edge of our scanner range," Kerra announced. "I bet that's a pirate ship in front of us and General Braxton is signaling us to play along," Sean advised Gavin.

"I think you're right. OK! Let's play along and see what comes of it," Gavin agreed.

"Cut engines and come to a complete stop. Signal the *Holcron Star* in the clear that we are surrendering and will not resist boarding."

A minute after Jonathan's shuttle docked with the *Halfling*, he sent the message everyone was waiting for.

"Sir!" Molly announced. "Jonathan has signaled the *Halfling* is successfully captured and requests permission to land in hangar bay 1."

"Great! Transmit permission granted," John said.

A few minutes later the *Halfling* and shuttle were brought into the *Holcron Star*'s main hangar.

Just as the *Halfling* was aboard, Molly announced an incoming message.

"Sir! We are receiving a message from the *Fire Hawk*. Captain Cregg Hatar requests a meeting with Captain Togg Gath."

John quickly scanned his data pad then replied, "Of course, welcome aboard. Captain Gath eagerly awaits your visit if you have the new replacements. Captain Hatar and his senior staff are invited to dine with him on the *Holcron Star*. He wishes to honor their victories and especially the recapture of the Cassarian freighter."

"Sir, the *Fire Hawk* replies they do have the replacements and look forward to some fine dining," Molly replied. "The new junior officers will transfer over with a shipment of aged Gamoran ale for the crew. They ask for assistance transporting the other requested supplies."

"Perfect. Great job, Molly."

"Thank you, sir!" Molly replied.

"Thank goodness the ship's computer contained a log of all the pirate ships, names of key officers and summaries of their meetings," John sighed. He was greatly relieved when Captain Hatar replied the *Fire Hawk* looked forward to the relaxation and fellowship.

"The *Fire Hawk* is the Gamoran pirates' most powerful ship next to the *Holcron Star*. The Cassarian fleet tried to destroy it on several occasions but the *Fire Hawk* always escaped to fight another day. Captain Hatar is more cunning than Captain Gath, but not as ruthless by all known accounts. He is very wary. If he gets the least suspicious of us, Captain Hatar could prove extremely dangerous," Aycana warned.

"I see," John agreed. "Molly, patch me through to Gavin and Cat. I guess we will have to make sure we are a step or two ahead of him at all times."

"Your patch to Gavin and Cat is ready, sir!" Molly replied.

"Their Captain and approximately five senior officers think they are coming aboard for a special dinner in about two hours," John explained.

'Let's make sure they receive a proper reception. Each of you will lead a team to capture them once they clear their shuttle. Take them out if you have too, but they must not be allowed to alert their ship or re-board their shuttle.

'Bert Anderson and Jonathan will simultaneously land assault teams on the *Fire Hawk*, incapacitate the crew and secure the ship. You two can work out the details. Brief me on the bridge when you are ready with your plan. Any questions?"

"We can get the job done. See you in an hour," Gavin replied.

The *Fire Hawk*'s shuttle eased into the *Holcron Star*'s hangar bay 1 to its assigned parking pad next to the *Halfling*. Once the outer doors closed and atmosphere restored, Deze, dressed in pirate clothing, entered the hangar, affixed the deck clamps to the landing gear, then waved the cockpit crew the customary welcome sign to begin disembarking. As the shuttle door opened, Captain Hatar proudly sauntered down the extended ramp followed by his senior officers. His attire was perfect for the occasion. The tall frame, typical Gamoran scars on his face, and gaunt features were not impressionable save his uniform for the occasion. He wore a white tunic and gold braid, a bright red, over the shoulder, sash filled with medals, and a polished brown belt with brown dress pants. The knee high brown polished boots finished the appearance. He gave the impression he was anything but a Gamoran Pirate. His officers were similarly, but more plainly dressed. Deze gave a smirk. The message was clear. Never dress better than your commander.

"Where is Captain Gath or the duty officer?" Captain Harter growled at Deze. "It is customary to be greeted aboard when a ship's captain arrives."

"I have no idea, sir," Deze replied nervously with a salute.

"All I know is to take care of the ship when it arrives. I'm not privy to the Captain's activities. Welcome aboard if that is all you want to hear."

"Why you insolent, little runt! How dare you talk to a superior in such a manner! I'm sure Captain Gath will have you whipped and put in chains for that remark," the captain snarled.

"Actually, you will be joining him very shortly… in the brig," Deze declared as he lay down on the deck.

"What…!" Captain Harter snarled again.

On cue, a cloud of gas poured out of the *Halfling*'s cargo bay engulfing the hangar. Within seconds Deze and all the pirates were unconscious. At the same time a security team with gas masks emerged from the *Halfling*, searched, disarmed and handcuffed the unconscious pirates while another team secured the inside of the shuttle.

"Hey Burt," Jonathan said. "I just got the go-ahead order." In minutes, they docked in the *Fire Hawk*'s hangar. Jonathan and his team were the first to race across the hangar. At the same time three pirates entered and were surprised.

"Take them out!" Jonathan ordered as he began firing. In a few seconds the blaster fire rendered them unconscious. One of Jonathan's team was hit as he raced down the ramp with the gas hose. He was stunned and temporarily out of action. Jonathan signaled the team to keep moving as he grabbed the gas hose, caught up with the team and tapped into the air circulation system. In less than ten seconds it was all over.

Burt's team raced through decks 2 and 3 while Jonathan's team cleared deck 1 and the bridge. The pirate crew were all quickly secured and accounted for before anyone regained consciousness. Five minutes later, Jonathan sent the code signal that the ship was secure and his team was maintaining the appearance of normal operations.

Admiral MacKay complemented John and Gavin on a job well done. "That worked perfectly."

"Sir," Molly reported. "We are receiving an encoded message from an unidentified sender. The transmission is originating from the shimmering anomaly. It is encrypted with an unknown code."

John reached for his data pad and went through the files that Captain Gath kept along with information he 'volunteered' to Cat Saunders. John found the encryption file and after entering the password was able to call up the message decoded and translated on his screen.

"Our mysterious anomaly is definitely the Outsiders. Captain Gath's encryption codes match up to prove it. They want to know why we were observed in the Earth space sector in violation of our orders and did we bother to make contact with their agents? The Outsiders also want to know why Captain

Gath has failed to maintain contact by way of the Secure Deep Space Transmitter system for the past three months?

'The lost shipment has displeased them greatly and they want to know if it was just recovered? They also remind Captain Gath not to fail again or he can be replaced with a more competent leader," John announced.

"Somewhere aboard this ship is a secret communications device that Capt. Gath hasn't told us about. I assume he is hoping they would rescue him," Admiral MacKay surmised.

"Yes!" John agreed. "I bet it's hidden in his quarters. We don't have time to find it. For now, let's see if we can deceive them into believing it's broken and let us off the hook."

John typed and encoded a message on his data pad.

Sir,

My most humble apology for your inconvenience, but your SDST device is a piece of junk that quit working some time ago. Suggest using this method of contact for the time being.

The freighter, which carried your cargo, was tracked through the Earth space sector to here. Though the freighter was recaptured, the cargo is unaccounted for. I will redouble efforts to recover said cargo.

No contact was made with your agents. I assumed their SDST device was defective as well. If you desire, I will return and deliver instructions as you wish.

Due to a mining mishap, it will be very difficult to meet your demand for a double shipment of Zannite crystals. However, I will direct the mining operation to make every effort to comply.

Looking forward to your complete victory.

Captain Togg Gath

"Molly, send this reply to the Outsider ship."

"Message sent, sir," Molly replied after she completed

the transmission.

A few minutes later another message was received. John repeated the decoding and translation process then shared it with Admiral MacKay.

Captain Gath,

We will forgive your incompetence this one last time. You were ordered not to have any contact with Earth. Your apology is accepted for now but demand no further failures.

We are already aware of the SDST transmitter issues, but most likely operator error. We will communicate through this system for now. Ensure codes are kept secure at all times.

No further contact with our agents is deemed necessary. Their operation is under way.

The few zannite crystals you previously provided met our quality standards and tested out on our flagship perfectly. Grand Viscount Zinge Horthnot is very pleased. The invasion force is on schedule to arrive and you must ensure the double shipment is at the rendezvous point on time.

There is a change in plans. You will transfer other cargo and slaves at that time as well. Do not disappoint him.

Captain Pinera Ditra

"Sir! The Outsider ship appears to be moving off our long range scope," Aycana announced.

"I think we did it. I think we really got them to buy off our deception. Thank you, God!" John sighed.

Gavin shook his head. "You know every time we solve a part of this puzzling plot we seem to find that there are more parts to it. Now we know who has zannite crystals besides us."

"And what's worse is we can't even get a target lock on them. Three pieces of good news out of this whole incident are: One, we know only their flagship, and this ship are equipped with zannite. Two, we now have a second pirate ship in our possession. Three, they still don't know about us," John said.

Susan was so deeply transfixed on the computer screen she barely noticed the door to the lab open and close. As she examined the body scan of Captain Gath, Khem silently walked up behind her and stood patiently waiting to be noticed.

"Well, if you help me finish going over the scan, I'll let you take me out to dinner," Susan offered without taking her eyes off the tissue scan.

"Do I get a kiss?" Khem teased.

"Daddy doesn't take kindly to lecherous men making passes at his little girl you know," Susan said sarcastically still focusing on the scan.

"OK! I'll settle for a late dinner," Khem said quickly in a tone of humorous surrender. "You looking for the implant?"

"Yes, I think he might have a different one here next to his rib," Susan said with excitement pointing to a piece of metal the size of a bean. It was surrounded by three smaller fragments.

"I think those are fragments from an old combat wound. However, notice the two tones of the bone structure on the neck vertebra where the implant is located whereas the other vertebrae are all the same color."

"Yes, I see. Its shape is slightly different too," Susan added as she looked closer. "The lighter material is obviously bone but what is the dark material making up the left side of the vertebra?"

Khem rotated the scan 90 degrees for a different view. "I think this is what you're looking for. See these two very faint strands extending from the dark area on the vertebra? They are wrapped around the spine and leading to the brain. One is connected to the temporal lobe and the other strand leads to the frontal lobe."

"Yes, I see. You're right, that's what we're looking for.

Should we remove it?"

Khem looked closer at the scan. "I think we need to do some more tests before we try surgery. With the way it's attached and wrapped around the spine I'm afraid we might do great harm by removing it."

Susan turned to the unconscious Capt. Gath on the examination table and asked, "Let's run your tests while he's unconscious. We can eat later."

"Agreed!" Khem said as he called a test protocol up on the medical computer.

Three hours later the tests were completed and analyzed. The results were not as hopeful as Susan and Khem originally thought. When John Braxton and Gavin were summoned to sick bay, both were surprised.

"We can surgically remove the device but it will most likely leave him permanently paralyzed. I can deactivate it with an electrical shock, but again it would most likely leave him severely brain damaged," Khem informed them.

"I see no reason to bother with it even if he is pond scum. We can use this knowledge to our advantage," Gavin said.

"I was thinking the same thing. As long as they think he is in charge we can keep our existence better concealed. I do, however, think it prudent to keep him completely isolated," John said.

On the observation deck people were socializing, playing games, laughing, and eating but Henry was oblivious to it all.

He just sat on one of the lounge chairs starring out the forward window seemingly lost in deep space.

Dexter walked up to Henry and, noticing his concentration, silently took a chair beside him. It wasn't long before he too joined Henry lost in deep thought. Now both were transfixed on the darkness of space as an hour went by without a word said between them.

Deze now appeared and noted the two men starring into space as if focused on something invisible. The screeching of the metal chair legs against the metal floor echoed around the observation deck as Deze pulled a chair up beside them. He wiggled himself into a comfortable position and joined them starring out the window. For a minute, he tried to find what they were staring at but could see nothing. The Gamoran could no longer keep his silence at the odd behavior.

"Is there something out there?" Deze whispered.

Expressionless, Henry nodded.

Deze resumed starring out into space but could still see nothing. He tried to see where in space they were looking but quickly realized they were staring at different areas of space.

"Is there something I'm supposed to see? Deze asked.

This time Dexter nodded while keeping his eyes fixed in space. Like fingernails on a chalkboard, Deze moved his screeching chair closer to Henry and resumed his search in space. Finally, after another 10 minutes of starring, his frustration factor peeked again. "Guys, I don't get it. What am I supposed to see?"

"A ship!" Henry whispered.

Deze raised his voice in frustration. "What? There's no ship."

"Yes, there is but we need to see it," Dexter whispered back. "Now think!"

Suddenly Deze realized what was going on. Without saying another word, he leaned back in his chair letting the darkness of space open up his mind. The duct tape engineers were now synchronized in thought.

Another three hours passed. The observation deck was now silent and empty except for the trio locked in thought.

Finally, Henry stood up. "Let's do it, fellas!

CHAPTER 15

A beautiful California coastal sunset of crimson and amber hued clouds gave way to dusk when passengers and crew stepped off the *Halfling* at Vandenberg AFB. General Klinedecker and Col. Perry were there to greet them at the bottom of the ramp. The somber mood of the arrivals did not go undetected by the two officers on the tarmac.

"Welcome home! Good to see all of you again," General Klinedecker greeted while shaking their hands.

"Jake, Arlin, glad to see you too," John said.

"We got your message last night. It seems you had a very eventful mission," Arlin said.

"As was expected, it revealed a lot of weaknesses, but we learned a lot too. Have you been able to assemble the new personnel and equipment?" John asked.

"We have everyone going through the processing line as we speak and the cargo is assembled in the two hangars next door ready for transport. My cargo handlers are standing by to assist with the loading," General Klinedecker pointed out.

John smiled."Thanks, our supply shuttles will arrive momentarily."

"Dr. Kremmel needs some assistance setting up the scanning stations.

Nobody and nothing is allowed aboard until scanned, not even myself. We appreciate everyone's patience and assistance. Please bear with us," Gavin said.

"What's with the unusual level of security and urgency to get under way again so quickly?" Arlin asked.

"Earth is under intermittent surveillance by an Outsider scout ship and we can't risk them finding us here. We learned they have lost contact with their agents on Earth due to faulty communication equipment. We could not determine how extensive the Outsider network is, but their fifth column plan for the invasion is already set in motion.

'On Earth the word is already out we have captured the *Holcron Star*. However, only a few key people know we've captured the *Fire Hawk*. Thankfully, when we encountered the Outsider ship, they didn't catch on to our ruse. One transmission from their spies on Earth and all is undone. If the Outsiders find us here it will compromise everything."

"I see. You'd better get out of here as fast as you can then," General Klinedecker agreed.

"Besides Capt. Gath, we discovered new implants in two Holcrons and a Cassarian with a non-functioning implant. They are able to silently communicate among themselves and Outsiders if they get close enough. You received the report about the two Americans. It leads us to believe there are possibly more Outsider agents already among us," General Klinedecker said.

"Arlin hand carried it to General Turnbull. He read it and hand carried it to the president personally," General Klinedecker explained.

"Yes, and they were both shocked. President Leatham authorized the FBI and CIA directors to read it. No one else is authorized to know unless they have been cleared by you aboard the *Holcron Star* and have a need to know for the time being. He is arranging a list of key people who will be paying you a visit under the guise of an orientation visit as soon as it can be arranged. Arlin said.

"What do we do with them after we identify them?" General Klinedecker asked.

"I wish we had an answer for that," John answered.

"Why not surgically remove them?" Col. Perry asked.

"So far, we haven't found a safe way to do so,"Khem

said. "The way the implant organically integrates into the host, they are effectively one and the same. The person is an extension of the implant devise and the integration is so smooth you can't tell the difference. Thus, when we refer to an implant, we are actually referring to them as one. For the moment separating them is impossible."

"That is scary to say the least," Arlin said shuddering his body.

"By the way, John. I read your report on the encounter with the outsider scout ship. That was real coolheaded thinking," Jake smiled as he patted John on the shoulder.

"Thanks, we uncovered they are the ones buying the slaves and after more. You can have Gath's SDST device to study," John said handing the small device to Arlin.

"Thanks, I'll pass it on to the right people for analysis. How do we locate all the implants without tipping our hand?" Arlin asked.

"The only means to identify them presently is to get them aboard the ship or through the scanners here. Dr. Kremmel and the duct tape engineers are trying to figure out a way to transfer the technology to Earth. A team of Air Force research engineers just arrived to help. We are working on it as hard and fast as we can," John replied scratching his head.

"You might as well start with those who claim they were alien abducted," Victoria offered half seriously.

Everyone laughed at Victoria's comment at first, but as the humor of the comment wore off, the possibility began to sink in.

"Victoria hit on an excellent point," Admiral MacKay said. "We do know both of the people were connected to claims of UFO abductions."

Jake shook his head. "It's the perfect cover for the Outsiders. Everybody dismisses the abduction stories out of hand as pure fiction. I mean, who hasn't written off those people as just a bunch of dingbats?"

Suddenly attention turned to Gavin, his sisters and the Braxton family. There was a long dead silence as everyone struggled for words. General Klinedecker's face turned red while Col. Perry's mouth hung open.

Siyana politely covered her mouth to hide her laughter. "General, if I were in your shoes as an Earthling before we arrived, I'd have thought the same thing,"

"Who knows how long the people with implants have been working themselves into positions of authority and building cells throughout the world. As sleeper agents, they can be activated and controlled to collect intelligence, commit sabotage or even direct or deflect public opinion," Victoria exclaimed.

John nodded agreement. "Good point. We have no idea how long they have been on Earth."

They are free to spread all over the world." General Klinedecker noted.

Gavin nodded. "Or on any other planet for that matter."

John shook his head. "You're right. They are an active underground force and their numbers are no doubt growing. We've got to solve this problem quickly."

Dr. Jerri Spinner was the State Department's last minute pick as Ambassador at Large for the mission. President Leatham decided to send Dr. Sanchez on a diplomatic mission to Nepal to make contact with the Free Chinese Peoples movement. The assignment went to another ambassador but he suddenly and conveniently fell very ill so she got the nod. Dr. Spinner had a reputation as a competent negotiator but her insufferable arrogance was well known throughout the diplomatic community.

Dr. Spinner stood tapping her right foot impatiently. She was furiously starring at a long processing line. *I'm a diplomat. I shouldn't be treated like everybody else. Having my belongings inspected and rummaged through like a dumpster diver looking for his next meal is absolutely humiliating.* Spotting an officer enter the hangar, she strutted over to him as if she were royalty.

"Major! I'm Dr. Jerri Spinner, the Ambassador at Large, for this mission. I have better things to do than stand in a processing line being searched and examined like a lab rat. I have diplomatic status and demand to be treated accordingly."

Traven looked down at a woman in her early 60s, short and thin with thinning gray hair in a bun. Her silver rimmed bifocals with an attached silver chain dangled from her neck. She reminded him of his rural Texas elementary schoolmarm. He swore she sucked a lemon before going to class every morning. That look haunted him his whole life and there before him was her toe tapping clone. He shook his head but the image just wouldn't go away.

"Well, Ms. Diplomat! As a security measure, orders are nobody gets aboard a shuttle until they go through screening and that includes diplomats. I apologize for the inconvenience, Ma'am," Traven said in his usual un-diplomatic manner.

Dr. Spinner to you. Don't ever call me Ma'am again."

"Yes, Ma'am!" Traven acknowledged trying not to smile.

Jerri's anger at Traven's insolence only made her more determined to get her way. "I don't think you understand my position, Major. You are interfering with a diplomatic mission. I demand treatment commensurate with my diplomatic rank immediately!" Jerri fumed.

"As you wish, Ma'am," Traven said. "Please follow me!"

Traven walked all the way to the end of the processing line with Dr. Spinner right on his heels and motioned a Security

Police Sergeant over to him.

"Sergeant, escort Ms. Diplomat through the processing line. When she's completed processing, see to it that she safely boards the shuttle. If she gets out of the processing line again, you will escort her off the base immediately."

"Yes, sir!" the sergeant answered snapping a salute.

"Are there any other problems you need assistance with?" Traven asked.

"Yes, who is going to carry all my luggage?"she angrily demanded, pointing to three large luggage carts piled with suitcases and trunks. "Well, Ma'am. You were told one suitcase and a trunk. If I were you, I'd do some fast decision making on what to leave behind. I don't think you can carry all that!" Traven responded then walked away.

Oooh! Jerri fumed. *You'll get yours when the time comes, Major. Just you wait and see.*

"What are you laughing at Sergeant?" Jerri snarled.

The sergeant smiled as he looked straight ahead saying nothing.

Cat was in her quarters on the *Holcron Star* when her flip com device beeped. Looking at the call screen she noticed it was Susan.

"Cat, we have an implant scanner alert on Dr. Jerri Spinner. She came aboard the ship about two minutes ago. All, and I mean all, of her luggage has been searched, scanned and found clean. Dad was right to think an implant would attempt to come aboard. Do you want us to arrest her now?" Susan asked.

"Not at this time. Victoria and I will handle her from here on out. Make sure no one else knows except Doctor Kremmel. I'll report the incident to Gen. Braxton personally," Cat replied.

"Will do! Out" Susan confirmed.

Cat immediately contacted John Braxton. Victoria and John were having lunch with General Klinedecker and his wife at their quarters. They approved Cat's plan. She couldn't help feeling excited about her first case under the newly formed Intelligence Branch.

Thomas Kasill was one step behind Agent Maxwell thanks to an anonymous phone tip. The caller alerted him to the name and location of a homeless person recently interviewed by the FBI. It didn't take long for Thomas to arrive near the vicinity the tipster identified. Driving around a couple blocks, he found a disheveled elderly black man, fitting the description, crawling into a dumpster behind a restaurant.

"Hey, you Sam Casey?" Thomas inquired as the man's head momentarily bobbed above the edge of the rusty green dumpster. The stench of the dumpster's contents was so strong Thomas found it difficult to speak.

The gaunt face never even looked at him as he disappeared into the dumpster again. "Depends on who's askin'!" a voice echoed.

"Thomas Kasill from the New York Daily Review. I understand you were interviewed by the FBI concerning the murder of Dr. Russell Long."

"What's it to ya?" Sam echoed tossing trash over his shoulder.

"Well, Sam, can you tell me what you told them?"

"Friends call me Sammy!"

"Sorry, Sammy. Can you please help me out?" Thomas asked again.

"We're not friends yet," Sammy gruffly retorted.

Thomas reached into his wallet and held a twenty-dollar bill over the edge of the dumpster. A wrinkly weathered hand reached up and snatched it away. There was a moment of silence.

"Okay, we're friends now. What do you want again?" Sammy asked as he continued to examine the bill.

"I'd like to know what you told the FBI," Thomas asked a bit annoyed at the game Sammy was playing.

Sammy finally leaned over the edge of the dumpster squinting his eyes with an air of suspicion. "That's classified. I need to see your ID?"

Thomas took out his wallet and handed Sammy his ID card. Sammy examined it front and back as carefully as if checking a lottery jackpot stub. Finally, Sammy handed it back. Like a fox, he carefully watched Thomas open his wallet, return the card and place the wallet into his hip pocket. While Thomas wasn't looking, Sam gave a little smirk and rolled his eyes.

"So, what can you tell me?" Thomas asked again. This time he produced a small pint bottle of whiskey from his trench coat and waved it in front of Sammy's face.

Sammy reeled away from the bottle expressing great indignation. "If ya want me to divulge classified information, you needs ta show more respect. I'm not some lowly street bum. I still have my dignity," he proudly declared thumping his chest.

"Sorry, Sammy. Forgive my bad manners my good friend. I should have known better," Thomas said apologetically. He produced a twenty-dollar bill out of his wallet and handed it to Sammy.

Sammy just glared at him as he negatively wagged his long boney finger.

Thomas added another twenty-dollar bill. Sammy again nodded disapproval while holding up five fingers. Thomas cringed as he pulled out three more twenty-dollar bills. "This ought to open up the classified vault don't you think?"

Sammy snatched the bills and stuffed them into his pants pocket. "OK! Now we're talking?" Sammy declared with delight.

He answered all of Thomas' questions concerning what he saw the night Dr. Long was murdered. Finally, Thomas asked, "Could you identify the woman if you saw her again?"

"Now you're askin' Top Secret stuff," Sammy said rubbing his scraggly chin.

Thomas sighed. Pulled out his wallet and produced three more twenties. Sam slyly held up ten fingers this time. "Sammy, you must come from a family of horse traders,"Thomas grumbled as he handed him two hundred dollar bills.

"Yep! Both my grand pappy and daddy were known far and wide as the best horse traders in the county," Sammy smiled puffing up his chest.

Thomas produced a picture of his sister and showed it to Sammy.

Once again Sammy shook his head. "Naw! That's not her. She looks more like your sister. The woman I saw was better lookin."

Thomas winced. He held up another photo of Loretta Sanchez. "OK, how about this woman?"

Sammy shook his head. "Nope, that's not her either. Say, the FBI had a better picture though. You fellas aren't working together are ya?"

"Not really, but we are after the same killer." Thomas said.

Sammy's eyes widened. "Say, that woman in the background looks a lot like her."

Thomas peered at the photo. "Are you sure it's her?"

Sammy scratched his head. "I'm not positive but she's as close as I've seen."

"Did the FBI show you her picture?" Thomas asked.

"Nope!" Sammy confidently replied.

Thomas shook his hand. "Thanks, Sammy, you've been a big help.

By the way, you weren't the tipster who called were you?" Thomas winked.

"Nah!" Sammy said sheepishly. "That was my buddy, Eli. You're the fella writes all them articles about Dr. Long's murder so I figured you'd be interested. I bet Eli I could get a hundred dollars outa you for my information."

Thomas smiled and shook his head. "You hustled me fair and square. Thanks again Sammy."

"By the ways, ya don't seem the whiskey type of fella. Ya care to make a small donation to the Sam Casey Charity Fund?"

Thomas laughed tossing Sammy the bottle. "Share that with Eli now!"

"Eli and I are real tight. We always share our good fortune." Sammy beamed.

Thomas could only shake his head in amazement as he drove away. *Used to be all you had to do was offer a bottle of cheap wine for information. Nowadays a twenty-dollar bill and a pint won't get you the time of day.*

Returning to his apartment, Thomas started reviewing his notes. Slowly a few more clues fell into place. Sitting on the couch with notes spread out on the coffee table, Thomas starred at them deep in thought.

In my gut, I know Dr. Sanchez is involved in the murder of Dr. Long, but why? The person Sammy picked out was a woman from the State Department that was present when he did the Sanchez interview. Sammy wasn't positive but it was enough to connect the dots. Who is she? Is she working with Dr. Sanchez or part of something bigger? I wonder if I can interview Gen. Braxton and his alien friends. I might pick some more clues.

Calls to FBI Headquarters and the White House Press Secretary got him nowhere. So, Thomas decided to go visit Press Secretary Melinda DuPont in person. He was surprised to find himself immediately ushered into her office.

Not likely a reporter gets this treatment every day, something's up.

"Mr. Kasill, welcome. Please have a seat. What brings you to the White House?" Melinda asked.

"As I'm sure you already know, I'm investigating the murder of Dr. Long. That investigation has led me to the alien issue. Not a single reporter has been allowed personal interviews with John Braxton or our off-world friends. I want to interview them and do the story nobody else has been allowed to do," Thomas stated.

"Going from space pirates, kidnapped aliens to Dr. Long's murder is quite a leap don't you think?" Melinda asked.

"Well, let's start with the fact I know who, within the administration leaked information about the aliens. I also know who they told and have evidence the same person was involved in killing Dr. Long. Why hasn't the FBI arrested anyone yet?" Thomas asked smiling as if he knew more than he was letting on.

"Impressive reporting," Melinda acknowledged. "You know withholding evidence in a murder could get you in a lot of trouble. I assume you want a deal for the information?" Melinda glared.

"I fork over my evidence. In return, I get access to General Braxton and the visitors and my paper's silence as long as we are allowed to break the story first."

"You know I don't have the authority to make any kind of deal."

"Then take me to who can," Thomas demanded.

Melinda grew pale. "Excuse me for a minute."

Melinda walked out of the room leaving Thomas alone to wonder what would happen next. When the door opened again Melinda was with a tall, athletic looking, female FBI agent in a black business suit. The look on her face told Thomas he was in deep trouble.

Silently, she took a position by the door with her hands folded in front of her. "Mr. Kasill, my name is Special Agent Maxine Maxwell of the FBI. I understand you are attempting to interfere in the investigation of Dr. Long's murder and trying to blackmail a government official."

"I… I wouldn't call it blackmail but…" Thomas stuttered in surprise before being cut off.

"Let me be very plain, you will tell me everything you know immediately," Agent Maxwell demanded. "If you refuse, it could be some time before anyone ever hears from you. Do you understand?"

"Hold on here. I know my rights. I don't have to tell you anything and you know it. Why don't you drop the strong-arm tactics and just back off?" Thomas retorted.

"I'm never friendly with terrorists, Mr. Kasill. Withholding information in a terrorist assassination makes you an accessory. Freedom of the press won't protect you from that and you know it."

"Do I get my deal or not?" Thomas demanded.

Maxine nodded. "I can recommend it but it's up to General Braxton if he wants to speak to you."

"OK!" sighed Thomas. "I have the same information you have according to Sam Casey. Dr. Sanchez's relationship with Dr. Long is well known in the beltway. However, Sammy identified a photo of a co-worker as the possible murderer. By the end of the day my paper will know her name. However, I do have information that leads me to suspect there is an alien connection that is far more troubling," Thomas declared.

"I see. What information do you have of this alien connection?"

"You mean to tell me you are unaware Dr. Sanchez's father claims the family was abducted by aliens? Why don't you ask her about it? I'm sure you won't learn much. She played dodgeball with me before she clammed up. Not the normal denial one would expect. If you want to know, read all about it in tomorrow's edition. It's sure to get lots of circulation."

Thomas was now playing his bluff and if they didn't buy into it soon he would be escorted out with an empty hat. It was time to stop talking and see if they believed enough of his story to assume there is more worth knowing.

Maxine and Melinda excused themselves from the room again. Thomas noted two Secret Service Agents were just outside the door.

Ms. DuPont escorted Maxine to the Oval Office. There a Secret Service agent checked Maxine's pass before allowing them to enter. President Leatham was at his desk. Sitting nearby were FBI Director Leon James and Chief of Staff Edward Cox.

"Well, what do you think of this reporter's information?" President Leatham asked.

"I think he's bluffing. He's hit a dead end and thinks if he mixes enough truth and innuendo, he can finagle an exclusive interview. On the other hand, he knows enough to seriously affect our investigation and throw every conspiracy nut into a panic followed by a press feeding frenzy."

"What if he really knows as much as he claims?" Director James asked.

He'll still accomplish the same thing if he prints it," Melinda reasoned. "Why not give him his wish?"

Edward Cox gave the president a wink. "Melinda has a good point. General Braxton is leaving in less than twelve hours. Mr. Kasill could arrive aboard the *Holcron Star* for the interviews and before he knows it, shanghaied into deep space for months."

"Great idea. Melinda, inform the young man and editor he gets his wish. Ed, make the arrangements with General Braxton and give him my deepest sympathies," the president smiled.

It was now thirty-six hours since John Braxton and the group of three ships returned to Earth. The prisoners were transferred and all the food, supplies, personnel, and equipment for the duct tape engineers were finally aboard. The final shuttle eased into the landing bay with a last-minute passenger. As Thomas stepped off the shuttle ramp, Jonathan Braxton greeted him.

"Welcome to the *Holcron Star*. I hope your flight was a pleasant one?" Jonathan said shaking his hand.

"Thank you! It was a better flight than last time I was aboard reporting on your wedding."

"Yes, we appreciated the great write up you gave us in the paper too. I'll escort you to your quarters and let you get settled. You're invited to join us for supper at 1800 hrs. in the Captain's Mess. We like to eat as a family whenever we can. By the way, you can watch our departure in one hour from the Observation Deck. It should be quite an impressive view."

"Departure?" Thomas asked completely surprised.

"Why from Earth, of course. You seem surprised. We were told you were joining us on this voyage. Didn't you know?" Jonathan asked.

"No, I asked for an interview with General Braxton, Ambassador Toburg and others and told I could take all the time I needed to do them. In return, I wouldn't go public until the arrests were made. The White House promised I would get to break the story first. They lied to me. Those dirty rotten..."

"They didn't lie to you," Jonathan interrupted. "You just didn't ask for all the details. That's your fault. You'll get your interviews just as the president promised. In fact, you'll get almost unlimited access to every part of the ship except the No Lone Zones.

'You're the only reporter on this mission so you get to break the story first just as the White House promised. A politician actually keeping his word. Amazing isn't it? How lucky can a reporter get anyway?"

"You're a sarcastic son of a gun, aren't you?" Thomas grumbled.

"I can't help it. I was born that way. Dad tried breaking me of the habit but gave up before resorting to violence," Jonathan teased.

"I can see why! Which way to my quarters?" Thomas asked resigning himself to his situation.

Two hours later, Thomas joined the Braxton and Toburg families for dinner. He was surprised at the closeness of the two families, especially David and Siyana. He was also pleased at the candidness of the answers to his questions. There were some questions John had no information to offer. Thomas sensed John was being honest and let it slide for the time being. In the end, everyone provided more information than he expected.

Thomas quickly realized during the interview the situation in space was far more dangerous than the people on Earth were told. All the tight security about what John Braxton and the alien allies were doing was meant to prevent a global panic. The survival and future of billions of people on several worlds truly rested on the success of this mission. He was also shocked at the hint of an independent colony on Terra. It was a bonus tidbit of information he hadn't expected.

After Thomas returned to his quarters, the full depth and breadth of the story struck him. *I have the most exclusive story in history. All I have to do is stay alive to report it.*

From the bridge of *Holcron Star,* Jonathan Braxton watched the shuttle depart for the *Fire Hawk* transferring its last crew member. Jonathan began to chuckle thinking back on his final instructions to the shuttle pilot. *Captain Reagan, welcome to space!*

The shuttle began to pitch, yaw and roll as the pilot over compensated on the flight controls. He leisurely recovered and when the shuttle was properly aligned for docking, the green light on the landing approach program began blinking. That allowed him to engage the autopilot for a programed landing in the hangar bay.

For the single passenger, Captain "Black" Jack Reagan was gripping the arms of his seat so tight his knuckles were white and every muscle in his body taunt. Jack began to take a reality check.

What were you thinking when you volunteered for this assignment? We're in the most unforgiving environment in the universe. We're so green, we glow in the dark. God help us, please!

Finally, the shuttle landed and Jack stepped onto the *Fire Hawk's* hangar deck. He looked around in amazement. He snapped a salute as Admiral MacKay entered the hangar and welcomed him.

Admiral MacKay returned the salute. "Jack, so nice to have you aboard."

Jack smiled, "I can hardly believe I'm here alive. That pilot is insane. What's he doing at the controls of a spacecraft? What have you gotten into and why isn't the Navy running this?"Jack sputtered.

"Stephen began laughing. It was the crew's way of welcoming you. He's actually one of our best instructor pilots. As to your other question, the long story short is the Cassarian Ambassador didn't trust foreign military on his ship. At the time, there were severe trust issues. He did trust John Braxton so here we are. One third of our crew are Cassarians and Holcrons and are very experienced. They will train the rest of our crew made up of U.S. and British military volunteers. I'll take you to your quarters, your things will be brought to you shortly."

Jonathan walked over to the command chair and noticed his father starring into deep space. "Watch where you're going or you could get sucked into a black hole."

John shook his head and smiled, "I was just trying to relax and think a bit."

"Thinking of what?" Jonathan asked.

"Of that dirty trick, you just pulled, Be careful, we can't afford to lose crew or shuttles, understand?" John admonished.

Jonathan nodded understanding.

John continued. "However, the pilot you picked was a great choice."

"Yes, sir! About the relaxing part of your thought, I'd rather do my relaxing on a warm sandy beach with Katrina, than on a starship wondering what could possibly go wrong next," Jonathan deadpanned.

John gave Jonathan a wry smile. "Guess I'll put some excitement into your sorry life. Plot a course for the Mentarus system. Once Aycana verifies it, send the coordinates to the *Fire Hawk* and *Halfling* for a 1500 hr. departure. After that, run practice fire and hull breach drills for the next hour. Everyone must know what to do blindfolded before we go into combat."

Jonathan's eyes lit up with excitement. "Yippee ki-yay! Let the fun begin!"

When Aycana came to the bridge to verify his course, she checked her data pad. After the ships took up the new heading, Jonathan sounded the fire alarm throughout the ship announcing the drill. It didn't take long before the new crew members discovered the Braxton definition of "fun."

The duct tape engineers were eating lunch at their usual table on the observation deck taking turns discussing different topics or problems. Henry pulled out a data pad and opened it to a short video of the Outsider ship encounter.

"Well guys, today's topic is the Outsider ship. What do we know and what weaknesses can we exploit?" Henry asked.

Dexter shrugged his shoulders. "All I ever got to see of it was the shimmering sensor image of it."

"I was on it once with Captain Gath," Deze announced.

"What? You never told us about this? Henry chided.

"I did tell General Braxton but I was ordered not to tell anyone else," Deze replied. "He wanted us to focus on the capture of the *Holcron Star.*"

"Okay, so we now have the ship, fill us in," Dexter grumbled.

Deze proceeded to tell them every detail he could remember but it only led to more questions and Deze could not answer any of them.

"Let's go look at the sensor data in the ship's computer. Maybe it can give us a clue," Dexter proposed.

The trio didn't even finish their lunch as they rushed off to the bridge. A few minutes later the bridge was invaded by the duct tape engineers.

"Hey, son! I mean General Braxton, or General, sir!" Henry stammered out in excitement.

"Dad, I'm forever your son and you're not in the military. Calling me son is OK," John replied. "I can tell by the gleam in your eyes something's up. What is it?"

"Sir, we need a copy of the archived sensor data of Outsider contacts," Dexter said.

"I see. Knock yourselves out," John said pointing at the computer terminal.

Dexter scratched his head. "Why would I do that?"

Henry grabbed Dexter's arm. "He's pulling your leg." "Never mind. It's just an expression," Henry quipped.

"Remember I told you about being on their ship?" Deze asked.

"Yes, I do. I discussed it with Admiral MacKay and Gavin. We decided to be on the lookout for it. When the *Halfling* did encounter it, they had no way to give us a heads up of their encounter without possibly giving away who we were. When we did encounter it, we decided to play innocent to avoid suspicion," John said. "What about it?"

"We're investigating a way to defeat the Outsiders," Deze said.

"Molly, please give them access to the archived sensor contacts with the Outsiders and let them copy whatever they think might be useful."

"Yes, sir!" Molly replied.

"You three can work on this project so long as it doesn't interfere with the duties of the crew. If you find a possible solution, report back to me directly. Understand?"

"Yes, sir!" Henry and Dexter replied. Once they had all the data from the computer archive they could collect, they rushed off to their workshop.

Admiral Dever was extremely frustrated by the series of events since his rendezvous with Gavin. First, two pirate ships attacked him. Fortunately, he was able to destroy one corvette and severely damage the light cruiser. Rather than surrender, the pirates scuttled their ship forcing Admiral Dever to spend more precious time recovering survivors. However, his flagship sustained serious damaged too. He was forced to return to Holcron. Since there was no other ship available, the admiral had to wait three weeks to complete repairs.

Admiral Dever realized the need to avoid any further contact with pirates until his mission to Cassaria and Katusium were accomplished. Another delay occurred when a distress call was received from a heavy freighter whose life support system was failing. It took two more days to repair the life support system. In the end, it took six weeks before the *HSS Torrent* finally made it to Cassaria.

King Adrian Toburg stood at the head of a small procession of staff and politicians waiting to greet his friend and most important ally. As he strode up the red carpet, Admiral Dever was taken aback by his friend's appearance. Instead of the strong, vibrant, energetic friend he remembered from their last meeting, Usus saw a gaunt, weak shell of a man who looked many years beyond his actual age. The strain of losing his four beloved children and the challenges of the past months had taken their toll on his health.

"Adrian, what have you done to yourself?" Usus cried as he hugged his closest friend. "I grieve your loss almost as much as you, but destroying yourself is no way to honor them. God will truly work things out for the better."

"I know they can't be dead. I just know it. The strain of the pirate situation and domestic politics is just more than I can bear anymore," Adrian sighed.

"Give yourself time to heal from this tragedy, Adrian. You are a great king and your people need you," Usus urged.

Adrian nodded as he placed his arm on his friend's shoulder. "As always, you are right. So, what brings you to Cassaria?"

"I decided to tag along with a couple inspectors from the Inspector General's Office for a routine Embassy inspection. While they are busy, I thought I might spend some time with you and Queen Pella, time permitting, of course?

'I also have the sad business of presenting this to you. We were attacked by two pirate ships and managed to destroy them. When searching the wreckage this necklace was found. I recognized it immediately and thought I should return it. Is it not Aycana's?" Usus asked.

As he handed it to Adrian, Usus again gave an embrace of comfort.

As he did so, Usus softly whispered in his ear, "Invite me to your home tonight and I will explain who really gave me the necklace. You are surrounded by traitors this very moment."

Adrian looked at the necklace, clutching it in his hands. "Oh God!" he cried out. "I feared this moment most of all. Please join us for supper. Tell Pella what you have told me. I can't bear tell her myself. I don't think I could find the words…" he feigned.

"Yes, of course, Adrian. I am honored. I need to take care of some embassy business first then join you. We will break the news together."

"Yes, yes, I will see you later then," King Toburg sighed.

King Toburg, now weak and overcome with grief could hardly walk. Admiral Dever took Adrian's arm to support him as they walked to the King's limousine. Along the way, Adrian clutched the necklace to his chest weeping inconsolably.

As the royal limousine drove off, General Nix Tayer rushed over to Admiral Dever with the customary greeting. Admiral Dever hid his feelings for the man he always secretly despised. Usus admitted Nix Tayer was rather handsome, tall, medium build with dark hair and sporting a flawless goatee. The eye patch over his left eye gave him a dashing appearance. However, Usus could not concede General Tayer was a hero of two battles against the pirates. It was rather pirate incompetence that decided the battles rather than his skills as a warrior leader.

Because he was the boyhood friend of Adrian, Usus

tolerated him. Tayer was a decent staff officer but Usus knew the truth, Nix was one of the most vain, self-promoting weasels Usus ever had the displeasure of meeting. His constant self-aggrandizing never quite rang true. Real heroes don't brag about their bravery every chance they get. With Gavin's information, it was now obvious the pirate victories were staged to make sure of his rise in power.

"Admiral Dever. Welcome to Cassaria. I hope your stay is a pleasant one," General Tayer announced with a limp handshake.

"General Tayer, it's never pleasant to tell a great friend his precious children were senselessly slaughtered," Usus admonished. "Nevertheless, I accept your welcome. I fear the queen will take this news harder than the king. There will be many tears shed in the Toburg home tonight."

General Tayer nodded agreement as he stroked his beard. "We are deeply concerned over Adrian's decline in health and personal loss. I fear he will be hospitalized and forced to resign if he doesn't recover soon. The council is very concerned."

It was all Admiral Dever could do to restrain his contempt. *How did this back stabbing idiot of a lackey ever become an advisor to the king? My stars, I don't know which is worse, his lack of military prowess or his fatuous vanity.*

"Well, I must be off to the embassy. Nice to see you again," Usus feigned before quickly entering his embassy car.

"Driver, to the embassy straight way. I don't think I can stand another minute of feigned politeness from that idiot,"Usus growled. Like a train in motion, the Holcron convoy sped off with its escort.

"Driver, drive slowly so I can enjoy the view. This estate is a planetary jewel," Usus declared.

"Yes, sir!"

Admiral Dever's limousine eased through the main gates of

the Toburg Estate and along the winding driveway. The beauty of the mansion, manicured grounds, and the largest collection of Cassaria's greatest carved statues always mesmerized Usus. The magnificently maintained flowerbeds, artfully trimmed shrubbery and hedges presented a masterpiece of gardening in their own right. The mansion was one of the greatest pieces of architecture on Cassaria yet not Cassarian in design at all.

Adrian's first wife, Alice, oversaw the design of the mansion and grounds. It stood in sharp contrast to the usually sterile white structures typical on Cassaria. The hand carved white marble of the finest quality was used to make the three-story structure.There were also many wonderfully carved marble statues, hanging gardens and balconies, stunning fountains and waterfalls that gave the whole view a wonderland-like effect on residents and visitors alike.

As he walked up the rose-colored marble steps, he was reminded of why King Adrian insisted on living on his estate rather than the state owned Royal Executive Manor.

Becoming a self-made billionaire before he entered military service, Adrian refused his military pay. His sense of honor, duty and patriotism just would not permit him to accept the people's money.

Adrian even refused a stipend offered by the legislature to help defray the expenses of his estate security. Yes, he still lived more richly than most Cassarians, but he refused to live off the hard-working citizens. He insisted on paying his own way in life.

He loved his country, and would sacrifice anything to protect the people. Trusting God to protect him, Adrian was a lion in battle. Usus recalled once after a battle one of his generals took him to task for taking so many risks.

Adrian stood his ground. "I fight for the people. My life means nothing if I fail in discharging my duty. It's by God's grace I win or lose. I fight with the prayer and hope God will spare my children from the hands of evil men and allow them to build a better world."

Usus couldn't wait to reveal God's providence.

When Usus reached the door, a servant greeted him and ushered him inside. Usus was surprised at the servant's appearance. The look just wasn't right. The servant's physique more resembled an elite Cassarian Space Ranger than a butler. He appeared in perfect physical condition, the typical ranger shaved head and the movement and alertness of a Cassarian Red Wolf.

The ultimate giveaway was the slight bulge underneath the right side of his jacket. It unmistakably hid a blaster pistol only noticeable to a trained eye. As Usus followed him to the living room another bodyguard stood by the door. Usus noted the obvious increase in security since his last visit.

"Usus, please come in and make yourself comfortable," Pella announced. "What would you like to drink? The usual iced Bocar tea?"

"Yes, Pella. That would be just fine," Usus said, taking a seat on the sofa. Pella looked at the servant across the room. He nodded and bowed as he backed out of the room closing the door behind him.

"Adrian is taking care of a small problem and will join us in a minute. Supper should be ready in about an hour so we have plenty of time to talk and revisit old times," Pella announced with her always gracious smile.

The living room was spacious with two interior walls and two exterior walls. The two exterior walls had large double glass doors framed with flowing lace curtains leading to a beautifully kept courtyard and swimming pool.

There were several chairs, sofas and small tables with lamps around the room. Along one interior wall was the door Usus used and three large illuminated display cases over eight feet high filled with some of the rarest pieces of Cassarian pottery, carvings and artifacts.

Four finely crafted wooden bookcases, eight-feet tall by twelve feet long, lined the walls around the room displaying an almost priceless book collection. Most of the books were Cassarian classics, the majority being original works by the finest authors and thinkers of the last five hundred years.

Centered on the other interior wall was a large fireplace and to the right of it, a door leading into Adrian's den. The rest of the wall was decorated with paintings of several generations of the Toburg family, especially the children whom Adrian and Pella cherished. Also, hanging about the room were artworks from some of the finest painters in Cassarian history.

Adrian burst into the room from the den with a mood far different from the one displayed when the admiral first arrived. "Usus, my dearest friend, welcome."

As Usus went to rise from his seat, the king motioned him to remain seated and relaxed.

"Pella, my dear, I hope you haven't been entertaining this rascal by yourself for too long," Adrian teased as he leaned over to give her a kiss on the cheek. "Usus has some very important news to share with us."

He reached into his pocket and pulled out Aycana's necklace. Adrian handed it to his wife. Pella almost fainted upon recognizing it.

"Usus, where did you get this?" Pella demanded clutching it to her breast. "It belongs to Aycana. I would know it anywhere. She was wearing it the day she left for Tigra with her brother and sisters."

"Six weeks ago, I was given it by Gavin aboard your transport he now calls the *Halfling*. Your children are all in good health and, for the time being, safe with special friends.

'I tried to come here sooner but was attacked by pirate

ships and forced to put in for repairs."

"Our precious gems are safe!" Adrian shouted with joy. "I knew they were alive! I just knew it!"

"If you met with him why didn't they return with you or at least send us a message sooner?" Pella inquired anxiously.

"Gavin told me if I gave you the necklace you would believe what I am about to report is true. To be honest with you, at first I could hardly believe his story but the truth is on his side."

"This is the most secure place on the planet for us to talk. Please tell us every detail. Leave nothing out. I will know the truth when I hear it," Adrian pleaded.

For the next two hours Usus repeated everything Gavin told him.

He told them of their capture, attempted escape, the downing of their transport, and the children's rescue by an Earthling named John Braxton and his family. He described their subsequent adventures including the capture of the *Holcron Star*. Usus also explained the discovery of large deposits of zannite crystals and of a galactic conspiracy.

Every key conspirator on Cassaria was named. He told them about the pending Quadas Day coup and invasion. Usus revealed the Tigrans were planning to betray the Katusians and the Gamoran pirates. He explained that wasn't the end of the treachery. The pirates were secretly in league with a far more powerful and dangerous foe called the Outsiders.

The admiral also explained the Outsider plan to turn the tables on the Tigrans and take over their whole region of the galaxy. Lastly, Usus revealed Braxton's plan for defeating the Tigrans then the Outsiders.

The king and queen were so engrossed in the report; Pella decided to have supper served to them on trays in the living room. However, the king and queen were so fixated on every word Usus spoke that no one thought to eat. By the time Usus finished answering all their questions it was very late, the food cold and barely touched.

"Usus, I beg of you do not spend a night here on Cassaria. What you say I know is true. That means you are not safe here either. Eliminating you would strengthen their hand and further isolate me. Go directly to your shuttle and leave Cassaria while you can.

'Finish your mission to Katusium and convince them of the impending betrayal. I'm sure they will listen to you. I will contact you again soon. Now go my friend," Adrian urged.

An hour later Admiral Dever left Cassarian orbit heading for Katusium.

After Adrian saw his friend off, he returned to the living room. Another visitor was already waiting next to the fireplace with a grim demeanor. He wore a plain Cassarian admiral's tunic, void of everything except for his rank and name. The gentleman was in his late 50's, short in stature, wire rimmed glasses, and slight of build. In fact, except for his red hair and mustache mixed with some gray, it would be difficult to pick him out of a crowd if out of uniform.

It was easy to underestimate Admiral Amboy Quanto. Except for the king and those who served under him, most military and political leaders did just that. The admiral relished being obscure. It allowed him to see and move about in a hostile environment virtually unnoticed and unfettered. The one person who trusted him most was also the one person who needed him now more than ever before.

"Did you hear everything Admiral Dever reported?" Adrian asked.

"Yes, his information fills in just about all the blanks in the conspiracy puzzle," Amboy said.

Adrian gave Amboy a slight bow of gratitude. "You have

been right all along about the conspiracy. I am greatly indebted to you, Amboy."

"I am dreadfully sorry General Tayer is so deeply involved," Amboy conceded.

"As a person, I find him ego centric but his loyalty I thought unquestionable. Since you spoke to me of the plot you uncovered, I realized a side of him I never noticed before. He craves power but has no clue how to use it," Adrian concluded.

'I have no doubt Council Elder Glaxis fears they might not be able to control him in the end.Tayer is not the biggest threat though. Council Assistant Quiller is the most cunning and dangerous of the conspirators. He trusts no one and I'm sure has plans to eliminate Tayer when the time comes. Why not let them think they are secure in their folly? If we foil the plotters at the right moment, we can roll up the whole lot of them," Admiral Quanto proposed.

Adrian rubbed his chin for a reflective moment then nodded in agreement, "Good point. We need to bag them all at the same time or the plot could still succeed in aiding the Tigran attack. We don't know everyone supporting them yet.

'This is what we will do…"

Well after the king and queen were fast asleep, two figures secretly prowled the Toburg estate surveying for security weaknesses. The security patrols were spread very thin and gaps existed in their patrols and camera sweeps. The Royal Guard consisted of about one hundred personal bodyguards used solely for protecting the king and royal family.

Domestic security was the responsibility of the Planetary Police Magistrate who, in turn, answered directly to the Council of Elders. The planetary police were responsible for all domestic law enforcement, and planetary security matters. Except for the King's Royal Guard, the military was responsible for security of military facilities and off world interests. In effect, the Royal Guard was totally dependent on the politically controlled police for information and threat assessment.

According to the Council, this arrangement was necessary to prevent the military from intimidating and alarming the public. What it really did was consolidate power within the council and weaken the King's traditional role as protector.

If anything went wrong on Cassaria, the king would be viewed as inept for failing to protect the people and the Council would be seen as the last line of defense that saves the day.

The two shadowy figures discovered there was only one route for King Toburg to travel to and from his office at the headquarters on base. There were also numerous places for ambush. It would be too obvious to attempt a coup at the military base where the king carried out his duties, but off base, he was an easy target.

As the sun came up, the shadowy team retreated into hiding.

Next to hangar 1 was a machine shop the crew nicknamed the Dark Pit. It was the home of the duct tape engineers and it didn't take long for the shop to reflect their personality. In various parts of the shop were workbenches covered with projects in various stages of completion. Everything a trio of inventors could need or want was at their fingertips. The smoke and aroma of burnt electrical wiring hung in the air around Dexter's workbench.

Henry was in the office and looked up in time to see a smoking electrical box fly past the office window. As he opened the office door a wiring harness just missed him and bounced off the doorframe.

"Hey, Dex! What's the matter?" Henry asked.

"I'm trying to come up with a way to circumvent the stealth technology of the Outsiders. Nothing's working." Dexter replied angrily.

Henry scratched his head. "So, what ya tried so far?"

"I've tried radioactive detector triggers and over twenty-five different ion wave triggering devices. Nothing works," Dexter sighed.

"Take a break and think outside the box?" Henry urged.

Dexter grumbled, "How about a manually operated drone packed with explosives to ram the ship."

"Ya got a good idea but what if what ya see is a projection and not the real thing?" Henry asked.

"Didn't think of that," Dexter nodded.

"The other problem is we don't have the right kind of drones nor materials to make them," Dexter conceded.

"What's that really tellin' us?" Henry asked.

"It tells us we have an enemy we can't destroy!" Dexter declared pounding his fist on the bench. "If we can't destroy them, don't you think we have a problem?"

"Dex, you're so obsessed with killin' everyone, ya can't see the forest for the trees," Henry said tapping his forehead.

"What?" Dexter asked confused.

"What I'm sayin' is there's more than one way to skin a cat," Henry chided.

Dexter sctatched his chin. "You lost me! What do forests, trees and dead cats got to do with killing the enemy?"

Henry sighed. "Dex, I've told ya before, ya gotta get rid of your hate. It makes ya blind. Hate is like flying a spaceship into the sun. Once it snares ya it takes ya where ya don't want to go."

"Where did you learn that?" Dexter asked.

"God taught me the hard way," Henry confessed. " Get out from hidin' behind your mask. Ya can't see or hear what he's tellin' ya."

"So, what's God telling you?" Dexter chided.

"I was blind but now I see," Henry smiled.

"What kind of gibberish is that?" Dexter grumbled.

"We just need to come up with a way to see 'em. My son and the *Holcron Star* can take care of the rest. Look at the space mine I just designed?" Henry said handing Dex the blueprints.

"Ah, now I understand," Dexter said.

"We're gonna flummox 'em, confound 'em, and confuse 'em till they can't see straight," Henry smiled. "Where did we store those empty barrels? We're gonna need a few for prototypes."

Just then the Dark Pit's door opened with Deze pushing a tool cart.

"I fixed Shuttle 1's power flux problem," Deze announced. "What's up?"

"We are going to flummox the Outsiders,"Dexter dryly answered.

"Now you're talking. What's a flummox?" Deze asked scratching his head.

It was midnight and the observation lounge was nearly empty except for a few crewmembers engaged in conversation and games. David and Siyana were sitting on a sofa playing a board game when Susan and Khem joined them.

"Hey, how's it going?" Susan asked.

"We were just finishing a game and about to turn in. What are you two doing?" David asked.

"We had to work late to finish up some lab work and thought we would grab some ice cream. Want to join us?" Khem offered.

Siyana looked at David and nodded. "Sure, why not?"

After raiding the food court to make their own ice cream concoctions, they returned to their table.

"So, what have you been doing lately?" Susan asked

David.

"Aycana's training Jonathan, myself and a few others as shuttle pilots in ground assault tactics. She's been working us to death."

"Well, if certain pilots weren't so slow in learning tactics you would have been done by now," Siyana teased.

"That's not true. Aycana says I'm the best pilot she has ever trained," David said defensively.

"I hate to burst your bubble, but you and Jonathan are the first and only pilots she's ever trained," Siyana laughed.

"OK, you got me. I surrender!" David replied holding his hands up. Everyone burst out laughing.

"David just might turn out to be a very good combat shuttle pilot. That is if he doesn't let it go to his head and get himself killed. I would be very unhappy if that happened," Siyana said winking an eye at David.

"Gee, sis. I think she cares for me," David teased.

"That's what I mean you lug head. In space, small mistakes add up to big consequences. You get your mind off your flying for even a split second you'll be dead in a flash," Siyana warned.

"Don't worry about David. The survival instinct runs strong in our family," Susan reassured her.

"I sure hope so. I really don't look forward to training another ship's pilot. This crash course stuff is really wearing me thin."

David gasped in mock surprise, "Gee, just when I thought we were getting along so well, I find out I'm stressing you out."

"Is there no letting up with him?" Siyana sighed.

Susan chuckled, "Just be glad Jonathan isn't here. There's no shutting him up once he gets on a roll."

Khem broke into the discussion. "To change the subject,

do you think we will come across the Outsiders again?"

David swallowed a bite of his banana split. "Nobody knows for sure. Dad wants to avoid them if possible for now. Why do you ask?"

"Susan and I are formulating a series of experiments testing how they communicate with each other and the implants. To do that we need a couple outsider test subjects. We suspect the Outsiders are capable of using telepathy with the implants," Khem said.

"Do the Outsiders have them too?" Siyana asked.

"If people with implants can communicate with others then it stands to reason Outsiders also have the devices," Susan said. "Of course, we won't know for sure until we capture one or get a body to examine.

'Only Deze and Capt. Gath know anything and that is limited to what they saw and experienced aboard their ship. Captain Gath was the only one to leave the shuttle. He was directed into a room and sat at a table waiting for someone to meet with him. He claims they rendered him unconscious. Later he regained consciousness still alone. The voice over the intercom said he could leave and thanked him for the meeting," Khem said.

"I bet that was when they injected the implant," Siyana guessed.

"Most likely. What I can't understand is why they wouldn't reveal themselves to him. There has to be some reason for the odd behavior. We'll figure it out," Khem pledged.

CHAPTER 16

The longer John Braxton endured the exercise briefing the angrier he became. The embarrassed team leaders, pilots and other key people sensed it too. The practice assault on the Mentarus moon was a disaster. First, the shuttle pilots did not follow the approach plan nor lay covering fire for each other as they simulated off-loading their troops. There was little coordination between the shuttle pilots and the aerial controllers. One collision was barely avoided when two shuttles ignored the controller and attempted to land in the same undesignated area. Because the plan was not properly followed the element of surprise was lost and shuttles were simulated destroyed. General Braxton was relieved when Admiral MacKay finished his briefing. John heard enough to know the root of the problem. Standing up he made eye contact with every person in the briefing room. As if on cue, Jonathan and David, sensing their father's anger, slid down in their seats realizing they'd let him down too.

"Thank you, Admiral MacKay, for the painfully honest and detailed analysis.

'Folks, had this been a real battle, we'd all be dead. I expect better discipline from our pilots. All of you pilots are from different worlds and are accustomed to different rules and procedures. All that is out the air lock, am I understood?" John growled.

"Yes, sir!" everyone shouted in reply.

"That was weak. We must fight as one. Am I understood?" John growled again.

This time the walls of the conference room reverberated as everyone shouted at the top of their lungs, "Yes, sir!"

"That's better. I was beginning to think some of you

wanted to die.

Listen, You're all excellent pilots on your home worlds. I know what we are attempting to do has not been done in recent memory. That is precisely why we are doing it.

No one is expecting the sky to fall on them like a thunderclap. It has got to shock the living daylights out of them with brutal overwhelming violence. It is how we will all survive. We are going to be outnumbered. Transitioning from space combat to ground combat requires critical timing, fearless reentry control and precision navigation. We don't land troops where they need to be, they die. Shuttles don't support each other with aerial cover, we die. Pilots think their job is done after unloading troops, we die. We are not just fighting to save Cassaria, Earth, Katusium or Holcron. One falls they all fall." John paused to let the point sink in.

"The blame rests on my shoulders. Obviously, I failed to ensure everyone clearly understood their mission and the need to follow it with exact precision and timing. I promise you I will not make that mistake again.

'All team leaders and crews will review their assignments, verify their nav-points and brief me on their flight execution in eight hours. We'll resume rehearsal tomorrow until it goes like clockwork. Everyone will do his or her duty flawlessly. No exceptions, no excuses, am I understood?"

"Yes, sir!" everyone shouted.

After the briefing, Stephen MacKay took John aside. "John, many of them haven't flown in a year or more. They will come around, but push them you must. I understand a space assault hasn't been attempted in over a hundred years by the other worlds and on Earth it has never been attempted. It is all new territory."

John nodded agreement. "I know. I have faith in them but this fiasco was my fault. I let them down."

"I'm sure you will make many more mistakes. Even the greatest generals and admirals made mistakes. Just don't beat yourself over it. Learn from the experience and move on," Admiral MacKay advised patting John on the shoulder.

"Thanks for the advice," John said nodding agreement.

After the briefing, John visited sick bay to check up on an experiment Khem and Susan were working on.

Passing the aid station, John saw Katrina treating some hand burns on one of the cooks.

"Hi, Katrina! How's my favorite daughter-in-law today?" John asked.

"What do you mean? I'm your only daughter-in-law!" Katrina replied a bit embarrassed.

"Well, see, you have the position all locked up." John teased.

"Things are a little slow today, but that is always good. It gives us more training and research time. Susan and Khem are in the lab if you want to see them," Katrina said with an upbeat smile.

"Thanks! See you later," John smiled.

When John entered the lab, he was surprised. On one of the computer screens was a heart shaped note with a birthday greeting from Susan. Across the room, Khem and Susan were intently studying a microscope screen and didn't seem to notice him.

"Well, I see you two have buried the hatchet," John observed starring at the screen.

"Oh, Dad! Hi! How's it going?" Susan said startled by his appearance.

"I thought I'd drop by and see how your research is going on the spinal bug? I'm not interrupting, am I?"

"No!" Khem replied. "Susan found out it was my birthday and wanted to cheer me up. I understand it is an Earth custom."

"In some places," John said with a feigned stern look. "How about your research?"

Khem shook his head. "Still nothing, everything we do to remove or kill the implant device in computer simulations result in the death or paralysis of the victim.

'The implant device we used was taken from one of our dead. It was the only one we had to test with. We discovered the one nonworking implant in one of our victims failed to activate at the time of insertion. It explains why she is still alive.

'We have also learned the device not only allows the victims to communicate with each other telepathically but directs their behavior in a very subliminal way. They are unaware they are being manipulated."

Susan interrupted. "I suspected the device is actually a living cell we have never encountered before."

Khem continued. "I think she's right and we have begun more in-depth testing to find out. We are also working on a device that can emit a very high-pitched sound wave. In effect, it shatters the implant device before it can self-destruct. It would require the victim not be aware of what is about to happen and the risk of being lethal is obviously very high."

"I assume asking for volunteers isn't going to happen?" John asked.

"Precisely!" Susan replied.

"I see. Thus, a moral dilemma I'm just not going to act on. It is incumbent for you two find a suitable solution." John said.

As John left the lab, Susan followed him down the short hallway. "Dad, can I talk to you for a second?"

"Sure?" John said.

Susan smiled. "I just want you to know Khem and I really have buried the hatchet."

"Well, that's good," John said with a smile.

"What I'm saying is our relationship is starting to change. Mom says I need to go slow and make sure this is what I want."

"Sounds like wise advice. Being isolated and working closely together has its plusses and minuses. Please keep us in the loop and make sure you don't get in over your head. Emotions can cloud one's vision, even for the best of us. I assume you told him how we do things?"

"We talked about it last night. He wants to talk with you very soon."

"Good! Why don't you invite Khem to supper tonight?"John said.

"Thanks, Dad, I will." Susan kissed her father on the cheek and with a wink returned to the lab like she was walking on a cloud.

Susan rejoined Khem still studying a sample under his microscope. "I assume you spoke to your father about us?"

"Yup! You're invited to join us for supper tonight. He said he looks forward to a meeting of the minds as he calls it." Susan smiled.

John was once again on his way to the bridge when a fire alarm sounded. "Explosion in hangar bay 1! Emergency teams respond!" Jonathan announced over the PA network.

"Bridge, I'm on the way to Hangar 1," John said as he stepped into the elevator.

Stepping through the hangar hatch, John froze in shock. In the middle of the hangar bay, were four beer kegs. One keg was split open and smoke coming out of a small box mounted on the top. Nearby stood Henry, Deze and Dexter unhurt but covered in black soot and dripping in a green, glowing goo. The goo was also splattered all over a large area of the hangar deck and oozing down one side of the *Halfling*.

Gavin appeared from inside the *Halfling*'s cargo bay. A glob of florescent goo oozed from the hull onto the ramp as he stepped out. Losing his footing, Gavin slid down the ramp, crumpling up in a heap on the hangar deck.

John was speechless. The fire and medic response teams right behind him rushed over to assist. Gavin was shaken and bruised but now lay haplessly covered in goo. The death-defying trio of duct tape engineers looked at each other then at John.

"What's going on here?" John demanded.

"We're sorry for the mess, John. We were about to test some space mines designed to expose cloaked ships. One apparently had a defective triggering device. We really are sorry!" Henry pleaded as he stood fidgeting. Black soot and glowing goo covered him head to toe.

"I told you there was too much propellant in the tank!" Dexter said glaring at Deze.

"That wasn't the problem. It was your motion sensor. It's too sensitive," Deze argued back.

"Enough! You were conducting an unauthorized experiment and could have gotten people injured." John fumed as he called two security personnel over. "Security, supervise these three as they clean up this mess. You are to ensure they jettison the remainder of their experiments. After they are done, escort them to the brig where they are to remain for 24 hours."

"Yes, sir!" the security officer answered.

Henry started to say something but John cut him off.

"Not now, Dad. Not now!" John growled as he turned and left the hangar.

Deze looked at Henry. "Is General Braxton upset with us?"

"That ain't the word for it," Henry said sheepishly lowering his head. "That ain't the word for it at all."

Special Agent Maxine Maxwell and her partner, Special

Agent Bill Wilson, just replaced the surveillance team when Dr. Sanchez left her apartment for her usual taxi ride to work. This time the taxi took a different route than usual. Fortunately, the driver was an agent with a bug and GPS device. Maxine followed a few cars behind for several miles before the taxi stopped in a large suburban park with numerous jogging trails.

Maxine parked nearby and followed on foot at a distance. Wilson stayed with the vehicle.

Dr. Sanchez took a leisurely walk down a short trail to an area where several trails intersected near a small pond filled with a flock of ducks and surrounded with several benches. Loretta stopped to feed the ducks some bread crumbs. She then paused for a drink at a fountain before returning to the taxi. Everything seemed so innocent but it was oh so out of character. Dr. Sanchez did nothing randomly.

Maxine was dumbfounded. She messaged Wilson to follow Dr. Sanchez and call for backup to assist her. Carefully Maxine solwly looked around the area. *Dr. Sanchez does nothing randomly. Her life revolves around a mental checklist. Nothing is done without purpose. Something just happened and I missed it.*

Maxine retraced Dr. Sanchez's movement through the park. There was nothing obvious. She fed the ducks and drank from a fountain. That had to be it. Walking over to the fountain, Maxine looked it over carefully. Underneath on one side near the knob was a small button sized object magnetically stuck next to it.

Taking out her small digital camera, Maxine snapped a picture of the device and left the area. She took a position on a park bench across the pond from the fountain pretending to read a newspaper while munching on a snack. When Agent Silas Wescott arrived, she had him mix in with a group of kids and parents on a nearby playground. His partner stayed with their vehicle.

About an hour later, a bald man in his mid-sixties meandered down a trail dressed in a brown oversized raincoat, rain boots and gloves.

He too fed the ducks a few pieces of bread from his pocket then went over to the fountain for a drink. The man didn't even look around to see who was watching as he bent over to   take a drink. Not even pretending to hide his actions, he crouched down, fumbled to remove the magnetic button and dropped it. He again fumbled around for it before finally slipping it into his coat pocket.

Silas chuckled to her over their radio net earpieces. "This guy has no field craft at all."

"No kidding!" Maxine whispered back. "It's as if he wants to make sure we see him take it. Are we being played or is he that inept?"

Silas shadowed him for several minutes to a bus stop. As the suspect boarded the public transportation, Silas hopped aboard. A moment later, Maxine and Silas's partner caught up to the bus tailing them for about three miles to a large twelve-story apartment complex. When the bus stopped, the elderly man exited with Silas close behind.

As Silas got off the bus he walked in the opposite direction towards Maxine. She quickly parked the car by the curb, grabbed a plastic shopping bag with some snacks in it from the back seat and picked up the tail. She followed after the suspect to the apartment entrance.

As he opened the front door with his security pass, Maxine walked up behind him. He kindly held the door open for her. She politely thanked him as she entered and rushed over to hold the closing empty elevator door. The man gave a grateful smile as he stepped inside.

"What floor?" Maxine asked. "Tenth floor, thank you!" he replied.

"Really, That's my floor too. What apartment do you live in?" Maxine asked as she pressed the tenth floor elevator button.

"Apartment 1025. I haven't seen you before. You must be new here?" the gentleman asked.

Maxine smiled. "I'm just helping my aunt for a couple of days. She just got out of the hospital."

"Are you related to that crabby old bat down the hall in Apartment 1010?" he asked.

Maxine sighed. "Yes, she can be quite a handful when she doesn't take her meds."

"You have my deepest sympathy, but I do hope she gets better," he grumbled.

When the elevator reached the tenth floor, they exited and went opposite directions down the hallway. As Maxine rounded the corner, she peeked around to confirm that the man entered the right apartment. It took a couple of hours before the FBI placed round the clock surveillance on the man and his apartment.

The next morning after the man left for work, Maxine obtained a warrant and rejoined her team. Drawing her weapon and holding it at the ready, she gave one of her team members the go ahead to pick the lock.

When ready she gave the order and her team burst into the apartment. As the team entered there was a violent explosion. The apartment was ripped apart. Four members of her team were instantly killed along with three elderly residents in neighboring apartments.

Maxine was to be the last one to enter. She was barely in the doorway when the blast blew her back out and across the hall. She was stunned and everything around her seemed to be moving. Her ears were ringing so loud she could barely think. She managed to check herself over and found her vest saved her life though she did have a few cuts and several bruises. As she managed to look around, the acrid smell of explosives, burning debris and flesh made her instantly sick in her stomach. Half her team was dead and two others severely injured. Her partner, Bill, and Agent Wescott were very shaken but not injured. They had been blocking the hallway when the bomb went off.

Maxine's anger washed over her. The senseless carnage overwhelmed her. She wanted to grieve for the loss of friends and teammates, however, her anger wouldn't let her. The grieving would have to come later. "If it's a war you want, you will regret it," Maxine cried out.

Captain Pell Hoss entered General Tayer's office and impatiently waited for the secretary to leave. Captain Hoss was an aide to General Tayer and reviled by everyone on the Cassarian Royal Headquarters Command staff. He was as arrogant as the general but content to ride on his boss' coattails.

Short of stature, white hair since youth, along with a gruff voice and mannerisms, Captain Hoss was the perfect "Black Hat" General Tayer needed to counter his "White Hat" image. Captain Hoss was quite adept at getting dirt on almost anyone and had no compunction to use it to General Tayer's advantage.

"Patience, captain, patience! I have to sign off on a few general orders and we will talk. Please have a seat," General Tayer calmly directed without looking up from his paperwork.

Captain Hoss took a seat and quietly waited as his feet excitedly bounced quietly on the carpet. A couple of minutes went by with the general exchanging a few questions and answers before the secretary left the room.

"Now, what brings you here all excited?" General Tayer asked.

"Sir, I found a very confidential memo from Admiral Quanto to Councilor Waddel expressing deep concern over

King Toburg's health and fitness to serve in his position," Pell explained as he handed a copy of the memo to him.

"I never thought I'd see the day this would happen even if it is within his rights and duty. However, it is very revealing of where he stands. If we can turn him to our side, he could prove very useful indeed," said General Tayer.

"Could this be a trick of some kind?" Pell suspeciously asked.

"I doubt it. Admiral Quanto is not capable of deception and has no aspirations of greatness. He is like a little puppy. He is more loyal to Cassaria and the office of king than to any particular person occupying the throne. I'm sure he does not suspect a plot or I would know about it from King Toburg. He trusts me more than anyone else and so does Councilor Waddel," General Tayer bragged with an air of confidence.

"Do you want me to do some digging on the admiral for future leverage?"

"Of course, nobody's squeaky clean. Everyone has a dark side. Go find it," General Tayer said dismissing his aide.

No sooner did Captain Hoss leave than the intercom beeped. His secretary announced Council Assistant Willett Quiller was on the secure line.

"Council Assistant Quiller, what can I do for you?" General Tayer inquired.

'We have a memo from Admiral Quanto to Councilor Waddel concerning the king. Are you aware of it?"

"I have heard some rumors of its contents. Why?"

"I am directed to advise you to make every effort to win Admiral Quanto to our side. He could be quite useful to us. However, if he does not back us, he must be removed from the equation. Do you understand?"

"I understand perfectly. Have a good day," General Tayer replied and hung up.

As was his custom, Admiral Quanto ate lunch at the headquarters cafeteria. Twice a week he ate in the Enlisted Mess Hall with his enlisted staff. Today, as with the other three days a week, he ate at the Officers Lounge. The meals served were typically bland but edible Cassarian fare. On those days he enjoyed reading old classical writings while he dined.

"May I join you, Amboy?" General Tayer asked.

Admiral Quanto meticulously marked his page, closed his book and gestured for his guest to join him.

"Nix, how are you doing? I haven't seen you in a while," the admiral replied.

"Paperwork, paperwork. A truly never-ending shuffle of paperwork only a bureaucrat could love. After a while the walls seem to close in trying to squeeze the very life out of you," Nix sighed.

"I agree. I miss being out with the fleet. It's a lot different out there," Amboy conceded.

"I feel the same way, but somebody has to keep on top of the paperwork so the king doesn't become over-stressed. It's been awfully tough for him the past few months."

"I agree. This morning I was in his office for a briefing and he was totally out of it. When the briefing was over, he had no clue what was just briefed. He froze when I asked for a decision. He declined and asked me to make an appointment for tomorrow. Before I left the room he changed his mind and told me to take care of it. I did what he asked.

'I'm afraid he'll forget directing me to take care of it and arrest me for usurping the throne," Amboy exclaimed shaking his head.

"You've noticed it too? I had a long conversation with him about his health and state of mind yesterday. He agreed to see the royal surgeon next week. Later, I'm talking to the royal surgeon who declared the king had seen him the day before,"

Nix explained.

It is not good. Not good at all," Amboy sighed as he stroked his scraggly goatee.

"Something needs to be done. Maybe King Adrian should take a temporary leave of absence and get some rest?" Nix craftily speculated.

Amboy leaned forward and in a hushed voice asked, "What about the Council of Elders, do they plan to take any action?" Amboy asked.

"Some would like to but are afraid to propose the motion without the required vote to legally remove him. They are afraid the military will step in and prevent it."

"That's crazy. The military will support whoever is elected king.

They just need to find someone the troops can trust. Like you for instance," Amboy stated in a successful attempt at flattery.

Nix took a deep breath and smiled. "I admit I'm highly qualified as king, but Adrian and I are lifelong friends. It wouldn't feel right being king as long as he is alive," Nix declared.

Amboy leaned forward and in a hushed voice asked, "What about the Council of Elders. Would they support you?"

"The council is ready to support me but at a price."

"You mean they want to own you." Amboy noted.

"When the time comes I'm made king, the council will learn that a king is meant to rule," Nix stated with an all-knowing smile.

Amboy looked at his watch. "Lunch is over for me. I have an intelligence assessment meeting to chair. Nice talking to you. We should get together for lunch and talk again sometime real soon."

"I look forward to it. You be very careful in the meantime.

You're a hard man to replace. If you need anything just ask. I'll do what little I can to help," Nix pledged.

"You are much too modest, Nix, but thank you for your offer," Amboy assured him as he patted his shoulder and left the officers lounge.

As he entered his office, Admiral Amboy Quanto smiled. He reached under his tunic, removed a recording device, and turned it off. *I own you now you arrogant, traitorous fool and you have no clue!*

The last of the shuttles landed on the *Holcron Star.* After rehearsing the assault exercise six times, everything finally went exactly according to plan. Just to impress on the crews the importance of discipline, John had them run the exercise perfectly two more times before standing down. John sat in the command chair very pleased with the results. John knew he had pushed them very hard but it had to be done. Next time it would be for real.

"Sir! We have a voice message from Admiral MacKay," Georgia announced.

John pressed the speaker button on his Command chair. "Yes, admiral?" John announced.

"Congratulations on a beautifully executed exercise. I believe we are ready for the real thing," the admiral announced.

"Thank you. I believe we are as ready as we're going to get. Let's take the fleet to the far edge of the system for a day to rest and repair before heading for Terra."

"I concur," the admiral agreed and ended the communication.

John wrote a message on his data pad congratulating the pilots for a job well done and handed the data pad to Georgia.

"Georgia, send this to the shuttle crews. They earned a rest after today. You have the bridge. Direct our ships to return to Sector 12 of the system for twenty-four-hour rest and repair. By the way, release our trio of mad scientists from the brig. I hope they have learned their lesson."

The next morning John was having breakfast with many of the Black Watch officers. They had just started eating when the call to "general quarters" sounded. John raced up the elevator to the bridge where Aycana was the duty officer. Siyana and David also arrived and replaced the pilots. Jonathan and Victoria arrived right behind them.

"Sir, we have sensor indications of an anomaly identical to that of the Outsider ship approaching on an intercept course from the far side of the system."

"Good job, Aycana. Estimated time of intercept?" "Approximately thirty minutes at present speed. They used the asteroid field just outside the system to hide their approach. They are also not using their customary shadow tactic," Aycana reported. "Aycana, open a secure channel to the *Fire Hawk and Halfling,*" John ordered.

John went over to the navigation station and showed Molly the course he wanted her to plot.

"Yes, John. I fear the cat is out of the bag. Surely, they witnessed our training and the *Halfling*'s actions," Admiral MacKay pointed out.

"I agree," Gavin said.

"We need to keep up the deception to the last possible moment. Admiral, I want us and the *Fire Hawk* to swing about to this location with the anomaly on our port side. I want the *Fire Hawk* to follow in left staggered formation.

'Gavin, maintain the *Halfling*'s present course," John instructed. "Yes, sir!" Gavin replied.

"Tactical: charge weapons, shield generators, and place on standby. Be ready to bring on line at a moment's notice."

"All weapons are charged and on standby!"Joshua Nevens replied.

Jonathan reported, "All shield generators are at one hundred percent and on standby."

About twenty minutes passed as the *Holcron Star* and *Fire Hawk* assumed their new course.

"Sir, I have an incoming message encoded. I'm transferring it to your data pad now," Georgia announced.

"What took them so long to make contact? I was beginning to wonder," John muttered aloud as he decoded the message.

The message read:

Capt. Gath,

You were ordered to proceed to your base and cease activity until time for the Cassarian invasion.

Why have you not followed orders? Return to your port immediately.

Captain Pinera Ditra

John was just about to reply when, without warning, there were three small explosions around the hull of the Outsider ship. The ship suddenly appeared in full view with an odd green florescent glowing substance highlighting it. It immediately fired the first salvo of proton plasma but missed. John was shocked as he realized immediately what had happened.

The outsider ship used their only zannite crystal to power its cannons.

"Shields up!" John shouted.

"Shields up!" Jonathan replied.

"Target their engines, shield generators and communications arrays. Fire when targets are acquired." John radioed the *Fire Hawk* with the same orders.

Within moments Aycana and Joshua opened fire with the *Fire Hawk* following less than a second later. Violet plasma cannon fire streaked from the two ships.

John muttered to himself. Henry's experiment worked after all. *And now we know how Captain Ditra chose to use his zannite crystal.* The crew of the Outsider ship was surprised and confused by the small explosions near their hull. At first the explosions seemed harmless. However, they quickly discovered their shields, targeting sensors and cloaking systems were temporarily disabled affecting the firing of its first salvo. The first hits from the *Holcron Star* severely damaged their shields.

The Outsiders fired a second salvo at the *Holcron Star* but to little effect. Captain Ditra was enraged. "The pirates have betrayed us. Let's teach them a lesson they won't forget."

The blinding effects of the florescent goo caused their shots to go wild but one shot did manage to strike the *Holcron Star*. By the third salvo from the *Fire Hawk and Holcron Star,* the hull was breached near the engine room, which knocked out their reactor core, power generators and life support systems. Defeat was now held off by the amount of remaining air.

In a final act of desperation, Captain Ditra gave his last order.

"Turn the ship 180 degrees, port. The shield generator is near critical, launch it at the pirate ships!" A large steel container about 40 feet long came shooting out the hangar bay. It was glowing red from the heat it was generating.

"Aycana, destroy that container NOW!" John ordered.

Without waiting for orders Jonathan shifted all power from the starboard shield generators to boost the port generators.

Aycana fired at it and the plasma beam just missed. She fired a second time and missed again. The third shot struck dead center causing a giant fireball. The blast sent out a shock wave that knocked everyone standing on the bridge to the deck but the shields managed to hold.

John looked to starboard and saw the *Halfling* was still

intact. The mass of the *Holcron Star* had shielded her from damage. The *Fire Hawk* was drifting slightly to starboard away from the explosion.

John called the *Fire Hawk*. "Admiral MacKay, report your situation."

"Captain Reagan here. The admiral was knocked out but is coming around and being taken to sick bay. Many systems went off line but are rebooting. Other injuries are coming in but appear to be minimal. We will be operational in about three minutes. I'll send a sitrep asap. *Fire Hawk* out!"

Before John could ask, the *Halfling* reported no injuries or damage.

John looked over at the Outsider scout ship. Its doom was sealed when a ruptured fuel cell near the engine room exploded, creating a hull breach large enough a small shuttle could fly through. With such a sudden and massive venting of atmosphere, it was too late for the crew to abandon ship or release a distress signal buoy. In less than a minute the battle was over. The drifting Outsider ship fell dark, silent and cold. The eerie green glow of the florescent goo covering the otherwise darkened hull added a surreal effect to the brief but deadly battle.

"Secure from general quarters," John ordered. "Damage report!"

"All stations report no damage except Cargo Hold 2. Minor damage occurred when some cargo shifted. *Fire Hawk* now reports one magnum plasma gun temporarily out of commission. A circuit board shorted. They expect repairs completed within the hour. Six crew have minor injuries, The worst casualty is Admiral MacKay. He suffered a concussion but has regained consciousness, sir," Aycana declared.

John looked at Jonathan. "Good move, you could have well saved us all."

Jonathan wiped his brow. "I was so scared I just did it without thinking."

That was what training is about. You did think. You just didn't know it," John nodded in approval.

John radioed the *Halfling*, "Gavin, see if you can dock with the Outsider ship. Recover the zannite crystal if you can. Strip the ship of any useful information or technology you can find. Also download everything from their computer if possible. Dr. Kremmel requests four intact bodies for study. When you are done, we'll tow it to the system's sun to dispose of the wreckage."

"Will do!" Gavin replied.

"That was totally unreal!" David exclaimed looking out the view port at the green glowing goo highlighting the wrecked scout ship. The search teams found the Outsider ship unusual in several ways proving Deze and Captain Gath's earlier information was fairly accurate. The ship was coated with a jet-black plastic-like outer hull substance never seen before.

There was a landing bay for shuttles in the rear lower section of the ship. The ship's apparent design was to rely on its stealth capability. With the huge warp engines, it was obviously designed as a deep space ghost. For a cruiser, it was under gunned compared to the firepower of the *Holcron Star* or *Fire Hawk*. With its stealth capability, the Outsider ship was designed to run not fight. John wondered, *Why, did Captain Ditra use the zannite crystal to boost fire power when speed was what he needed to survive?*

"Georgia, put me through to Captain Reagan," John said.

"Yes, John. I suggest the *Fire Hawk* take a position in Sector Six where the Outsider ship entered the system. We'll provide early warning for any more visitors." Jack offered.

"Sounds good!" John agreed. "We'll guard the boarding

party and *Halfling*. Once the boarding party is done searching the wreckage we'll put the *Halfling* in the hangar. We can then head home and pick up the troops. If any more Outsider ships appear, we run not fight."

"Roger that. By the way, what were those small explosions that started this whole thing? It totally blew their sensor systems bonkers."

"Simply put, the duct tape engineers struck again!" John said.

"Oh my!" Jack exclaimed.

Down in the Dark Pit the duct tape engineers were dancing around the workbenches, high fiving each other in celebration.

Three hundred Katusium senators and cabinet officials gathered for the special session in the parliament's amphitheater. The amphitheater was made of six half circle rows of simple hand finished burgundy colored hardwood tables and chairs. The walls were made of a white marble with fifty-one floor-length drapes of red velvet around the room. Between each drape was a golden crest representing each of the fifty states. As is customary, Admiral Usus Dever patiently kneeled on the hard, white marble floor in front of the rostrum. Enough politicians had done this over the last couple centuries, that a red pillow with gold tassels was made available to kneel on. Usus noted a simple but elegant chair of similar burgundy wood a few feet away for the prime minister to sit when yielding to another speaker.

Usus smiled noting the extra soft pillow on the seat. Old age does come with some perks even on Katusium. Glancing at the white ceiling, Usus could not miss the unique lighting. Embedded in the ceiling were rows of panels that appeared like glowing sheets of translucent pearl. The emitting light bathed everything in the theater, yet was so easy on the eyes it seemed to make one relax in its glow. Except for the plain bronze staff the Speaker held, there were no other symbols of power or ostentatious decoration.

Usus greatly admired the simple elegant ways of the Katusian people. Unlike on Holcron, Usus noted the prime minister is charged with conducting all Parliamentary meetings. Until the prime minister handed the staff to speak, all Usus could do was courteously wait for the formalities of the meeting to be completed.

Once the roll call was completed the prime minister called the special session to order by pounding his staff three times on a brass floor plate. The hall fell silent.

In the Katusium Parliament, members were required to remain totally silent showing respect and give thoughtful consideration to the speaker's words. Because of this custom, body language was a vital element of public speaking and show of good manners in Katusian culture.

Wealth, class or level of education did not earn the highest respect. It was simply earned by how one treated others. They were allowed to express their approval or disapproval only with a thumb up or down sign or even cover their ears with their hands if they vigorously objected but verbal interruptions were absolutely forbidden.

The prime minister no sooner called the meeting to order than a group of senators covered their faces in silent protest. Many Katusian senators did not want Usus to speak. To avoid the protest from spreading, the prime minister urged them to uncover their faces.

Admiral Dever in an effort to calm the protest, reached out with his palm open as a sign of friendship and peace. The prime minister finally saw the majority of senators relent and handed Usus the staff. The Admiral grasped the staff, then rose but did not stand behind the rostrum. By not doing so, he demonstrated his place as a foreigner honored to speak before the Katusian assembly. For the next thirty minutes, he carefully presented his case outlining the Tigran plan of divide and conquer, including the Outsider and Gamoran pirate plan of betrayal.

By tradition, questions were reserved for the end, whereupon senators would kneel on one knee next to where they sat. Admiral Dever's presentation went well until he asked for questions. Suddenly half the senators went to their knees. Patiently, Usus answered every question with candid honesty. Still the majority signaled with a thumb down gesture.

Some hand signs being shown Usus had no idea what they meant but from the facial expression it didn't look good for his cause. When two young senators interrupted verbally the prime minister quickly retrieved the staff, pounding it three times on the floor before the two became silent and resumed their seats. The disgraceful behavior could have resulted in forceful removal from the meeting. In fact, the Ceremonial guards stood nearby to enforce the parliamentary rules if needed. The silent anger the prime minister directed at them put them on notice of their imminent ejection.

To reinforce his displeasure he declared, "Katusians have a saying, "The greatest wisdom is demonstrated by one's actions, not words. Overt grandstanding is shameful and unbecoming for public servants in Katusian society. You are on notice!

'Admiral Dever came in friendship and peace to present the truth that we may decide our actions. He shall make his final statement and then we shall decide," he declared as he handed the staff once again to Usus.

"Thank you, prime minister," Usus said with a bow. "In closing I wish to recount the Gamoran pirate attack on the unarmed Katusian research vessel, *Wymeria*. It was not the Holcrons or Cassarians that attacked the ship, kill in cold blood the prime minister's son-in-law and fellow officers, or enslave the remaining Katusians including the prime minister's daughter and granddaughter. It was the Gamoran pirates aided by the Tigran Navy. Here is my proof!" The admiral then pointed his staff at the ceremonial guards who stepped aside to reveal Tierra and Geddy Kendra as proof of all his words.

Now the Katusian senators covered their eyes in sorrow. From that moment on there were vigorous hand signs calling for a vote and unanimous thumbs up throughout the chamber. When Admiral Dever finished his presentation one of the leaders of the senate was kneeling at his seat.

The prime minister stepped forward retrieved the staff and recognized the senator. He stood and directed his question to Tierra.

"Is all the Holcron leader spoken true in its entirety?"

"Yes, Senator, every word is true and more that he does not know. Of the one hundred men, forty-five women and thirty children who left on the peaceful research mission, only twenty men, ten women and one child remain alive. Tigran soldiers, our so-called trusted allies, murdered most of them. Most of the children starved to death while our so-called allies feasted nearby. The lowest animal on our planet is treated better than my daughter was in captivity. We, the people of Katusium, are watching our leaders. We wish to know if we are to be betrayed again and enslaved or are you brave enough to stand against such evil?"

The prime minister looked around the chamber and with no one kneeling and with unanimous gestures called for a very rare voice vote. There was a loud shout for an end to the Tigran Axis Treaty. The second vote was unanimous for the Katusium Navy to join forces with the Holcron Navy to aid Cassaria and Earth and bring an end to the treachery.

The Katusian Army and Navy moved quickly to seize Gamoran and Tigran ships and assets as well as prevent outside communication from the Tigran and Gamoran Embassies.

There were seventy-five days to go before the Quadas Day attack. Admiral Dever was pleased as he boarded his ship. He smiled, *Mission accomplished and just in time.*

Cat Saunders had her team of newly trained agents watching Dr. Jerri Spinner around the clock. It was good experience for them to learn the art of blending into a crowd and observing every detail of her activities. Cat went to the Braxton's quarters.

"Cat, have a seat, John will be along any second. Would you like a drink?" Victoria asked.

"Yes, some of that almond iced tea you are famous for if you have some," Cat answered with a big smile.

Almond ice tea it is," Victoria nodded.

As she handed Cat a glass of the tea, John entered.

"Yum! Can I have a glass too?" John asked.

"I knew you'd ask," Victoria smiled as she handed a glass to him. "Well, Cat, what have you got for us?" John inquired.

"I've had Dr. Spinner under surveillance since she came aboard. We slowly built a dossier detailing every idiosyncrasy, habit and personal contact. Daily routines, work habits and even what she ate and who with were recorded. A pattern started to form as she frequented the engineering deck and hangar. These are areas a person of her office would not normally venture, it was the route that aroused our attention. No matter where she was going, she always made it a point to pass right by the brig where Capt. Gath is still being held. We didn't think implants could communicate through walls but she was able to do so. We recorded Capt. Gath's reactions to prove it. We moved him to a cell across the room and they were not able to communicate. Capt. Gath became very agitated until we moved him back and she contacted him again."

"I see," Victoria said. "Did she have any reaction?"

"Yes, it was much subtler. She was observed walking the passage ways and running her hands along the walls like a school child searching for him. When communication was reestablished, she ceased the behavior," Cat explained.

"I see," John acknowledged. "Does any of this pose a threat?"

Cat shook her head. "It's possible. Who knows what could happen if the communication continues?"

"For security sake, I suggest we place him in the other cell so they can't hatch any plans for now," Victoria said.

"Let's do it," John agreed.

In the Dark Pit, Dexter, Henry and Deze were studying data recovered from the destroyed Outsider ship. They were able to put together a 3D projection of the ship and slowly studied each layer of the schematics. At first, they didn't know what to think. Deze verbalized his thoughts while Dexter kept advancing to a different area of the projection.

"This ship was poorly designed as a deep space scout ship. The weapons array only points forward. The upper half of the ship is more like a freighter with a large hangar added," Henry pointed out.

"Yes, the lower half of the ship was definitely an add on," Deze added. "You can see the seam where they had to joined the two hulls and had to adjust for the poor fit.

"Their captain was very brave to command that ship," Dexter declared. "I suspect it was a one-of-a-kind ship for this specific mission. It appears the zannite crystal was originally meant for their engines rather than for their plasma cannons or defensive shielding. Running was their best chance. When they diverted their power to the cannons it was a move of desperation. If we hadn't destroyed them the power overload would have."

"How so?" Henry asked.

"Because their power transfer system was not capable of handling the extra boost in power. It was burning out their systems. See here," Dexter said pointing to the power converter and generators. "They are too small to handle the load the zannite could create. Their engines could handle the load increase but the other systems could not. The *Holcron Star* is designed with all three systems independent, thus can handle the increase in power from the crystals with no problems. We can even shift additional power from one system to boost another by as much as twenty percent more for short periods." If they tried it, their ship would have turned into slag."

"So, they could engage small fry targets but otherwise flight or staying out of sight were their only real advantages?" Henry asked.

Deze nodded. "Yup, and our space mines nixed the cloaking advantage."

"Count our blessings, one defective mine caused the remaining mines to be jettisoned and just so happen end up in their ship's path. That isn't blind luck in my book," Henry smiled.

Deze pointed to a salvaged console sitting on the shop floor with a panel removed. "Hey fellas, I think this part here is the key to the whole stealth system. I can't read the control panel but I recognize an optical flux processor when I see one. I was asked to repair one for a deep space probe Captain Gath found. It can adjust for light distortions on deep space telescopes for sharper images. I bet they found a way to use it to create a reflective energy field that emulates the space around it like a mirror. The black coating of the hull is necessary to make certain no light reflects off the hull and distorts the mirror image."

"That is probably true, but why couldn't our sensors get a lock until the mirror image was broken?" Dexter argued.

"Maybe the energy field reflects more than the light around it to make it stealthy," Deze speculated.

"No, I think it is in the black coating. It probably acts just like the coating on our stealth bombers," Henry said while opening another access panel.

"You know you got a point there," Deze agreed.

Dexter reached inside the console with a pair of pliers. Suddenly there was a loud clanking sound as Dexter dropped the pliers and began gyrating his arms inside the panel access. Moments later he pulled out a two-foot long, egg shaped, spherical container and carried it over to the workbench.

All three of them were scratching their heads as they gazed at it. There were a series of lights that constantly blinked and a large blinking red button next to them that begged someone to press. Henry reached out to do just that when Deze slapped his hand away.

"What did you do that for? I was just going to press the button and see what happens," Henry said.

"I know and you would have killed us all," Deze scolded.

"You mean its booby trapped?" Henry asked.

"Yes, power is cut to the device, yet it still works as you can see by the lights," Dexter stated. "However this small button near the bottom is not as obvious. On some worlds, when you build something you don't want tampered with you install a sucker switch."

"A sucker switch?" Henry asked a bit confused.

"Yes, only a sucker would press it. The result is no more sucker," Deze said sarcastically.

"Oh!" Henry said as he grimaced and fidgeted.

Dexter pushed the smaller button and a spring-loaded panel opened to expose the inside. "This, gentlemen, is the heart of our targeting problem."

"It's a computer and I bet I know what it does," Deze

squealed with delight.

A few minutes later Deze had a makeshift connection to their shop computer and began analyzing the stealth computer data.

"Guys! I think I figured their stealth system out. When in stealth mode, their computer detects sensor signals striking the hull, it then analyses the signal and mirrors the return signals so nothing is detected.

'Essentially, the computer sends false sensor signals to fool our sensors into seeing nothing. Because our visual scopes are not sending a signal, they can't be scrambled. The black hull coating is also imbedded with trillions of tiny optical cells. The computer also tells the optical flux processor what mirror image to have the optical cells project. However, the mirror projection is under powered thus the visual distortions.

'The Outsiders are nearly invisible and impossible to target because our weapons are slaved to our sensors. Proximity fuses on our missiles won't work either, because they require a visual lock and don't recognize the distortions as a ship," Deze explained.

"Our mines worked because they had contact fuses and the magnetized iron fillings in our goo overloaded the stealth computer's sensors. Right?" Henry asked.

"Precisely. Though the florescent additive was dazzling, it was not absolutely necessary after all," Dexter concluded.

"If we continue with the mines, I think we need to keep using it," Henry noted. "The Outsiders were very confused by the goo and it does make it easier to visually identify the black hull."

"Good point," Deze and Dexter agreed.

"I do have an idea though that will solve the whole thing and it doesn't require a beer keg this time," Henry stated excitedly. "If we modify the ship's sensor computer to take the distortions from the long-range scopes and convert it into a filled in image, couldn't the targeting computer then lock on with missiles using contact or proximity fuses?"

"Yes, I think that would work nicely. It would also provide a target lock for the magnum laser cannons as well," Deze agreed. "I can write the program patch to do it but General Braxton had better be told before we do anything. I don't want to spend another day in the brig again," Deze exclaimed.

"What ya mean a day? Henry growled. "Your escape attempt caused us to have to stay an extra day in the brig."

Deze took offense. "All I did was sneak out and get us all some coffee. I did come back didn't I?"

"But you're not supposed to get caught!" Dexter glared.

"I also noticed you've been in the brig before. On the wall of my cell it has your name scrawled with twelve hash marks, Henry noted. "Does that mean you spent twelve days in the brig before?"

"Nope! It means I was in twelve times. I hold the record," Deze boasted.

Henry groaned. "Oh, great! We got us here a real junior Houdini. Don't worry about my son, guys. I can handle him."

Dexter in a moment of rare animation held up his hands to stop Henry. "Oh no you don't. I insist on talking to him."

"Yes, let Dex talk to him," Deze agreed.

Deze and Dexter starred at Henry as he fidgeted and finally agreed.

In sick bay, Khem and Susan stood on opposite sides of the operating table. The Outsider corpse was as strange as the ship itself. He was slightly below the average height of a human but of a husky build. The features were also human like but the skin was more similar to leather and totally hairless. The hands and feet were slightly webbed with fingernails similar to claws found on a cat, well-manicured but very sharp.

The facial features were human-like in general but the ears were long and reminded Susan of the ears on a goat. The nose was shaped like a human's but more flat and wide. The lips were puffed up and the tongue long. The teeth were thin and sharp like those of a cat.

"These Outsiders remind me of a movie I once saw years ago," Susan exclaimed.

"Was it any good?" Khem asked in passing while opening the chest cavity.

"Not really," Susan deadpanned as she strained to see the contents of the cavity.

"What was it about?" Khem asked in passing curiosity.

"On a secluded island a scientist experiments with human and animal DNA attempting to create the perfect human. His assistant tortures the part human, part animal creatures with electric shock to control them.

A young man crash lands his plane on the island and discovers the scientist's twisted research was putting all their lives in endanger. The scientist's daughter falls in love with him and tries to help the young man escape. The scientist murders his traitorous assistant for his cruelty then is killed by his own creations. The beautiful daughter turns back into an animal and eats the young man," Susan summarized.

"What was the point of the author's story?" Khem asked again.

"Man should not try to play God. The other point is love can cause people to do the dumbest things," Susan declared with a deadpan expression.

"I see!" Khem said holding back his smile.

"By the way, look at the heart and lungs on this guy. You'd think he was amphibian," Susan observed.

"Your right. Look here on the throat area. He can

breathe on land or water," Khem explained as he lifted two folds of skin revealing a set of gills.

Susan made a couple incisions in the abdomen and revealed the stomach contents. "Looks like the stomach contents are mostly raw flesh. Gee, amphibious flesh eaters. I wonder what his world is like?"

"We'll need to analyze the contents for sure," Khem said.

Susan grimaced, "I think I know why they want Earth."

"Why?"

"Earth is seventy percent water with a population of over seven billion people. To them Earth probably looks like the ideal galactic vacation resort complete with a global swimming pool and planetary smorgasbord."

CHAPTER 17

As the *Holcron Star* went into a stationary position above Terra, the bridge crew gazed in surprise and awe of the view. Terra was an inspiring view of beauty and tranquility. Landmasses of various sizes, polar ice caps, large blue lakes and stunning whit-capped mountains. The oceans reminded everyone of Earth.

The moon, Proto, was slightly smaller than the Earth's moon, with craters, mountains and jagged cliffs. Ancient volcanic tunnels, caves and cliffs honey-combed Proto. At the base of Proto's largest cliff they combined to make the ideal space repair port. Two of the largest landing bays each held a heavy cruiser undergoing repairs. The largest space dock was empty but large enough to accept the largest of deep space freighters for major repairs. On an other landing pad, the Katusian exploration ship, *Wymeria,* sat in shambles. One third of its outer hull plating was missing and two of its five engines were gone as well. It was obviously being stripped of parts to repair other ships. Two other derelict freighters could be seen a couple miles away in much worse condition.

"May God be with us," John prayed. "Aycana, begin your attack!" Deze's inside knowledge of the pirate space and ground defense system allowed Aycana to lock the pirates out and seize control of the defense network.

"We have control of their defense network," Aycana reported. John opened the channel to the *Fire Hawk.* "Admiral MacKay, the defenses are down, begin your assault." John switched channels. "Gavin, you may begin your assault." The *Halfling* and the four *Holcron Star* armored assault shuttles nosed down for re-entry.

John turned his attention to the vehicle yard containing about fifteen rail gun tanks and twenty armored personnel carriers. "Weapons! Target the vehicle yard. Fire two missiles when target is locked."

"Target locked. Missiles away," Georgia replied with a bit of excitement.

With his Captain's chair computer screen, John zoomed in on the target and watched as the missiles approached.

Some soldiers could be seen climbing into their vehicles but it was too late to escape the inevitable. The two explosions were quickly followed by many secondary explosions as the vehicles were torn apart like papier Mache models.

John Braxton and Stephen MacKay were relieved to see they achieved total surprise. However, they were surprised too. There was construction not shown in the most recent photos captured from the *Fire Hawk*.

With perfect timing, the *Fire Hawk*'s two shuttles completed their docking. Jonathan and Burt Armstrong led the two assault teams boarding the heavy cruisers. The cruiser Burt's team boarded turned out to be completely unmanned. However, the ship Jonathan was attempting to seize had a high number of maintenance personnel aboard who quickly armed themselves. Because of the thin air the maintenance people were wearing masks. Realizing it negated the use of the knockout gas, Jonathan came up with a new plan.

"Burt, link up asap. We can't use the gas. We'll have to do this the hard way," Jonathan explained.

"Be there in a minute," Burt replied.

The pirate maintenance people put up a very disorganized resistance. However, it was enough for the confined space of the ship to stall Jonathan's team. As the assault began to stall, Jonathan pushed his team forward.

Pointing at four of his team, he signaled them to throw stun grenades.

"Let's go!" he shouted and charged forward. Jonathan

grabbed a team member by the arm and pulled him to his feet shoving him onward. "They can die here on this rock but we sure aren't. Get moving!" Jonathan ordered.

The others quickly jumped up and followed screaming at the top of their lungs. As Jonathan charged forward leading his team, a pirate jumped up from among several of his stunned comrades and tried to stab him with a twelve-inch knife. Before Jonathan could react several shots from a pistol rang out. Jonathan turned to see Burt standing nearby with his pistol still smoking. The pirate crumpled up on the floor next to his unconscious friends. The ferocity of the charge rattled the remaining maintenance workers and resistance quickly melted.

In the meantime, the *Fire Hawk* docked and disgorged Alpha Company. They quickly overran and captured the control center and maintenance areas. What they ran into when they searched the rest of the base was not maintenance personnel or even pirate crew members, but a platoon of Tigran Space Marines anxious to put up a fight. They immediately counter attacked. Alpha Company was surprised but blocked their attack. The captain of Alpha Company divided his troops and pursued them down several tunnels. The Blue Watch aggressively pushed the marines deeper into the tunnels until there was no place left to retreat.

During the push the main group of retreating marines threw a barrage of grenades. When the smoke cleared, three Alpha Company soldiers lay dead, and six wounded, including the captain. A medic raced to help them. Jonathan's boarding team now arrived to help. Discovering the captain of Alpha Company was wounded and out of action. Jonathan's team responded with grenades of their own. There was silence as the smoke once again cleared.

Jonathan called out through an interpreter, "Let me speak with the officer in charge!"

A voice called back, "Your're speaking to him. What do

you want?"

Jonathan replied, "You have one minute to surrender or we will wipe you out."

There was a forty-five second pause when the voice replied, "We will never surrender. We will fight to the death."

A blast from a Tigran blaster rang out. There was a brief pause before a new voice spoke. "Our officer has fought to the death. I'm in charge now and we will surrender."

"Throw out all your weapons and step out into the open with your hands above your heads." Jonathan demanded.

There was a brief discussion between the Tigran and the interpreter. "What's he saying?" Jonathan asked.

"He is afraid they will be murdered." The interpreter said.

"Tell him he has a simple choice. Those who surrender will be treated with respect and their safety guaranteed. Don't surrender and we will collapse the tunnel and all of you will be entombed forever," Jonathan said.

The survivors quickly concluded there was no further point in resistance or negotiations.

Over twenty marines, many wounded, threw out their weapons in surrender. Jonathan signaled Proto was secure.

With the orbital and ground defense systems neutralized, the *Halfling* and three shuttles made their final approach on the airdrome-landing pad designated Landing Zone Gold.

Gavin looked at the base as it grew in size at their approach. The invasion of Terra began and there was no turning back. With the sun in their face, the enemy would not see them until the last possible second.

As the *Halfling* and shuttles touched down the ground fire was light and erratic. The Blue Watch began spreading out to reach their objectives, resistance began to build. With the troops off loaded, the ships took off to return to the *Holcron Star* for additional troops, supplies and equipment.

David, flying the fourth shuttle,broke off from the formation to insert two special teams as blocking forces. One team with mortars to the west of the base set up on a large hill designated Landing Zone Red. Landing Zone Blue was placed on a lower and smaller knoll to the south of the base. Between the fire teams and the base was a very large open plaza for landing large freighters.

John felt a cramp forming in his stomach.

"Something is wrong, Stephen. There are over 200 crewmembers unaccounted for. If the crews aren't on Proto then they must be at the base," John said in frustration.

"I think Major Rivers is about to discover the answer. Let's leave the boarding parties to guard the prisoners and facility. Implement Plan B. I'll have Alpha Company ready for the shuttles in ten minutes," Stephen proposed.

"Agreed," John said. "Go ahead and begin boarding Shuttle 2. Shuttle 1 just brought aboard the casualties and will arrive back to you shortly."

John turned to his communications officer. "Get Major Rivers on the phone, then notify *Halfling* and Shuttle 3 to pick up the rest of Alpha Company to reinforce Major Rivers at once. Our assault forces on Terra are about to find themselves in a hornet's nest. We need every soldier down there ASAP!"

The Terran sun rose over the mountain range lighting the way for the first wave of 106 troops forming Bravo Company. Major Rivers was the first to step on Terran soil. The troops raced to their objectives. Traven stood on the tarmac, looking at his map and the area around him.

Traven grumbled. "The map layout is way off.

Traven could see on the south side of LZ-Gold a maintenance barn and two shuttle hangars. Being secured by First Platoon from Company B. Third Platoon was closing in on the Command Headquarters building and zannite processing laboratories located about a hundred yards behind the shuttle hangars and facing the east end of the open plaza.

On the north side of LZ-Gold, Second Platoon secured the freighter hangar capable of housing two ships much larger than the *Halfling*. About a half mile behind the hangar was the shoreline of a very large lake. The lake stretched northwest for about four hundred miles to a large river that emptied into it.

Along the west side of LZ-Gold were stacks of storage containers and crates. Beside them stretching along the side of the freighter hangar were an operations building and two storage and maintenance barns. These buildings were also secured by Second Platoon. To that extent, the map was correct.

Through his field glasses Traven could see Third Platoon about to enter the more distant laboratory and the five story Command Headquarters building. Third Platoon can handle that problem. No sweat! Traven mused to himself.

No sooner did the soldiers reach the entrance than they set off charges blowing out the lobby entrance on the main floor of the buildings. A room by room, floor by floor brawl ensued. Third Platoon was specially trained for assaulting buildings. The lab facility had to be captured before the HQ building could be more quickly secured.

There was obviously some major construction since the *Holcron Star* or *Fire Hawk* last visited Terra. West of the vehicle buildings and storage containers and following along the north side of the plaza clearing were supposed to be two rows of warehouses, workshops, a vehicle yard and two troop barracks.

Traven counted three rows of structures and more troop barracks. He could see the vehicle storage yard burning with several rail gun tanks and personnel carriers destroyed.

However, there weren't two barracks but now six large barracks with large numbers of armed infantry racing between the buildings towards his position. There was also a vehicle barn opening up with five tanks emerging.

Traven no sooner shouted, "Take cover!" than a hail of fire erupted. Traven dived for cover while recalling his own words at the final briefing. *Who was the idiot that said this was going to be a cakewalk?*

John contacted Jonathan. "Jonathan, Plan B is in effect. Assist in transporting troops and supplies to LZ-Gold with shuttle 2. We need First Platoon to reinforce Major Rivers. The second platoon needs to reinforce LZ-Red and LZ-Blue.

John then called Traven, "Command 1 to Gold 1. Be advised approximately 200 pirates are at your location. Expect more resistance than planned."

Over the din of gunfire, Traven cupped his ear over the flip com. to block out the noise. "Gold 1 to Command 1. Be advised we have been formally introduced. We have also engaged an equal number of Tigran troops plus a platoon of rail gun tanks. Over!"

"Gold 1, Plan B in effect. Reinforcements in route. Command 1 out!"

Suddenly a shadow loomed over Traven. Looking up, he saw Sergeant Major Stone smile as blaster bursts whizzed around him. Traven shook his head. "Plan B is in effect. First Platoon/Alpha is on the way so make room for them. The pirate crews are here along with over 200 Tigran Marines."

"So, we're out-numbered. Now we got them wher we want them. Can do, sir!" Sergeant Major Stone replied.

Just before the firing erupted, David flew shuttle 4 to drop off Fire Team 6, a sniper team, and two mortar teams, on a large hill designated LZ-Red, near the base entrance to provide direct mortar fire and a blocking force to the West.

The next drop was LZ-Blue, located behind a knoll with a circular row of twelve granite columns reaching twelve feet high. The knoll overlooked the south end of the open plaza.

Behind the knoll was a mile long slopped clearing ending at the edge of a swift flowing river.

On the other side of the river was a fifty-mile wide flood plain of gently rolling fields leading to a forest. The forest butted up against a looming mountain range.

David flew the shuttle just a few feet above the trees along the riverbed, and then made a left turn heading directly for the knoll.

He landed at LZ-Blue and dismounted Fire Team 7. They scurried up the knoll to their position.

Corky looked at the twelve granite columns. "I wonder what those things are for?"

A Cassarian soldier beside him remarked, "This is a Tigran Holy Site. They construct it to call upon their gods to guarantee them victory. It is like claiming the ground here as their land. Now we claim it. They must do all they can to take it back or their gods will turn against them."

Corky grinned. "Well then, they are about to have their gods really angry at them because we aren't giving up one square inch of it. Start digging in."

When David cleared the top of the knoll, he was aghast at the sight before them. Spread across the plaza next to the barracks were five rail gun light tanks supporting at least 200 enemy troops. They were attempting to out flank LZ-Gold. When Fire Team 7 engaged them with machine gun fire and directing mortar fire from LZ-Red, the enemy immediately turned their attention to wiping out Fire Team 7.

David's copilot radioed Major Rivers. Unfortunately, Major Rivers was already engaged in a fierce firefight of his own. Three hundred Tigran Royal Marines and pirates pinned down his 106 Blue Watch troops. These Tigran fighters were considered the finest and fiercest fighting force in the known galaxy. Traven could send no aid. He was desperate for reinforcements as well. The second wave of fifty in the two shuttles from the *Fire Hawk*, can't arrive for at least an hour. The third wave of ninety soldiers wouldn't arrive for another thirty minutes behind them at best. The remainder of Alpha Company won't arrive until at least an hour after that.

In the meantime, Third Platoon was still struggling to capture the HQ building. As they captured one floor, the enemy would retreat to the next floor. Finally, Captain Wilson got word the Lab building was secure. He then sent a squad to the backside of the HQ building.

One of the team members was Japanese and very adept at free climbing buildings. He began his climb while the teams inside put up a distracting fire. Twenty minutes later he made it five floors to the top and lowered two ropes. Within minutes a squad and two sniper teams were in place. The squad entered the building from the roof access and as the teams below advanced and the enemy began to retreat they were quickly picked off. They bravely fought to the last man but in vain. The snipers began picking targets and taking them out, one by one.

David circled his shuttle around making three successive strafing runs on the tanks and troops threatening Fire Team 7. Concentrating his fire on the tanks, David managed to knock out all five tanks. He also began taking accurate, withering ground fire. The mortar team's rounds were accurate but two mortars were not enough to stall the enemy advance.

Another shuttle dropped off additional ammunition along with a fifty-caliber machine gun at LZ-Blue then sped off to supply LZ-Red. Fire Team 7 quickly put the new machine gun to good use in addition to the squad machine gun the team carried.

The Tigrans were relentless in their assault on both Fire Team 7 and the main assault force. Five hundred and fifty Tigran and Gamoran troops tried to overrun the main Blue Watch forces. With the lopsided odds in the Tigran colonel's favor it seemed the Blue Watch was on the verge of being wiped out if forced to retreat. The problem was the assault was such a surprise the marines fled their barracks and found themselves disorganized in the fire fight. He couldn't give orders to units that hardly existed. All he could do was tell his officers to take command of those soldiers in a given area to execute the battle. With the withering incoming fire, he found it almost impossible to mount an organized and coordinated attack. Try as they might, the Tigran and Gamoran forces could not force the Blue Watch to give an inch as his casualties were quickly mounting.

The Tigran commander decided to try to secure his rear and right flank, then concentrate everything he had on wiping out the larger force. Unfortunately, it was easier said than done.

Twice he sent the Gamoran contingent supported by his armor against the 12 Column knoll and twice they were driven back. One shuttle's daring strafing runs wiped out his remaining armor.

The Tigran commander ordered half his remaining pirates and two companies of Tigran marines to take the knoll at all costs. This allowed him to focus his efforts to destroy the enemy main force with his remaining larger yet less organized force.

With the Tigran armor destroyed, Fire Team 7 still needed more breaks if they were going to survive the blow the enemy was about to deliver.

David observed the enemy positions but the *Holcron Star* and *Fire Hawk* could do very little to stop the assaults. If they fired their magnum plasma cannons there was the risk of hitting the Blue Watch soldiers nearby. The troops of both sides were just too closely engaged. Realizing the dangers, General Braxton and Admiral MacKay had no alternative but to use the few shuttles they had to maintain aerial pressure on the enemy for as long as possible.

For Major Rivers, the arrival of First Platoon and Third

Platoon/Alpha was just in time to turn back the largest and most desperate attack yet on his position.

The Tigran commander fired a signal flare and the entire frontline charged the LZ Gold defenses of the Blue Watch. The snipers on the roof of the HQ building were joined by a Mark 19 grenade launcher which went into action with devastating effect. When a section of the defenses between two stacks of shipping containers was threatened, the 40 mm grenades rained down on the attackers. Still the Tigran and pirate attackers pressed on the attack. The center of the Blue Watch line was penetrated. It became a bottleneck of Tigran and pirate bodies and blood yet they were making the breach wider.

Traven called Sergeant Major Stone. "I need you to pull ten men from the left flank to help seal the breach or we'll be overrun any moment."

The Sergeant Major replied, "I'll be right there."

No sooner said than Traven heard the sound of two machine guns open up. Traven looked over his shoulder and there was Sergeant Major Stone and another sergeant standing in front of the breach firing two belt-fed machine guns into the enemy breach. Between them and the hail of 40 mm grenades the assault was stopped. What enemy was left retreated back to their positions. Traven looked across the breach in front of him. There were more bodies than he could count.

The sight so moved Traven, he stood, wiped a tear away and gave a slow-motion salute in their honor. A silence fell over the battlefield. "To the fallen brave I salute you," he declared.

The Tigran commander stood and copied the salute. Traven paused for a moment starring at his adversary before returning to cover.

No one could come to the aid of Fire Team 7 except David and his now badly battered shuttle.

"David, we need to get out of here before we get blown

to bits. We can't take much more damage," Bill, his copilot, warned.

"I don't care. We aren't leaving those guys. We have to help them hold on or they'll be wiped out. The enemy will then be able to out flank LZ-Gold. We are their only hope. You got that!"

"Affirmative!" Bill groaned.

"I'm with you too!"the loadmaster announced over the intercom from the back of the shuttle.

David brought the shuttle around for a sixth pass at a concentration of troops trying to set up a light rail cannon on the roof of a building looking down on the knoll. David fired a long burst at the roof. There was an explosion as the power generator for the rail gun disintegrated. As the shuttle passed overhead, a much larger secondary explosion ripped through the building. The exploding generator touched off an explosives cache inside the building. Shuttle 4 was fatally riddled with shrapnel. The back of the shuttle began filling with smoke.

"Brace for impact!" David shouted over the intercom to the copilot and loadmaster. David and his copilot fought at the controls to keep the shuttle airborne just long enough to bank around and behind the knoll of LZ-Blue.

David brought the nose of the shuttle up at the last second. The craft skidded across the ground sending dirt and debris aside like it was plowing a field. The shuttle came to rest about twenty yards behind the knoll. Smoke began billowing from a ruptured fuel cell. Shaking off the shock of the crash, David began shouting commands to his copilot while shutting down power before unbuckling his harness.

When he called to the copilot to evacuate there was no response. He looked over to see a limp body. He reached over and found a pulse.

"Bill, come on, we got to get out of here.The ship is

on fire!"David urged while gently shaking him. The copilot was still unresponsive. "OK! We will go together one way or the other." After fumbling with the harness for what seemed forever, David finally pulled out his folding knife and cut the copilot out of the restraints. Struggling with the limp body, David extracted the copilot from the seat and dragged him out the side hatch.

He laid Bill behind a large boulder a safe distance away. And removed his helmet. Looking around, David realized his loadmaster was missing.

Smoke was getting more intense. Flames began spreading from the fuel cell. He dashed back inside the shuttle. Through the flames, he could see the loadmaster still strapped in his seat. A long piece of shrapnel was protruding from his chest. Realizing there was nothing he could do, David retrieved the First Aid case and a large duffle bag strapped behind his seat, and exited the almost engulfed burning wreckage.

When David returned to his copilot, Bill was barely conscious. After ensuring Bill's airways were clear and breathing was normal, he checked for bleeding. There were no open wounds, however, both legs appeared broken. The copilot also mumbled about severe abdominal pain. David assumed there was some internal bleeding. Laying him on the ground, David placed an emergency blanket from the aid case over him. Locating a syringe of morphine, he injected it.

David touched his shoulder. "Bill, try to stay alert and don't try to move. Don't die on me you hear?

He took Bill's radio from the pocket on his chest but realized it was broken. David then took his radio and called for help over the emergency channel. There was no response. He tried two more times but heard no reply.

Behind David the sound of battle was intensifying. "Bill, I have to go but I'll be back. Hang on!"

Bill nodded as he opened his eyes. "Go, I got an angel to

watch me while you're gone." he whispered.

From the contents of the duffle bag David strapped on his body armor, checked his pistol, secured a knife to his belt, charged his carbine and made his way up the knoll to join Fire Team 7.

On the bridge of the *Holcron Star*, the holo-projector displayed the battlefield below with troop and aircraft movements. The reinforcements Traven received were slowly making the difference as the tide of the battle began shifting to their advantage. Fire Team 7 was barely holding on for dear life. LZ-Red was laying down fire that repeatedly broke every Tigran assault.

Gavin's voice boomed over the communications net chatter, "Command 1! Shuttle 4 is down. I say again, Shuttle 4 is down. I see no survivors."

Silence fell momentarily over the net. Siyana was piloting the *Holcron Star* and gasped at the news. "That David's shuttle!" She blurted out. She quickly covered her mouth with her hand as she turned to look at John and Victoria.

John felt his heart stop and his stomach churn into a bigger knot, but for the sake of everyone, he outwardly appeared stoic and resolute. *God, we are all in your hands.*

He smiled at Siyana and announced, "Pilot, steady as she goes. It's not over yet."

Victoria was in shock and speechless. She reached her hand out to hold John's for just a moment as if drawing on some of his strength. John gave her a confident smile of assurance.

"Command 1, I see one survivor carrying out another crew member from Shuttle 4. Its David, he's OK! I see him."

John gave a deep sigh then announced, *"Halfling,* Command 1. Thanks! Out."

Everyone on the bridge sighed relief and resumed their

duties. Now John's thoughts turned to Jonathan. He always had a low tolerance for those who messed with his brother and sister. They were like the three musketeers and John knew three things. First, with David down, there was no stopping Jonathan from coming to his rescue. Second, whoever got in his way was in for a world of hurt. Third, there was no one better to do the job.

Jonathan, flying one of the larger cargo shuttles, just delivered a load of munitions to LZ-Red, when he heard Shuttle 4 went down.

"No, that's not allowed!" Jonathan shouted. He looked toward LZ-Blue and could see the smoke and wreckage. Jonathan went through the same emotions as his father and mother but unlike them, he could and would do something about it.

"Loadmaster, check our cargo. What are we hauling?" Jonathan asked.

"Sir, we have five pallets of rifle ammo, grenades, smoke grenades, a Mark 307 automatic cannon with a pallet of 25 mm ammo, belted .30 cal. And .50 cal. machine gun ammo for LZ-Gold."

"Great! I'm going to fly very low over LZ-Blue. When I give you the green light, unload all of it. Make it quick before we start drawing fire. You understand?"

"Yes, sir! You got it," the loadmaster replied.

Shuttle 2 came speeding up the same riverbed approach Shuttle 4 had taken earlier. It came to a hover just a foot off the ground behind LZ-Blue. The rear ramp lowered and the cargo was quickly rolled out. No sooner than the last pallet hit the ground than the shuttle sped off again. Now Jonathan circled around making strafing runs. It was almost an air show of aerial acrobatics as Jonathan rolled, jinked and weaved to keep the shuttle over the target as much as possible to keep the enemy from reforming for another attack. That gave the fire team a chance to distribute their ammo.

From the moment Fire Team 7 hit the ground, Corky O'Brian sensed the team was in big trouble. There was 600 yards of open tarmac that formed a plaza with rows of buildings on the opposite side. To the left side of the plaza was another oblong and higher knoll designated LZ-Red.

On the right side of the plaza were the administrative and lab buildings. A mile behind LZ-Blue was a fast-moving river.

On the first assault on their position, the Tigran rail gun tanks appeared from behind the maintenance building. They raced across the open plaza firing as rapidly as they could, with marines right behind them. The tanks made short work of the granite columns but that ended up working against them. The fallen columns actually gave his fire team better protection and saved their lives more than once. It was at that point the crazy shuttle pilot that dropped them off made short work of the tanks forcing the assault to retreat for cover.

A second assault wave was entering the plaza when the shuttle made several more passes helping to drive them back once again. The pirates and Tigran Royal Marines mounted a third attack once again across the plaza despite the wide-open kill zone. Corky knew it was a matter of numbers. The enemy had the numbers and he didn't.

One of his soldiers suggested retreat. Another team member agreed. O'Brian lashed out, "The Blue Watch never retreats. We have a mission and we will accomplish it."

No sooner was the enemy beaten back a third time than David appeared. SSgt. O'Brian saw the shuttle attack an enemy roof top position that resulted in a huge explosion. The shuttle disappeared in the smoke and debris. Corky thought for sure the shuttle was blown to pieces. As the dust and smoke drifted away, he saw the shuttle circle around trailing smoke and crash land behind his position.

"Hey! I see you brought your sleeping bag. You planning

on camping out?" Corky asked as he put a fresh magazine in his rifle.

"Naw! I did bring some sandbox toys though. Mind if I play?" David asked as he unzipped the bag.

"We could use the help," Corky replied.

Corky took note of David's carbine, sidearm and a very wicked looking knife carried on his belt before looking inside the bag. Inside was a wild collection of weapons: a shotgun with a bandoleer of ammo, another .45 auto pistol, several pistol and rifle magazines, and half a dozen grenades.

"Have you ever been in combat before?" Corky asked.

"A couple minor skirmishes but nothing like this."

"Somehow I could tell. Welcome to our playground. Set up next to me on the right flank. Don't let anyone out flank you. Be careful, those guys play rough," Corky explained as he flinched from a random laser blast.

David took his position to the right of SSgt. O'Brian. No sooner did he get situated in his position than he spotted a group of Tigrans attempting to out flank his position.

At the same time a force of pirates and Tigrans began charging the knoll once again. The Tigrans trying to out flank Fire team 7 were surprised when David opened up on them.

A squad from LZ-Gold on the end of its left flank laid down withering fire. The rooftop snipers also began picking off the enemy.

As the enemy pressed their attack on the knoll, a shuttle came up low behind them, stopped long enough to drop some cargo pallets, then began a strafing run on the slow but steadily advancing troops. Jonathan's strafing run helped drive back the enemy and brought another lull in the battle.

This gave Corky and David a chance to retrieve more ammo for the beleaguered fire team.

"Another crazy pilot. Does he have a death wish too?"

Corky yelled at David as he turned to retrieve some rifle ammo from one of the pallets. "Naw! That's just my brother, Jonathan. He's the crazy one. I'm the cautious one."

"Then you must be David Braxton. That explains it all," Corky said as he picked up a .50 cal. ammo can and passed it to the Russian team member.

David opened the crate on the second pallet and found the M-307 automatic cannon. "All right, now we're talkin! Give me a hand."

Together they hauled the cannon to a good position among the fallen columns and hooked up the ammo box. Corky charged the gun and dialed in the range on the sights. David ran back for more ammo, which he distributed to wounded soldiers keeping them in the fight. He ran back a third time to resupply Corky.

Jonathan made another strafing run over the enemy held warehouses and realized the enemy was amassing for a fifth assault. Three of Fire Team Seven's members were wounded and one of them unconscious. David had a flash of genius.

As Jonathan made his third strafing run, David ran back to the pallets of supplies. He returned with two containers of smoke grenades just as the enemy launched its fifth and most violent assault. The Russian and David were throwing every smoke grenade they had while Corky opened fire with the automatic cannon with its airburst ammo.

The firing from both directions was ferocious and unrelenting. David saw a team member fall from a blaster bolt which struck him in the chest leaving one wounded Cassarian, the big burley Russian, Corky and David in the fight.

The enemy was halfway across the plaza and still advancing despite heavy casualties. Soon they would rush the position and it would be all over.

The Tigran Marines became disoriented from the thick

smoke enveloping the battlefield. Their blaster fire became erratic and ineffective in the dense smoke. Mortar fire from LZ-Red rained down in the dense swirling smoke to support Fire Team 7.

The Tigran officers shouted and urged their men onward. A do-or-die desperation settled over both sides of the battlefield. Time was running out. The Tigrans made a suicide charge across the remaining distance to the knoll but they were unable to accurately fire at the invaders desecrating their holy worship site. The Tigran Marines and remaining pirates desperately pressed on oblivious to the dead and dying around them. The instinct to survive was now in control of everyone.

With the last smoke grenade thrown, David fired his rifle at anything that moved until the gun was empty. Out of rifle ammo, he grabbed the shotgun and fired until its ammo was gone too.

The wounded Cassarian grabbed any weapon he could find from dead team members. He kept firing until he finally slumped down unconscious at his defensive position.

David began firing his two pistols at any Tigran emerging through the smoke. Running out of ammo again, David threw his last two grenades then reached for his knife.

In a flash of a thought he remembered his Dad once saying, "Only an absolute fool gets in a gunfight with a knife."

Dad, I sure hope you're wrong this time. From the left of David, a Tigran came charging the Russian who deftly grabbed him and threw him head long into a large piece of a column. Two more marines tackled him and a deadly wrestling match ensued. Corky was firing his pistol now at any one he could see. Two Tigrans charged him at once. Corky shot the first one who fell on top of him. He was now pinned down as the other Marine leaped on top of the other body attempting to stab Corky with a knife. David tried to come to his rescue when another Tigran charged out of the smoke to his right.

David deflected the blow and slashed at him across the chest. Right behind the bleeding marine another marine appeared. He stopped just short of David's reach with his knife. The marine paused to size up David and then charged. Thick smoke continued to swirl around the knoll as the last warriors went hand to hand.

Each slashed and parried each other's attacks failing to subdue the other until the marine made a mistake and feigned a low thrust while attempting to grab David's hand with the knife. David felt the deep sharp pain but the marine left an opening David took advantage of and finished off the marine. David felt another sharp pain from behind him and fell to one knee. The attacker let out a scream as he fell on top of David. The struggle for life took on an eerie silence as the muffled groans of wounded and dying ceased.

Traven's defensive center was on the verge of collapsing a second time from the sheer force of the enemy's assault, when the last of Alpha Company arrived. Now all of Blue Watch was in the battle.

The *Halfling* and two armored shuttles laid down a withering covering fire for LZ-Gold. Resistance was still fierce, but Traven could sense a change and despair in the enemy's efforts. His men were able to gain access to the roof of a hangar and post two more sniper teams. Now six teams of snipers from three positions produced devastating results on the enemy.

The snipers now spotted the Tigran commander race across an alley to join his second in command behind a couple of storage containers near the barracks.

Up to now, the forces at LZ-Red had been directing their mortar and rifle fire in support of LZ-Blue. The commander did not realize how exposed he was until now. It was too late as a sniper's bullet ended all concerns for victory. The Tigran senior officer next to him no sooner realized the commander was dead than another shot rang out. Seconds later, he was also relieved of command.

Over the next twenty minutes many more Tigrans and pirates were struck down by the snipers. Traven pressed home his attack on the rows of buildings. The Tigran and Gamoran defenders realized that with most of their officers and noncommissioned officers' dead or severely wounded and retreat impossible, there was no other option but surrender. Dying for a cause lost its importance with the destruction and capture of their god's symbol of promised victory. As it became obvious to the remaining Tigran and Gamoran combatants the battle was lost, they too laid down their arms in defeat.

Jonathan was nervous. The smoke prevented him from making any more strafing runs on the enemy. He couldn't see what was happening on the knoll. Sergeant Major Stone, leading a team across the plaza, reported no firing. Jonathan circled around and brought his shuttle to a landing on LZ-Blue next to the wreckage of Shuttle 4.

Jonathan stepped out with his pistol drawn and worked his way up the knoll. As the smoke slowly cleared, Sergeant Major Stone also arrived. Thomas Kasill shadowed Sergeant Major Stone throughout the battle now stood recording the carnage with his camera.

Jonathan first came upon David's copilot who was unconscious. Near the top, he found a dead fire team member surrounded by several dead Tigran soldiers. Bodies were so thick they had difficulty walking between them.

"Sergeant O'Brian! Where are you?" the sergeant major shouted. "Come on now, you can't die on me you crazy Irishman. You're alive around here somewhere, I know it. Answer me!"

Jonathan called out for his brother as well, but silence

was the only reply.

"Hey, sergeant major, I found one of ours, he's badly wounded.

Here's another one. He's unconscious too," another soldier shouted. "Get the medics and prepare stretchers to load them onto the shuttle." The sergeant major ordered.

Two more fire team members were found. One was seriously wounded and the other dead beneath several fallen Tigrans.

Jonathan searched the carnage. A hand protruded from underneath two fallen Tigran marines and seemed to be moving. He rushed over to see the hand move again. Then he heard a familiar muffled voice groan, "Over here!"

Jonathan's heart began beating rapidly. "I got ya David. I got ya!" Jonathan frantically called out as he dragged the bodies off his brother. David lay seriously wounded and barely able to move.

"Don't worry little brother. I'll get you out of here. Don't you dare die on me! Mom and Dad would be so ticked!" Tears ran down Jonathan's cheeks as he cradled his brother and shouted, "MEDIC! I need a medic NOW!"

Jonathan was holding David in his arms when he heard the clicking of a camera. Looking up he saw Thomas Kasill taking pictures. "You're not a medic. I need a medic."

Thomas scurried off and returned with a medic. Another voice called out, "I found him. I found Corky!"

Sergeant Major Stone rushed over to see a blood soaked Corky O'Brian slumped over the automatic cannon with two dead Tigrans on top of him. Pulling the dead Tigrans away, he began shouting, "Medic, over here ASAP!"

A second team of medics quickly began tending to the injured sergeant.

"You'd better not be dead you little pip-squeak." Stone

warned.

"Ah, now sergeant major!" Corky faintly replied opening one eye. "Ye think I'm dead do ya? I'll have ya know the good Lord personally told me I'm not goin' home today. I hope I didn't let ye down."

Sergeant Major Stone bent down and whispered in his ear, "Son, you could never let me down! Just don't let it go to your head." No one noticed the sergeant major fighting to hold back tears as Corky smiled before slipping into unconsciousness.

Jonathan eased Shuttle 2 to a gentle landing on the *Holcron Star*'s hangar deck. Medics and crew stood by to remove the wounded and rush them to sick bay. Twenty-three of the most serious casualties arrived for treatment while the rest were doctored on Terra.

John, Victoria and Siyana stood by as David was carried on a stretcher down the ramp. Victoria rushed to his side and grasped his good hand with John and Siyana beside her.

"You'll be all right!" Victoria said soothingly as she stroked his short brown hair.

"I'll make it, Mom, don't worry. Jonathan warned me you'd be upset if I didn't," David smiled weakly.

"I am upset but don't you worry. We have the best doctors in the galaxy. In the meantime, we have someone to keep an eye on you." Siyana stepped forward as Victoria took their hands and joined them; then stepped aside. Jonathan on the other side of David's stretcher smiled. John placed his fingers gently on David's shoulder.

"No more heroics for a while. We need you," John assured him.

"I just did what you taught us, Dad. Do the right thing and let God take care of the rest."

John struggled to keep his composure. "You did fine, son,

just fine."

Two orderlies came to take David to sick bay.

"I'll catch up with you two after surgery," John said urging Siyana to stay with David.

In sick bay, Khem, Susan and Katrina were overwhelmed with the constant stream of wounded soldiers. Susan knew David was badly injured and on his way. For now, she needed to block out her anxiety to focus on her patient. She just finished with her patient when two orderlies rushed in with another wounded warrior and carefully laid him on the operating table.

The wounded soldier turned his head to meet her horrified stare. "Hey Sis! I'm on a tight schedule, can you patch me up quick?" David asked still groggy from the pain meds.

Susan, gasping in shock and staggered backwards. Khem seeing what happened quickly caught her while giving a cutting glare of disapproval to the orderlies. Katrina helped her to a chair.

"I'll take care of David. You finish closing up my patient. Trust me, I'll make sure he is as good as new again," Khem reassured her.

Susan shook off the shock and nodded. She began finishing up Khem's patient. A nurse wiped away the tears welling up in her eyes.

"Don't worry Susan. David will be fine," Katrina assured her.

Khem and two nurses operated on David for over five hours. After carefully making sure all internal bleeding was stopped, Khem closed up his wounds and injected the healing nano cells. Afterwards, David was moved to the recovery room.

Siyana and Victoria took turns staying by his side while he lay unconscious for several hours. When David regained consciousness, the fog seemed to lift as he slowly gazed around the room.

His eyes gradually focused on Siyana asleep in a chair beside the bed. His stirring startled her awake.

"You're awake!" Siyana whispered while gently stroking his hair. "How do you feel?"

"Like I got run over by a Mack Truck," David weakly replied.

"Khem says you'll be just fine," Siyana assured him.

"I guess I'll have to take Khem's word for it, but my whole body feels like it's crawling from the inside out," David complained.

"Go back to sleep. The nano cells are healing your body. I'll be here when you wake up. I promise!" Siyana whispered.

David smiled, slowly closed his eyes and drifted back into the cloud of sleep.

Once the Tigran and Gamoran forces surrendered, Gavin joined up with Major Rivers to free prisoners held in the mines. They found a horrifying scene reminiscent of the liberated people on the *Holcron Star*. Even before they entered the mine, the stench wafted out, sickening all who came near.

Four hundred men and women, filthy, half-starved and sick, welcomed being rescued from the mineshafts. It was an emotional time for many of the Cassarians, Holcrons and Katusians liberated from the *Holcron Star* who were reunited with former shipmates, friends, and family.

Robin Lefleur, anticipating the condition of the people, prepared special meals for them in advance. The medical personnel from the *Fire Hawk* were sent to supervise the relief program on Terra. Several crew members from both ships, cross-trained as medics, were flown to Terra to assist.

John Braxton and Stephen MacKay arrived to inspect the scene with Gavin and Traven.

John could hardly contain his anger. "I want every surviving enemy officer and civilian leader detained in a separate holding area. I want to know who is responsible for this inhumanity. Document everything. This cannot be tolerated."

"Are you wanting to hold military tribunals?" Stephen asked.

John shook his head. "Oooh, I'd love to do it, but we just aren't there yet. It could be a year or more before we could do anything. If a government requests any of the prisoners for trial for crimes against their people, they are welcome to come get them.

"As an ambassador of Cassaria, I officially request transfer of pirate prisoners into custody once the battle of Cassaria is settled," Gavin said.

"Request approved!" John agreed. "They're all yours as soon as a Cassarian ship arrives. You have to take the Tigran prisoners too."

Gavin nodded. "They'll most likely be repatriated in the end anyway."

"Good enough," John agreed.

'Traven, All of Blue Watch will remain here on Terra, along with the construction team. You know what to do."

Traven nodded. "Yep! We'll clean up here."

"In five days, Admiral Dever will rendezvous with us. We'll know if he successfully brought the Katusians to our side and destroyed the Gamoran pirate base on Betarus Minor along the way."

"What if he didn't destroy the base or turn the Katusians?" Traven asked.

"Then we have no choice. We'll have to leave sooner than planned, make a detour to Betarus Minor, fight another battle against the pirates before racing to Cassaria," Gavin replied.

"How can we do it with the force we have!" Traven asked.

"We're getting spread thin but we need to think positive," John reminded everyone.

"Gavin, can you put together a volunteer crew from those we just liberated to man the captured cruisers? We need every ship possible if there are enough people up to it before we leave."

"Many are in poor condition, but I have no doubt there will be no shortage of experienced volunteers for at least one ship, possibly both. I'll get right on it," Gavin replied.

"Do we have a casualty report yet?" John asked Traven.

"The Blue Watch causalities were higher than anticipated: twenty-one killed and seventy-seven wounded. The use of ceramic body armor greatly reduced the severity of injuries against their laser weapons. The Black Watch suffered the loss of one shuttle and another severely damaged. One crewmember was killed and two seriously wounded.

'The enemy casualties were much worse. Our use of projectile weapons versus their laser weapons really made a difference. The Tigrans and Gamorans had 297 killed, 179 wounded plus twelve missing in action and presumed dead from the huge explosion that brought down Shuttle 4. We are holding another 225 Gamoran and Tigran prisoners, mostly civilians in a makeshift prison at the mine. There are another 149 prisoners on Proto. We also captured 2 heavy cruisers, ten shuttles and two large freighters."

"Those are the top of the line, 60 passenger, armored Holcron assault shuttles previously captured by the pirates," Gavin interjected.

"The two freighters are Tigran supply transports. They are about five times larger than the *Halfling*. They each brought 250 Tigran space marines, tanks, personnel carriers, and construction equipment here four months ago."

"By the way, the two cruisers were in the process of

having the zannite upgrade installed. We arrived just in time," Stephen said grimly.

"Were any other Gamoran or Tigran ships upgraded before these?" John asked.

"We are researching that issue as we speak. There are enough zannite crystals on hand to upgrade at least 90 to 100 ships. I get the feeling the Tigrans were suspicious the Gamoran pirates were double crossing them and sent troops to protect their interests."

Stephen MacKay's flip com.beeped and after a short conversation hung up. "Gentlemen, the maintenance logs show three Tigran heavy cruisers were upgraded and left about three week ago to join the Tigran fleet. No more ships are expected to arrive before the attack on Cassaria."

"What about the pirate fleet? Where are they, and are they upgraded with zannite?" John asked.

Admiral MacKay smiled.

The pirates are massing most of their ships at Betarus Minor. They are due to arrive tomorrow and upgraded there so the Tigrans wouldn't know their true strength. If Admiral Dever arrives on time, he will catch them with their ships shut down for the changeover."

"Well, Stephen, every dark cloud has a silver lining. Let's pray Admiral Dever exacts his revenge," John smiled.

The next morning, John and Victoria visited the make shift hospital on Terra. As they visited each Blue Watch soldier, John prayed with them and thanked them for their service, while Victoria pinned a medal to their pillow. The silver, heart shaped medal had a raised cross in the center attached to a purple ribbon. On the backside was inscribed: In honor of the sacrifice of some for the freedom of all.

When John decided to visit the prisoner ward, the two guards hesitated to let Victoria, John and an interpreter enter for their own protection. However, John insisted and the guards relented.

A Gamoran prisoner turned out to be a doctor and agreed to help tend to the wounded prisoners. He followed them from patient to patient. He was amazed that John and Victoria were genuinely interested in the care of each prisoner.

John asked each patient if they were comfortable and if they were getting the care they needed.

One patient appeared very uncomfortable as he kept moving his head on the pillow.

"You need another pillow?" John asked.

The Tigran was frightened to answer but nervously nodded his head.

John smiled. "Allow me to help you?"

John called for a pillow and with one hand held it above him. Gently, John shifted his head forward and slipped the pillow in behind him. The Tigran's dark brown eyes continued to show fear.

"You have nothing to fear," John said as he gently adjusted the pillow behind him for more elevation.

'Does that make you feel more comfortable?"

The Tigran smiled and nodded his head in gratitude. The other Tigran and Gamoran patients watched in amazement. Many started whispering to each other and nodded in silent agreement.

"What are they whispering about?"Victoria asked the interpreter.

The interpreter thought for a moment. "Tigran mrines are expected to fight to the death. The Tigran commander would have ordered them put to death rather than waste resources on wounded soldiers who are considered cowards for failing to make greater sacrifices.

'The patients are saying, 'General Braxton not only gives aid and comfort to his wounded soldiers, but to his wounded enemies as well.' They expected death, but General Braxton extends mercy and respect. They are not sure what to think of Earthlings," the interpreter replied.

"They needn't worry. We don't practice the brutality and savagery of their leaders. As long as they are peaceful, we will treat them with the respect and kindness due any being. When we win this war, they will be repatriated to their homes in peace," Victoria assured the doctor.

"You fail to understand," the interpreter said. "They can never go home. Blood honor is one of the tenets of their society. Their own families will kill them to wipe away the shame of defeat."

In the midnight blackness, two dark figures crept quietly along the shadows of the garden wall and shrubs of King Toburg's estate. Unnoticed by a bodyguard, one of them crept up behind the guard and silently ended his life. One figure hid the body under some nearby bushes and resumed the guard's duties as if all was well.

The other figure worked his way up to the mansion, deftly crept up the steps to the second-floor veranda, and climbed a lattice onto the third-floor balcony. Reaching into a pouch on his belt, he produced a tool to pick the lock. Once the door unlocked, he carefully slipped inside.

The king and queen were in a deep sleep as the figure crept across the room and approached the bed. The assassin raised his blaster pistol to fire.

Slick step out from behind a curtain and deftly followed him across the room. With one hand over the assassin's mouth from behind and a quick thrust of a knife the assassination attempt ended. Slick quietly lowered the body onto the floor and placed a small folded piece of paper into the dead assassin's shirt pocket. He then left the bedroom as silently as he entered.

Retracing the assassin's path, Slick made his way to where the lookout was stationed. Sandi had already overpowered the lookout and dispatched him just as efficiently.

Looking at the body and then at Sandi he could see she was shaking with an adrenalin surge. He whispered to her, "Good job!"

A minute later, they were on the other side of the wall and heading back to their hide out.

Twenty minutes later, a horrifying scream jolted Adrian out of bed followed by another scream. Turning on the nightstand light Adrian grabbed a blaster pistol from the drawer.

A petrified Pella was on the floor atop a body dressed in black. She screamed again upon seeing the body and fled to her husband's side. Blood soaked her nightgown.

The king's bodyguards, alerted by her scream, burst into the room with their weapons drawn. Adrian lowered his pistol while his bodyguards checked the body on the floor and swiftly searched the room and balcony. The Chief of Security radioed each guard around the estate; one guard failed to report. He lay dead along with the body of another intruder near the garden.

"What is going on here? A body is found in the middle of the night in my bedroom and nobody knows a thing?" the king asked his chief of security.

"This doesn't make sense. How did he get in here to assassinate you only to be murdered instead? I don't get it," the chief of security said scratching his head.

"Sire! There is no identification on the body but this piece of paper was found in his shirt pocket. It appears to be a phone number," reported one of the security guards as he handed the piece of paper to the chief of security.

"Your Majesty, I insist we move you and Queen Pella to a more secure location until we know more about what is going on," the chief of security urged.

"I disagree. Something very strange is going on for sure. However, I don't want to tip anyone off about what we know or don't know. Double the guard detail for now. Let us see if curiosity exposes the cat." Adrian ordered.

"I see your point. I'll make the arrangements right away, sire," his chief of security nodded in agreement.

"Darling, I don't feel safe here. Can we please sleep somewhere else?" Queen Pella pleaded.

"I agree. Let's get you cleaned up and take one of the guest rooms for tonight, my dear," Adrian said wrapping his robe around his wife.

After studying the evidence from the apartment explosion and recovered data from the bomber's hard drive, Special Agent Maxine Maxwell at first thought they recovered a gold mine. The woman in the picture Sammy identified was Dr. Jerri Spinner a co-worker of Dr. Sanchez. A report from *Holcron Star* security was passed on to her identifying Doctors Sanchez and Spinner as Outsider Implants. The dots were now starting to connect. In the recovered hard drive were the names of tens of thousands of implant members and locations of implant cells. A cursory check revealed some of the people were average citizens going about their daily lives. Others were at every level of local, state and federal government, including police departments, military, Homeland Security and FBI.

Studying cell locations and implant names, Maxine laughed. *It's like looking at Who's who in America. These Outsiders are so smart they can travel across the galaxy but can't run a spy ring? This doesn't pass the smell test, something's wrong.*

What if they were smart enough to run one? What if this was all a diversion, including the data recovered. Could they have played us the fools and succeeded? Just how involved is

Dr. Sanchez? Is all this really intended to keep us out of the way of their real plan? If so, what are they really planning?

The only way to know is to bring in a couple suspected implants on the list and check them out. A knot tightened in the pit of her stomach as she realized how overconfident she and her team of agents had become.

"Now half of my team is dead," Maxine said aloud.

"What are you saying?" Her partner asked.

"They know we will follow every lead. They are slowing us down and we are wasting time and lives," Maxine explained. "Somehow we have to get a step ahead of them. If these people are not implants, three precious weeks of investigative work and the lives of agents wasted. Call the field office in New York and bring in the two special agents. Let's find out who they really are."

"You got it!" her partner agreed.

Five hours later, Maxine received a call from the New York office. It was everything she feared. Both of the FBI agents were clean. When she informed her remaining team members and supervisor of the results they began to realize a lot more manpower was needed. Maxine not only realized how clever Dr. Sanchez was, but how dangerous.

Maxine threw her coffee cup into the trash can in frustration. *All right. Dr. Sanchez, you got me this time, but even the best criminals eventually make a mistake. Dead or alive, you're goin' down.*

CHAPTER 18

Six days after the capture of Terra, life was still anything but normal routine. Worried unfriendly forces might show up, John Braxton pushed to restore the Terran base to operational status. The engineering teams rushed to repair damaged facilities and cleanup from the battle.

The Blue Watch troops referred to their new base as "Twelve Points" referring to the 12 shattered granite columns on the knoll where Fire Team 7 made their heroic stand. The name caught on quickly. When General Braxton heard the reference he made it official.

Every facility was searched, weapons and explosives secured, and inventories taken. Camouflaged bunkers were under construction and a defensive perimeter was established to enhance security.

A funeral service was held for those soldiers killed in the assault. They were given temporary burial in a meadow overlooking the lake. Under heavy guard, Tigrans and Gamorans were permitted to honor their fallen according to their customs, and ashes stored until it was possible to return them home.

John Braxton anxiously paced the bridge of the *Holcron Star*. "Dad, please, you're driving us nuts with your pacing," Jonathan pleaded.

"I'm sorry, I didn't realize it was distracting," John replied as he returned to his command chair only to get up again a few seconds later.

"What's troubling you?" Jonathan asked.

"Admiral Dever was supposed to be here almost two days ago and we haven't heard from him. Did the Holcrons and Katusians take out the remaining pirate base?"

"Dad, we have been in trouble since we got involved in this mess. We'll hear from him soon enough. Besides there isn't a whole lot we can do about it at the moment." Jonathan reasoned.

John nodded agreement. "Good point! One battle cruiser and a heavy cruiser aren't a lot against a whole fleet even with zannite upgrades,"

Jonathan agreed. "Can we find enough people to get the other two cruisers up and running?"

"I asked Gavin to help us with that. We'll have to wait and see what he can come up with."

"Sir! I have a large formation of ships entering sensor buoy range.

Estimated arrival in two hours," Georgia announced. "Have they identified themselves?" John asked.

"I have an incoming message from Admiral Dever," Molly replied. "I just sent it to your data pad."

John called up the message.

General Braxton,

The combined Holcron and Katusium fleet has arrived. I apologize for the delay. The Gamoran pirate base on Betarus Minor no longer exists. Their fleet of seven light cruisers and three corvettes no longer exist.

Our fleet consists of:

1 Battle carrier with 100 fighters

10 converted light carriers w/ 25 fighters each

10 Heavy cruisers

10 Light cruisers

32 Corvettes

35 Heavy Freighters

I hope this will do. Look forward to meeting you.

Regards, Admiral Usus Dever

John took a deep breath then wrote a reply of thanks and

asked Molly send it.

"Dad, now will you relax?" Jonathan asked.

John nodded, "Yes, and thank God too."

Maxine Maxwell sat in the pew for Sunday morning church service but couldn't keep her mind on the sermon. Her thoughts kept wandering off to the most puzzling case of her career. Usually she took notes on the message, but for once she had brought her job to church. She tried to shake her mind clear of the case and refocus on the sermon but to no avail.

Every lead we get seems to come to a dead end. Every intercept the National Security Agency finds fails to get them one step closer to finding a single cell. Dr. Sanchez has managed to disappear too. And on top of that, an unidentified hit and run driver killed Sammy, our only witness in the case. I should have seen that one coming.

Whoever is leading this alien operation has always stayed two steps ahead of them no matter what we do. They always seem to know what we're going to do before we do it. How do they do it? Nobody is that clever…or… are they?

Maxine shook her head to refocus her mind on the sermon.

"Old Satan never shows his real face to us," the fiery, white haired preacher proclaimed as he waved his black robed arms.

'He has to take other forms or we would know who he really is. He knows we would flee his hatred and ugliness. He is the wolf in sheep's clothing, the great deceiver, the trickster, and the beguiling voice of a serpent. He knows our every weakness. He knows how to blind us and lead us into temptation. Only with the shield of faith can we resist his fiery darts…"

As people in the pews shouted, "Amen!" and "Hallelujah!" Maxine received an epiphany.

The preacher is right. I have been blind but now I see. Dr.

Sanchez or someone else could have followed the reporter and learned of poor Sam Casey. The poor guy never hurt anyone in his whole life yet was run over like common road kill. However, that doesn't explain the other problems in the case.

The problem is one of our own hiding behind smoke and mirrors. There are Implants in the FBI all right, just not in New York. Having Implants in Washington D.C. was obvious, but till now I was blind to see my team is likely compromised.

"Hallelujah! Now I see! Hallelujah!" Maxine shouted.

"Come in, captain," King Toburg urged his chief of security. Pointing to the brown leather seat in front of his beautifully hand carved Cassarian walnut desk.

"Please sit," the king gestured. "What have you learned so far?"

"I'd rather stand if you don't mind, sire!"

"As you wish," Adrian nodded. "Go on with your report, please!"

"We have learned the names of the two assassins and traced the phone number to a secure phone belonging to Captain Pell Hoss, the personal aide of Admiral Nix Tayer. A search of the assassins' apartment turned up encrypted messages from Captain Pell Hoss' computer on their data pads. The most recent one was received the same day as the assassination attempt.

'We know a message using the same encryption code was sent to Captain Hoss' computer a couple hours after the failed assassination attempt. This security code is reserved for inter-Home Fleet use. Headquarters staff are not authorized access," the chief of security explained.

"You've made excellent progress. I want Captain Hoss arrested immediately and thoroughly interrogated," King Adrian ordered.

"There is one more bit of bad news that I'm afraid is even more disturbing, sire!" the captain stated hesitantly.

"More bad news? Go on!" the king sighed.

"About the same time the message was sent to Captain Hoss' computer after the assassination attempt, an encrypted message was sent from the same computer to Admiral Nix Tayer's personal computer at his residence.

'The general left an hour later for an unscheduled tour of several army and marine bases. According to his secretary, he is not expected to return until just before the Quadas Day Parade."

King Toburg grabbed his chest and fell back in his chair in despair. "You're right. It's the worst kind of news. The conspiracy appears to extend to at least some senior commanders in the Home Fleet." There was a long pause and deep sadness in the king's eyes.

Taking a deep breath and clenching his fist, King Toburg declared, "I will take care of him myself. I want Captain Hoss quietly arrested and taken under maximum security to the *C.S.S. Tarentino*. No one is to have access to the ship and no outside contact except through Admiral Quanto, head of intelligence and myself. Understand?"

"Yes, sire! Isn't that ship decommissioned?"

"Yes, it still has sub-light engines and life support but is modified with slave controls. It is a target ship for an upcoming exercise," King Adrian said.

'It's the most secure and last place anyone would look for a conniving little land crab. You and your men are the only ones to know where Captain Hoss is located and keep it that way. Dismissed!"

"Yes, sire!" the chief of security replied and quickly left.

Moments later, Admiral Quanto stepped out from a secret door behind the king's desk and took a nearby seat.

"Sire, if you ever decide to retire from the military, you should consider acting as a new career. That was a superb performance."

"Thank you!" the king replied. "By the way, I really liked the way you set the stage for getting Captain Hoss out of the way. However, I would love to know how you learned of the assassination attempt and thwarted it?"

"Honestly, sire! General Tayer really did plan to kill you using those two assassins. A little birdie told me of the attempt. The evidence was real and exposed by surreptitious means I had nothing to do with. Now the remaining conspirators will come to me for help. I guarantee you it will be their undoing."

"Excellent! However, why didn't you tell me of the assassination attempt? Whose side are you really on? Pella and I could have been killed."

"I don't know who the person was that thwarted the assassination attempt. Two nights ago, I went for one of my nightly walks and this person jogs up to me with a hood over his head. I couldn't recognize him in the darkness. He told me about the assassination plot and handed me a data card with an encryption access code matching the code in Captain Hoss' computer.

'He said in Hoss' computer I would find all the incriminating names, messages, computer addresses and phone numbers. I didn't know whom the assassins were or when they planned to strike. The gentleman cautioned me not to tell anyone especially you."

'He said and I quote, 'Be patient. We are sent to protect the king.' He wouldn't reveal himself to me but he did show me the ring you gave Estron at her commissioning. I recognized it and decided to trust him. By the way, he is not from Cassaria or any other planet we know."

Something caught the admiral's eye on the wall behind the king's desk. It was a picture of a much younger Adrian Toburg posing with some of the crew of his first command and a group of freed pirate captives. "Now I remember! When I was your executive officer on that converted freighter, we freed some pirate captives. Alice spoke a language we never heard before. The man spoke a few words in the same language mixed with Cassarian before switching to a universal translator. The female working with him was definitely Cassarian. I'd say she was from the Spritan Highlands. Her accent is identical to yours."

Adrian smiled. "My children never cease to amaze me, Amboy. They always seem to find the best of friends wherever they go. We must continue to be vigilant. It's not over yet.

'The Marine Commander of Xandra Marine Base is on our list of most loyal officers. Arrange a very secret meeting with me. I have two special missions for him I'm sure he will enjoy immensely."

Admiral Usus Dever lumbered down the shuttle ramp. Gavin, Aycana, Estron and Siyana rushed to greet him. The towering figure opened both arms wide enough to embrace the four. The Braxton family and a few key people stood behind them watching the reunion.

"Uncle!" the three sisters shouted as they embraced him. "Gavin, I'm so glad to see you again. I notice your ship is still in one piece too.

'You ladies never looked lovelier to my old and tired eyes. You have all grown so much since I saw you last, especially you little Siyana. I see the blush of love on your cheeks," he teased.

Siyana shyly blushed. "I see my brother told you too much about our adventures."

"I see you have all grown more beautiful and I sense much wiser. Your father has a right to be proud you." Admiral Dever smiled.

"How is Father?" Aycana asked.

"All of Cassaria mourns with him over your supposed deaths but I tell you a little secret. He never stopped believing you were alive and safe. When I told him of your good fortune he wept for joy. He knew in his heart all was well and anxious to have you at his side again."

"Great!" Estron shouted. "When do we go home?"

"I'm sorry Estron, but I was given explicit instructions. Under no circumstances are any of you to return home until this is over.

'As we speak, his enemies are plotting how to destroy Cassaria. I feel sorry for those fools. They haven't a chance if we arrive in time. Later we will talk more. Now introduce me to our new friends."

Aycana hooked her arm around her uncle's left arm and led him over to John Braxton. "Uncle Usus! This is our rescuer, friend and chosen leader, General John Braxton from Earth.

'John, this is our godfather, Admiral Usus Dever. We think of him as our uncle. We are all kindred spirits here," Aycana said.

Usus grasped John's hand firmly while peering deep in his eyes for a long moment before speaking. "Tell me John Braxton, if I don't join you what will you do?"

Everyone around the two men gasped in dreaded silence at the unexpected question. An awkward tension crackled in the air.

"I came to save my friends, my planet and the planets of my friends. I came to fight for a new world where we can come together in freedom. If I fight alone, then so be it. If I die, so be it. But you, sir, will miss a great and glorious fight," John countered.

Admiral Dever paused in contemplation before breaking out in boisterous laughter.

"You are a man who knows his destiny. I see it in your eyes. Yes, we will fight well and bravely together."

Usus placed his free hand around John's shoulder then asked, "Is this your family?"

"Yes, this is my wife, Victoria," John beamed.

"Allow me to ask, how did such a beautiful woman decide to marry a man that gets you into so much trouble?" Usus teased.

"Believe me, it was a hard sell. Life is anything but normal around John but you get used to it," Victoria bantered back.

"A beautiful woman with whit is a rare treasure," Usus graciously smiled.

John continued the introductions. "This is our oldest son, Jonathan and his wife, Katrina and our daughter, Susan. Our youngest son, David is in sick bay recuperating from his wounds."

Usus bowed slightly. "I see your children are very busy keeping you out of trouble. Your family brings you much honor."

John continued the introductions, "This is retired Admiral Stephen MacKay, commander of the *U.S.S. Fire Hawk.* Admiral, meet Admiral Usus Dever, Commander of the Combined Holcron and Katusian Fleet."

Admiral Dever shook his hand. "Admiral MacKay, if you are retired, I wonder what it is like to be a working admiral on your home world."

"What can I say, retirement is over rated." Stephen laughed. "Gavin told us some of your exploits over the years. I look forward to our victory together."

"And Dr. Jerri Spinner is our diplomatic advisor," Victoria said ending the introductions.

"Nice to meet you Dr. Spinner," the admiral said.

"I'd like some time at your convenience to discuss

planetary relations?" Dr. Spinner asked.

"I'm afraid that is not an area of expertise for me but you are free to get with my Officer of Protocol. She loves discussing such topics."

Before Dr. Springer could say more Victoria interrupted.

"Admiral Dever, please join us for dinner this evening. We are preparing a grand meal in your honor," Victoria offered. "Your officers are also welcome. Dr. Spinner and I have lunch together every day. Maybe your Protocol officer would like to join us for lunch tomorrow?"

"Great idea. Will you be serving hot mocha lattes tonight?" Usus excitedly asked. "I swear there is nothing like them anywhere in the known galaxy," Usus whispered to Victoria.

"Admiral, we have mocha lattes and much more," Victoria replied to the admiral's delight.

"I do have one other request. Before tonight's dinner, I would like to meet your young David. I understand he is a good, brave young man. If Siyana has her eyes on him then he is very fortunate indeed. I'm tasked to deliver a special message from a loving father."

"Sure, Gavin and Siyana can escort you to sick bay," John said.

"Good! Good! I'd like that very much. By the way, my government was pleased to find the *Holcron Star* no longer in pirate hands. By galactic law, your capture of the *Holcron Star* in free space makes it yours to keep as a prize of war. You honored us by offering to return it, however, your trade proposal has taken us in another direction.

'Your generous trade proposal is accepted and implementation of our trade package is underway. We will trade for the zannite crystals as agreed. The zannite crystals will enable us to build ships greater than the *Holcron Star*. Our government looks forward to doing business with you in the future providing you live that long," Admiral Dever replied.

"Thank you as well. I too pray we all live long lives," John nodded.

As they ascended the elevator to sick bay on deck 2, Gavin and Siyana briefed Admiral Dever on their recent exploits, the capture of Terra and particularly the Battle of Twelve Points.

"You really know how to stir up a fire hornet's nest don't you? Did you not realize the columns on the knoll were vital Tigran religious symbols?" Usus asked.

"The *Holcron Star*'s computer maps showed no such religious site or even a strong Tigran presence. We had no idea until our attack was under way," Gavin said.

The admiral shook his head. "The columns are like the proverbial line in the sand. For five hundred years, everywhere they built the columns; they never gave ground even once and were always victorious in battle.

The Tigrans are fiercely dedicated to their religious shrines. Having your soldiers among the religious columns was defilement to the extreme to them. With heavy losses and failure to drive the fire team and David off the knoll, and their leaders killed, they lost heart believing their gods were false or had abandoned them."

Gavin scratched his head. "This was just a small outpost. How could it be such a monumental loss?"

"John Braxton has sown the seeds of doubt and defeat into a society that does not know how to deal with such terms. I have no doubt this will have grave repercussions throughout Tigran society. For the Tigrans, it exposed their priesthood's false prophecy. Earth's appearance as a galactic player was not foreseen much less the presence of Outsiders. In their minds he is a harbinger of doom."

'The zannite crystals and General Braxton's fortuitous

victory changes the balance of power in the region. I hope John Braxton's charmed life doesn't end until this is over, nor young David's for that matter," Usus said with a wink at Siyana.

When the three entered David's room, Gavin made the customary introductions then left. Usus talked with Siyana and David for almost an hour, taking the measure of the relationship before getting to his purpose for the visit.

"As Siyana's godfather, I have a message to deliver to the both of you," Usus said. "Cassarian customs of courtship are for the purpose of testing the honor, love and growth of a relationship. The custom is not often practiced in modern times except by the Spritan Highland clans. The traditions are a means of demonstrating to the parents both parties are truly willing to dedicate their lives to one another. With great honor of trust, I deliver this message from a loving father.

'David, do you freely chose to pursue this relationship…'"

As the admiral held their hands together he repeated the message in accordance with Cassarian custom. There were smiles, laughter and tears as the message and blessings were given. With a foreboding of things to come, Usus could not help wonder if his task had greater meaning.

The next morning key officers of the newly formed fleet began to gather for a planning session at the Command Center on Terra. John Braxton, Admiral MacKay, and Captain Jack Reagan were already seated in the room going over some notes.

Admiral Dever and four of his officers followed their escort to the briefing room. Gavin and Jonathan were waiting in the hallway to welcome them.

They were shocked at the sight of the group. The one Katusian and four Holcron officers appeared dizzy and unsteady. Their eyes were bloodshot with dilated pupils and their hands shook uncontrollably.

"Forgive me, Uncle Usus, but you and your staff look awful! Didn't you get any sleep?" Gavin asked.

"I didn't sleep a wink last night. I lay in bed starring at the ceiling or running up and down the deck for something to do. My officers didn't do much better. I can get a chocolate latte? I'm thirsty."

"I think all of you have the caffeine jitters. How many lattes did you have last night, sir?" Jonathan asked.

"About twelve. My officers had as many too. Those drinks are fantastic!" declared Admiral Dever.

Jonathan and Gavin burst out laughing.

"Admiral, you and your men are on a major caffeine high. I suggest you lay off the caffeine drinks for 24 hours. I bet your heart is racing like a mad dog's right now?" Jonathan chuckled.

"How did you know about my heart? You are very wise for a young man, Jonathan Braxton. I think I will take your advice while I am able."

"Admiral, I suggest you and your men return to quarters for a few more hours of rest. I'll ask Dr. Kremmel to come by to make sure everything is OK."

"Yes, I think that is a good idea for now. Thank you for the advice but what about the meeting?"

Gavin ushered the Holcron officers back in the direction of their quarters.

"Uncle, I'm sure General Braxton won't mind delaying the meeting until you and your staff are more rested. Please go get some rest, you really look like you need it."

"You are so kind," the admiral muttered. As the group walked down the corridor, Jonathan and Gavin could hear Admiral Dever still extolling his newfound passion for coffee.

Eight hours later everyone again gathered for the meeting. The metallic ringing sound of a ceremonial brass hammer against a softball-sized cup fashioned from a nickel meteorite caught everyone's attention.

John Braxton looked around the room. "If everyone will please take a seat I'd like to get started. I'd like to thank Admiral Dever for the gift. It has a nice ring to it and looks cool too."

"Beats wrapping your knuckles to death too!" Admiral Dever joked.

"Yes, indeed. I'd like to remind everyone this meeting is classified Top Secret. No one outside this room is cleared for any of this information for the time being. As far as anyone outside this room is concerned, we are discussing plans for a galactic picnic.

'I hope everyone had a chance to read the brief I sent to each of your data pads. It allows us to dispense with a lengthy briefing,"John said as he called up a holo-projection map never seen before. This is a map of the new galaxy as we uncovered from an engagement with an Outsider scout ship in the Mentarus system. What caused the engagement is a story we will not go into for now."

Many in the room were taken aback from the enormity of the map and its implications. Admiral Dever leaned foreword and tried to grasp every detail.

"As you can see, what we know of the galaxy just increased by more than a thousand fold. There are at least 300 inhabited and habitable planets and thousands more solar systems. The extent of the Outsider territory is shown in the yellow area on the map. We have learned the Outsiders originate from the planet, Uvaria.

'The Uvarian Empire, is made up of fifteen inhabited planets with approximately twenty-five billion people. The empire has expanded to a point they are experiencing difficulty maintaining effective political and economic control. Two planets recently attempted revolts that were brutally suppressed revealing serious weaknesses in the Empire.

'Resources are stretched to their breaking point and the Uvarian leaders believe the problem must be solved soon. Terror or breakthrough technologies are their only options.

'To sustain and expand their empire they need to dramatically improve warp drive performance. The key to that accomplishment is a rich source of zannite.

'After a decade of searching, they discovered six sources. Four planets were found with small to moderate amounts of zannite, but under conditions impossible to mine. Another planet has a fair amount of the zannite, but the environment so inhospitable it is regarded as too high risk for present mining technology.

'That leaves the richest source, Terra. Two problems exist that must be overcome. Five planets in the region have space combat capability that must be neutralized. Secondly, the logistics and manpower necessary to sustain long-term operations from Uvaria are impossible. The operation must be secure and self-sustaining.

'Their plan is to conquer Earth first to support a base of operations with a sustainable environment of food and labor. All the Uvarian subterfuge and intrigue are designed to deceive, divide, isolate and conquer the five planets ensuring victory before the first shot. We need to come up with a plan to gum up the works and gather enough force to stop them.

Surprise and the zannite are the only things in our favor for the moment.

"What food sources do they require?" asked Commodore Lynx Montell, commander of the Katusian contingent.

John slowly looked around the room at each person before raising his eyebrows at the commander from Katusium.

"Never mind, I get it," Commodore Montell cringed. "They are going to wish they were vegans before this is over."

"Admiral MacKay would you like to provide us your analysis?" John asked.

"Thank you! The Uvarian force consists of two fleets. An advance combat fleet consisting of thirty-six heavy cruisers. Only their flagship is zannite equipped. We destroyed the other one though it only had zannite-enhanced engines. The invasion fleet has over one hundred heavy transport ships with 1.5 million troops along with another hundred supply ships for support.

'The Uvarians rely on sizeable Assault Transport Ships (ATS), each carrying about fifteen thousand assault troops and equipment. The ships are designed to batter down planetary defenses and support the ground assault troops. They are not designed to engage in space combat.

'The Uvarians have the advantage of a large fleet of stealth equipped heavy cruisers to eliminate any space threat before the ATSs arrive. Uvarian cruisers are equipped with multiple laser cannons and heavy shield generators. However, the stealth system, shield generators, and weapon systems rely on such enormous power requirements they can't operate simultaneously without zannite enhancements. In our battle we discovered they have to drop stealth mode to engage in combat. They have to drop their shields to half strength or cease defensive weapons to fire their laser cannons. They are definitely inferior to our zannite-enhanced magnum plasma cannons. If our ships maneuver in pairs, we can engage Uvarian cruisers one at a time with overwhelming firepower.

'We believe the ATS ships are especially vulnerable to attacks by fighters equipped with hyper velocity kinetic energy missiles. If we can strike their engines or reactors, we can severely cripple or destroy them. Any questions?"

Everyone in the room suddenly realized the Achilles heel of the Uvarians laid before them.

"In other words, the battle for Cassaria is part of their

plan. No matter if we win or loose the battle, if the losses are too high we can't win the war," Admiral Dever surmised.

"If the Tigrans are made to realize they are being used in this war, might they be persuaded to unite with us?" a Holcron officer asked.

"Wishful thinking," Admiral Dever charged. "The Tigrans are already committed to war or they would not have sent the Royal Marines to Terra and built the twelve pillars. They have lost their first battle, their blood drawn and their religious site desecrated. Even if you lived long enough to reach Tigra and spoke to their leaders, they would reject any proof of a conspiracy. They will merely claim we started this war and their gods demand revenge."

"The wrench in the whole plan is Earth," Admiral MacKay said. "We have to find a way to foil the attack on Cassaria and still get to Earth fast enough and with enough strength to foil their attack."

"I can get the fleet to Cassaria and together defeat the Tigrans. However, it will take almost six weeks to get to Earth. I'm afraid we will be too late. We will never reach Earth fast enough to engage the Uvarians before Earth is conquered no matter how large our fleet. Do we know if there is another fleet behind this one?" Admiral Dever asked.

"I doubt they have another fleet to spare, at least in the near future. Without zannite crystals they are overextended and know it," Admiral MacKay replied.

"I read a book once about a battle in the Pacific during World War II. A few destroyers and escort carriers took on a Japanese fleet. They put up such a ferocious fight the Japanese thought they were up against a superior force and retreated. Why can't we do the same?" Jonathan asked.

Everyone paused a moment waiting for John Braxton to respond to the question. John appeared oblivious to everyone's focus on him. Instead, he was focused on some calculations on his data pad.

"Dad? Hello! Are you with us?" Jonathan asked.

Without saying a word or looking up, he held up one finger while he pecked away. Finally John laid down the data pad.

John looked around the table. "Gentlemen, we have the means and the time to engage both the Tigrans and Uvarians. We just have to use all of our resources very carefully."

"What do you mean?" Gavin asked.

John smiled, "Admiral Dever, how would you like to take an early delivery of zannite crystals for your government per our trade agreement?"

Admiral Dever cleared his throat, "Sure, but there is no way to get them installed in time to do any good. It would take weeks to install them."

"That's not quite true, admiral," Jonathan interrupted. "With the crystals installed you can arrive in a fourth the normal time required. I was with Dexter, Deze and Grandpa two days ago as they were making some modifications on the zannite module to the reactor core.

'They discovered the Uvarians had a more efficient way of using the zannite crystals to maximize warp engine performance. Deze claims integrating some of their changes will give us 10 percent more power, less maintenance upkeep and longer fuel life. It also allows a safer, easier and faster installation."

'The new upgrade only takes two days rather than a week to install. The zannite upgrade for the shields and weapons can be done while under way within a couple of days if need be."

Gavin interjected, "I get where the Braxtons are going with this. We can take a small, very fast but powerful blocking force hidden in the Laylar System, make a surprise attack, and then fight delaying actions all the way to Earth. After the first couple of hit and run attacks they will be very wary and slow their approach. It could buy the time needed for Admiral Dever's fleet to reach Earth in time."

"Hopefully then we'll have sufficient forces to defeat the Uvarians," John proposed while studying the holographic map.

"I sense an opportunity!" Admiral Dever observed as he leaned forward in his chair.

"You agree?" John smiled looking at Admiral Dever and his officers.

"There are enough crystals to modify your whole fleet. We will show your engineers how to install them. Your modifications would be completed in five or so days."

"On behalf of my government, I accept delivery of our share of the crystals. I'm sure the Katusium government will reimburse my government for the crystals installed in their ships," Admiral Dever replied, turning to Commodore Montell.

The Katusian officer smiled and nodded agreement. After the meeting was concluded John asked Jonathan to stay behind until Admiral Dever and his staff left.

"Why wasn't I informed of the engine enhancements of our duct tape engineers?" John asked.

"You were busy. I was Officer of the Watch. It was classified as category B maintenance so I authorized it and entered it into the ship's log.

I haven't had the chance to brief you yet because of the meeting," Jonathan replied confident he'd made the right decision.

"That was a command decision affecting the operational performance of the ship. I should have been informed before, not after the fact," John sternly stated.

"You're right. I'm sorry. It won't happen again," Jonathan said apologetically.

"You just don't get it do you, son."

"What?" Jonathan asked totally confused.

"When I put someone in command, I expect them to command. You were in command and made a command decision. I expect you to defend your decisions. You like to make decisions don't you?" John asked.

"I was wondering when you were going to lay it on him," Admiral MacKay smiled.

"Tell me what?" Jonathan asked still very confused.

"You are going to be so sorry you ever made a command decision, Jonathan," Gavin teased.

"Captain Reagan is taking command of the cruiser, *Fire Brand.*

However, I need someone to command the cruiser *Fire Fox*, someone who knows how to give orders as well as take them. I know you don't have experience but I don't have a lot of options.

The truth is we don't have any ship officers much less experienced, so I have to look for the next best thing. I need someone with the ability to lead, a quick study, and someone everyone can trust."

"What about Gavin? He knows more than all of us," Jonathan asked nervously.

"John needs me on the *Holcron Star* as an advisor and to run the *Halfling* for special missions," Gavin answered.

"The fact remains the *Fire Fox* has a crew but no captain at the moment. We need all the firepower we can get. Admiral Dever has agreed to loan a few officers and crew to help you. Either you take command or it gets left behind. That is the crux of our manpower problem. You want the job?"

"Do you trust me?" Jonathan asked.

"Son, of course I trust you. Everything about our situation is far from ideal but it's the hand we're dealt. Are you going to step up to the plate or not?" John challenged.

Jonathan looked into the faces of everyone. Each of them

nodded in agreement. "OK, I'm your man," Jonathan finally replied.

"Well, Captain, you'd better get to your ship. You got a lot to do and little time."

"Do I get David?" Jonathan asked.

"No! Don't push your luck. Dr. Kremmel says he wants to hold him for a few days of rehab. I already have plans for him," John said.

"Nuts! Can't blame a new ship's captain for trying?"

Estron looked at the paper sign taped to the door to the Dark Pit. It read:

Danger! Warning! We're busy. Keep out!

Henry Braxton

PS: Can't say we didn't warn ya!

Shaking her head, she tore off the sign and entered the Dark Pit. Tossing it in the trash can next to the door she went over to the workbench where the duct tape engineers were absorbed in their work. They were huddled around an access panel to a large metal box. It looked like they were performing surgery on the strange piece of technology.

"How's it going, guys?" Estron asked trying to peer over Dex's shoulder to see what they were doing.

"Don't have time to talk," Henry muttered. "Can't ya read the sign?"

Estron gave up trying to see what they were doing and began looking at the parts laying on the bench. "You mean the one I took down?"

"Well, what's your problem?" Henry asked as he strained

to reach deeper into the box.

"Yes, what's your problem?" Deze echoed.

Ignoring Henry's question, Estron began picking up parts on the bench and examining them.

Henry tried to shout a warning. "Hey, don't mess with them. You could get…"

There was a loud crackle of electricity and a puff of oily smoke as Estron reeled backwards across the room. With a muffled thud she landed splayed out on her back on a nearby workbench. A small puff of smoldering smoke rose from her jacket sleeve, as she lay barely conscious from the shock. For a moment all she could do was lay dazed as the room slowly revolved around her.

The trio raced to her aid.

"Estron, are you all right?" Deze asked.

"What do you think?" Estron groaned trying to move. "I can't find a part of me that doesn't hurt."

"Can't say we didn't warn ya!" Henry quipped as he helped her slowly sit up.

"That…you did. I'm sorry for…my arrogance." Estron groaned as she brushed her static charged hair away and held her head in an effort to hold back the pain.

"Dex brought over a chair. "Estron, you need to sit for a while.

Do you need a medic?" Henry asked.

Estron paused for a minute. "I think I'll be OK…I'll just sit here for a spell. Thanks."

Deze handed Estron a mug of coffee. "Here work on this for a bit. It might help."

"Thank you, Deze. I appreciate it.

'What was…that thing! What are you guys doing?" Estron slowly asked.

"That was a backup power pack for the Uvarian Cloaking computer," Dex said. We were trying to see if or how our mine affected it before the ship was destroyed. We've been looking into a different approach."

"What different approach?" Estron asked.

Deze pointed to one of the experimental mines. "The mines work but it requires the ship to pass near the mine. We want something that seeks out the ship and makes it visible."

Estron's interest piqued. "OK, since you have the computer to study, why not find a way to hack into it? We can insert a virus to make the ship visible but also continue drawing power preventing them from bringing their shields and laser weapons to full power?"

Henry scratched his head. "I don't know nothin' about hacking but if someone comes up with a program I'll find a way to deliver it."

"I'm with Henry," Dex said. "Deze, you know anything about hacking?"

"That's what got me thrown into the brig a few times," Deze said. "I'm good but not that good with the time we have."

The three men turned their attention to Estron.

Estron pushed up her sleeves and smiled. "I haven't found a system I couldn't hack yet. Let's get to work."

Dex nodded his approval.

"Welcome to the Dark Pit!" Henry declared.

"Yep! Welcome to the Dark Pit," Deze echoed.

In sick bay, David and his roommate were packing up their things.

It was now mid-morning and the next day both fleets were to depart on their missions.

"It was sure great getting to know you," David exclaimed.

"By the way, congratulations on your field promotion."

"Thanks! It was great getting to know you too. Next time, though, we need to find some guys that don't play so rough. Those guys had no playground manners at all," Second Lieutenant Corky O'Brian complained.

"No kidding. They were quite poor weren't they? If there is a next time, I promise to bring more and better toys. Grandpa is working on something special for me. He promised I'd get a real blast out of it once he gets it working right."

"For your sake, I hope it works. Take care, mate, I have to report to Lt. Col. Rivers for my new assignment."

As they were about to depart, a nurse stopped them. "I've been instructed to have you report to hangar 1 in thirty minutes. Both of you will be available for light duty for a couple of days then ready to return to regular duty. Take advantage of the break."

"Thanks a lot." Corky replied.

When David and Corky arrived at the hangar deck, Siyana was standing next to the small Hummingbird shuttle.

"There you are.I've tried to get a hold of you for the last 30 minutes. I can't seem to find any of my family either," David exclaimed.

"You'd better not get a hold of me, David Braxton. That is forbidden on my world unless we're married," Siyana scolded with a coy smile.

"Oops, mate!" Corky teased.

"I'm sorry! That is not what I meant. On Earth it means I was trying to find you."

David looked around at the hangar and noted all the other shuttles were gone.

"Where is everyone? The ship is almost empty and all the shuttles are out."

Siyana flashed her blue eyes. "Oh, Jonathan came up with

a training exercise and your Dad ordered everyone to participate. They're all planet side but should be back in a few hours."

"Now that you found me, we have to get going. I volunteered to take you for twenty-four hours of rest and recuperation. Let's get going, the rental fee for the shuttle is by the hour," Siyana teased.

Minutes later the shuttle was skimming along Terra's surface. The scenery below left David and Siyana speechless. Corky closed his eyes after retrieving an airbag. The snow capped mountains glistened in the cloudless sunlight. The rich, emerald grassy plains, dark green forests, blue oceans and pristine lakes and meandering rivers were more beautiful than any tourist advertising video. They also saw majestic glaciers, over a mile thick, slowly grinding the landscape creating valleys, streams, lakes and rivers. The valleys of enormously tall fir and cedar like trees interspersed with groves of broadleaf trees were a painter's palette of greens and browns. Fields of meadow flowers and blooming shrubs added to the rainbow of colors.

Siyana eased the shuttle down to a few hundred feet above a large plateau teeming with wildlife grazing in great herds. The shuttle continued following a large, wide river meandering through the plateau.

"Hey, Corky, you gotta see this!" David shouted excitedly.

Corky opened his eyes just as the shuttle came to the end of the river then sharply plunge a thousand feet over the river's massive waterfall.

Siyana pulled up just two hundred feet short of the huge lake at the bottom and shot through a misty rainbow. David and Siyana squealed with excitement as he filmed the whole event. Corky groaned as he clutched the barf bag close to his face.

They continued flying along the vast lake to the other end into a broad and long grand valley. The lush valley boasted towering fir like trees, a variety of immense hardwoods, large grassy fields and hundreds of smaller lakes, ponds and streams. From the vast lake, the river continued for another three hundred miles until it reached the sandy beaches of the largest of Terra's seven oceans.

Siyana and David took turns taking pictures of the water cascading over the edge of the plateau creating a glistening rainbow. David spotted something white moving in a field off in the distance. Siyana decided to check it out. Taking the shuttle down to almost treetop level, she eased up on the throttle and clearing a couple of low hills, brought the shuttle to a hover. Before them was a majestic herd of large, white animals calmly grazing on lush fields of grass.

"Wow! They look like the bison on Earth except they are taller and stockier, with a silvery white curly coat. This is absolutely awesome!" David exclaimed.

Corky unbuckled himself to lean over David's shoulder for a better view. All he could say was, "Amazing!"

"There is nothing even close to this on Cassaria. Trust me," Siyana said in awe.

They watched the herd for a while longer then moved on. A few miles further a column of smoke was seen rising and Siyana suggested they check it out. Siyana again brought the shuttle down to treetop level and followed a stream around a bend to where the smoke emanated. To David's surprise there before him on the ground was the *Halfling* and a few large shuttles.

A short distance away was a large campfire with a campsite complete with open air dinning tents, picnic tables, food and a large crowd waving at him and holding large signs. Some signs read, "We Love You, David!" Other signs read, "Heroes welcome!" A couple signs had nothing but a bright green shamrock superimposed over a big red heart."

One sign that caught David's eye, made him laugh till it

hurt. Jonathan held it high. It read, "Don't Do That Again!" A large banner behind them stretched between two poles read, "Welcome To Terran Command BBQ."

David and Siyana soon joined the family, Gavin, Aycana, and Estron and as many personnel as could be spared, along with their guests, Admiral Dever, some of his staff, and many who were rescued. Those who could not come initially were rotated out during the all day event. Everyone got to spend time relaxing, fishing and playing various games.

Henry had the time of his life teaching Aycana and Estron how to fish in the stream. He was quite proud when their first catches were some of the largest salmon he'd ever seen.

Robin Lefleur supervised the meal, which composed of a barbecued side of bison, local fowl similar to turkey, and fresh fish that looked like a cross between a rainbow Trout and a salmon baked on wooden planks around a fire. There were vegetables, salads, native fruit compote, various desserts including David's favorite, Boston cream pie. Beverages offered were a selection of lemonade, iced tea, and to Admiral Dever's delight, an endless supply of coffee and fresh fruit smoothies.

As sundown approached, some of the people gathered wood and piled it onto the fire until there was a huge bonfire. Gavin waited until everyone gathered around the fire before addressing them.

"I don't know what everyone else thinks, but you Earthlings really know how to throw a down-home party. So many of us have been through so much in such a short time together, I think we really have become a family of sorts.

'When the Braxton family rescued my sisters and I, they risked everything for five strangers from another world. They had no idea if we were friendly or hostile. They just knew they were doing the right thing. It didn't stop there.

'As events kept unfolding, problems kept growing. They

didn't care. They just kept giving all they had. They didn't whine or quit, they just kept giving. They treated us like part of their family. To them we weren't aliens, just friends needing help. As that family grew so did their hearts. We learned from them how to overcome adversity as a family.

'When David was shot down you could sense the power of that family come together like I never witnessed in my life. The news was felt like a shock wave throughout the battlefield and fleet. It energized everyone with even more determination and strength. Crowds of shipmates gathered around sick bay praying for him and all the other wounded. Crew members on duty waited anxiously for word of recovery of their friends and loved ones.

'We are a family who cares like none other I've ever known. We keep growing as a family and always digging a little deeper finding even more to give. Never quitting, always finding a way, no sacrifice too small, no obstacle too big, and the power of faith are just a few of the values the Braxtons taught us and united us in spirit. They also taught us what good food really is." Gavin paused as everyone applauded.

"Tomorrow some of us will separate to our assignments for the battles to come, but always remember we are still family. No matter where we are, we have one cause, one duty, one calling: freedom for all!"

Everyone cheered and clapped as Gavin took a seat on a nearby log. John and Victoria were deeply moved by Gavin's speech. A chant began calling on John to speak. As he rose the group cheered then fell silent as he spoke.

"Thank you, thank you, Gavin for those kind words. They are deeply appreciated. I also want to thank Robin. You and your food service people worked tirelessly to make this a memorable day for all of us. Thank you!" John paused for a moment for a round of applause then spoke again.

"I also want to thank Victoria for supporting me through

thick and thin. Dear, you always know my weaknesses and fill in the gaps. I couldn't have gotten us this far without you.

'My children, what can I say? You always keep me going if for no other reason than to keep up.

'Dad, your sourdough spirit and creativity provided both victories and unintended humor and always at the right time.

'Gavin, Aycana, Estron and Siyana, Dexter and Deze, words can't describe what each of you mean to us. In such a short time you have become part of a special family.

'Through trials, hardships and sacrifice we became a band of brothers and sisters, a family bonded together. Sadly, we lost some of our brothers and sisters along the way. Their sacrifice will not be in vain. We must harden our resolve even more to ensure freedom for billions of people.

'Soon, we depart on another mission with even greater dangers. The most challenging and dangerous mission any of us can imagine. We will adapt…overcome…and prevail. Everything is at stake. We have our families, our freedom and planets to save."

Everyone stood and cheered. For the many who were liberated from the bonds of slavery, freedom had new understanding. The price of their freedom was paid and now it was up to them to pay it forward.

CHAPTER 19

Assistant Councilor Willett Quiller rushed his spindly body up the long white marble steps leading to the Great Hall of Unity in the Cassarian capitol city of Kysandia. Once inside, he rushed to the elevator and selected the top floor. As he went up the elevator, he leaned over with his hands on his knees breathing heavily. Loosening his collar, Willett was trying to cool down on the hottest day of the summer so far. Not a good day to be running up the marble steps, he noted to himself. It was then he noticed he was sweating through his dark suit jacket. Oh well, they will just have to put up with the body odor. Usually fastidious about promptness, this time he was unusually late for the councilors meeting but found it necessary to confirm the report.

The magnificent edifice was considered the grandest example of Cassarian architecture on the planet. It was an imposing regal structure rising ten stories and made of the finest polished granite and marble on Cassaria. The facade was decorated with striking white marble columns finished with finely carved statues and ornaments depicting Cassarian culture.

Reminiscent of a very large centuries old temple, wings were added with the growth of government and increased the structure's grander. At the top of a long flight of marble stairs was the great hall lined with statues and paintings of famous Cassarian leaders, folk heroes and historical events.

Two large finely inlayed hand-carved wooden doors opened into the grand assembly hall where the Council Elders conducted Cassaria's legislative business. The wings housed offices for councilors and their staff. Several legislative agencies and administrative departments were located in the many buildings throughout the capitol. In the eyes of visitors, it was obvious Kysandia was the ultimate seat of Cassarian power.

Senior Council Elders offices were located on the tenth floor, commonly known as the "Tenth Cloud," not because it was that high up, but because the egos of those on the tenth floor were that lofty.

The centuries old law required any building in the capitol of Kysandia be no more than nine stories high so no one could look down on the seat of government. The people of Cassaria looked upon the rule as pure arrogance and thus used the term "Tenth Cloud" to express their distain.

Councilor Druck Waddel and Councilor Taxis Glaxis were seated in a "Tenth Cloud" executive conference room near their offices.

"The Quadas Day Parade starts in three hours. All is going according to plan," Councilor Waddel assured his fellow councilors.

"I assume General Tayer will lead the military units along the parade route?" Councilor Glaxis asked.

"Yes, just before the marching units round the corner to approach the reviewing stands, I will announce to the audience and cameras the crowning of our new king. He will pause before us, dismount his horse and approach the stage. Once we crown him king and he makes a few remarks the parade will resume.

'We hired thousands of people to line the route and cheer during the ceremony. Just in case, plenty of law enforcement officers will be positioned behind the crowds and quickly arrest anyone who makes a scene," Councilor Waddel confirmed.

"Oh! This will be the greatest day in Cassarian history, a new government for a better world. What about King Toburg? Has he been arrested yet?" Glaxis said.

Waddel continued, "He should have been arrested about

twenty minutes ago on his way to the parade. The press release has already been issued stating that due to his failing health, he is resigning for the good of Cassaria. His bodyguards will be arrested later and tried for treason."

The vigorous pounding on the conference room door caught everyone's attention. Not even waiting for permission to enter, Assistant Councilor Quiller thrust the doors open still panting out of breath, "King Toburg escaped!"

"What?" Councilor Waddel shrieked.

"When the royal motorcade reached the road block, the police went to arrest King Toburg as ordered," Quiller declared. "However, when they opened the door to his vehicle it turned out the vehicle was a decoy. The twelve law enforcers were gunned down and the assailants escaped.

The king and his bodyguards are reportedly in hiding."

"What are we going to do now?" Councilor Glaxis cried out.

"Absolutely nothing," a calm, confident voice announced brushing aside the panic as the person entered the chamber.

"Admiral Quanto! Thank the gods you are here. What do we do now? You must help us!" Councilor Glaxis begged.

"Why are you fretting? I have already taken care of everything, gentlemen. When I heard the law enforcers were killed attempting to arrest the King, I gave orders to have military security forces search for king Toburg and the Royal Guard. I also ordered extra security to surround the parade route and reviewing stands to ensure nothing untoward happens. Actually, the king's actions and the deaths of the law enforcers helps prove the charges," Admiral Quanto explained.

"Having the military armed around the capitol is strictly forbidden. You know that!" Councilor Waddel challenged.

"Nonsense. The people will want a traitorous king arrested promptly. They will also see that the military is supporting you publicly. All you have to do is have the Directorate of

Law Enforcement issue a statement appreciating the military's prompt assistance and all will be well. The troops will return to their base once this crisis is over, I promise. Besides, with your plan to declare martial law, a military presence will help demonstrate their support for your vast power when the time comes."

Councilor Waddel agreed. "Yes! Yes! A press release stating the king was to resign because of poor health, then goes mad, commits treason and kills several law enforcers before fleeing into hiding makes it all the more believable. The masses will suck it up without question.

'After our enemy's attack and defeat our fleet and ground forces, it will be discovered General Tayer is also involved and arrested. The planet is invaded and we declare martial law with emergency powers. Yes, that is a great plan. Good job, Admiral Quanto."

"One thing more if I may suggest? It is an absolute must to make sure every politician, government official and leading business people supporting this action be visible in the reviewing stands. Every broadcast station on the planet is covering the event. There is no better time to convince them you are the man of the hour that can save them," Amboy suggested.

"Yes, I see your point. It's brilliant, Admiral Quanto. The people will be shocked by all the bloodshed and destruction. They need to see real leadership rise out of the ashes and restore order and peace," Councilor Glaxis agreed. "The people will beg us to rule and we will gladly do it."

"Agreed! Quickly, contact all our supporters to assemble," Councilor Waddel instructed Council Assistant Quiller.

The guard mount assembled for shift change at the Kardena Defense Base, ninety miles from the capitol, where the planetary shield generators operated. The duty officer ceremoniously inspected each row of enforcers, carefully inspecting their uniforms and weapons. He was visibly upset with the inspection and began chewing out each of the oncoming enforcers. Many of the uniforms were ill fitting on the muscular enforcers with some uniforms about to burst the seams. The new Sergeant at Arms informed him they were newly assigned and the quartermaster refused to issue proper fitting uniforms to his platoon.

"Sergeant at Arms! Notify the Quartermaster's office they are on report and to issue proper fitting uniforms to our enforcers ASAP! This is not acceptable."

"Yes,sir!"the sergeant replied with a wink at the new replacements.

As soon as the shift change was completed, a alone figure strode up the short drive to the main gate. His stride had the precision expected of a well-disciplined Royal Marine officer.

When he reached the gate, the law enforcer on duty snapped to attention. General Exis Yeager returned the salute and identified himself. There was a quick exchange of passwords and gate guards opened the main gate.

The general calmly gave the signal for the convoy of vehicles containing two hundred Royal Marines to proceed. The convoy raced past the guard shack to their objectives. The general flagged down the last armored troop carrier. Once the general was aboard the vehicle sped away.

With the shift change complete and weapons of the relieved guards checked in at the armory, their replacements promptly arrested them and took control of the armory and security headquarters.

At the same time the marines seized the generator plant and shield projector. An Explosive Ordinance Team deactivated the explosive charges. There would be no failure of the planetary shields today.

General Yeager smiled at his watch and knew the Quadas Day parade was starting. Everything was going according to schedule. The signal for mission accomplished was broadcast over a secure radio frequency to the fleet. The planet defenses were now secure and the fleet released from their space docks to reform and prepare to receive the imminent attack.

Broadcasting live throughout Cassaria, the Quadas Day parade started down the main avenue. Floats and marching bands led the way. News commentators reported the tragic news of King Toburg's mental breakdown and murder of several law enforcers. The wild speculation of who would be the next king fueled even greater interest than the parade and its proceedings.

Behind the last float was a long gap and the intended suspense rose in the crowd. Rounding the corner, the Cassarian Royal Military Band led by the color guard played patriotic music as they marched in flawless order down Main Street, stopping near the reviewing stand.

This was the moment for which Councilors Waddel and Glaxis anxiously awaited. Both strode proudly to the podium. Councilor Waddel spoke a few words of welcome, then introduced Councilor Glaxis to address the audience.

"My fellow patriotic Cassarians,"Glaxis boomed over the speaker. An assistant rushed up to adjust the volume. Glaxis smiled and resumed. "It is my honor and duty to announce the formation of a new kingdom.   I present to you our new king… King Nix Tayer! May his reign restore honor to our great planet of Cassaria."

The crowd gave a less than overwhelming response. Military commanders in the distance could be heard shouting orders for their troops to advance in parade march.

The sound of a thousand marching soldiers echoed down

the street as they rounded the corner. The first sight to come into view was not at all what everyone expected, especially those in the official reviewing stands.

Leading the formation was General Nix Tayer mounted backwards on a black ox instead of a prancing white horse. Bound hand and foot, wearing nothing but pants, tee shirt, and socks the traditional symbol of a coward and traitor. The crowd began murmuring in confusion at the scene.

Behind the disgraced general followed a thousand marching soldiers in full battle gear. Next a hundred armored troop carriers thundered down the street. The troops quickly fanned out along the street and around the reviewing stands. The crowds now stood in shock. The broadcasting cameras caught the shock and confusion of the moment.

Councilors Waddel and Glaxis, along with their fellow conspirators, attempted to flee in panic but one hundred soldiers with rifles at the ready prevented them from leaving the reviewing stand. Other soldiers stationed along the parade route quickly disarmed the law enforcers.

Admiral Quanto strode confidently to the podium. The television cameras zoomed in on him as he announced, "Councilors Druck Waddel and Taxis Glaxis, I charge you and your fellow conspirators with treason, murder, attempted murder of the king and attempted insurrection against the king and the good people of Cassaria. In the name of the king, you are hereby under arrest!"

Now the unmistakable sound of prancing horse hoofs echoed down the boulevard announcing a new arrival. A white horse decked out with glossy black leather and gold trimmed tack rounded the corner with a steady proud gait making its way past the crowds and troops.

It's rider in splendid full dress uniform stopped in front of the reviewing stand. The news cameras closed in on the horse and rider and in shocked surprise announced King Adrian

Toburg's arrival.

He dismounted his horse. With his white-gloved hand resting on the pommel of his ceremonial sword and the plumed feathers of his ceremonial helmet fluttering in the breeze, the king strode with military precision up the steps to the reviewing stand's podium. Metal taps on his polished black boots made a steady tapping sound on the metal steps breaking the silence. A sense of awe permeated the crowd while fear overwhelmed the traitors. Admiral Quanto bowed and stepped aside, inviting King Toburg to approach the podium.

"My beloved Cassarians! Despite rumors of my demise, it is my duty to report to you that I am quite well and proud to remain your faithful servant."

A genuine, spontaneous roar of cheer and applause rose up from the crowd that no amount of money could purchase. King Toburg paused until the crowd became quiet and pointed to the captured conspirators. "These traitors have done their best to weaken our military and planetary defenses to allow Tigran and Gamoran pirate forces the opportunity to destroy us.

'Our military forces have thwarted their plans and are now preparing to defend against an imminent attack. I urge you to take shelter immediately and pray for our fleet and allies as we save our world, our homes and our families from the destruction these evil men plotted to bring upon all Cassaria. This day we fight for our freedom!"

The crowd cheered again before dispersing to their homes. Soldiers restraining the conspirators led them away to a high security prison to await trial. The law enforcers were rounded up and led away as well. They would be imprisoned until it was determined their involvement in the conspiracy.

Three shuttles landed nearby awaiting their passengers. King Toburg walked over to General Tayer.

"Nix, you and I were lifelong friends. We grew up together, sharing everything. We went to school together, attended the academy together and were commissioned together, even our children played together. You have thrown everything away and brought great shame to your clan and children. Why and for what? I don't understand?"

Nix attempted to be defiant but failed. "You never cared to understand. You were the king and I was always the King's errand boy. Always in the shadows, ignored and my talents wasted. Nobody respected me for who I was. I was a great general and could have been a great king but you were in the way."

Adrian cut him off. "Enough! I was chosen king. I never sought the position. I shared all I could with you like a brother and now you tell me it wasn't enough? You plotted to murder your best friend and betray your people for what? For more power, a lousy title and a crown that doesn't even fit? You want to be the great general? I'll give you the glory you deserve but not the glory you seek. For the rest of our planet's existence your name will be remembered with a curse and disdain. You will lead the attack on the Tigran fleet aboard the *C.S.S. Tarentino*."

"That wreck? That ship has no shields or weapons. Nothing but sub light engines and life support. What is this?" Nix said in a panicked voice.

"You will lead our attack. We have slaved the controls so the ship will be directed remotely. Someone has to identify the Tigran ships equipped with zannite crystals. What better way than to use a decoy ship?" Adrian asked.

"What? How did you find…" Nix replied in horror.

Adrian scowled as he cut him off. "Yes, I know about the zannite. I know everything about your little rebellion and every move you and your traitorous cohorts planned. I know about your deal with the Gamoran pirates and Tigrans. I know about your assassination attempt. I know that Councilors Waddel and Glaxis were going to blame you for the defeat and replace you with themselves when you were no longer needed. Nix, you were just a useful fool to them all along. You never had a chance."

General Tayer stood speechless, his body wracked with fear and trembling. Now the full measure of his betrayal struck him like a sucker punch to the gut. In his jealous quest for power, the consequences of treason and betrayal never crossed his mind. It was oblivious to him his lifelong friend just showed mercy, sparring him from the hideous torture and beheading the law allowed. Adrian's faith in God would not allow him that option.

"The Tigrans will try to demonstrate their superior firepower to make us afraid. We will not fear them. You and your traitorous friends will know what fear is just before all of you are vaporized at the hands of your fellow evil doers."

"You can't do that, what about the law? I have a right to a trial," Nix cried out.

"Nix, remember in school you were always getting in trouble for not doing your homework? You still haven't learned to do your homework.

'According to an ancient law I have the right during war to pass sentence on all capital crimes without trial. I asked the Council of Unity numerous times to change it but they never took action. They unwisely kept the old law hopping to use it against me. Now I am duty bound to use the law as it was intended and the sentence will be carried out.

'Farewell, Nix, and enjoy your imaginary glory while it lasts." "Guards! Escort General Tayer along with Counselors Waddel and Glaxis to one of the shuttles for transport to *CSS Tarentino*."

King Toburg turned to Admiral Quanto, "Amboy, thank you for your faithfulness and devotion to duty. Never has a Cassarian king had a more loyal officer and defender than you. Let's go spring our trap!"

Field Marshal Victor Kanseu saw himself silently gliding over fields of grain waving in the breeze, orchards full of fruit, and irrigated fields filled with vegetables. Approaching the highlands, he saw a flock of thousands of six legged sherpons grazing on the mountain meadow and a young boy, looking like himself, sitting under an old tree carving a piece of wood. His herding dog, Dargo, sat nearby overlooking the flock.

A pack of black wolves appeared on a rocky ledge. They leaped from the ledge and viciously ripped into the flock. Victor jumped up to drive them off. The wolves saw him dressed in his sherpon wool vest and turned upon him. Dozens of sharp teeth ripped into his flesh as he let out a horrific scream.

Bolting upright in his bed, Victor was in a full sweat, wide-awake and shaking with fear. It was only a nightmare he realized as he tried to shake it off. Victor fought this dream for almost two years but this time it ended with himself being attacked by a black wolf pack bent on a killing frenzy. The sherpon were valued for their fine rich wool and lean flavorful meat. They were also so docile they were easily herded without any sense of danger. Many times, he witnessed one stand in frozen fear as a pack of black wolves tore it to pieces. It would merely cry out in pain while being devoured.

As he shook off the effects of the nightmare he realized his communicator was beeping loudly.

"Yes!" Victor answered.

"Sir, you asked to be called when we approached the Cassarian system," the duty officer reported.

"Excellent! I'll be on the bridge shortly. Order the fleet out of warp and continue at .8 sub-light speed," Victor ordered.

Prime Minister Nikola Penasee was already present when Victor arrived on the bridge. The Tigran battle fleet was forming up into their assigned positions for the attack. It was a battle he planned for over two years and poured over every detail dozens of times. It was also a battle all his instincts told him not to fight. That accounted for his nightmares.

The prime minister was obsessed with ruling the known galaxy. He preached the gods of war ordained Tigra's destiny. Many Tigrans believed his fiery rhetoric, but some citizens and leaders of a few states refused to support him unless he demonstrated what they called "Blessing of the gods." Win the first battle and the opposition would call upon the "Blessing of the gods" and they would sacrifice themselves. If the first battle were lost there would be sudden vacancies for a prime minister, twelve chief priests and field marshal. This was a rare call because few ever wanted to risk coming out on the wrong side. Usually leaders just let things play out and live another day.

In Tigran culture, invoking bloodshed in the name of the gods was a very powerful yet risky affair. If victorious, you were declared a god among gods, and worshiped for life. If you failed, your name would be cursed forever. You and your family would be stoned to death, their bodies left in the desert for the buzzards.

In Penesee's mind, power is raw and absolute. Like in a wolf pack, power goes to the one who seizes it and remains until someone takes it. He experienced war first hand and realized the randomness of death had nothing to do with fickle gods playing celestial games with men's lives. Destiny was his god and would do his duty to the end.

For some people, death comes sooner than to others, but death comes to all. Do you die bravely like a wolf or as a frightened sherpon?

That was the only choice one need make. A soldier does his duty hopping glory will shine upon him and fate crush his enemy. Soldiers are tools of the state, instruments to be wielded carefully and wisely. For the instruments, once destroyed, can never be used again. Victor made his choice long ago to side with the prime minister, but now the thought haunted him, is the prime minister a god in the making or just one Bocar nut short of a dozen? Why am I having doubts now? The pit in his stomach began to churn.

"Field Marshall Kanseu, you may begin your attack. Sensors show a small fleet forming in our rear. It should be the assault force. Your plan has worked perfectly," Prime Minister Penasee informed him.

"I don't see the Gamoran pirates or the Katusians, where are they?" Victor asked.

The prime minister scoffed. "I wouldn't worry about them too much. They are always late. You know that."

Victor sighed. "True! The troop ships will be arriving shortly and we need to start the attack. With Cassaria's planetary shields down, they can land while we destroy Cassaria's fleet."

"Field Marshal! The Cassarian fleet is advancing in front of us. We have also identified the ships to our rear are Holcron heavy cruisers, corvettes and the Katusian fleet," the Intel officer reported.

"Are the planetary shields down?" the field marshal asked. "Cassaria is just coming within sensor range. The shields are up."

"What's going on here!" the prime minister exclaimed in a confused voice.

"In short, we are betrayed by the Katusians. We are outnumbered, out gunned and surrounded. The troop ships will arrive any minute and find themselves overwhelmed," Victor answered calmly.

"Sir, I have an incoming voice message from King Adrian Toburg," the communications officer declared.

"Play it over the speakers!" Prime Minister Penasee ordered. "They most assuredly wish to surrender."

Victor closed his eyes in disgust. *Such an arrogant*

fool, even a blind man can see those we counted on to betray Cassaria have betrayed us instead. It is all over but the dying.

King Toburg's voice announced, "Prime Minister Penasee. The 12 Pillars of the Gods holy site is desecrated and smashed along with the Tigran Royal Marines you sent to protect the Gamoran zannite mines. Your commander is dead along with most of his troops. The Gamoran pirates are destroyed and no longer exist.

'The lies you told the Katusians have been revealed and the treachery you planned upon them foiled. Your gods will not bless you in this battle nor in this war. You must surrender and face trial for galactic war crimes or you and thousands of Tigrans will be needlessly slaughtered without mercy or honor this day."

"What? How can this be?" Prime Minister Penasee cried out in anger as he shook his fists.

"This is Cassarian trickery. Our plans were perfect and blessed by the temple gods of war. The gods promised we would be victorious. We cannot be defeated. Our ships are more powerful than theirs. Attack! Field Marshall Kanseu, you must attack now!" Prime Minister Penasee ordered.

"As you command. However, it is my duty to inform you we are out maneuvered and trapped. If we stay, most of the fleet will be lost. If we fight our way out of the trap and return to Tigra we might save most of the fleet to live and fight another day."

"What cowardice is this? Tigrans never retreat. You were ordered to attack. Obey or die, Field Marshall Kanseu."

"Your order will be obeyed, prime minister," Field Marshall Kanseu replied without emotion. The command went out to the whole fleet. "All ships, begin the attack!"

Out of the Cassarian battle line a lone aged Cassarian heavy cruiser advanced toward the Tigran fleet. General Tayer watched on the large surround screen on the bridge.

The controls at the engineering console moved as if a ghost was in command. All the power available was applied to the forward shields. Try as hard as he might he could not over ride them. All the prisoners could do was watch the Tigrans begin their advance.

"General Tayer, do something. Save us before we are destroyed," Counselor Waddell pleaded.

"It's too late for that. All the controls are locked out. All we can do is watch," Nix sighed.

"Sure, you can. You are a general and hero. Save us!" Counselor Glaxis screamed.

Nix shook his head. "Gentlemen, less than two hours ago you were plotting to betray me. Now you want me to save you. Are you joking? I can't even save myself."

"Well, what can you do?" Glaxis shouted in anger.

"I can tell you what is happening right up to the moment we all die in a massive explosion," Nix replied.

Captain Hoss laughed. "Nix, you've lied all your life. You sure you can get the blow by blow, right?"

Nix ignored the insult. "Well if I don't, whoever survives can sue me."

"Fair point. I trust at least the general can get enough of the attack right that we won't need to quibble over the details," Willett pointed out.

General Tayer bowed. "Thank you, Mr. Quiller. We might as well pass the time calmly than all running around screaming.

'Our ship will be turning about and aim for the Tigran Flagship any moment." The Tigran ships began to shift as the flagship took the center of the forward screen.

"The remote pilot is excellent. The maneuver was dead center," Nix Tayer said.

Taxis Glaxis grumbled. "Can we suspense with the jokes

please."

Nix smiled. "It wasn't meant as a joke but at this point I don't really care."

"Look, our ships are breaking formation," Counselor Waddell said as he pointed at the Cassarian formation.

"Not really. General Tayer said. "They are shifting into three ship formations so as to overlap their shields for optimum protection. At the same time, it also allows them to focus their firepower for greater effect.

Once you batter the shields down on an enemy ship, it's game over. That is how we will die.

'We will be in range of their weapons momentarily. Adrian is trying to use this ship to expose which of their ships are equipped with zannite. Once he knows where they are he will focus on them." Several violet laser flashes raced across space from four Tigran heavy cruisers converging on the lone Cassarian ship. The missiles followed right behind them.

Everyone on the bridge covered their eyes in a futile gesture as the laser beams broke down the shields and sliced through the hull venting atmosphere. Seconds later the missiles tore into the ship. The massive explosions tore the ship apart. *CSS Tarentino* had successfully accomplished its final mission.

Instead of making the enemy tremble, the Cassarians and allies unleashed a barrage of plasma cannons, laser fire and missiles at the Tigran fleet. A look of horror fell on the faces of both Prime Minister Penasee and Field Marshall Kanseu as giant flashes of violet plasma from twenty Allied cruisers converge on their center force of thirty-five cruisers. Three Allied volleys of fire took a toll no one expected. Two of the Tigran zannite equipped ships took the brunt of the attack. After two volleys, the ships lost their shields and began to vent atmosphere. The next volley left them drifting wreckage. The third ship's shields were damaged but held. Two decks were venting atmosphere including engineering causing a decrease in firepower and maneuvering. The flagship shields momentarily dropped but were back online before the next volley struck. Hull integrity remained but starboard laser cannons went off line. Four other Tigran cruisers not in range to fire could do nothing as the longer ranged Zannite powered plasma from the Allies left them in shambles.

Magnum plasma cannons and missiles flashed across space in every direction with devastating effect. Admiral Kanseu had no choice but to order his fleet to close the distance with the Cassarian fleet. He tried to get all of his ships in range to break up the attack by the two allied fleets surrounding him.

Both sides tried to hold their formations as the distance closed between them. Some of the ships on the left flank closed so quickly, ships began slugging it out toe to toe. Now the Tigran carriers launched 200 fighters to turn the right flank of the Cassarian and Allied fleets.

King Toburg countered by launching 350 fighters from Cassaria's moon base to engage them.

A gigantic dogfight ensued. Tigran fighters were unable to prevent forty Katusian and Holcron corvettes from attacking the carriers. Despite a powerful array of defensive weapons the carriers suffered explosions in their hangar bays that quickly spread to other decks.

Wreckage of ships and remains of lifeless bodies littered the battlefield adrift in space. Within an hour, carriers were exploding wrecks as flaming bulkheads gave way and internal atmosphere vented into space. Horrified crews screamed only briefly before being frozen in place or sucked out of their doomed ships. It was a macabre scene of silent death! With the carriers neutralized and the Tigran fighters running out of fuel with no place to land, the Holcron and Katusian corvettes fired on any damaged Tigran ship they could find, like jackals attacking wounded prey separated from the herd. Three severely damaged Tigran heavy cruisers disintegrated in a series of massive explosions shredding most of the fleeing escape capsules. The scene of carnage was no different for the Cassarian fleet.

The Tigran Field Marshall was not deterred. He spotted a Cassarian Heavy Cruiser flanked by two light cruisers trying to press their attack on two damaged Tigran light cruisers on his port side. Fifteen enemy cruisers to his rear were closing in and firing deadly volleys into his quickly dwindling fleet. He ordered his flagship to maneuver to port and fire a broadside into the lead Cassarian heavy cruiser hoping it would force the trio to break off their attack. Again, his magnum lasers flashed their violet light and struck their intended target.

King Adrian Toburg was on the bridge of his flagship leading a three-ship formation against two Tigran light cruisers when suddenly a powerful broadside from the Tigran flagship weakened his shields. The second broadside crushed his shields and missiles struck his ship in numerous places. One blast struck close to the bridge and atmosphere began to vent. The hull was breached in several places.

Debris pinned Adrian to the floor. A steel section of bulkhead was on top of his chest He tried to push it off but it would not budge.

"Help!" Adrian cried out in agony.

Two crewmembers rushed to his aid. They tried to lift the bulkhead but it would not budge. Looking around one of them saw a long piece of pipe. As he went to retrieve it there was a loud sound of steel buckling and hissing of air escaping. Using the pipe as a lever, he pried on the bulkhead and was able to lift it while the other crewmember pulled the king free.

The crew member who pulled him out declared, "Sire, we will get you out here, hang on."

The king nodded as they lifted him up and dragged him off the bridge into the passageway just as the last of the bridge atmosphere escaped. Putting an arm around the king on each side they made their way to the end of the passageway to a turbo-lift. It was jammed. Taking another short passageway, they came to another turbo-lift. It was working and they make it down two decks only to find the damage to the doors blocked their exit. Back up a deck and down another passageway they found another working turbo-lift that took them to the third deck and sick bay.

Over half of the crew were either killed or wounded. The engineering section activated the secondary bridge and struggled to get the mortally wounded ship to safety within the planetary shields. They sent out a call on the emergency channel calling for help.

The Tigran Field Marshall grinned with satisfaction as he saw numerous bodies being thrown into space along with venting atmosphere from the blast holes in the doomed ship.

Admiral Dever saw the Cassarian flagship take the volleys of laser and missile fire. Several escape pods were seen fleeing the ship. He knew the ship was out of the battle and fighting to survive as it withdrew. It was the only hope for many of the crew. With the ship's communications temporarily disrupted, there was no way of knowing the extent of casualties.

Just before the Tigran flagship fired its third volley at the stricken Cassarian vessel, Admiral Dever ordered three of his ships to fire broadsides of Plasma cannons and missiles of their own. Previous hits plus three successive volleys on the Tigran flagship left it a shattered hulk.

The fourth volley of plasma cannons and missiles struck the ship so violently that numerous secondary explosions were set off throughout the ship. Within seconds the last of the Tigran zannite equipped cruisers exploded and ceased to exist along with all hands.

By now the Tigran fleet was to have destroyed Cassarian defenses allowing the troop ships to pass through and land troops, tanks and additional fighters on Cassaria. Instead, there were so few Tigran combat ships left in the fight the troop and supply ships were now vulnerable. Admiral Dever saw the weakness and wheeled his left flank about to confront them. The transports found themselves in a hornet's nest of withering fire that their shields could not hope to withstand. Realizing their hopeless situation, the Tigran invasion force tried to scatter in hope of escaping the onslaught.

Now pinned by Dever's left flanking movement the allied fighters and corvettes began flitting among them firing at every target of opportunity. Some ships attempted to avoid the pursuing fighters and corvettes only to collide into other troop ships. As the transports were ripped open like ripened fruit, thousands of Tigran soldiers, the pride of Tigran society, began drifting out of the wreckage into lifeless space.

Admiral Dever looked about the carnage from his bridge. It was a savage and sickening sight, even for a warrior of his experience. It all seemed such a waste of life but necessary to end the bloodlust of twisted tyrants.

"Communications! Open a channel to the Tigran ships," Usus ordered.

"Channel open, sir." The communications officer responded.

"To commander of remaining Tigran forces. This is Admiral Usus Dever. Continued conflict is futile. Your ships are surrounded and situation untenable. Your surrender will end the useless deaths of good people on both sides. I await your favorable and unconditional response."

An eerie lull overcame the battlefield as all ships waited for a response. There was a crackling on the speakers as the enemy responded. "I'm Captain Sesque!" a female voice announced. "I'm the senior surviving commander. I have ordered my ships to stand down and prepare to receive boarders. There will be no further hostilities. We are at your mercy.

'I also request recovery and medical assistance for our

forces in pursuant to galactic law."

"Captain Sesque, your surrender is graciously accepted. Standby to coordinate rescue and medical attention as needed. Ensure all weapon systems on remaining ships are powered down and weapon stores secured. Failure to do so will result in the instant destruction of offending vessel."

"Understood, admiral. There will be no resistance, Captain Sesque, out!"

Admiral Dever ordered all allied ships to cease-fire as well. Rescue ships were dispatched to sort through the darkened hulks of once proud fighting ships looking for remaining life.

An emergency voice message came through to Admiral Dever announcing King Toburg's serious wounds and requesting transfer to his ship for immediate medical care.

Admiral Dever quickly dispatched a shuttle for the transfer along with a medical team to help the other wounded. When King Adrian was brought aboard, the doctors quickly assessed his injuries. The crushing weight of the debris that fell on his body resulted in extensive internal damage beyond treatment. The surgeons could only keep him comfortable until the end. Admiral Dever rushed to his friend's side.

"Usus, my good friend! The doctors tell me I haven't … long to live. Are any of my children with you?" Adrian asked under labored breath.

"They obeyed your orders. They are far away preparing for another battle I fear will be even greater than this one," Usus replied as he fought the lump forming in his throat and tears in his eyes.

"I'm pleased. When they disappeared, I begged God to spare them. I offered myself instead. From that moment on I knew they were safe, but I would probably never see them again in this life." Adrian paused as he choked on some blood and struggled to breath.

Usus smiled. "They have grown in courage and wisdom. Gavin has grown into a fine leader. Aycana has become the warrior you always dreamed she'd be. Estron has a caring heart and a beauty under all that grease. Little Siyana is no longer that little girl. She has grown into a true princess in both beauty and brains. The young man she has chosen is a most courageous warrior. He is so much like you. Together they remind me of you and Alice. You have every right to be proud of them. They bring great honor to the Toburg clan."

Adrian's breathing became more labored. "Thank you. You have always been…like a true brother. Tell my wife… and children I love them dearly. I leave…them a new Cassaria. We will meet again in a happier time and place."

"I promise to tell them, my brother. I also promise to do all in my power to bring them home safely. I swear with my life."

"I know you will. I…didn't even…have to ask." Adrian struggled to breath even more as he whispered, "I'll be watching…from Heaven. We…will meet soon enough. So long…good friend." With a final sigh, the greatest king of Cassaria went limp and life left him.

"Yes, we will meet again all too soon my friend!" Usus whispered. "I just pray I can fulfill my promise first."

When Admiral Amboy Quanto received the news of King Toburg's death, he clutched his chest as he struggled for words that would not come. The admiral fought to regain his composure and requested a com-channel to ships throughout the Cassarian fleet.

"Today Cassaria achieved its greatest victory due to the leadership of our greatest king, King Adrian Toburg. With his death, we have also received our greatest loss. I never served a greater leader or a man who loved being a servant to his people more. He was everything a great king should be yet he yearned for the day Cassaria no longer had one. God rest his soul as he takes his place in Heaven!"

Hearing these words, men and women throughout the fleet found it difficult to rejoice in their victory as they mourned their loss.

Even the people on Cassaria rejoiced in the victory until word of the king's death was reported, their joy turned to weeping and sorrow.

Everyone knew they had lost a truly great leader and servant.

Admiral Quanto welcomed Admiral Dever to a seat in his office. Though Admiral Quanto was serving as the temporary king he refused to use the King's office.

"Welcome Admiral Dever. Please, have a seat. The final report of the battle was just passed to me."

Admiral Dever took a chair covered in soft leather and sighed. "This was the most brutal battle I have ever fought. I'm stunned at the price we have paid. There will be much crying on our home worlds tonight. What was the final tally?"

Admiral Quanto cleared his throat. "Ninety percent of the Tigran fleet is destroyed or damaged beyond repair. Only five of the fifty-three Tigran cruisers are combat capable. Of the 315 troop transports and support ships, 220 were lost with 400,000 troops. We captured 175,000 troops. Both of their carriers, thirty corvettes and 200 fighters were also lost. The allies suffered forty percent lost or severely damaged, just about all were Cassarian heavy or light cruisers. Zannite definitely made the difference."

Admiral Dever sighed, "Our losses were still severe considering the battle we are about to fight. We won and lost at the same time."

"What do you mean?" Amboy asked.

"General Braxton will be going up against a force far greater than his own unless we arrive in time to join him. Even then we will be fighting a series of hit and run battles against a superior force in numbers. The goal is to delay them until your carrier and converted transports arrived with 400 fighters," Usus explained.

"We captured about fifteen freighters that can be easily and quickly convert to carry forty fighters each. That gives you a thousand fighters total. I think we can do it in time." Amboy offered.

"Well take whatever we can get," Usus smiled.

Admiral Dever readied his fleet for the race to Herrac 2. The zannite-equipped cruisers suffered minor damage that could be quickly repaired and launched as soon as they were ready to join John Braxton's tiny fleet. Repair crews frantically set to work making repairs and installing the zannite upgrades on the remaining ships that would head to Earth. It wasn't as many as they hoped for but it was all they could get ready in time. Admiral Quanto sent a ship on the diplomatic mission to negotiate the Tigran Peace Treaty and introduce a new world of freedom. He also sent the cremated remains of their prime minister and the many thousands of fallen Tigrans. The Tigran prisoners were held on Cassaria until assurances were made they would not be sacrificed in atonement to their false gods.

Tigra wasn't the only planet that had a change in government. The day after the battle, remaining members of the Council of Unity met with Admiral Quanto and his senior staff. The Councilors offered Admiral Quanto the kingship fully expecting him to accept it.

Highly insulted by the offer, Admiral Quanto exploded in rage. "You traitors! You come to me and offer power you do not have the authority of the people to give thinking I can be controlled. The people who put their lives at risk saving your worthless skins, and the many who died doing so cry out for freedom. All you can offer is continued second-class citizenship under another master. How dare you! How dare you mock their great sacrifices!

'I refuse the kingship. Nor will I allow anyone else to hold the office. Our greatest king is dead and not yet even buried. All you politicians can think about is how to jockey for more power." Admiral Quanto paused to withdraw a document from his case and unrolled it on the table.

"King Adrian Toburg wrote this document some time ago and after the battle, planned to present it to the people. It proposes a new government giving equal citizenship and equal voice to all the people no matter their birth, religion or social status. No more inherited membership in the Council of Unity. No more kings and no more crooked government agencies used to line your pockets and those of the life sucking leaches that follow you. Read this document carefully, gentlemen.

'Not only are you resigning from office, you are donating all of your estates and wealth to the new government. You will do it without protest. You will sign it before you leave this room or face an immediate military tribunal and found guilty of treason, graft, corruption and conspiracy against the Cassarian people.

'King Toburg and I spent the better part of the last ten years collecting evidence and documenting your sins against the people. Sign and be free men or be assured you will be executed before the sun comes up again."

The politicians were speechless. They balked at signing until Admiral Quanto presented another document listing all the charges against them. The new leader of the council silently read the extensive charges against him. Seeing the steely resolve in Admiral Quanto's eyes, his body shook with fear. He quickly took the pen from the Admiral's hand, signed the document, removed the chain and symbol of office from around his neck and with head held low, silently left the room into exile.

The others followed in turn then escorted out of the capitol city and banished. Senior officers cheered as the last politician signed. Admiral Quanto smiled and held the document up for all to see.

"No more kings. No more crooked elitists who think only they know what is best for the people of Cassaria. Gentlemen, we have given our people true freedom, let them make the most of it. Let the people know their freedom was purchased this day with blood of our bravest countrymen. The price of freedom has been paid in full."

Late that evening, Admiral Quanto was finishing up some paperwork in his den. He signed a general order retiring several senior officers who had displayed support for General Nix Tayer's revolt. They too would be banished from the capitol city, and barred from ever holding public office.

They all knew on Cassaria, banishment from the capitol was a very public and grave punishment. Every corporation and associate would shun them for fear of being thought of as supporters of traitors. Unemployable for life most would take the hint and seek exile on another planet.

They would adopt as low a profile as possible and start a quiet new life out of fear of being considered a troublemaker and forced to move on. Many communities would not allow them entry or do business in their jurisdiction. Violation of the banishment would result in a trial on the original charges. Execution would be swift and certain. After ten years if they behaved themselves, they could apply for a conditional pardon as the law provided even though in practice a pardon was not likely.

He returned the pen to its holder on the desktop. Amboy felt a gentle breeze on his neck.

"About time you showed up. I was running out of things to keep me busy until you arrived. Please have a seat. All of you," the admiral offered.

"You are most gracious, admiral," Slick replied.

Slick and his four companions came around to the front of the desk and took a seat on the leather chairs and matching sofa.

"Cassaria is greatly indebted for your service. You foiled two assassination attempts on King Toburg; helped expose the traitorous General Tayer, along with his cohorts; and above all, prevented massive genocide of the Cassarian people. One day soon the people of Cassaria will be told how indebted we are to General Braxton, you and your assistants. You have done a great service."

"I appreciate your kind words, but you and Admiral Dever must keep our identities a secret. It must be kept that way," Slick urged.

"You know I could have you arrested as spies?" Admiral Quanto said with a slight grin.

"You could, but then we could never help you again. That would spoil a wonderful relationship," Slick responded with a sly wink of his eye.

"Yes, indeed, it would spoil a great relationship, wouldn't it?" Amboy smiled.

"I do understand your point. Be assured, I have no plans to return to Cassaria unless invited," Slick replied.

"That is reassuring, believe me. Tell me are all spies in your country on Earth as good as you?"

"There's always someone better. In the spy business, you just do your best to never run into them."

"My, a humble master spy. I never met one before," the admiral exclaimed as both burst out laughing. "Will you take back a message to General Braxton?"

"Of course. I will be departing with Admiral Dever when his ship is ready."

"If it's not too late by the time you catch up to him, tell General Braxton Cassaria is greatly indebted to him. Also warn him at least two of the Cassarians and Holcrons he freed are spies. They can still undo all we have accomplished so far."

"Thank you for the heads up," Slick said.

"Is there anything I can do before you depart?" Amboy asked.

Slick cleared his throat. "Yes, we would be very grateful for any support you can provide in the establishment of a free Terran colony."

Admiral Quanto nodded. "Of course, I don't know how things will shake out but I pledge to do whatever I can."

"Thank you very much," Slick said.

A moment later the group left the way they came. Admiral Quanto was left alone thanking the God of Heaven for his gift of providence.

As Estron walked down the corridor to her room she heard a loud crashing sound in the nearby room. It was Dexter's room and it sounded like a brawl was taking place.

Estron pounded on the door. "Dexter! Is everything alright? This is Estron. Let me in?"

There was more crashing and yelling but no response.

"Dexter, this is Estron. Please let me in?" she called out again.

She called Henry on her flip com.

"Henry, come quick to Dexter's room there is something terribly wrong!"

"OK, I'll be right there," Henry replied.

Henry was a few doors down. When he joined Estron there was another loud crash and some groaning.

"What on Earth!" Henry said punching a few keys on the lock pad. Nothing happened. Henry tried again. This time the door opened. On the floor, Dexter was face down banging his fists and weeping uncontrollably. Estron knelt down beside Dexter and gently placed her hands on his shoulders trying to comfort him.

"Dex, please let me help you?" She softly pleaded. "This is not the way to remember."

Dex tried to bring himself under control but was still in obvious pain.

"Estron, Please, go away. Leave me alone!" Dex said gritting his teeth.

"What's this about?" Henry asked.

"Estron pointed around the room, "This happens every year on the anniversary of his wife and daughter's murders." Estron said.

"I see!" Henry noted.

"We are here for you," Estron said comforting Dex in her arms. "We didn't know what the date meant until a couple years ago. Dex has always kept his emotions private but on this date, it all comes out.

"Please go away!" Dex pleaded. "I don't want anybody's help."

"I think you do with all this mess to clean up. Dex, you definitely need help." Henry said.

"Who says I need help?" Dex angrily replied. "I can clean up the room myself."

"That isn't the only help you need and you know it." Henry said as he set a bookshelf upright and began putting the books back in place.

"Dude, I've been where you're at and it's an ugly place,"

Henry said. "We both know nothing good comes out of this."

"Henry, Dex is hurting and you're not helping," Estron scolded.

"Quite the contrary. He knows I'm right, he just want's something that can't happen." Henry said.

Estron was about to reply when Dexter put a finger to her lips.

Dexter sighed in despair. "Henry, there is no truth just pain. Pain never goes away."

Henry shook his head. "So, you finally hit bottom?"

"Yes!" Dexter nodded.

"Then close your eyes. Tell me what you see?" Henry calmly pleaded.

"No. What's that got to do with anything?" Dexter sighed forcing his anger to subside.

"Ya once told me your wife and daughters were Christians, right?"

"Yes, so what?" Dexter asked.

Henry looked around the room. "So, you know they are watching your antics right this minute. You think they're proud of this?"

Dexter hung his head low but said nothing.

"Just what I thought," Henry said. "Dex, you can't ride no horse sitting in the saddle backwards. Ya gotta focus on where you're going not where ya been."

Estron and Dexter looked at Henry totally dumfounded.

"Dex, it takes faith to get where they are, not this," Henry said with a flick of his finger against the forehead of Dexter's mask.

Now Estron realized what Henry was saying. She nodded at Henry but said nothing more.

Dexter said nothing either as the trio restored order to the room. By the time Henry and Estron left, Dexter was so deep in thought he barely noticed them wave good-bye. In reflective solitude, he sat on the carpeted floor leaning against the sofa with his eyes closed.

He breathed deeply and slowly allowed the anger and pain to evaporate. It didn't take long before it was replaced with a smiling countenance the mask could not hide.

"Thank you, Henry! Thank you!" he whispered.

CHAPTER 20

Braxton's small fleet left Terra a few days earlier to provide the crews more time to train on the way to the Laylar System. There, John Braxton and Admiral MacKay planned to intercept the Uvarian fleet. If possible they wanted to lure the Uvarians away from Earth to buy time needed for the Allied Main Fleet's arrival. Hopefully, they would arrive in time and with enough strength to defeat the Uvarians.

On the bridge, John was deep in thought. *On Earth, an army could use delaying tactics by clever use of terrain, weather or even leaking false intelligence to confuse or mask real intentions. In space, it was much more difficult. A planet or an asteroid field might be big enough to hide behind, but they were far and few between. In the vastness of deep space there simply was no opportunity to lay a trap... or was there?*

John didn't seem to notice the hailing signal or Admiral McKay's appearance on the communication screen. Stephen could see John was deep in thought but grew impatient.

Like an epiphany, an idea took shape in his mind. There were risks, but the payoff would be worthwhile if it worked and no loss if it didn't. It was all in the timing.

"Stephen, I have an idea," John finally announced.

"Did you notice I was waiting?" Stephen smiled. "For a moment I was beginning to wonder if something was wrong."

"Sorry, I needed to finish my thought. Can we talk privately?"

"Sure, call me back on a secure line, out," Stephen said.

John looked at his communications officer in training. "Comm., when hailed, inform the senior officer on deck. Never open the channel until directed. It is an important procedure that must be followed at all times no matter who is hailing us. Am I understood?"

"Yes, sir!" the embarrassed trainee replied.

"Very good. I'll be in my quarters. Set up a secure channel to my screen with Admiral MacKay. Thank you," John announced and left.

A minute later they were on a secure channel.

"Stephen," John exclaimed. "What, if we could set up our Uvarian spy to help us? She is fed false information and allowed to steal the Uvarian shuttle we have. She is later rescued by the Uvarian fleet. She convinces them to divert course to attack us at another location that forces them to waste time yet gives Admiral Dever a chance to join up and turn the tables to our advantage. What do you think? Will it buy the time we need?" John asked.

"You're not the only one who studied Robert E. Lee," Stephen winked. "If it doesn't work then our task force risks being as useful as a gnat trying to stop a bull elephant. However, I think your point is valid. Our Uvarian spy can be useful with the proper nudge.

"Let me get back with you after I nail down a few things," John said. When John returned to the bridge. Two of the male bridge crew appeared to be joking with the female Communications trainee.

"What is going on here? Nobody has time to stand around joking. If you think you know everything maybe we ought to run some drills and find out. I expect professionalism on the bridge at all times. If there are any distractions on the bridge I can remove them," John barked as he glanced at the trainees.

The demeanor on the bridge changed instantly as everyone quickly began finding something to do.

Siyana looked at David.

He shrugged his shoulders and without saying a word

called up a flight training scenario. Without missing a beat the two were going through checklist exercises. Before the day was over the other bridge crew would get the same treatment.

Satisfied discipline was restored on the bridge, John began studying a couple holographic star charts, did a few calculations on his data pad, and then called up another chart. After some more calculations he called Victoria.

"Hi! Can you meet me in our quarters in ten minutes?"

"In the middle of the day?" Victoria teased.

"Sure, why not?" John asked. "I got a problem only you can help me with."

"Well that's comforting to know but can't it wait?" Victoria asked.

John let his guard down and let his frustration show. "If it could wait, I'd call you later don't you think?"

"I'll be right there!" Victoria replied a bit hurt by her husband's demeanor.

John returned the flip com. to his belt, while looking around the bridge. Most of the crew was busy trying to ignore what happened but one crewmember had a grin on his face.

John pointed his finger at him. Officer of the Deck, put that man on report for conduct unbecoming. He is to remain in his quarters for 24 hours. Get him off this bridge now!"

"Yes, sir!" Aycana answered sharply.

After discussing his plan with Victoria, John went down to hangar bay 1 and found the duct tape engineers and Estron working on another of their wild experiments.

"Dad, how are we doing today?" John inquired.

"Just fine, son. Our space mine is improved and we should have at least a hundred completed within the next three days. We are also working on a new weapon I promised David for his birthday. If the demo version works, we will make more of them," Henry said with a bit of pride pointing to his latest invention on the workbench.

"General, we took the Tigran rail gun concept and figured a way to scale it down as a shoulder fired weapon," Deze pointed out.

"That is interesting. How does it work?" John asked.

"We designed it to shoot a .17 caliber copper coated steel ball. The power coil around the barrel pushes the ball down the barrel. By the time it exits the barrel it is traveling at over five times the velocity of a normal rifle bullet. In our trial it pierced one inch armored plating out to 500 yards. If you can see it, you can kill it.

'If we can get the recharge rate on the coil to work faster and a lighter, longer lasting power pack, we should get this baby to fire up to 500 rounds per minute. A soldier will have select fire, carry over 1000 rounds and still carry at least ten to fifteen pounds less than they carry now," Dexter added.

"That's fantastic. Just don't shoot up the hangar bay while perfecting it. OK?" John warned.

"Don't worry about us. You won't ever need to send us to the brig again. I promise!" Henry assured him.

"I hope not! It doesn't look good when the ship's captain has to put his own father in the brig for endangering the crew, does it? Now, I have a question for you. We saved the captured Uvarian shuttle to study. Is it possible to get it flyable on a one time, one way mission in deep space?"

"I suppose so," Henry sighed. "We can plug the leaks but I wouldn't trust it with my life. The only systems that are fully working are the life support and navigation systems. The propulsion system is at fifty percent power at best. The coolant system has so many leaks it can't hold warp speed for more than a few hours. I can't emphasize enough about the damage to the hull."

"How about remote piloting?" John asked Dexter.

"That is about the only reliable thing that operates. Whoever flies it is a dead man," Dexter emphasized.

"Then it will meet my needs. Can you get it ready within three days?" John asked.

"No problem. We will get on it right away," Henry promised. "I can tell you're up to somethin."

Dr. Jerri Spinner was working her way through the lunch line on the observation deck. She was lonely and frustrated but learned to put up a good front. Though she managed to alienate most of the crew with her arrogant, superior attitude, the cause and effect were totally oblivious to her. If it weren't for her friendship with Victoria she would have no friends at all.

A tray bumped into her back. Jerri spun around like a cat but checked herself just in time.

"Oh! Victoria, I didn't see you behind me. How are you today?" Jerri said with a rehearsed smile and fake politeness.

Victoria apologized, "I'm so sorry. Please forgive me? I was trying to decide between soup, sandwich or both. I wasn't paying attention. It's been a stressful morning. Yourself ?"

"I've been trying to keep busy. Space travel is so boring. I don't know how you can stand it, honestly! Your husband's suggestion of learning a couple of languages before making diplomatic contact was a good idea. Fortunately, my services haven't been needed yet so there is little else to do," Jerri exclaimed as she placed a small bowl of mixed fruit on her tray.

"It does have its moments, but usually I'm too busy to think about it when I'm on duty. He's working on some scheme or plan, I think," Victoria exclaimed with irritation.

Jerri pointed to a far table, "Our usual table is taken. Let's take a table over in the corner where it's more quiet."

They found a table and began eating. Jerri picked up the

conversation again. "So tell me Chief of Morale and Welfare, what's been happening?"

"John has me doing it full time now to keep the crew's stress level down.

"Why did he do that?" Jerri asked.

"The crew is getting restless. A couple of fights broke out last night and wrecked my sleep. He doesn't think I'm smart enough to handle it. I'm a top architect not the crew's den mother," Victoria stated with obvious disdain.

'What really gets me angry is being replaced by some bumbling, boy chasing blond," she stressed rolling her eyes and waving a few strands of her long, silky, jet-black hair.

"Men think women are so stupid. I ran into the same thing at the State Department. I have a Ph.D. in political science and another in economic development. You'd think I'd get some respect. Instead, I've been asked to fetch coffee more often than I care to remember. What did he do to get you so upset, anyway?" Jerri asked innocently.

"Well, he was planning some trick to play on the Uvarians. When I asked what he was doing, he said it was too complicated for me to understand. Two can play that game. A few sweet nothings in his ear and he was babbling everything. He is planning to launch a shuttle with a dead implant with false information to fool the Uvarians.

'It's supposed to look like he escaped with some secret plans. I told him they would catch on to his ruse in no time. Dead men can't talk, so how is he supposed to fool them," Victoria lamented.

Admiral Mackay, the Katusian commander, and John got in a big argument over it. In the end they agreed if it didn't work no loss but if it succeeded it could cause heavy losses for the Uvarians. 'He rolled his eyes at me and told me that it was best to leave the planning up to men. I got so mad I told him he could sleep on the couch for a while if he didn't straighten up," Victoria said getting herself worked up again.

"My stars! Does he treat you like that all the time?" Jerri asked in feigned shock.

"He has his ups and downs. He is under a lot of stress and he doesn't handle stress very well. When he gets stressed out he becomes very demanding and patronizing. Men are such emotional wrecks."

Jerri scoffed. "If women ruled the universe instead of men, things would run so much smoother, don't you think? Any woman with even the least intelligence can make a smart man spill his guts. After all, we've had men wrapped around our fingers for thousands of years have we not?"

Victoria broke out laughing and nodded agreement. "You free for lunch again tomorrow?"

"Sure. Same time, same place?" Jerri asked.

"Sounds good," Victoria said and left to make her rounds.

In the meeting room John brought up a holo-projection of space stretching from Sepious Minor to Earth to Terra.

"Gentlemen, this is a summary of our battlefield. The two Uvarian fleets are about three days from the Laylar System. The Uvarian Combat Fleet will be in the lead to sweep away any opposition ahead of their Assault Transport (AT) Fleet. They assume our Allied forces are still at Cassaria battling the Tigran and Gamoran Pirate fleet.

'The AT Fleet is expecting feeble opposition. They will be disappointed. Our goal is to buy time for the Allied Main Fleet to arrive and help us finish the job?" John explained.

The commander of the Katusian carrier, Commodore Montell, stood to speak. "Their weaknesses are obvious, but how do we exploit them without wiping ourselves out in the process?

'Although Uvarian magnum lasers are impractical for defending against close-in fighters, they are still very dangerous. One hit from a magnum laser can vaporize a small fighter no matter how powerful its shields. With the allied cruisers outnumbered five to one, the covering fire will just not be enough. It would be suicide."

"You are right, captain. Admiral MacKay and I have come up with a plan called Operation Snake Eyes. We propose to split the fleet into two task forces.

'Task Force Hammer will consist of eight cruisers. Its mission is to attack the Uvarian Combat Fleet at Laylar then draw them away from Earth. Nine of the heavy replenishment freighters will go to Herrac 2 to replenish Task Force Hammer when it arrives from the Laylar raid with the enemy in pursuit.

'Task Force Anvil will consist of the Katusian carrier, the *Fire Hawk*, the six heavy freighters ferrying three-hundred additional fighters. and twenty Katusian heavy freighters delivering orbital Anti-Space Missile defense systems. This task force will head directly to Earth and engage the Uvarian ATF once they enter the system.

'I must stress the ATF be wiped out in its entirety. Not one ship of their assault fleet can escape. Ram them if you must. Can you do that?" John challenged.

With a wry smile the Katusian Captain shook his head. "You're taking on the largest military force in the known galaxy with a mostly inexperienced force one-fifth the size and the only advantage you have is courage? No wonder Admiral Dever is so excited about you Earthlings. You are right, it will be a defeat the Uvarian Empire will never see coming."

"Good!" John declared. "I believe we can do this but lets not fool ourselves. This will cost us dearly. We will prevail but it won't be over. They are a desperate empire seeking to survive. They are on the brink of disintegration or victory. Their defeat must be so overwhelming their oppressed planets see hope for freedom causing the empire to disintegrate. The alternative is for them to give up the idea of obtaining zannite and watch their empire crumble.

Everyone in the room now realized what John was seeing. Saving the allied worlds and Earth was just the beginning. Freedom was hanging in the balance on many more planets.

"How are you going to handle the Uvarian cruisers?" Captain Reagan asked with a concerned tone. "With our forces divided we will be weaker than we are now."

"As I mentioned before, Task Force Hammer will make a hit and run attack in the Laylar System and try to lure the Uvarian Combat Fleet to follow. If it works, we will lure them to the Herrac 2 System. The Allied fleet from Cassaria can arrive in time to spring our trap."

"What if the trap doesn't work?" Captain Reagan asked.

Admiral Mackay replied, "If we fail to lure the Uvarian Combat Fleet away, we fight a series of hit and run attacks as we retreat to Earth. The plan is to buy enough time for help to arrive from Cassaria. If Task Force Hammer succeeds in luring the Uvarian cruisers away and defeat them it makes the job of destroying the ATF that much easier."

"Let us all hope so. This is definitely our best shot. If our plan doesn't work, billions of people will endure unbelievable misery and suffering for a long time to come," Jonathan concluded.

John turned to the Katusian commander. "I am putting Admiral MacKay in overall command of Task Force Anvil. I mean no offense, however, Earth has not yet completely adjusted to the idea of life on other planets. He can secure the cooperation and support your task force will need."

"I understand completely," Commodore Montell replied. "The people of our planet would feel the same way."

"Great!" John said. "Task Force Anvil needs to leave

ASAP. You will arrive at Earth in three days and have seventeen days to setup your defense plan. I need you to place Katusian deep space communication buoys along the way to establish a communications network. Signal me your status when you arrive. We will get there as fast as we can from Herrac 2.”

A few remaining details were ironed out before everyone returned to their ships for final preparations. Five hours later the two task forces separated and a final message was sent to Terra providing additional details for Admiral Dever and the Allied Main Fleet.

The computer finished running the series of tests. The results were another failure. Khem banged his fist on the table in frustration. His quest to discover a way to remove or neutralize the Uvarian implants without surgery was not working.

A computer simulation of the procedure was a complete failure. When the simulated implant was detached from the spine, the patient slipped into a coma and died. No matter how they tried to remove the implant, the degree of risk proved greater than Khem could accept.

“We have tried just about everything possible to remove the implants but the risk factor is just way too high. Even dissolving the implant seems to work at first, but then the process reverses itself. The electrical shock treatment has a temporary effect and surgery is not an option. A twenty percent survival rate just isn’t acceptable,” Khem exclaimed.

“Maybe we are not looking at this problem from the right angle,” Susan replied.

“What do you mean?” Khem asked.

“There used to be the question, “Do you starve the cold and feed the fever or do you starve the fever and feed the cold?”

“I see where you are going,” Khem replied.

Susan smiled. “Right, the doctor win’s a cookie. Instead

of trying to remove it why not rewire it? What if we gave it a different power source then cut the connection to the brain. It should keep working but no longer communicating with the brain. As the power source runs out it dies a peaceful death.

"You have a point. Let's go over our data again," Khem agreed.

While both silently reflected on what they knew about the implants, Susan's flip com. began beeping.

"Hi, Mom! What's up?" Susan asked.

"Hey!" Victoria exclaimed. "We're planning dinner with the whole family tonight. Are you and Khem able to join us?"

"Mom is planning a family dinner for tonight. Want to come along?" Susan asked Khem.

"Of course."

"Yes, Mom, we'll be there. About what time?"

"How about 1830 hours in the VIP dining room,"Victoria replied. "See you then. Bye."

As Susan closed her flip com. she suddenly gasped.

"What's wrong?" Khem asked.

"What if once we redirected the power and wiring we could communicate with it and that way reprogram it to shut down.

"I see where you're going. The two strands serve as wiring but also as an antenna directing the brain's thoughts and actions. We graft on new wiring to a different source then disconnect the strands to the brain. We then use the new source to reprogram it to shut itself down. It doesn't have to be removed, just made inert," Khem exclaimed.

"I bet once the power is cut, normal behavior is restored."

"With the power source cut won't the device try to repair itself?" Susan added.

Gavin shrugged his shoulders. "Only one way to find out and we need an implant to prove it. I should have figured this out a long time ago. We make a pretty good team don't we?"

'If you have anything other than medicine in mind, you'd better talk to Dad about it. Otherwise you might find yourself with something else implanted," Susan teased.

"Good point!" Khem agreed. "Maybe it is time your father and I have that serious chat. The problem is every time I try to talk to him he changes the subject."

"If he didn't approve he'd tell you right out. He's testing you. Persistence wins respect, don't give up," Susan smiled.

Special Agent Maxine Maxwell spent weeks sniffing around Washington D.C. on the hunch that Dr. Sanchez was still in the area. Though she didn't get any leads on Dr. Sanchez, she did find two other contacts that drew suspicion. Both had past claims of Alien abduction. It struck Maxine odd that someone who publically seemed hostile to alien abduction conspiracies would associate with some who made such claims. The other lead was found almost by accident.

A search of Dr. Jerri Spinner's apartment turned up a phone number and address of an individual totally out of Dr. Sanchez's circle of associates. On a hunch, Maxine did a background check and found the person died two years ago. Her partner, Bill Wilson remembered some news stories of homeless people disappearing in the area late at night. A stakeout ensued.

The very reclusive man came out of his rundown bungalow only at night. Dressed in loose fitting jogging pants and a heavy hoodie covering most of his face, he jogged around the neighborhood a few times then went back inside. The jogging routine was always at the exact same time and route with exactly six laps. This went on for two weeks then suddenly the routine changed with one less lap each night for the past five nights.

"Why are we watching this guy?" her partner asked. "He does the same routine every night and no one comes or goes except him." "Because this is the only lead we have," Maxine said. "Dr. Sanchez and Dr. Spinner have the same tight circle of friends with the exception of this guy. Could it be he is the contact for a different cell? Don't you think it's strange that no one ever comes to visit and he never visits anyone?"

"Not really. He's weird off the bat. How many people do you know that go jogging in 80-degree weather like it was the middle of winter? The only thing stranger is he jogs one lap less each night. Three nights ago it was hotter and he ran four laps. Since then he has jogged one less lap each night. Why jog one lap?" Bill asked.

Maxine looked over at Bill. "Think of the significance of what you just said."

"I got it. I'm thinking what you're thinking now. It's a countdown signal." Bill said as he picked up the radio.

"We need more backup," Maxine said. "Radio it in and ask for some more coffee and food. We're here for the long haul," Bill added.

The early morning drizzling rain turned into a torrential down pour by mid-morning. The radio weather report predicted the storm would break up and turn to muggy sunshine over the next couple of hours. Maxine was growing impatient with the surveillance when the suspect exited the house with his usual attire.

"Bill, wake up!" Maxine prodded her partner. "Something is definitely going down."

The rain didn't seem to bother him in the least. In one hand he carried a five foot long and ten inch wide black plastic shipping tube and in the other hand a heavy duffle bag. He placed the items in the back of the van and drove off.

With Bill driving, Maxine summoned two nearby teams

to join in tailing him. They followed the suspect's van through town and onto the parkway towards Baltimore.

About half way there he turned off into the Patuxent Research Refuge. He continued driving until he turned off into a small clearing along the river.

When the suspect pulled off, Maxine directed Bill to slow down but drive on by. The storm had subsided and the clouds were beginning to break up improving visibility. Coming to a nearby turnout, they turned around and drove by the vehicle again. They spotted the suspect parked in the middle of the clearing. The suspect was just sitting motionless in the driver's seat.

"I wonder if he is planning to meet someone. Pull over down there out of view. I'll try to work my way through the woods to his site. I'll keep in touch by radio and use the video camera to record whoever shows up."

"Got it," Bill remarked. "I'll inform the other teams to prepare to follow any vehicle that shows up."

"Good, keep your radio channel open," Maxine added as she exited the car.

It took her a few minutes to work herself through the wet woods and mud to the edge of the clearing. She was still about fifty feet away and could barely see through the passenger side window but it was as close as she could get.

Through the zoom camera lens, she spied the man just sitting motionless in the driver's seat. Despite the hood, something seemed strange about him.

"People don't sit motionless, they like to move. What's he up to?" she whispered. "Be patient, Maxie. Be patient."

Marine 1 lifted off with two escort helicopters and climbed to their assigned altitude for the short flight to Baltimore for a fundraising rally. Higher above were two F-35s for added protection.

After the rally, President Leatham was looking forward to some rest and escaping the pressures of Washington at Camp David. So much happened in the last six months he was desperate for some rest. A getaway was long overdue.

The rear van doors opened. The open doors prevented Maxine from a clear view of what was happening. She was about to work herself to a better position when he stepped into view holding a strange looking shoulder fired rocket launcher. Before she could react, he stepped around to the other side of the van out of view. In the distance, Maxine heard the unmistakable sound of two other missiles being launched in the distance.

She drew her pistol and charged the assassin. It was too late. Maxine hadn't run half the distance when a missile launched in a cloud of smoke.

Virginia Leatham, the First Lady, looked out the side window of *Marine 1* and saw the smoke trails of the oncoming missiles. Tugging on the sleeve of a nearby Secret Service Agent, she pointed out the window. "What are those things?" she asked.

Before the agent could answer, the three helicopters began a series of wild maneuvers to evade the oncoming missiles. The onboard electronic countermeasures tried to confuse the missiles' targeting systems but had little effect. The aircraft deployed chaff and flares but confused the missiles for a few seconds. When the two F-35s dove to intercept them, two more missiles appeared.

The helicopter pilots, in a last-ditch effort, put their helicopters into a steep left bank and dove as steeply as the craft could stand. The three missiles overshot their targets. The two fighters dove at *Marine 1* hoping the missiles would lock onto them instead. Two missiles did and the pilots hit afterburners to lure them away from *Marine 1.*

The missiles followed. It appeared the fighter pilots were

going to escape when the missiles began to accelerate. The pilots tried every maneuver they could but time ran out and the missiles struck their targets. The copilot of *Marine 1* looked at the pilot and both began breathing deeply as the third missile homed in on one of the escorting helicopters. There was an explosion and wreckage began raining from the sky.

The last two missiles acquired their remaining targets. Flairs and chaff again filled the air to no effect. The pilots jinked to the right then the left, then right again. It was to no avail. The pilot dove for the trees but there was just not enough time. Both missiles slammed into their targets at virtually the same instant. There were two large exploding fireballs, as the two helicopters were violently ripped apart. Flames and debris filled the air. There were no survivors.

Loretta Sanchez could see the flames and debris falling in the distance. When the other teams are done the major leaders of the world will be dead. They will be the lucky ones. Wait until the invasion fleet arrives. There won't be a city left un-torched."

Her body guard nodded. "When our Combat Fleet meets up with their hero, he will be dead and so will all their hope."

Maxine looked up and saw the explosions. On her radio Maxine shouted for her partner's assistance. She rounded the side of the van aiming her gun. The man wheeled around and looked at her as she ordered him to drop the launcher and lay on the ground. He appeared to obey her at first. The man gazed at her for a moment, dropped the launcher, then bolted for the nearby river.

Maxine raced towards him shouting again for him to stop. The man turned and falling to one knee fired a strange looking weapon at her. A green bolt of energy zipped through the air barely missing Maxine's head and sliced through the van's rear doors like a hot knife slicing through butter. Sparks of hot metal showered over and around Maxine as she returned fire.

The man took two shots in the chest but still managed to get up. He struggled to keep his balance then staggered toward the river a few yards away. Maxine again ordered him to stop. He didn't. She fired several more shots. This time the man's legs buckled under him as he slumped to the ground at the water's edge.

Her partner ran up behind her and yelled, "*Marine 1* was just shot down!"

"Better call and report the location and need for help. We have a lot of crime scene to secure. Send the other teams to locate where the other missiles were launched. There are four other launchers involved." Maxine bent down to check the man's pulse on his neck. As she felt for a pulse she suddenly shrieked and jumped away in shock.

Bill reached down and pulled the hoodie away revealing a man with a gray leathery face, no facial hair, large eyes, and small ears. They also saw a set of gills on his neck below and behind the jaw. Blood was slowly oozing out of them.

"Well, I bet immigration doesn't know about this guy!" Bill calmly mused.

"You never miss the obvious do you, Sherlock?" Maxine growled.

Vice President Gary Koppel was on his way to Number One Observatory Circle when the Secret Service driver made a violent U-turn on Massachusetts Ave. The tires left a cloud of smoke as rockets, bullets and blaster gunfire erupted around them. The rockets missed their mark exploding into nearby vehicles and store fronts sending flames and debris high into the air.

The evasive action saved the vice president but two escorting officers went tumbling from their motorcycles. One officer lay fatally wounded in the street but the other officer, even with two broken legs struggled to remain in the fight. She crawled to her cycle using it for cover while returning fire. Her brave fight was cut short in a flaming explosion when a bolt of blaster fire struck the gas tank.

The vice president's vehicle raced to avoid the gauntlet of fire for the next fifty yards. Two capitol police cruisers set up a blocking position to shield the vice president and his Secret Service escorts escape. The four officers took cover behind their patrol cars and began to provide covering fire. Two more rockets slammed into the police cruisers leaving wreckage and carnage. Their bold sacrifice allowed the vice president to escape to safety.

"Mr. Vice President!" the lead Secret Service Agent called out from the front passenger seat. "*Marine 1* was just shot down by a missile.

"Were they able to land safely? Are the president and his wife OK?" Vice President Koppel asked trying to shake off the shock of all that was happening.

The agent shook his head. "Sorry, sir!" "No confirmation yet but wreckage is strewn over a large area."

Vice President Koppel leaned back in his seat, and closed his eyes in prayer. His limousine made it to the safety of the White House where he was escorted to the presidential underground command center. That night, after he was sworn in as the new president, he was secreted out of Washington D.C. to a more secure location.

Victoria set her lunch tray on the table opposite Dr. Jerri Spinner. "How are you doing today, Dr. Spinner?" Victoria asked.

"Oh please! Call me Jerri. There is no need for formality among friends. I'm doing fine. Yourself?"

"I'm all right," Victoria sighed as she spread her napkin

across her lap.

Jerri looked very concerned. "Victoria, you sound tired. Have you been on duty long?"

Victoria sighed. "Time wise, not very long, otherwise, it has been a very demanding and frustrating shift so far. Everyone wants just a minute of your time to solve problems they could easily solve themselves. This person doesn't like burgers every meal. I tell them to order something else. On and on and on, you know what I mean? 'Everyone thinks because I'm the general's wife, I can put in a good word for them for a promotion or job. I'm getting burned out doing this human relations stuff."

"I know what you mean." Jerri noted. "John is probably causing some strain too, I bet?"

"Well," Victoria nodded. "He was doing well until he received a message from Earth a few minutes ago. The report said President Leatham and his wife were assassinated forty-eight hours ago along with other key foreign leaders by suicide teams of suspected Uvarian commandos. They also damaged numerous civilian and military facilities around the world. Many countries are so ill prepared to fight an alien invasion, they have made formal requests for the United Nations to declare a world government to negotiate with the Uvarian government. President Koppel declared the United States would not support any move towards a world government. The Security Council is deeply divided on how to respond.

Some congressional members threaten to impeach the new president if he doesn't support U.N. Resolution 1421 for forming a world government.

'President Koppel refused to cave. He also ordered the military to prepare for long term resistance."

"Oh my word! I can't believe they would do such a thing," Jerri agreed in shock. "How is John taking all of this?"

"He is in our quarters throwing the worst temper tantrum I've ever seen. He swears he will not stand down no matter who orders him."

"You mean he still plans to attack them? Isn't he outnumbered?" Jerri gasped in feigned astonishment.

Victoria shook her head in agreement. "You're right on both counts. Our first attack should be sometime tomorrow morning. He thinks some miracle will happen I guess. The problem is Admiral Dever sent a message to Terra, which was relayed just before we got out of communications range. Admiral MacKay is urging him not to go through with the plan to launch the shuttle with the dead Uvarian. He believes tricking the Uvarians to follow our fleet to Herrac 2 will end like Custer's last Stand.

'The Battle of Cassaria went badly. Both sides took heavy losses and ended in a devastating draw. There are only ten cruisers available to meet us at Herrac 2 and some of them are barely combat effective. They will arrive almost a day late. John is trying to come up with a plan to delay the Uvarians an extra day."

"I'd better not say any more. It only gets worse," Victoria sighed as she struggled to calm herself. "John would be furious if all this leaked out."

"How can it get worse? Victoria, you can trust me. I work for the State Department. I know how to keep secrets."

"I'm sorry I forgot about your security clearance," Victoria apologized. "Well, most of the Katusian forces were recalled three days ago to protect their home world. We don't have much of a force left. The remaining Katusian cruisers will leave after the Laylar raid. When this is all over, we will be the only ones left and barely able to defend ourselves."

Jerri reached over the table and grasped Victoria's hands. "Don't worry," Jerri reassured her. "We may loose Earth but maybe God has a plan we need to search out and follow. In the end peace will find a way. I'm sure of it."

"Thanks, I needed to hear that. Sometimes it is hardest to follow our own advice," Victoria agreed while holding back her tears.

Jerri looked puzzled. "You mentioned using an implant body before, why the switch to a Uvarian body?"

"John changed the body thinking the Uvarian body in a Uvarian shuttle would be more believable. He should have thought of that from the beginning." Victoria sighed shaking her head.

"John says we really have nothing to loose. We will launch the shuttle before the battle and pretend it is hiding. When the Uvarians try to retrieve the shuttle, we will pretend we are trying to destroy it. That will convince the Uvarians we didn't want it to fall into their hands and add credibility to the ruse.

'John thinks fooling the Uvarians will be our best hope of survival. The problem is John's plan is so transparent, I fear all John will succeed in doing is put us in even more danger. Earth is lost and defeat of the Allies is not far behind."

'I suggested we flee to uncharted space and try to find a planet we can colonize. Hopefully the Uvarians will never find us. John said he would consider it later," Victoria said with a glimmer of hope.

"I doubt the Uvarians would let a ship like the *Holcron Star* remain on the loose. They will hunt us down no matter where we go. It's for the best if we follow the U.N.'s example and try to make peace with them. On the bright side, it's better than being dead," Jerri optimistically advised.

"It's probably better than living on some desert planet living like a bunch of starving cavemen too," Victoria said a little light heartedly.

"It's probably better than living on some ice planet like a frozen Eskimo," Jerri added teasingly.

They both laughed and changed the subject. Both knew in the back of their mind the danger they were soon to face.

Victoria continued to be downcast and worried.

For Jerri's part, she realized that the Uvarians needed to be warned of the trap. Maybe it was possible to eliminate both forces. How to warn them was easy to figure out. All she had to do was get aboard that shuttle before it launched. She was sure the Uvarians would reward her generously for her information.

It was late at night and John was going over some details with his commanders making sure each one knew their assignment and formation position. The commanders had to be totally clear what was required and how to do it.

John was expecting to make contact with the Uvarian Combat Fleet sometime around late morning.

The message from Admiral MacKay confirmed they had arrived at Earth but the announcement of President Leatham's assassination sent shockwaves through the ship. Those in Terran Command greatly admired his strength and positive vision for the future.

John believed President Koppel possessed those same virtues and was confident American resolve would stand firm.

John decided to make a round of the ship before turning in for the night. As he stepped off the elevator onto deck 1, Chaplain Boyle greeted him.

"John, I was on my way to the bridge to see you. I know you like to make the rounds before a battle. You mind if I join you?" Chaplain Boyle asked.

"Not at all, I could use the company," John smiled.

It was almost midnight when Henry entered hangar 1 to find Estron and Deze busy finishing the modifications to the battered Shuttle 2.

"How's it goin'? Henry asked.

"We've been working on this thing since 5 o'clock this morning. I just finished tuning the joystick controls. It's ready to go, no thanks to Dex," Estron grumbled.

Yep, since 5 o'clock!" Deze wearily emphasized.

"Why didn't you guys call fer me?" Henry asked.

Estron closed up the toolbox. "Henry, with all due respect, shuttle controls aren't your area of expertise. I figured we could handle it and we did. We sure could have used Dex though."

"Where is he?" Henry asked.

"I assume he was the person who reassembled the captured Uvarian shuttle. Someone was working on it last night but when I arrived they were all ready done," Estron explained.

"He did a good job too!" Deze added.

"Nobody knows how to fly that thing. Why bother?" Henry asked.

"If anyone can figure it out it would be Dex," Deze said.

"Deze and I haven't seen him since his meltdown three days ago. Have you?" Estron asked.

Henry shook his head. "Not really. I talked to him on the flip com yesterday morning. He said he was sleeping in and appreciated the call. He said he'd been working on a special project for Gavin."

"I haven't heard of a special project and I'm sure Gavin would have at least told me about it," Estron said.

"Somethin' fishy goin' on here," Henry agreed. "I'll talk to John about it in the morning. For now we need to get some sleep. It's going to be a big day tomorrow."

Henry helped Deze stow away the tools in the hangar bay tool locker while Estron made sure the Uvarian shuttle controls were set and the autopilot on standby. The medical team would come by later and setup the decoy and then all would be ready for launch. A few minutes later the hangar was empty.

CHAPTER 21

The klaxon reverberated throughout the *Holcron Star* as crewmembers raced to their battle stations. John Braxton was already on the bridge and noted the crew's response was the fastest he'd ever timed.

"All stations report action ready!" Georgia called out.

"Thanks, Comm.," John replied. He studied the holo-projection of the Laylar System, taking note as his cruisers nestled up behind their designated asteroids. From the intelligence, they recovered from the Uvarian scout ship, the fleet was to drop out of warp and reassemble when all ships arrived and accounted for.

The large asteroids blocked the Uvarian sensors preventing the Uvarian Combat Fleet from detecting them. Task Force Hammer was under a communications blackout with all sensors operating in passive mode to avoid possible detection. The plan was to pounce on the enemy fleet at the last possible moment.

Surveying the bridge, John noted Gavin was serving as First Officer, Aycana as the Weapons Officer and Joshua Nevens assisted at the Defense Systems Console. David and Siyana were at the flight controls.

Dr. Jerri Spinner, taking advantage of the rush to battle stations quickly made her way to hangar bay 1. Victoria, anticipating her actions, shadowed her. "Everything is going as planned," Victoria whispered just loud enough for her ear bud to pick it up.

"Good!" John replied on his ear bud.

As Victoria followed she noticed a tall, slender Holcron, in a dark green Engineering work uniform, follow Jerri toward the hangar. Jerri weaved her way through the rushing maze of people and finally made it to a secondary hangar entrance hatch. She pressed the hatch actuator button and entered the hangar. The hatch automatically closed behind her.

"What is this guy doing? His duty station is on the next deck in Engineering," Victoria whispered.

Victoria alerted Security. Lt. O'Brian acknowledged a four-man security team was on the way to assist.

The Holcron crewmember arrived at the hangar hatch and reached out to press the hatch actuator button. Victoria stepped behind him, pulled a compact pistol and pressed it against his back.

"Freeze!" Victoria commanded.

"Please, don't shoot!" the Holcron pleaded.

"Place your hands behind your head, slowly get on your knees and cross your legs," Victoria instructed.

"Yes, sir!" the man said as he quickly complied.

"What is your name and why are you here instead of at your duty station?" Victoria commanded.

"My name is Chief Master Sergeant Kieran Tossa. I was on my way there when I noticed Dr. Spinner was going in the opposite direction of her quarters. She has been in the reactor room a lot lately and I suspected she was up to something. I thought I'd follow her and see where she was going," Kieran answered.

"Why should you care where she goes?"

"I don't trust her," he replied.

"Why?"

"Why would this unfriendly arrogant diplomat with no science background suddenly show up in a reactor control room asking questions about its intricate workings? I reported it to my supervisor but he didn't think it was a big deal. He dismissed it as Earthling curiosity. I didn't buy it."

Just then the security team arrived. They drew their weapons and surrounded Chief Tossa.

John heard the conversation. "Victoria, I know this guy. He's trustworthy. If Dr. Spinner tried to sabotage anything, he will know. I'll alert Lt. O'Brian for additional assistance."

Victoria looked at the security team leader. "You can relax. Let him up," Victoria said.

"Yes, ma'am!" the team leader replied.

"Can Dexter and Deze help in the search? They are now very familiar with the system," Chief Tossa explained.

John over heard the request and replied to Victoria they were on the way.

Cat Saunders, concealed on the *Halfling*'s command deck, took over tracking Dr. Spinner as she entered the shuttle with the dead Uvarian at the controls. Cat confirmed Dr. Spinner boarded the shuttle.

Lt. Corky O'Brian posted security teams at all the exits then joined Victoria.

She let out a sigh. "Okay, Corky, it's now a waiting game."

Corky nodded, "Does Jerri leave a message to tip off the Uvarians, become a stowaway, or chicken out?"

Three hours had gone by since the call to battle stations. Jerri was becoming impatient. Where was the Uvarian fleet?

She could tell the dead Uvarian was an officer. He had been carefully preserved and the blood around the shuttle made it appear he'd bled out during his escape. The false information was planted on a memory stick hidden inside his tunic. She reasoned the scene was real enough. It was up to her to arrive in person to make sure the Uvarians got the right information.

Jerri was quite proud of herself. *When I foil their plan and the Uvarians turn the tables on them, the Braxtons are going to go down in history as the fools that made Allied defeat possible.*

John Braxton kept questioning himself. *Human nature such as it is, even with the best plan, Murphy's Law can turn victory into defeat in a second. Did I underestimate the resourcefulness of Dr. Spinner? Maybe I should have come up with a less risky plan. No, stick to the plan and trust your crew, especially Victoria and Cat. If we're not on God's side it won't matter.*

John smiled at Gavin. "Let's do it!"

"Launching now!" Gavin replied. He sent a signal from a handheld control box to the decoy shuttle's computer. The engines powered up and the autopilot followed the preprogrammed flight plan. The shuttle rose off the deck, slowly rotated 180 degrees and launched.

John looked at Gavin. "Now there's no turning back. Gavin couldn't hide the excitement of something finally happening."

After a brief flight, the shuttle nestled itself among a concentration of small asteroids. Another two hours went by and everyone on the bridge grew restless again. Finally, Estron announced several ships were detected.

"Deze's program is working!" she exclaimed. "They are just entering our Intel buoy's range. We can track them clearly now."

"How many ships?" John asked.

"Twelve cruisers in four formations approaching at warp 4. They should arrive in the Laylar System in an hour and a half," Estron reported.

"That's not all of them. Stay alert, people," John announced to the crew. We've sighted lead ships of the Uvarian fleet."

On the holo-projector, John watched the fleet approach near the Laylar System. The groups of Uvarian cruisers were flying in "V" formations. John hoped the Uvarian sensors would detect the hidden shuttle without sensing his ships.

The first ships of the Uvarian fleet dropped out of warp with their shields up. The lead ship then altered course towards the decoy shuttle.

"John, The Uvarian cruiser has launched a recovery ship to retrieve the decoy," Gavin reported.

"Great. Now where is the rest of the fleet?" John replied.

It took another ten minutes for the Uvarian recovery ship to attach a magnetic cable to the shuttle and begin returning to the command ship.

John was ready to order the attack when Dexter called excitedly from the reactor room.

"John!" Victoria shouted into John's ear bud. "Do not raise shields or fire any energy weapons. We will be space dust if you do. Chief Tossa found a case with an explosive device attached to the #2 reactor maintenance console. The power fluctuation will trigger detonation. We cannot go to warp either.

"How soon can the bomb be deactivated?" John asked.

"Chief Tossa says it will take a couple minutes once he re-routes power from reactor 1 maintenance console. You will have only weapons and shields until he can bring #2 reactor back on line. Our missiles are unaffected and safe to fire. You'll have no warp capability though."

"How long will that take?" John asked as options raced through his mind.

"Give me thirty minutes. Is that enough?" Dexter asked.

"Do I have any choice?" John asked rhetorically. "Do it."

"Aycana, when you have shields and forward plasma guns let me know. Target our forward missiles just behind the decoy shuttle. Do not hit it. I repeat do not hit the shuttle. Also, target missiles on the closest cruisers except their flagship."

"Yes, sir!" Aycana replied.

To everyone on the bridge time seemed to stand still as the seconds ticked by.

"Sir," Dexter announced over the ship's com. net, "power transfer is complete."

"Yes!" Aycana shouted with glee as she powered up the magnum plasma cannons.

"Shields and forward defense lasers on line," Joshua reported.

John was at the holo-projector map noting the updated ship formations. He touched the Communications button for the task force channel on the Command cuff on his left forearm.

"Sir," Estron shouted. "Twelve more Uvarian cruisers are coming up on sensors. No! Wait, a third group of twelve more are also just coming up on sensors.

"Hold fire, do not activate shields," John ordered.

"What's wrong?" Gavin asked.

"I'm not sure," John answered. "Are they expecting us or is coming out of warp with shields up, standard procedure? Has our trap become their trap? The last group of ships are projected to drop out of warp right behind us.

"They are on to us," John called out.

Grand Viscount Zinge Horthnot stood on the bridge of his flagship, relishing the sight of his planet's greatest victory. The bridge was small and cramped for such a large cruiser. About ten personnel monitored all ship functions from a series of consoles in the shape of a horseshoe.

The consoles created a soft glow of blinking lights in rainbow colors around the darkened bridge. A revolving command chair with a holographic projector was situated in the center behind the pilot's chair. A walk area between the forward observation port and the flight console allowed the bridge crew to take an occasional stretch in the cramped work area.

The forward observation port gave a limited view of space, but Zinge enjoyed the view all the same. With great pride, he gazed at the stars while reflecting on the past and future to come.

Conquest of the planets in this sector of space would be the crowning jewel in a long and bloody series of empire building wars. The leaders of Uvaria had his family to thank for building the largest empire in the known galaxy.

His father had the vision of a great Uvarian empire. High Admiral Xavian Horthnot spent three decades of careful planning, shipbuilding and training to set the stage for this glorious victory now just days away. As Zinge rose from the ranks in his father's footsteps, he realized his father was a great visionary. However, he lacked the ruthlessness necessary to carry the plan to ultimate victory. Zinge was determined to make up for his father's shortcomings and achieve the greatest victory.

Zinge felt the nudge of his First Officer. "Sorry, sir! We are approaching the Laylar System. Everything is going as planned."

"Zinge wrinkled his nose in disgust. "Not really. The last report from Scout ship 1 is almost two months old. Our Implant force on Earth hasn't been heard from in eight months. We still don't have our zannite shipment either. My stomach is telling me something is amiss."

"Sir, we just received a message from Scout Ship 3." The communications officer reported.

"What is it," Zinge asked.

The First Officer retrieved the message, read it and handed it to the Grand Viscount. "They just arrived at the Laylar System. The captain reports a Uvarian shuttle is adrift at the rendezvous point. It is sending a distress signal with the proper code," the First Officer stated handing him a copy of the message.

"Can they identify the shuttle and is there any life aboard?" Zinge asked.

The Communications officer responded. "Sir, the shuttle is from Scout Ship 1. The life support signal reports one life is aboard and one is deceased. Scout Ship 3 reports they are unable to recover the shuttle at this time."

"How interesting!" Zinge noted. When we arrive, we will recover the shuttle. They are to remain on station and cloaked."

"Comm., notify the fleet to come out of warp with shields up and in assigned coordinates and intervals," Zinge ordered. "If this is a trap it will be on them."

"Yes, sir!" the Communications Officer replied. Message sent!"

As the Viscount's flagship and three escorting cruisers came out of warp, Zinge ordered the recovery operation to begin.

Everyone on the bridge was looking at John. John didn't flinch. He kept starring at the scene before them. Another fifteen minutes went by and still John didn't give the order to fire. Victoria returned to the bridge and stood boldly beside him.

"John, are you OK?" Victoria asked, noticing his fixation on the flagship.

"Patience, Victoria, patience!" We need to give our rat time to complete her mission," John murmured.

Another ten minutes later, Estron called out, "Sir, another flight of four cruisers are about to come out of warp. Sensors show the shimmering effect of a Uvarian scout ship fifty degrees, starboard. Wait a minute, another one is 320 degrees, port. They are holding just out of plasma cannon range. How did they get that close?"

"They are on to us," John called out as he flipped on the Task Force comm. link. "They know we are here. All ships, advance and open fire. Focus on the flagship that recovered the shuttle on your first salvo then concentrate your fire on the ship on the port side. Ignore the scout ships for now."

"Aycana, keep firing forward plasma cannons on the port side ship next to the Uvarian flagship. I want them to scatter so we can cut through the formation. Once we are between them, fire a broadside of everything we got into both ships," John ordered.

"Aye, sir!" Aycana acknowledged.

"Gavin, keep an eye on our ships. If anyone gets into trouble let me know," John directed as he had David alter course.

"Sir, hangar bay 1 wants to know if they can launch the mines yet?" Estron asked.

John studied the Uvarian ships around them and the locations of the Allied cruisers then paused for a few moments.

"Sir! Should they begin launching?" Estron asked again.

John took another long pause and finally gave the command. "All ships begin launching three mines every five-seconds until they are all released."

Down in hangar bay 1, Henry and his crew began launching his latest improved mines. Only time would tell if they were effective.

In the first salvo of missiles and magnum plasma cannon fire, one Uvarian cruiser was seriously damaged. The flagship was slightly damaged but appeared to be having trouble maintaining course. The second flight of four ships were just coming out of warp to the rear of the Allied ships.

The *Holcron Star* led the Allied cruisers on a blitz through the Uvarian formation with seemingly total reckless abandon. Each Allied cruiser followed right behind the *Holcron Star* straight through the enemy formation, firing their missiles and plasma cannon broadsides as they passed. There was no quarter given to any Uvarian ships. The enemy had to get out of the way, be blown to bits, or rammed.

John Braxton was pleased as he saw each of the ships push

their way through the Uvarian formation. The maneuver caused complete confusion. Within minutes the Uvarian ships were scattered in total disarray. Befuddled by the unconventional tactic, one Uvarian ship made a series of wild maneuvers of its own, fired a missile salvo on *Fire Fox,* as it closely passed another already damaged Uvarian cruiser.

Fire Fox immediately performed a roll, over the other Uvarian ship causing the missiles from the first Uvarian ship to hit it instead. The fatally struck ship began to break apart with a rippling effect along the length of its hull. Task Force Hammer had fought its way through the Uvarian formation emerging on the opposite side of the demoralized Uvarian fleet.

"Helm, good job getting us through," John called out. "Take us out just beyond their range and bring us about for another pass once our ships are back in formation."

As the tiny task force regrouped, John called for damage reports. "The cruiser, *K.S.S. Gershan,* took two hits which damaged the rear shields and started an electrical fire in the hangar bay. The fire was quickly put out but four crewmembers lost their lives and five were injured in the process. The captain reports repairs to the rear shields expected in one hour. The hangar should be usable in twenty-four hours," Gavin reported. "Five cruisers report only minor damage and remain combat ready. Jonathan reports the *Fire Fox* sustained no damage or casualties."

"Good news, Gavin, and thanks for the good report on Jonathan. How about the Uvarians?"

"This is what we have confirmed. two cruisers destroyed, one was destroyed by friendly fire. Two were severely damaged and at least temporarily out of the fight. Three are damaged and still in the fight. We have their fleet in total disarray. I must say, we have done far more damage than we ever hoped for," Gavin replied a bit excited.

"Excellent! They will be expecting us this time," John noted.

"Sir!" Georgia called out. "There is a flight of four Uvarian cruisers coming out of warp just in front of the main formation. There is another flight of six cruisers coming in. Sensors report they will be coming out of warp in front of the asteroid field joining up with the other three ships."

"I expect a fourth flight will be right behind us. We will then be boxed in. There are too may for us to do another blitz now. Now the flight that came out of warp behind the asteroids started to advance and join up with the main body. It didn't get far before running into Henry's improved mines. Silently they began attaching themselves to the hulls of the three cruisers. In a short time, the other six inbound ships will find themselves with mines attached.

Chief Tossa, Deze and Dexter were working feverishly to get the bomb dismantled. The more they studied the makeup of the bomb the more roadblocks prevented them from dismantling it.

Victoria returned to the #2 Reactor Control Room. "How are we doing?"

Dexter sighed. "I'm not sure we can dismantle this bomb without jettisoning the reactor core first," Dexter stated in frustration.

"What do you mean? We can't just sit here trapped in the middle of battle waiting to be blown to bits. We must find a way to dismantle the bomb and restore warp capability. Once the Uvarians discover our dilemma, the whole Uvarian fleet will focus their attack on us," Victoria retorted.

"Dr. Spinner took her metal briefcase everywhere on the ship. Everyone got so used to seeing her with it no one got suspicious when she brought it into the reactor room. She feigned so much interest in the job we do here, we thought she got distracted, left it behind, and would be back for it.

That is all of us except for Chief Tossa. We had no idea how she figured a way of integrating it into the console," a reactor technician explained.

"Don't worry, you weren't the only one fooled," Victoria stated a bit perturbed with herself. "An investigation will be held later to find out what happened and how to prevent it in the future. In the meantime let's focus on getting rid of the bomb."

Deze crawled out from under the console shaking his head. "This bomb is a nightmare to dismantle," he declared. "What do you mean?" Dexter asked.

"The bomb is something I've never seen before. I have to assume Dr. Spinner somehow smuggled it aboard from Terra. The bomb is attached to the #2 reactor control console with two thread like filaments. As far as I can determine, the case contains a sensor that locks out the console control settings and locks in preprogrammed override settings. The two thin threads leading from the case are intertwined into the console wiring. It's a mess. If the override signal is broken, we are dead. If we tamper with the magnetic field around the case, we're dead. If there is a power surge in the reactor, we are dead. If we jettison the reactor which will circumvent it, even then we are dead," Deze explained.

"Wait a minute. I've heard that description before. These Uvarians are tricky," Victoria said. She grasped her flip com. and contacted Khem in sick bay.

"I have you on speaker. How do you dismantle an implant?" Victoria urgently asked.

"The only way we have found to neutralize the implant is to splice it to a different power source then cut the primary optical threads to the original power source. We can then command it to shut down without killing the host. Why do you ask?" Khem inquired, very puzzled by the question.

Great! If we live long enough I'll tell you about it later.

Bye!" Victoria exclaimed as she ended the call.

"You heard him, there is another way. Will that work?" Victoria asked.

"It sounds simple enough," Dexter replied.

Chief Kieran Tossa smiled. "When we have to repair a control console, we lock it out and assume control from the other reactor's console. It is a backup system that we hardly ever use because such maintenance is rare, but it does work."

"It's not so simple," Khem interjected as he and Susan entered the room. "Let me look at it?"

"Be my guest!" Chief Tossa agreed.

Khem crawled underneath the console and saw the threads leading from the case into the console.

"Just as I thought. You people touch those threads we are all dead.

You need a surgeon, not a mechanic. Chief, you stay. Everyone else out. Susan, go to the lab and bring the threads we cloned, the power pack we use to keep them alive, and the surgical tools we made to handle them. Make it fast."

Susan didn't say a word as she ran to the sick bay lab.

"Chief, I overheard you say console #1 can lock out this console. Correct?" Khem asked.

"Yes," Chief Tossa replied.

"Great. Go there and call me when you are ready. Don't lock this console out until I say so. Got it?" Khem asked.

"You got it!" Chief Tossa said and raced to the other console.

A couple minutes later Susan returned with the items. "Here we go," Susan said a bit winded.

"Ok, I need you to put on surgical gloves and get on the other side of the console. You will need to copy every move I make on your thread at almost the exact time. We need to be careful that we don't cause any power flux surge or the wedding is off," Khem cautioned as he put on his surgical gloves.

"So, you did talk to Dad?" Susan ask a bit surprised.

"Not yet, he is a bit preoccupied. We'll get to it, I promise," Khem smiled. "Take one of the cloned threads and cut into two 18 inch lengths." The sound of the scissors making a snip sound echoed in the otherwise silent room.

Khem's flip com buzzed and he opened it up.

"Yes, Chief, stand by for my order to isolate the #2 console," Khem said.

"Here is yours," Susan said handing Khem one of the cloned threads.

"Take yours and hold it about half an inch from the thread like this." Khem demonstrated.

Susan carefully copied Khem's every move. As the cloned threads came closer and closer they started to vibrate like they recognized each other. Suddenly the cloned threads stretched out and wrapped around the other threads connecting with a slight spark as they bonded together.

"Wow! Was that supposed to happen?" Susan asked surprised. "I didn't expect the spark for sure."

"Well we are still here so I guess so. I was hoping they would connect but I wasn't expecting a spark," Khem sighed in relief. "Can you hand me the power pack?"

On her side, Susan reached over to the tray and retrieved the power pack. Khem inserted the remaining end of each cloned thread in a port in the power pack.

"Chief, are you ready?" Khem shouted.

"Susan, take the scissors and cut both threads above the connections at the same time I give the signal," Khem instructed.

"I am ready to flip the switch," Chief Tossa replied. Khem placed his finger on the button of the power pack.

Susan murmured, "God, we could use a lot of grace right now!"

"Everyone is ready…NOW!" Khem shouted. The threads were snipped, the power pack became the power source, and the console cut out at the same instant.

"Great job everyone, we are still here,"Khem announced excitedly. "The first successful implant surgery was a lifesaving success."

A voice came over the ship's intercom: "On behalf of the crew, we thank God's grace and all three of you for a job well done.

Dr. Jerri Spinner sat in the room with her hands handcuffed to a metal table. Her interrogator lacked any form of subtlety during her initial interrogation. The room continued to spin around her as the pain in her temples slowly subsided. Bit by bit, her senses allowed her to register the extent of her injuries. Her jaw ached and her cheeks were swollen from the brutal beating. The left side of her face was covered with blood from a cut above the eye and blood from a broken nose trickled off her chin and down her chest.

As Jerri looked around the stark, dimly lit room, all thoughts of being welcomed as a hero vanished. She wondered if she would be beaten to death or end up a new addition to the slave trade. A husky guard wearing a forest green jumpsuit, heavy leather vest and black helmet stood blocking the only exit to the barren room.

She asked the guard, "Please, can I have a drink of water?"

The guard stood silent and made no indication she was even in the room. A few more minutes went by and she asked again. Again, the guard made no acknowledgment or movement. Suddenly the door opened and an Uvarian officer walked in who was obviously an officer of high rank. The guard immediately came to attention and snapping a salute. The officer sat down in a chair opposite Jerri and ordered the guard to remove her restraints.

"Dr. Spinner, I am Grand Viscount Zinge Horthnot. I apologize for your treatment. If my incompetent interrogator had followed procedures, he would have found the implant device and saved you much pain and suffering."

"I understand, Master," Jerri painfully conceded.

"What is going on here? We retrieve a scout ship shuttle way out here in space and inside we find one of my best commanders dead, plans for a trap against our fleet and one of our Earthling agents. Why was the *Holcron Star* shooting at both of us?"

"Master, all things are not as they seem. Six months ago, General John Braxton and his family captured a freighter with your shipment of zannite crystals and the Cassarian royal family. They then managed to capture the *Holcron Star* by pretending to be pirates. Their deception allowed them to capture additional pirate ships, and recruit help from Holcron and Katusium.

'Your dead commander and his crew encountered the *Holcron Star* in the Mentarus system. Not knowing the *Holcron Star* was captured; they were surprised by General Braxton and destroyed. A few bodies and the damaged shuttle were retrieved. General Braxton used your commander's body to plant false plans and used the shuttle to deceive you.

'The Gamoran pirates are wiped out. The zannite mines on the planet they call Terra are now under General Braxton's control. The battle of Cassaria did take place and both sides suffered severe losses."

"I see!" Zinge replied. "What about Earth? We lost communications with them some time ago."

Jerri nodded. "On Earth, your agents successfully assassinated the president of the United States. Along with other attacks around the planet, they have caused much disruption, confusion and fear. The remaining leaders of Earth have decided not to resist your invasion to save lives in a battle they are convinced is futile.

'General Braxton refuses to surrender and is attempting to lure your combat fleet to Herrac 2. His plan was to trap you between his task force and the remnant forces from the battle of Cassaria. That plan has, however, unraveled because the forces from Cassaria are few and will arrive later than General Braxton planned. It is true they are equipped with zannite but the crews are very inexperienced. I planted a bomb on the *Holcron Star.* If pressed in an attack it will explode the reactor when they attempt warp travel.

'I sneaked onto the shuttle to warn you. The Katusians have withdrawn all of their ships to protect their home world except for four cruisers that were left behind as a token show of support. If General Braxton is attacked at Herrac 2 within thirteen days, his task force will be wiped out before they can unite with the Cassarian remnant. The remaining ships can easily be destroyed ending any meaningful resistance.

'All the other planets will surrender to avoid destruction," Jerri reported.

"You risked everything to warn us. Thank you! This General Braxton is a great risk taker. Within six months a man with not so much as a space suit, has managed to reveal our invasion plans, defeat the pirates, steals our zannite, unite the other planets and now attacks my fleet. I must make an example of him and crush his resistance movement less other worlds think they can do the same," Zinge declared.

"I hope my mission was successful enough to please you, Master?" Jerri begged.

Zinge reached out to put his hand gently on top of her head and stroked her hair like he was petting a dog. "You have done well my dear, very well indeed."

A few minutes later the Grand Viscount was again

on the bridge in communication with Vice Admiral Baya Mutaka. Zinge was mindful of her ruthless and sometimes reckless behavior but her planning was superb. Zinge liked her frankness and courage to speak her mind. Zinge informed her of Dr. Spinner's report.

"Sir, I do not believe any of this. Are we supposed to believe some backwater Earthling has successfully and single handedly wiped out the Gamoran pirates? In the last thirty years, the other planets united couldn't do it. The whole story just doesn't wash," Baya exclaimed.

"At first I thought so as well. The problem is the implant device prevents our human agents from deceiving us. It also explains why the *Holcron Star* is leading a mixed force against us," Zinge added.

"I see your point. Then we must pursue them and wipe them out. The use of zannite crystals makes them a very dangerous threat despite their size. We cannot let them attack the invasion fleet."

"Precisely! We must pursue them, and attack them wherever they go. We must wipe them out before they unite with the remaining ships from Cassaria. I will order the invasion fleet to proceed to Earth while we pursue the enemy cruisers. They may be faster and better armed but we have more ships, greater combined firepower and most importantly, combat experience.

'We must destroy the *Holcron Star* now while we have an advantage. They must be destroyed before they find a way to dismantle the bomb and restore warp drive. Then we will proceed to Herrac 2 to wipe out the survivors. We must be there in thirteen days."

John Braxton sat in his command chair with an air of calm serenity. Inside, he was about to scream. The dismantling of the bomb was a success. Now Chief Tossa had to sync the two warp drive engines and warp drive would be restored. It was only a matter of time before the Uvarian commander believed Dr. Spinner's report and came gunning for him. Now would be their best shot at eliminating the *Holcron Star*. They can't afford to pass it up.

"Sir, sensors are indicating the Uvarian fleet is moving in our direction. We will be in their combat range in about five minutes," Georgia reported.

"Status on the warp sync?" John asked.

"Dexter reports the warp sync failed and has to be rebooted. It will be another ten minutes," Victoria replied.

"If we are alive by then," John quipped. "Gavin, maintain our distance for as long as we can. Let's see if we can shake something loose."

"Can do!" Gavin replied and began plotting a new course. He relayed the change to the task force.

"Sir, ten Uvarian cruisers are appearing on our sensors just ahead of us. Distance is closing fast. They will be in combat range in five minutes," Georgia stated.

" They found out about the bomb. The cat is out of the bag. They know we can't out run them."

"Do you really want to fight them here?" Gavin asked.

"Not really. Our plan was to bait them into following us. Not get wiped out in a last stand. We must keep to our plan and not play their game. The *Holcron Star* can't run but the rest of the force can and must. We can't beat them here. We have to save what ships we can to fight another day. The battle must be fought at Herrac 2 with the Main Allied Fleet arriving from Cassaria," John stressed.

"Even without the *Holcron Star*?" Gavin asked.

"We are expendable for the greater good, if necessary. We can't hope to win here. We knew that from the beginning.

We are outnumbered and being surrounded.

Their entire Combat Fleet has arrived ahead of their own plan. We are outnumbered four to one. Even with our superior fire power, it is only a matter of time. That said, I do not plan to die today. I'm not in the mood. We only have to hold them off until the warp drives on both engines are re-synced," John declared.

"Why do we have to wait for the engines to be re-synced?" Victoria asked.

"Because if they are out of sync the ship will be ripped apart," Gavin explained.

"I see, let's not do that then," Victoria nodded.

"I'm not in the mood to die either. Today we beat the odds," Gavin agreed with a determined voice.

"Aycana, I want all available weapons aimed at their flagship. When it is in range open fire!" John ordered.

"Victoria, tell Dexter and Deze they are going to be sucking space if they don't get warp drive back on line fast," John directed with obvious frustration.

Victoria relayed the message.

"Tell General Braxton we are doing the best we can," Dexter replied.

"Dexter, you don't understand. The Uvarian cruisers will solve the problem very shortly if we don't get warp capability fast," Victoria retorted.

"I get the picture!" Dexter said shaking his head in frustration.

Meanwhile, John directed the task force to advance on the oncoming Uvarian cruisers. They were to make one pass at the enemy and then proceed to Herrac 2.

"What about you? You can't break contact without warp engines. You'll be cut to pieces," Jonathan replied over the communications net.

"We expect to have warp power by then," John replied optimistically. "You have your orders, now do your duty! Out."

"Gavin, I think it is time to activate Henry's little toys," John said with a mischievous grin.

"With pleasure, sir!" Gavin then pressed a series of numbers on a code pad on a remote device carried on his belt.

Seconds later there were numerous minor explosions on the exterior hulls of many Uvarian cruisers.

The mines Henry's team launched during the first attack had magnetically attached themselves to the hulls of several Uvarian cruisers as they struggled to reorganize their formations. When the code signal was sent, they went active and created havoc.

The explosions didn't breach the ship hulls. Instead, they released Henry's slimy concoction of florescent, magnetic goo rendering Uvarian sensor and targeting systems useless. The affected ships were forced to cease firing their energy weapons. Missiles could still launch but, with the friend or foe signals masked, everyone was now a potential target. This forced the Uvarians to severely limit their missile attack for fear of striking their own ships. For now they were effectively out of the fight.

The Allied cruisers were able to open fire first and fired two salvos of plasma cannons. The allied missiles homed in on the magnetic goo and struck before the Uvarians were able to return fire. Several Uvarian cruisers took heavy damage. The *Holcron Star*, however, continued to focus its power of destruction on the Uvarian flagship.

"Sir, our shields are about to fail. We must withdraw and let the rest of the fleet destroy them," the Defensive Countermeasures Officer reported.

"We stay and fight. A fleet commander never withdraws

while in battle. Never!" Zinge declared. "Steady on course and keep firing everything we got! I want all weapons directed at the *Holcron Star*!

"Yes, sir!" the First Officer replied as he assisted the Weapons Officer to direct fire.

Suddenly there was a massive jolt like the crew had never felt before. The whole ship shuddered and alarm systems throughout the ship began blaring.

"Damage report!" Zinge ordered.

"Sir, the shields are gone and a missile ruptured the aft auxiliary fuel storage tank. It is venting fuel into the hangar bay and generator room," the Engineering Officer replied.

"Get all personnel out of those areas and begin ventilation of atmosphere now. If the fuel ignites the ship will be torn apart."

"We are trying, sir! However, the ventilation controls are jammed. We can't come close to venting fast enough."

Now a second greater explosion rocked the ship followed by a groan that reverberated throughout the hull of the mighty Uvarian flagship. Grand Viscount Zinge Horthnot suddenly realized the grand empire he envisioned would not include him after all. Sadly, but calmly, he made the announcement that every ship's captain deep down in his soul dreads.

"Abandon ship! Abandon ship!" he ordered over the ship's intercom. "Rear Admiral Baya Mutaka the command is yours. Proceed to Herrac 2 and wipe them out including the fleet from Cassaria. Make Uvaria proud."

Those on the bridge looked at Zinge serenely sitting in his command chair gazing into space ready to accept his imminent death with dignity. Realizing they could not save themselves, the bridge crew resolved to stay at their posts and die with their great leader. The end came quickly.

With the ventilation system open and the controls

destroyed, the explosive yellow fumes continued spreading into every part of the ship. The crewmembers in Engineering valiantly began shutting down power in areas of the ship where the fumes were entering. In a last-ditch effort, the First Officer ordered the airlocks opened on the lower decks. It seemed to work as some contamination alarms began turning off. Some of the surviving crew began to cheer, thinking they were going to save the ship after all. However, when the fumes reached the electrical generator room, the resultant explosion destroyed the adjacent reactor control room. This set off a chain reaction the ship could not survive.

Those on the bridge of the *Holcron Star* could see the air locks open on the Uvarian flagship as yellow fumes began to escape. A moment later there was an almost blinding flash from the Uvarian flagship. The massive explosion lit up the bridge of the *Holcron Star* despite the protective screen filters of the bridge view ports.

David and Siyana reflexively covered their eyes with their arms as the blinding light lit up the bridge.

Siyana let out a gasp. "Oh my! Those people never had a chance to escape."

David looked at Siyana. "In an instant three hundred crewmembers and as many dreams ceased to exist. We'll join them if we don't find a way out of this mess. Look for an escape route."

Siyana nodded.

A moment later another similar explosion of another Uvarian cruiser took place.

Siyana pointed over to where the ship had been. "There is our escape route."

David agreed as he brought the ship about.

John looked at Gavin and Victoria and smiled. "Two down," John declared optimistically.

The other Allied cruisers successfully fought their way through the blocking force of Uvarian cruisers then went to maximum warp speed for Herrac 2. Now alone, the crippled *Holcron Star* faced eight Uvarian cruisers with the rest of the Uvarian fleet closing in fast for the kill.

"Sir, the shields are holding but with the fire we are taking we can't hold for much longer," Joshua reported.

John shook his head and contacted #1 reactor control room. "Dexter, I need warp drive now! We can't hold any longer."

"Just one more minute, general."

"In a minute and two-seconds the Uvarians will solve our warp drive problem for us. Do you understand?" John pleaded.

"Yes, sir!" Dexter replied.

A close by Uvarian missile explosion rocked the ship giving more urgency to Dexter and his team.

"Sir, the shields are about to collapse. I'm not sure how much more we can take," Joshua declared.

"Aycana, route power from the plasma guns to the shield generator.

That will buy us some extra time," John ordered. "Concentrate your missiles on the closest ships."

"Yes, sir!" Aycana responded with renewed determination.

Jonathan pounded his fist on the armrest of his command chair.

The remainder of Task Force Hammer successfully withdrew from the battle leaving the *Holcron Star* behind and hopelessly trapped.

"Dad taught us better than this. He should know better than to think I would leave family behind. Reverse course. The *Fire Fox* is going back to assist the *Holcron Star*," Jonathan told his Cassarian First Officer, Seth Briggans.

"But what can we do alone against so many?" he asked. "Be a shield for as long as we can," Jonathan declared.

"That doesn't sound very healthy," the First Officer advised with a bit of sarcasm.

"Actually, it can prove very unhealthy but someone's gota do it. Now, let's go!" Jonathan commanded.

Another missile tried to penetrate the *Holcron Star*'s shields but failed. However, the effect was telling. The shields quivered for a few more seconds then finally collapsed.

"Sir, the shields just failed and we have a power failure with the defensive targeting sensors. It will take at least two minutes to bring them back up," Joshua reported with frustration in his voice.

John looked out the forward port and saw three missiles coming straight for them. Standing behind John, Victoria instinctively placed her hands on John's shoulders, closed her eyes and began to pray. The bridge crew stood transfixed as they waited for the inevitable explosions.

From out of nowhere the *Fire Fox* appeared right in front of the *Holcron Star* firing its defensive lasers at the missiles and using its shields to absorb the simultaneous blasts.

"Fire a spread of three missiles on each of those two closest ships," Jonathan ordered pointing them out. Focus the plasma cannons at the closest one too."

"Yes, sir," the Weapons officer replied. "Missiles away."

As the missiles struck the shields of the first cruiser the shields began to buckle. When the plasma fire from four cannons struck, the shields could not hold. The plasma burned through the hull and hit one of the missile storage holds causing a rippling explosion. Within seconds another Uvarian cruiser was breaking apart in a series of secondary explosions.

"Looks like you could use a helping hand! How long do you intend to play around with these guys?" Jonathan called out.

"We were doing just fine, thank you!" John replied with a voice of mock indignation.

"Sir, the rest of the Uvarian fleet is in range and has launched at least twenty missiles. Impact in fifteen seconds," Joshua reported.

"Son, really, you'd better get out of here. There is nothing you can do against that many missiles," John pleaded.

John's flip com. beeped.

"Sir, warp capability restored," Dexter calmly reported.

"*Fire Fox*, max warp now. We are with you!" John ordered. "David, max warp now!"

Just seconds before the missiles reached their intended targets, the *Holcron Star* and *Fire Fox* warped out of the battle.

John was frustrated with himself. "We lost the battle. I failed to follow my plan and almost got us all killed. The objective was to hit and run. Instead I chose to get greedy and try to take out a few more cruisers. It wasn't worth the damage we took."

Gavin shook his head. You were right on the hit and run plan but I disagree with your idea of failure. We destroyed at least seven ships total and damaged as many more and no losses. True, we almost died but God was with us and we escaped to fight another day. Though the Allies withdrew from the battle, we clearly dished out far more than we took by any measure. The fact that such a small force inflicted so much damage is an even greater blow to Uvarian pride."

Rear Admiral Baya Mutaka now assumed command of the fleet. "Uvarian blood was spilt and must be avenged," Baya cried out. "Grand Viscount Horthnot's last orders were to continue to Herrac 2, wipe out this tiny task force and then set a trap for the fleet from Cassaria. However, we must strike where they are weakest. The mission must come first then revenge.

'We will continue pursuit for the next 24 hours. Then I want the fleet to alter course to Earth," Admiral Mutaka ordered her new Operations Officer.

"We're not going to pursue the enemy to Herrac 2?" he cautiously inquired.

"No! Our mission is to secure Earth then the zannite mines. That mission is secondary nothing more. We will only engage the enemy fleet if they interfere with that mission. Soon enough we will take care of their puny fleet."

"I don't understand," the operations officer countered. "They already have control of the mines.Is not our mission a failure already?"

"And you wonder why you are not an admiral after all these years?"

"You are a good tactician but need a vision of the larger conflict. A trick or two up one's sleeve can make the difference between success and failure. Once we capture Earth and are replenished, we will proceed to Mentarus. Then we will show our enemies how Uvarians rule."

CHAPTER 22

Attention all hands. Stand down from General quarters. We have made good our escape from the Uvarian cruisers and heading to Herrac 2. All of you are commended for an exceptional job well done especially in handling of the bomb in #2 reactor control room. Return to normal duties at this time," John announced.

"Sir!" Georgia reported. "We're receiving a distress call from *K.S.S. Gershan* requesting immediate assistance. They report severe damage to their warp engines and a failing reactor core. They are leaking radiation and must abandon ship."

"Gavin! How soon can we reach them?" John asked.

Gavin checked the navigation computer, "We should be there in ten minutes."

"Georgia, notify the *K.S.S. Gershan* that the *Fire Fox* and *Holcron Star* are responding and give them our arrival time," John said. "Tell them to hold on till then if possible. Also notify the *Fire Fox* to assist in the rescue."

"Victoria, get the medical staff and emergency response teams ready to receive the crew for decontamination processing and radiation treatment."

"'Will do!" Victoria replied and left the bridge for sick bay.

"Should I get the *Halfling* ready to help shuttle the crew over?" Gavin asked.

"Good idea! Go ahead and get your crew ready. Have David take Shuttle 3. I'll have *Fire Fox* send two of their shuttles as well. That should get the whole crew off in one trip," John replied.

A few minutes later, the ships arrived and began evacuating the *K.S.S. Gershan* crew. Three of the ship's shuttles were already loaded with many of the worst casualties. There were many more that needed stretchers and there were not enough. Over a dozen wounded were placed on the *Halfling*'s deck so more could be brought aboard. The ship's captain was the last to leave the dying ship. Once the rescue ships withdrew, John Braxton gave Aycana the order to destroy the mortally damaged cruiser.

As the rescued crew arrived on board the *Holcron Star*, Susan directed a decontamination team to process the survivors through the decontamination protocols. Two nurses were doing triage and ensuring decontamination was complete on each patient before directing the orderlies on where to take the patients.

A shuttle from the *Fire Fox* landed with two medical teams to assist. Susan waved at Katrina as she stepped out of the shuttle with four of *Fire Fox*'s nurses. "Glad to see you. Send one of your teams to help Khem in sick bay. Sick bay is already overloaded so the rest of us are going to need to treat non-surgical patients here. I'm set up for burn victims in front of Shuttle Space B. You and your team can treat what patients are left wherever you can find space."

"You got it," Katrina acknowledged and began directing her team to their duties.

Susan took two of her nurses over to a portable treatment center. "This machine is the latest technology Dr. Kremmel developed. We are the first to use it. The machine generates synthetic skin coverings infused with nano cells. The synthetic skin treatments allow burns to heal quickly and prevent pain and infection. All you need to do is provide a small piece of the patient's damaged skin onto a test slide and place it in the test slide slot. Then slowly wave the hand scanner over the wound area and press the blue button to input the scan data. A tray on the other end delivers the coverings specific to the patient's DNA and blood type. Make sure the wound area is clean of debris and dry before you place the covering on the wound area. You understand what to do?" Both nurses nodded.

"Good, I'll watch you do one and then let's get going,"Susan said. The nurses went through the steps but forgot the blue button. Susan showed where the button was on the hand-held scanner.

Within ten minutes the synthetic skin covering was complete and placed on the patient. The patient felt almost immediate relief.

Katrina was trying feverishly to stop the bleeding from a wounded crew member in triage when suddenly blood from a main artery in the leg started to spray into the air. A nurse quickly assisted Katrina in clamping the severed artery then had orderlies rush the crew member to sick bay.

The Gershan's captain was nearby in a state of shock from burns covering his hands and arms. Many crew lay on the hangar deck moaning in agony waiting their turn for treatment.

The Gershan's first officer was badly burned on one side of his face and sat in shock on the deck slowly surveying the chaos and sounds around him with his one good eye. When he saw a wounded crew member scream in agony from her wounds his mind suddenly snapped.

The Katusian first officer jumped up and pushed past a nurse beside Katrina to attack a nearby security guard. In the ensuing struggle he tried to wrestle away the guard's blaster rifle. The guard valiantly defended himself against the adrenaline high attacker. However, the crazed Katusian officer flung him around in a circle and succeeded in wrenching the rifle away.

During the struggle, a few wild blaster bursts flashed about the hangar as he staggered to keep his balance. Katrina, just a few feet away, took one of the stray blasts in the back and collapsed on the floor as she tried to shield a patient from the attack.

Susan was focused on helping with some severely wounded crew members nearby. She just finished preparing an injection of painkiller for a badly wounded patient when the attack began.

Hearing the shots, she looked up in time to see Katrina fall over a patient. He wheeled around to fire at her, but never got the chance.

Susan gave him a swift high kick that knocked the rifle out of his hands, followed by a crushing right handed chop to the left shoulder. Susan's left hand still holding the prepared syringe instinctively followed her right chop with a left-handed stab of the needle. At the same moment, Victoria fired her blaster pistol from twenty feet away stunning the deranged officer. The Katusian officer fell forward collapsing into Susan's arms.

"Well, between your stun shot and my injection he won't be up and around for quite a while," Susan declared looking at Victoria.

Two nurses helped Katrina to her feet. She was dazed from the stun shot and her legs were wobbly, but otherwise she was fine.

"It was a good thing the guard's rifle was set for stun," Katrina moaned as she tried to rub her back. "That shot really hurts."

Victoria stormed over to where they were standing. "Susan! You don't know how lucky you are? After shooting Katrina, he changed the setting. His next shot would have put a hole in you large enough for a football to pass through," Victoria growled showing the rifle setting to her. "Next time think twice about being a hero. Doctors are scarce around here. You are not expendable."

"Yes, ma-am!" Susan replied sheepishly.

Admiral Stephen MacKay and Commodore Linx Montell exited their shuttle at Vandenberg AFB and were quickly ushered to an office inside the hangar. There, General Turnbull, General Klinedecker and Col. Perry were waiting. Two other generals from Russia and Great Britain along with some of their key staff were also present. After introductions were made, everyone sat down around the conference table.

Stephen sensed something was wrong, but waited to see how things unfolded before speaking up. Col. Perry went to the podium and started the briefing.

"This is the present state of readiness around the world," he said as he revealed a global map on the large projector screen. "Each country is given a color showing their defensive readiness posture. The green countries are considered ready and on alert. The yellow countries are not capable of more than modest national defense. The red coded countries are not combat-capable for more than token resistance to invading Uvarian forces. Some of the red countries have opted for no resistance.

'As you can see Earth has huge defensive gaps. Europe, Russia, North America, and Japan are about as ready as possible. There are some weaknesses but, in general, they are ready to put up a vigorous defense. Africa, along with parts of Asia and Latin America..."

When the briefing ended, there were grim faces around the room except for Commodore Montell and Admiral MacKay.

"What are you two grinning about?" General Turnbull asked.

"The defense of Earth looks simple to us," Commodore Montell replied confidently. "Our fighters will blast them to bits in space and your ground forces get to clean up any stragglers. What's so hard about that?"

"I greatly admire Katusian courage and confidence, but your fighters are vastly out gunned. If any Uvarian assault vessels are able make their landings in the wrong areas, we will have more than a clean-up operation on our hands. Worse, our weapons are definitely inferior to theirs," General Turnbull noted.

"Then again the solution is the same. We must defeat them in space," Commodore Montell exclaimed with a more serious expression.

"General Turnbull!" Admiral MacKay added. The Uvarian assault ships are very large, but lack the maneuverability of our missiles and fighters. They will pound Earth's military assets from space with impunity. Then they will pound population centers like the pirates did in China. In seconds forty-four million people vanished. Imagine what a hundred and fifty ships will do?

'They will not send invasion forces until they have pounded any detectable resistance. If, and I mean if, you have any air or anti-air assets left you can use them to attack invasion forces during initial re-entry if you are even in range. After that they will rule the skies and resistance will quickly be dealt with.

'If they do manage to land, their troops will lack air cover until their ships are airborne again. Their assault ships are vulnerable to attack while on the ground if they happen to land within striking distance. Don't forget they will use some ships in space to cover their own landing craft."

"OK, I concede your point, space is our first line of defense. How do you propose to stop them there?" General Turnbull replied.

"We have set up intel buoys around the outer edge of the solar system. They will give us advance warning of their approach. We will have some idea of their trajectory and where they might come out of warp. It will take a while for them to reassemble their fleet. While they are doing so, we plan to attack them in a series of hit and run attacks and take out stragglers. As the Uvarians approach Earth, our forces will hit them with everything we have until one side is wiped out.

It's up to you to mop up anything that gets past us. We can't come to your rescue until the enemy fleet is destroyed.

Somewhere along the way we expect General Braxton to join us in the attack," Admiral MacKay declared.

"Not a complicated plan is it?" Col. Perry asked.

"What other plan can there be with the resources we have?" Commodore Montell retorted.

"Are you sure Braxton can get here in time?" General Turnbull inquired apprehensively.

Admiral MacKay confidently smiled, "At the moment, he is only out numbered four to one so it will be a little tight with the timing. I'm sure he will show up though, he hasn't missed a fight yet."

General Turnbull turned to his staff. With a wry smile declared, "We had better redouble our defensive efforts, gentlemen. These guys have been in deep space far too long. They've all gone mad."

As John and Victoria visited the various workstations it became noticeable the stress was beginning to wear on the crew. The crew came from a wide variety of cultures and many of them suffered horrific experiences that added to the mental stress. To counter these stresses, John and Victoria made a point to give words of encouragement and assurance of their valuable teamwork. Everyone had a valuable contribution to the mission and it was greatly appreciated. In the depths of space there were no replacements, no vacations and no quitters.

Once the rounds were completed they visited sick bay, checking up on the survivors of the *KSS Gershan*. Afterwards, John and Victoria returned to the bridge. The next twelve hours passed tediously. John grew impatient. Not a single Intel buoy reported any Uvarian movement.

Gavin had relieved Aycana on the bridge and sensed

something was amiss too. He ran repeated checks on the sensor equipment and visual scanners in the hope of a positive report. The Intel buoys remained silent.

"Gavin, something has gone wrong. It's been eighteen hours since the Uvarians should have appeared but still no sign of them. We should have picked up something on our Intel buoys by now," John stated pounding his fist on the arm of his command chair.

"I agree! But where are they?" Gavin asked as he called up a hologram of their region of space.

"After we attacked them at Laylar, they took our bait and altered course to follow us to Herrac 2. Our first Intel buoy reported the Uvarian Combat Fleet was on course to our location," John stated pointing to the last known location on the holo projector.

"Yes, but if they altered course somewhere just past the range of the Intel buoy, they could still arrive before their invasion fleet arrives at Earth," Gavin explained.

"Is it possible we misinterpreted their plans? Could they be going to Terra and the zannite mines with Earth as a diversion?" John asked.

"It's possible but I doubt it. They have a large fleet with over half a million people that took nine months to get to Earth. I suspect their supplies would be low and Earth is going to be used as a supply base for the final push to Terra and beyond. Remember they were expecting to have the pirates provide them with a zannite shipment before Earth was attacked," Gavin concluded.

"That seals it then. Contact Admiral Dever of the situation and to head for Earth at full speed. Tell him to bring his fleet up behind the Uvarian fleet and attack with all haste. Our task force will make for Earth immediately. I pray we arrive in time," John grimly stated.

Admiral MacKay was getting impatient. Neither the Uvarians or General Braxton's fleet had been detected by the Intel buoys.

Where is General Braxton? He should be here by now! Admiral MacKay wondered to himself. He was about to pace around the bridge one more time when an Intel buoy signaled several ships were dropping out of warp. The Uvarian combat Fleet had arrived. Admiral MacKay felt his stomach tighten into a twisted knot. It was the worst possible time. With his tiny task force, he was about to face the wrath of Uvarian might.

"Admiral, another Intel buoy has detected a group of ships coming out of warp. It's a very large group," his first officer reported as his voice quivered. The pain in Stephen's stomach went to a numbness he'd never experienced.

"How long before the cruisers are within range?" "About twenty minutes, sir," the first officer replied.

Fifteen minutes later the first officer reported another group of ships were breaking warp.

To his delight, Admiral MacKay watched John Braxton's task force appear in formation in front of his own task force. He also noted the Katusian cruiser was missing. "Glad you could make it." MacKay called.

"Wouldn't miss this for the world." Braxton called back. "As you can see we are outnumbered," Stephen sighed.

"All the more likely to hit something," John answered.

"Form up your cruisers in a staggered formation facing the Uvarian right flank," Stephen ordered.

"Will do!" John replied

In reaction, the Uvarian cruisers shifted to their left without even slowing down to make a strike at the carrier and modified heavy freighters. A minute later Stephen smiled as the Uvarians shifted right into a mine field. He commanded the freighters to launch their fighters for the attack. A hundred fighters emerged to attack the cruisers trying to extricate themselves from the mine field. Missiles streaked to their targets and three cruisers erupted in fireballs and debris. Two more Uvarian cruisers were adrift. Now the cruisers from both sides began to engage each other. The missiles and magnum cannon fire crisscrossed the gulf between them in a horrifying light show.

Defensive lasers lashed out at incoming missiles with some good effect. With zannite enhancements, the allied forces were able to draw first blood. Admiral Mackay skillfully guided the fleet grudgingly giving ground in an effort to keep just out of range of the Uvarian cruisers while keeping in range with their own magnum plasma cannons. Still the Uvarians advanced. Now Stephen had a large but loose field of asteroids at his back causing the Uvarians to become more aggressive. Stephen ordered the fleet to stand their ground at this point.

"All Fighters attack!" Admiral MacKay ordered over the fleet comm. net.

From behind asteroids all across his rear, two hundred and fifty allied fighters now rose to engage the Uvarian cruisers.

The fighters proved difficult to destroy as they deftly worked their way through the enemy defenses. The enemy cruisers began to break formation. That allowed the Allied corvettes to attack the stragglers and damaged ships. The problem was evident from the beginning. The allied forces were out numbered, but not out gunned.

Brilliant flashes erupted from a Katusian cruiser on Stephen's left flank. He quickly ordered the cruisers to close formation and continue concentrating on the Uvarian flanks. Admiral MacKay saw numerous escape pods jettison away from the ship but not as many as he hopped for. He watched the ship break apart, but could do nothing to help in its final death throws.

Three more enemy cruisers exploded but the damage to the allied cruisers was also taking a toll as three suffered damage. Stephen saw one Holcron cruiser struggling to keep its shields up. He ordered the ship to retire and get help from a repair ship on the other side of Earth's moon. The remaining Allied cruisers wheeled about and closed in on the left flank focusing its fire at the center of the formation in an effort to divide the enemy forces.

John formed his remaining cruisers into a line formation with overlapping fields of fire and shield protection. Their missiles fired in a ripple effect on the center ship. At the same time a wave of fifteen Uvarian missiles streaked towards his own formation. The defensive lasers of his ships streaked out to intercept them. Four managed to get through but were picked off by fighters.

A barrage of allied missiles closed in on the lead Uvarian cruiser.

Its shields and defensive lasers absorbed the first wave of missiles. The second wave battered the shields down, blinding the defensive sensors. The next wave found their mark. Allied missiles rippled along the side of the enemy cruiser, followed by venting hot gasses and debris. Finally a huge explosion rendered the drifting cruiser a useless hulk of giant debris.

The Uvarian force once again began slowly advancing, unrelenting in its drive towards Earth.

John watched two missiles strike the *Fire Hound*. Its shields were already weakened. The first missile collapsed the shields and the second struck the starboard engines.

"David, bring us closer to the *Fire Hound* for more shield support. Her shields are gone!" John ordered.

"I'll try but we are already supporting the *Fire Fox* with our shields," David responded.

"We can't support both," Gavin replied. "It's impossible."

With a flash of brilliant light, there was a large explosion near the *Fire Hound*'s engine room. Slowly, the ship began dropping out of formation. Several more secondary explosions followed. Escape pods deployed from the forward section of the once proud ship. John tried counting them but realized they were too few to account for most of the crew.

"Delay that order, it's too late. Maintain our present course," John sighed.

John opened a com. link to Admiral MacKay. "Stephen, we have lost the *Fire Hound* and two more are barely in the fight. Now is the time to commit your remaining force and get some of the pressure off us or it will be too late."

"I've already given the order. We will engage momentarily," Admiral MacKay replied.

"God bless, Stephen. See you when it's over," John declared.

"Now would be a good time for Admiral Dever to show up," Gavin quipped.

"Look at that! The *K.S.S. Jerigin* and the six converted mini-carriers have launched their remaining fighters and now are headed straight into the Uvarian formation. He is forcing them to break up their formation," Gavin gasped.

"Yes," John said. "We will take up flanking positions and shield them.

Gavin said, "Sir, the shields on the *Fire Fox* just failed."

"Damage Control! Evacuate deck 3 then vent atmosphere to put the fire out. I want a team to assist Engineering in restoring power to the shield generator. I need the shields back on line ASAP!" Jonathan ordered.

"Sir, we just restored power to the missile targeting system and have launch capability restored!" Seth reported.

"Great!" Jonathan declared. "Once we have our shields restored, we will follow the *Holcron Star*."

"You think we can get through their defenses?" Seth asked nervously.

"We will charge through as they struggle to reform. We'll launch everything we've got at their command ship. Our shields should last that long," Jonathan explained.

"Captain, Engineering reports shields fully restored, but not sure how long they can keep it together," the Communications Officer reported.

"That's all we need. Let's do it," Jonathan ordered.

The *Fire Fox* moved into position to make its attack. The K.S.S.Jerigin's audacious maneuver succeeded in breaking up the Uvarian formation. It allowed the fighters to attack the ships more effectively. The maneuver came with a price as two of the converted carriers took severe damage and began drifting out of control.

Three severely damaged Uvarian cruisers broke formation. The *Holcron Star* and two nearby cruisers immediately finished them off.

"Now! All ahead at maximum sub light speed for that hole in the Uvarian ranks straight for their command ship," Jonathan ordered.

"Aye, sir!" Helm replied.

John ordered his remaining ships into two, threeship formations. Each to concentrate on securing the flanks while the carriers directed their heavy cannons at the center.

The *Holcron Star* turned about with its formation to attack the Uvarian right flank when he saw the *Fire Fox* make a dash for the hole in the center of the Uvarian fleet. At first he wanted to order Jonathan to cease his attack and return to his assigned position in the formation. However, when he spotted

Jonathan's obvious target he changed his mind.

"Command 1 to *Fire Fox* 1." Target approved and God's speed!"

Gavin turned to John and gasped, "Is he mad? The *Fire Fox* will be cut to pieces."

"Not if we can help it. We are going to destroy them from the inside out."

It was now John received a call that brought tears to his eyes. "General Braxton, I hope you left some glory for the rest of us. It would be in poor taste not to share victory with your friends," Admiral Dever said breaking radio silence with a roar of laughter.

"Admiral, you can have all the glory you can find," John replied with a serious but relieved tone. "We could use some help here. Send a formation to block any Uvarian retreat."

"No problem. We will engage momentarily."

John turned to Gavin and nodded. "Just in time."

"In the nick of time if there's any left," Gavin added.

The *Fire Fox* slipped through the gap in the Uvarian defense and drew down on the enemy command cruiser. Both ships launched their salvo of missiles and cannon fire at the same time.

At that moment, a severely damaged Uvarian cruiser lost flight control and found itself between the *Fire Fox* and the Uvarian command ship just in time to absorb the salvos from each side. With their shields already weakened, the initial strikes had minor effect but the second wave of strikes broke the shields down and missiles raked the port side of the Uvarian cruiser. The primary explosions left the ship mortally wounded.

The secondary explosions in the reactor room caused a violent rupture along the entire ship, shattering the hull into thousands of red-hot, glowing pieces of debris.

Jonathan had only seconds to bring the *Fire Fox* about and cross the stern of the Uvarian command cruiser. A massive burst of magnum plasma cannon fire raked the engines setting the enemy adrift.

A third enemy cruiser from the formation lost its bridge and targeting system, but was able to launch its missiles. Three missile strikes broke down the fragile shields and the last missile struck the *Fire Fox* in the mid section. The impact and explosions shook the ship to its core. Power faded throughout the mortally wounded ship. It began drifting away from the battle.

"Captain, Engineering reports the reactors are down for good. Reactor #1, engineering, storage holds A and B, and sick bay are venting atmosphere," Seth announced as the emergency lighting came on line.

"Order evacuation from those areas. Any radiation leakage?" Jonathan asked as he picked himself up from the floor.

"Negative, sir," Seth replied. "Engineering sensors indicate atmosphere venting extinguished the fire and the core safety system locked the reactor down. Most of Engineering made it out, however, sick bay reports they're trapped and need help getting the injured out."

"Sick bay!" Jonathan called on his communications cuff.

"Yes, Jonathan," Katrina replied.

"Can you make it to the shuttle bay?"

"No! We have sealed ourselves off from the damaged area but can't exit from this deck in either direction. We don't have much air left either," Katrina reported.

"Can you make it to the escape capsules?"

"No, they are on the other side of the fire wall," Katrina replied with fear in her voice. "Got any other ideas besides the ones we've already tried?"

The ship shook violently as one of the fuel cells ruptured. Metal bulkheads began creaking and giving way throughout the ship.

"That does it!" Jonathan groaned. He gave the dreaded order, "Abandon ship!"

"Aye, sir." Seth replied. "What about sick bay?"

"Order everyone off the ship while they can. We will suit up and go get them. We leave no one behind," Jonathan replied with determination.

"Katrina, can you make it to Storage C?" Jonathan asked as he looked at a hologram projection of the ship.

"Yes, but there is no exit there. That won't do any good!" Katrina desperately replied.

"Don't worry about that. Just get everyone you can to that hold along with any oxygen bottles you can find and seal yourselves in. I'm coming to get you. Just hold on," Jonathan pleaded.

Jonathan and Seth suited up for their space walk. As they exited the airlock, both of them were captivated by the view before them. In the eerie panoramic view of space the battle raged.

Missiles, laser, and plasma cannon fire arced streaks of colored light between the two decimated fleets. Small escape pods with blinking lights and glowing rocket engines desperately maneuvered to avoid the crossfire and debris of once proud and mighty warships. Of the nine allied cruisers only four were left and one of them severely damaged. One carrier, two converted carriers and MacKay's cruiser were all that was left of Admiral MacKay's force. The Uvarians were not abandoning their attack. It was then Jonathan noticed streaks of light as many ships started coming out of warp.

"Yes, Admiral Dever has finally arrived. Thank you, God," Jonathan sighed. Others formed up with the *Holcron*

Star and began pressing their attack to finish off the Uvarian cruisers.

Jonathan could see in the distance the large armada of Uvarian Assault Transports closing in on Earth and the little flashes of light from the fighters. Many of Admiral Dever's ships began attacking the Assault Transports with devastating effect. It reminded Jonathan of lightening bugs flitting about. It all seemed so surreal in the vastness of space.

Jonathan tapped Seth on the shoulder and motioned him to follow. They made their way aft to an airlock that allowed them access to the hangar bay. Once inside they were shocked by the damage to the hangar. A missile had ripped a hole on deck three that also punctured a fuel storage tank.

Before the atmosphere was completely vented, flames buckled the hull plating on the whole side of the hangar destroying the nearest of two shuttles. The third shuttle, to Jonathan's relief, was scorched by the flames but otherwise untouched. The hull breach vented the atmosphere just in time to put the fire out and prevent any real damage to it.

Seth found a cutting torch cart and with the assistance of zero gravity easily brought it into the shuttle.

Jonathan, in the meantime, tried to open the hangar doors but could not get them to budge. He finally gave up and entered the shuttle with Seth and closed the hatch. Once the atmosphere was restored they removed their helmets.

"What are we going to do if we can't get the doors open?" Seth asked as he sat in the copilot's seat.

"We blast them open," Jonathan replied as he strapped himself into his seat and brought the shuttle to life.

"OK! Guess we don't have much choice if we're going to get out of here." Seth agreed.

Once the shuttle engines were online, Jonathan carefully lifted the shuttle a few inches off the deck and powered up the forward cannons. A few blasts and suddenly one of the doors broke away allowing the shuttle to escape.

Carefully, Jonathan guided the shuttle along the length of *Fire Fox's* shattered hull until he came to hover above Storage C. Seth extended the shuttle's airlock tube the 2 feet between the two vessels and tried to seal the coupling lock.

"Captain, I can't get a good seal!" Seth cried out.

"Keep trying till you do. We have to get a good seal. We didn't get this far only to fail," Jonathan growled with determination.

On the fifth try Seth finally got a solid lock. Jonathan opened the airlock hatch. Lighting up the torch, he began cutting through the hull. After about twenty minutes, he had just a couple of inches to go when the torch stopped.

"We're out of gas. Give me a hand!" Jonathan called out to Seth.

Together they tried to pry the metal away but couldn't get it to budge. In desperation Seth and Jonathan jumped on the piece of hull plating. Still nothing.

"God, don't you think there have been enough obstacles for one day? I could use a hand ya know? That's my wife and crew on the other side," Jonathan pleaded in desperation.

Inspiration struck him. Jonathan drew his pistol and changed the setting from stun to full. He aimed at the last couple of inches of hull plating and fired several blasts. Jonathan then grabbed one of the empty tanks and repeatedly bashed it against the cutout. Grudgingly the metal began to pry away.

"Anybody down there?" Jonathan shouted through the hole.

There was a scraping noise as an object on the other side was pushed out of the way and some shouting from those trapped inside. A pair of hands and the head of a crewmember appeared. Seth and Jonathan grabbed her and pulled her through the opening.

"Ten more are coming. They just have to stack some crates to get up to the hole you made. It's near the ceiling of the hold," she explained.

"Sorry about that, ma'am! Seth apologized.

Jonathan retrieved a coil of rope from a storage locker and threw one end through the hole. Send up three more able bodied first," He shouted through the opening. Four more made it through the hole and into the shuttle.

"Ok! All of you pull people up through the hole. I'm going down to get the wounded ready to move. When I tug on the rope three times pull them up."

Jonathan descended down the dark hole with nothing but a glow light to see with. He found Katrina and a nurse struggling with tying the rope in a way to get the patient safely ready. Jonathan tugged on the rope and guided the patient carefully over the crates and wrecked equipment through the hole. He repeated the process six more times then sent the nurse up. There was another explosion that rocked the ship and the sound of more bulkheads collapsing.

"Hurry up, we need to get out of here now," Jonathan urged.

Katrina slipped the rope over her head and around her waist. Jonathan tugged on the rope and she quickly disappeared through the hole.

The rope was lowered again. As he tied the rope off, another explosion shook the ship and the rapid hissing of air ventilating from the storage room became more like a wind tunnel. He tugged on the rope and made it through the hole.

As Jonathan lay sprawled on the floor of the shuttle, Seth secured the hatch just in time. Jonathan raced to the pilot seat and released the shuttle from the hull just as the section collapsed. He quickly strapped himself into the seat and powered up the engines.

Jonathan looked about to get his bearings and saw the

Holcron Star fire it's plasma cannons at a Uvarian cruiser bearing down on the *Fire Fox*. It exploded in a show of fireworks. He raced to get away. The debris, wreckage of ships, and cannon fire made an obstacle course as he jinked and weaved desperately trying to reach the safety of the *Holcron Star*.

Jonathan sighed relief when he finally touched down on the hangar deck. Seth came up to the cockpit and reported they had twenty crewmen aboard.

"I wish there were more," Jonathan sighed as he patted his first officer on the shoulder. He made his way to where Katrina was helping a critically injured crew member. He patiently waited until the orderlies came, put her on a gurney, and rushed her off to sick bay.

Jonathan put his arms around Katrina and holding her close whispered, "Don't scare me like that again. How could I go on without you?" Jonathan declared as he stroked her hair.

"Let's not do this again," Katrina nodded.

Susan and Victoria stepped into the shuttle with a medical team. "You two had me worried when I heard your ship was hit,"

Victoria said choking back tears as she hugged them both. "You weren't the only one," Katrina declared.

"Well, I'd better report to the bridge," Jonathan said. "There is still a battle to win."

CHAPTER 23

Victoria and others repeatedly urged him to rest, but John Braxton refused. Following twelve hours of intense battle and another twenty-four hours of rescue operations, John Braxton finally allowed himself to leave the bridge. It wasn't until everyone alive was rescued that he finally relinquished the bridge to Gavin and left for his quarters.

John wearily made his way to his bedroom. The last thing he remembered was sitting on the bed taking off his shoes.

John awoke to a gentle nudge from his beloved wife as she softly called his name.

"John…John! I hate to disturb you, but you need to wake up," Victoria said.

Wearily, John opened his eyes and rolled over. He could not remember removing his clothes. Victoria sat on the side of the bed nudging his shoulders. He turned his head to see Victoria's bright smile. As he looked around the room he noticed a fresh uniform hanging on a wall hook and realized she had taken care of him.

"How long was I asleep?" John asked still in a daze.

"About fourteen hours. I don't ever remember you sleeping so long. It is definitely not your nature. Sorry, I had to wake you up, but the White House has tried to contact you four times in the past four hours. I gave strict orders to the bridge not to disturb you unless the president himself calls. I imagine they're getting a bit impatient by now."

"Yes, I guess so. How are my special heroes?"

"All are doing well. We have already evacuated most of them to Vandenberg AFB. The most serious cases are still in sick bay until they are stable enough to be transported. The last caller from the White House told Jonathan you would want to call him right away.”

“Did he leave a name and number?” John asked.

“Oh! Nobody I ever heard of before. He said his name was Ed Cox,” Victoria teased with a smile.

John chuckled. I’ll call him but first I need to visit sick bay.

“Jonathan bet the caller you wouldn’t get back to him until you did. The caller said he understood. Everyone is learning your priorities. Jonathan will be delighted to know he won his bet.”

“Jonathan is right. I’m not doing anything until I visit my special heroes. At the moment the galaxy can wait.”

John showered and dressed then headed to sick bay where he visited each of the injured to express appreciation and ensured every need was attended too.

After leaving sick bay, John made his call to the White House then paid a visit to the Dark Pit. John found Estron, Deze, Dexter, and Henry busy on a new project.

“Dad, how are you doing?” John asked.

“Fine, just fine,” Henry stammered.

John took Estron aside. “There is far too much for the duct tape engineers to do and they need a fourth member. I’m reassigning you to the Dark Pit until further notice if you want the job?”

Estron’s green eyes sparkled as she broke out into a rare dimpled smile.

“I was thinking of going home but now I can’t stop thinking this is home and I’m part of a special family. I can’t imagine being anywhere else. Thank you!” she replied.

Henry held out a gift-wrapped box. “We just finished a project we’ve been working on for several weeks. It took some time to develop and we were almost done when we had to stop to work on mines with the help of Engineering. This is the first one and we want you to have it.”

"Yes, we want you to have the first one. It is so cold," Deze exclaimed.

"The term is 'cool' not 'cold' but you're catching on," Henry kindly corrected.

"Gee, guys. I'm touched. What is it?" John asked.

"Well, open it up and find out!" Henry excitedly responded.

John tore open the wrapper on the small box and lifted the lid. Inside was a gold wristwatch like none John had ever seen. It had a digital face displaying military time with two small buttons on each side.

"This is really a nice watch. Thanks!" John said appreciatively.

"That is not just any watch, sir," Deze explained. "The watch is designed to detect implants if they are within about 30 feet of you. If an implant comes within range, the background will go from a cobalt blue to a pale red. If more than one implant is nearby, it will flash a number indicating how many. The two stems on the left side are reset controls. The two buttons on the right side are normal watch controls. Real slippery isn't it?"

Henry almost burst out laughing.

"I believe you mean slick and yes it's really slick. Thank you all for the gift. I'll wear it from now on," John stated replacing his old watch with the new one on his wrist. "Can we get more of these devices?"

"It will be awhile as that was the first one, but we will be able to have a hundred more made within a month or two. With your permission we can send the specs to Cassaria and have them made faster," Estron said with a proud smile.

"Permission granted. Please excuse me as I need to get to the hangar before our guests arrive," John exclaimed as he hurried on his way.

John arrived at the hangar in time to welcome Admirals Usus Dever and Stephen MacKay just as their shuttle settled onto the deck. The six security guards snapped to attention as the two men stepped down the shuttle ramp.

"Gentlemen, welcome aboard," John said as he shook their hands and smiled.

"General, it truly is good to see you alive again," Usus said a bit subdued. I grieve for our losses but the Uvarians will remember this battle with much anguish and sorrow. Not a single Uvarian ship survived."

"I doubt we have seen the last of them. This was the first battle they ever lost. I can't imagine not trying to even the score," Stephen added.

"I agree! Some of their ground forces did manage to land, but they were few. It was a close call for us. I was just visiting sick bay and plan to visit the remaining wounded before we head to Washington tomorrow.

'Our wounded in sick bay are in good spirits. They kept asking how bad we whooped them," John said a bit amused. "God was truly with us."

Everyone nodded agreement.

Early the next morning two shuttles from the *Holcron Star* arrived at Vandenberg AFB. One shuttle landed on the landing pad at the hospital with the last of the wounded. The second shuttle eased into the cavernous hangar and settled to a gentle landing, the whole Braxton family, Admiral Dever, Gavin and his sisters, Admiral MacKay and his daughter Molly exited the shuttle to a host of VIPs, reporters, lights and cameras.

General Klinedecker and Col. Perry greeted them. After a few handshakes and introductions, the guests were whisked off in staff cars to the hospital where the wounded allies were being treated. Each of the injured was questioned about their needs. Whatever they asked for or needed was written down in a notebook by a burly chief master sergeant standing behind General Braxton. Whatever the patients wanted, he would make sure they got it. John chatted with each of them for a minute or two, sometimes prayed with them, pined a medal on their pillow or on their chest, snapped a salute, then moved on to the next special hero.

"General Braxton really takes their care personally doesn't he?" a doctor asked Victoria as they were going from room to room.

"Yes, he does. He was once where they are now. In the War of Russian Aggression, John was seriously injured in a missile attack. He spent months in a hospital in Germany. John literally had to learn to walk all over again. While still in a wheelchair, he insisted on visiting every one of his people. It is a duty he will never give up. You'd better make sure they get the very best treatment or you will find he has a dark side," Victoria warned.

"Yes, we've already discovered that. No one is complaining either," the doctor said with a smile.

A couple of hours later, John and the others gathered at Gen.

Klinedecker's home for an informal working luncheon.

"John, President Koppel called me personally this morning. He has some concerns he wanted you aware of before you arrive in Washington this evening. He said some members of Congress have decided you have become a threat to their power. It is more than just the usual anti-military trash talk. They have powerful friends in the media and are preparing the ultimate hatchet job on you.

'In the public's eye you have gained much respect and popularity. That is viewed as a threat by the swamp in Washington. An outside-the-beltway hero in possession of power can't be tolerated at the expense of the Washington elite. In their minds, you must play their game or be politically destroyed. Julius Caesar never had enemies like those organizing against you.

'The president wants you to avoid the press at all costs

until the White House has held its planned press conference tonight. His public relations people will keep things under control.”

“Thanks for the heads up. Ed Cox mentioned something about a storm starting to stir among some Washington power brokers and advised me to keep a low profile for now. I deplore the politics of personal destruction they play in Washington. I haven’t been on Earth for the last four months much less talked to the press about anything. I don’t get it!” John said helplessly confused.

“Oh, you have done far more than you realize,” Arlin pointed out. “Your tag-along reporter, Thomas Kasill, has been sending dispatches quite regularly and the public has been eating them up. Thomas was sent to do a hatchet job on you. Instead, he made you almost a cult hero along with everyone in your command. The New York Daily Review fired him two months ago for not destroying you. He’s been freelancing from deep space ever since.”

“You’re kidding?” John replied. “I was not aware he was fired. We placed no restrictions on his articles except the publishing of classified plans. When I first met him, I told him we wouldn’t baby sit him but did have open airlocks for those who leaked classified information.

‘He was required to clear his dispatches for classified info but otherwise was free to write whatever he wanted. I never liked the press in general, but I support their freedom of the press. I allowed him a twenty minute interview once a week and free access to any part of the ship as long as he didn’t interfere with the ship’s operations.”

“His recounting of the invasion of Terra and especially the Battle of Twelve Points has everyone around the world still talking,” Arlin stated. “Corky O’Brian, Jonathan and David Braxton almost have cult followings as well. Sergeant Major Stone has become a legend. A first edition Terran Command comic book about them was just released."

"Don't underestimate your accomplishments or the political capital you have gained from it," General Klinedecker continued. "Spend it wisely."

Arlin explained, "Senator Pickering is Queen Weasel in Washington and I suggest you stay away from her at all costs. She values power more than anything and is as contemptible a person as I've ever had the displeasure of meeting. The president is a good man and will do whatever is in his power to protect you. However, some on his staff are just too naive for the gutters of Washington."

"Thanks for the heads up. By the way, how is our recruiting of settlers for Terra going?" John asked.

"It had a slow start but is coming together nicely. I had to setup a nonprofit foundation called the New World Institute. Officially I'm only a voluntary advisor for now," Arlin stated.

"What do you mean?" Gavin asked.

Arlin explained, "In three weeks my retirement from the Air Force will be official. If I try to do both jobs while in uniform, Senator Pickering will find a way to ruin me to get to you. In civilian clothes, she will find me much harder to deal with. Senator Pickering has sponsored a bill formally calling on recognition of Terra as a protectorate colony of the United Nations.

'Twice in the last three weeks Senator Pickering dragged me before the Homeland Security Senate hearings to answer questions about your activities. So far I have avoided giving her any ammunition, but her spies are digging into everything about you.

'Last time before the committee, she tried to accuse you of fomenting a war with China by killing one of its citizens working in Detroit. She blew her top when I refused to answer her questions on the matter, as I was not cleared to divulge classified information. She immediately demanded a closed-door session and I again told her I couldn't answer, as it was not a military operation I knew nothing. 'She went berserk again and demanded to know who did run the operation and to what extent you or your people were involved in her murder. When I told her it was a CIA operation, she called in CIA Director Mike Richards.

He told her he couldn't answer either as the agents in the field had yet to make a report. Senator Pickering then demanded the agents appear before the committee and Richards told her that was impossible.

The senator was totally exasperated and demanded they appear to testify.

'Director Richards informed her the agents were many light years away on another planet and could not be debriefed or appear before the committee any time soon. The chairwoman at that point cut Senator Pickering off and accused her of leading the committee on a wild goose chase. I tell you, if looks could kill, the look Senator Pickering gave would have instantly incinerated us.

'Since that day I've had three separate investigations for unspecified charges of misconduct. One of the FBI agents wanted to know who I ticked off in Washington to cause such a stir and the other agent said he could smell Pickering's henchmen all over the complaints."

"Unbelievable!" John sighed shaking his head. "We risk our lives and those from other worlds to save this planet and all some people can do is complain we won. May God help us!"

After another two hours of discussion covering replenishment and support needs, the working luncheon broke up. Everyone returned to the shuttle for departure to Joint Base Andrews. Three hours later the shuttle set down in a specially prepared hangar where a convoy of black limousines awaited to take them to their meeting at the White House. As the Braxtons stepped off the shuttle, two Secret Service Agents, along with a White House aide, met them. The first limousine was parked separately from the others with four body guards posted around it. A woman in a very well-designed black business suit stepped out of the rear compartment and approached John Braxton.

"You are Mr. John Braxton, I presume?" she curtly asked.

"No, not really," John stated a bit perturbed pointing to his nametag and rank.

"I apologize. General John Braxton then?" she asked again. John just nodded in agreement.

"Please step into the limousine here. The Senator would like to welcome you to Washington."

John knew something was up when the White House aide couldn't make his way to John fast enough to stop him. John waved him off and entered the vehicle's back seat.

"Please General, have a seat for a few moments. I wish to welcome you to Washington. I won't keep you long, but I did want to meet America's first intergalactic hero. My name is Senator Francis Pickering."

John reached out to shake her hand but said nothing as he glanced at his watch then slid into the seat offered him.

"Don't worry about the time, General Braxton. I will be brief. On behalf of a grateful nation, and moreover, a grateful world, I want to thank you for your heroic accomplishments. We are indebted to you and your brave galactic friends."

John smiled, nodded appreciatively but again said nothing.

The Senator continued. "This entirely sordid affair has been highly irregular but I understand. Nothing like this has ever happened before in our entire history. In Washington, however, we are most interested in finding out exactly what happened that led to this nasty event and determine how best to prevent it from happening again. Since time is of the essence, please allow me to get to the point."

John again nodded and smiled politely.

"Terra must be brought under United Nations control so all nations can benefit equally. We want you to publicly support that proposal. I am certain that if you cooperate with us things will go well for you. You and your family can return to your Michigan home and live a quiet, normal life again. How does that sound?" the senator smiled.

John blankly starred at the senator but again said nothing.

"I think you do not appreciate the storm that is about to descend upon you and your family. There have been allegations of murder, theft of government property, money laundering, misappropriation of government funds, violations of international treaties, piracy and even kidnapping.

Even if these charges prove false, I'm afraid you and your family could be financially ruined and disgraced. You wouldn't want that would you?"

Again, John starred at the senator blankly but did not respond.

There was a long pregnant pause as the two of them starred at each other without expression. Finally the senator broke the deadlock.

"Well, I thought we could come to an amicable agreement but I see that is impossible. General Braxton, you may fancy yourself a great warrior, but let me assure you, here you are on my turf. Here I am the master. Even the president has no idea what is about to happen.

'I want Terra under a new United Nations Charter and the sole representative for Earth on the proposed Galactic Council. It would be a kind gesture to not stand in my way. Have a good evening, general," Senator Pickering stated as she pointed to the door.

John just smiled as he exited the limo but refused to shake

the senator's extended hand. As he walked away he glanced at his watch. It flashed a red 6 on the screen. He walked over to the White House aide and smiled.

"General, I'm so sorry, the senator showed up at the last possible second and…"

"No need to apologize," John interrupted waving him off. The senator just wanted to meet me. I was glad to indulge her with a couple of minutes. She is a very interesting person," John smiled as he entered the limo with his family waiting.

"Who was that in the other limo?" Victoria asked.

"Senator Pickering and five of her puppets," John replied.

"Oh my!" Victoria gasped. "She was certainly bold to meet you here."

"I almost expected it. It was important to her to get to me before I arrived at the White House. She tried to persuade me to support her proposals."

"Well, how did it go?" Jonathan asked a bit amused.

"I hope you all brought your flame retardant suits," John warned.

"John, you didn't say anything to tick her off did you?" Victoria asked with a stern look.

"Dear, I let her do all the talking. I didn't say a single word. Boy Scout's honor," John pledged holding up his right hand and giving the Boy Scout sign.

"You should have at least punched her lights out!" Henry grumbled as he scratched his beard.

"Grandpa, are you advocating violence against a U.S. Senator?" Susan asked with feigned admonishment.

"Sorry, but in this case it was the most polite thing I could think of," the old sourdough replied sheepishly.

Everyone broke out in laughter as Henry's face turned red with embarrassment.

"Let's enjoy the moment. This is a time for healing and

rejoicing for our family and nation. The future has more dark days ahead and they will come soon enough," John said.

Yes, many more dark days. How many more implants are there?

The war on Earth is not even close to being over. John thought to himself.

On the observation deck of the *Holcron Star*, the Braxtons, Toburg siblings, special guests Admiral Dever, Vice Admiral MacKay along with most of the officers and a hundred personnel of Terran Command gathered for a special ceremony. A camera crew located in the room was ready to begin broadcasting the event for those Terran Command members not able to attend as well as to the public. People were dressed in the formal attire of their respective branch or service for the solemn occasion.

Through the large portal windows, they gazed at the stunning vastness of Terra below. The beautiful blues of its vast oceans, pure white polar caps, the shades of green forests and brown deserts laced with white wisps of clouds and scattered darker storm clouds gave a dramatic backdrop for the gathering. The people stood engaging in reverent whispers or silence next to their seats waiting for the ceremony to begin.

Standing at the head table and observing it was at the top of the hour, General Braxton, wearing white gloves, took a small polished brass gavel and gave a single tap to the ship's glistening meteorite bell in front of him. The ringing sound signaled everyone's attention to begin the ceremony. They turned to face the special gold trimmed, white cloth covered table to John's right and came to attention. Centered on the table was a golden torch with a bright yellow flame and a ceremonial scroll beside it. Chaplain Boyle gave the opening invocation.

Lt. Col. Rivers stepped forward. Wearing white gloves, carefully removed the golden ribbon from the scroll and began calling out the name of each fallen warrior of Terran Command.

Throughout the calling of the names, the room was silent save for an occasional soft muffled cry for a lost friend or loved one. When Lt. Col. Rivers read the last name, he ceremoniously carried the golden torch to the head table. He first presented the scroll to General Braxton. John slowly placed the scroll on a special golden platter held up by a tripod then turned to face Lt. Col. Rivers again. Traven then handed John the torch and placed it in a stand next to the scroll. Traven then gave a slow measured salute. John returned the salute in the same manner. Traven then took a step back, did an about face and returned to his place.

General Braxton rang the ship's bell three times and called out: "Duty, Honor, Country!"

Taking the torch, he held it high with his left hand. With his right hand, he raised high his crystal goblet and proclaimed, "To those who have fallen in battle, we salute your most precious sacrifice. You lived, loved, fought, and sacrificed your lives for freedom. May your sacrifices never be forgotten or in vain. We accept your charge to protect and preserve the freedom you have purchased. May freedom's light forever shine forth and evil cower at its mighty power!"

Everyone raised their crystal goblet high and in unison loudly proclaimed: "Here! Here!"

After downing their drink, they broke the stem of their goblets to signify there was no retreat from the pledge just made to their fallen comrades.

Thus, was born the Passing of the Torch Ceremony. It was meant as a memorial to future generations of the price that must be paid for freedom and the duty of the living to preserve it.

www.ingramcontent.com/pod-product-compliance
Lightning Source LLC
Chambersburg PA
CBHW071419190726

48292CB00001B/45